HARLEQUIN

Also by Bernard Cornwell

The SHARPE series
(in chronological order)

THE LAST KINGDOM

The GRAIL QUEST Series

STONEHENGE: A NOVEL OF 2000 BC

The STARBUCK Chronicles

The WARLORD Chronicles

GALLOWS THIEF

By Bernard Cornwell and Susannah Kells

HARLEQUIN

VAGABOND

BERNARD CORNWELL

HarperCollins*Publishers*

HarperCollins*Publishers*
77–85 Fulham Palace Road,
Hammersmith, London W6 8JB

www.harpercollins.co.uk

This omnibus edition published in 2006 by HarperCollins*Publishers*

Harlequin
Copyright © Bernard Cornwell 2000
Vagabond
Copyright © Bernard Cornwell 2002

Bernard Cornwell asserts the moral right to
be identified as the author of this work

ISBN 0 00 777777 9

Set in PostScript Linotype Meridien with Photina display by
Rowland Phototypesetting Limited,
Bury St Edmunds, Suffolk

Printed and bound in Great Britain by
Clays Ltd, St Ives plc

HARLEQUIN

is for

Richard and Julie Rutherford-Moore

English

Lannion La Roche-Derrien
Guingamp

BRITTANY

Finistère

RENNES

Channel

Le Crotoy
Crécy

Abbeville

Somme

Rouen

Seine

Caen

PARIS

NORMANDY

Poissy

Fougères

'. . . many deadly battles have been fought, people slaughtered, churches robbed, souls destroyed, young women and virgins deflowered, respectable wives and widows dishonoured; towns, manors and buildings burned, and robberies, cruelties and ambushes committed on the highways. Justice has failed because of these things. The Christian faith has withered and commerce has perished and so many other wickednesses and horrid things have followed from these wars that they cannot be spoken, numbered or written down.'

JEAN II, KING OF FRANCE, 1360

Harlequin, probably derived from the Old French *hellequin:* a troop of the devil's horsemen.

CONTENTS

Prologue

The treasure of Hookton was stolen on Easter morning 1342.

It was a holy thing, a relic that hung from the church rafters, and it was extraordinary that so precious an object should have been kept in such an obscure village. Some folk said it had no business being there, that it should have been enshrined in a cathedral or some great abbey, while others, many others, said it was not genuine. Only fools denied that relics were faked. Glib men roamed the byways of England selling yellowed bones that were said to be from the fingers or toes or ribs of the blessed saints, and sometimes the bones were human, though more often they were from pigs or even deer, but still folk bought and prayed to the bones. 'A man might as well pray to St Guinefort,' Father Ralph said, then snorted with mocking laughter. 'They're praying to ham bones, ham bones! The blessed pig!'

It had been Father Ralph who had brought the treasure to Hookton and he would not hear of it being taken away to a cathedral or abbey, and so for eight years it hung in the small church, gathering dust and growing spider webs that shone silver when the sunlight slanted through the high window of the western tower. Sparrows perched on the treasure and some mornings there were bats hanging from its shaft. It was rarely cleaned and hardly ever brought down, though once in a while Father Ralph would demand that ladders be fetched and the treasure unhooked from its chains and he would pray over it and stroke it. He never boasted of it. Other churches or monasteries, possessing such a prize, would have used it to attract pilgrims, but Father Ralph turned visitors away. 'It is nothing,' he would say if a stranger enquired after the relic, 'a bauble. Nothing.' He became angry if the visitors persisted. 'It is nothing, nothing, nothing!' Father Ralph was a frightening man even when he was not angry, but in his temper he was a wild-haired fiend, and his flaring anger protected the treasure, though Father Ralph himself believed that ignorance was its best protection for if men did not know of it then God would guard it. And so He did, for a time.

Hookton's obscurity was the treasure's best protection. The tiny village lay on England's south coast where the Lipp, a stream that was almost a river, flowed to the sea across a shingle beach. A half-dozen fishing boats worked from the village, protected at night by the Hook itself, which was a tongue of shingle that curved around the Lipp's last reach, though in the famous storm of 1322 the sea had roared across the Hook and pounded the boats to splinters on the upper beach. The village had never really recovered from that tragedy. Nineteen boats had sailed from the Hook before the storm, but twenty years later only six small craft worked the waves beyond the Lipp's treacherous bar. The rest of the villagers worked in the saltpans, or else herded sheep and cattle on the hills behind the huddle of thatched huts which clustered about the small stone

4

church where the treasure hung from the blackened beams. That was Hookton, a place of boats, fish, salt and livestock, with green hills behind, ignorance within and the wide sea beyond.

Hookton, like every place in Christendom, held a vigil on the eve of Easter, and in 1342 that solemn duty was performed by five men who watched as Father Ralph consecrated the Easter Sacraments and then laid the bread and wine on the white-draped altar. The wafers were in a simple clay bowl covered with a piece of bleached linen, while the wine was in a silver cup that belonged to Father Ralph. The silver cup was a part of his mystery. He was very tall, pious and much too learned to be a village priest. It was rumoured that he could have been a bishop, but that the devil had persecuted him with bad dreams and it was certain that in the years before he came to Hookton he had been locked in a monastery's cell because he was possessed by demons. Then, in 1334, the demons had left him and he was sent to Hookton where he terrified the villagers by preaching to the gulls, or pacing the beach weeping for his sins and striking his breast with sharp-edged stones. He howled like a dog when his wickedness weighed too heavily on his conscience, but he also found a kind of peace in the remote village. He built a large house of timber, which he shared with his house-keeper, and he made friends with Sir Giles Marriott, who was the lord of Hookton and lived in a stone hall three miles to the north.

Sir Giles, of course, was a gentleman, and so it seemed was Father Ralph, despite his wild hair and angry voice. He collected books which, after the treasure he had brought to the church, were the greatest marvels in

Hookton. Sometimes, when he left his door open, people would just gape at the seventeen books that were bound in leather and piled on a table. Most were in Latin, but a handful were in French, which was Father Ralph's native tongue. Not the French of France, but Norman French, the language of England's rulers, and the villagers reckoned their priest must be nobly born, though none dared ask him to his face. They were all too scared of him, but he did his duty by them; he christened them, churched them, married them, heard their confessions, absolved them, scolded them and buried them, but he did not pass the time with them. He walked alone, grim-faced, hair awry and eyes glowering, but the villagers were still proud of him. Most country churches suffered ignorant, pudding-faced priests who were scarce more educated than their parishioners, but, Hookton, in Father Ralph had a proper scholar, too clever to be sociable, perhaps a saint, maybe of noble birth, a self-confessed sinner, probably mad, but undeniably a real priest.

Father Ralph blessed the Sacraments, then warned the five men that Lucifer was abroad on the night before Easter and that the devil wanted nothing so much as to snatch the Holy Sacraments from the altar and so the five men must guard the bread and wine diligently and, for a short time after the priest had left, they dutifully stayed on their knees, gazing at the chalice, which had an armorial badge engraved in its silver flank. The badge showed a mythical beast, a yale, holding a grail, and it was that noble device which suggested to the villagers that Father Ralph was indeed a high-born man who had fallen low through being possessed of devils. The silver chalice seemed to shimmer in the light of two

6

immensely tall candles which would burn through the whole long night. Most villages could not afford proper Easter candles, but Father Ralph purchased two from the monks at Shaftesbury every year and the villagers would sidle into the church to stare at them. But that night, after dark, only the five men saw the tall unwavering flames.

Then John, a fisherman, farted. 'Reckon that's ripe enough to keep the old devil away,' he said, and the other four laughed. Then they all abandoned the chancel steps and sat with their backs against the nave wall. John's wife had provided a basket of bread, cheese and smoked fish, while Edward, who owned a saltworks on the beach, had brought ale.

In the bigger churches of Christendom knights kept this annual vigil. They knelt in full armour, their surcoats embroidered with prancing lions and stooping hawks and axe heads and spread-wing eagles, and their helmets mounted with feathered crests, but there were no knights in Hookton and only the youngest man, who was called Thomas and who sat slightly apart from the other four, had a weapon. It was an ancient, blunt and slightly rusted sword.

'You reckon that old blade will scare the devil, Thomas?' John asked him.

'My father said I had to bring it,' Thomas said.

'What does your father want with a sword?'

'He throws nothing away, you know that,' Thomas said, hefting the old weapon. It was heavy, but he lifted it easily; at eighteen, he was tall and immensely strong. He was well liked in Hookton for, despite being the son of the village's richest man, he was a hard-working boy. He loved nothing better than a day at sea hauling tarred nets that left his hands raw and bleeding. He knew how to sail a boat, had the strength to pull a good oar when the wind failed; he could lay snares, shoot a bow, dig a grave, geld a calf, lay thatch or cut hay all day long. He was a big, bony, black-haired country boy, but God had given him a father who wanted Thomas to rise above common things. He wanted the boy to be a priest, which was why Thomas had just finished his first term at Oxford.

'What do you do at Oxford, Thomas?' Edward asked him.

'Everything I shouldn't,' Thomas said. He pushed black hair away from his face that was bony like his father's. He had very blue eyes, a long jaw, slightly hooded eyes and a swift smile. The girls in the village reckoned him handsome.

'Do they have girls at Oxford?' John asked slyly.

'More than enough,' Thomas said.

'Don't tell your father that,' Edward said, 'or he'll be whipping you again. A good man with a whip, your father.'

'There's none better,' Thomas agreed.

'He only wants the best for you,' John said. 'Can't blame a man for that.'

Thomas did blame his father. He had always blamed his father. He had fought his father for years, and nothing so raised the anger between them as Thomas's obsession with bows. His mother's father had been a bowyer in the Weald, and Thomas had lived with his grandfather until he was nearly ten. Then his father had brought him to Hookton, where he had met Sir Giles Marriott's huntsman, another man skilled in archery, and the huntsman had become his new tutor.

Thomas had made his first bow at eleven, but when his father found the elmwood weapon he had broken it across his knee and used the remnants to thrash his son. 'You are not a common man,' his father had shouted, beating the splintered staves on Thomas's back and head and legs, but neither the words nor the thrashing did any good. And as Thomas's father was usually preoccupied with other things, Thomas had plenty of time to pursue his obsession.

By fifteen he was as good a bowyer as his grandfather, knowing instinctively how to shape a stave of yew so that the inner belly came from the dense heartwood while the front was made of the springier sapwood, and when the bow was bent the heartwood was always trying to return to the straight and the sapwood was the muscle that made it possible. To Thomas's quick mind there was something elegant, simple and beautiful about a good bow. Smooth and strong, a good bow was like a girl's flat belly, and that night, keeping the Easter vigil in Hookton church, Thomas was reminded of Jane, who served in the village's small alehouse.

John, Edward and the other two men had been speaking of village things: the price of lambs at Dorchester fair, the old fox up on Lipp Hill that had taken a whole flock of geese in one night and the angel who had been seen over the rooftops at Lyme.

'I reckon they's been drinking too much,' Edward said.

'I sees angels when I drink,' John said.

'That be Jane,' Edward said. 'Looks like an angel, she does.'

'Don't behave like one,' John said. 'Lass is pregnant,' and all four men looked at Thomas, who stared innocently up at the treasure hanging from the rafters. In truth Thomas was frightened that the child was indeed his and terrified of what his father would say when he found out, but he pretended ignorance of Jane's pregnancy that night. He just looked at the treasure that was half obscured by a fishing net hung up to dry, while the four older men gradually fell asleep. A cold draught flickered the twin candle flames. A dog howled somewhere in the village, and always, never ending, Thomas could hear the sea's heartbeat as the waves thumped on the shingle then scraped back, paused and thumped again. He listened to the four men snoring and he prayed that his father would never find out about Jane, though that was unlikely for she was pressing Thomas to marry her and he did not know what to do. Maybe, he thought, he should just run away, take Jane and his bow and run, but he felt no certainty and so he just gazed at the relic in the church roof and prayed to its saint for help.

The treasure was a lance. It was a huge thing, with a shaft as thick as a man's forearm and twice the length of a man's height and probably made of ash though it was so old no one could really say, and age had bent the blackened shaft out of true, though not by much, and its tip was not an iron or steel blade, but a wedge of tarnished silver which tapered to a bodkin's point. The shaft did not swell to protect the handgrip, but was smooth like a spear or a goad; indeed the relic looked very like an oversized ox-goad, but no farmer would ever tip an ox-goad with silver. This was a weapon, a lance.

But it was not any old lance. This was the very lance which St George had used to kill the dragon. It was

England's lance, for St George was England's saint and that made it a very great treasure, even if it did hang in Hookton's spidery church roof. There were plenty of folk who said it could not have been St George's lance, but Thomas believed it was and he liked to imagine the dust churned by the hooves of St George's horse, and the dragon's breath streaming in hellish flame as the horse reared and the saint drew back the lance. The sunlight, bright as an angel's wing, would have been flaring about St George's helmet, and Thomas imagined the dragon's roar, the thrash of its scale-hooked tail, the horse screaming in terror, and he saw the saint stand in his stirrups before plunging the lance's silver tip down through the monster's armoured hide. Straight to the heart the lance went, and the dragon's squeals would have rung to heaven as it writhed and bled and died. Then the dust would have settled and the dragon's blood would have crusted on the desert sand, and St George must have hauled the lance free and some-how it ended up in Father Ralph's possession. But how? The priest would not say. But there it hung, a great dark lance, heavy enough to shatter a dragon's scales.

So that night Thomas prayed to St George while Jane, the black-haired beauty whose belly was just rounding with her unborn child, slept in the taproom of the ale-house, and Father Ralph cried aloud in his nightmare for fear of the demons that circled in the dark, and the vixens screamed on the hill as the endless waves clawed and sucked at the shingle on the Hook. It was the night before Easter.

Thomas woke to the sound of the village cockerels and saw that the expensive candles had burned down almost to their pewter holders. A grey light filled the window above the white-fronted altar. One day, Father Ralph had promised the village, that window would be a blaze of coloured glass showing St George skewering the dragon with the silver-headed lance, but for now the stone frame was filled with horn panes that turned the air within the church as yellow as urine.

Thomas stood, needing to piss, and the first awful screams sounded from the village.

For Easter had come, Christ was risen and the French were ashore.

The raiders came from Normandy in four boats that had sailed the night's west wind. Their leader, Sir Guillaume d'Evecque, the Sieur d'Evecque, was a seasoned warrior who had fought the English in Gascony and Flanders, and had twice led raids on England's southern coast. Both times he had brought his boats safe home with cargoes of wool, silver, livestock and women. He lived in a fine stone house on Caen's Île St Jean, where he was known as the knight of the sea and of the land. He was thirty years old, broad in the chest, wind-burned and fair-haired, a cheerful, unreflective man who made his living by piracy at sea and knight-service on shore, and now he had come to Hookton.

It was an insignificant place, hardly likely to yield any great reward, but Sir Guillaume had been hired for the task and if he failed at Hookton, if he did not snatch so much as one single poor coin from a villager, he would still make his profit for he had been promised one thousand livres for this expedition. The contract was signed and sealed, and it promised Sir Guillaume the one thousand livres together with any other plunder he could find in Hookton. One hundred livres had already been paid and the rest was in the keeping of Brother Martin in Caen's Abbaye aux Hommes, and all Sir Guillaume had to do to earn the remaining nine hundred livres was bring his boats to Hookton, take what he wanted, but leave the church's contents to the man who had offered him such a generous contract. That man now stood beside Sir Guillaume in the leading boat.

He was a young man, not yet thirty, tall and black-haired, who spoke rarely and smiled less. He wore an expensive coat of mail that fell to his knees and over it a surcoat of deep black linen that bore no badge, though Sir Guillaume guessed the man was nobly born for he had the arrogance of rank and the confidence of privilege. He was certainly not a Norman noble, for Sir Guillaume knew all those men, and Sir Guillaume doubted the young man came from nearby Alençon or Maine, for he had ridden with those forces often enough, but the sallow cast of the stranger's skin suggested he came from one of the Mediterranean provinces, from Languedoc perhaps, or Dauphine, and they were all mad down there. Mad as dogs. Sir Guillaume did not even know the man's name.

'Some men call me the Harlequin,' the stranger had answered when Sir Guillaume had asked.

'Harlequin?' Sir Guillaume had repeated the name, then made the sign of the cross for such a name was hardly a boast. 'You mean like the hellequin?'

'Hellequin in France,' the man had allowed, 'but in Italy they say harlequin. It is all the same.' The man had smiled, and something about that smile had suggested Sir Guillaume had best curb his curiosity

13

if he wanted to receive the remaining nine hundred livres.

The man who called himself the Harlequin now stared at the misty shore where a stumpy church tower, a huddle of vague roofs and a smear of smoke from the smouldering fires of the saltpans just showed. 'Is that Hookton?' he asked.

'So he says,' Sir Guillaume answered, jerking his head at the shipmaster.

'Then God have mercy on it,' the man said. He drew his sword, even though the four boats were still a half-mile from shore. The Genoese crossbowmen, hired for the voyage, made the sign of the cross, then began winding their cords as Sir Guillaume ordered his banner raised to the masthead. It was a blue flag decorated with three stooping yellow hawks that had outspread wings and claws hooked ready to savage their prey. Sir Guillaume could smell the salt fires and hear the cockerels crowing ashore.

The cockerels were still crowing as the bows of his four ships ran onto the shingle.

Sir Guillaume and the Harlequin were the first ashore, but after them came a score of Genoese crossbowmen, who were professional soldiers and knew their business. Their leader took them up the beach and through the village to block the valley beyond, where they would stop any of the villagers escaping with their valuables. Sir Guillaume's remaining men would ransack the houses while the sailors stayed on the beach to guard their ships.

It had been a long, cold and anxious night at sea, but now came the reward. Forty men-at-arms invaded Hookton. They wore close-fitting helmets and had mail

14

shirts over leather-backed hacquetons, they carried swords, axes or spears, and they were released to plunder. Most were veterans of Sir Guillaume's other raids and knew just what to do. Kick in the flimsy doors and start killing the men. Let the women scream, but kill the men, for it was the men who would fight back hardest. Some women ran, but the Genoese crossbowmen were there to stop them. Once the men were dead the plundering could begin, and that took time for peasants everywhere hid whatever was valuable and the hiding places had to be ferreted out. Thatch had to be pulled down, wells explored, floors probed, but plenty of things were not hidden. There were hams waiting for the first meal after Lent, racks of smoked or dried fish, piles of nets, good cooking pots, distaffs and spindles, eggs, butter churns, casks of salt – all humble enough things, but sufficiently valuable to take back to Normandy. Some houses yielded small hoards of coins, and one house, the priest's, was a treasure-trove of silver plate, candlesticks and jugs. There were even some good bolts of woollen cloth in the priest's house, and a great carved bed, and a decent horse in the stable. Sir Guillaume looked at the seventeen books, but decided they were worthless and so, having wrenched the bronze locks from the leather covers, he left them to burn when the houses were fired.

He had to kill the priest's housekeeper. He regretted that death. Sir Guillaume was not squeamish about killing women, but their deaths brought no honour and so he discouraged such slaughter unless the woman caused trouble, and the priest's housekeeper wanted to fight. She slashed at Sir Guillaume's men-at-arms with a roasting spit, called them sons of whores and devils' grubs, and in the end Sir Guillaume cut her down with his sword because she would not accept her fate.

'Stupid bitch,' Sir Guillaume said, stepping over her body to peer into the hearth. Two fine hams were being smoked in the chimney. 'Pull them down,' he ordered one of his men, then left them to search the house while he went to the church.

Father Ralph, woken by the screams of his parishioners, had pulled on a cassock and run to the church. Sir Guillaume's men had left him alone out of respect, but once inside the little church the priest had begun to hit the invaders until the Harlequin arrived and snarled at the men-at-arms to hold the priest. They seized his arms and held him in front of the altar with its white Easter frontal.

The Harlequin, his sword in his hand, bowed to Father Ralph. 'My lord Count,' he said.

Father Ralph closed his eyes, perhaps in prayer, though it looked more like exasperation. He opened them and gazed into the Harlequin's handsome face. 'You are my brother's son,' he said, and did not sound mad at all, merely full of regret.

'True.'

'How is your father?'

'Dead,' the Harlequin said, 'as is his father and yours.'

'God rest their souls,' Father Ralph said piously.

'And when you are dead, old man, I shall be the Count and our family will rise again.'

Father Ralph half smiled, then just shook his head and looked up at the lance. 'It will do you no good,' he said, 'for its power is reserved for virtuous men. It will not work for evil filth like you.' Then Father Ralph gave a curious mewing noise as the breath rushed from him

16

and he stared down to where his nephew had run the sword into his belly. He struggled to speak, but no words came, then he collapsed as the men-at-arms released him and he slumped by the altar with blood puddling in his lap.

The Harlequin wiped his sword on the wine-stained altar cloth, then ordered one of Sir Guillaume's men to find a ladder.

'A ladder?' the man-at-arms asked in confusion.

'They thatch their roofs, don't they? So they have a ladder. Find it.' The Harlequin sheathed his sword, then stared up at the lance of St George.

'I have put a curse on it.' Father Ralph spoke faintly. He was pale-faced, dying, but sounded oddly calm.

'Your curse, my lord, worries me as much as a tavern maid's fart.' The Harlequin tossed the pewter candlesticks to a man-at-arms, then scooped the wafers from the clay bowl and crammed them into his mouth. He picked up the bowl, peered at its darkened surface and reckoned it was a thing of no value so left it on the altar. 'Where's the wine?' he asked Father Ralph.

Father Ralph shook his head. *'Calix meus inebrians,'* he said, and the Harlequin just laughed. Father Ralph closed his eyes as the pain griped his belly. 'Oh God,' he moaned.

The Harlequin crouched by his uncle's side. 'Does it hurt?'

'Like fire,' Father Ralph said.

'You will burn in hell, my lord,' the Harlequin said, and he saw how Father Ralph was clutching his wounded belly to staunch the flow of blood and so he pulled the priest's hands away and then, standing, kicked him hard in the stomach. Father Ralph gasped

17

with pain and curled his body. 'A gift from your family,' the Harlequin said, then turned away as a ladder was brought into the church.

The village was filled with screams, for most of the women and children were still alive and their ordeal had scarcely begun. All the younger women were briskly raped by Sir Guillaume's men and the prettiest of them, including Jane from the alehouse, were taken to the boats so they could be carried back to Normandy to become the whores or wives of Sir Guillaume's soldiers. One of the women screamed because her baby was still in her house, but the soldiers did not understand her and they struck her to silence then pushed her into the hands of the sailors, who lay her on the shingle and lifted her skirts. She wept inconsolably as her house burned. Geese, pigs, goats, six cows and the priest's good horse were herded towards the boats while the white gulls rode the sky, crying.

The sun had scarcely risen above the eastern hills and the village had already yielded more than Sir Guillaume had dared hope for.

'We could go inland,' the captain of his Genoese crossbowmen suggested.

'We have what we came for,' the black-dressed Harlequin intervened. He had placed the unwieldy lance of St George on the graveyard grass, and now stared at the ancient weapon as though he was trying to understand its power.

'What is it?' the Genoese crossbowman asked.

'Nothing that is of use to you.'

Sir Guillaume grinned. 'Strike a blow with that,' he said, 'and it'll shatter like ivory.'

The Harlequin shrugged. He had found what he

18

wanted, and Sir Guillaume's opinion was of no interest.

'Go inland,' the Genoese captain suggested again.

'A few miles, maybe,' Sir Guillaume said. He knew that the dreaded English archers would eventually come to Hookton, but probably not till midday, and he wondered if there was another village close by that would be worth plundering. He watched a terrified girl, maybe eleven years old, being carried towards the beach by a soldier. 'How many dead?' he asked.

'Ours?' The Genoese captain seemed surprised by the question. 'None.'

'Not ours, theirs.'

'Thirty men? Forty? A few women?'

'And we haven't taken a scratch!' Sir Guillaume exulted. 'Pity to stop now.' He looked at his employer, but the man in black did not seem to care what they did, while the Genoese captain just grunted, which surprised Sir Guillaume for he thought the man was eager to extend the raid, but then he saw that the man's sullen grunt was not caused by any lack of enthusiasm, but by a white-feathered arrow that had buried itself in his breast. The arrow had slit through the mail shirt and padded hacqueton like a bodkin sliding through linen, killing the crossbowman almost instantly.

Sir Guillaume dropped flat and a heartbeat later another arrow whipped above him to thump into the turf. The Harlequin snatched up the lance and was running towards the beach while Sir Guillaume scrambled into the shelter of the church porch. 'Crossbows!' he shouted. 'Crossbows!'

Because someone was fighting back.

*　　*　　*

Thomas had heard the screams and, like the other four men in the church, he had gone to the door to see what they meant, but no sooner had they reached the porch than a band of armed men, their mail and helmets dark grey in the dawn, appeared in the graveyard.

Edward slammed the church door, dropped the bar into its brackets, then crossed himself. 'Sweet Jesus,' he said in astonishment, then flinched as an axe thumped into the door. 'Give me that!' He seized the sword from Thomas.

Thomas let him take it. The church door was shaking now as two or three axes attacked the old wood. The villagers had always reckoned that Hookton was much too small to be raided, but the church door was splintering in front of Thomas's eyes, and he knew it must be the French. Tales were told up and down the coast of such landings, and prayers were said to keep folk from the raids, but the enemy was here and the church echoed with the crash of their axe blows.

Thomas was in panic, but did not know it. He just knew he had to escape from the church and so he ran and jumped onto the altar. He crushed the silver chalice with his right foot and kicked it off the altar as he climbed onto the sill of the great east window where he beat at the yellow panes, shattering the horn down into the churchyard. He saw men in red and green jackets running past the alehouse, but none looked his way as he jumped down into the churchyard and ran to the ditch where he ripped his clothes as he wriggled through the thorn hedge on the other side. He crossed the lane, jumped the fence of his father's garden, and hammered on the kitchen door, but no one responded and a crossbow bolt smacked into the lintel just inches from his face. Thomas ducked and ran through the bean plants to the cattle shed where his father stabled a horse. There was no time to rescue the beast, so instead Thomas climbed into the hay loft where he hid his bow and arrows. A woman screamed close by. Dogs were howling. The French were shouting as they kicked down doors. Thomas seized his bow and arrow bag, ripped the thatch away from the rafters, squeezed through the gap and dropped into the neighbour's orchard.

He ran then as though the devil was on his heels. A crossbow bolt thumped into the turf as he came to Lipp Hill and two of the Genoese archers started to follow him, but Thomas was young and tall and strong and fast. He ran uphill through a pasture bright with cowslips and daisies, leaped a hurdle that blocked a gap in a hedge, then twisted right towards the hill's crest. He went as far as the wood on the hill's far side and there he dropped to catch his breath amidst a slope drifted with a haze of bluebells. He lay there, listening to the lambs in a nearby field. He waited, hearing nothing untoward. The crossbowmen had abandoned their pursuit.

Thomas lay in the bluebells for a long time, but at last he crept cautiously back to the hilltop from where he could see a straggle of old women and children scattering on the further hill. Those folk had somehow evaded the crossbowmen and would doubtless flee north to warn Sir Giles Marriott, but Thomas did not join them. Instead he worked his way down to a hazel copse where dog's mercury bloomed and from where he could see his village dying.

Men were carrying plunder to the four strange boats that were grounded on the Hook's shingle. The first thatch was being fired. Two dogs lay dead in the street beside a woman, quite naked, who was being held down while Frenchmen hitched up their mail shirts to take their turns with her. Thomas remembered how, not long ago, she had married a fisherman whose first wife had died in childbirth. She had been so coy and happy, but now, when she tried to crawl off the road, a Frenchman kicked her in the head, then bent with laughter. Thomas saw Jane, the girl he feared he had made pregnant, being dragged towards the boats and was ashamed that he felt a sense of relief that he would not have to confront his father with her news. More cottages were fired as Frenchmen hurled burning straw onto their thatch, and Thomas watched the smoke curl and thicken, then worked his way through the hazel saplings to a place where hawthorn blossom was thick, white and concealing. It was there he strung his bow.

It was the best bow he had ever made. It had been cut from a stave that had washed ashore from a ship that had foundered in the channel. A dozen staves had come to Hookton's shingle on the south wind and Sir Giles Marriott's huntsman reckoned they must have been Italian yew, for it was the most beautiful wood he had ever seen. Thomas had sold eleven of the tight-grained staves in Dorchester, but kept the best one. He'd carved it, steamed the ends to give them a slight bend against the wood's grain, then painted the bow with a mix of soot and flax-seed oil. He had boiled the mix in his mother's kitchen on days when his father was away, and Thomas's father had never known what he was doing, though sometimes he would complain of the smell and Thomas's mother would say she had been making a potion to poison the rats. The bow had had to be painted to stop it from drying out, for then the wood would become brittle and shatter under the stress of the taut string. The paint had dried a deep golden colour, just like the bows Thomas's grandfather used to make in the Weald, but Thomas had wanted it to be darker and so he had rubbed more soot into the wood and smeared it with beeswax, and he'd gone on doing it for a fortnight until the bow was as black as the shaft of St George's lance. He'd tipped the bow with two pieces of nocked horn to hold a cord that was made from woven hemp strands that had been soaked in hoof-glue, then he'd whipped the cord where the arrow would rest with still more hemp. He'd stolen coins from his father to buy arrow heads in Dorchester, then made the shafts from ash and goose feathers and on that Easter morning he had twenty-three of those good arrows in his bag.

Thomas strung the bow, took a white-fledged arrow from the bag, then looked at the three men beside the church. They were a long way off, but the black bow was as big a weapon as any ever made and the power in its yew belly was awesome. One of the men had a simple mail coat, another a plain black surcoat while the third had a red and green jacket over his mail shirt, and Thomas decided that the most gaudily dressed man must be the raid's leader and so he should die.

Thomas's left hand shook as he drew the bow. He was dry-mouthed, frightened. He knew he would shoot wild so he lowered his arm and released the cord's tension. Remember, he told himself, remember everything you have ever been taught. An archer does not aim, he kills. It is all in the head, in the arms, in the eyes, and killing a man is no different from shooting a hind. Draw

and loose, that was all, and that was why he had practised for over ten years so that the act of drawing and
loosing was as natural as breathing and as fluent as
water flowing from a spring. Look and loose, do not
think. Draw the string and let God guide the arrow.

Smoke thickened above Hookton, and Thomas felt
an immense anger surge like a black humour and he
pushed his left hand forward and drew back with the
right and he never took his eyes off the red and green
coat. He drew till the cord was beside his right ear and
then he loosed.

That was the first time Thomas of Hookton ever shot
an arrow at a man and he knew it was good as soon as
it leaped from the string, for the bow did not quiver.
The arrow flew true and he watched it curve down,
sinking from the hill to strike the green and red coat
hard and deep. He let a second arrow fly, but the man
in the mail coat dropped and scurried to the church
porch while the third man picked up the lance and ran
towards the beach where he was hidden by the smoke.

Thomas had twenty-one arrows left. One each for the
holy trinity, he thought, and another for every year
of his life, and that life was threatened, for a dozen
crossbowmen were running towards the hill. He loosed
a third arrow, then ran back through the hazels. He was
suddenly exultant, filled with a sense of power and
satisfaction. In that one instant, as the first arrow slid
into the sky, he knew he wanted nothing more from
life. He was an archer. Oxford could go to hell for all
he cared, for Thomas had found his joy. He whooped
with delight as he ran uphill. Crossbow bolts ripped
through the hazel leaves and he noted that they made
a deep, almost humming noise as they flew. Then he

was over the hill's crest where he ran west for a few yards before doubling back to the summit. He paused long enough to loose another arrow, then turned and ran again.

Thomas led the Genoese crossbowmen a dance of death – from hill to hedgerow, along paths he had known since childhood – and like fools they followed him because their pride would not let them admit that they were beaten. But beaten they were, and two died before a trumpet sounded from the beach, summoning the raiders to their boats. The Genoese turned away then, stopping only to fetch the weapon, pouches, mail and coat of one of their dead, but Thomas killed another of them as they stooped over the body and this time the survivors just ran from him.

Thomas followed them down to the smoke-palled village. He ran past the alehouse, which was an inferno, and so to the shingle where the four boats were being shoved into the sea-reach. The sailors pushed off with long oars, then pulled out to sea. They towed the best three Hookton boats and left the others burning. The village was also burning, its thatch whirling into the sky in sparks and smoke and flaming scraps. Thomas shot one last useless arrow from the beach and watched it plunge into the sea short of the escaping raiders, then he turned away and went back through the stinking, burning, bloody village to the church, which was the only building the raiders had not set alight. The four companions of his vigil were dead, but Father Ralph still lived. He was sitting with his back against the altar. The bottom of his gown was dark with fresh blood and his long face was unnaturally white.

Thomas kneeled beside the priest. 'Father?'

Father Ralph opened his eyes and saw the bow. He grimaced, though whether in pain or disapproval, Thomas could not tell.

'Did you kill any of them, Thomas?' the priest asked.

'Yes,' Thomas said, 'a lot.'

Father Ralph grimaced and shuddered. Thomas reckoned the priest was one of the strongest men he had ever known, flawed perhaps, yet tough as a yew stave, but he was dying now and there was a whimper in his voice. 'You don't want to be a priest, do you, Thomas?' He asked the question in French, his mother tongue.

'No,' Thomas answered in the same language.

'You're going to be a soldier,' the priest said, 'like your grandfather.' He paused and whimpered as another bolt of pain ripped up from his belly. Thomas wanted to help him, but in truth there was nothing to be done. The Harlequin had run his sword into Father Ralph's belly and only God could save the priest now. 'I argued with my father,' the dying man said, 'and he disowned me. He disinherited me and I have refused to acknowledge him from that day to this. But you, Thomas, you are like him. Very like him. And you have always argued with me.'

'Yes, Father,' Thomas said. He took his father's hand and the priest did not resist.

'I loved your mother,' Father Ralph said, 'and that was my sin, and you are the fruit of that sin. I thought if you became a priest you could rise above sin. It floods us, Thomas, it floods us. It is everywhere. I have seen the devil, Thomas, seen him with my own eyes and we must fight him. Only the Church can do that. Only the Church.' The tears flowed down his hollow unshaven cheeks. He looked past Thomas into the roof of the nave. 'They stole the lance,' he said sadly.

'I know.'

'My great-grandfather brought it from the Holy Land,' Father Ralph said, 'and I stole it from my father and my brother's son stole it from us today.' He spoke softly. 'He will do evil with it. Bring it home, Thomas. Bring it home.'

'I will,' Thomas promised him. Smoke began to thicken in the church. The raiders had not fired it, but the thatch was catching the flames from the burning scraps that filled the air. 'You say your brother's son stole it?' Thomas asked.

'Your cousin,' Father Ralph whispered, his eyes closed. 'The one dressed in black. He came and stole it.'

'Who is he?' Thomas asked.

'Evil,' Father Ralph said, 'evil.' He moaned and shook his head.

'Who is he?' Thomas insisted.

'*Calix meus inebrians*.' Father Ralph said in a voice scarce above a whisper. Thomas knew it was a line from a psalm and meant 'my cup makes me drunk' and he reckoned his father's mind was slipping as his soul hovered close to his body's end.

'Tell me who your father was!' Thomas demanded. Tell me who I am, he wanted to say. Tell me who you are, Father. But Father Ralph's eyes were closed though he still gripped Thomas's hand hard. 'Father?' Thomas asked. The smoke dipped in the church and sifted out through the window Thomas had broken to make his escape. 'Father?'

But his father never spoke again. He died, and Thomas, who had fought against him all his life, wept like a child. At times he had been ashamed of his father, but in that smoky Easter morning he learned that he loved him. Most priests disowned their children, but Father Ralph had never hidden Thomas. He had let the world think what it wanted and he had freely confessed to being a man as well as a priest and if he sinned in loving his housekeeper then it was a sweet sin that he never denied even if he did say acts of contrition for it and feared that in the life hereafter he would be punished for it.

Thomas pulled his father away from the altar. He did not want the body to be burned when the roof collapsed. The silver chalice that Thomas had accidentally crushed was under the dead man's blood-soaked robe and Thomas pocketed it before dragging the corpse out into the graveyard. He lay his father beside the body of the man in the red and green coat and Thomas crouched there, weeping, knowing that he had failed in his first Easter vigil. The devil had stolen the Sacraments and St George's lance was gone and Hookton was dead.

At midday Sir Giles Marriott came to the village with a score of men armed with bows and billhooks. Sir Giles himself wore mail and carried a sword, but there was no enemy left to fight and Thomas was the only person left in the village.

'Three yellow hawks on a blue field,' Thomas told Sir Giles.

'Thomas?' Sir Giles asked, puzzled. He was the lord of the manor and an old man now, though in his time he had carried a lance against both the Scots and the French. He had been a good friend to Thomas's father, but he did not understand Thomas, whom he reckoned had grown wild as a wolf.

'Three yellow hawks on a blue field,' Thomas said vengefully, 'are the arms of the man who did this.' Were they the arms of his cousin? He did not know. There were so many questions left by his father.

'I don't know whose badge that is,' Sir Giles said, 'but I shall pray by God's bowels he screams in hell for this work.'

There was nothing to be done until the fires had burned themselves out, and only then could the bodies be dragged from the ashes. The burned dead had been blackened and grotesquely shrunk by the heat so that even the tallest men looked like children. The dead villagers were taken to the graveyard for a proper burial, but the bodies of the four crossbowmen were dragged down to the beach and there stripped naked.

'Did you do this?' Sir Giles asked Thomas.

'Yes, sir.'

'Then I thank you.'

'My first dead Frenchmen,' Thomas said angrily.

'No,' Sir Giles said, and he lifted one of the men's tunics to show Thomas the badge of a green chalice embroidered on its sleeve. 'They're from Genoa,' Sir Giles said. 'The French hire them as crossbowmen. I've killed a few in my time, but there are always more where they come from. You know what the badge is?'

'A cup?'

Sir Giles shook his head. 'The Holy Grail. They reckon they have it in their cathedral. I'm told it's a great green thing, carved from an emerald and brought back from the crusades. I should like to see it one day.'

'Then I shall bring it to you,' Thomas said bitterly, 'just as I shall bring back our lance.'

Sir Giles stared to sea. The raiders' boats were long

gone and there was nothing out there but the sun on the waves. 'Why would they come here?' he asked.

'For the lance.'

'I doubt it was even real,' Sir Giles said. He was red-faced, white-haired and heavy now. 'It was just an old spear, nothing more.'

'It's real,' Thomas insisted, 'and that's why they came.'

Sir Giles did not argue. 'Your father,' he said instead, 'would have wanted you to finish your studies.'

'My studies are done,' Thomas said flatly. 'I'm going to France.'

Sir Giles nodded. He reckoned the boy was far better suited to be a soldier than a priest. 'Will you go as an archer?' he asked, looking at the great bow on Thomas's shoulder, 'or do you want to join my house and train to be a man-at-arms?' He half smiled. 'You're gently born, you know?'

'I'm bastard born,' Thomas insisted.

'Your father was of good birth.'

'You know what family?' Thomas asked.

Sir Giles shrugged. 'He would never tell me, and if I pressed him he would just say that God was his father and his mother was the Church.'

'And my mother,' Thomas said, 'was a priest's house-keeper and the daughter of a bowyer. I shall go to France as an archer.'

'There's more honour as a man-at-arms,' Sir Giles observed, but Thomas did not want honour. He wanted revenge.

Sir Giles let him choose what he wanted from the enemy's dead and Thomas picked a mail coat, a pair of long boots, a knife, a sword, a belt and a helmet. It was all plain gear, but serviceable, and only the mail coat needed mending, for he had driven an arrow clean through its rings. Sir Giles said he owed Thomas's father money, which may or may not have been true, but he paid it to Thomas with the gift of a four-year-old gelding. 'You'll need a horse,' he said, 'for nowadays all archers are mounted. Go to Dorchester,' he advised Thomas, 'and like as not you'll find someone recruiting bowmen.'

The Genoese corpses were beheaded and their bodies left to rot while their four heads were impaled on stakes and planted along the Hook's shingle ridge. The gulls fed on the dead men's eyes and pecked at their flesh until the heads were flensed down to bare bones that stared vacantly to the sea.

But Thomas did not see the skulls. He had gone across the water, taken his black bow and joined the wars.

PART ONE

Brittany

It was winter. A cold morning wind blew from the sea bringing a sour salt smell and a spitting rain that would inevitably sap the power of the bowstrings if it did not let up.

'What it is,' Jake said, 'is a waste of goddamn time.'

No one took any notice of him.

'Could have stayed in Brest,' Jake grumbled, 'been sitting by a fire. Drinking ale.'

Again he was ignored.

'Funny name for a town,' Sam said after a long while. 'Brest. I like it, though.' He looked at the archers. 'Maybe we'll see the Blackbird again?' he suggested.

'Maybe she'll put a bolt through your tongue,' Will Skeat growled, 'and do us all a favour.'

The Blackbird was a woman who fought from the town walls every time the army made an assault. She was young, had black hair, wore a black cloak and shot a crossbow. In the first assault, when Will Skeat's archers had been in the vanguard of the attack and had lost four men, they had been close enough to see the Blackbird clearly and they had all thought her beautiful, though after a winter campaign of failure, cold, mud and hunger, almost any woman looked beautiful. Still, there was something special about the Blackbird.

'She doesn't load that crossbow herself,' Sam said, unmoved by Skeat's surliness.

'Of course she bloody doesn't,' Jake said. 'There ain't a woman born that can crank a crossbow.'

'Dozy Mary could,' another man said. 'Got muscles like a bullock, she has.'

'And she closes her eyes when she shoots,' Sam said, still talking of the Blackbird. 'I noticed.'

'That's because you weren't doing your goddamn job,' Will Skeat snarled, 'so shut your mouth, Sam.'

Sam was the youngest of Skeat's men. He claimed to be eighteen, though he was really not sure because he had lost count. He was a draper's son, had a cherubic face, brown curls and a heart as dark as sin. He was a good archer though; no one could serve Will Skeat without being good.

'Right, lads,' Skeat said, 'make ready.'

He had seen the stir in the encampment behind them. The enemy would notice it soon and the church bells would ring the alarm and the town walls would fill with defenders armed with crossbows. The crossbows would rip their bolts into the attackers and Skeat's job today was to try to clear those crossbowmen off the wall with his arrows. Some chance, he thought sourly. The defenders would crouch behind their crenellations and so deny his men an opportunity to aim, and doubtless this assault would end as the five other attacks had finished, in failure.

It had been a whole campaign of failure. William Bohun, the Earl of Northampton, who led this small English army, had launched the winter expedition in hope of capturing a stronghold in northern Brittany, but the assault on Carhaix had been a humiliating failure, the defenders of Guingamp had laughed at the English, and the walls of Lannion had repulsed every attack. They had captured Tréguier, but as that town had no walls it was not much of an achievement and no place to make a fortress. Now, at the bitter end of the year, with nothing better to do, the Earl's army had fetched up outside this small town, which was scarcely more than a walled village, but even this miserable place had defied the army. The Earl had launched attack after attack and all had been beaten back. The English had been met by a storm of crossbow bolts, the scaling ladders had been thrust from the ramparts and the defenders had exulted in each failure.

'What is this goddamn place called?' Skeat asked.

'La Roche-Derrien,' a tall archer answered.

'You would know, Tom,' Skeat said, 'you know everything.'

'That is true, Will,' Thomas said gravely, 'quite literally true.' The other archers laughed.

'So if you know so bloody much,' Skeat said, 'tell me what this goddamn town is called again.'

'La Roche-Derrien.'

'Daft bloody name,' Skeat said. He was grey-haired, thin-faced and had known nearly thirty years of fighting. He came from Yorkshire and had begun his career as an archer fighting against the Scots. He had been as lucky as he was skilled, and so he had taken plunder, survived battles and risen in the ranks until he was wealthy enough to raise his own band of soldiers. He now led seventy men-at-arms and as many archers, whom he had contracted to the Earl of Northampton's service which was why he was crouching behind a wet hedge a hundred and fifty paces from the walls of a town whose name he still could not remember. His men-at-arms were in the camp, given a day's rest after leading the last failed assault. Will Skeat hated failure.

'La Roche what?' he asked Thomas.

'Derrien.'

'What does that goddamn mean?'

'That, I confess, I do not know.'

'Sweet Christ,' Skeat said in mock wonder, 'he doesn't know everything.'

'It is, however, close to *derrière*, which means arse,' Thomas added. 'The rock of the arse is my best translation.'

Skeat opened his mouth to say something, but just then the first of La Roche-Derrien's church bells sounded the alarm. It was the cracked bell, the one that sounded so harsh, and within seconds the other churches added their tolling so that the wet wind was filled with their clangour. The noise was greeted by a subdued English cheer as the assault troops came from the camp and pounded up the road towards the town's southern gate. The leading men carried ladders, the rest had swords and axes. The Earl of Northampton led the assault, as he had led all the others, conspicuous in his plate armour half covered by a surcoat showing his badge of the lions and stars.

'You know what to do!' Skeat bellowed.

The archers stood, drew their bows and loosed. There were no targets on the walls, for the defenders were staying low, but the rattle of the steel-tipped arrows on the stones should keep them crouching. The white-feathered arrows hissed as they flew. Two other archer bands were adding their own shafts, many of them firing high into the sky so that their missiles dropped vertically onto the wall's top, and to Skeat it seemed impossible that anyone could live under that hail of feather-tipped steel, yet as soon as the Earl's attacking column came within a hundred paces the crossbow bolts began to spit from the walls.

There was a breach close to the gate. It had been made by a catapult, the only siege machine left in decent repair, and it was a poor breach, for only the top third of the wall had been dismantled by the big stones and the townsfolk had crammed timber and bundles of cloth into the gap, but it was still a weakness in the wall and the ladder men ran towards it, shouting, as the crossbow bolts whipped into them. Men stumbled, fell, crawled and died, but enough lived to throw two ladders against the breach and the first men-at-arms began to climb. The archers were loosing as fast as they could, overwhelming the top of the breach with arrows, but then a shield appeared there, a shield that was immediately stuck by a score of shafts, and from behind the shield a crossbowman shot straight down one of the ladders, killing the leading man. Another shield appeared, another crossbow was loosed. A pot was shoved onto the breach's top, then toppled over, and a gush of steaming liquid spilled down to make a man scream in agony. Defenders were hurling boulders over the breach and their crossbows were snapping.

'Closer!' Skeat shouted, and his archers pushed through the hedge and ran to within a hundred paces of the town ditch, where they again loosed their long war bows and slashed their arrows into the embrasures. Some defenders were dying now, for they had to show themselves to shoot their crossbows down into the crowd of men who jostled at the foot of the four ladders that had been laid against the breach or walls. Men-at-arms climbed, a forked pole shoved one ladder back and Thomas twitched his left hand to change his aim and released his fingers to drive an arrow into the breast of a man pushing on the pole. The man had been covered by a shield held by a companion, but the shield shifted for an instant and Thomas's arrow was the first through the small gap, though two more followed before the dying man's last heartbeat ended. Other men succeeded in toppling the ladder. 'St George!' the English shouted, but the saint must have been sleeping for he gave the attackers no help.

More stones were hurled from the ramparts, then a great mass of flaming straw was heaved into the crowded attackers. A man succeeded in reaching the top of the breach, but was immediately killed by an axe that split his helmet and skull in two. He slumped on the rungs, blocking the ascent, and the Earl tried to haul him free, but was struck on the head by one of the boulders and collapsed at the ladder's foot. Two of his men-at-arms carried the stunned Earl back to the camp and his departure took the spirit from the attackers. They no longer shouted. The arrows still flew, and men still tried to climb the wall, but the defenders sensed they had repelled this sixth attack and their crossbow bolts spat relentlessly. It was then Thomas saw the Blackbird on the tower above the gate. He laid the steel arrow tip on her breast, raised the bow a fraction and then jerked his bow hand so that the arrow flew wild. Too pretty to kill, he told himself and knew he was a fool for thinking it. She shot her bolt and vanished. A half-dozen arrows clattered onto the tower where she had been standing, but Thomas reckoned all six archers had let her shoot before they loosed.

'Jesus wept,' Skeat said. The attack had failed and the men-at-arms were running from the crossbow bolts. One ladder still rested against the breach with the dead man entangled in its upper rungs. 'Back,' Skeat shouted, 'back.'

The archers ran, pursued by quarrels, until they could push through the hedge and drop into the ditch. The defenders were cheering and two men bared their back-sides on the gate tower and briefly shoved their arses towards the defeated English.

'Bastards,' Skeat said, 'bastards.' He was not used to failure. 'There has to be a bloody way in,' he growled.

Thomas unlooped the string from his bow and placed it under his helmet. 'I told you how to get in,' he told Skeat, 'told you at dawn.'

Skeat looked at Thomas for a long time. 'We tried it, lad.'

'I got to the stakes, Will. I promise I did. I got through them.'

'So tell me again,' Skeat said, and Thomas did. He crouched in the ditch under the jeers of La Roche-Derrien's defenders and he told Will Skeat how to unlock the town, and Skeat listened because the York-shireman had learned to trust Thomas of Hookton.

Thomas had been in Brittany for three years now, and though Brittany was not France its usurping Duke brought a constant succession of Frenchman to be killed and Thomas had discovered he had a skill for killing. It was not just that he was a good archer – the army was full of men who were as good as he and there was a handful who were better – but he had discovered he could sense what the enemy was doing. He would watch them, watch their eyes, see where they were looking, and as often as not he anticipated an enemy move and was ready to greet it with an arrow. It was like a game, but one where he knew the rules and they did not.

It helped that William Skeat trusted him. Skeat had been unwilling to recruit Thomas when they first met by the gaol in Dorchester where Skeat was testing a score of thieves and murderers to see how well they could shoot a bow. He needed recruits and the King needed archers, so men who would otherwise have faced the gallows were being pardoned if they would serve abroad, and fully half of Skeat's men were such felons. Thomas, Skeat had reckoned, would never fit in with such rogues. He had taken Thomas's right hand, seen the callouses on the two bow fingers which said he was an archer, but then had tapped the boy's soft palm.

'What have you been doing?' Skeat had asked.

'My father wanted me to be a priest.'

'A priest, eh?' Skeat had been scornful. 'Well, you can pray for us, I suppose.'

'I can kill for you too.'

Skeat had eventually let Thomas join the band, not least because the boy brought his own horse. At first Skeat thought Thomas of Hookton was little more than another wild fool looking for adventure – a clever fool, to be sure – but Thomas had taken to the life of an archer in Brittany with alacrity. The real business of the civil war was plunder and, day after day, Skeat's men rode into land that gave fealty to the supporters of Duke Charles and they burned the farms, stole the harvest and took the livestock. A lord whose peasants cannot pay rent is a lord who cannot afford to hire soldiers, so Skeat's men-at-arms and mounted archers were loosed on the enemy's land like a plague, and Thomas loved the life. He was young and his task was not just to fight the enemy, but to ruin him. He burned farms, poisoned wells, stole seed-grain, broke ploughs, fired the mills, ring-barked the orchards and lived off his plunder. Skeat's men were the lords of Brittany, a scourge from hell, and the French-speaking villagers in the east of the Duchy called them the *hellequin*, which meant the devil's horsemen. Once in a while an enemy war band would seek to trap them and Thomas had learned that the English archer, with his great long war bow, was the king of those skirmishes. The enemy hated the archers. If they captured an English bowman they killed him. A man-at-arms might be imprisoned, a lord would be ransomed, but an archer was always murdered. Tortured first, then murdered.

Thomas thrived on the life, and Skeat had learned the lad was clever, certainly clever enough to know better than to fall asleep one night when he should have been standing guard and, for that offence Skeat had thumped the daylights out of him. 'You were goddamn drunk!' he had accused Thomas, then beat him thoroughly, using his fists like blacksmith's hammers. He had broken Thomas's nose, cracked a rib and called him a stinking piece of Satan's shit, but at the end of it Will Skeat saw that the boy was still grinning, and six months later he made Thomas into a vintenar, which meant he was in charge of twenty other archers.

Those twenty were nearly all older than Thomas, but none seemed to mind his promotion for they reckoned he was different. Most archers wore their hair cropped short, but Thomas's hair was flamboyantly long and wrapped with bowcords so it fell in a long black plait to his waist. He was clean-shaven and dressed only in black. Such affectations could have made him unpopular, but he worked hard, had a quick wit and was generous. He was still odd, though. All archers wore talismans, maybe a cheap metal pendant showing a saint, or a dried hare's foot, but Thomas had a desiccated dog's paw hanging round his neck which he claimed was the hand of St Guinefort, and no one dared dispute him because he was the most learned man in Skeat's band. He spoke French like a nobleman and Latin like a priest, and Skeat's archers were perversely proud of him because of those accomplishments. Now, three years after joining Will Skeat's band, Thomas was one of his chief archers. Skeat even asked his advice sometimes; he rarely took it, but he asked, and Thomas still had the dog's paw, a crooked nose and an impudent grin.

And now he had an idea how to get into La Roche-Derrien.

That afternoon, when the dead man-at-arms with the split skull was still tangled in the abandoned ladder, Sir Simon Jekyll rode towards the town and there trotted his horse back and forth beside the small, dark-feathered crossbow bolts that marked the furthest range of the defenders' weapons. His squire, a daft boy with a slack jaw and puzzled eyes, watched from a distance. The squire held Sir Simon's lance, and should any warrior in the town accept the implicit challenge of Sir Simon's mocking presence, the squire would give his master the lance and the two horsemen would fight on the pasture until one or the other yielded. And it would not be Sir Simon for he was as skilled a knight as any in the Earl of Northampton's army.

And the poorest.

His destrier was ten years old, hard-mouthed and sway-backed. His saddle, which was high in pommel and cantle so that it held him firm in its grip, had belonged to his father, while his hauberk, a tunic of mail that covered him from neck to knees, had belonged to his grandfather. His sword was over a hundred years old, heavy, and would not keep its edge. His lance had warped in the wet winter weather, while his helmet, which hung from his pommel, was an old steel pot with a worn leather lining. His shield, with its escutcheon of a mailed fist clutching a war-hammer, was battered and faded. His mail gauntlets, like the rest of his armour, were rusting, which was why his squire had a thick, reddened ear and a frightened face, though the real reason for the rust was not that the squire did not try to clean the mail, but that Sir Simon could not afford the vinegar and fine sand that was used to scour the steel. He was poor.

Poor and bitter and ambitious.

And good.

No one denied he was good. He had won the tournament at Tewkesbury and received a purse of forty pounds. At Gloucester his victory had been rewarded by a fine suit of armour. At Chelmsford it had been fifteen pounds and a fine saddle, and at Canterbury he had half hacked a Frenchman to death before being given a gilded cup filled with coins, and where were all those trophies now? In the hands of the bankers and lawyers and merchants who had a lien on the Berkshire estate that Sir Simon had inherited two years before, though in truth his inheritance had been nothing but debt, and the moment his father was buried the moneylenders had closed on Sir Simon like hounds on a wounded deer.

'Marry an heiress,' his mother had advised, and she had paraded a dozen women for her son's inspection, but Sir Simon was determined his wife should be as beautiful as he was handsome. And he was handsome. He knew that. He would stare into his mother's mirror and admire his reflection. He had thick fair hair, a broad face and a short beard. At Chester, where he had unhorsed three knights inside four minutes, men had mistaken him for the King, who was reputed to fight anonymously in tournaments, and Sir Simon was not going to throw away his good royal looks on some wrinkled hag just because she had money. He would marry a woman worthy of himself, but that ambition would not pay the estate's debts and so Sir Simon, to defend himself against his creditors, had sought a letter of protection from King Edward III. That letter shielded Sir Simon from all legal proceedings so long as he served the King in a foreign war, and when Sir Simon had crossed the Channel, taking six men-at-arms, a dozen archers and a slack-jawed squire from his encumbered estate, he had left his creditors helpless in England. Sir Simon had also brought with him a certainty that he would soon capture some French or Breton nobleman whose ransom would be sufficient to pay all he owed, but so far the winter campaign had not yielded a single prisoner of rank and so little plunder that the army was now on half rations. And how many well-born prisoners could he expect to take in a miserable town like La Roche-Derrien? It was a shit hole.

Yet he rode up and down beneath its walls, hoping some knight would take the challenge and ride from the town's southern gate that had so far resisted six English assaults, but instead the defenders jeered him and called him a coward for staying out of their crossbows' range and the insults piqued Sir Simon's pride so that he rode closer to the walls, his horse's hoofs sometimes clattering on one of the fallen quarrels. Men shot at him, but the bolts fell well short and it was Sir Simon's turn to jeer.

'He's just a bloody fool,' Jake said, watching from the English camp. Jake was one of William Skeat's felons, a murderer who had been saved from the gallows at Exeter. He was cross-eyed, yet still managed to shoot straighter than most men. 'Now what's he doing?'

Sir Simon had stopped his horse and was facing the gate so that the men who watched thought that perhaps a Frenchman was coming to challenge the English knight who taunted them. Instead they saw that a lone crossbowman was standing on the gate turret and beckoning Sir Simon forward, daring him to come within range.

Only a fool would respond to such a dare, and Sir Simon dutifully responded. He was twenty-five years old, bitter and brave, and he reckoned a display of careless arrogance would dishearten the besieged garrison and encourage the dispirited English and so he spurred the destrier deep into the killing ground where the French bolts had torn the heart out of the English attacks. No crossbowman fired now; there was just the lone figure standing on the gate tower, and Sir Simon, riding to within a hundred yards, saw it was the Blackbird.

This was the first time Sir Simon had seen the woman every archer called the Blackbird and he was close enough to perceive that she was indeed a beauty. She stood straight, slender and tall, cloaked against the winter wind, but with her long black hair loose like a young girl's. She offered him a mocking bow and Sir Simon responded, bending awkwardly in the tight saddle, then he watched as she picked up her crossbow and put it to her shoulder.

And when we're inside the town, Sir Simon thought, I'll make you pay for this. You'll be flat on your arse, Blackbird, and I'll be on top. He stood his horse quite still, a lone horseman in the French slaughter ground, daring her to aim straight and knowing she would not. And when she missed he would give her a mocking salute and the French would take it as a bad omen.

But what if she did aim straight?

Sir Simon was tempted to lift the awkward helmet from his saddle's pommel, but resisted the impulse. He had dared the Blackbird to do her worst and he could show no nerves in front of a woman and so he waited as she levelled the bow. The town's defenders were watching her and doubtless praying. Or perhaps making wagers.

Come on, you bitch, he said under his breath. It was cold, but there was sweat on his forehead.

She paused, pushed the black hair from her face, then rested the bow on a crenellation and aimed again. Sir Simon kept his head up and his gaze straight. Just a woman, he told himself. Probably could not hit a wagon at five paces. His horse shivered and he reached out to pat its neck. 'Be going soon, boy,' he told it.

The Blackbird, watched by a score of defenders, closed her eyes and shot.

Sir Simon saw the quarrel as a small black blur against the grey sky and the grey stones of the church towers showing above La Roche-Derrien's walls.

He knew the quarrel would go wide. Knew it with an absolute certainty. She was a woman, for God's sake! And that was why he did not move as he saw the blur coming straight for him. He could not believe it. He was waiting for the quarrel to slide to left or right, or to plough into the frost-hardened ground, but instead it was coming unerringly towards his breast and, at the very last instant, he jerked up the heavy shield and ducked his head and felt a huge thump on his left arm as the bolt slammed home to throw him hard against the saddle's cantle. The bolt hit the shield so hard that it split through the willow boards and its point gouged a deep cut through the mail sleeve and into his forearm. The French were cheering and Sir Simon, knowing that other crossbowmen might now try to finish what the Blackbird had begun, pressed his knee into his destrier's flank and the beast obediently turned and then responded to the spurs.

'I'm alive,' he said aloud, as if that would silence the French jubilation. Goddamn bitch, he thought. He would pay her right enough, pay her till she squealed, and he curbed his horse, not wanting to look as though he fled.

An hour later, after his squire had put a bandage over the slashed forearm, Sir Simon had convinced himself that he had scored a victory. He had dared, he had survived. It had been a demonstration of courage, and he lived, and for that he reckoned he was a hero and he expected a hero's welcome as he walked toward the tent that housed the army's commander, the Earl of Northampton. The tent was made from two sails, their linen yellow and patched and threadbare after years of service at sea. They made a shabby shelter, but that was typical of William Bohun, Earl of Northampton who, though cousin to the King and as rich a man as any in England, despised gaudiness.

The Earl, indeed, looked as patched and threadbare as the sails that made his tent. He was a short and squat man with a face, men said, like the backside of a bull, but the face mirrored the Earl's soul, which was blunt, brave and straightforward. The army liked William Bohun, Earl of Northampton, because he was as tough as they were themselves. Now, as Sir Simon ducked into the tent, the Earl's curly brown hair was half covered with a bandage where the boulder thrown from La Roche-Derrien's wall had split his helmet and driven a ragged edge of steel into his scalp. He greeted Sir Simon sourly. 'Tired of life?'

'The silly bitch shut her eyes when she pulled the trigger!' Sir Simon said, oblivious to the Earl's tone.

'She still aimed well,' the Earl said angrily, 'and that will put heart into the bastards. God knows, they need no encouragement.'

'I'm alive, my lord,' Sir Simon said cheerfully. 'She wanted to kill me. She failed. The bear lives and the dogs go hungry.' He waited for the Earl's companions to congratulate him, but they avoided his eyes and he interpreted their sullen silence as jealousy.

Sir Simon was a bloody fool, the Earl thought, and

50

shivered. He might not have minded the cold so much had the army been enjoying success, but for two months the English and their Breton allies had stumbled from failure to farce, and the six assaults on La Roche-Derrien had plumbed the depths of misery. So now the Earl had called a council of war to suggest one final assault, this one to be made that same evening. Every other attack had been in the forenoon, but perhaps a surprise escalade in the dying winter light would take the defenders by surprise. Only what small advantages that surprise might bring had been spoiled because Sir Simon's foolhardiness must have given the townsfolk a new confidence and there was little confidence among the Earl's war captains who had gathered under the yellow sailcloth.

Four of those captains were knights who, like Sir Simon, led their own men to war, but the others were mercenary soldiers who had contracted their men to the Earl's service. Three were Bretons who wore the white ermine badge of the Duke of Brittany and led men loyal to the de Montfort Duke, while the others were English captains, all of them commoners who had grown hard in war. William Skeat was there, and next to him was Richard Totesham, who had begun his service as a man-at-arms and now led a hundred and forty knights and ninety archers in the Earl's service. Neither man had ever fought in a tournament, nor would they ever be invited, yet both were wealthier than Sir Simon, and that rankled. My hounds of war, the Earl of Northampton called the independent captains, and the Earl liked them, but then the Earl had a curious taste for vulgar company. He might be cousin to England's King, but William Bohun happily drank with men like Skeat

51

and Totesham, ate with them, spoke English with them, hunted with them and trusted them, and Sir Simon felt excluded from that friendship. If any man in this army should have been an intimate of the Earl it was Sir Simon, a noted champion of tournaments, but Northampton would rather roll in the gutter with men like Skeat.

'How's the rain?' the Earl asked.

'Starting again,' Sir Simon answered, jerking his head at the tent's roof, against which the rain pattered fitfully.

'It'll clear,' Skeat said dourly. He rarely called the Earl 'my lord', addressing him instead as an equal which, to Sir Simon's amazement, the Earl seemed to like.

'And it's only spitting,' the Earl said, peering out from the tent and letting in a swirl of damp, cold air. 'Bowstrings will pluck in this.'

'So will crossbow cords,' Richard Totesham interjected. 'Bastards,' he added. What made the English failure so galling was that La Roche-Derrien's defenders were not soldiers but townsfolk: fishermen and boatbuilders, carpenters and masons, and even the Blackbird, a woman! 'And the rain might stop,' Totesham went on, 'but the ground will be slick. It'll be bad footing under the walls.'

'Don't go tonight,' Will Skeat advised. 'Let my boys go in by the river tomorrow morning.'

The Earl rubbed the wound on his scalp. For a week now he had assaulted La Roche-Derrien's southern wall and he still believed his men could take those ramparts, yet he also sensed the pessimism among his hounds of war. One more repulse with another twenty or thirty dead would leave his army dispirited and with the prospect of trailing back to Finisterre with nothing accomplished. 'Tell me again,' he said.

Skeat wiped his nose on his leather sleeve. 'At low tide,' he said, 'there's a way round the north wall. One of my lads was down there last night.'

'We tried it three days ago,' one of the knights objected.

'You tried the down-river side,' Skeat said. 'I want to go up-river.'

'That side has stakes just like the other,' the Earl said.

'Loose,' Skeat responded. One of the Breton captains translated the exchange for his companions. 'My boy pulled a stake clean out,' Skeat went on, 'and he reckons half a dozen others will lift or break. They're old oak trunks, he says, instead of elm, and they're rotted through.'

'How deep is the mud?' the Earl asked.

'Up to his knees.'

La Roche-Derrien's wall encompassed the west, south and east of the town, while the northern side was defended by the River Jaudy, and where the semicircular wall met the river the townsfolk had planted huge stakes in the mud to block access at low tide. Skeat was now suggesting there was a way through those rotted stakes, but when the Earl's men had tried to do the same thing at the eastern side of the town the attackers had got bogged down in the mud and the townsfolk had picked them off with bolts. It had been a worse slaughter than the repulses in front of the southern gate.

'But there's still a wall on the riverbank,' the Earl pointed out.

'Aye,' Skeat allowed, 'but the silly bastards have

broken it down in places. They've built quays there, and there's one right close to the loose stakes.'

'So your men will have to remove the stakes and climb the quays, all under the gaze of men on the wall?' the Earl asked sceptically.

'They can do it,' Skeat said firmly.

The Earl still reckoned his best chance of success was to close his archers on the south gate and pray that their arrows would keep the defenders cowering while his men-at-arms assaulted the breach, yet that, he conceded, was the plan that had failed earlier in the day and on the day before that. And he had, he knew, only a day or two left. He possessed fewer than three thousand men, and a third of those were sick, and if he could not find them shelter he would have to march back west with his tail between his legs. He needed a town, any town, even La Roche-Derrien.

Will Skeat saw the worries on the Earl's broad face. 'My lad was within fifteen paces of the quay last night,' he asserted. 'He could have been inside the town and opened the gate.'

'So why didn't he?' Sir Simon could not resist asking. 'Christ's bones!' he went on. 'But I'd have been inside!'

'You're not an archer,' Skeat said sourly, then made the sign of the cross. At Guingamp one of Skeat's archers had been captured by the defenders, who had stripped the hated bowman naked then cut him to pieces on the rampart where the besiegers could see his long death. His two bow fingers had been severed first, then his manhood, and the man had screamed like a pig being gelded as he bled to death on the battlements.

The Earl gestured for a servant to replenish the cups

of mulled wine. 'Would you lead this attack, Will?' he asked.

'Not me,' Skeat said. 'I'm too old to wade through boggy mud. I'll let the lad who went past the stakes last night lead them in. He's a good boy, so he is. He's a clever bastard, but an odd one. He was going to be a priest, he was, only he met me and came to his senses.'

The Earl was plainly tempted by the idea. He toyed with the hilt of his sword, then nodded. 'I think we should meet your clever bastard. Is he near?'

'Left him outside,' Skeat said, then twisted on his stool. 'Tom, you savage! Come in here!'

Thomas stooped into the Earl's tent, where the gathered captains saw a tall, long-legged young man dressed entirely in black, all but for his mail coat and the red cross sewn onto his tunic. All the English troops wore that cross of St George so that in a mêlée they would know who was a friend and who an enemy. The young man bowed to the Earl, who realized he had noticed this archer before, which was hardly surprising for Thomas was a striking-looking man. He wore his black hair in a pigtail, tied with bowcord, he had a long bony nose that was crooked, a clean-shaven chin and watchful, clever eyes, though perhaps the most noticeable thing about him was that he was clean. That and, on his shoulder, the great bow that was one of the longest the Earl had seen, and not only long, but painted black, while mounted on the outer belly of the bow was a curious silver plate which seemed to have a coat of arms engraved on it. There was vanity here, the Earl thought, vanity and pride, and he approved of both things.

'For a man who was up to his knees in river mud last

55

night,' the Earl said with a smile, 'you're remarkably clean.'

'I washed, my lord.'

'You'll catch cold!' the Earl warned him. 'What's your name?'

'Thomas of Hookton, my lord.'

'So tell me what you found last night, Thomas of Hookton.'

Thomas told the same tale as Will Skeat. How, after dark, and as the tide fell, he had waded out into the Jaudy's mud. He had found the fence of stakes ill-maintained, rotting and loose, and he had lifted one out of its socket, wriggled through the gap and gone a few paces towards the nearest quay. 'I was close enough, my lord, to hear a woman singing,' he said. The woman had been singing a song that his own mother had crooned to him when he was small and he had been struck by that oddity.

The Earl frowned when Thomas finished, not because he disapproved of anything the archer had said, but because the scalp wound that had left him unconscious for an hour was throbbing. 'What were you doing at the river last night?' he asked, mainly to give himself more time to think about the idea.

Thomas said nothing.

'Another man's woman,' Skeat eventually answered for Thomas, 'that's what he was doing, my lord, another man's woman.'

The assembled men laughed, all but Sir Simon Jekyll, who looked sourly at the blushing Thomas. The bastard was a mere archer yet he was wearing a better coat of mail than Sir Simon could afford! And he had a confidence that stank of impudence. Sir Simon shuddered.

There was an unfairness to life which he did not understand. Archers from the shires were capturing horses and weapons and armour while he, a champion of tournaments, had not managed anything more valuable than a pair of goddamned boots. He felt an irresistible urge to deflate this tall, composed archer.

'One alert sentinel, my lord,' Sir Simon spoke to the Earl in Norman French so that only the handful of well-born men in the tent would understand him, 'and this boy will be dead and our attack will be floundering in river mud.'

Thomas gave Sir Simon a very level look, insolent in its lack of expression, then answered in fluent French. 'We should attack in the dark,' he said, then turned back to the Earl. 'The tide will be low just before dawn tomorrow, my lord.'

The Earl looked at him with surprise. 'How did you learn French?'

'From my father, my lord.'

'Do we know him?'

'I doubt it, my lord.'

The Earl did not pursue the subject. He bit his lip and rubbed the pommel of his sword, a habit when he was thinking.

'All well and good if you get inside,' Richard Totesham, seated on a milking stool next to Will Skeat, growled at Thomas. Totesham led the largest of the independent bands and had, on that account, a greater authority than the rest of the captains. 'But what do you do when you're inside?'

Thomas nodded, as though he had expected the question. 'I doubt we can reach a gate,' he said, 'but if I can put a score of archers onto the wall beside the river then they can protect it while ladders are placed.'

'And I've got two ladders,' Skeat added. 'They'll do.'

The Earl still rubbed the pommel of his sword. 'When we tried to attack by the river before,' he said, 'we got trapped in the mud. It'll be just as deep where you want to go.'

'Hurdles, my lord,' Thomas said. 'I found some in a farm.' Hurdles were fence sections made of woven willow that could make a quick pen for sheep or could be laid flat on mud to provide men with footing.

'I told you he was clever,' Will Skeat said proudly. 'Went to Oxford, didn't you, Tom?'

'When I was too young to know better,' Thomas said drily.

The Earl laughed. He liked this boy and he could see why Skeat had such faith in him. 'Tomorrow morning, Thomas?' he asked.

'Better than dusk tonight, my lord. They'll still be lively at dusk.' Thomas gave Sir Simon an expressionless glance, intimating that the knight's display of stupid bravery would have quickened the defenders' spirits.

'Then tomorrow morning it is,' the Earl said. He turned to Totesham. 'But keep your boys closed on the south gate today. I want them to think we're coming there again.' He looked back to Thomas. 'What's the badge on your bow, boy?'

'Just something I found, my lord,' Thomas lied, handing the bow to the Earl, who had held out his hand. In truth he had cut the silver badge out of the crushed chalice that he had found under his father's robes, then pinned the metal to the front of the bow where his left hand had worn the silver almost smooth.

The Earl peered at the device. 'A yale?'

'I think that's what the beast is called, my lord,' Thomas said, pretending ignorance.

'Not the badge of anyone I know,' the Earl said, then tried to flex the bow and raised his eyebrows in surprise at its strength. He gave the black shaft back to Thomas then dismissed him. 'I wish you Godspeed in the morning, Thomas of Hookton.'

'My lord,' Thomas said, and bowed.

'I'll go with him, with your permission,' Skeat said, and the Earl nodded, then watched the two men leave. 'If we do get inside,' he told his remaining captains, 'then for God's sake don't let your men cry havoc. Hold their leashes tight. I intend to keep this town and I don't want the townsfolk hating us. Kill when you must, but I don't want an orgy of blood.' He looked at their sceptical faces. 'I'll be putting one of you in charge of the garrison here, so make it easy for yourselves. Hold them tight.'

The captains grunted, knowing how hard it would be to keep their men from a full sack of the town, but before any of them could respond to the Earl's hopeful wishes, Sir Simon stood.

'My lord? A request?'

The Earl shrugged. 'Try me.'

'Would you let me and my men lead the ladder party?'

The Earl seemed surprised at the request. 'You think Skeat cannot manage on his own?'

'I am sure he can, my lord,' Sir Simon said humbly, 'but I still beg the honour.'

Better Sir Simon Jekyll dead than Will Skeat, the Earl thought. He nodded. 'Of course, of course.'

The captains said nothing. What honour was there

59

in being first onto a wall that another man had captured? No, the bastard did not want honour, he wanted to be well placed to find the richest plunder in town, but none of them voiced his thought. They were captains, but Sir Simon was a knight, even if a penniless one.

The Earl's army threatened an attack for the rest of that short winter's day, but it never came and the citizens of La Roche-Derrien dared to hope that the worst of their ordeal was over, but made preparations in case the English did try again the next day. They counted their crossbow bolts, stacked more boulders on the ramparts and fed the fires which boiled the pots of water that were poured onto the English. Heat the wretches up, the town's priests had said, and the townsfolk liked that jest. They were winning, they knew, and they reckoned their ordeal must finish soon, for the English would surely be running out of food. All La Roche-Derrien had to do was endure and then receive the praise and thanks of Duke Charles.

The small rain stopped at nightfall. The townsfolk went to their beds, but kept their weapons ready. The sentries lit watch fires behind the walls and gazed into the dark.

It was night, it was winter, it was cold and the besiegers had one last chance.

The Blackbird had been christened Jeanette Marie Halevy, and when she was fifteen her parents had taken her to Guingamp for the annual tournament of the apples. Her father was not an aristocrat so the family could not sit in the enclosure beneath St Laurent's

60

tower, but they found a place nearby, and Louis Halevy made certain his daughter was visible by placing their chairs on the farm wagon which had carried them from La Roche-Derrien. Jeanette's father was a prosperous shipmaster and wine merchant, though his fortune in business had not been mirrored in life. One son had died when a cut finger turned septic and his second son had drowned on a voyage to Corunna. Jeanette was now his only child.

There was calculation in the visit to Guingamp. The nobility of Brittany, at least those who favoured an alliance with France, assembled at the tournament where, for four days, in front of a crowd that came as much for the fair as for the fighting, they displayed their talents with sword and lance. Jeanette found much of it tedious, for the preambles to each fight were long and often out of earshot. Knights paraded endlessly, their extravagant plumes nodding, but after a while there would be a brief thunder of hoofs, a clash of metal, a cheer, and one knight would be tumbled in the grass. It was customary for every victorious knight to prick an apple with his lance and present it to whichever woman in the crowd attracted him, and that was why her father had taken the farm wagon to Guingamp. After four days Jeanette had eighteen apples and the enmity of a score of better-born girls.

Her parents took her back to La Roche-Derrien and waited. They had displayed their wares and now the buyers could find their way to the lavish house beside the River Jaudy. From the front the house seemed small, but go through the archway and a visitor found himself in a wide courtyard reaching down to a stone quay where Monsieur Halevy's smaller boats could be

61

moored at the top of the tide. The courtyard shared a wall with the church of St Renan and, because Monsieur Halevy had donated the tower to the church, he had been permitted to drive an archway through the wall so that his family did not need to step into the street when they went to Mass. The house told any suitor that this was a wealthy family, and the presence of the parish priest at the supper table told him it was a devout family. Jeanette was to be no aristocrat's plaything, she was to be a wife.

A dozen men condescended to visit the Halevy house, but it was Henri Chenier, Comte d'Armorique, who won the apple. He was a prime catch, for he was nephew to Charles of Blois, who was himself a nephew to King Philip of France, and it was Charles whom the French recognized as Duke and ruler of Brittany. The Duke allowed Henri Chenier to present his fiancée, but afterwards advised his nephew to discard her. The girl was a merchant's daughter, scarce more than a peasant, though even the Duke admitted she was a beauty. Her hair was shining black, her face was unflawed by the pox and she had all her teeth. She was graceful, so that a Dominican friar in the Duke's court clasped his hands and exclaimed that Jeanette was the living image of the Madonna. The Duke agreed she was beautiful, but so what? Many women were beautiful. Any tavern in Guingamp, he said, could throw up a two-livre whore who could make most wives look like hogs. It was not the job of a wife to be beautiful, but to be rich. 'Make the girl your mistress,' he advised his nephew, and virtually ordered Henri to marry an heiress from Picardy, but the heiress was a pox-faced slattern and the Count of Armorica was besotted by Jeanette's beauty and so he defied his uncle.

He married the merchant's daughter in the chapel of his castle at Plabennec, which lay in Finisterre, the world's end. The Duke reckoned his nephew had listened to too many troubadours, but the Count and his new wife were happy and a year after their wedding, when Jeanette was sixteen, their son was born. They named him Charles, after the Duke, but if the Duke was complimented, he said nothing. He refused to receive Jeanette again and treated his nephew coldly.

Later that same year the English came in force to support Jean de Montfort, whom they recognized as the Duke of Brittany, and the King of France sent reinforcements to his nephew Charles, whom he recognized as the real Duke, and so the civil war began in earnest. The Count of Armorica insisted that his wife and baby son went back to her father's house in La Roche-Derrien because the castle at Plabennec was small, in ill repair and too close to the invader's forces.

That summer the castle fell to the English just as Jeanette's husband had feared, and the following year the King of England spent the campaigning season in Brittany, and his army pushed back the forces of Charles, Duke of Brittany. There was no one great battle, but a series of bloody skirmishes, and in one of them, a ragged affair fought between the hedgerows of a steep valley, Jeanette's husband was wounded. He had lifted the face-piece of his helmet to shout encouragement to his men and an arrow had gone clean through his mouth. His servants brought the Count to the house beside the River Jaudy where he took five days to die; five days of constant pain during which he was unable to eat and scarce able to breathe as the wound festered and the blood congealed in his gullet.

He was twenty-eight years old, a champion of tournaments, and he wept like a child at the end. He choked to death and Jeanette screamed in frustrated anger and grief.

Then began Jeanette's time of sorrow. She was a widow, *la veuve Chenier*, and not six months after her husband's death she became an orphan when both her parents died of the bloody flux. She was just eighteen and her son, the Count of Armorica, was two, but Jeanette had inherited her father's wealth and she determined to use it to strike back at the hated English who had killed her husband, and so she began outfitting two ships that could prey on English shipping.

Monsieur Belas, who had been her father's lawyer, advised against spending money on the ships. Jeanette's fortune would not last for ever, the lawyer said, and nothing soaked up cash like outfitting warships that rarely made money, unless by luck. Better, he said, to use the ships for trade. 'The merchants in Lannion are making a fine profit on Spanish wine,' he suggested. He had a cold, for it was winter, and he sneezed. 'A very fine profit,' he said wistfully. He spoke in Breton, though both he and Jeanette could, if needs be, speak French.

'I do not want Spanish wine,' Jeanette said coldly, 'but English souls.'

'No profit in those, my lady,' Belas said. He found it strange to call Jeanette 'my lady'. He had known her since she was a child, and she had always been little Jeanette to him, but she had married and become an aristocratic widow, and a widow, moreover, with a temper. 'You cannot sell English souls,' Belas pointed out mildly.

'Except to the devil,' Jeanette said, crossing herself. 'But I don't need Spanish wine, Belas. We have the rents.'

'The rents!' Belas said mockingly. He was tall, thin, scanty-haired and clever. He had served Jeanette's father well and long, and was resentful that the merchant had left him nothing in his will. Everything had gone to Jeanette except for a small bequest to the monks at Pontrieux so they would say Masses for the dead man's soul. Belas hid his resentment. 'Nothing comes from Plabennec,' he told Jeanette. 'The English are there, and how long do you think the rents will come from your father's farms? The English will take them soon.' An English army had occupied unwalled Tréguier, which was only an hour's walk northwards, and they had pulled down the cathedral tower there because some crossbowmen had shot at them from its summit. Belas hoped the English would retreat soon, for it was deep in the winter and their supplies must be running low, but he feared they might ravage the countryside about La Roche-Derrien before they left. And if they did, Jeanette's farms would be left worthless. 'How much rent can you get from a burned farm?' he asked her.

'I don't care!' she snapped. 'I shall sell everything if I have to, everything!' Except for her husband's armour and weapons. They were precious and would go to her son one day.

Belas sighed for her foolishness, then huddled in his black cloak and leaned close to the small fire which spat in the hearth. A cold wind came from the nearby sea, making the chimney smoke. 'You will permit me, madame, to offer you advice? First, the business.' Belas paused to wipe his nose on his long black sleeve. 'It ails, but I can find you a good man to run it as your father did, and I would draw up a contract which would ensure the man would pay you well from the profits. Second, madame, you should think of marriage.' He paused, half expecting a protest, but Jeanette said nothing. Belas sighed. She was so lovely! There were a dozen men in town who would marry her, but marriage to an aristocrat had turned her head and she would settle for nothing less than another titled man. 'You are, madame,' the lawyer continued carefully, 'a widow who possesses, at the moment, a considerable fortune, but I have seen such fortunes drain away like snow in April. Find a man who can look after you, your possessions and your son.'

Jeanette turned and stared at him. 'I married the finest man in Christendom,' she said, 'and where do you think I will find another like him?'

Men like the Count of Armorica, the lawyer thought, were found everywhere, more was the pity, for what were they but brute fools in armour who believed war was a sport? Jeanette, he thought, should marry a prudent merchant, perhaps a widower who had a fortune, but he suspected such advice would be wasted. 'Remember the old saying, my lady,' he said slyly. 'Put a cat to watch a flock and the wolves eat well.'

Jeanette shuddered with anger at the words. 'You go beyond yourself, Monsieur Belas.' She spoke icily, then dismissed him, and the next day the English came to La Roche-Derrien and Jeanette took her dead husband's crossbow from the place where she hid her wealth and she joined the defenders on the walls. Damn Belas's advice! She would fight like a man and Duke Charles, who despised her, would learn to admire her, to support her and restore her dead husband's estates to her son.

So Jeanette had become the Blackbird and the English had died in front of her walls and Belas's advice was forgotten, and now, Jeanette reckoned, the town's defenders had so rattled the English that the siege would surely be lifted. All would be well, in which belief, for the first time in a week, the Blackbird slept well.

Thomas crouched beside the river. He had broken through a stand of alders to reach the bank where he now pulled off his boots and hose. Best to go barelegged, he reckoned, so the boots did not get stuck in the river mud. It was going to be cold, freezing cold, but he could not remember a time when he had been happier. He liked this life, and his memories of Hookton, Oxford and his father had almost faded.

'Take your boots off,' he told the twenty archers who would accompany him, 'and hang your arrow bags round your necks.'

'Why?' someone challenged him from the dark.

'So it bloody throttles you,' Thomas growled.

'So your arrows don't get wet,' another man explained helpfully.

Thomas tied his own bag round his neck. Archers did not carry the quivers that hunters used, for quivers were open at the top and their arrows could fall out when a man ran or stumbled or clambered through a hedge. Arrows in quivers got wet when it rained, and wet feathers made arrows fly crooked, so real archers used linen bags that were water-proofed with wax and sealed by laces. The bags were bolstered by withy frames that spread the linen so the feathers were not crushed.

Will Skeat edged down the bank where a dozen men were stacking the hurdles. He shivered in the cold wind that came from the water. The sky to the east was still dark, but some light came from the watch fires that burned within La Roche-Derrien.

'They're nice and quiet in there,' Skeat said, nodding towards the town.

'Pray they're sleeping,' Thomas said.

'In beds too. I've forgotten what a bed's like,' Skeat said, then edged aside to let another man through to the riverbank. Thomas was surprised to see it was Sir Simon Jekyll, who had been so scornful of him in the Earl's tent. 'Sir Simon,' Will Skeat said, barely bothering to disguise his own scorn, 'wants a word with thee.'

Sir Simon wrinkled his nose at the stench of the river mud. Much of it, he supposed, was the town's sewage and he was glad he was not wading barelegged through the muck.

'You are confident of passing the stakes?' he asked Thomas.

'I wouldn't be going otherwise,' Thomas said, not bothering to sound respectful.

Thomas's tone made Sir Simon bridle, but he controlled his temper. 'The Earl,' he said distantly, 'has given me the honour of leading the attack on the walls.' He stopped abruptly and Thomas waited, expecting more, but Sir Simon merely looked at him with an irritated face.

'So Thomas takes the walls,' Skeat finally spoke, 'to make it safe for your ladders?'

'What I do not want,' Sir Simon ignored Skeat and spoke to Thomas, 'is for you to take your men ahead of mine into the town itself. We see armed men, we're likely to kill them, you understand?'

Thomas almost spat in derision. His men would be armed with bows and no enemy carried a long-stave bow like the English so there was hardly any chance of being mistaken for the town's defenders, but he held his tongue. He just nodded.

'You and your archers can join our attack,' Sir Simon went on, 'but you will be under my command.'

Thomas nodded again and Sir Simon, irritated by the implied insolence, turned on his heel and walked away.

'Goddamn bastard,' Thomas said.

'He just wants to get his nose into the trough ahead of the rest of us,' Skeat said.

'You're letting the bastard use our ladders?' Thomas asked.

'If he wants to be first up, let him. Ladders are green wood, Tom, and if they break I'd rather it was him tumbling than me. Besides, I reckon we'll be better off following you through the river, but I ain't telling Sir Simon that.' Skeat grinned, then swore as a crash sounded from the darkness south of the river. 'Those bloody white rats,' Skeat said, and vanished into the shadows.

The white rats were the Bretons loyal to Duke John, men who wore his badge of a white ermine, and some sixty Breton crossbowmen had been attached to Skeat's soldiers, their job to rattle the walls with their bolts as the ladders were placed against the ramparts. It was those men who had startled the night with their noise and now the noise grew even louder. Some fool had tripped in the dark and thumped a crossbowman with a pavise, the huge shield behind which the crossbows were laboriously reloaded, and the crossbowman struck back, and suddenly the white rats were having a brawl in the dark. The defenders, naturally, heard them and started to hurl burning bales of straw over the ramparts and then a church bell began to toll, then another, and all this long before Thomas had even started across the mud.

Sir Simon Jekyll, alarmed by the bells and the burning straw, shouted that the attack must go in now. 'Carry the ladders forward!' he bellowed. Defenders were running onto La Roche-Derrien's walls and the first crossbow bolts were spitting off the ramparts that were lit bright by the burning bales.

'Hold those goddamn ladders!' Will Skeat snarled at his men, then looked at Thomas. 'What do you reckon?'

'I think the bastards are distracted,' Thomas said.

'So you'll go?'

'Got nothing better to do, Will.'

'Bloody white rats!'

Thomas led his men onto the mud. The hurdles were some help, but not as much as he had hoped, so that they still slipped and struggled their way towards the great stakes and Thomas reckoned the noise they made was enough to wake King Arthur and his knights. But the defenders were making even more noise. Every church bell was clanging, a trumpet was screaming, men were shouting, dogs barking, cockerels were crowing, and the crossbows were creaking and banging as their cords were inched back and released.

The walls loomed to Thomas's right. He wondered if the Blackbird was up there. He had seen her twice now and been captivated by the fierceness of her face and her wild black hair. A score of other archers had seen

71

her too, and all of them men who could thread an arrow through a bracelet at a hundred paces, yet the woman still lived. Amazing, Thomas thought, what a pretty face could do.

He threw down the last hurdle and so reached the wooden stakes, each one a whole tree trunk sunk into the mud. His men joined him and they heaved against the timber until the rotted wood split like straw. The stakes made a terrible noise as they fell, but it was drowned by the uproar in the town. Jake, the cross-eyed murderer from Exeter gaol, pulled himself alongside Thomas. To their right now was a wooden quay with a rough ladder at one end. Dawn was coming and a feeble, thin, grey light was seeping from the east to outline the bridge across the Jaudy. It was a handsome stone bridge with a barbican at its further end, and Thomas feared the garrison of that tower might see them, but no one called an alarm and no crossbow bolts thumped across the river.

Thomas and Jake were first up the quay ladder, then came Sam, the youngest of Skeat's archers. The wooden landing stage served a timberyard and a dog began barking frantically among the stacked trunks, but Sam slipped into the blackness with his knife and the barking suddenly stopped. 'Good doggy,' Sam said as he came back.

'String your bows,' Thomas said. He had looped the hemp cord onto his own black weapon and now untied the laces of his arrow bag.

'I hate bloody dogs,' Sam said. 'One bit my mother when she was pregnant with me.'

'That's why you're daft,' Jake said.

'Shut your goddamn faces,' Thomas ordered. More archers were climbing the quay, which was swaying alarmingly, but he could see that the walls he was supposed to capture were thick with defenders now. English arrows, their white goose feathers bright in the flamelight of the defenders' fires, flickered over the wall and thumped into the town's thatched roofs. 'Maybe we should open the south gate,' Thomas suggested.

'Go through the town?' Jake asked in alarm.

'It's a small town,' Thomas said.

'You're mad,' Jake said, but he was grinning and he meant the words as a compliment.

'I'm going anyway,' Thomas said. It would be dark in the streets and their long bows would be hidden. He reckoned it would be safe enough.

A dozen men followed Thomas while the rest started plundering the nearer buildings. More and more men were coming through the broken stakes now as Will Skeat sent them down the riverbank rather than wait for the wall to be captured. The defenders had seen the men in the mud and were shooting down from the end of the town wall, but the first attackers were already loose in the streets.

Thomas blundered through the town. It was pitch-black in the alleys and hard to tell where he was going, though by climbing the hill on which the town was built he reckoned he must eventually go over the summit and so down to the southern gate. Men ran past him, but no one could see that he and his companions were English. The church bells were deafening. Children were crying, dogs howling, gulls screaming, and the noise was making Thomas terrified. This was a daft idea, he thought. Maybe Sir Simon had already climbed the walls? Maybe he was wasting his time? Yet white-feathered arrows still thumped into the town roofs, suggesting the walls were untaken, and so he forced himself to keep going. Twice he found himself in a blind alley and the second time, doubling back into a wider street, he almost ran into a priest who had come from his church to fix a flaming torch in a wall bracket.

'Go to the ramparts!' the priest said sternly, then saw the long bows in the men's hands and opened his mouth to shout the alarm.

He never had time to shout for Thomas's bow stave slammed point-first into his belly. He bent over, gasping, and Jake casually slit his throat. The priest gurgled as he sank to the cobbles and Jake frowned when the noise stopped.

'I'll go to hell for that,' he said.

'You're going to hell anyway,' Sam said, 'we all are.'

'We're all going to heaven,' Thomas said, 'but not if we dawdle.' He suddenly felt much less frightened, as though the priest's death had taken his fear. An arrow struck the church tower and dropped into the alley as Thomas led his men past the church and found himself on La Roche-Derrien's main street, which dropped down to where a watch fire burned by the southern gate. Thomas shrank back into the alley beside the church, for the street was thick with men, but they were all running to the threatened side of the town, and when Thomas next looked the hill was empty. He could only see two sentinels on the ramparts above the gate arch. He told his men about the two sentries.

'They're going to be scared as hell,' he said. 'We kill the bastards and open the gate.'

'There might be others,' Sam said. 'There'll be a guard house.'

'Then kill them too,' Thomas said. 'Now, come on!'

They stepped into the street, ran down a few yards and there drew their bows. The arrows flew and the two guards on the arch fell. A man stepped out of the guard house built into the gate turret and gawped at the archers, but before any could draw their bows he stepped back inside and barred the door.

'It's ours!' Thomas shouted, and led his men in a wild rush to the arch.

The guard house stayed locked so there was no one to stop the archers from lifting the bar and pushing open the two great gates. The Earl's men saw the gates open, saw the English archers outlined against the watch fire and gave a great roar from the darkness that told Thomas a torrent of vengeful troops was coming towards him.

Which meant La Roche-Derrien's time of weeping could begin. For the English had taken the town.

Jeanette woke to a church bell ringing as though it was the world's doom when the dead were rising from their graves and the gates of hell were yawning wide for sinners. Her first instinct was to cross to her son's bed, but little Charles was safe. She could just see his eyes in the dark that was scarcely alleviated by the glowing embers of the fire.

'Mama?' he cried, reaching up to her.

'Quiet,' she hushed the boy, then ran to throw open the shutters. A faint grey light showed above the eastern roofs, then steps sounded in the street and she leaned from the window to see men running from their houses with swords, crossbows and spears. A trumpet was calling from the town centre, then more church bells began tolling the alarm into a dying night. The bell of the church of the Virgin was cracked and made a harsh, anvil-like noise that was all the more terrifying.

'Madame!' a servant cried as she ran into the room.

'The English must be attacking.' Jeanette forced herself to speak calmly. She was wearing nothing but a linen shift and was suddenly cold. She snatched up a cloak, tied it about her neck, then took her son into her arms. 'You will be all right, Charles,' she tried to console him. 'The English are attacking again, that is all.'

Except she was not sure. The bells were sounding so wild. It was not the measured tolling that was the usual signal of attack, but a panicked clangour as though the men hauling the ropes were trying to repel an attack by their own efforts. She looked from the window again and saw the English arrows flitting across the roofs. She could hear them thumping into the thatch. The children of the town thought it was a fine sport to retrieve the enemy arrows and two had injured themselves sliding from the roofs. Jeanette thought about getting dressed, but decided she must find out what was happening first so she gave Charles to the servant, then ran downstairs.

One of the kitchen servants met her at the back door. 'What's happening, madame?'

'Another attack, that is all.'

She unbarred the door to the yard, then ran to the private entrance to Renan's church just as an arrow struck the church tower and clattered down into the yard. She pulled open the tower door, then groped up the steep ladders that her father had built. It had not been mere piety that had inspired Louis Halevy to construct the tower, but also the opportunity to look down-river to see if his boats were approaching, and the high stone parapet offered one of the best views in La Roche-Derrien. Jeanette was deafened by the church bell that swung in the gloom, each clapper stroke thumping her ears like a physical blow. She climbed past the bell, pushed open the trapdoor at the top of the ladders and clambered onto the leads.

The English had come. She could see a torrent of men flowing about the river edge of the wall. They waded through the mud and swarmed over the broken stakes like a torrent of rats. Sweet Mother of Christ, she thought, sweet Mother of Christ, but they were in the town! She hurried down the ladders. 'They're here!' she called to the priest who hauled the bell rope. 'They're in the town!'

'Havoc! Havoc!' the English shouted, the call that encouraged them to plunder.

Jeanette ran across the yard and up the stairs. She pulled her clothes from the cupboard, then turned when the voices shouted havoc beneath her window. She forgot her clothes and took Charles back into her arms. 'Mother of God,' she prayed, 'look after us now, look after us. Sweet Mother of God, keep us safe.' She wept, not knowing what to do. Charles cried because she was holding him too tight and she tried to soothe him. Cheers sounded in the street and she ran back to the window and saw what looked like a dark river studded with steel flowing towards the town centre. She collapsed by the window, sobbing. Charles was screaming. Two more servants were in the room, somehow thinking that Jeanette could shelter them, but there was no shelter now. The English had come. One of the servants shot the bolt on the bedroom door, but what good would that do?

Jeanette thought of her husband's hidden weapons and of the Spanish sword's sharp edge, and wondered if she would have the courage to place the point against her breast and heave her body onto the blade. It would be better to die than be dishonoured, she thought, but then what would happen to her son? She wept helplessly, then heard someone beating on the big gate which led to her courtyard. An axe, she supposed, and she listened to its crunching blows that seemed to shake the whole house. A woman screamed in the town, then another, and the English voices cheered rampantly. One by one the church bells fell silent until only the cracked bell hammered its fear across the roofs. The axe still bit at the door. Would they recognize her, she wondered. She had exulted in standing on the ramparts, shooting her husband's crossbow at the besiegers, and her right shoulder was bruised because of it, but she had welcomed the pain, believing that every bolt fired made it less likely that the English would break into the town.

No one had thought they could. And why besiege La Roche-Derrien anyway? It had nothing to offer. As a port it was almost useless, for the largest ships could not make it up the river even at the top of the tide. The English, the townspeople had believed, were making a petulant demonstration and would soon give up and slink away.

But now they were here, and Jeanette screamed as the sound of the axe blows changed. They had broken through, and doubtless were trying to lift the bar. She closed her eyes, shaking as she heard the gate scrape on the cobbles. It was open. It was open. Oh, Mother of God, she prayed, be with us now.

The screams sounded downstairs. Feet thumped on the stairs. Men's voices shouted in a strange tongue.

Be with us now and at the hour of our death for the English had come.

Sir Simon Jekyll was annoyed. He had been prepared to climb the ladders if Skeat's archers ever gained the walls, which he doubted, but if the ramparts were captured then he intended to be first into the town. He foresaw cutting down a few panicked defenders then finding some great house to plunder.

But nothing happened as he had imagined it. The town was awake, the wall manned, and the ladders never went forward, but Skeat's men still got inside by simply wading through the mud at the river's edge. Then a cheer at the southern side of the town suggested that gate was open, which meant that the whole damned army was getting into La Roche-Derrien ahead of Sir Simon. He swore. There would be nothing left!

'My lord?' One of his men-at-arms prompted Sir Simon, wanting a decision as to how they were to reach the women and valuables beyond the walls, which were emptying of their defenders as men ran to protect their homes and families. It would have been quicker, far quicker, to have waded through the mud, but Sir Simon did not want to dirty his new boots and so he ordered the ladders forward.

The ladders were made of green wood and the rungs bent alarmingly as Sir Simon climbed, but there were no defenders to oppose him and the ladder held. He clambered into an embrasure and drew his sword. A half-dozen defenders lay spitted with arrows on the rampart. Two were still alive and Sir Simon stabbed the nearest one. The man had been roused from his bed and had no mail, not even a leather coat, yet still the old sword made hard work of the killing stroke. It was not designed for stabbing, but for cutting. The new swords, made from the finest southern European steel, were renowned for their ability to pierce mail and leather, but this ancient blade required all Sir Simon's brute force to penetrate a rib cage. And what chance, he wondered sourly, would there be of finding a better weapon in this sorry excuse for a town?

There was a flight of stone steps down into a street that was thronged by English archers and men-at-arms smeared with mud to their thighs. They were breaking into houses. One man was carrying a dead goose, another had a bolt of cloth. The plundering had begun and Sir Simon was still on the ramparts. He shouted at his men to hurry and when enough of them had gathered on the wall's top, he led them down into the street. An archer was rolling a barrel from a cellar door, another dragged a girl by an arm. Where to go? That was Sir Simon's problem. The nearest houses were all being sacked, and the cheers from the south suggested the Earl's main army was descending on that part of the town. Some townsfolk, realizing all was lost, were fleeing in front of the archers to cross the bridge and escape into the countryside.

Sir Simon decided to strike east. The Earl's men were to the south, Skeat's were staying close to the west wall so the eastern quarter offered the best hope of plunder. He pushed past Skeat's muddy archers and led his men towards the bridge. Frightened people ran past him, ignoring him and hoping he would ignore them. He crossed the main street, which led to the bridge, and saw a roadway running alongside the big houses that fronted the river. Merchants, Sir Simon thought, fat merchants with fat profits, and then, in the growing light, he saw an archway that was surmounted by a coat of arms. A noble's house.

'Who has an axe?' he asked his men.

One of the men-at-arms stepped forward and Sir Simon indicated the heavy gate. The house had windows on the ground floor, but they were covered by heavy iron bars, which seemed a good sign. Sir Simon stepped back to let his man start work on the gate.

The axeman knew his business. He chopped a hole where he guessed the locking bar was, and when he had broken through he put a hand inside and pushed the bar up and out of its brackets so that Sir Simon and his archers could heave the gates open. Sir Simon left two men to guard the gate, ordering them to keep every other plunderer out of the property, then led the rest into the yard. The first things he saw were two boats tied at the river's quay. They were not large ships, but all hulls were valuable and he ordered four of his archers to go aboard.

'Tell anyone who comes that they're mine, you understand? Mine!'

He had a choice now: storerooms or house? And a stable? He told two men-at-arms to find the stable and stand guard on whatever horses were there, then he kicked in the house door and led his six remaining men into the kitchen. Two women screamed. He ignored them; they were old, ugly servants and he was after richer things. A door led from the back of the kitchen and he pointed one of his archers towards it, then, holding his sword ahead of him, he went through a small dark hall into a front room. A tapestry showing Bacchus, the god of wine, hung on one wall and Sir Simon had an idea that valuables were sometimes hidden behind such wall-coverings so he hacked at it with his blade, then hauled it down from its hooks, but there was only a plaster wall behind. He kicked the chairs, then saw a chest that had a huge dark padlock.

'Get it open,' he ordered two of his archers, 'and whatever's inside is mine.' Then, ignoring two books which were of no use to man or beast, he went back into the hall and ran up a flight of dark wooden stairs.

Sir Simon found a door leading to a room at the front of the house. It was bolted and a woman screamed from the other side when he tried to force the door. He stood back and used the heel of his boot, smashing the bolt on the far side and slamming the door back on its hinges. Then he stalked inside, his old sword glittering in the dawn's wan light, and he saw a black-haired woman.

Sir Simon considered himself a practical man. His father, quite sensibly, had not wanted his son to waste time on education, though Sir Simon had learned to read and could, at a pinch, write a letter. He liked useful things – hounds and weapons, horses and armour – and he despised the fashionable cult of gentility. His mother was a great one for troubadours, and was forever listening to songs of knights so gentle that Sir Simon reckoned they would not have lasted two minutes in a tourney's mêlée. The songs and poems celebrated love as though it was some rare thing that gave a life enchantment, but Sir Simon did not need poets to define love, which to him was tumbling a peasant girl in a harvest field or thrusting at some ale-reeking whore in a tavern, but when he saw the black-haired woman he suddenly understood what the troubadours had been celebrating.

It did not matter that the woman was shaking with fear or that her hair was wildly awry or that her face was streaked with tears. Sir Simon recognized beauty and it struck him like an arrow. It took his breath away. So this, then, was love! It was the realization that he could never be happy until this woman was his – and that was convenient, for she was an enemy, the town was being sacked and Sir Simon, clad in mail and fury, had found her first.

'Get out!' he snarled at the servants in the room. 'Get out!'

The servants fled in tears and Sir Simon booted the broken door shut, then advanced on the woman, who crouched beside her son's bed with the boy in her arms.

'Who are you?' Sir Simon asked in French.

The woman tried to sound brave. 'I am the Countess of Armorica,' she said. 'And you, monsieur?'

Sir Simon was tempted to award himself a peerage to impress Jeanette, but he was too slow-witted and so heard himself uttering his proper name. He was slowly becoming aware that the room betrayed wealth. The bed hangings were thickly embroidered, the candlesticks were of heavy silver and the walls either side of the stone hearth were expensively panelled in beautifully carved wood. He pushed the smaller bed against the door, reckoning that should ensure some privacy, then went to warm himself at the fire. He tipped more sea-coal onto the small flames and held his chilled gloves close to the heat.

'This is your house, madame?'

'It is.'

'Not your husband's?'

'I am a widow,' Jeanette said.

A wealthy widow! Sir Simon almost crossed himself out of gratitude. The widows he had met in England had been rouged hags, but this one . . . ! This one was different. This one was a woman worthy of a tournament's champion and seemed rich enough to save him from the ignominy of losing his estate and knightly rank. She might even have enough cash to buy a baronage. Maybe an earldom?

He turned from the fire and smiled at her. 'Are those your boats at the quay?'

'Yes, monsieur.'

'By the rules of war, madame, they are now mine. Everything here is mine.'

Jeanette frowned at that. 'What rules?'

'The law of the sword, madame, but I think you are fortunate. I shall offer you my protection.'

Jeanette sat on the edge of her curtained bed, clutching Charles. 'The rules of chivalry, my lord,' she said, 'ensure my protection.' She flinched as a woman screamed in a nearby house.

'Chivalry?' Sir Simon asked. 'Chivalry? I have heard it mentioned in songs, madame, but this is a war. Our task is to punish the followers of Charles of Blois for rebelling against their lawful lord. Punishment and chivalry do not mix.' He frowned at her. 'You're the Blackbird!' he said, suddenly recognizing her in the light of the revived fire.

'The blackbird?' Jeanette did not understand.

'You fought us from the walls! You scratched my

arm!' Sir Simon did not sound angry, but astonished. He had expected to be furious when he met the Blackbird, but her reality was too overpowering for rage. He grinned. 'You closed your eyes when you shot the crossbow, that's why you missed.'

'I did not miss!' Jeanette said indignantly.

'A scratch,' Sir Simon said, showing her the rent in his mail sleeve. 'But why, madame, do you fight for the false duke?'

'My husband,' she said stiffly, 'was nephew to Duke Charles.'

Sweet God, Sir Simon thought, sweet God! A prize indeed. He bowed to her. 'So your son,' he said, nodding at Charles, who was peering anxiously from his mother's arms, 'is the present Count?'

'He is,' Jeanette confirmed,

'A fine boy.' Sir Simon forced himself to the flattery. In truth he thought Charles was a pudding-faced nuisance whose presence inhibited him from a natural urge to thrust the Blackbird onto her back and thus show her the realities of war, but he was acutely aware that this widow was an aristocrat, a beauty, and related to Charles of Blois, who was nephew to the King of France. This woman meant riches and Sir Simon's present necessity was to make her see that her best interest lay in sharing his ambitions. 'A fine boy, madame,' he went on, 'who needs a father.'

Jeanette just stared at him. Sir Simon had a blunt face. It was bulbous-nosed, firm-chinned, and showed not the slightest sign of intelligence or wit. He had confidence, though, enough to have persuaded himself that she would marry him. Did he really mean that? She gaped, then gave a startled cry as angry shouting erupted beneath her window. Some archers were trying to get past the men guarding the gate. Sir Simon pushed open the window. 'This place is mine,' he snarled in English. 'Go find your own chickens to pluck.' He turned back to Jeanette. 'You see, madame, how I protect you?'

'So there is chivalry in war?'

'There is opportunity in war, madame. You are wealthy, you are a widow, you need a man.'

She gazed at him with disturbingly large eyes, hardly daring to believe his temerity. 'Why?' she asked simply.

'Why?' Sir Simon was astonished by the question. He gestured at the window. 'Listen to the screams, woman! What do you think happens to women when a town falls?'

'But you said you would protect me,' she pointed out.

'So I will.' He was getting lost in this conversation. The woman, he thought, though beautiful, was remarkably stupid. 'I will protect you,' he said, 'and you will look after me.'

'How?'

Sir Simon sighed. 'You have money?'

Jeanette shrugged. 'There is a little downstairs, my lord, hidden in the kitchen.'

Sir Simon frowned angrily. Did she think he was a fool? That he would take that bait and go downstairs, leaving her to climb out of the window? 'I know one thing about money, madame,' he said, 'and that is that you never hide it where the servants can find it. You hide it in the private rooms. In a bedchamber.' He pulled open a chest and emptied its linens onto the floor, but there was nothing hidden there, and then, on an inspiration, he began rapping the wooden panelling. He had heard that such panels often concealed a hiding place and he was rewarded almost instantly by a satisfyingly hollow sound.

'No, monsieur!' Jeanette said.

Sir Simon ignored her, drawing his sword and hacking at the limewood panels that splintered and pulled away from their beams. He sheathed the blade and tugged with his gloved hands at the shattered wood.

'No!' Jeanette wailed.

Sir Simon stared. Money was concealed behind the panelling, a whole barrel of coins, but that was not the prize. The prize was a suit of armour and a set of weapons such as Sir Simon had only ever dreamed of. A shining suit of plate armour, each piece chased with subtle engravings and inlaid with gold. Italian work? And the sword! When he drew it from the scabbard it was like holding Excalibur itself. There was a blue sheen to the blade, which was not nearly as heavy as his own sword but felt miraculously balanced. A blade from the famous swordsmiths of Poitiers, perhaps, or, even better, Spanish?

'They belonged to my husband,' Jeanette appealed to him, 'and it is all I have of his. They must go to Charles.'

Sir Simon ignored her. He traced his gloved finger down the gold inlay on the breastplate. That piece alone was worth an estate!

'They are all he has of his father's,' Jeanette pleaded.

Sir Simon unbuckled his sword belt and let the old weapon drop to the floor, then fastened the Count of Armorica's sword about his waist. He turned and stared at Jeanette, marvelling at her smooth unscarred face. These were the spoils of war that he had dreamed about and had begun to fear would never come his way: a barrel of cash, a suit of armour fit for a king, a blade made for a champion and a woman that would be the envy of England. 'The armour is mine,' he said, 'as is the sword.'

'No, monsieur, please.'

'What will you do? Buy them from me?'

'If I must,' Jeanette said, nodding at the barrel.

'That too is mine, madame,' Sir Simon said, and to prove it he strode to the door, unblocked it and shouted for two of his archers to come up the stairs. He gestured at the barrel and the suit of armour. 'Take them down,' he said, 'and keep them safe. And don't think I haven't counted the cash, because I have. Now go!'

Jeanette watched the theft. She wanted to weep for pity, but forced herself to stay calm. 'If you steal everything I own,' she said to Sir Simon, 'how can I buy the armour back?'

Sir Simon shoved the boy's bed against the door again, then favoured her with a smile. 'There is something you can use to buy the armour, my dear,' he said winningly. 'You have what all women have. You can use that.'

Jeanette closed her eyes for a few heartbeats. 'Are all the gentlemen of England like you?' she asked.

'Few are so skilled in arms,' Sir Simon said proudly.

He was about to tell her of his tournament triumphs, sure that she would be impressed, but she interrupted him. 'I meant,' she said icily, 'to discover whether the knights of England are all thieves, poltroons and bullies.'

Sir Simon was genuinely puzzled by the insult. The woman simply did not seem to appreciate her good fortune, a failing he could only ascribe to innate stupidity. 'You forget, madame,' he explained, 'that the winners of war get the prizes.'

'I am your prize?'

She was worse than stupid. Sir Simon thought, but who wanted cleverness in a woman? 'Madame,' he said, 'I am your protector. If I leave you, if I take away my protection, then there will be a line of men on the stairs waiting to plough you. Now do you understand?'

'I think,' she said coldly, 'that the Earl of Northampton will offer me better protection.'

Sweet Christ, Sir Simon thought, but the bitch was obtuse. It was pointless trying to reason with her for she was too dull to understand, so he must force the breach. He crossed the room fast, snatched Charles from her arms and threw the boy onto the smaller bed. Jeanette cried out and tried to hit him, but Sir Simon caught her arm and slapped her face with his gloved hand and, when she went immobile with pain and astonishment, he tore her cloak's cords apart and then, with his big hands, ripped the shift down the front of her body. She screamed and tried to clutch her hands over her nakedness, but Sir Simon forced her arms apart and stared in astonishment. Flawless!

'No!' Jeanette wept.

Sir Simon shoved her hard back onto the bed. 'You want your son to inherit your traitorous husband's armour?' he asked. 'Or his sword? Then, madame, you had better be kind to their new owner. I am prepared to be kind to you.' He unbuckled the sword, dropped it on the floor, then hitched up his mail coat and fumbled with the strings of his hose.

'No!' Jeanette wailed, and tried to scramble off the

bed, but Sir Simon caught hold of her shift and yanked the linen so that it came down to her waist. The boy was screaming and Sir Simon was fumbling with his rusted gauntlets and Jeanette felt the devil had come into her house. She tried to cover her nakedness, but the Englishman slapped her face again, then once more hauled up his mail coat. Outside the window the cracked bell of the Virgin's church was at last silent, for the English had come, Jeanette had a suitor and the town wept.

Thomas's first thought after opening the gate was not plunder, but somewhere to wash the river muck off his legs, which he did with a barrel of ale in the first tavern he encountered. The tavern-keeper was a big bald man who stupidly attacked the English archers with a club, so Jake tripped him with his bowstave, then slit his belly.

'Silly bastard,' Jake said. 'I wasn't going to hurt him. Much.'

The dead man's boots fitted Thomas, which was a welcome surprise, for very few did, and once they had found his cache of coins they went in search of other amusement. The Earl of Northampton was spurring his horse up and down the main street, shouting at wild-eyed men not to set the town alight. He wanted to keep La Roche-Derrien as a fortress, and it was less useful to him as a heap of ashes.

Not everyone plundered. Some of the older men, even a few of the younger, were disgusted by the whole business and attempted to curb the wilder excesses, but they were wildly outnumbered by men who saw nothing but opportunity in the fallen town. Father Hobbe, an English priest who had a fondness for Will Skeat's men, tried to persuade Thomas and his group to guard a church, but they had other pleasures in mind. 'Don't spoil your soul, Tom,' Father Hobbe said in a reminder that Thomas, like all the men, had said Mass the day before, but Thomas reckoned his soul was going to be spoiled anyway so it might as well happen sooner than later. He was looking for a girl, any girl really, for most of Will's men had a woman in camp. Thomas had been living with a sweet little Breton, but she had caught a fever just before the beginning of the winter campaign and Father Hobbe had said a funeral Mass for her. Thomas had watched as the girl's unshrouded body had thumped into the shallow grave and he had thought of the graves at Hookton and of the promise he had made to his dying father, but then he had pushed the promise away. He was young and had no appetite for burdens on his conscience.

La Roche-Derrien now crouched under the English fury. Men tore down thatch and wrecked furniture in their search for money. Any townsman who tried to protect his women was killed, while any woman who tried to protect herself was beaten into submission. Some folk had escaped the sack by crossing the bridge, but the small garrison of the barbican fled from the inevitable attack and now the Earl's men-at-arms manned the small tower and that meant La Roche-Derrien was sealed to its fate. Some women took refuge in the churches and the lucky ones found protectors there, but most were not lucky.

Thomas, Jake and Sam finally discovered an unplundered house that belonged to a tanner, a stinking fellow with an ugly wife and three small children. Sam, whose innocent face made strangers trust him on sight, held his knife at the throat of the youngest child and the tanner suddenly remembered where he had hidden his cash. Thomas had watched Sam, fearing he really would slit the boy's throat, for Sam, despite his ruddy cheeks and cheerful eyes, was as evil as any man in Will Skeat's band. Jake was not much better, though Thomas counted both as friends.

'The man's as poor as we are,' Jake said in wonderment as he raked through the tanner's coins. He pushed a third of the pile towards Thomas. 'You want his wife?' Jake offered generously.

'Christ, no! She's cross-eyed like you.'

'Is she?'

Thomas left Jake and Sam to their games and went to find a tavern where there would be food, drink and warmth. He reckoned any girl worth pursuing had been caught already, so he unstrung his bow, pushed past a group of men tearing the contents from a parked wagon and found an inn where a motherly widow had sensibly protected both her property and her daughters by welcoming the first men-at-arms, showering them with free food and ale, then scolding them for dirtying her floor with their muddy feet. She was shouting at them now, though few understood what she said, and one of the men growled at Thomas that she and her daughters were to be left alone.

Thomas held up his hands to show he meant no harm, then took a plate of bread, eggs and cheese. 'Now pay her,' one of the men-at-arms growled, and Thomas dutifully put the tanner's few coins on the counter.

'He's a good-looking one,' the widow said to her daughters, who giggled.

Thomas turned and pretended to inspect the daughters. 'They are the most beautiful girls in Brittany,' he said to the widow in French, 'because they take after you, madame.'

That compliment, though patently untrue, raised squeals of laughter. Beyond the tavern were screams and tears, but inside it was warm and friendly. Thomas ate the food hungrily, then tried to hide himself in a window bay when Father Hobbe came bustling in from the street. The priest saw Thomas anyway.

'I'm still looking for men to guard the churches, Thomas.'

'I'm going to get drunk, father,' Thomas said happily. 'So goddamn drunk that one of those two girls will look attractive.' He jerked his head at the widow's daughters.

Father Hobbe inspected them critically, then sighed. 'You'll kill yourself if you drink that much, Thomas.' He sat at the table, waved at the girls and pointed at Thomas's pot. 'I'll have a drink with you,' the priest said.

'What about the churches?'

'Everyone will be drunk soon enough,' Father Hobbe said, 'and the horror will end. It always does. Ale and wine, God knows, are great causes of sin but they make it short-lived. God's bones, but it's cold out there.' He smiled at Thomas. 'So how's your black soul, Tom?'

Thomas contemplated the priest. He liked Father Hobbe, who was small and wiry, with a mass of untamed black hair about a cheerful face that was thick-scarred from a childhood pox. He was low born, the son of a Sussex wheelwright, and like any country lad

93

he could draw a bow with the best of them. He sometimes accompanied Skeat's men on their forays into
Duke Charles's country and he willingly joined the
archers when they dismounted to form a battleline.
Church law forbade a priest from wielding an edged
weapon, but Father Hobbe always claimed he used
blunt arrows, though they seemed to pierce enemy mail
as efficiently as any other. Father Hobbe, in short, was
a good man whose only fault was an excessive interest
in Thomas's soul.

'My soul,' Thomas said, 'is soluble in ale.'

'Now there's a good word,' Father Hobbe said. 'Soluble, eh?' He picked up the big black bow and prodded
the silver badge with a dirty finger. 'You've discovered
anything about that?'

'No.'

'Or who stole the lance?'

'No.'

'Do you not care any more?'

Thomas leaned back in the chair and stretched
his long legs. 'I'm doing a good job of work, father.
We're winning this war, and this time next year? Who
knows? We might be giving the King of France a bloody
nose.'

Father Hobbe nodded agreement, though his face
suggested Thomas's words were irrelevant. He traced
his finger through a puddle of ale on the table top. 'You
made a promise to your father, Thomas, and you made
it in a church. Isn't that what you told me? A solemn
promise, Thomas? That you would retrieve the lance?
God listens to such vows.'

Thomas smiled. 'Outside this tavern, father, there's
so much rape and murder and theft going on that all

the quills in heaven can't keep up with the list of sins. And you worry about me?'

'Yes, Thomas, I do. Some souls are better than others. I must look after them all, but if you have a prize ram in the flock then you do well to guard it.'

Thomas sighed. 'One day, father, I'll find the man who stole that goddamn lance and I'll ram it up his arse until it tickles the hollow of his skull. One day. Will that do?'

Father Hobbe smiled beatifically. 'It'll do, Thomas, but for now there's a small church that could do with an extra man by the door. It's full of women! Some of them are so beautiful that your heart will break just to gaze at them. You can get drunk afterwards.'

'Are the women really beautiful?'

'What do you think, Thomas? Most of them look like bats and smell like goats, but they still need protection.'

So Thomas helped guard a church, and afterwards, when the army was so drunk it could do no more damage, he went back to the widow's tavern where he drank himself into oblivion. He had taken a town, he had served his lord well and he was content.

Thomas was woken by a kick. A pause, then a second kick and a cup of cold water in his face. 'Jesus!'

'That's me,' Will Skeat said. 'Father Hobbe told me you'd be here.'

'Oh, Jesus,' Thomas said again. His head was sore, his belly sour and he felt sick. He blinked feebly at the daylight, then frowned at Skeat. 'It's you.'

'It must be grand to be so clever,' Skeat said. He grinned at Thomas, who was naked in the straw of the tavern stables that he was sharing with one of the widow's daughters. 'You must have been drunk as a lord to sheathe your sword in that,' Skeat added, looking at the girl who was pulling a blanket over herself.

'I was drunk,' Thomas groaned. 'Still am.' He staggered to his feet and put on his shirt.

'The Earl wants to see you,' Skeat said with amusement.

'Me?' Thomas looked alarmed. 'Why?'

'Perhaps he wants you to marry his daughter,' Skeat said. 'Christ's bones, Tom, but look at the state of you!'

Thomas pulled on his boots and mail coat, then retrieved his hose from the baggage camp and donned a cloth jacket over his mail. The jacket bore the Earl of Northampton's badge of three green and red stars being pounced on by a trio of lions. He splashed water on his face, then scraped at his stubble with a sharp knife.

'Grow a beard, lad,' Skeat said, 'it saves trouble.'

'Why does Billy want to see me?' Thomas asked, using the Earl's nickname.

'After what happened in the town yesterday?' Skeat suggested thoughtfully. 'He reckons he's got to hang someone as an example, so he asked me if I had any useless bastards I wanted to be rid of and I thought of you.'

'The way I feel,' Thomas said, 'he might as well hang me.' He retched drily, then gulped down some water.

He and Will Skeat went back into the town to find the Earl of Northampton sitting in state. The building where his banner hung was supposed to be a guildhall, though it was probably smaller than the guardroom in the Earl's own castle, but the Earl was sitting at one end as a succession of petitioners pleaded for justice. They were complaining about being robbed, which was pointless considering they had refused to surrender the town, but the Earl listened politely enough. Then a lawyer, a weasel-snouted fellow called Belas, bowed to the Earl and declaimed a long moan about the treatment offered to the Countess of Armorica. Thomas had been letting the words slide past him, but the insistence in Belas's voice made him take notice.

'If your lordship,' Belas said, smirking at the Earl, 'had not intervened, then the Countess would have been raped by Sir Simon Jekyll.'

Sir Simon stood to one side of the hall. 'That is a lie!' he protested in French.

The Earl sighed. 'So why were your breeches round your ankles when I came into the house?'

97

Sir Simon reddened as the men in the hall laughed. Thomas had to translate for Will Skeat, who nodded, for he had already heard the tale.

'The bastard was about to roger some titled widow,' he explained to Thomas, 'when the Earl came in. Heard her scream, see? And he'd seen a coat of arms on the house. The aristocracy look after each other.'

The lawyer now laid a long list of charges against Sir Simon. It seemed he was claiming the widow and her son as prisoners who must be held for ransom. He had also stolen the widow's two ships, her husband's armour, his sword and all the Countess's money. Belas made the complaints indignantly, then bowed to the Earl. 'You have a reputation as a just man, my lord,' he said obsequiously, 'and I place the widow's fate in your hands.'

The Earl of Northampton looked surprised to be told his reputation for fairness. 'What is it you want?' he asked.

Belas preened. 'The return of the stolen items, my lord, and the protection of the King of England for a widow and her noble son.'

The Earl drummed his fingers on the arm of the chair, then frowned at Sir Simon. 'You can't ransom a three-year-old,' he said.

'He's a count!' Sir Simon protested. 'A boy of rank!'

The Earl sighed. Sir Simon, he had come to realize, had a mind as simple as a bullock seeking food. He could see no point of view but his own and was single-minded about pursuing his appetites. That, perhaps, was why he was such a formidable soldier, but he was still a fool. 'We do not hold three-year-old children to ransom,' the Earl said firmly, 'and we don't hold women as prisoners, not unless there is an advantage which outweighs the courtesy, and I see no advantage here.' The Earl turned to the clerks behind his chair. 'Who did Armorica support?'

'Charles of Blois, my lord,' one of the clerks, a tall Breton cleric, answered.

'Is it a rich fief?'

'Very small, my lord,' the clerk, whose nose was running, spoke from memory. 'There is a holding in Finisterre which is already in our hands, some houses in Guingamp, I believe, but nothing else.'

'There,' the Earl said, turning back to Sir Simon. 'What advantages will we make from a penniless three-year-old?'

'Not penniless,' Sir Simon protested. 'I took a rich armour there.'

'Which the boy's father doubtless took in battle!'

'And the house is wealthy.' Sir Simon was getting angry. 'There are ships, storehouses, stables.'

'The house,' the clerk sounded bored, 'belonged to the Count's father-in-law. A dealer in wine, I believe.'

The Earl raised a quizzical eyebrow at Sir Simon, who was shaking his head at the clerk's obstinacy. 'The boy, my lord,' Sir Simon responded with an elaborate courtesy which bordered on insolence, 'is kin to Charles of Blois.'

'But being penniless,' the Earl said, 'I doubt he provokes fondness. More of a burden, wouldn't you think? Besides, what would you have me do? Make the child give fealty to the real Duke of Brittany? The real Duke, Sir Simon, is a five-year-old child in London. It'll be a nursery farce! A three-year-old bobbing down to a five-year-old! Do their wet nurses attend them? Shall we feast on milk and penny-cakes after? Or maybe we can enjoy a game of hunt the slipper when the ceremony is over?'

'The Countess fought us from the walls!' Sir Simon attempted a last protest.

'Do not dispute me!' the Earl shouted, thumping the arm of his chair. 'You forget that I am the King's deputy and have his powers.' The Earl leaned back, taut with anger, and Sir Simon swallowed his own fury, but could not resist muttering that the Countess had used a crossbow against the English.

'Is she the Blackbird?' Thomas asked Skeat.

'The Countess? Aye, that's what they say.'

'She's a beauty.'

'After what I found you prodding this morning,' Skeat said, 'how can you tell?'

The Earl gave an irritated glance at Skeat and Thomas, then looked back to Sir Simon. 'If the Countess did fight us from the walls,' he said, 'then I admire her spirit. As for the other matters . . .' He paused and sighed. Belas looked expectant and Sir Simon wary. 'The two ships,' the Earl decreed, 'are prizes and they will be sold in England or else taken into royal service, and you, Sir Simon, will be awarded one-third of their value.' That ruling was according to the law. The King would take a third, the Earl another and the last portion went to the man who had captured the prize. 'As to the sword and armour . . .' The Earl paused again. He had rescued Jeanette from rape and he had liked her, and he had seen the anguish on her face and listened to her impassioned plea that she owned nothing that had belonged to her husband except the precious armour and the beautiful sword, but such things, by their very

100

nature, were the legitimate plunder of war. 'The armour and weapons and horses are yours, Sir Simon,' the Earl said, regretting the judgement but knowing it was fair. 'As to the child, I decree he is under the protection of the Crown of England and when he is of age he can decide his own fealty.' He glanced at the clerks to make sure they were noting down his decisions. 'You tell me you wish to billet yourself in the widow's house?' he asked Sir Simon.

'I took it,' Sir Simon said curtly.

'And stripped it bare, I hear,' the Earl observed icily. 'The Countess claims you stole money from her.'

'She lies.' Sir Simon looked indignant. 'Lies, my lord, lies!'

The Earl doubted it, but he could hardly accuse a gentleman of perjury without provoking a duel and, though William Bohun feared no man except his king, he did not want to fight over so petty a matter. He let it drop. 'However,' he went on, 'I did promise the lady protection against harassment.' He stared at Sir Simon as he spoke, then looked at Will Skeat, and changed to English. 'You'd like to keep your men together, Will?'

'I would, my lord.'

'Then you'll have the widow's house. And she is to be treated honourably, you hear me? Honourably! Tell your men that, Will!'

Skeat nodded. 'I'll cut their ears off if they touch her, my lord.'

'Not their ears, Will. Slice something more suitable away. Sir Simon will show you the house and you, Sir Simon,' the Earl spoke French again, 'will find a bed elsewhere.'

Sir Simon opened his mouth to protest, but one look

from the Earl quietened him. Another petitioner came forward, wanting redress for a cellar full of wine that had been stolen, but the Earl diverted him to a clerk who would record the man's complaints on a parchment which the Earl doubted he would ever find time to read.

Then he beckoned to Thomas. 'I have to thank you, Thomas of Hookton.'

'Thank me, my lord?'

The Earl smiled. 'You found a way into the town when everything else we'd tried had failed.'

Thomas reddened. 'It was a pleasure, my lord.'

'You can claim a reward of me,' the Earl said. 'It's customary.'

Thomas shrugged. 'I'm happy, my lord.'

'Then you're a lucky man, Thomas. But I shall remember the debt. And thank you, Will.'

Will Skeat grinned. 'If this lump of a daft fool don't want a reward, my lord, I'll take it.'

The Earl liked that. 'My reward to you, Will, is to leave you here. I'm giving you a whole new stretch of countryside to lay waste. God's teeth, you'll soon be richer than me.' He stood. 'Sir Simon will guide you to your quarters.'

Sir Simon might have bridled at the curt order to be a mere guide, but surprisingly he obeyed without showing any resentment, perhaps because he wanted another chance to meet Jeanette. And so, at midday, he led Will Skeat and his men through the streets to the big house beside the river. Sir Simon had put on his new armour and wore it without any surcoat so that the polished plate and gold embossment shone bright in the feeble winter sun. He ducked his helmeted head

102

under the yard's archway and immediately Jeanette came running from the kitchen door, which lay just to the gate's left.

'Get out!' she shouted in French, 'get out!'

Thomas, riding close behind Sir Simon, stared at her. She was indeed the Blackbird and she was as beautiful at close range as she had been when he had glimpsed her on the walls.

'Get out, all of you!' She stood, hands on her hips, bareheaded, shouting.

Sir Simon pushed up the pig-snout visor of the helmet. 'This house is commandeered, my lady,' he said happily. 'The Earl ordered it.'

'The Earl promised I would be left alone!' Jeanette protested hotly.

'Then his lordship has changed his mind,' Sir Simon said.

She spat at him. 'You have already stolen everything else of mine, now you would take the house too?'

'Yes, madame,' Sir Simon said, and he spurred the horse forward so that it crowded her. 'Yes, madame,' he said again, then wrenched the reins so that the horse twisted and thumped into Jeanette, throwing her onto the ground. 'I'll take your house,' Sir Simon said, 'and anything else I want, madame.' The watching archers cheered at the sight of Jeanette's long bare legs. She snatched her skirts down and tried to stand, but Sir Simon edged his horse forward to force her into an undignified scramble across the yard.

'Let the lass up!' Will Skeat shouted angrily.

'She and I are old friends, Master Skeat,' Sir Simon answered, still threatening Jeanette with the horse's heavy hoofs.

'I said let her up and leave her be!' Will snarled.

Sir Simon, offended at being ordered by a commoner and in front of archers, turned angrily, but there was a competence about Will Skeat that gave the knight pause. Skeat was twice Sir Simon's age and all those years had been spent in fighting, and Sir Simon retained just enough sense not to make a confrontation. 'The house is yours, Master Skeat,' he said condescendingly, 'but look after its mistress. I have plans for her.' He backed the horse from Jeanette, who was in tears of shame, then spurred out of the yard.

Jeanette did not understand English, but she recognized that Will Skeat had intervened on her behalf and so she stood and appealed to him. 'He has stolen everything from me!' she said, pointing at the retreating horseman. 'Everything!'

'You know what the lass is saying, Tom?' Skeat asked.

'She doesn't like Sir Simon,' Thomas said laconically. He was leaning on his saddle pommel, watching Jeanette.

'Calm the girl down, for Christ's sake,' Skeat pleaded, then turned in his saddle. 'Jake? Make sure there's water and hay for horses. Peter, kill two of them heifers so we can sup before the light goes. Rest of you? Stop gawping at the lass and get yourselves settled!'

'Thief!' Jeanette called after Sir Simon, then turned on Thomas. 'Who are you?'

'My name is Thomas, madame.' He slid out of the saddle and threw his reins to Sam. 'The Earl has ordered us to live here,' Thomas went on, 'and to protect you.'

'Protect me!' Jeanette blazed at him. 'You are all thieves! How can you protect me? There is a place in hell for thieves like you and it is just like England. You are thieves, every one of you! Now, go! Go!'

'We're not going,' Thomas said flatly.

'How can you stay here?' Jeanette demanded. 'I am a widow! It is not proper to have you here.'

'We're here, madame,' Thomas said, 'and you and us will have to make the best of it. We'll not encroach. Just show me where your private rooms are and I'll make sure no man trespasses.'

'You? Make sure? Ha!' Jeanette turned away, then immediately turned back. 'You want me to show you my rooms, yes? So you know where my valuable properties are? Is that it? You want me to show you where you can thieve from me? Why don't I just give you everything?'

Thomas smiled. 'I thought you said Sir Simon had already stolen everything?'

'He has taken everything, everything! He is no gentleman. He is a pig. He is,' Jeanette paused, wanting to contrive a crushing insult, 'he is English!' Jeanette spat at Thomas's feet and pulled open the kitchen door. 'You see this door, Englishman? Everything beyond this door is private. Everything!' She went inside, slammed the door, then immediately opened it again. 'And the Duke is coming. The proper Duke, not your snivelling puppet child, so you will all die. Good!' The door slammed again.

Will Skeat chuckled. 'She don't like you either, Tom. What was the lass saying?'

'That we're all going to die.'

'Aye, that's true enough. But in our beds, by God's grace.'

'And she says we're not to go past that door.'

'Plenty of room out here,' Skeat said placidly,

watching as one of his men swung an axe to kill a heifer. The blood flowed over the yard, attracting a rush of dogs to lap at it while two archers began butchering the still twitching animal.

'Listen!' Skeat had climbed a mounting block beside the stables and now shouted at all his men. 'The Earl has given orders that the lass who was spitting at Tom is not to be molested. You understand that, you whoresons? You keep your britches laced up when she's around, and if you don't, I'll geld you! You treat her proper, and you don't go through that door. You've had your frolic, so now you can knuckle down to a proper bit of soldiering.'

The Earl of Northampton left after a week, taking most of his army back to the fortresses in Finisterre, which was the heartland of Duke John's supporters. He left Richard Totesham as commander of the new garrison, but he also left Sir Simon Jekyll as Totesham's deputy.

'The Earl doesn't want the bastard,' Will Skeat told Thomas, 'so he's foisted him on us.'

As Skeat and Totesham were both independent captains, there could have been jealousy between them, but the two men respected each other and, while Totesham and his men stayed in La Roche-Derrien and strengthened its defences, Skeat rode out into the country to punish the folk who paid their rents and owed their allegiance to Duke Charles. The hellequin were thus released to be a curse on northern Brittany.

It was a simple business to ruin a land. The houses and barns might be made of stone, but their roofs would burn. The livestock was captured and, if there were too many beasts to herd home, then the animals were slaughtered and their carcasses tipped down wells to poison the water. Skeat's men burned what would burn, broke what would break and stole what could be sold. They killed, raped and plundered. Fear of them drove men away from their farms, leaving the land desolate. They were the devil's horsemen, and they did King Edward's will by harrowing his enemy's land.

They wrecked village after village – Kervec and Lanvellec, St Laurent and Les Sept Saints, Tonquedec and Berhet, and a score of other places whose names they never learned. It was Christmas time, and back home the yule logs were being dragged across frost-hardened fields to high-beamed halls where troubadours sang of Arthur and his knights, of chivalrous warriors who allied pity to strength, but in Brittany the hellequin fought the real war. Soldiers were not paragons; they were scarred, vicious men who took delight in destruction. They hurled burning torches onto thatch and tore down what had taken generations to build. Places too small to have names died, and only the farms in the wide peninsula between the two rivers north of La Roche-Derrien were spared because they were needed to feed the garrison. Some of the serfs who were torn from their land were put to work heightening La Roche-Derrien's walls, clearing a wider killing ground in front of the ramparts and making new barriers at the river's edge. It was a winter of utter misery for the Bretons. Cold rains whipped from the wild Atlantic and the English scoured the farmlands.

Once in a while there would be some resistance. A brave man would shoot a crossbow from a wood's edge, but Skeat's men were experts in trapping and killing such enemies. A dozen archers would dismount and stalk the enemy from the front while a score of others galloped about his rear, and in a short while there would be a scream and another crossbow was added to the plunder. The crossbow's owner would be stripped, mutilated and hanged from a tree as a warning to other men to leave the hellequin alone, and the lessons worked, for such ambushes became fewer. It was the wrecking time and Skeat's men became rich. There were days of misery, days of slogging through cold rain with chapped hands and wet clothes, and Thomas always hated it when his men fetched the duty of leading the spare horses and then driving the captured livestock home. Geese were easy – their necks were wrung and the dead birds hung from the saddles – but cows were slow, goats wayward, sheep stupid and pigs obstinate. There were, however, enough farm-bred boys in the ranks to ensure that the animals reached La Roche-Derrien safely. Once there they were taken to a small square that had become a slaughteryard and stank of blood. Will Skeat also sent cartloads of plunder back to the town and most of that was shipped home to England. It was usually humble stuff: pots, knives, plough-blades, harrow-spikes, stools, pails, spindles, anything that could be sold, until it was said that there was not a house in southern England which did not possess at least one object plundered from Brittany.

In England they sang of Arthur and Lancelot, of Gawain and Perceval, but in Brittany the hellequin were loose.

And Thomas was a happy man.

*   *   *

Jeanette was loath to admit it, but the presence of Will Skeat's men was an advantage to her. So long as they were in the courtyard she felt safe in the house and she began to dread the long periods they spent away from the town, for it was then that Sir Simon Jekyll would haunt her. She had begun to think of him as the devil, a stupid devil to be sure, but still a remorseless, unfeeling lout who had convinced himself Jeanette must wish nothing so much as to be his wife. At times he would force himself to a clumsy courtesy, though usually he was bumptious and crude and always he stared at her like a dog gazing at a haunch of beef. He took Mass in the church of St Renan so he could woo her, and it seemed to Jeanette she could not walk in the town without meeting him. Once, encountering Jeanette in the alley beside the church of the Virgin, he crowded her against the wall and slid his strong fingers up to her breasts.

'I think, madame, you and I are suited,' he told her in all earnestness.

'You need a wife with money,' she told him, for she had learned from others in the town the state of Sir Simon's finances.

'I have your money,' he pointed out, 'and that has settled half my debts, and the prize money from the ships will pay much of the rest. But it is not your money I want, sweet one, but you.' Jeanette tried to wrench away, but he had her trapped against the wall. 'You need a protector, my dear,' he said, and kissed her tenderly on the forehead. He had a curiously full mouth, big-lipped and always wet as though his tongue was too large, and the kiss was wet and stank of stale wine. He pushed a hand down her belly and she struggled harder, but he just pressed his body against hers and took hold of her hair beneath her cap. 'You would like Berkshire, my dear.'

'I would rather live in hell.'

He fumbled at the laces of her bodice and Jeanette vainly tried to push him away, but she was only saved when a troop of men rode into the alley and their leader called a greeting to Sir Simon, who had to turn away to respond and that allowed Jeanette to wrench herself free. She left her cap in his grasp as she ran home, where she barred the doors, then sat weeping and angry and helpless. She hated him.

She hated all the English, yet as the weeks passed she watched the townsfolk come to approve of their occupiers, who spent good money in La Roche-Derrien. English silver was dependable, unlike the French, which was debased with lead or tin. The presence of the English had cut the town off from its usual trade with Rennes and Guingamp, but the shipowners were now free to trade with both Gascony and England and so their profits rose. Local ships were chartered to import arrows for the English troops, and some of the shipmasters brought back bales of English wool that they resold in other Breton ports that were still loyal to Duke Charles. Few folk were willing to travel far from La Roche-Derrien by land, for they needed to secure a pass from Richard Totesham, the commander of the garrison, and though the scrap of parchment protected them from the hellequin it was no defence against the outlaws who lived in the farms emptied by Skeat's men. But boats from La Roche-Derrien and Tréguier could still sail east to Paimpol or west to Lannion and so trade with England's enemies. That was how letters were sent out of

La Roche-Derrien, and Jeanette wrote almost weekly to Duke Charles with news of the changes the English were making to the town's defences. She never received a reply, but she persuaded herself that her letters were useful.

La Roche-Derrien prospered, but Jeanette suffered. Her father's business still existed, but the profits mysteriously vanished. The larger ships had always sailed from the quays of Tréguier, which lay an hour upriver, and though Jeanette sent them to Gascony to fetch wine for the English market, they never returned. They had either been taken by French ships or, more likely, their captains had gone into business for themselves. The family farms lay south of La Roche-Derrien, in the countryside laid waste by Will Skeat's men, and so those rents disappeared. Plabennec, her husband's estate, was in English-held Finisterre and Jeanette had not seen a penny from that land in three years, so by the early weeks of 1346 she was desperate and thus summoned the lawyer Belas to the house.

Belas took a perverse pleasure in telling her how she had ignored his advice, and how she should never have equipped the two boats for war. Jeanette suffered his pomposity, then asked him to draw up a petition of redress which she could send to the English court. The petition begged for the rents of Plabennec, which the invaders had been taking for themselves. It irked Jeanette that she must plead for money from King Edward III of England, but what choice did she have? Sir Simon Jekyll had impoverished her.

Belas sat at her table and made notes on a scrap of parchment. 'How many mills at Plabennec?' he asked.

'There were two.'

'Two,' he said, noting the figure. 'You do know,' he added cautiously, 'that the Duke has made a claim for those rents?'

'The Duke?' Jeanette asked in astonishment. 'For Plabennec?'

'Duke Charles claims it is his fief,' Belas said.

'It might be, but my son is the Count.'

'The Duke considers himself the boy's guardian,' Belas observed.

'How do you know these things?' Jeanette asked.

Belas shrugged. 'I have had correspondence from the Duke's men of business in Paris.'

'What correspondence?' Jeanette demanded sharply.

'About another matter,' Belas said dismissively, 'another matter entirely. Plabennec's rents were collected quarterly, I assume?'

Jeanette watched the lawyer suspiciously. 'Why would the Duke's men of business mention Plabennec to you?'

'They asked if I knew the family. Naturally I revealed nothing.'

He was lying, Jeanette thought. She owed Belas money, indeed she was in debt to half of La Roche-Derrien's tradesmen. Doubtless Belas thought his bill was unlikely to be paid by her and so he was looking to Duke Charles for eventual settlement. 'Monsieur Belas,' she said coldly, 'you will tell me exactly what you have been telling the Duke, and why.'

Belas shrugged. 'I have nothing to tell!'

'How is your wife?' Jeanette asked sweetly.

'Her aches are passing as winter ends, thank God. She is well, madame.'

'Then she will not be well,' Jeanette said tartly, 'when

she learns what you do with your clerk's daughter? How old is she, Belas? Twelve?'

'Madame!'

'Don't madame me!' Jeanette thumped the table, almost upsetting the flask of ink. 'So what has passed between you and the Duke's men of business?'

Belas sighed. He put the cap on the ink flask, laid down the quill and rubbed his thin cheeks. 'I have always,' he said, 'looked after the legal matters of this family. It is my duty, madame, and sometimes I must do things that I would rather not, but such things are also a part of my duty.' He half smiled. 'You are in debt, madame. You could rescue your finances easily enough by marrying a man of substance, but you seem reluctant to follow that course and so I see nothing but ruin in your future. Ruin. You wish some advice? Sell this house and you will have money enough to live for two or three years, and in that time the Duke will surely drive the English from Brittany and you and your son will be restored to Plabennec.'

Jeanette flinched. 'You think the devils will be defeated that easily?' She heard hoofs in the street and saw that Skeat's men were returning to her courtyard. They were laughing as they rode. They did not look like men who would be defeated soon; indeed, she feared they were unbeatable for they had a blithe confidence that galled her.

'I think, madame,' Belas said, 'that you must make up your mind what you are. Are you Louis Halevy's daughter? Or Henri Chenier's widow? Are you a merchant or an aristocrat? If you are a merchant, madame, then marry here and be content. If you are an aristocrat then raise what money you can and go to

113

the Duke and find yourself a new husband with a title.'

Jeanette considered the advice impertinent, but did not bridle. 'How much would we make on this house?' she asked instead.

'I shall enquire, madame,' Belas said. He knew the answer already, and knew that Jeanette would hate it, for a house in a town occupied by an enemy would fetch only a fraction of its proper value. So now was not the time to give Jeanette that news. Better, the lawyer thought, to wait until she was truly desperate, then he could buy the house and its ruined farms for a pittance.

'Is there a bridge across the stream at Plabennec?' he asked, drawing the parchment towards him.

'Forget the petition,' Jeanette said.

'If you wish, madame.'

'I shall think about your advice, Belas.'

'You will not regret it,' he said earnestly. She was lost, he thought, lost and defeated. He would take her house and farms, the Duke would claim Plabennec and she would be left with nothing. Which was what she deserved, for she was a stubborn and proud creature who had risen far above her proper station. 'I am always,' Belas said humbly, 'at your ladyship's service.' From adversity, he thought, a clever man could always profit, and Jeanette was ripe for plucking. Put a cat to guard the sheep and the wolves would eat well.

Jeanette did not know what to do. She was loath to sell the house for she feared it would fetch a low price, but nor did she know how else she could raise money. Would Duke Charles welcome her? He had never shown any sign of it, not since he had opposed her marriage to his nephew, but perhaps he had softened

114

since then? Perhaps he would protect her? She decided she would pray for guidance; so she wrapped a shawl around her shoulders, crossed the yard, ignoring the newly returned soldiers, and went into St Renan's church. There was a statue of the virgin there, sadly shorn of her gilded halo, which had been ripped away by the English, and Jeanette often prayed to the image of Christ's mother, whom she believed had a special care for all women in trouble.

She thought at first that the dimly lit church was empty. Then she saw an English bow propped against a pillar and an archer kneeling at the altar. It was the good-looking man, the one who wore his hair in a long pigtail bound with bowcord. It was, she thought, an irritating sign of vanity. Most of the English wore their hair cropped, but a few grew it extravagantly long and they were the ones who seemed most flamboyantly confident. She wished he would leave the church; then she was intrigued by his abandoned bow and so she picked it up and was astonished by its weight. The string hung loose and she wondered how much strength would be needed to bend the bow and hook the string's free loop on the empty horn tip. She pressed one end of the bow on the stone floor, trying to bend it, and just then an arrow span across the flagstones to lodge against her foot.

'If you can string the bow,' Thomas said, still on his knees at the altar, 'you can have a free shot.'

Jeanette was too proud to be seen to fail and too angry not to try, though she attempted to disguise her effort which barely flexed the black yew stave. She kicked the arrow away. 'My husband was killed by one of these bows,' she said bitterly.

'I've often wondered,' Thomas said, 'why you Bretons or the French don't learn to shoot them. Start your son at seven or eight years, madame, and in ten years he'll be lethal.'

'He'll fight as a knight, like his father.'

Thomas laughed. 'We kill knights. They haven't made an armour strong enough to resist an English arrow.'

Jeanette shuddered. 'What are you praying for, Englishman?' she asked. 'Forgiveness?'

Thomas smiled. 'I am giving thanks, madame, for the fact that we rode six days in enemy country and did not lose one man.' He climbed from his knees and pointed to a pretty silver box that sat on the altar. It was a reliquary and had a small crystal window that was rimmed with drops of coloured glass. Thomas had peered through the window and seen nothing more than a small black lump about the size of a man's thumb. 'What is it?' he asked.

'The tongue of St Renan,' Jeanette said defiantly. 'It was stolen when you came to our town, but God was good and the thief died next day and the relic was recovered.'

'God is indeed good,' Thomas said drily. 'And who was St Renan?'

'He was a great preacher,' she said, 'who banished the *nains* and *gorics* from our farmlands. They still live in the wild places, but a prayer to St Renan will scare them away.'

'*Nains* and *gorics*?' Thomas asked.

'They are spirits,' she said, 'evil ones. They once haunted the whole land, and I pray daily to the saint that he will banish the hellequin as he drove out the *nains*. You know what the hellequin are?'

'We are,' Thomas said proudly.

She grimaced at his tone. 'The hellequin,' she said icily, 'are the dead who have no souls. The dead who were so wicked in life that the devil loves them too much to punish them in hell and so he gives them his horses and releases them on the living.' She hefted his black bow and pointed to the silver plate tacked to its belly. 'You even have the devil's picture on your bow.'

'It's a yale,' Thomas said.

'It is a devil,' she insisted, and threw the bow at him. Thomas caught it and, because he was too young to resist showing off, casually strung it. He made it appear effortless. 'You pray to St Renan,' he said, 'and I shall pray to St Guinefort. We shall see which saint is the stronger.'

'Guinefort? I've not heard of her.'

'Him,' Thomas corrected her, 'and he lived in the Lyonnaise.'

'You pray to a French saint?' Jeanette asked, intrigued.

'All the time,' Thomas said, touching the desiccated dog's paw that hung about his neck. He did not tell Jeanette anything more about the saint, who had been a favourite of his father's – who, in his better moments, would laugh at the story. Guinefort had been a dog and, so far as Thomas's father knew, the only animal ever to be canonized. The beast had saved a baby from a wolf, then been martyred by his owner, who thought the dog had eaten the baby when in truth he had hidden it beneath the cot. 'Pray to the blessed Guinefort!' had been Father Ralph's reaction to every domestic crisis, and Thomas had adopted the saint as his own. He sometimes wondered whether the saint was an efficient intercessor in heaven, though perhaps Guinefort's whining and barking were as effective as the pleas of any other saint, but Thomas was sure that few other folk used the dog as their representative to God and perhaps that meant he received special protection. Father Hobbe had been shocked to hear of a holy dog, but Thomas, though he shared his father's amusement, now genuinely thought of the animal as his guardian.

Jeanette wanted to know more about the blessed St Guinefort, but she did not want to encourage an intimacy with any of Skeat's men and so she forgot her curiosity and made her voice cold again. 'I have been wanting to see you,' she said, 'to tell you that your men and their women must not use the yard as a latrine. I see them from the window. It is disgusting! Maybe you behave like that in England, but this is Brittany. You can use the river.'

Thomas nodded, but said nothing. Instead he carried his bow down the nave, which had one of its long sides obscured by fishing nets hung up for mending. He went to the church's western end, which was gloomily decorated by a painting of the doom. The righteous were vanishing into the rafters, while the condemned sinners were tumbling to a fiery hell cheered on by angels and saints. Thomas stopped in front of the painting.

'Have you ever noticed,' he said, 'how the prettiest women are always falling down to hell and the ugly ones are going up to heaven?'

Jeanette almost smiled for she had often wondered about that same question, but she bit her tongue and said nothing as Thomas walked back up the nave beside a painting of Christ walking on a sea that was grey and white-crested like the ocean off Brittany. A shoal of mackerel were poking their heads from the water to watch the miracle.

'What you must understand, madame,' Thomas said, gazing up at the curious mackerel, 'is that our men do not like being unwelcome. You won't even let them use the kitchen. Why not? It's big enough, and they'd be glad of a place to dry their boots after a wet night's riding.'

'Why should I have you English in my kitchen? So you can use that as a latrine as well?'

Thomas turned and looked at her. 'You have no respect for us, madame, so why should we have respect for your house?'

'Respect!' She mocked the word. 'How can I respect you? Everything that is precious to me was stolen. Stolen by you!'

'By Sir Simon Jekyll,' Thomas said.

'You or Sir Simon,' Jeanette asked, 'what is the difference?'

Thomas picked up the arrow and dropped it into his bag. 'The difference, madame, is that once in a while I talk to God, while Sir Simon thinks he is God. I shall ask the lads to piss in the river, but I doubt they'll want to please you much.' He smiled at her, then was gone.

Spring was greening the land, giving a haze to the trees and filling the twisting laneways with bright flowers. New green moss grew on thatch, there was white stitchwort in the hedgerows, and kingfishers whipped between the new yellow leaves of the riverside sallows.

Skeat's men were having to go further from La Roche-Derrien to find new plunder and their long rides took them dangerously close to Guingamp, which was Duke Charles's headquarters, though the town's garrison rarely came out to challenge the raiders. Guingamp lay to the south, while to the west was Lannion, a much smaller town with a far more belligerent garrison that was inspired by Sir Geoffrey de Pont Blanc, a knight who had sworn an oath that he would lead Skeat's raiders back to Lannion in chains. He announced that the Englishmen would be burned in Lannion's marketplace because they were heretics, the devil's men.

Will Skeat was not worried by such a threat. 'I might lose a wink of sleep if the silly bastard had proper archers,' he told Tom, 'but he ain't, so he can blunder about as much as he likes. Is that his real name?'

'Geoffrey of the White Bridge.'

'Daft bastard. Is he Breton or French?'

'I'm told he's French.'

'Have to teach him a lesson then, won't we?'

Sir Geoffrey proved an unwilling pupil. Will Skeat dragged his coat closer and closer to Lannion, burning houses within sight of its walls in an effort to lure Sir Geoffrey out into an ambush of archers, but Sir Geoffrey had seen what English arrows could do to mounted knights and so he refused to lead his men in a wild charge that would inevitably finish as a pile of screaming horses and bleeding men. He stalked Skeat instead, looking for some place where he could ambush the Englishmen, but Skeat was no more of a fool than Sir Geoffrey, and for three weeks the two war bands circled and skirted each other. Sir Geoffrey's presence slowed

Skeat, but did not stop the destruction. The two forces clashed twice, and both times Sir Geoffrey threw his crossbowmen forward on foot, hoping they could finish off Skeat's archers, but both times the longer arrows won and Sir Geoffrey drew off without forcing a fight he knew he must lose. After the second inconclusive clash he even tried appealing to Will Skeat's honour. He rode forward, all alone, dressed in an armour as beautiful as Sir Simon Jekyll's, though Sir Geoffrey's helmet was an old-fashioned pot with perforated eye holes. His surcoat and his horse's trapper were dark blue on which white bridges were embroidered and the same device was blazoned on his shield. He carried a blue-painted lance from which he had hung a white scarf to show he came in peace. Skeat rode forward to meet him with Thomas as interpreter. Sir Geoffrey lifted off his helmet and pushed a hand through his sweat-flattened hair. He was a young fellow, golden-haired and blue-eyed, with a broad, good-humoured face, and Thomas felt he would probably have liked the man if he had not been an enemy. Sir Geoffrey smiled as the two Englishmen curbed their horses.

'It is a dull thing,' he said, 'to shoot arrows at each other's shadows. I suggest you bring your men-at-arms into the field's centre and meet us there on equal terms.'

Thomas did not even bother to translate, for he knew what Skeat's answer would be. 'I have a better idea,' he said, 'you bring your men-at-arms and we'll bring our archers.'

Sir Geoffrey looked puzzled. 'Do you command?' he asked Thomas. He had thought that the older and grizzled Skeat was the captain, but Skeat stayed silent.

'He lost his tongue fighting the Scots,' Thomas said, 'so I speak for him.'

'Then tell him I want an honourable fight,' Sir Geoffrey said spiritedly. 'Let me pit my horsemen against yours.' He smiled as if to suggest his suggestion was as reasonable as it was chivalrous as it was ridiculous.

Thomas translated for Skeat, who twisted in his saddle and spat into the clover.

'He says,' Thomas said, 'that our archers will meet your men. A dozen of our archers against a score of your men-at-arms.'

Sir Geoffrey shook his head sadly. 'You have no sense of sport, you English,' he said, then put his leather-lined pot back on his head and rode away. Thomas told Skeat what had passed between them.

'Silly goddamn bastard,' Skeat said. 'What did he want? A tournament? Who does he think we are? The knights of the round bloody table? I don't know what happens to some folk. They put a sir in front of their names and their brains get addled. Fighting fair! Whoever heard of anything so daft? Fight fair and you lose. Bloody fool.'

Sir Geoffrey of the White Bridge continued to haunt the hellequin, but Skeat gave him no chance for a fight. There was always a large band of archers watching the Frenchman's forces, and whenever the men from Lannion became too bold they were likely to have the goose-feathered arrows thumping into their horses. So Sir Geoffrey was reduced to a shadow, but he was an irritating and persistent shadow, following Skeat's men almost back to the gates of La Roche-Derrien.

The trouble occurred the third time that he trailed

Skeat and so came close to the town. Sir Simon Jekyll had heard of Sir Geoffrey and, warned by a sentinel on the highest church tower that Skeat's men were in sight, he led out a score of the garrison's men-at-arms to meet the hellequin. Skeat was just over a mile from the town and Sir Geoffrey, with fifty men-at-arms and as many mounted crossbowmen, was just another half-mile behind. The Frenchman had caused no great problems to Skeat and if Sir Geoffrey wanted to ride home to Lannion and claim that he had chased the hellequin back to their lair then Skeat was quite happy to give the Frenchman that satisfaction.

Then Sir Simon came and it was all suddenly display and arrogance. The English lances went up, the helmet visors clanged shut and their horses were prancing. Sir Simon rode towards the French and Breton horsemen, bellowing a challenge. Will Skeat followed Sir Simon and advised him to let the bastards be, but the Yorkshireman was wasting his breath.

Skeat's men-at-arms were at the front of the column, escorting the captured livestock and three wagons filled with plunder, while the rearguard was formed by sixty mounted archers. Those sixty men had just reached the big woods where the army had camped during the siege of La Roche-Derrien and, at a signal from Skeat, they split into two groups and rode into the trees either side of the road. They dismounted in the woods, tied their horses' reins to branches, then carried their bows to the edge of the trees. The road ran between the two groups, edged by wide grassy verges.

Sir Simon wheeled his horse to confront Will Skeat. 'I want thirty of your men-at-arms, Skeat,' he demanded peremptorily.

'You can want them,' Will Skeat said, 'but you'll not have them.'

'Good Christ, man, I outrank you!' Sir Simon was incredulous at Skeat's refusal. 'I outrank you, Skeat! I'm not asking, you fool, I'm ordering.'

Skeat looked up at the sky. 'Looks like rain, don't you think? And we could do with a drop. Fields are right dry and streams are low.'

Sir Simon reached out and gripped Skeat's arm, forcing the older man to turn to him. 'He has fifty knights,' Sir Simon spoke of Sir Geoffrey de Pont Blanc, 'and I have twenty. Give me thirty men and I'll take him prisoner. Just give me twenty!' He was pleading, all arrogance gone, for this was a chance for Sir Simon to fight a proper skirmish, horseman against horseman, and the winner would have renown and the prize of captured men and horses.

But Will Skeat knew everything about men, horses and renown. 'I'm not out here to play games,' he said, shaking his arm free, 'and you can order me till the cows sprout wings, but you'll not have a man of mine.'

Sir Simon looked anguished, but then Sir Geoffrey de Pont Blanc decided the matter. He saw how his men-at-arms outnumbered the English horsemen and so he ordered thirty of his followers to ride back and join the crossbowmen. Now the two troops of horsemen were evenly matched and Sir Geoffrey rode forward on his big black stallion that was swathed in its blue and white trapper and had a boiled leather mask for face armour, a chanfron. Sir Simon rode to meet him in his new armour, but his horse had no padded trapper and no chanfron, and he wanted both, just as he wanted this fight. All winter he had endured the misery of a peasant's war, all muck and murder, and now the enemy was offering honour, glory and the chance to capture some fine horses, armour and good weapons. The two men saluted each other by dipping their lances, then exchanged names and compliments.

Will Skeat had joined Thomas in the woods. 'You might be a woolly-headed fool, Tom,' Skeat said, 'but there's plenty more stupid than you. Look at the daft bastards! Not a brain between either of them. You could shake them by the heels and nothing would drop out of their ears but dried muck.' He spat.

Sir Geoffrey and Sir Simon agreed on the rules of the fight. Tournament rules, really, only with death to give the sport spice. An unhorsed man was out of the fight, they agreed, and would be spared, though such a man could be taken prisoner. They wished each other well then turned and rode back to their men.

Skeat tied his horse to a tree and strung his bow. 'There's a place in York,' he said, 'where you can watch the mad folk. They keep them caged up and you pay a farthing to go and laugh at them. They should put those two silly bastards in with them.'

'My father was mad for a time,' Thomas said.

'Don't surprise me, lad, don't surprise me at all.' Skeat said. He looped his bowcord onto a stave that had been carved with crosses.

His archers watched the men-at-arms from the edge of the woods. As a spectacle it was wondrous, like a tournament, only on this spring meadow there were no marshals to save a man's life. The two groups of horsemen readied themselves. Squires tightened girths, men hefted lances and made sure their shield straps were tight. Visors clanged shut, turning the horsemen's world into a dark place slashed with slitted daylight. They dropped their reins, for from now on the well-trained destriers would be guided by the touch of spur and the pressure of knees; the horsemen needed both hands for their shields and weapons. Some men wore two swords, a heavy one for slashing and a thinner blade for stabbing, and they made certain the weapons slid easily from their scabbards. Some gave their lances to squires to leave a hand free to make the sign of the cross, then took the lances back. The horses stamped on the pasture, then Sir Geoffrey lowered his lance in a signal that he was ready and Sir Simon did the same, and the forty men spurred their big horses forward. These were not the light-boned mares and geldings that the archers rode, but the heavy destriers, stallions all, and big enough to carry a man and his armour. The beasts snorted, tossed their heads and lumbered into a trot as the riders lowered their long lances. One of Sir Geoffrey's men made the beginner's mistake of lowering the lance too much so that the point struck the dry turf and he was lucky not be unhorsed. He left the lance behind and drew his sword. The horsemen spurred into the canter and one of Sir Simon's men swerved to the left, probably because his horse was ill trained, and it bumped the next horse and the ripple of colliding horses went down the line as the spurs rowelled back to demand the gallop. Then they struck.

The sound of the wooden lances striking shields and mail was a crunch like splintering bones. Two horsemen were rammed back out of their high saddles, but most of the lance thrusts had been parried by shields and now the horsemen dropped the shivered weapons as they galloped past their opponents. They sawed on the reins and drew their swords, but it was plain to the watching archers that the enemy had gained an advantage. Both of the unhorsed riders were English, and Sir Geoffrey's men were much more closely aligned so that when they turned to bring their swords to the mêlée they came as a disciplined group that struck Sir Simon's men in a clangour of sword against sword. An Englishman reeled from the mêlée with a missing hand. Dust and turf spewed up from hoofs. A riderless horse limped away. The swords clashed like hammers on anvils. Men grunted as they swung. A huge Breton, with no device on his plain shield, was wielding a falchion, a weapon that was half sword and half axe, and he used the broad blade with a terrible skill. An English man-at-arms had his helmet split open and his skull with it, so that he rode wavering from the fight, blood pouring down his mail coat. His horse stopped a few paces from the turmoil and the man-at-arms slowly, so slowly, bent forward and then slumped down from the saddle. One foot was trapped in a stirrup as he died but his horse did not seem to notice. It just went on cropping the grass.

Two of Sir Simon's men yielded and were sent back to be taken prisoner by the French and Breton squires. Sir Simon himself was fighting savagely, turning his horse to beat off two opponents. He sent one reeling out of the fight with a useless arm, then battered the other with swift cuts from his stolen sword. The French had fifteen men still fighting, but the English were down to ten when the great brute with the falchion decided to finish Sir Simon off. He roared as he charged, and Sir Simon caught the falchion on his shield and lunged his sword into the mail under the Breton's armpit. He yanked the sword free and there was blood pouring from the rent in the enemy's mail and leather tunic. The big man twitched in the saddle and Sir Simon hammered the sword onto the back of his head, then turned his horse to beat off another assailant, before wheeling back to drive his heavy weapon in a crushing blow against the big Breton's adam's apple. The man dropped his falchion and clutched his throat as he rode away.

'He's good, isn't he?' Skeat said flatly. 'Got suet for brains, but he knows how to fight.'

But, despite Sir Simon's prowess, the enemy was winning and Thomas wanted to advance the archers. They only needed to run about thirty paces and then would have been in easy range of the rampaging enemy horsemen, but Will Skeat shook his head. 'Never kill two Frenchmen when you can kill a dozen, Tom,' he said reprovingly.

'Our men are getting beat,' Thomas protested.

'Then that'll teach 'em not to be bloody fools, won't it?' Skeat said. He grinned. 'Just wait, lad, just wait, and we'll skin the cat proper.'

The English men-at-arms were being beaten back and only Sir Simon was fighting with spirit. He was indeed good. He had driven the huge Breton from the fight and was now holding off four of the enemy, and doing it with a ferocious skill, but the rest of his men, seeing that their battle was lost and that they could not reach Sir Simon because there were too many enemy horsemen around him, turned and fled.

'Sam!' Will shouted across the road. 'When I give you the word, take a dozen men and run away! You hear me, Sam?'

'I'll run away!' Sam shouted back.

The English men-at-arms, some bleeding and one half falling from his tall saddle, thundered back down the road towards La Roche-Derrien. The French and Bretons had surrounded Sir Simon, but Sir Geoffrey of the White Bridge was a romantic fellow and refused to take the life of a brave opponent, and so he ordered his men to spare the English knight.

Sir Simon, sweating like a pig under the leather and iron plate, pushed up the snoutlike visor of his helmet. 'I don't yield,' he told Sir Geoffrey. His new armour was scarred and his sword edge chipped, but the quality of both had helped him in the fight. 'I don't yield,' he said again, 'so fight on!'

Sir Geoffrey bowed in his saddle. 'I salute your bravery, Sir Simon,' he said magnanimously, 'and you are free to go with all honour.' He waved his men-at-arms aside and Sir Simon, miraculously alive and free, rode away with his head held high. He had led his men into disaster and death, but he had emerged with honour.

Sir Geoffrey could see past Sir Simon, down the long road that was thick with fleeing men-at-arms and, beyond them, the captured livestock and the heaped carts of plunder that were being escorted by Skeat's men. Then Will Skeat shouted at Sam and suddenly Sir Geoffrey could see a bunch of panicked archers riding northwards as hard as they could. 'He'll fall for it,' Skeat said knowingly, 'you just see if he don't.'

Sir Geoffrey had proved in the last few weeks that he was no fool, but he lost his wits that day. He saw a chance to cut down the hated hellequin archers and recapture three carts of plunder and so he ordered his remaining thirty men-at-arms to join him and, leaving his four prisoners and nine captured horses in the care of his crossbowmen, waved his knights forward. Will Skeat had been waiting weeks for this.

Sir Simon turned in alarm as he heard the sound of hooves. Nearly fifty armoured men on big destriers charged towards him and, for a moment, he thought they were trying to capture him and so he spurred his horse towards the woods only to see the French and Breton horsemen crash past him at full gallop. Sir Simon ducked under branches and swore at Will Skeat, who ignored him. He was watching the enemy.

Sir Geoffrey de Pont Blanc led the charge and saw only glory. He had forgotten the archers in the woods, or else believed they had all fled after the defeat of Sir Simon's men. Sir Geoffrey was on the cusp of a great victory. He would take back the plunder and, even better, lead the dreaded hellequin to a fiery fate in Lannion's marketplace.

'Now!' Skeat shouted through cupped hands. 'Now!'

There were archers on both sides of the road and they stepped out from the new spring foliage and loosed their bowstrings. Thomas's second arrow was in the air before the first even struck. Look and loose, he thought, do not think, and there was no need to aim, for the enemy was a tight group and all the archers did was pour their long arrows into the horsemen so that in an eyeblink the charge was reduced to a tangle of rearing stallions, fallen men, screaming horses and splashing blood. The enemy had no chance. A few at the back managed to turn and gallop away, but the majority were trapped in a closing ring of bowmen who drove their arrows mercilessly through mail and leather. Any man who even twitched invited three or four arrows. The pile of iron and flesh was spiked with feathers, and still the arrows came, cutting through mail and driving deep into horseflesh. Only the handful of men at the rear and a single man at the very front of the charge survived.

That man was Sir Geoffrey himself. He had been ten paces in front of his men and maybe that was why he was spared, or perhaps the archers had been impressed by the manner in which he had treated Sir Simon, but for whatever reason he rode ahead of the carnage like a charmed soul. Not an arrow flew close, but he heard the screams and clatter behind and he slowed his horse then turned to see the horror. He watched with disbelief for an instant, then walked his stallion back towards the arrow-stuck pile that had been his men. Skeat shouted at some of his bowmen to turn and face the enemy's crossbowmen, but they, seeing the fate of their men-at-arms, were in no mood to face the English arrows. They retreated southwards.

There was a curious stillness then. Fallen horses twitched and some beat at the road with their hooves. A man groaned, another called on Christ and some just whimpered. Thomas, an arrow still on his bowstring, could hear larks, the call of plovers and the whisper of wind in the leaves. A drop of rain fell, splashing the dust on the road, but it was a lone outrider of a shower that went to the west. Sir Geoffrey stood his horse beside his dead and dying men as if inviting the archers to add his corpse to the heap that was streaked with blood and flecked with goose feathers.

'See what I mean, Tom?' Skeat said. 'Wait long enough and the bloody fools will always oblige you. Right, lads! Finish the bastards off!' Men dropped their bows, drew their knives and ran to the shuddering heap, but Skeat held Thomas back. 'Go and tell that stupid white bridge bastard to make himself scarce.'

Thomas walked to the Frenchman, who must have thought he was expected to surrender for he pulled off his helmet and extended his sword handle. 'My family cannot pay a great ransom,' he said apologetically.

'You're not a prisoner,' Thomas said.

Sir Geoffrey seemed perplexed by the words. 'You release me?'

'We don't want you,' Thomas said. 'You might think about going to Spain,' he suggested, 'or the Holy Land. Not too many hellequin in either place.'

Sir Geoffrey sheathed his sword. 'I must fight against the enemies of my king so I shall fight here. But I thank you.' He gathered his reins and just at that moment Sir Simon Jekyll rode out of the trees, pointing his drawn sword at Sir Geoffrey.

'He's my prisoner!' he called to Thomas. 'My prisoner!'

'He's no one's prisoner,' Thomas said. 'We're letting him go.'

'You're letting him go?' Sir Simon sneered. 'Do you know who commands here?'

'What I know,' Thomas said, 'is that this man is no prisoner.' He thumped the trapper-covered rump of Sir Geoffrey's horse to send it on its way. 'Spain or the Holy Land!' he called after Sir Geoffrey.

Sir Simon turned his horse to follow Sir Geoffrey, then saw that Will Skeat was ready to intervene and stop any such pursuit so he turned back to Thomas. 'You had no right to release him! No right!'

'He released you,' Thomas said.

'Then he was a fool. And because he is a fool, I must

be?' Sir Simon was quivering with anger. Sir Geoffrey might have declared himself a poor man, hardly able to raise a ransom, but his horse alone was worth at least fifty pounds, and Skeat and Thomas had just sent that money trotting southwards. Sir Simon watched him go, then lowered the sword blade so that it threatened Thomas's throat. 'From the moment I first saw you,' he said, 'you have been insolent. I am the highest-born man on this field and it is I who decides the fate of prisoners. You understand that?'

'He yielded to me,' Thomas said, 'not to you. So it don't matter what bed you were born in.'

'You're a pup!' Sir Simon spat. 'Skeat! I want recompense for that prisoner. You hear me?'

Skeat ignored Sir Simon, but Thomas did not have enough sense to do the same.

'Jesus,' he said in disgust, 'that man spared you, and you'd not return the favour? You're not a bloody knight, you're just a bully. Go and boil your arse.'

The sword rose and so did Thomas's bow. Sir Simon looked at the glittering arrow point, its edges feathered white through sharpening and he had just enough wit not to strike with his sword. He sheathed it instead, slamming the blade into the scabbard, then wheeled his destrier and spurred away.

Which left Skeat's men to sort out the enemy's dead. There were eighteen of them and another twenty-three grievously wounded. There were also sixteen bleeding horses and twenty-four dead destriers, and that, as Will Skeat remarked, was a wicked waste of good horseflesh.

And Sir Geoffrey had been taught his lesson.

There was a fuss back in La Roche-Derrien. Sir Simon Jekyll complained to Richard Totesham that Will Skeat had failed to support him in battle, then also claimed to have been responsible for the death or wounding of forty-one enemy men-at-arms. He boasted he had won the skirmish, then returned to his theme of Skeat's perfidy, but Richard Totesham was in no mood to endure Sir Simon's querulousness. 'Did you win the fight or not?'

'Of course we won!' Sir Simon blinked indignantly. 'They're dead, ain't they?'

'So why did you need Will's men-at-arms?' Totesham asked.

Sir Simon searched for an answer and found none. 'He was impertinent,' he complained.

'That's for you and him to settle, not me,' Totesham said in abrupt dismissal, but he was thinking about the conversation and that night he talked with Skeat.

'Forty-one dead or wounded?' he wondered aloud. 'That must be a third of Lannion's men-at-arms.'

'Near as maybe, aye.'

Totesham's quarters were near the river and from his window he could watch the water slide under the bridge arches. Bats flittered about the barbican tower that guarded the bridge's further side, while the cottages beyond the river were lit by a sharp-edged moon. 'They'll be short-handed, Will,' Totesham said.

'They'll not be happy, that's for sure.'

'And the place will be stuffed with valuables.'

'Like as not,' Skeat agreed. Many folk, fearing the hellequin, had taken their belongings to the nearby fortresses, and Lannion must be filled with their goods. More to the point, Totesham would find food there. His garrison received some food from the farms north of La Roche-Derrien and more was brought across the Channel from England, but the hellequin's wastage of the countryside had brought hunger perilously close.

'Leave fifty men here?' Totesham was still thinking aloud, but he had no need to explain his thoughts to an old soldier like Skeat.

'We'll need new ladders,' Skeat said.

'What happened to the old ones?'

'Firewood. It were a cold winter.'

'A night attack?' Totesham suggested.

'Full moon in five or six days.'

'Five days from now, then,' Totesham decided. 'And I'll want your men, Will.'

'If they're sober by then.'

'They deserve their drink after what they did today,' Totesham said warmly, then gave Skeat a smile. 'Sir Simon was complaining about you. Says you were impertinent.'

'That weren't me, Dick, it was my lad Tom. Told the bastard to go and boil his arse.'

'I fear Sir Simon was never one for taking good advice,' Totesham said gravely.

Nor were Skeat's men. He had let them loose in the

town, but warned them that they would feel rotten in the morning if they drank too much and they ignored that advice to make celebration in La Roche-Derrien's taverns. Thomas had gone with a score of his friends and their women to an inn where they sang, danced and tried to pick a fight with a group of Duke John's white rats, who were too sensible to rise to the provocation and slipped quietly into the night. A moment later two men-at-arms walked in, both wearing jackets with the Earl of Northampton's badge of the lions and the stars. Their arrival was jeered, but they endured it with patience and asked if Thomas was present.

'He's the ugly bastard over there,' Jake said, pointing to Thomas, who was dancing to the music of a flute and drum. The men-at-arms waited till he had finished his dance, then explained that Will Skeat was with the garrison's commander and wanted to talk with him.

Thomas drained his ale. 'What it is,' he told the other archers, 'is that they can't make a decision without me. Indispensable, that's me.' The archers mocked that, but cheered good-naturedly as Thomas left with the two men-at-arms.

One of them came from Dorset and had actually heard of Hookton. 'Didn't the French land there?' he asked.

'Bastards wrecked it. I doubt there's anything left,' Thomas said. 'So why does Will want me?'

'God knows and He ain't telling,' one of the men said. He had led Thomas towards Richard Totesham's quarters, but now he pointed down a dark alley. 'They're in a tavern at the end there. Place with the anchor hanging over the door.'

'Good for them,' Thomas said. If he had not been half

drunk he might have realized that Totesham and Skeat were unlikely to summon him to a tavern, let alone the smallest one in town at the river end of the darkest alley, but Thomas suspected nothing until he was half-way down the narrow passage and two men stepped from a gateway. The first he knew of them was when a blow landed on the back of his head. He pitched forward onto his knees and the second man kicked him in the face, then both men rained kicks and blows on him until he offered no more resistance and they could seize his arms and drag him through the gate into a small smithy. There was blood in Thomas's mouth, his nose had been broken again, a rib was cracked and his belly was churning with ale.

A fire burned in the smithy. Thomas, through half-closed eyes, could see an anvil. Then more men surrounded him and gave him a second kicking so that he rolled into a ball in a vain attempt to protect himself.

'Enough,' a voice said, and Thomas opened his eyes to see Sir Simon Jekyll. The two men who had fetched him from the tavern, and who had seemed so friendly, now came through the smithy gate and stripped off their borrowed tunics showing the Earl of North-ampton's badge. 'Well done,' Sir Simon told them, then looked at Thomas. 'Mere archers,' Sir Simon said, 'do not tell knights to boil their arse.'

A tall man, a huge brute with lank yellow hair and blackened teeth, was standing beside Thomas, wanting to kick him if he offered an insolent reply, so Thomas held his tongue. Instead he offered a silent prayer to St Sebastian, the patron saint of archers. This plight, he reckoned, was too serious to be left to a dog.

'Take his breeches down, Colley,' Sir Simon ordered,

and turned back to the fire. Thomas saw there was a great three-legged pot standing in the red-hot charcoal. He swore under his breath, realizing that he was the one who was to get a boiled arse. Sir Simon peered into the pot. 'You are to be taught a lesson in courtesy,' he told Thomas, who whimpered as the yellow-haired brute cut through his belt, then dragged his breeches down. The other men searched Thomas's pockets, taking what coins they found and a good knife, then they turned him onto his belly so that his naked arse was ready for the boiling water.

Sir Simon saw the first wisps of steam float from the pot. 'Take it to him,' he ordered his men.

Three of Sir Simon's soldiers were holding Thomas down and he was too hurt and too weak to fight them, so he did the only thing he could. He screamed murder. He filled his lungs and bellowed as loud as he could. He reckoned he was in a small town that was crowded with men and someone must hear and so he shrieked the alarm. 'Murder! Murder!' A man kicked his belly, but Thomas went on shouting.

'For Christ's sake, silence him,' Sir Simon snarled, and Colley, the yellow-haired man, kneeled beside Thomas and tried to stuff straw into his mouth, but Thomas managed to spit it out.

'Murder!' he screamed. 'Murder!'

Colley swore, took a handful of filthy mud and slapped it into Thomas's mouth, muffling his noise. 'Bastard,' Colley said, and thumped Thomas's skull. 'Bastard!'

Thomas gagged on the mud, but he could not spit it out.

Sir Simon was standing over him now. 'You are to

be taught good manners,' he said, and watched as the steaming pot was carried across the smithy yard.

Then the gate opened and a newcomer stepped into the yard. 'What in God's name is happening here?' the man asked, and Thomas could have sung a *Te Deum* in praise of St Sebastian if his mouth had not been crammed with mud, for his rescuer was Father Hobbe, who must have heard the frantic shouting and come running down the alley to investigate. 'What are you doing?' the priest demanded of Sir Simon.

'It is not your business, father,' Sir Simon said.

'Thomas, is it you?' He turned back to the knight. 'By God, it is my business!' Father Hobbe had a temper and he lost it now. 'Who the devil do you think you are?'

'Be careful, priest,' Sir Simon snarled.

'Be careful! Me? I will have your soul in hell if you don't leave.' The small priest snatched up the smith's huge poker and wielded it like a sword. 'I'll have all your souls in hell! Leave! All of you! Out of here! Out! In the name of God, get out! Get out!'

Sir Simon backed down. It was one thing to torture an archer, but quite another to get into a fight with a priest whose voice was loud enough to attract still more attention. Sir Simon snarled that Father Hobbe was an interfering bastard, but he retreated all the same.

Father Hobbe knelt beside Thomas and hooked some of the mud from his mouth, along with tendrils of thick blood and a broken tooth. 'You poor lad,' Father Hobbe said, then helped Thomas stand. 'I'll take you home, Tom, take you home and clean you up.'

Thomas had to vomit first, but then, holding his breeches up, he staggered back to Jeanette's house, supported all the way by the priest. A dozen archers greeted him, wanting to know what had happened, but Father Hobbe brushed them aside. 'Where's the kitchen?' he demanded.

'She won't let us in there,' Thomas said, his voice indistinct because of his swollen mouth and bleeding gums.

'Where is it?' Father Hobbe insisted. One of the archers nodded at the door and the priest just pushed it open and half carried Thomas inside. He sat him on a chair and pulled the rush lights to the table's edge so he could see Thomas's face. 'Dear God,' he said, 'what have they done to you?' He patted Thomas's hand, then went to find water.

Jeanette came into the kitchen, full of fury. 'You are not supposed to be here! You will get out!' Then she saw Thomas's face and her voice trailed away. If someone had told her that she would see a badly beaten English archer she would have been cheered, but to her surprise she felt a pang of sympathy. 'What happened?'

'Sir Simon Jekyll did this,' Thomas managed to say.

'Sir Simon?'

'He's an evil man.' Father Hobbe had heard the name and came from the scullery with a big bowl of water. 'He's an evil thing, evil.' He spoke in English. 'You have some cloths?' he asked Jeanette.

'She doesn't speak English,' Thomas said. Blood was trickling down his face.

'Sir Simon attacked you?' Jeanette asked. 'Why?'

'Because I told him to boil his arse,' Thomas said, and was rewarded with a smile.

'Good,' Jeanette said. She did not invite Thomas to stay in the kitchen, but nor did she order him to leave. Instead she stood and watched as the priest washed his face, then took off Thomas's shirt to bind up the cracked rib.

'Tell her she could help me,' Father Hobbe said.

'She's too proud to help,' Thomas said.

'It's a sinful sad world,' Father Hobbe declared, then knelt down. 'Hold still, Tom,' he said, 'for this will hurt like the very devil.' He took hold of the broken nose and there was the sound of cartilage scraping before Thomas shouted in pain. Father Hobbe put a cold wet cloth over his nose. 'Hold that there, Tom, and the pain will go. Well, it won't really, but you'll get used to it.' He sat on an empty salt barrel, shaking his head. 'Sweet Jesus, Tom, what are we going to do with you?'

'You've done it,' Thomas said, 'and I'm grateful. A day or two and I'll be leaping about like a spring lamb.'

'You've been doing that for too long, Tom,' Father Hobbe said earnestly. Jeanette, not understanding a word, just watched the two men. 'God gave you a good head,' the priest went on, 'but you waste your wits, Tom, you do waste them.'

'You want me to be a priest?'

Father Hobbe smiled. 'I doubt you'd be much credit to the Church, Tom. You'd like as not end up as an archbishop because you're clever and devious enough, but I think you'd be happier as a soldier. But you have debts to God, Tom. Remember that promise you made to your father! You made it in a church, and it would be good for your soul to keep that promise, Tom.'

Thomas laughed, and immediately wished he had not, for the pain whipped through his ribs. He swore, apologized to Jeanette, then looked back to the priest. 'And how in the name of God, father, am I supposed to keep that promise? I don't even know what bastard stole the lance.'

'What bastard?' Jeanette asked, for she had picked up that one word. 'Sir Simon?'

'He is a bastard,' Thomas said, 'but he's not the only one,' and he told her about the lance, about the day his village had been murdered, about his father dying, and about the man who carried a banner showing three yellow hawks on a blue field. He told the story slowly, through bloody lips, and when he had finished Jeanette shrugged.

'So you want to kill this man, yes?'

'One day.'

'He deserves to be killed,' Jeanette said.

Thomas stared at her through half-closed eyes, astonished by those words. 'You know him?'

'He is called Sir Guillaume d'Evecque,' Jeanette said.

'What's she saying?' Father Hobbe asked.

'I know him,' Jeanette said grimly. 'In Caen, where he comes from, he is sometimes called the lord of the sea and of the land.'

'Because he fights on both?' Thomas guessed.

'He is a knight,' Jeanette said, 'but he is also a sea-raider. A pirate. My father owned sixteen ships and Guillaume d'Evecque stole three of them.'

'He fought against you?' Thomas sounded surprised.

Jeanette shrugged. 'He thinks any ship that is not French is an enemy. We are Bretons.'

Thomas looked at Father Hobbe. 'There you are, father,' he said lightly, 'to keep my promise all I must do is fight the knight of the sea and of the land.'

Father Hobbe had not followed the French, but he shook his head sadly. 'How you keep the promise,

Thomas, is your business. But God knows you made it, and I know you are doing nothing about it.' He fingered the wooden cross he wore on a leather lace about his neck. 'And what shall I do about Sir Simon?'

'Nothing,' Thomas said.

'I must tell Totesham, at least!' the priest insisted.

'Nothing, father.' Thomas was just as insistent. 'Promise me.'

Father Hobbe looked suspiciously at Thomas. 'You're not thinking of taking your own revenge, are you?'

Thomas crossed himself and hissed because of the pain in his rib. 'Doesn't our Mother Church tell us to turn the other cheek?' he asked.

'It does,' Father Hobbe said dubiously, 'but it wouldn't condone what Sir Simon did tonight.'

'We shall turn away his wrath with a soft answer,' Thomas said, and Father Hobbe, impressed by this display of genuine Christianity, nodded his acceptance of Thomas's decision.

Jeanette had been following the conversation as best she could and had at least gathered the gist of their words. 'Are you discussing what to do to Sir Simon?' she asked Thomas.

'I'm going to murder the bastard,' Thomas said in French.

She offered him a sour grimace. 'That is a very clever idea, Englishman. So you will be a murderer and they will hang you. Then, thanks be to God, there will be two dead Englishmen.'

'What's she saying, Thomas?' Father Hobbe asked.

'She's agreeing that I ought to forgive my enemies, father.'

'Good woman, good woman,' Father Hobbe said.

'Do you really want to kill him?' Jeanette demanded coldly.

Thomas shuddered with the pain, but he was not so hurt that he could not appreciate Jeanette's closeness. She was a hard woman, he reckoned, but still as lovely as the spring and, like the rest of Will Skeat's men, he had harboured impossible dreams of knowing her better. Her question gave him that chance. 'I'll kill him,' he assured her, 'and in killing him, my lady, I'll fetch you your husband's armour and sword.'

Jeanette frowned at him. 'You can do that?'

'If you help me.'

She grimaced. 'How?'

So Thomas told her and, to his astonishment, she did not dismiss the idea in horror, but instead nodded a grudging acceptance. 'It might really work,' she said after a while, 'it really might work.'

Which meant that Sir Simon had united his enemies and Thomas had found himself an ally.

Jeanette's life was encompassed by enemies. She had her son, but everyone else she loved was dead, and those who were left she hated. There were the English, of course, occupying her town, but there was also Belas, the lawyer, and the shipmasters who had cheated her, and the tenants who used the presence of the English to default on their rent, and the town's merchants who dunned her for money she did not have. She was a countess, yet her rank counted for nothing. At night, brooding on her plight, she would dream of meeting a great champion, a duke perhaps, who would come to La Roche-Derrien and punish her enemies one by one.

She saw them whimpering with terror, pleading for mercy and receiving none. But in each dawn there was no duke and her enemies did not cringe, and Jeanette's troubles were unrelieved until Thomas promised to help her kill the one enemy she hated above the rest.

To which end, early in the morning after her conversation with Thomas, Jeanette went to Richard Totesham's headquarters. She went early because she hoped Sir Simon Jekyll would still be in bed, and though it was essential he knew the purpose of her visit, she did not want to meet him. Let him learn from others what she planned.

The headquarters, like her own house, fronted the River Jaudy, and the waterfront yard, despite the early hour, already held a score of petitioners seeking favours from the English. Jeanette was told to wait with the other petitioners. 'I am the Countess of Armorica,' she told the clerk.

'You must wait like the rest,' the clerk answered in poor French, then cut another notch in a tally stick on which he was counting arrow sheaves that were being unloaded from a lighter that had come upriver from the deepwater harbour at Tréguier. A second lighter held barrels of red herrings, and the stench of the fish made Jeanette shudder. English food! They did not even gut the herrings before smoking them and the red fish came from the barrels covered in yellow-green mould, yet the archers ate them with relish. She tried to escape the reeking fish by crossing the yard to where a dozen local men trimmed great lengths of timber propped on sawhorses. One of the carpenters was a man who had sometimes worked for Jeanette's father, though he was usually too drunk to hold a job for more than a few days.

He was barefoot, ragged, hump-backed and hare-lipped, though when he was sober he was as good a labourer as any in the town.

'Jacques!' Jeanette called. 'What are you doing?' She spoke in Breton.

Jacques tugged his forelock and bobbed down. 'You're looking well, my lady.' Only a few folk could understand his speech for his split lip mangled the sounds. 'Your father always said you were his angel.'

'I asked what you are doing.'

'Ladders, my lady, ladders.' Jacques cuffed a stream of mucus from his nose. There was a weeping ulcer on his neck and the stink of it was as bad as the red herrings. 'They want six ever so long ladders.'

'Why?'

Jacques looked left and right to make sure no one could overhear him. 'What he says,' he jerked his head at the Englishman who was supposedly supervising the work, 'what he says is that they're taking them to Lannion. And they're long enough for that big wall, ain't they?'

'Lannion?'

'He likes his ale, he does,' Jacques said, explaining the Englishman's indiscretion.

'Hey! Handsome!' the supervisor shouted at Jacques. 'Get to work!' Jacques, with a grin to Jeanette, picked up his tools.

'Make the rungs loose!' Jeanette advised Jacques in Breton, then turned because her name had been called from the house. Sir Simon Jekyll, looking heavy-eyed and sleepy, was standing in the doorway and Jeanette's heart sank at the sight of him.

'My lady,' Sir Simon offered Jeanette a bow, 'you should not be waiting with common folk.'

'Tell that to the clerk,' Jeanette said coldly.

The clerk tallying the arrow sheaves squealed when Sir Simon caught him by the ear. 'This clerk?' he asked.

'He told me to wait out here.'

Sir Simon cuffed the man across the face. 'She's a lady, you bastard! You treat her like a lady.' He kicked the man away, then pulled the door fully open. 'Come, my lady,' he invited her.

Jeanette went to the door and was relieved to see four more clerks busy at tables inside the house. 'The army,' Sir Simon said as she brushed past him, 'has almost as many clerks as archers. Clerks, farriers, masons, cooks, herdsmen, butchers, anything else on two legs that can take the King's coin.' He smiled at her, then brushed a hand down his threadbare wool robe that was trimmed with fur. 'If I had known you were gracing us with a visit, my lady, I would have dressed.'

Sir Simon, Jeanette noted gladly, was in a puppy mood this morning. He was always either boorish or clumsily polite and she hated him in either mood, but at least he was easier to deal with when he tried to impress her with his manners. 'I came,' she told him, 'to request a pass from Monsieur Totesham.' The clerks watched her surreptitiously, their quills scratching and spluttering on the scraped parchment.

'I can give you a pass,' Sir Simon said gallantly, 'though I trust you are not leaving La Roche-Derrien permanently?'

'I just wish to visit Louannec,' Jeanette said.

'And where, dear lady, is Louannec?'

'It is on the coast,' Jeanette said, 'north of Lannion.'

'Lannion, eh?' He perched on a table's edge, his bare

147

leg swinging. 'Can't have you wandering near Lannion. Not this week. Next, maybe, but only if you can persuade me that you have good reason to travel.' He smoothed his fair moustache. 'And I can be very persuadable.'

'I wish to pray at the shrine there,' Jeanette said.

'I would not keep you from your prayers,' Sir Simon said. He was thinking that he should have invited her through into the parlour, but in truth he had small appetite for love's games this morning. He had consoled himself for his failure to boil Thomas of Hookton's backside by drinking deep into the darkness, and his belly felt liquid, his throat was dry and his head was banging like a kettledrum. 'Which saint will have the pleasure of hearing your voice?' he asked.

'The shrine is dedicated to Yves who protects the sick. My son has a fever.'

'Poor boy,' Sir Simon said in mock sympathy, then peremptorily ordered a clerk to write the pass for her ladyship. 'You will not travel alone, madame?' he asked.

'I shall take servants.'

'You would be better with soldiers. There are bandits everywhere.'

'I do not fear my own countrymen, Sir Simon.'

'Then you should,' he said tartly. 'How many servants?'

'Two.'

Sir Simon told the clerk to note two companions on the pass, then looked back to Jeanette. 'You really would be much safer with soldiers as escort.'

'God will preserve me,' Jeanette said.

Sir Simon watched as the ink on the pass was sanded dry and a blob of hot wax was dropped onto the parchment. He pressed a seal into the wax, then held the document to Jeanette. 'Maybe I should come with you, madame?'

'I would rather not travel at all,' Jeanette said, refusing to take the pass.

'Then I shall relinquish my duties to God,' Sir Simon said.

Jeanette took the pass, forced herself to thank him, then fled. She half expected that Sir Simon would follow her, but he let her go unmolested. She felt dirty, but also triumphant because the trap was baited now. Well and truly baited.

She did not go straight home, but went instead to the house of the lawyer, Belas, who was still eating a breakfast of blood sausage and bread. The aroma of the sausage put an edge to Jeanette's hunger, but she refused his offer of a plate. She was a countess and he was a mere lawyer and she would not demean herself by eating with him.

Belas straightened his robe, apologized that the parlour was cold, and asked whether she had at last decided to sell the house. 'It is the sensible thing to do, madame. Your debts mount.'

'I shall let you know my decision,' she said, 'but I have come on other business.'

Belas opened the parlour shutters. 'Business costs money, madame, and your debts, forgive me, are mounting.'

'It is Duke Charles's business,' Jeanette said. 'Do you still write to his men of business?'

'From time to time,' Belas said guardedly.

'How do you reach them?' Jeanette demanded.

Belas was suspicious of the question, but finally saw

no harm in giving an answer. 'The messages go by boat to Paimpol,' he said, 'then overland to Guingamp.'

'How long does it take?'

'Two days? Three? It depends if the English are riding the country between Paimpol and Guingamp.'

'Then write to the Duke,' Jeanette said, 'and tell him from me that the English will attack Lannion at the end of this week. They are making ladders to scale the wall.' She had decided to send the message through Belas, for her own couriers were two fishermen who only came to sell their wares in La Roche-Derrien on a Thursday, and any message sent through them must arrive too late. Belas's couriers, on the other hand, could reach Guingamp in good time to thwart the English plans.

Belas dabbed egg from his thin beard. 'You are sure, madame?'

'Of course I'm sure!' She told him about Jacques and the ladders and about the indiscreet English supervisor, and how Sir Simon had forced her to wait a week before venturing near Lannion on her expedition to the shrine at Louannec.

'The Duke,' Belas said as he ushered Jeanette to the house door, 'will be grateful.'

Belas sent the message that day, though he did not say it came from the Countess, but instead claimed all the credit for himself. He gave the letter to a shipmaster who sailed that same afternoon, and next morning a horseman rode south from Paimpol. There were no hellequin in the wasted country between the port and the Duke's capital so the message arrived safely. And in Guingamp, which was Duke Charles's headquarters, the farriers checked the war horses' shoes, the crossbowmen greased their weapons, squires scrubbed mail till it shone and a thousand swords were sharpened.

The English raid on Lannion had been betrayed.

Jeanette's unlikely alliance with Thomas had soothed the hostility in her house. Skeat's men now used the river as their lavatory instead of the courtyard, and Jeanette allowed them into the kitchen, which proved useful, for they brought their rations with them and so her household ate better than it had since the town had fallen, though she still could not bring herself to try the smoked herrings with their bright red, mould-covered skins. Best of all was the treatment given to two importunate merchants who arrived demanding payment from Jeanette and were so badly manhandled by a score of archers that both men left hatless, limping, unpaid and bloody.

'I will pay them when I can,' she told Thomas.

'Sir Simon's likely to have money on him,' he told her.

'He is?'

'Only a fool leaves cash where a servant can find it,' he said.

Four days after the beating his face was still swollen and his lips black with blood clots. His rib hurt and his body was a mass of bruises, but he had insisted to Skeat that he was well enough to ride to Lannion. They would leave that afternoon. At midday Jeanette found him in St Renan's church.

'Why are you praying?' she asked him.

'I always do before a fight.'

'There will be a fight today? I thought you were not riding till tomorrow?'

'I love a well-kept secret,' Thomas said, amused. 'We're going a day early. Everything's ready, why wait?'

'Going where?' Jeanette asked, though she already knew.

'To wherever they take us,' Thomas said.

Jeanette grimaced and prayed silently that her message had reached Duke Charles. 'Be careful,' she said to Thomas, not because she cared for him, but because he was her agent for taking revenge on Sir Simon Jekyll. 'Perhaps Sir Simon will be killed?' she suggested.

'God will save him for me,' Thomas said.

'Perhaps he won't follow me to Louannec?'

'He'll follow you like a dog,' Thomas said, 'but it will be dangerous for you.'

'I shall get the armour back,' Jeanette said, 'and that is all that matters. Are you praying to St Renan?'

'To St Sebastian,' Thomas said, 'and to St Guinefort.'

'I asked the priest about Guinefort,' Jeanette said accusingly, 'and he said he had never heard of him.'

'He probably hasn't heard of St Wilgefortis either,' Thomas said.

'Wilgefortis?' Jeanette stumbled over the unfamiliar name. 'Who is he?'

'She,' Thomas said, 'and she was a very pious virgin who lived in Flanders and grew a long beard. She prayed every day that God would keep her ugly so that she could stay chaste.'

Jeanette could not resist laughing. 'That isn't true!'

'It is true, my lady,' Thomas assured her. 'My father was once offered a hair of her holy beard, but he refused to buy it.'

'Then I shall pray to the bearded saint that you survive your raid,' Jeanette said, 'but only so you can help me against Sir Simon. Other than that I hope you all die.'

The garrison at Guingamp had the same wish, and to make it come true they assembled a strong force of crossbowmen and men-at-arms to ambush the Englishmen on their way to Lannion, but they, like Jeanette, were convinced that La Roche-Derrien's garrison would make their sally on the Friday and so they did not leave till late on Thursday, by which time Totesham's force was already within five miles of Lannion. The shrunken garrison did not know the English were coming because Duke Charles's war captains, who commanded his forces in Guingamp while the Duke was in Paris, decided not to warn the town. If too many people knew that the English had been betrayed then the English themselves might hear of it, abandon their plans and so deny the Duke's men the chance of a rare and complete victory.

The English expected victory themselves. It was a dry night and, near midnight, a full moon slid out from behind a silver-edged cloud to cast Lannion's walls in sharp relief. The raiders were hidden in woods from where they watched the few sentinels on the ramparts. Those sentinels grew sleepy and, after a time, went to the bastions where fires burned and so they did not see the six ladder parties creep across the night fields, nor the hundred archers following the ladders. And still they slept as the archers climbed the rungs and Totesham's main force erupted from the woods, ready to burst through the eastern gate that the archers would open.

The sentinels died. The first dogs awoke in the town,

then a church bell began to ring and Lannion's garrison came awake, but too late for the gate was open and Totesham's mail-clad soldiers were crying havoc in the dark alleys while still more men-at-arms and archers were pouring through the narrow gate.

Skeat's men were the rearguard and so waited outside the town as the sack began. Church bells were clanging wildly as the town's parishes woke to nightmare, but gradually the clangour ceased.

Will Skeat stared at the moon-glossed fields south of Lannion. 'I hear it was Sir Simon Jekyll who improved your looks,' he said to Thomas.

'It was.'

'Because you told him to boil his arse?' Skeat grinned. 'You can't blame him for thumping you,' Skeat said, 'but he should have talked to me first.'

'What would you have done?'

'Made sure he didn't thump you too much, of course,' Skeat said, his gaze moving steadily across the landscape. Thomas had acquired the same habit of watchfulness but all the land beyond the town was still. A mist rose from the low ground. 'So what do you plan to do about it?' Skeat asked.

'Talk to you.'

'I don't fight your goddamn battles, boy,' Skeat growled. 'What do you plan to do about it?'

'Ask you to lend me Jake and Sam on Saturday. And I want three crossbows.'

'Crossbows, eh?' Skeat asked flatly. He saw that the rest of Totesham's force had now entered the town so he put two fingers to his lips and sounded a piercing whistle to signal that his own men could follow. 'Onto the walls!' he shouted as the hellequin rode forward.

154

'Onto the walls!' That was the rearguard's job: to man the fallen town's defences. 'Half the bloody bastards will still get drunk,' Skeat growled, 'so you stay with me, Tom.'

Most of Skeat's men did their duty and climbed the stone steps to the town's ramparts, but a few slipped away in search of plunder and drink, so Skeat, Thomas and a half-dozen archers scoured the town to find those laggards and drive them back to the walls. A score of Totesham's men-at-arms were doing much the same – dragging men out of taverns and setting them to loading the many wagons that had been stored in the town to keep them from the hellequin. Totesham particularly wanted food for his garrison, and his more reliable men-at-arms did their best to keep the English soldiers from drink, women or anything else that would slow the plunder.

The town's garrison, woken and surprised, had done their best to fight back, but they had responded much too late, and their bodies now lay in the moonlit streets. But in the western part of the town, close to the quays which fronted the River Léguer, the battle still went on, and Skeat was drawn to the sound. Most men were ignoring it, too intent on kicking down house doors and ransacking warehouses, but Skeat reckoned no one in town was safe until all the defenders were dead.

Thomas followed him to find a group of Totesham's men-at-arms who had just retreated from a narrow street. 'There's a mad bastard down there,' one of them told Skeat, 'and he's got a dozen crossbowmen.'

The mad bastard and his crossbowmen had already killed their share of Englishmen, for the red-crossed bodies lay where the street bent sharply towards the river.

'Burn them out,' one of the men-at-arms suggested.

'Not before we've searched the buildings,' Skeat said, then sent two of his archers to fetch one of the ladders that had been used to scale the ramparts. Once the ladder was fetched he propped it against the nearest house and looked at Thomas, who grinned, climbed the rungs and then clambered up the steep thatch. His broken rib hurt, but he gained the ridge and there took the bow from his shoulder and fitted an arrow onto the cord. He walked along the rooftop, his mooncast shadow long on the sloping straw. The roof ended just above the place where the enemy waited and so, before reaching the ridge's peak, he drew the bow to its full extent, then took two steps forward.

The enemy saw him and a dozen crossbows jerked up, but so did the unhelmeted face of a fair-haired man who had a long sword in his hand. Thomas recognized him. It was Sir Geoffrey de Pont Blanc, and Thomas hesitated because he admired the man. But then the first bolt whipped so close to his face that he felt the wind of its passing on his cheek and so he loosed, and he knew the arrow would go straight into the open mouth of Sir Geoffrey's upturned face. He did not see it strike, though, for he had stepped back as the other crossbows twanged and their bolts seared up towards the moon.

'He's dead!' Thomas shouted.

There was a tramp of feet as the men-at-arms charged before the crossbowmen could reload their clumsy weapons. Thomas stepped back to the ridge's end and saw the swords and axes rise and fall. He saw the blood splash up onto the plastered house fronts. Saw the men hacking at Sir Geoffrey's corpse just to make certain he was really dead. A woman shrieked in the house that Sir Geoffrey had been defending.

Thomas slithered down the thatch and jumped into the street where Sir Geoffrey had died and there he picked up three of the crossbows and a bag of bolts that he carried back to Will Skeat.

The Yorkshireman grinned. 'Crossbows, eh? That means you'll be pretending to be the enemy, and you can't do that in La Roche-Derrien, so you're waylaying Sir Simon somewhere outside the town. Am I right?'

'Something like that.'

'I could read you like a bloody book, boy, if I could read, which I can't on account of having too much sense.' Skeat walked on towards the river where three ships were being plundered and another two, their holds already emptied, were burning fiercely. 'But how do you get the bastard out of town?' Skeat asked. 'He's not a complete fool.'

'He is when it comes to the Countess.'

'Ah!' Skeat grinned. 'And the Countess, she's suddenly being nice to us all. So it's you and her, is it?'

'It is not her and me, no.'

'Soon will be, though, won't it?' Skeat said.

'I doubt it.'

'Why? Because she's a countess? Still a woman, boy. But I'd be careful of her.'

'Careful?'

'Hard bitch, that one. Looks lovely on the outside, but it's all flint inside. She'll break your heart, boy.'

Skeat had stopped on the wide stone quays where men were emptying warehouses of leather, grain, smoked fish, wine and bolts of cloth. Sir Simon was among them, shouting at his men to commandeer more wagons. The town was yielding a vast fortune. It was a much bigger place than La Roche-Derrien and, because it had successfully fought off the Earl of Northampton's winter siege, it had been reckoned a safe place for Bretons to store their valuables. Now it was being gutted. A man staggered past Thomas with an armload of silver plate, another man was dragging a half-naked woman by the shreds of her nightdress. One group of archers had broken open a vat and were dipping their faces to drink the wine.

'It was easy enough getting in here,' Skeat said, 'but it'll be the devil's own job to get these sodden bastards back out again.'

Sir Simon beat his sword on the backs of two drunks who were getting in the way of his men emptying a storehouse of its bolts of cloth. He saw Thomas and looked surprised, but he was too wary of Will Skeat to say anything. He just turned away.

'Bastard must have paid off his debts by now,' Skeat said, still staring at Sir Simon's back. 'War's a good way to get rich, so long as you ain't taken prisoner and ransomed. Not that they'd ransom you or me, boy. Slit our bellies and prick our eyes out, more like. Have you ever shot a crossbow?'

'No.'

'Ain't quite as easy as it looks. Not as hard as shooting a real bow, of course, but it still takes practice. Goddamn things can pitch a bit high if you're not used to them. Do Jake and Sam want to help you?'

'They say so.'

'Of course they do, evil bastards that they are.' Skeat

still stared at Sir Simon, who was wearing his new, shining armour. 'I reckon the bastard will carry his cash with him.'

'I would think so, yes.'

'Half mine, Tom, and I'll ask no questions come Saturday.'

'Thanks, Will.'

'But do it proper, Tom,' Skeat said savagely, 'do it proper. I don't want to watch you hang. I don't mind watching most fools doing the rope dance with the piss running down their legs, but it'd be a shame to watch you twitching your way to the devil.'

They went back to the walls. Neither man had collected any plunder, but they had already taken more than enough from their raids on the north Breton farms and it was now the turn of Totesham's men to gorge themselves on a captured town.

One by one the houses were searched and the tavern barrels were drained. Richard Totesham wanted his force to leave Lannion at dawn, but there were too many captured carts waiting to get through the narrow eastern gate and not nearly enough horses to pull the carts, so men were harnessing themselves the shafts rather than leave their pickings behind. Other men were drunk and senseless, and Totesham's men-at-arms scoured the town to find them, but it was fire that drove most of the drunks from their refuges. The townsfolk fled south as the English set the thatched roofs alight.

The smoke thickened into a vast dirty pillar that drifted south on the small sea wind. The pillar glowed a lurid red on its underside, and it must have been that sight which first told the approaching force from Guingamp that they had arrived too late to save the town. They had marched through the night, expecting to find some place where they could lay an ambush for Totesham's men, but the damage was already done. Lannion was burning and its wealth was piled on carts that were still being manhandled through the gate. But if the hated English could not be ambushed on their way to the town, then they could be surprised as they left and so the enemy commanders swung their forces eastwards towards the road which led back to La Roche-Derrien.

Cross-eyed Jake saw the enemy first. He was gazing south through the pearly mist that lay over the flat land and he saw the shadows in the vapour. At first he thought it was a herd of cows, then he decided it had to be refugees from the town. But then he saw a banner and a lance and the dull grey of a mail coat, and he shouted to Skeat that there were horsemen in sight.

Skeat peered over the ramparts. 'Can you see anything, Tom?'

It was just before dawn proper and the countryside was suffused with greyness and streaked with mist. Thomas stared. He could see a thick wood a mile or more to the south and a low ridge showing dark above the mist. Then he saw the banners and the grey mail in the grey light, and a thicket of lances.

'Men-at-arms,' he said, 'a lot of the bastards.'

Skeat swore. Totesham's men were either still in the town or else strung along the road to La Roche-Derrien, and strung so far that there could be no hope of pulling them back behind Lannion's walls – though even if that had been possible it was not practical for the whole western side of the town was burning furiously and the flames were spreading fast. To retreat behind the walls

160

was to risk being roasted alive, but Totesham's men were hardly in a fit condition to fight: many were drunk and all were laden with plunder.

'Hedgerow,' Skeat said curtly, pointing to a ragged line of blackthorn and elder that ran parallel to the road where the carts rumbled. 'Archers to the hedge, Tom. We'll look after your horses. Christ knows how we'll stop the bastards,' he made the sign of the cross, 'but we ain't got much choice.'

Thomas bullied a passage at the crowded gate and led forty archers across a soggy pasture to the hedgerow that seemed a flimsy barrier against the enemy massing in the silvery mist. There were at least three hundred horsemen there. They were not advancing yet, but instead grouping themselves for a charge, and Thomas had only forty men to stop them.

'Spread out!' he shouted. 'Spread out!' He briefly went onto one knee and made the sign of the cross. St Sebastian, he prayed, be with us now. St Guinefort, protect me. He touched the desiccated dog's paw, then made the sign of the cross again.

A dozen more archers joined his force, but it was still far too small. A score of pageboys, mounted on ponies and armed with toy swords, could have massacred the men on the road, for Thomas's hedge did not provide a complete screen, but rather straggled into nothingness about half a mile from the town. The horsemen only had to ride round that open end and there would be nothing to stop them. Thomas could take his archers into the open ground, but fifty men could not stop three hundred. Archers were at their best when they were massed together so that their arrows made a hard, steel-tipped rain. Fifty men could make a shower, but they would still be overrun and massacred by the horsemen.

'Crossbowmen,' Jake grunted, and Thomas saw the men in green and red jackets emerging from the woods behind the enemy men-at-arms. The new dawn light reflected cold from mail, swords and helmets. 'Bastards are taking their time,' Jake said nervously. He had planted a dozen arrows in the base of the hedge, which was just thick enough to stop the horsemen, but not nearly dense enough to slow a crossbow bolt.

Will Skeat had gathered sixty of his men-at-arms beside the road, ready to countercharge the enemy whose numbers increased every minute. Duke Charles's men and their French allies were riding eastwards now, looking to advance about the open end of the hedge where there was an inviting swathe of green and open land leading all the way to the road. Thomas wondered why the hell they were waiting. He wondered if he would die here. Dear God, he thought, but there were not nearly enough men to stop this enemy. The fires continued to burn in Lannion, pouring smoke into the pale sky.

He ran to the left of the line, where he found Father Hobbe holding a bow. 'You shouldn't be here, father,' he said.

'God will forgive me,' the priest said. He had tucked his cassock into his belt and had a small stand of arrows stuck into the hedgebank. Thomas gazed at the open land, wondering how long his men would last in that immensity of grass. Just what the enemy wanted, he thought, a stretch of bare flat land on which their horses could run hard and straight. Only the land was not entirely flat for it was dotted with grassy hummocks through which two grey herons walked stiff-legged as

162

they hunted for frogs or ducklings. Frogs, Thomas thought, and ducklings. Sweet God, it was a marsh! The spring had been unusually dry, yet his boots were soaking from the damp field he had crossed to reach the hedgerow. The realization burst on Thomas like the rising sun. The open land was marsh! No wonder the enemy was waiting. They could see Totesham's men strung out for slaughter, but they could see no way across the swampy ground.

'This way!' Thomas shouted at the archers. 'This way! Hurry! Hurry! Come on, you bastards!'

He led them round the end of the hedge into the swamp where they leaped and splashed through a maze of marsh, tussocks and streamlets. They went south towards the enemy and once in range Thomas spread his men out and told them to indulge in target practice. His fear had gone, replaced by exaltation. The enemy was balked by the marsh. Their horses could not advance, but Thomas's light archers could leap across the tussocks like demons. Like hellequin.

'Kill the bastards!' he shouted.

The white-fledged arrows hissed across the wetland to strike horses and men. Some of the enemy tried to charge the archers, but their horses floundered in the soft ground and became targets for volleys of arrows. The crossbowmen dismounted and advanced, but the archers switched their aim to them, and now more archers were arriving, dispatched by Skeat and Totesham, so that the marsh was suddenly swarming with English and Welsh bowmen who poured a steel-tipped hell on the befuddled enemy. It became a game. Men wagered on whether or not they could strike a particular target. The sun rose higher, casting shadows from the dead horses. The enemy was edging back to the trees. One brave group tried a last charge, hoping to skirt the marsh, but their horses stumbled in the soft ground and the arrows spitted and sliced at them so that men and beasts screamed as they fell. One horseman struggled on, flailing his beast with the flat of his sword. Thomas put an arrow into the horse's neck and Jake skewered its haunch, and the animal screeched piteously as it thrashed in pain and collapsed into the swamp. The man somehow extricated his feet from his stirrups and stumbled cursing towards the archers with his sword held low and shield high, but Sam buried an arrow in his groin and then a dozen more bowmen added their arrows before swarming over the fallen enemy. Knives were drawn, throats cut, then the business of plunder could begin. The corpses were stripped of their mail and weapons and the horses of their bridles and saddles, then Father Hobbe prayed over the dead while the archers counted their spoils.

The enemy was gone by mid-morning. They left two score of dead men, and twice that number had been wounded, but not a single Welsh or English archer had died.

Duke Charles's men slunk back to Guingamp. Lannion had been destroyed, they had been humiliated and Will Skeat's men celebrated in La Roche-Derrien. They were the hellequin, they were the best and they could not be beaten.

The following morning Thomas, Sam and Jake left La Roche-Derrien before daybreak. They rode west towards Lannion, but once in the woods they swerved off the road and picketed their horses deep among the trees. Then, moving like poachers, they worked their way back to the wood's edge. Each had his own bow slung on his shoulder, and carried a crossbow too, and they practised with the unfamiliar weapons as they waited in a swathe of bluebells at the wood's margin from where they could see La Roche-Derrien's western gate. Thomas had only brought a dozen bolts, short and stub-feathered, so each of them shot just two times. Will Skeat had been right: the weapons did kick up as the archers loosed so that their first bolts went high on the trunk that was their target. Thomas's second shot was more accurate, but nothing like as true as an arrow shot from a proper bow. The near miss made him apprehensive of the morning's risks, but Jake and Sam were both cheerful at the prospect of larceny and murder.

'Can't really miss,' Sam said after his second shot had also gone high. 'Might not catch the bastard in the belly, but we'll hit him somewhere.' He levered the cord back, grunting with the effort. No man alive could haul a crossbow's string by arm-power alone and so a mechanism had to be employed. The most expensive crossbows, those with the longest range, used a jackscrew. The archer would place a cranked handle on the screw's end and wind the cord back, inch by creaking inch, until the pawl above the trigger engaged the string. Some crossbowmen used their bodies as a lever. They wore thick leather belts to which a hook was attached and by bending down, attaching the hook to the cord and then straightening, they could pull the twisted strings back, but the crossbows Thomas had brought from Lannion used a lever, shaped like a goat's hind leg, that forced the cord and bent the short bow shaft,

165

which was a layered thing of horn, wood and glue. The lever was probably the fastest way of cocking the weapon, though it did not offer the power of a screw-cocked bow and was still slow compared to a yew shaft. In truth there was nothing to compare with the English bow and Skeat's men debated endlessly why the enemy did not adopt the weapon. 'Because they're daft,' was Sam's curt judgement, though the truth, Thomas knew, was that other nations simply did not start their sons early enough. To be an archer meant starting as a boy, then practising and practising until the chest was broad, the arm muscles huge and the arrow seemed to fly without the archer giving its aim any thought.

Jake shot his second bolt into the oak and swore horribly when it missed the mark. He looked at the bow. 'Piece of shit,' he said. 'How close are we going to be?'

'Close as we can get,' Thomas said.

Jake sniffed. 'If I can poke the bloody bow into the bastard's belly I might not miss.'

'Thirty, forty feet should be all right,' Sam reckoned.

'Aim at his crotch,' Thomas encouraged them, 'and we should gut him.'

'It'll be all right,' Jake said, 'three of us? One of us has got to skewer the bastard.'

'In the shadows, lads,' Thomas said, gesturing them deeper into the trees. He had seen Jeanette coming from the gate where the guards had inspected her pass then waved her on. She sat sideways on a small horse that Will Skeat had lent her and was accompanied by two grey-haired servants, a man and a woman, both of whom had grown old in her father's service and now walked beside their mistress's horse. If Jeanette had truly planned to ride to Louannec then such a feeble and aged escort would have been an invitation for trouble, but trouble, of course, was what she intended, and no sooner had she reached the trees than the trouble appeared as Sir Simon Jekyll emerged from the archway's shadow, riding with two other men.

'What if those two bastards stay close to him?' Sam asked.

'They won't,' Thomas said. He was certain of that, just as he and Jeanette had been certain that Sir Simon would follow her and that he would wear the expensive suit of plate he had stolen from her.

'She's a brave lass,' Jake grunted.

'She's got spirit,' Thomas said, 'knows how to hate someone.'

Jake tested the point of a quarrel. 'You and her?' he asked Thomas. 'Doing it, are you?'

'No.'

'But you'd like to. I would.'

'I don't know,' Thomas said. He thought Jeanette beautiful, but Skeat was right, there was a hardness in her that repelled him. 'I suppose so,' he admitted.

'Of course you would,' Jake said, 'be daft not to.'

Once Jeanette was among the trees Thomas and his companions trailed her, staying hidden and always conscious that Sir Simon and his two henchmen were closing quickly. Those three horsemen trotted once they reached the wood and succeeded in catching up with Jeanette in a place that was almost perfect for Thomas's ambush. The road ran within yards of a clearing where a meandering stream had undercut the roots of a willow. The fallen trunk was rotted and thick with disc-like fungi. Jeanette, pretending to make way for the three armoured horsemen, turned into the clearing and waited beside the dead tree. Best of all there was a stand of young alders close to the willow's trunk that offered cover to Thomas.

Sir Simon turned off the road, ducked under the branches and curbed his horse close to Jeanette. One of his companions was Henry Colley, the brutal yellow-haired man who had hurt Thomas so badly, while the other was Sir Simon's slack-jawed squire, who grinned in expectation of the coming entertainment. Sir Simon pulled off the snouted helmet and hung it on his saddle's pommel, then smiled triumphantly.

'It is not safe, madame,' he said, 'to travel without an armed escort.'

'I am perfectly safe,' Jeanette declared. Her two servants cowered beside her horse as Colley and the squire hemmed Jeanette in place with their horses.

Sir Simon dismounted with a clank of armour. 'I had hoped, dear lady,' he said, approaching her, 'that we could talk on our way to Louannec.'

'You wish to pray to the holy Yves?' Jeanette asked. 'What will you beg of him? That he grants you courtesy?'

'I would just talk with you, madame,' Sir Simon said.

'Talk of what?'

'Of the complaint you made to the Earl of Northampton. You fouled my honour, lady.'

'Your honour?' Jeanette laughed. 'What honour do you have that could be fouled? Do you even know the meaning of the word?'

Thomas, hidden behind the straggle of alders, was whispering a translation to Jake and Sam. All three crossbows were cocked and had their wicked little bolts lying in the troughs.

168

'If you will not talk to me on the road, madame, then we must have our conversation here,' Sir Simon declared.

'I have nothing to say to you.'

'Then you will find it easy enough to listen,' he said, and reached up to haul her out of the saddle. She beat at his armoured gauntlets, but no resistance of hers could prevent him from dragging her to the ground. The two servants shrieked protests, but Colley and the squire silenced them by grabbing their hair, then pulling them out of the clearing to leave Jeanette and Sir Simon alone.

Jeanette had scrabbled backwards and was now standing beside the fallen tree. Thomas had raised his crossbow, but Jake pushed it down, for Sir Simon's escort was still too near.

Sir Simon pushed Jeanette hard so that she sat down on the rotting trunk, then he took a long dagger from his sword belt and drove its narrow blade hard through Jeanette's skirts so that she was pinned to the fallen willow. He hammered the knife hilt with his steel-shod foot to make sure it was deep in the trunk. Colley and the squire had vanished now and the noise of their horses' hooves had faded among the leaves.

Sir Simon smiled, then stepped forward and plucked the cloak from Jeanette's shoulders. 'When I first saw you, my lady,' he said, 'I confess I thought of marriage. But you have been perverse, so I have changed my mind.' He put his hands at her bodice's neckline and ripped it apart, tearing the laces from their embroidered holes. Jeanette screamed as she tried to cover herself and Jake again held Thomas's arm down.

'Wait till he gets the armour off,' Jake whispered.

They knew the bolts could pierce mail, but none of the three knew how strong the plate armour would prove.

Sir Simon slapped Jeanette's hands away. 'There, madame,' he said, gazing at her breasts, 'now we can have discourse.'

Sir Simon stepped back and began to strip himself of the armour. He pulled off the plated gauntlets first, unbuckled the sword belt, then lifted the shoulder pieces on their leather harness over his head. He fumbled with the side buckles of the breast and back plates that were attached to a leather coat that also supported the rerebraces and vambraces that protected his arms. The coat had a chain skirt, which, because of the weight of the plate and ring mail, made it a struggle for Sir Simon to drag over his head. He staggered as he pulled at the heavy armour and Thomas again raised the crossbow, but Sir Simon was stepping back and forward as he tried to steady himself and Thomas could not be sure of his aim and so kept his finger off the trigger.

The armour-laden coat thumped onto the ground, leaving Sir Simon tousle-haired and bare-chested, and Thomas again put the crossbow stock into his shoulder, but now Sir Simon sat down to strip off the cuisses, greaves, poleyns and boots, and he sat in such a way that his armoured legs were towards the ambush and kept getting in the way of Thomas's aim. Jeanette was struggling with the knife, scared out of her wits that Thomas had not stayed close, but tug as she might the dagger would not move.

Sir Simon pulled off the sollerets that covered his feet, then wriggled out of the leather breeches to which the leg plates were attached. 'Now, madame,' he said, standing whitely naked, 'we can talk properly.'

Jeanette heaved a last time at the dagger, hoping to plunge it into Sir Simon's pale belly, and just then Thomas pulled his trigger.

The bolt scraped across Sir Simon's chest. Thomas had aimed at the knight's groin, hoping to send the short arrow deep into his belly, but the bolt had grazed one of the whiplike alder boughs and been deflected. Blood streaked on Sir Simon's skin and he dropped to the ground so fast that Jake's bolt whipped over his head. Sir Simon scrambled away, going first to his discarded armour. Then he realized he had no time to save the plate and so he ran for his horse, and it was then that Sam's bolt caught him in the flesh of his right thigh so that he yelped, half fell and decided there was no time to rescue his horse either and just limped naked and bleeding into the woods. Thomas loosed a second bolt that rattled past Sir Simon to whack into a tree, and then the naked man vanished. Thomas swore. He had meant to kill, but Sir Simon was all too alive.

'I thought you weren't here!' Jeanette said as Thomas appeared. She was clutching her torn clothing to her breasts.

'We missed the bastard,' Thomas said angrily. He heaved the dagger free of her skirts while Jake and Sam thrust the armour into two sacks. Thomas threw down the crossbow and took his own black bow from his shoulder. What he should do now, he thought, was track Sir Simon through the trees and kill the bastard. He could pull out the white-feathered arrow and put a crossbow bolt into the wound so that whoever found him would believe that bandits or the enemy had killed the knight.

'Search the bastard's saddle pouches,' he told Jake

and Sam. Jeanette had tied the cloak round her neck and her eyes widened as she saw the gold pour from the pouches. 'You're going to stay here with Jake and Sam,' Thomas told her.

'Where are you going?' she asked.

'To finish the job,' Thomas said grimly. He loosed the laces of his arrow bag and dropped one crossbow bolt in among the longer arrows. 'Wait here,' he told Jake and Sam.

'I'll help you,' Sam said.

'No,' Thomas insisted, 'wait here and look after the Countess.' He was angry with himself. He should have used his own bow from the start and simply removed the telltale arrow and shot a bolt into Sir Simon's corpse, but he had fumbled the ambush. But at least Sir Simon had fled westwards, away from his two men-at-arms, and he was naked, bleeding and unarmed. Easy prey, Thomas told himself as he followed the blood drops among the trees. The trail went west and then, as the blood thinned, southwards. Sir Simon was obviously working his way back towards his companions and Thomas abandoned caution and just ran, hoping to cut the fugitive off. Then, bursting through some hazels, he saw Sir Simon, limping and bent. Thomas pulled the bow back, and just then Colley and the squire came into view, both with swords drawn and both spurring their horses at Thomas. He switched his aim to the nearest and loosed without thinking. He loosed as a good archer should, and the arrow went true and fast, smack into the mailed chest of the squire, who was thrown back in his saddle. His sword dropped to the ground as his horse swerved hard to its left, going in front of Sir Simon.

Colley wrenched his reins and reached for Sir Simon, who clutched at his outstretched hand and then half ran and was half carried away into the trees. Thomas had dragged a second arrow from the bag, but by the time he loosed it the two men were half hidden by trees and the arrow glanced off a branch and was lost among the leaves.

Thomas swore. Colley had stared straight at Thomas for an instant. Sir Simon had also seen him and Thomas, a third arrow on his string, just stared at the trees as he understood that everything had just fallen apart. In one instant. Everything.

He ran back to the clearing by the stream. 'You're to take the Countess to the town,' he told Jake and Sam, 'but for Christ's sake go carefully. They'll be searching for us soon. You'll have to sneak back.'

They stared at him, not understanding, and Thomas told them what had happened. How he had killed Sir Simon's squire, and how that made him both a murderer and a fugitive. He had been seen by Sir Simon and by the yellow-haired Colley, and they would both be witnesses at his trial and celebrants at his execution.

He told Jeanette the same in French. 'You can trust Jake and Sam,' he told her, 'but you mustn't be caught going home. You have to go carefully!'

Jake and Sam argued, but Thomas knew well enough what the consequences of the killing arrow were. 'Tell Will what happened,' he told them. 'Blame it all on me and say I'll wait for him at Quatre Vents.' That was a village the hellequin had laid waste south of La Roche-Derrien. 'Tell him I'd like his advice.'

Jeanette tried to persuade him that his panic was

173

unnecessary. 'Perhaps they did not recognize you?' she suggested.

'They recognized me, my lady,' Thomas said grimly. He smiled ruefully. 'I am sorry, but at least you have your armour and sword. Hide them well.' He pulled himself into Sir Simon's saddle. 'Quatre Vents,' he told Jake and Sam, then spurred southwards through the trees.

He was a murderer, a wanted man and a fugitive, and that meant he was any man's prey, alone in the wilderness made by the hellequin. He had no idea what he should do or where he could go, only that if he was to survive then he must ride like the devil's horseman that he was.

So he did.

Quatre Vents had been a small village, scarce larger than Hookton, with a gaunt barn-like church, a cluster of cottages where cows and people had shared the same thatched roofs, a water mill, and some outlying farms crouched in sheltered valleys. Only the stone walls of the church and mill were left now, the rest was just ashes, dust and weeds. The blossom was blowing from the untended orchards when Thomas arrived on a horse sweated white by its long journey. He released the stallion to graze in a well-hedged and overgrown pasture, then took himself into the woods above the church. He was shaken, nervous and frightened, for what had seemed like a game had twisted his life into darkness. Not a few hours before he had been an archer in England's army and, though his future might not have appealed to the young men with whom he had rioted in Oxford, Thomas had been certain he would at least rise as high as Will Skeat. He had imagined himself leading a band of soldiers, becoming wealthy, following his black bow to fortune and even rank, but now he was a hunted man. He was in such panic that he began to doubt Will Skeat's reaction, fearing that Skeat would be so disgusted at the failure of the ambush that he would arrest Thomas and lead him back to a rope-dancing end in La Roche-Derrien's marketplace. He worried that Jeanette would have been caught going back to the town. Would they charge her with murder too? He shivered as night fell. He was twenty-two years old, he had failed utterly, he was alone and he was lost.

He woke in a cold, drizzling dawn. Hares raced across the pasture where Sir Simon Jekyll's destrier cropped the grass. Thomas opened the purse he kept under his mail coat and counted his coins. There was the gold from Sir Simon's saddle pouch and his own few coins, so he was not poor, but like most of the hellequin he left the bulk of his money in Will Skeat's keeping; even when they were out raiding, there were always some men left in La Roche-Derrien to keep an eye on the hoard. What would he do? He had a bow and some arrows, and perhaps he could walk to Gascony, though he had no idea how far that was, but at least he knew there were English garrisons there who would surely welcome another trained archer. Or perhaps he could find a way to cross the Channel? Go home, find another name, start again – except he had no home. What he must never do was find himself within a hanging rope's distance of Sir Simon Jekyll.

The hellequin arrived shortly after midday. The archers rode into the village first, followed by the men-at-arms, who were escorting a one-horse wagon that had wooden hoops supporting a flapping cover of brown cloth. Father Hobbe and Will Skeat rode beside the wagon, which puzzled Thomas, for he had never known the hellequin use such a vehicle before. But then Skeat and the priest broke away from the men-at-arms and spurred their horses towards the field where the stallion grazed.

The two men stopped by the hedge, and Skeat cupped his hands and shouted towards the woods, 'Come on out, you daft bastard!' Thomas emerged very sheepishly, to be greeted with an ironic cheer from the archers. Skeat regarded him sourly. 'God's bones, Tom,' he said, 'but the devil did a bad thing when he humped your mother.'

Father Hobbe tutted at Will's blasphemy, then raised a hand in blessing. 'You missed a fine sight, Tom,' he said cheerfully: 'Sir Simon coming home to La Roche, half naked and bleeding like a stuck pig. I'll hear your confession before we go.'

'Don't grin, you stupid bastard,' Skeat snapped. 'Sweet Christ, Tom, but if you do a job, do it proper. Do it proper! Why did you leave the bastard alive?'

'I missed.'

'Then you go and kill some poor bastard squire instead. Sweet Christ, but you're a goddamn bloody fool.'

'I suppose they want to hang me?' Thomas asked.

'Oh no,' Skeat said in feigned surprise, 'of course not! They want to feast you, hang garlands round your neck and give you a dozen virgins to warm your bed. What the hell do you think they want to do with you? Of course they want you dead and I swore on my mother's life I'd bring you back if I found you alive. Does he look alive to you, father?'

Father Hobbe examined Thomas. 'He looks very dead to me, Master Skeat.'

'He bloody deserves to be dead, the daft bastard.'

'Did the Countess get safe home?' Thomas asked.

'She got home, if that's what you mean,' Skeat said, 'but what do you think Sir Simon wanted the moment he'd covered up his shrivelled prick? To have her house searched, Tom, for some armour and a sword that were legitimately his. He's not such a daft fool; he knows you and she were together.' Thomas cursed and Skeat repeated the blasphemy. 'So they pressed her two servants and they admitted the Countess planned everything.'

'They did what?' Thomas asked.

'They pressed them,' Skeat repeated, which meant that the old couple had been put flat on the ground and had stones piled on their chests. 'The old girl squealed everything at the first stone, so they were hardly hurt,' Skeat went on, 'and now Sir Simon wants to charge her ladyship with murder. And naturally he had her house searched for the sword and armour, but they found nowt because I had them and her hidden well away, but she's still as deep in the shit as you are. You can't just go about sticking crossbow bolts into knights and slaughtering squires, Tom! It upsets the order of things!'

'I'm sorry, Will,' Thomas said.

'So the long and the brief of it,' Skeat said, 'is that the Countess is seeking the protection of her husband's uncle.' He jerked a thumb at the cart. 'She's in that, together with her bairn, two bruised servants, a suit of armour and a sword.'

'Sweet Jesus,' Thomas said, staring at the cart.

'You put her there,' Skeat growled, 'not Him. And I had the devil's own business keeping her hid from Sir Simon. Dick Totesham suspects I'm up to no good and he don't approve, though he took my word in the end, but I still had to promise to drag you back by the scruff of your miserable neck. But I haven't seen you, Tom.'

'I'm sorry, Will,' Thomas said again.

'You bloody well should be sorry,' Skeat said, though he was exuding a quiet satisfaction that he had managed to clean up Thomas's mess so efficiently. Jake and Sam had not been seen by Sir Simon or his surviving man-at-arms, so they were safe, Thomas was a fugitive and Jeanette had been safely smuggled out of La Roche-Derrien before Sir Simon could make her life into utter misery. 'She's travelling to Guingamp,' Skeat went on, 'and I'm sending a dozen men to escort her and God only knows if the enemy will respect their flag of truce. If I had a lick of bloody sense I'd skin you alive and make a bow-cover out of your hide.'

'Yes, Will,' Thomas said meekly.

'Don't bloody "yes, Will" me,' Skeat said. 'What are you going to do with the few days you've got left to live?'

'I don't know.'

Skeat sniffed. 'You could grow up, for a start, though there's probably scant chance of that happening. Right, lad.' He braced himself, taking charge. 'I took your money from the chest, so here it is.' He handed Thomas a leather pouch. 'And I've put three sheaves of arrows in the lady's cart and that'll keep you for a few days. If you've got any sense, which you ain't, then you'd go south or north. You could go to Gascony, but it's a hell of a long walk. Flanders is closer and has plenty of English troops who'll probably take you in if they're desperate. That's my advice, lad. Go north and hope Sir Simon never goes to Flanders.'

'Thank you,' Thomas said.

'But how do you get to Flanders?' Skeat asked.

'Walk?' Thomas suggested.

'God's bones,' Will said, 'but you're a useless worm-eaten piece of lousy meat. Walk dressed like that and carrying a bow, and you might just as well just cut your own throat. It'll be quicker than letting the French do it.'

'You might find this useful,' Father Hobbe intervened, and offered Thomas a black cloth bundle which, on unrolling, proved to be the robe of a Dominican friar. 'You speak Latin, Tom,' the priest said, 'so you could pass for a wandering preacher. If anyone challenges you, say you're travelling from Avignon to Aachen.'

Thomas thanked him. 'Do many Dominicans travel with a bow?' he asked.

'Lad,' Father Hobbe said sadly, 'I can unbutton your breeches and I can point you down wind, but even with the Good Lord's help I can't piss for you.'

'In other words,' Skeat said, 'work it out for yourself. You got yourself in this bloody mess, Tom, so you get yourself out. I enjoyed your company, lad. Thought you'd be useless when I first saw you and you weren't, but you are now. But be lucky, boy.' He held out his hand and Thomas shook it. 'You might as well go to Guingamp with the Countess,' Skeat finished, 'and then find your own way, but Father Hobbe wants to save your soul first. God knows why.'

Father Hobbe dismounted and led Thomas into the roofless church where grass and weeds now grew between the flagstones. He insisted on hearing a confession and Thomas was feeling abject enough to sound contrite.

Father Hobbe sighed when it was done. 'You killed a man, Tom,' he said heavily, 'and it is a great sin.'

'Father –' Thomas began.

'No, no, Tom, no excuses. The Church says that to

kill in battle is a duty a man owes to his lord, but you killed outside the law. That poor squire, what offence did he give you? And he had a mother, Tom; think of her. No, you've sinned grievously and I must give you a grievous penance.'

Thomas, on his knees, looked up to see a buzzard sliding between the thinning clouds above the church's scorched walls. Then Father Hobbe stepped closer, looming above him. 'I'll not have you muttering paternosters, Tom,' the priest said, 'but something hard. Something very hard.' He put his hand on Thomas's hair. 'Your penance is to keep the promise you made to your father.' He paused to hear Thomas's response, but the young man was silent. 'You hear me?' Father Hobbe demanded fiercely.

'Yes, father.'

'You will find the lance of St George, Thomas, and return it to England. That is your penance. And now,' he changed into execrable Latin, 'in the name of the Father, and of the Son, and of the Holy Spirit, I absolve you.' He made the sign of the cross. 'Don't waste your life, Tom.'

'I think I already have, father.'

'You're just young. It seems like that when you're young. Life's nothing but joy or misery when you're young.' He helped Thomas up from his knees. 'You're not hanging from a gibbet, are you? You're alive, Tom, and there's a deal of life in you yet.' He smiled. 'I have a feeling we shall meet again.'

Thomas made his farewells, then watched as Will Skeat collected Sir Simon Jekyll's horse and led the hellequin eastwards, leaving the wagon and its small escort in the ruined village.

The leader of the escort was called Hugh Boltby, one

181

of Skeat's better men-at-arms, and he reckoned they would likely meet the enemy the next day somewhere close to Guingamp. He would hand the Countess over, then ride back to join Skeat. 'And you'd best not be dressed as an archer, Tom,' he added.

Thomas walked beside the wagon that was driven by Pierre, the old man who had been pressed by Sir Simon. Jeanette did not invite Thomas inside, indeed she pretended he did not exist, though next morning, after they had camped in an abandoned farm, she laughed at the sight of him dressed in the friar's robe.

'I'm sorry about what happened,' Thomas said to her.

Jeanette shrugged. 'It may be for the best. I probably should have gone to Duke Charles last winter.'

'Why didn't you, my lady?'

'He hasn't always been kind to me,' she said wistfully, 'but I think that might have changed by now.' She had persuaded herself that the Duke's attitude might have altered because of the letters she had sent to him, letters that would help him when he led his troops against the garrison at La Roche-Derrien. She also needed to believe the Duke would welcome her, for she desperately needed a safe home for her son, Charles, who was enjoying the adventure of riding in a swaying, creaking wagon. Together they would both start a new life in Guingamp and Jeanette had woken with optimism about that new life. She had been forced to leave La Roche-Derrien in a frantic hurry, putting into the cart just the retrieved armour, the sword and some clothes, though she had some money that Thomas suspected Will had given to her, but her real hopes were pinned on Duke Charles who, she told Thomas, would surely find her a house and lend her money in advance of the missing rents from Plabennec. 'He is sure to like Charles, don't you think?' she asked Thomas.

'I'm sure,' Thomas said, glancing at Jeanette's son, who was shaking the wagon's reins and clicking his tongue in a vain effort to make the horse go quicker.

'But what will you do?' Jeanette asked.

'I'll survive,' Thomas said, unwilling to admit that he did not know what he would do. Go to Flanders, probably, if he could ever reach there. Join another troop of archers and pray nightly that Sir Simon Jekyll never came his way again. As for his penance, the lance, he had no idea how he was to find it or, having found it, retrieve it.

Jeanette, on that second day of the journey, decided Thomas was a friend after all.

'When we get to Guingamp,' she told him, 'you find somewhere to stay and I shall persuade the Duke to give you a pass. Even a wandering friar will be helped by a pass from the Duke of Brittany.'

But no friar ever carried a bow, let alone a long English war bow, and Thomas did not know what to do with the weapon. He was loath to abandon it, but the sight of some charred timbers in the abandoned farmhouse gave him an idea. He broke off a short length of blackened timber and lashed it crosswise to the unstrung bowstave so that it resembled a pilgrim's cross-staff. He remembered a Dominican visiting Hookton with just such a staff. The friar, his hair cropped so short he looked bald, had preached a fiery sermon outside the church until Thomas's father became tired of his ranting and sent him on his way, and Thomas now reckoned he would have to pose as just such a man. Jeanette suggested he tied flowers to the staff to disguise it further, and so he wrapped it with clovers that grew tall and ragged in the abandoned fields.

The wagon, hauled by a bony horse that had been plundered from Lannion, lurched and lumbered southwards. The men-at-arms became ever more cautious as they neared Guingamp, fearing an ambush of crossbow bolts from the woods that pressed close to the deserted road. One of the men had a hunting horn that he sounded constantly to warn the enemy of their approach and to signal that they came in peace, while Boltby had a strip of white cloth hanging from the tip of his lance. There was no ambush, but a few miles short of Guingamp they came in sight of a ford where a band of enemy soldiers waited. Two men-at-arms and a dozen crossbowmen ran forward, their weapons cocked, and Boltby summoned Thomas from the wagon. 'Talk to them,' he ordered.

Thomas was nervous. 'What do I say?'

'Give them a bloody blessing, for Christ's sake,' Boltby said, disgusted, 'and tell them we're here in peace.'

So, with a beating heart and a dry mouth, Thomas walked down the road. The black gown flapped awkwardly about his ankles as he waved his hands at the crossbowmen. 'Lower your weapons,' he called in French, 'lower your weapons. The Englishmen come in peace.'

One of the horsemen spurred forward. His shield bore the same white ermine badge that Duke John's men carried, though these supporters of Duke Charles had surrounded the ermine with a blue wreath on which fleurs-de-lis had been painted.

'Who are you, father?' the horseman demanded.

Thomas opened his mouth to answer, but no words

came. He gaped up at the horseman, who had a reddish moustache and oddly yellow eyes. A hard-looking bastard, Thomas thought, and he raised a hand to touch St Guinefort's paw. Perhaps the saint inspired him, for he was suddenly possessed of devilment and began to enjoy playing a priest's role. 'I am merely one of God's humbler children, my son,' he answered unctuously.

'Are you English?' the man-at-arms demanded suspiciously. Thomas's French was near perfect, but it was the French spoken by England's rulers rather than the language of France itself.

Thomas again felt panic fluttering in his breast, but he bought time by making the sign of the cross, and as his hand moved so inspiration came to him. 'I am a Scotsman, my son,' he said, and that allayed the yellow-eyed man's suspicions; the Scots had ever been France's ally. Thomas knew nothing of Scotland, but doubted many Frenchmen or Bretons did either, for it was far away and, by all accounts, a most uninviting place. Skeat always said it was a country of bog, rock and heathen bastards who were twice as difficult to kill as any Frenchman. 'I am a Scotsman,' Thomas repeated, 'who brings a kinswoman of the Duke out of the hands of the English.'

The man-at-arms glanced at the wagon. 'A kinswoman of Duke Charles?'

'Is there another duke?' Thomas asked innocently. 'She is the Countess of Armorica,' he went on, 'and her son, who is with her, is the Duke's grandnephew and a count in his own right. The English have held them prisoner these six months, but by God's good grace they have relented and set her free. The Duke, I know, will want to welcome her.'

Thomas laid on Jeanette's rank and relationship to the Duke as thick as newly skimmed cream and the enemy swallowed it whole. They allowed the wagon to continue, and Thomas watched as Hugh Boltby led his men away at a swift trot, eager to put as much distance as possible between themselves and the crossbowmen. The leader of the enemy's men-at-arms talked with Jeanette and seemed impressed by her hauteur. He would, he said, be honoured to escort the Countess to Guingamp, though he warned her that the Duke was not there, but was still returning from Paris. He was said to be at Rennes now, a city that lay a good day's journey to the east.

'You will take me as far as Rennes?' Jeanette asked Thomas.

'You want me to, my lady?'

'A young man is useful,' she said. 'Pierre is old,' she gestured at the servant, 'and has lost his strength. Besides, if you're going to Flanders then you will need to cross the river at Rennes.'

So Thomas kept her company for the three days that it took the painfully slow wagon to make the journey. They needed no escort beyond Guingamp for there was small danger of any English raiders this far east in Brittany and the road was well patrolled by the Duke's forces. The countryside looked strange to Thomas, for he had become accustomed to rank fields, untended orchards and deserted villages, but here the farms were busy and prosperous. The churches were bigger and had stained glass, and fewer and fewer folk spoke Breton. This was still Brittany, but the language was French.

They stayed in country taverns that had fleas in the straw. Jeanette and her son were given what passed for the best room while Thomas shared the stables with the two servants. They met two priests on the road, but neither suspected that Thomas was an imposter. He greeted them in Latin, which he spoke better than they did, and both men wished him a good day and a fervent Godspeed. Thomas could almost feel their relief when he did not engage them in further conversation. The Dominicans were not popular with parish priests. The friars were priests themselves, but were charged with the suppression of heresy so a visitation by the Dominicans suggested that a parish priest has not been doing his duty and even a rough, wild and young friar like Thomas was unwelcome.

They reached Rennes in the afternoon. There were dark clouds in the east against which the city loomed larger than any place Thomas had ever seen. The walls were twice as high as those at Lannion or La Roche-Derrien, and had towers with pointed roofs every few yards to serve as buttresses from which crossbowmen could pour bolts on any attacking force. Above the walls, higher even than the turrets, the church towers or the cathedral, was the citadel, a stronghold of pale stone hung with banners. The smell of the city wafted westwards on a chill wind, a stink of sewage, tanneries and smoke.

The guards at the western gate became excited when they discovered the arrows in the wagon, but Jeanette persuaded them that they were trophies she was taking to the Duke. Then they wanted to levy a custom's duty on the fine armour and Jeanette harangued them again, using her title and the Duke's name liberally. The soldiers eventually gave in and allowed the wagon into the narrow streets where shopwares protruded onto the roadway. Beggars ran beside the wagon and soldiers jostled Thomas, who was leading the horse. The city was crammed with soldiers. Most of the men-at-arms were wearing the wreathed white ermine badge, but many had the green grail of Genoa on their tunics, and the presence of so many troops confirmed that the Duke was indeed in the city and readying himself for the campaign that would eject the English from Brittany.

They found a tavern beneath the cathedral's looming twin towers. Jeanette wanted to ready herself for her audience with the Duke and demanded a private room, though all she got for her cash was a spider-haunted space beneath the tavern's eaves. The innkeeper, a sallow fellow with a twitch, suggested Thomas would be happier in the Dominican friary that lay by the church of St Germain, north of the cathedral, but Thomas declared his mission was to be among sinners, not saints, and so the innkeeper grudgingly said he could sleep in Jeanette's wagon that was parked in the inn yard.

'But no preaching, father,' the man added, 'no preaching. There's enough of that in the city without spoiling the Three Keys.'

Jeanette's maid brushed her mistress's hair, then coiled and pinned the black tresses into ram's horns that covered her ears. Jeanette put on a red velvet dress that had escaped the sack of her house and which had a skirt that fell from just beneath her breasts to the floor, while the bodice, intricately embroidered with cornflowers and daisies, hooked tight up to her neck. Its sleeves were full, trimmed with fox fur, and dropped to her red shoes, which had horn buckles. Her hat matched the dress and was trimmed with the same fur and a blue-black veil of lace. She spat on her son's face and rubbed off the dirt, then led him down to the tavern yard.

'Do you think the veil is right?' she asked Thomas anxiously.

Thomas shrugged. 'It looks right to me.'

'No, the colour! Is it right with the red?'

He nodded, hiding his astonishment. He had never seen her dressed so fashionably. She looked like a countess now, while her son was in a clean smock and had his hair wetted and smoothed.

'You're to meet your great-uncle!' Jeanette told Charles, licking a finger and rubbing at some more dirt on his cheek. 'And he's nephew to the King of France. Which means you're related to the King! Yes, you are! Aren't you a lucky boy?'

Charles recoiled from his mother's fussing, but she did not notice for she was busy instructing Pierre, her manservant, to stow the armour and sword in a great sack. She wanted the duke to see the armour. 'I want him to know,' she told Thomas, 'that when my son comes of age he will fight for him.'

Pierre, who claimed to be seventy years old, lifted the sack and almost fell over with the weight. Thomas offered to carry it to the citadel instead, but Jeanette would not hear of it.

'You might pass for a Scotsman among the common folk, but the Duke's entourage will have men who may have visited the place.' She smoothed wrinkles from the red velvet skirt. 'You wait here,' she told Thomas, 'and I'll send Pierre back with a message, maybe even some money. I'm sure the Duke is going to be generous. I shall demand a pass for you. What name shall I use? A Scot's name? Just Thomas the friar? As soon as he sees you,' she was now talking to her son, 'he'll open his purse, won't he? Of course he will.'

Pierre managed to hoist the armour onto his shoulder without falling over and Jeanette took her son's hand. 'I shall send you a message,' she promised Thomas.

'God's blessing, my child,' Thomas said, 'and may the blessed St Guinefort watch over you.'

Jeanette wrinkled her nose at that mention of St Guinefort, who, she had learned from Thomas, was really a dog. 'I shall put my trust in St Renan,' she said reprovingly, and with those words she left. Pierre and his wife followed her, and Thomas waited in the yard, offering blessings to ostlers, stray cats and tapmen. Be mad enough, his father had once said, and they will either lock you away or make you a saint.

The night fell, damp and cold, with a gusting wind sighing in the cathedral's towers and rustling the tavern's thatch. Thomas thought of the penance that Father Hobbe had demanded.

Was the lance real? Had it truly smashed through a dragon's scales, pierced the ribs and riven a heart in which cold blood flowed? He thought it was real. His father had believed and his father, though he might have been mad, had been no fool. And the lance had looked old, so very old. Thomas had used to pray to St George, but he no longer did and that made him feel guilty so that he dropped to his knees beside the wagon and asked the saint to forgive him his sins, to forgive him for the squire's murder and for impersonating a friar. I do not mean to be a bad person, he told the dragon killer, but it is so easy to forget heaven and the saints. And if you wish, he prayed, I will find the lance, but you must tell me what to do with it. Should he restore it to Hookton that, so far as Thomas knew, no longer existed? Or should he return it to whoever had owned it before his grandfather stole it? And who was his grandfather? And why had his father hidden from his family? And why had the family sought him out to take the lance back? Thomas did not know and, for the past three years, he had not cared, but suddenly, in the tavern yard, he found himself consumed by curiosity. He did have a family somewhere. His grandfather had been a soldier and a thief, but who was he? He added a prayer to St George to allow him to discover them.

'Praying for rain, father?' one of the ostlers suggested. 'I reckon we're going to get it. We need it.'

Thomas could have eaten in the tavern, but he was suddenly nervous of the crowded room where the Duke's soldiers and their women sang, boasted and brawled. Nor could he face the landlord's sly suspicions. The man was curious why Thomas did not go to the friary, and even more curious why a friar should travel with a beautiful woman. 'She is my cousin,' Thomas had told the man, who had pretended to believe the lie, but Thomas had no desire to face more questions and so he stayed in the yard and made a poor meal from the dry bread, sour onions and hard cheese that was the only food left in the wagon.

It began to rain and he retreated into the wagon and listened to the drops patter on the canvas cover. He thought of Jeanette and her little son being fed sugared delicacies on silver plates before sleeping between clean linen sheets in some tapestry-hung bedchamber, and then began to feel sorry for himself. He was a fugitive, Jeanette was his only ally and she was too high and mighty for him.

Bells announced the shutting of the city's gates. Watchmen walked the streets, looking for fires that could destroy a city in a few hours. Sentries shivered on the walls and Duke Charles's banners flew from the citadel's summit. Thomas was among his enemies, protected by nothing more than wit and a Dominican's robe. And he was alone.

Jeanette became increasingly nervous as she approached the citadel, but she had persuaded herself that Charles of Blois would accept her as a dependant once he met her son who was named for him, and Jeanette's husband had always said that the Duke would like Jeanette if only he could get to know her better. It was true that the Duke had been cold in the past, but her letters must have convinced him of her allegiance and, at the very least, she was certain he would possess the chivalry to look after a woman in distress.

To her surprise it was easier to enter the citadel than it had been to negotiate the city gate. The sentries waved her across the drawbridge, beneath the arch and so into a great courtyard ringed with stables, mews and storehouses. A score of men-at-arms were practising with their swords which, in the gloom of the late afternoon, generated bright sparks. More sparks flowed from a smithy where a horse was being shoed, and Jeanette caught the whiff of burning hoof mingling with the stink of a dungheap and the reek of a decomposing corpse, which hung in chains high on the courtyard wall. A laconic and misspelled placard pronounced the man to have been a thief.

A steward guided her through a second arch and so

into a great cold chamber where a score of petitioners waited to see the Duke. A clerk took her name, raising an eyebrow in silent surprise when she announced herself. 'His grace will be told of your presence,' the man said in a bored voice, then dismissed Jeanette to a stone bench that ran along one of the hall's high walls.

Pierre lowered the armour to the floor and squatted beside it while Jeanette sat. Some of the petitioners paced up and down, clutching scrolls and silently mouthing the words they would use when they saw the Duke, while others complained to the clerks that they had already been waiting three, four or even five days. How much longer? A dog lifted its leg against a pillar, then two small boys, six or seven years old, ran into the hall with mock wooden swords. They gazed at the petitioners for a second, then ran up some stairs that were guarded by men-at-arms. Were they the Duke's sons, Jeanette wondered, and she imagined Charles making friends with the boys.

'You're going to be happy here,' she told him.

'I'm hungry, Mama.'

'We shall eat soon.'

She waited. Two women strolled along the gallery at the head of the stairs wearing pale dresses made of expensive linen that seemed to float as they walked and Jeanette suddenly felt shabby in her wrinkled red velvet. 'You must be polite to the Duke,' she told Charles, who was getting fretful from hunger. 'You kneel to him, can you do that? Show me how you kneel.'

'I want to go home,' Charles said.

'Just for Mama, show me how you kneel. That's good!'

Jeanette ruffled her son's hair in praise, then immediately tried to stroke it back into place. From upstairs came the sound of a sweet harp and a breathy flute, and Jeanette thought longingly of the life she wanted. A life fit for a countess, edged with music and handsome men, elegance and power. She would rebuild Plabennec, though with what she did not know, but she would make the tower larger and have a staircase like the one in this hall. An hour passed, then another. It was dark now and the hall was dimly lit by two burning torches that sent smoke into the fan tracery of the high roof. Charles became ever more petulant so Jeanette took him in her arms and tried to rock him to sleep. Two priests, arm in arm, came slowly down the stairs, laughing, and then a servant in the Duke's livery ran down and all the petitioners straightened and looked at the man expectantly. He crossed to the clerk's table, spoke there for a moment, then turned and bowed to Jeanette.

She stood. 'You will wait here,' she told her two servants.

The other petitioners stared at her resentfully. She had been the last to enter the hall, yet she was the first to be summoned. Charles dragged his feet and Jeanette struck him lightly on the head to remind him of his manners. The servant walked silently beside her. 'His grace is in good health?' Jeanette asked nervously.

The servant did not reply, but just led her up the stairs, then turned right down the gallery where rain spat through open windows. They went under an arch and up a further flight of steps at the top of which the servant threw open a high door. 'The Count of Armorica,' he announced, 'and his mother.'

The room was evidently in one of the citadel's turrets

194

for it was circular. A great fireplace was built into one side, while cruciform arrow slits opened onto the grey wet darkness beyond the walls. The circular chamber itself was brilliantly lit by forty or fifty candles that cast their light over hanging tapestries, a great polished table, a chair, a prie-dieu carved with scenes from Christ's passion, and a fur-covered couch. The floor was soft with deerskins. Two clerks worked at a smaller table, while the Duke, gorgeous in a deep blue robe edged with ermine and with a cap to match, sat at the great table. A middle-aged priest, gaunt, white-haired and narrow faced, stood beside the prie-dieu and watched Jeanette with an expression of distaste.

Jeanette curtsied to the Duke and nudged Charles. 'Kneel,' she whispered.

Charles began crying and hid his face in his mother's skirts.

The Duke flinched at the child's noise, but said nothing. He was still young, though closer to thirty than to twenty, and had a pale, watchful face. He was thin, had a fair beard and moustache, and long, bony white hands that were clasped in front of his down-turned mouth. His reputation was that of a learned and pious man, but there was a petulance in his expression that made Jeanette wary. She wished he would speak, but all four men in the room just watched her in silence.

'I have the honour of presenting your grace's grand-nephew,' Jeanette said, pushing her crying son forward, 'the Count of Armorica.'

The Duke looked at the boy. His face betrayed nothing.

'He is named Charles,' Jeanette said, but she might as well have stayed silent for the Duke still said nothing.

The silence was broken only by the child's whimpering and the crackle of flames in the great hearth. 'I trust your grace received my letters,' Jeanette said nervously.

The priest suddenly spoke, making Jeanette jump with surprise. 'You came here,' he said in a high voice, 'with a servant carrying a burden. What is in it?'

Jeanette realized they must have thought she had brought the Duke a gift and she blushed for she had not thought to bring one. Even a small token would have been a tactful gesture, but she had simply not remembered that courtesy. 'It contains my dead husband's armour and sword,' she said, 'which I rescued from the English who have otherwise left me with nothing. Nothing. I am keeping the armour and sword for my son, so that one day he can use them to fight for his liege lord.' She bowed her head to the Duke.

The Duke steepled his fingers. To Jeanette it seemed he never blinked and that was as unsettling as his silence.

'His grace would like to see the armour,' the priest announced, though the Duke had shown no sign of wishing anything at all. The priest snapped his fingers and one of the clerks left the room. The second clerk, armed with a small pair of scissors, went round the big chamber trimming the wicks of the many candles in their tall iron holders. The Duke and the priest ignored him.

'You say,' the priest spoke again, 'that you wrote letters to his grace. Concerning what?'

'I wrote about the new defences at La Roche-Derrien, father, and I warned his grace of the English attack on Lannion.'

'So you say,' the priest said, 'so you say.' Charles was

still crying and Jeanette jerked his hand hard in the hope of stilling him, but he just whined more. The clerk, head averted from the Duke, went from candle to candle. The scissors snipped, a puff of smoke would writhe for a heartbeat, then the flame would brighten and settle. Charles began crying louder.

'His grace,' the priest said, 'does not like snivelling infants.'

'He is hungry, father,' Jeanette explained nervously.

'You came with two servants?'

'Yes, father,' Jeanette said.

'They can eat with the boy in the kitchens,' the priest said, and snapped his fingers towards the candle-trimming clerk, who, abandoning his scissors on a rug, took the frightened Charles by the hand. The boy did not want to leave his mother, but he was dragged away and Jeanette flinched as the sound of his crying receded down the stairs.

The Duke, other than steepling his fingers, had not moved. He just watched Jeanette with an unreadable expression.

'You say,' the priest took up the questioning again, 'that the English left you with nothing?'

'They stole all I had!'

The priest flinched at the passion in her voice. 'If they left you destitute, madame, then why did you not come for our help earlier?'

'I did not wish to be a burden, father.'

'But now you do wish to become a burden?'

Jeanette frowned. 'I have brought his grace's nephew, the Lord of Plabennec. Or would you rather that he grew up among the English?'

'Do not be impertinent, child,' the priest said placidly.

The first clerk re-entered the room carrying the sack, which he emptied on the deerskins in front of the Duke's table. The Duke gazed at the armour for a few seconds, then settled back in his high carved chair.

'It is very fine,' the priest declared.

'It is most precious,' Jeanette agreed.

The Duke peered again at the armour. Not a muscle of his face moved.

'His grace approves,' the priest said, then gestured with a long white hand and the clerk, who seemed to understand what was wanted without words, gathered up the sword and armour and carried them from the room.

'I am glad your grace approves,' Jeanette said, and dropped another curtsy. She had a confused idea that the Duke, despite her earlier words, had assumed the armour and sword were a gift, but she did not want to enquire. It could all be cleared up later. A gust of cold wind came through the arrow slits to bring spots of rain and to flicker the candles in wild shudders.

'So what,' the priest asked, 'do you require of us?'

'My son needs shelter, father,' Jeanette said nervously. 'He needs a house, a place to grow and learn to be a warrior.'

'His grace is pleased to grant that request,' the priest said.

Jeanette felt a great wash of relief. The atmosphere in the room was so unfriendly that she had feared she would be thrown out as destitute as she had arrived, but the priest's words, though coldly stated, told her that she need not have worried. The Duke was taking his responsibility and she curtsied for a third time. 'I am grateful, your grace.'

The priest was about to respond, but, to Jeanette's surprise, the Duke held up one long white hand and the priest bowed. 'It is our pleasure,' the Duke said in an oddly high-pitched voice, 'for your son is dear to us and it is our desire that he grows to become a warrior like his father.' He turned to the priest and inclined his head, and the priest gave another stately bow then left the room.

The Duke stood and walked to the fire where he held his hands to the small flames. 'It has come to our notice,' he said distantly, 'that the rents of Plabennec have not been paid these twelve quarters.'

'The English are in possession of the domain, your grace.'

'And you are in debt to me,' the Duke said, frowning at the flames.

'If you protect my son, your grace, then I shall be for ever in your debt,' Jeanette said humbly.

The Duke took off his cap and ran a hand through his fair hair. Jeanette thought he looked younger and kinder without the hat, but his next words chilled her. 'I did not want Henri to marry you.' He stopped abruptly.

For a heartbeat Jeanette was struck dumb by his frankness. 'My husband regretted your grace's disapproval,' she finally said in a small voice.

The Duke ignored Jeanette's words. 'He should have married Lisette of Picard. She had money, lands, tenants. She would have brought our family great wealth. In times of trouble wealth is a . . .' he paused, trying to find the right word, 'it is a cushion. You, madame, have no cushion.'

'Only your grace's kindness,' Jeanette said.

'Your son is my charge,' the Duke said. 'He will be raised in my household and trained in the arts of war and civilization as befits his rank.'

'I am grateful.' Jeanette was tired of grovelling. She wanted some sign of affection from the Duke, but ever since he had walked to the hearth he would not meet her eyes.

Now, suddenly, he turned on her. 'There is a lawyer called Belas in La Roche-Derrien?'

'Indeed, your grace.'

'He tells me your mother was a Jewess.' He spat the last word.

Jeanette gaped at him. For a few heartbeats she was unable to speak. Her mind was reeling with disbelief that Belas would say such a thing, but at last she managed to shake her head. 'She was not!' she protested.

'He tells us, too,' the Duke went on, 'that you petitioned Edward of England for the rents of Plabennec?'

'What choice did I have?'

'And that your son was made a ward of Edward's?' the Duke asked pointedly.

Jeanette opened and closed her mouth. The accusations were coming so thick and fast she did not know how to defend herself. It was true that her son had been named a ward of King Edward's, but it had not been Jeanette's doing; indeed, she had not even been present when the Earl of Northampton made that decision, but before she could protest or explain the Duke spoke again.

'Belas tells us,' he said, 'that many in the town of La Roche-Derrien have expressed satisfaction with the English occupiers?'

'Some have,' Jeanette admitted.

'And that you, madame, have English soldiers in your own house, guarding you.'

'They forced themselves on my house!' she said indignantly. 'Your grace must believe me! I did not want them there!'

The Duke shook his head. 'It seems to us, madame, that you have given a welcome to our enemies. Your father was a vintner, was he not?'

Jeanette was too astonished to say anything. It was slowly dawning on her that Belas had betrayed her utterly, yet she still clung to the hope that the Duke would be convinced of her innocence. 'I offered them no welcome,' she insisted. 'I fought against them!'

'Merchants,' the Duke said, 'have no loyalties other than to money. They have no honour. Honour is not learned, madame. It is bred. Just as you breed a horse for bravery and speed, or a hound for agility and ferocity, so you breed a nobleman for honour. You cannot turn a plough-horse into a destrier, nor a merchant into a gentleman. It is against nature and the laws of God.' He made the sign of the cross. 'Your son is Count of Armorica, and we shall raise him in honour, but you, madame, are the daughter of a merchant and a Jewess.'

'It is not true!' Jeanette protested.

'Do not shout at me, madame,' the Duke said icily. 'You are a burden on me. You dare to come here, tricked out in fox fur, expecting me to give you shelter? What else? Money? I will give your son a home, but you, madame, I shall give you a husband.' He walked towards her, his feet silent on the deerskin rugs. 'You are not fit to be the Count of Armorica's mother. You have offered comfort to the enemy, you have no honour.'

'I –' Jeanette began to protest again, but the Duke slapped her hard across the cheek.

'You will be silent, madame,' he commanded, 'silent.' He pulled at the laces of her bodice and, when she dared to resist, he slapped her again. 'You are a whore, madame,' the Duke said, then lost patience with the intricate cross-laces, retrieved the discarded scissors from the rug and used them to cut through the laces to expose Jeanette's breasts. She was so astonished, stunned and horrified that she made no attempt to protect herself. This was not Sir Simon Jekyll, but her liege lord, the King's nephew and her husband's uncle. 'You are a pretty whore, madame,' the Duke said with a sneer. 'How did you enchant Henri? Was it Jewish witchcraft?'

'No,' Jeanette whimpered, 'please, no!'

The Duke unhooked his gown and Jeanette saw he was naked beneath.

'No,' she said again, 'please, no.'

The Duke pushed her hard so that she fell on the bed. His face still showed no emotion – not lust, not pleasure, not anger. He hauled her skirts up, then knelt on the bed and raped her with no sign of enjoyment. He seemed, if anything, angry, and when he was done he collapsed on her, then shuddered. Jeanette was weeping. He wiped himself on her velvet skirt. 'I shall take that experience,' he said, 'as payment of the missing rents from Plabennec.' He crawled off her, stood and hooked the ermine edges of his gown. 'You will be placed in a chamber here, madame, and tomorrow I shall give you in marriage to one of my men-at-arms. Your son will stay here, but you will go wherever your new husband is posted.'

202

Jeanette was whimpering on the bed. The Duke grimaced with distaste, then crossed the room and kneeled on the prie-dieu. 'Arrange your gown, madame,' he said coldly, 'and compose yourself.'

Jeanette rescued enough of the cut laces to tie her bodice into place, then looked at the Duke through the candle flames. 'You have no honour,' she hissed, 'you have no honour.'

The Duke ignored her. He rang a small handbell, then clasped his hands and closed his eyes in prayer. He was still praying when the priest and a servant came and, without a word, took Jeanette by her arms and walked her to a small room on the floor beneath the Duke's chamber. They thrust her inside, shut the door and she heard a bolt slide into place on the far side. There was a straw-filled mattress and a stack of brooms in the makeshift cell, but no other furnishing.

She lay on the mattress and sobbed till her broken heart was raw.

The wind howled at the window and rain beat on its shutters, and Jeanette wished she was dead.

The city's cockerels woke Thomas to a brisk wind and pouring rain that beat on the cart's leaking cover. He opened the flap and sat watching the puddles spread across the cobbles of the inn yard. No message had come from Jeanette, nor, he thought, would there be one. Will Skeat had been right. She was as hard as mail and, now she was in her proper place – which, in this cold, wet dawn, was probably a deep bed in a room warmed by a fire tended by the Duke's servants – she would have forgotten Thomas.

And what message, Thomas asked himself, had he been expecting? A declaration of affection? He knew that was what he wanted, but he persuaded himself he merely waited so Jeanette could send him the pass signed by the Duke, yet he knew he did not need a pass. He must just walk east and north, and trust that the Dominican's robe protected him. He had little idea how to reach Flanders, but had a notion that Paris lay somewhere close to that region so he reckoned he would start by following the River Seine, which would lead him from Rennes to Paris. His biggest worry was that he would meet some real Dominican on the road, who would quickly discover Thomas had only the haziest notion of the brotherhood's rules and no knowledge at all of their hierarchy, but he consoled himself that Scottish Dominicans were probably so far from civilization that such ignorance would be expected of them. He would survive, he told himself.

He stared at the rain spattering in the puddles. Expect nothing from Jeanette, he told himself, and to prove that he believed that bleak prophecy he readied his small baggage. It irked him to leave the mail coat behind, but it weighed too much, so he stowed it in the wagon, then put the three sheaves of arrows into a sack. The seventy-two arrows were heavy and their points threatened to tear open the sack, but he was reluctant to travel without the sheaves that were wrapped in hempen bowstring cord and he used one cord to tie his knife to his left leg where, like his money pouch, it was hidden by the black robe.

He was ready to go, but the rain was now hammering the city like an arrow storm. Thunder crackled to the west, the rain pelted on the thatch, poured off the roofs and overflowed the water butts to wash the inn's night-soil out of the yard. Midday came, heralded by the city's rain-muffled bells, and still the city drowned. Wind-driven dark clouds wreathed the cathedral's towers and Thomas told himself he would leave the moment the rain slackened, but the storm just became fiercer. Lightning flickered above the cathedral and a clap of thunder rocked the city. Thomas shivered, awed by the sky's fury. He watched the lightning reflected in the cathedral's great west window and was amazed by the sight. So much glass! Still it rained and he began to fear that he would be trapped in the cart till the next day. And then, just after a peal of thunder seemed to stun the whole city with its violence, he saw Jeanette.

He did not know her at first. He just saw a woman standing in the arched entrance to the inn's yard with the water flowing about her shoes. Everyone else in Rennes was huddling in shelter, but this woman suddenly appeared, soaked and miserable. Her hair, which had been looped so carefully over her ears, hung lank and black down the sopping red velvet dress, and it was that dress that Thomas recognized, then he saw the grief on her face. He clambered out of the wagon.

'Jeanette!'

She was weeping, her mouth distorted by grief. She seemed incapable of speaking, but just stood and cried.

'My lady!' Thomas said. 'Jeanette!'

'We must go,' she managed to say, 'we must go.' She had used soot as a cosmetic about her eyes and it had run to make grey streaks down her face.

'We can't go in this!' Thomas said.

'We must go!' she screamed at him angrily. 'We must go!'

'I'll get the horse,' Thomas said.

'There's no time! There's no time!' She plucked at his robe. 'We must go. Now!' She tried to tug him through the arch into the street.

Thomas pulled away from her and ran to the wagon where he retrieved his disguised bow and the heavy sack. There was a cloak of Jeanette's there and he took that too and wrapped it about her shoulders, though she did not seem to notice.

'What's happening?' Thomas demanded.

'They'll find me here, they'll find me!' Jeanette declared in a panic, and she pulled him blindly out of the tavern's archway. Thomas turned her eastwards onto a crooked street that led to a fine stone bridge across the Seine and then to a city gate. The big gates were barred, but a small door in one of the gates was open and the guards in the tower did not care if some fool of a drenched friar wanted to take a madly sobbing woman out of the city. Jeanette kept looking back, fearing pursuit, but still did not explain her panic or her tears to Thomas. She just hurried eastwards, insensible to the rain, wind and thunder.

The storm eased towards dusk, by which time they were close to a village that had a poor excuse for a tavern. Thomas ducked under the low doorway and asked for shelter. He put coins on a table.

'I need shelter for my sister,' he said, reckoning that anyone would be suspicious of a friar travelling with a woman. 'Shelter, food and a fire,' he said, adding another coin.

'Your sister?' The tavern-keeper, a small man with a face scarred by the pox and bulbous with wens, peered at Jeanette, who was crouched in the tavern's porch.

Thomas touched his head, suggesting she was mad. 'I am taking her to the shrine of St Guinefort,' he explained.

The tavern-keeper looked at the coins, glanced again at Jeanette, then decided the strange pair could have the use of an empty cattle byre. 'You can put a fire there,' he said grudgingly, 'but don't burn the thatch.'

Thomas lit a fire with embers from the tavern's kitchen, then fetched food and ale. He forced Jeanette to eat some of the soup and bread, then made her go close to the fire. It took over two hours of coaxing before she would tell him the story, and telling it only made her cry again. Thomas listened, appalled.

'So how did you escape?' he asked when she was finished.

A woman had unbolted the room, Jeanette said, to fetch a broom. The woman had been astonished to see Jeanette there, and even more astonished when Jeanette ran past her. Jeanette had fled the citadel, fearing the soldiers would stop her, but no one had taken any notice of her and now she was running away. Like Thomas she was a fugitive, but she had lost far more than he. She had lost her son, her honour and her future.

'I hate men,' she said. She shivered, for the miserable fire of damp straw and rotted wood had scarcely dried her clothes. 'I hate men,' she said again, then looked at Thomas. 'What are we going to do?'

'You must sleep,' he said, 'and tomorrow we'll go north.'

She nodded, but he did not think she had understood his words. She was in despair. The wheel of fortune that had once raised her so high had taken her into the utter depths.

She slept for a time, but when Thomas woke in the grey dawn he saw she was crying softly and he did not know what to do or say, so he just lay in the straw until he heard the tavern door creak open, then went to fetch some food and water. The tavern-keeper's wife cut some bread and cheese while her husband asked Thomas how far he had to walk.

'St Guinefort's shrine is in Flanders,' Thomas said.

'Flanders!' the man said, as though it was on the far side of the moon.

'The family doesn't know what else to do with her,' Thomas explained, 'and I don't know how to reach Flanders. I thought to go to Paris first.'

'Not Paris,' the tavern-keeper's wife said scornfully, 'you must go to Fougères.' Her father, she said, had often traded with the north countries and she was sure that Thomas's route lay through Fougères and Rouen. She did not know the roads beyond Rouen, but was certain he must go that far, though to begin, she said, he must take a small road that went north from the village. It went through woods, her husband added, and he must be careful for the trees were hiding places for terrible men escaping justice, but after a few miles he would come to the Fougères highway, which was patrolled by the Duke's men.

Thomas thanked her, offered a blessing to the house, then took the food to Jeanette, who refused to eat. She seemed drained of tears, almost of life, but she followed Thomas willingly enough as he walked north. The road, deep rutted by wagons and slick with mud from the previous day's rain, twisted into deep woods that dripped with water. Jeanette stumbled for a few miles, then began to cry. 'I must go back to Rennes,' she insisted. 'I want to go back to my son.'

Thomas argued, but she would not be moved. He finally gave in, but when he turned to walk south he just began to cry even harder. The Duke had said she was not a fit mother! She kept repeating the words, 'Not fit! Not fit!' She screamed at the sky. 'He made me his whore!' Then she sank onto her knees beside the road and sobbed uncontrollably. She was shivering again and Thomas thought that if she did not die of an ague then the grief would surely kill her.

'We're going back to Rennes,' Thomas said, trying to encourage her.

'I can't!' she wailed. 'He'll just whore me! Whore

me!' She shouted the words, then began rocking back and forwards and shrieking in a terrible high voice. Thomas tried to raise her up, tried to make her walk, but she fought him. She wanted to die, she said, she just wanted to die. 'A whore,' she screamed, and tore at the fox-fur trimmings of her red dress, 'a whore! He said I shouldn't wear fur. He made me a whore.' She threw the tattered fur into the undergrowth.

It had been a dry morning, but the rain clouds were heaping in the east again, and Thomas was nervously watching as Jeanette's soul unravelled before his eyes. She refused to walk, so he picked her up and carried her until he saw a well-trodden path going into the trees. He followed it to find a cottage so low, and with its thatch so covered with moss that at first he thought it was just a mound among the trees until he saw blue-grey woodsmoke seeping from a hole at its top. Thomas was worried about the outlaws who were said to haunt these woods, but it was beginning to rain again and the cottage was the only refuge in sight, so Thomas lowered Jeanette to the ground and shouted through the burrow-like entrance. An old man, white-haired, red-eyed and with skin blackened by smoke, peered back at Thomas. The man spoke a French so thick with local words and accent that Thomas could scarcely understand him, but he gathered the man was a forester and lived here with his wife, and the forester looked greedily at the coins Thomas offered, then said that Thomas and his woman could use an empty pig shelter. The place stank of rotted straw and shit, but the thatch was almost rainproof and Jeanette did not seem to care. Thomas raked out the old straw, then cut Jeanette a bed of bracken. The forester, once the money was in his hands, seemed little interested in his guests, but in the middle of the afternoon, when the rain had stopped, Thomas heard the forester's wife hissing at him and, a few moments later, the old man left and walked towards the road, but without any of the tools of his trade; no axe, billhook or saw.

Jeanette was sleeping, exhausted, so Thomas stripped the dead clover plants from his black bow, unlashed the crosspiece and put back the horn tips. He strung the yew, thrust half a dozen arrows into his belt and followed the old man as far as the road, and there he waited in a thicket.

The forester returned towards evening with two young men whom Thomas presumed were the outlaws of whom he had been warned. The old man must have reckoned that Thomas and his woman were fugitives, for though they carried bags and money, they had sought a hiding place and that was enough to raise anyone's suspicions. A friar did not need to skulk in the trees, and women wearing dresses trimmed with torn remnants of fur did not seek a forester's hospitality. So doubtless the two young men had been fetched to help slit Thomas's throat and then divide whatever coins they found on his body. Jeanette's fate would be similar, but delayed.

Thomas put his first arrow into the ground between the old man's feet and the second into a tree close by. 'The next arrow kills,' he said, though they could not see him for he was in the thicket's shadows. They just stared wide-eyed at the bushes where he was hiding and Thomas made his voice deep and slow. 'You come with murder in your souls,' he said, 'but I can raise the hellequin from the deeps of hell. I can make the devil's claws cut to your heart and have the dead haunt your daylight. You will leave the friar and his sister alone.'

The old man dropped to his knees. His superstitions were as old as time and scarcely touched by Christianity. He believed there were trolls in the forest and giants in the mist. He knew there were dragons. He had heard of black-skinned men who lived on the moon and who dropped to earth when their home shrank to a sickle. He understood there were ghosts who hunted among the trees. All this he knew as well as he knew ash and larch, oak and beech, and he did not doubt that it was a demon who had spat the strangely long arrow from the thicket.

'You must go,' he told his companions, 'you must go!' The two fled and the old man touched his forehead to the leaf mould. 'I meant no harm!'

'Go home,' Thomas said.

He waited till the old man had gone, then he dug the arrow out of the tree and that night he went to the forester's cottage, crawled through the low doorway and sat on the earthen floor facing the old couple.

'I shall stay here,' he told them, 'until my sister's wits are recovered. We wish to hide her shame from the world, that is all. When we go we shall reward you, but if you try to kill us again I shall summon demons to torment you and I will leave your corpses as a feast for the wild things that lurk in the trees.' He put another small coin on the earth floor. 'You will bring us food each night,' he told the woman, 'and you will thank God that though I can read your hearts I still forgive you.'

They had no more trouble after that. Every day the old man went off into the trees with his billhook and axe, and every night his wife brought her visitors gruel or bread. Thomas took milk from their cow, shot a deer and thought Jeanette would die. For days she refused to eat, and sometimes he would find her rocking back and forth in the noxious shed and making a keening noise. Thomas feared she had gone mad for ever. His father would sometimes tell him how the mad were treated, how he himself had been treated, how starvation and beating were the only cures. 'The devil gets into the soul,' Father Ralph had said, 'and he can be starved out or he can be thrashed out, but there is no way he will be coaxed out. Beat and starve, boy, beat and starve, it is the only treatment the devil understands.' But Thomas could neither starve nor beat Jeanette, so he did his best by her. He kept her dry, he persuaded her to take some warm milk fresh from the cow, he talked with her through the nights, he combed her hair and washed her face and sometimes, when she was sleeping and he was sitting by the shed and staring at the stars through the tangled trees, he would wonder whether he and the hellequin had left other women as broken as Jeanette. He prayed for forgiveness. He prayed a lot in those days, and not to St Guinefort, but to the Virgin and to St George.

The prayers must have worked for he woke one dawn to see Jeanette sitting in the shed's doorway with her thin body outlined by the bright new day. She turned to him and he saw there was no madness in her face any more, just a profound sorrow. She looked at him a long time before she spoke.

'Did God send you to me, Thomas?'

'He showed me great favour if He did,' Thomas replied.

She smiled at that, the first smile he had seen on her face since Rennes. 'I have to be content,' she said very earnestly, 'because my son is alive and he will be properly cared for and one day I shall find him.'

'We both shall,' Thomas said.

'Both?'

He grimaced. 'I have kept none of my promises,' he said. 'The lance is still in Normandy, Sir Simon lives, and how I shall find your son for you, I do not know. I think my promises are worthless, but I shall do my best.'

She held out her hand so he could take it and she let it stay there. 'We have been punished, you and I,' she said, 'probably for the sin of pride. The Duke was right. I am no aristocrat. I am a merchant's daughter, but thought I was higher. Now look at me.'

'Thinner,' Thomas said, 'but beautiful.'

She shuddered at that compliment. 'Where are we?'

'Just a day outside Rennes.'

'Is that all?'

'In a pig shed,' Thomas said, 'a day out of Rennes.'

'Four years ago I lived in a castle,' she said wistfully. 'Plabennec wasn't large, but it was beautiful. It had a tower and a courtyard and two mills and a stream and an orchard that grew very red apples.'

'You will see them again,' Thomas said, 'you and your son.'

He regretted mentioning her son for tears came to her eyes, but she cuffed them away. 'It was the lawyer,' she said.

'Lawyer?'

'Belas. He lied to the Duke.' There was a kind of wonderment in her voice that Belas had proved so traitorous. 'He told the Duke I was supporting Duke Jean. Then I will, Thomas, I will. I will support your duke. If that is the only way to regain Plabennec and find my son then I shall support Duke Jean.' She squeezed Thomas's hand. 'I'm hungry.'

They spent another week in the forest while Jeanette recovered her strength. For a while, like a beast struggling to escape a trap, she devised schemes that would give her instant revenge on Duke Charles and restore her son, but the schemes were wild and hopeless and, as the days passed, she accepted her fate.

'I have no friends,' she said to Thomas one night.

'You have me, my lady.'

'They died,' she said, ignoring him. 'My family died. My husband died. Do you think I am a curse on those I love?'

'I think,' Thomas said, 'that we must go north.'

She was irritated by his practicality. 'I'm not sure I want to go north.'

'I do,' Thomas said stubbornly.

Jeanette knew that the further north she went, the further she went from her son, but she did not know what else to do, and that night, as if accepting that she would now be guided by Thomas, she came to his bracken bed and they were lovers. She wept afterwards, but then made love to him again, this time fiercely, as though she could slake her misery in the consolations of the flesh.

Next morning they left, going north. Summer had come, clothing the countryside in thick green. Thomas had disguised the bow again, lashing the crosspiece to the stave and hanging it with bindweed and willowherb instead of clover. His black robe had become ragged and

215

no one would have taken him for a friar, while Jeanette had stripped the remains of the fox fur from the red velvet, which was dirty, creased and threadbare. They looked like vagabonds, which they were, and they moved like fugitives, skirting the towns and bigger villages to avoid trouble. They bathed in streams, slept beneath the trees and only ventured into the smallest villages when hunger demanded they buy a meal and cider in some slatternly tavern. If they were challenged they claimed to be Bretons, brother and sister, going to join their uncle who was a butcher in Flanders, and if anyone disbelieved the tale they were unwilling to cross Thomas, who was tall and strong and always kept his knife visible. By preference, though, they avoided villages and stayed in the woods where Thomas taught Jeanette how to tickle the trout out of their streams. They would light fires, cook their fish and cut bracken for a bed.

They kept close to the road, though they were forced to a long detour to avoid the drum-like fortress of St-Aubin-du-Cormier, and another to skirt the city of Fougères, and somewhere north of that city they entered Normandy. They milked cows in their pastures, stole a great cheese from a wagon parked outside a church and slept under the stars. They had no idea what day of the week it was, nor even what month it was any more. Both were browned by the sun and made ragged by travelling. Jeanette's misery was dissolved in a new happiness, and nowhere more than when they discovered an abandoned cottage – merely cob walls of mud and straw decaying without a roof – in a spinney of hazel trees. They cleared away the nettles and brambles and lived in the cottage for more than a week, seeing no one, wanting to see no one, delaying their future because the present was so blissful. Jeanette could still weep for her son and spent hours devising exquisite revenges to be taken against the Duke, against Belas and against Sir Simon Jekyll, but she also revelled in that summer's freedom. Thomas had fitted his bow again so he could hunt and Jeanette, growing ever stronger, had learned to pull it back almost to her chin.

Neither knew where they were and did not much care. Thomas's mother used to tell him a tale of children who ran away into the forest and were reared by the beasts. 'They grow hair all over their bodies,' she would tell him, 'and have claws and horns and teeth,' and now Thomas would sometimes examine his hands to see if claws were coming. He saw none. Yet if he was becoming a beast then he was happy. He had rarely been happier, but he knew that the winter, even though far off, was nevertheless coming and so, perhaps a week after midsummer, they moved gently north again in search of something that neither of them could quite imagine.

Thomas knew he had promised to retrieve a lance and restore Jeanette's son, but he did not know how he was to do either of those things. He only knew he must go to a place where a man like Will Skeat would employ him, though he could not talk of such a future with Jeanette. She did not want to hear about archers or armies, or of men and mail coats, but she, like him, knew they could not stay for ever in their refuge.

'I shall go to England,' she told him, 'and appeal to your king.' Out of all the schemes she had dreamed of, this was the only one that made sense. The Earl of Northampton had placed her son under the King of

England's protection, so she must appeal to Edward and hope he would support her.

They walked north, still keeping the road to Rouen in sight. They forded a river and climbed into a broken country of small fields, deep woods and abrupt hills, and somewhere in that green land, unheard by either of them, the wheel of fortune creaked again. Thomas knew that the great wheel governed mankind, it turned in the dark to determine good or evil, high or low, sickness or health, happiness or misery. Thomas reckoned God must have made the wheel to be the mechanism by which He ruled the world while He was busy in heaven, and in that midsummer, when the harvest was being flailed on the threshing floors, and the swifts were gathering in the high trees, and the rowan trees were in scarlet berry, and the pastures were white with ox-eye daisies, the wheel lurched for Thomas and Jeanette.

They walked to the wood's edge one day to check that the road was still in view. They usually saw little more than a man driving some cows to market, a group of women following with eggs and vegetables to sell. A priest might pass on a poor horse, and once they had seen a knight with his retinue of servants and men-at-arms, but most days the road lay white, dusty and empty under the summer sun. Yet this day it was full. Folk were walking southwards, driving cows and pigs and sheep and goats and geese. Some pushed handcarts, others had wagons drawn by oxen or horses, and all the carts were loaded high with stools, tables, benches and beds. Thomas knew he was seeing fugitives.

They waited till it was dark, then Thomas beat the worst dirt off the Dominican's gown and, leaving Jeanette in the trees, walked down to the road where some of the travellers were camping beside small, smoky fires.

'God's peace be on you,' Thomas said to one group.

'We have no food to spare, father,' a man answered, eyeing the stranger suspiciously.

'I am fed, my son,' Thomas said, and squatted near their fire.

'Are you a priest or a vagabond?' the man asked. He had an axe and he drew it towards him protectively, for Thomas's tangled hair was wildly long and his face as dark as any outlaw's.

'I am both,' Thomas said with a smile. 'I have walked from Avignon,' he explained, 'to do penance at the shrine of St Guinefort.'

None of the refugees had ever heard of the Blessed Guinefort, but Thomas's words convinced them, for the idea of pilgrimage explained his woebegone condition while their own sad condition, they made clear, was caused by war. They had come from the coast of Normandy, only a day's journey away, and in the morning they must be up early and travelling again to escape the enemy.

Thomas made the sign of the cross. 'What enemy?' he asked, expecting to hear that two Norman lords had fallen out and were ravaging each other's estates.

But the ponderous wheel of fortune had turned unexpectedly. King Edward III of England had crossed the Channel. Such an expedition had long been expected, but the King had not gone to his lands in Gascony, as many had thought he would, nor to Flanders where other Englishmen fought, but had come to Normandy. His army was just a day away and, at the news, Thomas's mouth dropped open.

'You should flee them, father,' one of the women advised Thomas. 'They know no pity, not even for friars.'

Thomas assured them he would, thanked them for their news, then walked back up the hill to where Jeanette waited. All had changed.

His king had come to Normandy.

They argued that night. Jeanette was suddenly convinced they should turn back to Brittany and Thomas could only stare at her in astonishment.

'Brittany?' he asked faintly.

She would not meet his eyes, but stubbornly stared at the campfires that burned all along the road, while further north, on the night's horizon, great red glows showed where larger fires burned, and Thomas knew that English soldiers must have been ravaging the fields of Normandy just as the hellequin had harrowed Brittany. 'I can be near Charles if I'm in Brittany,' Jeanette said.

Thomas shook his head. He was dimly aware that the sight of the army's destruction had forced them both into a reality from which they had been escaping in these last weeks of freedom, but he could not connect that with her sudden wish to head back to Brittany.

'You can be near Charles,' he said carefully, 'but can you see him? Will the Duke let you near him?'

'Maybe he will change his mind,' Jeanette said without much conviction.

'And maybe he'll rape you again,' Thomas said brutally.

'And if I don't go,' she said vehemently, 'maybe I will never see Charles again. Never!'

'Then why come this far?'

'I don't know, I don't know.' She was angry as she used to be when Thomas first met her in La Roche-Derrien. 'Because I was mad,' she said sullenly.

'You say you want to appeal to the King,' Thomas said, 'and he's here!' He flung a hand towards the livid glow of the fires. 'So appeal to him here.'

'Maybe he won't believe me,' Jeanette said stubbornly.

'And what will we do in Brittany?' Thomas asked, but Jeanette would not answer. She looked sulky and still avoided his gaze. 'You can marry one of the Duke's men-at-arms,' Thomas went on, 'that's what he wanted, isn't it? A pliant wife of a pliant follower so that when he feels like taking his pleasure, he can.'

'Isn't that what you do?' she challenged him, looking him in the face at last.

'I love you,' Thomas said.

Jeanette said nothing.

'I do love you,' Thomas said, and felt foolish for she had never said the same to him.

Jeanette looked at the glowing horizon that was tangled by the leaves of the forest. 'Will your king believe me?' she asked him.

'How can he not?'

'Do I look like a countess?'

She looked ragged, poor and beautiful. 'You speak like a countess,' Thomas said, 'and the King's clerks will make enquiries of the Earl of Northampton.' He did not know if that was true, but he wanted to encourage her.

Jeanette sat with her head bowed. 'Do you know

what the Duke told me? That my mother was a Jewess!'
She looked up at him, expecting him to share her indignation.

Thomas frowned. 'I've never met a Jew,' he said.

Jeanette almost exploded. 'You think I have? You need to meet the devil to know he is bad? A pig to discover he stinks?' She began to weep. 'I don't know what to do.'

'We shall go to the King,' Thomas said, and next morning he walked north and, after a few heartbeats, Jeanette followed him. She had tried to clean her dress, though it was so filthy that all she could manage was to brush the twigs and leaf mould from the velvet. She coiled her hair and pinned it with slivers of wood.

'What kind of man is the King?' she asked Thomas.

'They say he's a good man.'

'Who says?'

'Everyone. He's straightforward.'

'He's still English,' Jeanette said softly, and Thomas pretended not to hear. 'Is he kind?' she asked him.

'No one says he's cruel,' Thomas said, then held up a hand to silence Jeanette.

He had seen horsemen in mail.

Thomas had often found it strange that when the monks and scriveners made their books they painted warfare as gaudy. Their squirrel-hair brushes showed men in brightly coloured surcoats or jupons, and their horses in brilliantly patterned trappers. Yet for most of the time war was grey until the arrows bit, when it became shot through with red. Grey was the colour of a mail coat, and Thomas was seeing grey among the green leaves. He did not know if they were Frenchmen or Englishmen, but he feared both. The French were his enemy, but so were the English until they were convinced that he was English too, and convinced, moreover, that he was not a deserter from their army.

More horsemen came from the distant trees and these men were carrying bows, so they had to be English. Still Thomas hesitated, reluctant to face the problems of persuading his own side that he was not a deserter. Beyond the horsemen, hidden by the trees, a building must have been set on fire for smoke began to thicken above the summer leaves. The horsemen were looking towards Thomas and Jeanette, but the pair were hidden by a bank of gorse and after a while, satisfied that no enemy threatened, the troops turned and rode eastwards.

Thomas waited till they were out of sight, then led Jeanette across the open land, into the trees and out to where a farm burned. The flames were pale in the bright sun. No one was in sight. There was just a farm blazing and a dog lying next to a duck pond that was surrounded by feathers. The dog was whimpering and Jeanette cried out for it had been stabbed in the belly. Thomas stooped beside the beast, stroked its head and fondled its ears and the dying dog licked his hand and tried to wag its tail and Thomas rammed his knife deep into its heart so that it died swiftly.

'It would not have lived,' he told Jeanette. She said nothing, just stared at the burning thatch and rafters. Thomas pulled out the knife and patted the dog's head. 'Go to St Guinefort,' he said, cleaning the blade. 'I always wanted a dog when I was a child,' he told Jeanette, 'but my father couldn't abide them.'

'Why?'

'Because he was strange.' He sheathed the knife and

stood. A track, imprinted with hoofmarks, led north from the farm, and they followed it cautiously between hedges thick with cornflowers, ox-eye and dogwood. They were in a country of small fields, high banks, sudden woods and lumpy hills, a country for ambush, but they saw no one until, from the top of a low hill, they glimpsed a squat stone church tower in a valley and then the unburned roofs of a village and after that the soldiers. There were hundreds of them camped in the fields beyond the cottages, and more in the village itself. Some large tents had been raised close to the church and they had the banners of nobles planted by their entrances.

Thomas still hesitated, reluctant to finish these good days with Jeanette, yet he knew there was no choice and so, bow on his shoulder, he took her down to the village. Men saw them coming and a dozen archers, led by a burly man in a mail hauberk, came to meet them.

'What the hell are you?' was the burly man's first question. His archers grinned wolfishly at the sight of Jeanette's ragged dress. 'You're either a bleeding priest who stole a bow,' the man went on, 'or an archer who filched a priest's robe.'

'I'm English,' Thomas said.

The big man seemed unimpressed. 'Serving who?'

'I was with Will Skeat in Brittany,' Thomas said.

'Brittany!' The big man frowned, not certain whether or not to believe Thomas.

'Tell them I'm a countess,' Jeanette urged Thomas in French.

'What's she saying?'

'Nothing,' Thomas said.

'So what are you doing here?' the big man asked.

'I got cut off from my troop in Brittany,' Thomas said weakly. He could hardly tell the truth – that he was a fugitive from justice – but he had no other tale prepared. 'I just walked.'

It was a lame explanation and the big man treated it with the scorn it deserved. 'What you mean, lad,' he said, 'is that you're a bloody deserter.'

'I'd hardly come here if I was, would I?' Thomas asked defiantly.

'You'd hardly come here from Brittany if you just got lost!' the man pointed out. He spat. 'You'll have to go to Scoresby, let him decide what you are.'

'Scoresby?' Thomas asked.

'You've heard of him?' the big man asked belligerently.

Thomas had heard of Walter Scoresby who, like Skeat, was a man who led his own band of men-at-arms and archers, but Scoresby did not have Skeat's good reputation. He was said to be a dark-humoured man, but he was evidently to decide Thomas's fate, for the archers closed around him and walked the pair towards the village. 'She your woman?' one of them asked Thomas.

'She's the Countess of Armorica,' Thomas said.

'And I'm the bloody Earl of London,' the archer retorted.

Jeanette clung to Thomas's arm, terrified of the unfriendly faces. Thomas was equally unhappy. When things had been at their worst in Brittany, when the hellequin were grumbling and it was cold, wet and miserable, Skeat liked to say 'be happy you're not with Scoresby' and now, it seemed, Thomas was.

'We hang deserters,' the big man said with relish.

Thomas noted that the archers, like all the troops he could see in the village, wore the red cross of St George on their tunics. A great crowd of them were gathered in a pasture that lay between the small village church and a Cistercian monastery or priory that had somehow escaped destruction, for the white-robed monks were assisting a priest who said Mass for the soldiers. 'Is it Sunday?' Thomas asked one of the archers.

'Tuesday,' the man said, taking off his hat in honour of the sacraments, 'St James's day.'

They waited at the pasture's edge, close to the village church where a row of new graves suggested that some villagers had died when the army came, but most had probably fled south or west. One or two remained. An old man, bent double from work and with a white beard that almost reached the ground, mumbled along with the distant priest while a small boy, perhaps six or seven years old, tried to draw an English bow to the amusement of its owner.

The Mass ended and the mail-clad men climbed from their knees and walked towards the tents and houses. One of the archers from Thomas's escort had gone into the dispersing crowd and he now reappeared with a group of men. One stood out because he was taller than the others and had a new coat of mail that had been polished so it seemed to shine. He had long boots, a green cloak and a gold-hilted sword with a scabbard wrapped in red cloth. The finery seemed at odds with the man's face, which was pinched and gloomy. He was bald, but had a forked beard, which he had twisted into plaits. 'That's Scoresby,' one of the archers muttered and Thomas had no need to guess which of the approaching soldiers he meant.

Scoresby stopped a few paces away and the big archer who had arrested Thomas smirked. 'A deserter,' he announced proudly, 'says he walked here from Brittany.'

Scoresby gave Thomas a hard glance and Jeanette a much longer look. Her ragged dress revealed a length of thigh and a ripped neckline and Scoresby clearly wanted to see more. Like Will Skeat he had begun his military life as an archer and had risen by dint of shrewdness, and Thomas guessed there was not much mercy in his soul's mix.

Scoresby shrugged. 'If he's a deserter,' he said, 'then hang the bastard.' He smiled. 'But we'll keep his woman.'

'I'm not a deserter,' Thomas said, 'and the woman is the Countess of Armorica, who is related to the Count of Blois, nephew to the King of France.'

Most of the archers jeered at this outrageous claim, but Scoresby was a cautious man and he was aware of a small crowd that had gathered at the churchyard's edge. Two priests and some men-at-arms wearing noblemen's escutcheons were among the spectators, and Thomas's confidence had put just enough doubt in Scoresby's mind. He frowned at Jeanette, seeing a girl who looked at first glance like a peasant, but despite her tanned face she was undoubtedly beautiful and the remnants of her dress suggested she had once known elegance.

'She's who?' Scoresby demanded.

'I told you who she was,' Thomas said belligerently, 'and I will tell you more. Her son has been stolen from her, and her son is a ward of our king's. She has come for His Majesty's help.' Thomas hastily told Jeanette what he had said and, to his relief, she nodded her agreement.

Scoresby gazed at Jeanette and something about her increased his doubt. 'Why are you with her?' he asked Thomas.

'I rescued her,' Thomas said.

'He says,' a voice spoke in French from the crowd and Thomas could not see the speaker, who was evidently surrounded by men-at-arms, all wearing a green and white livery. 'He says that he rescued you, madame, is that true?'

'Yes,' Jeanette said. She frowned, unable to see who was questioning her.

'Tell us who you are,' the unseen man demanded.

'I am Jeanette, dowager Countess of Armorica.'

'Your husband was who?' The voice suggested a young man, but a very confident young man.

Jeanette bridled at the tone of the question, but answered it. 'Henri Chenier, Comte d'Armorique.

'And why are you here, madame?'

'Because Charles of Blois has kidnapped my child!' Jeanette answered angrily. 'A child who was placed under the protection of the King of England.'

The young man said nothing for a while. Some in the crowd were edging nervously away from the liveried men-at-arms who surrounded him, and Scoresby was looking apprehensive. 'Who placed him under that protection?' he eventually asked.

'William Bohun,' Jeanette said, 'Earl of Northampton.'

'I believe her,' the voice said, and the men-at-arms stepped aside so that Thomas and Jeanette could see the speaker, who proved to be scarce more than a boy.

Indeed, Thomas doubted he had even begun to shave, though he was surely full grown for he was tall – taller even than Thomas – and had only stayed hidden because his men-at-arms had been wearing green and white plumes in their helmets. The young man was fair-haired, had a face slightly burned by the sun, was dressed in a green cloak, plain breeches and a linen shirt, and nothing except his height explained why men were suddenly kneeling on the grass. 'Down,' Scoresby hissed at Thomas who, perplexed, went on one knee. Now only Jeanette, the boy and his escort of eight tall men-at-arms were standing.

The boy looked at Thomas. 'Did you really walk here from Brittany?' he asked in English, though, like many noblemen, his English was touched with a French accent.

'We both did, sire,' Thomas said in French.

'Why?' he demanded harshly.

'To seek the protection of the King of England,' Thomas said, 'who is the guardian of my lady's son, who has been treacherously taken prisoner by England's enemies.'

The boy looked at Jeanette with much the same wolfish appreciation that Scoresby had shown. He might not shave, but he knew a beautiful woman when he saw one. He smiled. 'You are most welcome, madame,' he said. 'I knew of your husband's reputation, I admired him, and I regret that I will never have a chance to meet him in combat.' He bowed to Jeanette, then untied his cloak and walked to her. He placed the green cape over her shoulders to cover the torn dress. 'I shall ensure, madame,' he said, 'that you are treated with the courtesy your rank demands and will vow to keep whatever promises England made on your son's behalf.' He bowed again.

Jeanette, astonished and pleased by the young man's manner, put the question that Thomas had been wanting answered. 'Who are you, my lord?' she asked, offering a curtsey.

'I am Edward of Woodstock, madame,' he said, offering her his arm.

It meant nothing to Jeanette, but it astonished Thomas. 'He is the King's eldest son,' he whispered to her.

She dropped to one knee, but the smooth-cheeked boy raised her and walked her towards the priory. He was Edward of Woodstock, Earl of Chester, Duke of Cornwall and Prince of Wales. And the wheel of fate had once again spun Jeanette high.

The wheel seemed indifferent towards Thomas. He was left alone, abandoned. Jeanette walked away on the Prince's arm and did not so much as glance back at Thomas. He heard her laugh. He watched her. He had nursed her, fed her, carried her and loved her, and now, without a thought, she had discarded him. No one else was interested in him. Scoresby and his men, cheated of a hanging, had gone to the village, and Thomas wondered just what he was supposed to do.

'Goddamn,' he said aloud. He felt conspicuously foolish in his tattered robe. 'Goddamn,' he said again. Anger, thick as the black humour that could make a man sick, rose in him, but what he could do? He was a fool in a ragged robe and the Prince was the son of a king.

The Prince had taken Jeanette to the low grassy ridge

where the big tents stood in a colourful row. Each tent had a flagpole, and the tallest flew the quartered banner of the Prince of Wales, which showed the golden lions of England on the two red quarters and golden fleur-de-lis on the two blue. The fleur-de-lis were there to show the King's claim to the French throne while the whole flag, which was that of England's king, was crossed with a white-toothed bar to show that this was the banner of the King's eldest son. Thomas was tempted to follow Jeanette, to demand the Prince's help, but then one of the lower banners, the one furthest away from him, caught the small warm wind and sluggishly lifted its folds. He stared at it.

The banner had a blue field and was slashed diagonally with a white band. Three rampant yellow lions were emblazoned on either side of the bar, which was decorated with three red stars that had green centres. It was a flag Thomas knew well, but he scarcely dared believe that he was seeing it here in Normandy, for the arms were those of William Bohun, Earl of Northampton. Northampton was the King's deputy in Brittany, yet his flag was unmistakable and Thomas walked towards it, fearing that the wind-rippled flag would turn out to be a different coat of arms, similar to the Earl's, but not the same.

But it was the Earl's banner, and the Earl's tent, in contrast to the other stately pavilions on the low ridge, was still the grubby shelter made from two worn-out sails. A half-dozen men-at-arms wearing the Earl's livery barred Thomas's way as he neared the tent. 'Have you come to hear his lordship's confession or put an arrow in his belly?' one asked.

'I would speak to his lordship,' Thomas said, barely

suppressing the anger provoked by Jeanette's abandonment of him.

'But will he talk to you?' the man asked, amused at the ragged archer's pretensions.

'He will,' Thomas said with a confidence he did not entirely feel. 'Tell him the man who gave him La Roche-Derrien is here,' he added.

The man-at-arms looked startled. He frowned, but just then the tent flap was thrown back and the Earl himself appeared, stripped to the waist to reveal a muscled chest covered in tight red curls. He was chewing on a goose-bone and peered up at the sky as though fearing rain. The man-at-arms turned to him, indicated Thomas, then shrugged as if to say he was not responsible for a madman showing up unannounced.

The Earl stared at Thomas. 'Good God,' he said after a while, 'have you taken orders?'

'No, my lord.'

The Earl stripped a piece of flesh from the bone with his teeth. 'Thomas, ain't that right?'

'Yes, my lord.'

'Never forget a face,' the Earl said, 'and I have cause to remember yours, though I hardly expected you to fetch up here. Did you walk?'

Thomas nodded. 'I did, my lord.' Something about the Earl's demeanour was puzzling, almost as though he was not really surprised to see Thomas in Normandy.

'Will told me about you,' the Earl said, 'told me all about you. So Thomas, my modest hero from La Roche-Derrien, is a murderer, eh?' He spoke grimly.

'Yes, my lord,' Thomas said humbly.

The Earl threw away the stripped bone, then snapped his fingers and a servant tossed him a shirt from within the tent. He pulled it on and tucked it into his hose. 'God's teeth, boy, do you expect me to save you from Sir Simon's vengeance? You know he's here?'

Thomas gaped at the Earl. Said nothing. Sir Simon Jekyll was here? And Thomas had just brought Jeanette to Normandy. Sir Simon could hardly hurt her so long as she was under the Prince's protection, but Sir Simon could harm Thomas well enough. And delight in it.

The Earl saw Thomas blanch and he nodded. 'He's with the King's men, because I didn't want him, but he insisted on travelling because he reckons there's more plunder to be had in Normandy than in Brittany and I dare say he's right, but what will truly put a smile on his face is the sight of you. Ever been hanged, Thomas?'

'Hanged, my lord?' Thomas asked vaguely. He was still reeling from the news that Sir Simon had sailed to Normandy. He had just walked all this way to find his enemy waiting?

'Sir Simon will hang you,' the Earl said with indecent relish. 'He'll let you strangle on the rope and there'll be no kindly soul tugging on your ankles to make it quick. You could last an hour, two hours, in utter agony. You could choke for even longer! One fellow I hanged lasted from matins till prime and still managed to curse me. So I suppose you want my help, yes?'

Thomas belatedly went onto one knee. 'You offered me a reward after La Roche-Derrien, my lord. Can I claim it now?'

The servant brought a stool from the tent and the Earl sat, his legs set wide. 'Murder is murder,' he said, picking his teeth with a sliver of wood.

'Half Will Skeat's men are murderers, my lord,' Thomas pointed out.

The Earl thought about that, then reluctantly nodded. 'But they're pardoned murderers,' he answered. He sighed. 'I wish Will was here,' he said, evading Thomas's demand. 'I wanted him to come, but he can't come until Charles of Blois is put back into his cage.' He scowled at Thomas. 'If I give you a pardon,' the Earl went on, 'then I make an enemy out of Sir Simon. Not that he's a friend now, but still, why spare you?'

'For La Roche-Derrien,' Thomas said.

'Which is a great debt,' the Earl agreed, 'a very great debt. We'd have looked bloody fools if we hadn't taken that town, miserable goddamn place though it be. God's teeth, boy, but why didn't you just walk south? Plenty of bastards to kill in Gascony.' He looked at Thomas for a while, plainly irritated by the undeniable debt he owed the archer and the nuisance of paying it. He finally shrugged. 'I'll talk to Sir Simon, offer him money, and if it's enough he'll pretend you're not here. As for you,' he paused, frowning as he remembered his earlier meetings with Thomas, 'you're the one who wouldn't tell me who your father was, ain't I right?'

'I didn't tell you, my lord, because he was a priest.'

The Earl thought that was a fine jest. 'God's teeth! A priest? So you're a devil's whelp, are you? That's what they say in Guyenne, that the children of priests are the devil's whelps.' He looked Thomas up and down, amused again at the ragged robe. 'They say the devil's whelps make good soldiers,' he said, 'good soldiers and better whores. I suppose you've lost your horse?'

'Yes, my lord.'

'All my archers are mounted,' the Earl said, then turned to one of his men-at-arms. 'Find the bastard a sway-backed nag till he can filch something better, then

234

give him a tunic and offer him to John Armstrong.' He looked back to Thomas. 'You're joining my archers, which means you'll wear my badge. You're my man, devil's whelp, and perhaps that will protect you if Sir Simon wants too much money for your miserable soul.'

'I shall try to repay your lordship,' Thomas said.

'Pay me, boy, by getting us into Caen. You got us into La Roche-Derrien, but that little place is nothing compared to Caen. Caen is a true bastard. We go there tomorrow, but I doubt we'll see the backside of its walls for a month or more, if ever. Get us into Caen, Thomas, and I'll forgive you a score of murders.' He stood, nodded a dismissal and went back into the tent.

Thomas did not move. Caen, he thought, Caen. Caen was the city where Sir Guillaume d'Evecque lived, and he made the sign of the cross for he knew fate had arranged all this. Fate had determined that his crossbow arrow would miss Sir Simon Jekyll and it had brought him to the edge of Caen. Because fate wanted him to do the penance that Father Hobbe had demanded. God, Thomas decided, had taken Jeanette from him because he had been slow to keep his promise.

But now the time for the keeping of promises had come, for God had brought Thomas to Caen.

Normandy

The Earl of Northampton had been summoned from Brittany to be one of the Prince of Wales's advisers. The Prince was just sixteen, though John Armstrong reckoned the boy was as good as any grown man. 'Ain't nothing wrong with young Edward,' he told Thomas. 'Knows his weapons. Headstrong, maybe, but brave.'

That, in John Armstrong's world, was high praise. He was a forty-year-old man-at-arms who led the Earl's personal archers and was one of those hard, common men that the Earl liked so much. Armstrong, like Skeat, came from the north country and was said to have been fighting the Scots since he had been weaned. His personal weapon was a falchion, a curved sword with a heavy blade as broad as an axe, though he could draw a bow with the best of his troop. He also commanded three score of hobelars, light horsemen mounted on shaggy ponies and carrying spears.

'They don't look up to much,' he said to Thomas, who was gazing at the small horsemen, who all had long shaggy hair and bent legs, 'but they're rare at scouting. We send swarms of yon bastards into the Scottish hills to find the enemy. Be dead else.' Armstrong had been at La Roche-Derrien and remembered Thomas's achievement in turning the town's river flank and, because of that, he accepted Thomas readily enough. He gave him a lice-ridden hacqueton – a padded jacket that might stop a feeble sword cut – and a short surcoat, a jupon, that had the Earl's stars and lions on its breast and bore the cross of St George on its right sleeve. The hacqueton and jupon, like the breeches and arrow bag that completed Thomas's outfit, had belonged to an archer who had died of the fever shortly after reaching Normandy. 'You can find yourself better stuff in Caen,' Armstrong told him, 'if we ever get into Caen.'

Thomas was given a sway-backed grey mare that had a hard mouth and an awkward gait. He watered the beast, rubbed her down with straw, then ate red herrings and dry beans with Armstrong's men. He found a stream and washed his hair, then twisted the bowcord round the wet pigtail. He borrowed a razor and scraped off his beard, tossing the stiff hairs into the stream so that no one could work a spell on them. It seemed strange to spend the night in a soldiers' encampment and to sleep without Jeanette. He still felt bitter about her and that bitterness was like a sliver of iron in his soul when he was roused in the night's dark heart. He felt lonely, chill and unwanted as the archers began their march. He thought of Jeanette in the Prince's tent, and remembered the jealousy he had felt in Rennes when she had gone to the citadel to meet Duke Charles. She was like a moth, he thought, flying to the brightest candle in the room. Her wings had been scorched once, but the flame drew her still.

The army advanced on Caen in three battles, each of about four thousand men. The King commanded one, the Prince of Wales the second while the third was under the orders of the Bishop of Durham, who much preferred slaughter to sanctity. The Prince had left the encampment early to stand his horse beside the road where he could watch his men pass in the summer dawn. He was in black armour, with a lion crest on his helm, and escorted by a dozen priests and fifty knights. As Thomas approached, he saw Jeanette was among those green-and-white-blazoned horsemen. She was wearing the same colours, a dress of pale green cloth with white cuffs, hems and bodice, and was mounted on a palfrey that had silver curb chains, green and white ribbons plaited into its mane and a white saddle cloth embroidered with the lions of England. Her hair had been washed, brushed and coiled, then decorated with cornflowers, and as Thomas came nearer he thought how ravishing she looked. There was a radiant happiness on her face and her eyes were bright. She was just to one side of the Prince and a pace or so behind him, and Thomas noted how often the boy turned to speak to her. The men in front of Thomas were pulling off their helmets or caps to salute the Prince, who looked from Jeanette to them, sometimes nodding or calling out to a knight he recognized.

Thomas, riding his borrowed horse that was so small his long legs hung almost to the ground, raised a hand to greet Jeanette. She stared into his smiling face, then looked away without showing any expression. She spoke with a priest who was evidently the Prince's chaplain. Thomas let his hand drop. 'If you're a bloody prince,' the man beside Thomas said, 'you get the cream, don't you? We get lice and he gets that.'

Thomas said nothing. Jeanette's dismissal had left him embarrassed. Had the last weeks been a dream? He twisted in his saddle to look at her and saw she was

241

laughing at some comment of the Prince's. You are a fool, Thomas told himself, a fool, and he wondered why he felt so hurt. Jeanette had never declared any love for him, yet her abandonment bit his heart like a snake. The road dropped into a hollow where sycamore and ash grew thick and Thomas, turning again, could not see Jeanette.

'There'll be plenty of women in Caen,' an archer said with relish.

'If we ever get in,' another commented, using the five words that were always spoken whenever the city was named.

The previous night Thomas had listened to the campfire talk that had all been about Caen. It was, he gathered, a huge city, one of the biggest in France, and protected by a massive castle and a great wall. The French, it seemed, had adopted a strategy of retreating into such citadels rather than face England's bowmen in the open fields, and the archers feared they could be stranded in front of Caen for weeks. The city could not be ignored, for if it was left untaken its huge garrison would threaten the English supply lines. So Caen had to fall and no one believed it would be easy, though some men reckoned the new guns that the King had fetched to France would knock down the city's ramparts as easily as Joshua's trumpets had felled the walls of Jericho.

The King himself must have been sceptical of the guns' power for he had decided to scare the city into surrender by the sheer numbers of his army. The three English battles moved eastward on every road, track or stretch of meadow that offered a path, but an hour or two after dawn the men-at-arms who served as marshals began halting the various contingents. Sweaty horsemen galloped up and down the masses of men, shouting at them to move into a rough line. Thomas, wrestling with his stubborn mare, understood that the whole army was being formed into a huge crescent. A low hill lay in front and a hazy smear beyond the hill betrayed the thousands of cooking fires in Caen. When the signal was given the whole clumsy crescent of mailed men would be advanced to the hilltop so that the defenders, instead of seeing a few English scouts trickle from the woods, would be presented with an overwhelming host and, to make the army seem double its real size, the marshals were pushing and shouting the camp followers into the curved line. Cooks, clerks, women, masons, farriers, carpenters, scullions, anyone who could walk, crawl, ride or stand was being added to the crescent, and a host of bright flags were raised over those bemused masses. It was a hot morning and the leather and mail made men and horses sweat. Dust blew in the wind. The Earl of Warwick, Marshal of the Host, was galloping up and down the crescent, red-faced and cursing, but slowly the cumbersome line formed to his satisfaction.

'When the trumpet sounds,' a knight shouted at Armstrong's men, 'advance to the hilltop. When the trumpet sounds! Not before!'

That army of England must have looked like twenty thousand men when the trumpets tore the summer sky with their massed defiance. To Caen's defenders it was a nightmare. One moment the horizon was empty, even though the sky beyond had long been blanched by the dust kicked up by hoofs and boots, and then there was a sudden host, a horde, a swarm of men glinting iron-hard in the sun and topped by a forest of raised lances and flags. The whole north and east of the city was ringed with men who, when they saw Caen, gave a great roar of incoherent scorn. There was plunder ahead of them, a whole rich city waiting to be taken.

It was a fine and famous city, bigger even than London and that was the biggest city in England. Caen, indeed, was one of the great cities of France. The Conqueror had endowed it with the wealth he stole from England, and it still showed. Within the city walls the church spires and towers stood as close as the lances and flags in Edward's army, while on either side of the city were two vast abbeys. The castle lay to the north, its ramparts, like the pale stone of the city's high walls, hung with war banners. The English roar was answered with a defiant cheer from the defenders, who clustered thick on the ramparts. So many crossbows, Thomas thought, remembering the heavy bolts thumping from La Roche-Derrien's embrasures.

The city had spread beyond its walls, but instead of placing the new houses beside the ramparts, as most towns did, here they had been built on a sprawling island that lay to the south of the old city. Formed by a maze-like tangle of tributaries that fed the two main rivers which flowed by Caen, the island had no walls, for it was protected by the waterways. It needed such protection, for even from the hilltop Thomas could see that the island was where the wealth of Caen lay. The old city within its high walls would be a labyrinth of narrow alleys and cramped houses, but the island was filled with large mansions, big churches and wide gardens. But even though it appeared to be the wealthiest part of Caen, it did not seem to be defended. No troops were visible there. Instead they were all on the ramparts of the old city. The town's boats had been moored on the island's bank, opposite the city wall, and Thomas wondered if any of them belonged to Sir Guillaume d'Evecque.

The Earl of Northampton, released from the Prince's entourage, joined John Armstrong at the head of the archers and nodded towards the city walls.

'Brute of a place, John!' the Earl said cheerfully.

'Formidable, my lord,' Armstrong grunted.

'The island's named for you,' the Earl said glibly.

'For me?' Armstrong sounded suspicious.

'It's the Île St Jean,' the Earl said, then pointed to the nearer of the two abbeys, a great monastery that was surrounded by its own ramparts, which were joined to the city's higher walls. 'The Abbaye aux Hommes,' the Earl said. 'You know what happened when they buried the Conqueror there? They left him in the abbey for too long and when the time came to put him in the vault he was rotted and swollen. His body burst and they reckon the stench of it drove the congregation out of the abbey.'

'God's vengeance, my lord,' Armstrong said stoically.

The Earl gave him a quizzical look. 'Maybe,' he said uncertainly.

'There's no love of William in the north country,' Armstrong said.

'Long time ago, John.'

'Not so long that I won't spit on his grave,' Armstrong declared, then explained himself. 'He might have been our king, my lord, but he were no Englishman.'

'I suppose he wasn't,' the Earl allowed.

'Time for revenge,' Armstrong said loudly enough for the nearest archers to hear. 'We'll take him, we'll take his city and we'll take his goddamn women!'

The archers cheered, though Thomas did not see how the army could possibly take Caen. The walls were huge and well-buttressed with towers, and the ramparts were thick with defenders who looked as confident as the attackers. Thomas was searching the banners for the one showing three yellow hawks on a blue field, but there were so many flags and the wind was stirring them so briskly that he could not pick Sir Guillaume d'Evecque's three hawks from the other gaudy ripples that swirled beneath the embrasures.

'So what are you, Thomas?' The Earl had dropped back to ride beside him. His horse was a big destrier so that the Earl, despite being much shorter than Thomas, towered above him. He spoke in French. 'English or Norman?'

Thomas grimaced. 'English, my lord. Right to my sore arse.' It had been so long since he had ridden that his thighs were chafed raw.

'We're all English now, aren't we?' The Earl sounded mildly surprised.

'Would you want to be anything else?' Thomas asked, and looked around at the archers. 'God knows, my lord, I wouldn't want to fight them.'

'Nor me,' the Earl grunted, 'and I've saved you a fight with Sir Simon. Or rather I've saved your miserable life. I talked to him last night. I can't say he was very willing to spare you a throttling and I can't blame him for that.' The Earl slapped at a horsefly. 'But in the end his greed overcame his hatred of you. You've cost me my share of the prize money for the Countess's two ships, young Thomas. One ship for his dead squire and the other for the hole you put in his leg.'

'Thank you, my lord,' Thomas said effusively. He felt the relief surge through him. 'Thank you,' he said again.

'So you're a free man,' the Earl said. 'Sir Simon shook on it, a clerk made a note of it and a priest witnessed it. Now for God's sake don't go and kill another of his fellows.'

'I won't, sir,' Thomas promised.

'And you're in my debt now,' the Earl said.

'I acknowledge it, my lord.'

The Earl made a dismissive noise, suggesting it was unlikely Thomas could ever pay such a debt, then he shot the archer a suspicious look. 'And speaking of the Countess,' he went on, 'you never mentioned that you brought her north.'

'It didn't seem important, my lord.'

'And last night,' the Earl continued, 'after I'd growled at Jekyll for you, I met her ladyship in the Prince's quarters. She says you treated her with complete chivalry. It seems you behaved with discretion and respect. Is that really true?'

Thomas reddened. 'If she says so, my lord, it must be true.'

The Earl laughed, then touched his spurs to his destrier. 'I've bought your soul,' he said cheerfully, 'so fight well for me!' He curved away to rejoin his men-at-arms.

'He's all right, our Billy,' an archer said, nodding at the Earl, 'a good one.'

'If only they were all like him,' Thomas agreed.

'How come you talk French?' the archer asked suspiciously.

'Picked it up in Brittany,' Thomas said vaguely.

The army's vanguard had now reached the cleared

247

space in front of the walls and a crossbow bolt slammed into the turf as a warning. The camp followers, who had helped give the illusion of overwhelming force, were pitching tents on the hills to the north, while the fighting men spread out in the plain that surrounded the city. Marshals were galloping between the units, shouting that the Prince's men were to go clear about the walls to the Abbaye aux Dames on the city's further side. It was still early, about mid-morning, and the wind brought the smell of Caen's cooking fires as the Earl's men marched past deserted farms. The castle loomed above them.

They went to the western side of the town. The Prince of Wales, mounted on a big black horse and followed by a standard-bearer and a troop of men-at-arms, galloped to the convent, which, because it lay well outside the city walls, had been abandoned. He would make it his home for the duration of the siege and Thomas, dismounting where Armstrong's men would camp, saw Jeanette following the Prince. Following him like a puppy, he thought sourly, then chided himself for jealousy. Why be jealous of a prince? A man might as well resent the sun or curse the ocean. There are other women, he told himself as he hobbled his horse in one of the abbey pastures.

A group of archers was exploring the deserted buildings that lay close to the convent. Most were cottages, but one had been a carpenter's workshop and was piled with wood-shavings and sawdust, while beyond it was a tannery, still stinking of the urine, lime and dung that cured the leather. Beyond the tannery was nothing but a waste ground of thistles and nettles that ran clear to the city's great wall, and Thomas saw that dozens of archers were venturing into the weeds to stare at the ramparts. It was a hot day so that the air in front of the walls seemed to shiver. A small north wind drifted some high clouds and rippled the long grass that grew in the ditch at the base of the battlements. About a hundred archers were in the waste ground now and some were within long crossbow range, though no Frenchman shot at them. A score of the inquisitive bowmen were carrying axes to cut firewood, but morbid curiosity had driven them towards the ramparts instead of outwards to the woods and Thomas now followed them, wanting to judge for himself what horrors the besiegers faced. The screeching sound of ungreased axles made him turn to see two farm wagons being dragged towards the convent. They both held guns, great bulbous things with swollen metal bellies and gaping mouths. He wondered if the guns' magic could blast a hole through the city's ramparts, but even if it did then men would still have to fight through the breach. He made the sign of the cross. Maybe he would find a woman inside the city. He had almost everything a man needed. He had a horse, he had a hacqueton, he had his bow and arrow bag. He just needed a woman.

Yet he did not see how an army twice the size could cross Caen's great walls. They reared up from their boggy ditch like cliffs, and every fifty paces there was a conical roofed bastion that would give the garrison's crossbowmen the chance to slash their quarrels into the flanks of the attackers. It would be carnage, Thomas thought, far worse than the slaughter that had occurred each time the Earl of Northampton's men had assailed the southern wall at La Roche-Derrien.

More and more archers came into the waste ground

to stare at the city. Most were just inside crossbow range, but the French still ignored them. Instead the defenders began hauling in the gaudy banners that hung from the embrasures. Thomas looked for Sir Guillaume's three hawks, but could not see them. Most of the banners were decorated with crosses or the figures of saints. One showed the keys of heaven, another the lion of St Mark and a third had a winged angel scything down English troops with a flaming sword. That banner disappeared.

'What the hell are the goddamn bastards doing?' an archer asked.

'The bastards are running away!' another man said. He was staring at the stone bridge that led from the old city to the Île St Jean.

That bridge was thronged with soldiers, some mounted, most on foot, and all of them streaming out of the walled city onto the island of big houses, churches and gardens. Thomas walked a few paces southwards to get a better view and saw crossbowmen and men-at-arms appear in the alleys between the island's houses.

'They're going to defend the island,' he said to anyone in earshot.

By now carts were being pushed over the bridge and he could see women and children being chivvied on their way by men-at-arms.

More defenders crossed the bridge and still more banners vanished from the walls until there was only a handful left. The big flags of the great lords still flew from the castle's topmost towers, and pious banners hung down the keep's long walls, but the city ramparts were almost bare and there must have been a thousand archers from the Prince of Wales's battle watching those walls now. They should have been cutting firewood, building shelters or digging latrines, but a slow suspicion was dawning on them that the French were not planning to defend both the city and the island, but only the island. Which meant the city had been abandoned. That seemed so unlikely that no one even dared mention it. They just watched the city's inhabitants and defenders crowd across the stone bridge and then, as the last banner was hauled from the ramparts, someone began walking towards the nearest gate.

No one gave any orders. No prince, earl, constable or knight ordered the archers forward. They simply decided to approach the city themselves. Most wore the Prince of Wales's green and white livery, but a good few, like Thomas, had the Earl of Northampton's stars and lions. Thomas half expected crossbowmen to appear and greet the straggling advance with a terrible volley of spitting quarrels, but the embrasures stayed empty and that emboldened the archers who saw birds settling on the crenellations, a sure sign that the defenders had abandoned the wall. The men with axes ran to the gate and started to hack at its timbers, and no crossbow bolts flew from the flanking bastions. The great walled city of William the Conqueror had been left unguarded.

The axemen broke through the iron-studded planks, lifted the bar and pulled the big gates open to reveal an empty street. A handcart with one broken wheel was abandoned on the cobbles, but no Frenchmen were visible. There was a pause as the archers stared in disbelief, then the shouting began. 'Havoc! Havoc!' The first thought was plunder, and men eagerly broke into the houses, but found little except chairs, tables and

251

cupboards. Everything of real value, like every person in the city, was gone to the island.

Still more archers were coming into the city. A few climbed towards the open ground surrounding the castle where two died from crossbow bolts spat from the high ramparts, but the rest spread through the city to find it bare, and so more and more men were drawn towards the bridge that spanned the River Odon and led to the Île St Jean. At the bridge's southern end, where it reached the island, there was a barbican tower that was thick with crossbows, but the French did not want the English getting close to the barbican and so they had hastily thrown up a barricade on the bridge's northern side out of a great heap of wagons and furniture and they had garrisoned the barrier with a score of men-at-arms reinforced by as many crossbowmen. There was another bridge at the island's further side, but the archers did not know of its existence and, besides, it was a long way off and the barricaded bridge was the quickest route to the enemy's riches.

The first white-fledged arrows began to fly. Then came the harder sounds of the enemy's crossbows discharging and the crack of bolts striking the stones of the church beside the bridge. The first men died.

There were still no orders. No man of rank was inside the city yet, just a mass of archers as mindless as wolves smelling blood. They poured arrows at the barricade, forcing its defenders to crouch behind the overturned wagons, then the first group of English gave a cheer and charged at the barricade with swords, axes and spears. More men followed as the first tried to climb the ungainly pile. The crossbows banged from the barbican and men were thrown back by the heavy bolts. The

French men-at-arms stood to repel the survivors and swords clashed on axes. Blood was slick on the bridge approach and one archer slipped and was trampled underfoot by his colleagues going to the fight. The English were howling, the French were shouting, a trumpet was calling from the barbican and every church bell on the Île St Jean was tolling the alarm.

Thomas, having no sword of his own, was standing in the porch of a church which stood hard beside the bridge from where he was shooting arrows up at the barbican tower, but his aim was obscured because a thatch in the old city was on fire and the smoke was curling over the river like a low cloud.

The French held all the advantages. Their crossbowmen could shoot from the barbican and from the shelter of the barricade, and to attack them the English had to funnel onto the narrow bridge approach, which was littered with bodies, blood and bolts. Still more enemy crossbowmen were stationed in the line of boats that was moored along the island's bank, stranded there by the falling tide, and the defenders of those boats, sheltered by the stout wooden gunwales, could shoot up at any archer foolish enough to show himself on those parts of the city wall that were not smoke-shrouded. More and more crossbowmen were coming to the bridge until it seemed as if the air above the river was as thick with quarrels as a flock of starlings.

Another rush of archers charged from the alleys to fill the narrow street leading to the barricade. They screamed as they charged. They were not fighting with their bows, but rather with axes, swords, billhooks and spears. The spears were mostly carried by the hobelars, many of them Welshmen who uttered a high-shrieked howl as they ran with the archers. A dozen of the new attackers must have fallen to crossbow bolts, but the survivors leaped the bodies and closed right up to the barricade that was now defended by at least thirty men-at-arms and as many crossbowmen. Thomas ran and picked up the arrow bag of a dead man. The attackers were crammed up against the arrow-stuck barricade with little room to wield their axes, swords and spears. The French men-at-arms stabbed with lances, hacked with swords and flailed with maces, and as the front rank of archers died, the next rank was pushed onto the enemy weapons, and all the time the crossbow quarrels thumped down from the barbican's crenellated tower and flew up from the grounded ships in the river. Thomas saw a man reeling from the bridge with a crossbow bolt buried in his helmet. Blood poured down his face as he made a strange incoherent mewing before falling to his knees and then, slowly, collapsing on the road where he was trampled by another rush of attackers. A few English archers found their way onto the roof of the church and they killed a half-dozen of the barricade's defenders before the crossbowmen on the barbican swept them away with stinging volleys. The bridge approach was thick with bodies now, so many corpses that they obstructed the charging English, and a half-dozen men began heaving the dead over the parapet. A tall archer, armed with a long-handled axe, managed to reach the barricade's summit, where he chopped the heavy blade again and again, beating down at a Frenchman who had ribbons on his helmet, but then he was struck by two crossbow bolts and he folded over, letting the axe fall and clutching at his belly, and the French hauled him down to their side of the barricade where three men hacked at him with swords, then used the archer's own axe to sever his head. They thrust the bloody trophy onto a spear and waved it above the barricade to taunt their attackers.

A mounted man-at-arms, wearing the Earl of Warwick's badge of a bear and ragged staff, shouted at the archers to retreat. The Earl himself was in the city now, sent by the King to pull his bowmen back from their unequal fight, but the archers were not willing to listen. The French were jeering them, killing them, but still the archers wanted to break through the bridge's defences and slake themselves on Caen's wealth. And so still more blood-maddened men charged at the barricade – so many that they filled the road as the bolts whipped down from the smoky sky. The attackers at the back heaved forward and the men at the front died on French lances and blades.

The French were winning. Their crossbow bolts were smacking into the crush of men and those at the front began to push backwards to escape the slaughter while those at the back still shoved forward and the ones in between, threatened with a crushing death, broke through a stout wooden fence that let them spill off the bridge's approach onto a narrow strip of ground that lay between the river and the city walls. More men followed them.

Thomas was still crouching in the church porch. He sent an occasional arrow up towards the barbican, but the thickening smoke hung like fog and he could scarcely see his targets. He watched the men streaming off the bridge onto the narrow riverbank, but did not follow, for that seemed just another way of committing suicide. They were trapped there with the high city wall at their backs and the swirling river in front, and the far bank of the river was lined with boats from which crossbowmen poured quarrels into these new and inviting targets.

The spillage of men off the bridge opened the roadway to the barricade again and newly arrived men, who had not experienced the carnage of the first attacks, took up the fight. A hobelar managed to climb onto an overturned wagon and stabbed down with his short spear. There were crossbow bolts sticking from his chest, but still he screeched and stabbed and tried to go on fighting even when a French man-at-arms disembowelled him. His guts spilled out, but somehow he found the strength to raise the spear and give one last lunge before he fell into the defenders. A half-dozen archers were trying to dismantle the barricade, while others were throwing the dead off the bridge to clear the roadway. At least one living man, wounded, was thrown into the river. He screamed as he fell.

'Get back, you dogs, get back!' The Earl of Warwick had come to the chaos and he flailed at men with his marshal's staff. He had a trumpeter sounding the four falling notes of the retreat while the French trumpeter was blasting out the attack signal, brisk couplets of rising notes that stirred the blood, and the English and Welsh were obeying the French rather than the English trumpet. More men – hundreds of them – were streaming into the old city, dodging the Earl of Warwick's constables and closing on the bridge where, unable to get past the barricade, they followed the men down to the riverbank from where they shot their arrows at the crossbowmen in the barges. The Earl of Warwick's men started pulling archers away from the street that led to the bridge, but for every one they hauled away another two slipped past.

A crowd of Caen's menfolk, some armed with nothing more than staves, waited beyond the barbican, promising yet another fight if the barricade was ever overcome. A madness had gripped the English army, a madness to attack a bridge that was too well defended. Men went screaming to their deaths and still more followed. The Earl of Warwick was bellowing at them to pull back, but they were deaf to him. Then a great roar of defiance sounded from the riverbank and Thomas stepped out from the porch to see that groups of men were now trying to wade the River Odon. And they were succeeding. It had been a dry summer, the river was low and the falling tide made it lower still, so that at its deepest the water only came up to a man's chest. Scores of men were now plunging into the river. Thomas, dodging two of the Earl's constables, leaped the remnants of the fence and slithered down the bank, which was studded with embedded crossbow quarrels. The place stank of shit, for this was where the city emptied its nightsoil. A dozen Welsh hobelars waded into the river and Thomas joined them, holding his bow high above his head to keep its string dry. The crossbowmen had to stand up from their shelter behind the barge gunwales to shoot down at the attackers in the river, and once they were standing they made easy targets for those archers who had stayed on the city bank.

The current was strong and Thomas could only take short steps. Bolts splashed about him. A man just in front was hit in the throat and was snatched down by the weight of his mail coat to leave nothing but a swirl of bloody water. The ships' gunwales were stuck with white-feathered arrows. A Frenchman was draped over the side of one boat and his body twitched whenever an arrow hit his corpse. Blood trickled from a scupper.

'Kill the bastards, kill the bastards,' a man muttered next to Thomas, who saw it was one of the Earl of Warwick's constables; finding he could not stop the attack, he had decided to join it. The man was carrying a curved falchion, half sword and half butcher's cleaver.

The wind flattened the smoke from the burning houses, dipping it close to the river and filling the air with scraps of burning straw. Some of those scraps had lodged in the furled sails of two of the ships that were now burning fiercely. Their defenders had scrambled ashore. Other enemy bowmen were retreating from the first mud-streaked English and Welsh soldiers who clambered up the bank between the grounded boats. The air was filled with the quick-fluttering hiss of arrows flying overhead. The island's bells still clamoured. A Frenchman was shouting from the barbican's tower, ordering men to spread along the river and attack the groups of Welsh and English who struggled and slithered in the river mud.

Thomas kept wading. The water reached his chest, then began to recede. He fought the clinging mud of the riverbed and ignored the crossbow bolts that drove into the water about him. A crossbowman stood up from behind a boat's gunwale and aimed straight at Thomas's chest, but then two arrows struck the man and he fell backwards. Thomas pushed on, climbing now. Then suddenly he was out of the river, and he stumbled up the slick mud into the shelter of the over-hanging stern of the closest barge. He could see that men were still fighting at the barricade, but he could also see that the river was now swarming with archers and hobelars who, mud-spattered and soaking, began to haul themselves onto the boats. The remaining defenders had few weapons other than their crossbows, while most of the archers had swords or axes. The fight on the moored boats was one-sided, the slaughter brief, and then the disorganized and leaderless mass of attackers surged off the blood-soaked decks and up from the river onto the island.

The Earl of Warwick's man-at-arms went ahead of Thomas. He clambered up the steep grassy bank and was immediately hit in the face by a crossbow bolt so that he jerked backwards with a fine mist of blood encircling his helmet. The bolt had driven clean through the bridge of his nose, killing him instantly and leaving him with an offended expression. His falchion landed in the mud at Thomas's feet, so he slung his bow and picked the weapon up. It was surprisingly heavy. There was nothing sophisticated about a falchion; it was simply a killing tool with an edge designed to cut deep because of the weight of the broad blade. It was a good weapon for a mêlée. Will Skeat had once told Thomas how he had seen a Scottish horse decapitated with a single blow of a falchion, and just to see one of the brutal blades was to feel terror in the gut.

The Welsh hobelars were on the barge, finishing off its defenders, then they gave a shout in their strange language and leaped ashore and Thomas followed them, to find himself in a loose rank of crazed attackers who ran towards a row of tall and wealthy houses defended by the men who had escaped from the barges and by the citizens of Caen. The crossbowmen had time to loose one bolt apiece, but they were nervous and most shot wide, and then the attackers were onto them like hounds onto a wounded deer.

Thomas wielded the falchion two-handed. A crossbowman tried to defend himself with his bow but the heavy blade sliced through the weapon's stock as if it had been made of ivory, then buried itself in the Frenchman's neck. A spurt of blood jetted over Thomas's head as he wrenched the heavy sword free and kicked the crossbowman between the legs. A Welshman was grinding a spear blade into a Frenchman's ribs. Thomas stumbled on the man he had struck down, caught his balance and shouted the English war cry. 'St George!' He swung the blade again, chopping through the forearm of a man wielding a club. He was close enough to smell the man's breath and the stink of his clothes. A Frenchman was swinging a sword while another was beating at the Welsh with an iron-studded mace. This was tavern fighting, outlaw fighting, and Thomas was screaming like a fiend. God damn them all. He was spattered with blood as he kicked and clawed and slashed his way down the alley. The air seemed unnaturally thick, moist and warm; it stank of blood. The iron-studded mace missed his head by a finger's breadth and struck the wall instead, and Thomas swung the falchion upwards so it cut into the man's groin. The man yelled out and Thomas kicked the back of the blade to drive it home. 'Bastard,' he said, kicking the blade again, 'bastard.' A Welshman speared the man and two more leaped his body and, their long hair and beards smeared with blood, lunged their red-bladed spears at the next rank of defenders.

There must have been twenty or more enemy in the alley, and Thomas and his companions were fewer than a dozen, but the French were nervous and the attackers were confident and so they ripped into them with spear and sword and falchion; just hacking and stabbing, slicing and cursing them, killing in a welter of summer hatred. More and more English and Welsh were swarming up from the river, and the sound they made was a keening noise, a howl for blood and a wail of derision for a wealthy enemy. These were the hounds of war that had escaped from their kennels and they were taking this great city that the lords of the army had supposed would hold the English advance for a month.

The defenders in the alley broke and ran. Thomas hacked a man down from behind and wrenched the blade free with a scraping noise of steel on bone. The hobelars kicked in a door, claiming the house beyond as their property. A rush of archers in the Prince of Wales's green and white livery poured down the alley, following Thomas into a long and pretty garden where pear trees grew about neat plots of herbs. Thomas was struck by the incongruity of such a beautiful place under a sky filled with smoke and terrible with screams. The garden had a border of sweet rocket, wallflowers and peonies, and seats under a vine trellis and for an instant it looked like a scrap of heaven, but then the archers trampled the herbs, threw down the grape arbour and ran across the flowers.

A group of Frenchmen tried to drive the invaders out of the garden. They approached from the east, from out of the mass of men waiting behind the bridge's barbican. They were led by three mounted men-at-arms, who all wore blue surcoats decorated with yellow stars. They jumped their horses over the low fences and shouted as they raised their long swords ready to strike.

The arrows smacked into the horses. Thomas had not unslung his bow, but some of the Prince's archers had arrows on their cords and they aimed at the horses instead of the riders. The arrows bit deep, the horses screamed, reared and fell, and the archers swarmed over the fallen men with axes and swords. Thomas went to the right, heading off the Frenchmen on foot, most of whom seemed to be townsfolk armed with anything from small axes to thatch-hooks to ancient two-handed swords. He cut the falchion through a leather coat, kicked the blade free, swung it so that blood streamed in droplets from the blade, then hacked again. The French wavered, saw more archers coming from the alley and fled back to the barbican.

The archers were hacking at the unsaddled horsemen. One of the fallen men screamed as the blades chopped at his arms and trunk. The blue and yellow surcoats were soaked in blood. Then Thomas saw that it was not yellow stars on a blue field, but hawks. Hawks with their wings raised and their claws outstretched. Sir Guillaume d'Evecque's men! Maybe Sir Guillaume himself! But when he looked at the grimacing, blood-spattered faces Thomas saw that all three had been young men. But Sir Guillaume was here in Caen, and the lance, Thomas thought, must be near. He broke through the fence and headed down another alley. Behind him, in the house that the hobelars had commandeered, a woman cried, the first of many. The church bells were falling silent.

Edward the Third, by the Grace of God, King of England, led close to twelve thousand fighting men and by now a fifth of them were on the island and still more were coming. No one had led them there. The only orders they had received were to retreat. But they had disobeyed and so they had captured Caen, though the enemy still held the bridge barbican from where they were spitting crossbow bolts.

Thomas emerged from the alley into the main street, where he joined a group of archers who swamped the crenellated tower with arrows and, under their cover, a howling mob of Welsh and English overwhelmed the Frenchmen cowering under the barbican's arch before charging the defenders of the bridge barricade, who were now assailed on both sides. The Frenchmen, seeing their doom, threw down their weapons and shouted that they yielded, but the archers were in no mood for quarter. They just howled and attacked. Frenchmen were tossed into the river, and then scores of men hauled the barricade apart, tipping its furniture and wagons over the parapet.

The great mass of Frenchmen who had been waiting behind the barbican scattered into the island, most, Thomas assumed, going to rescue their wives and daughters. They were pursued by the vengeful archers who had been waiting at the bridge's far side, and the grim crowd went past Thomas, going into the heart of the Île St Jean where the screams were now constant. The cry of havoc was everywhere. The barbican tower was still held by the French, though they were no longer using their crossbows for fear of retaliation by the English arrows. No one tried to take the tower, though a small group of archers stood in the bridge's centre and stared up at the banners hanging from the ramparts.

Thomas was about to go into the island's centre when he heard the clash of hooves on stone and he looked back to see a dozen French knights who must have been concealed behind the barbican. Those men now erupted from a gate and, with visors closed and lances couched, spurred their horses towards the bridge. They plainly wanted to charge clean through the old city to reach the greater safety of the castle.

Thomas took a few steps towards the Frenchmen, then thought better of it. No one wanted to resist a dozen fully armoured knights. But he saw the blue and yellow surcoat, saw the hawks on a knight's shield and he unslung his bow and took an arrow from the bag. He hauled the cord back. The Frenchmen were just spurring onto the bridge and Thomas shouted, 'Evecque! Evecque!' He wanted Sir Guillaume, if it was he, to see his killer, and the man in the blue and yellow surcoat did half turn in the saddle though Thomas could not see his enemy's face because the visor was down. He loosed, but even as he let the cord snap he saw that the arrow was warped. It flew low, smacking into the man's left leg instead of the small of his back where Thomas had aimed. He pulled a second arrow out, but the dozen knights were on the bridge now, their horses' hooves striking sparks from the cobbles, and the leading men lowered their lances to batter the handful of archers aside, and then they were through and galloping up the further streets towards the castle. The white-fledged arrow still jutted from the knight's thigh where it had sunk deep and Thomas sent a second arrow after it, but that one vanished in the smoke as the French fugitives disappeared in the old city's tight streets.

The castle had not fallen, but the city and the island belonged to the English. They did not belong to the King yet, because the great lords – the earls and the barons – had not captured either place. They belonged to the archers and the hobelars, and they now set about plundering the wealth of Caen.

The Île St Jean was, other than Paris itself, the fairest, plumpest and most elegant city in northern France. Its houses were beautiful, its gardens fragrant, its streets wide, its churches wealthy and its citizens, as they should be, civilized. Into that pleasant place came a savage horde of muddy, bloody men who found riches beyond their dreams. What the hellequin had done to countless Breton villages was now visited on a great city. It was a time for killing, for rape and wanton cruelty. Any Frenchman was an enemy, and every enemy was cut down. The leaders of the city garrison, magnates of France, were safe in the upper floors of the barbican tower and they stayed there until they recognized some English lords to whom they could safely surrender, while a dozen knights had escaped to the castle. A few other lords and knights managed to outgallop the invading English and flee across the island's southern bridge, but at least a dozen titled men whose ransoms could have made a hundred archers rich as princelings were cut down like dogs and reduced to mangled meat and weltering blood. Knights and men-at-arms, who could have paid a hundred or two hundred pounds for their freedom, were shot with arrows or clubbed down in the mad rage which possessed the army. As for the humbler men, the citizens armed with lengths of timber, mattocks or mere knives, they were just slaughtered. Caen, the city of the Conqueror that had become rich on English plunder, was killed that day and the wealth of it was given back to Englishmen.

And not just its wealth, its women too. To be a

woman in Caen that day was to be given a foretaste of hell. There was little fire, for men wanted the houses to be plundered rather than burned, but there were devils aplenty. Men begged for the honour of their wives and daughters, then were forced to watch that honour being trampled. Many women hid, but they were found soon enough by men accustomed to riddling out hiding places in attics or under stairs. The women were driven to the streets, stripped bare and paraded as trophies. One merchant's wife, monstrously fat, was harnessed to a small cart and whipped naked up and down the main street which ran the length of the island. For an hour or more the archers made her run, some men laughing themselves to tears at the sight of her massive rolls of fat, and when they were bored with her they tossed her into the river where she crouched, weeping and calling for her children until an archer, who had been trying out a captured crossbow on a pair of swans, put a quarrel through her throat. Men laden with silver plate were staggering over the bridge, others were still searching for riches and instead found ale, cider or wine, and so the excesses grew worse. A priest was hanged from a tavern sign after he tried to stop a rape. Some men-at-arms, very few, tried to stem the horror, but they were hugely outnumbered and driven back to the bridge. The church of St Jean, which was said to contain the fingerbones of St John the Divine, a hoof of the horse St Paul was riding to Damascus and one of the baskets that had held the miraculous loaves and fishes, was turned into a brothel where the women who had fled to the church for sanctuary were sold to grinning soldiers. Men paraded in silks and lace and threw dice for the women from whom they had stolen the finery.

Thomas took no part. What happened could not be stopped, not by one man nor even by a hundred men. Another army could have quelled the mass rape, but in the end Thomas knew it would be the stupor of drunkenness that would finish it. Instead he searched for his enemy's house, wandering from street to street until he found a dying Frenchman and gave him a drink of water before asking where Sir Guillaume d'Evecque lived. The man rolled his eyes, gasped for breath and stammered that the house was in the southern part of the island. 'You cannot miss it,' the man said, 'it is stone, all stone, and has three hawks carved above the door.'

Thomas walked south. Bands of the Earl of Warwick's men-at-arms were coming in force to the island to restore order, but they were still struggling with the archers close to the bridge, and Thomas was going to the southern part of the island which had not suffered as badly as the streets and alleys closer to the bridge. He saw the stone house above the roofs of some plundered shops. Most other buildings were half-timbered and straw-roofed, but Sir Guillaume d'Evecque's two-storey mansion was almost a fortress. Its walls were stone, its roof tiled and its windows small, but still some archers had got inside, for Thomas could hear screams. He crossed a small square where a large oak grew through the cobbles, strode up the house steps and under an arch that was surmounted by the three carved hawks. He was surprised by the depth of anger that the sight of the escutcheon gave him. This was revenge, he told himself, for Hookton.

He went through the hallway to find a group of archers and hobelars squabbling over the kitchen pots.

Two menservants lay dead by the hearth in which a fire still smouldered. One of the archers snarled at Thomas that they had reached the house first and its contents were theirs, but before Thomas could answer he heard a scream from the upper floor and he turned and ran up the big wooden stairway. Two rooms opened from the upper hallway and Thomas pushed open one of the doors to see an archer in the Prince of Wales's livery struggling with a girl. The man had half torn off her pale blue dress, but she was fighting back like a vixen, clawing at his face and kicking his shins. Then, just as Thomas came into the room, the man managed to subdue her with a great clout to the head. The girl gasped and fell back into the wide and empty hearth as the archer turned on Thomas. 'She's mine,' he said curtly, 'go and find your own.'

Thomas looked at the girl. She was fair-haired, thin and weeping. He remembered Jeanette's anguish after the Duke had raped her and he could not stomach seeing such pain inflicted on another girl, not even a girl in Sir Guillaume d'Evecque's mansion.

'I think you've hurt her enough,' he said. He crossed himself, remembering his sins in Brittany. 'Let her go,' he added.

The archer, a bearded man a dozen years older than Thomas, drew his sword. It was an old weapon, broad-bladed and sturdy, and the man hefted it confidently. 'Listen, boy,' he said, 'I'm going to watch you go through that door, and if you don't I'll string your goddamn guts from wall to wall.'

Thomas hefted the falchion. 'I've sworn an oath to St Guinefort,' he told the man, 'to protect all women.'

'Goddamn fool.'

The man leaped at Thomas, lunged, and Thomas stepped back and parried so that the blades struck sparks as they rang together. The bearded man was quick to recover, lunged again, and Thomas took another backwards step and swept the sword aside with the falchion. The girl was watching from the hearth with wide blue eyes. Thomas swung his broad blade, missed and was almost skewered by the sword, but he stepped aside just in time, then kicked the bearded man in the knee so that he hissed with pain, then Thomas swept the falchion in a great haymaking blow that cut into the bearded man's neck. Blood arced across the room as the man, without a sound, dropped to the floor. The falchion had very nearly severed his head and the blood still pulsed from the open wound as Thomas knelt beside his victim.

'If anyone asks,' he said to the girl in French, 'your father did this, then ran away.' He had got into too much trouble after murdering a squire in Brittany and did not want to compound the crime by the death of an archer. He took four small coins from the archer's pouch then smiled at the girl, who had remained remarkably calm while a man was almost decapitated in front of her eyes. 'I'm not going to hurt you,' Thomas said, 'I promise.'

She watched him from the hearth. 'You won't?'

'Not today,' he said gently.

She stood, shaking the dizziness from her head. She pulled her dress close at her neck and tied the torn parts together with loose threads. 'You may not hurt me,' she said, 'but others will.'

'Not if you stay with me,' Thomas said. 'Here,' he took the big black bow from his shoulder, unstrung it and tossed it to her. 'Carry that,' he said, 'and everyone will know you're an archer's woman. No one will touch you then.'

She frowned at the weight of the bow. 'No one will hurt me?'

'Not if you carry that,' Thomas promised her again. 'Is this your house?'

'I work here,' she said.

'For Sir Guillaume d'Evecque?' he asked and she nodded. 'Is he here?'

She shook her head. 'I don't know where he is.'

Thomas reckoned his enemy was in the castle where he would be trying to extricate an arrow from his thigh. 'Did he keep a lance here?' he asked, 'a great black lance with a silver blade?'

She shook her head quickly. Thomas frowned. The girl, he could see, was trembling. She had shown bravery, but perhaps the blood seeping from the dead man's neck was unsettling her. He also noted she was a pretty girl despite the bruises on her face and the dirt in her tangle of fair hair. She had a long face made solemn by big eyes. 'Do you have family here?' Thomas asked her.

'My mother died. I have no one except Sir Guillaume.'

'And he left you here alone?' Thomas asked scornfully.

'No!' she protested. 'He thought we'd be safe in the city, but then, when your army came, the men decided to defend the island instead. They left the city! Because all the good houses are here.' She sounded indignant.

'So what do you do for Sir Guillaume?' Thomas asked her.

'I clean,' she said, 'and milk the cows on the other

side of the river.' She flinched as men shouted angrily from the square outside.

Thomas smiled. 'It's all right, no one will hurt you. Hold on to the bow. If anyone looks at you, say, "I am an archer's woman."' He repeated it slowly, then made her say the phrase over and over till he was satisfied. 'Good!' He smiled at her. 'What's your name?'

'Eleanor.'

He doubted it would serve much purpose to search the house, though he did, but there was no lance of St George hidden in any of the rooms. There was no furniture, no tapestries, nothing of any value except the spits and pots and dishes in the kitchen. Everything precious, Eleanor said, had gone to the castle a week before. Thomas looked at the shattered dishes on the kitchen flagstones.

'How long have you worked for him?' he asked.

'All my life,' Eleanor said, then added shyly, 'I'm fifteen.'

'And you never saw a great lance that he brought back from England?'

'No,' she said, eyes wide, but something about her expression made Thomas think she was lying, though he did not challenge her. He decided he would question her later, when she had learned to trust him.

'You'd better stay with me,' he told Eleanor, 'then you won't get hurt. I'll take you to the encampment and when our army moves on you can come back here.' What he really meant was that she could stay with him and become a true archer's woman, but that, like the lance, could wait a day or two.

She nodded, accepting that fate with equanimity. She must have prayed to be spared the rape that tortured

271

Caen and Thomas was her prayer's answer. He gave her his arrow bag so that she looked even more like an archer's woman. 'We'll have to go through the city,' he told Eleanor as he led her down the staircase, 'so stay close.'

He went down the house's outer steps. The small square was now crowded with mounted men-at-arms wearing the badge of the bear and ragged staff. They had been sent by the Earl of Warwick to stop the slaughter and robbery, and they stared hard at Thomas, but he lifted his hands to show he was carrying nothing, then threaded between the horses. He had gone perhaps a dozen paces when he realized that Eleanor was not with him. She was terrified of the horsemen in dirty mail, their grim faces framed in steel and so she had hesitated at the house door.

Thomas opened his mouth to call her and just then a horseman spurred at him from under the branches of the oak. Thomas looked up, then the flat of a sword blade hammered into the side of his head and he was pitched forward, his ear bleeding, onto the cobblestones. The falchion fell from his hand, then the man's horse stepped on his forehead and Thomas's vision was seared with lightning.

The man climbed from the saddle and stamped his armoured foot on Thomas's head. Thomas felt the pain, heard the protests from the other men-at-arms, then felt nothing as he was kicked a second time. But in the few heartbeats before he lost consciousness he had recognized his assailant.

Sir Simon Jekyll, despite his agreement with the Earl, wanted revenge.

Perhaps Thomas was lucky. Perhaps his guardian saint, whether dog or man, was looking after him, for if he had been conscious he would have suffered torture. Sir Simon might have put his signature to the agreement with the Earl the previous night, but the sight of Thomas had driven any mercy from his mind. He remembered the humiliation of being hunted naked through the trees and he recalled the pain of the crossbow bolt in his leg, a wound that still made him limp, and those memories provoked nothing except a wish to give Thomas a long, slow hurting that would leave the archer screaming. But Thomas had been stunned by the flat of the sword and by the kicks to his head and he did not know a thing as two men-at-arms dragged him towards the oak. At first the Earl of Warwick's men had tried to protect Thomas from Sir Simon, but when he assured them that the man was a deserter, a thief and a murderer they had changed their minds. They would hang him.

And Sir Simon would let them. If these men hanged Thomas as a deserter then no one could accuse Sir Simon of executing the archer. He would have kept his word and the Earl of Northampton would still have to forfeit his share of the prize money. Thomas would be dead and Sir Simon would be both richer and happier.

The men-at-arms were willing enough once they heard Thomas was a murderous thief. They had orders to hang enough rioters, thieves and rapists to cool the army's ardour, but this quarter of the island, being furthest from the old city, had not seen the same atrocities as the northern half and so these men-at-arms had been denied the opportunity to use the ropes which the Earl had issued. Now they had a victim and so one man tossed the rope over an oak branch.

Thomas was aware of little of it. He felt nothing as Sir Simon searched him and cut away the money pouch from under his tunic; he did not know a thing when the rope was knotted about his neck, but then he was dimly aware of the stench of horse urine and suddenly there was a tightening at his gullet and his slowly recovering sight was sheeted with red. He felt himself hauled into the air, then tried to gasp because of a dreadful gripping pain in his throat, but he could not gasp and he could scarcely breathe; he could only feel a burning and choking as the smoky air scraped in his windpipe. He wanted to scream in terror but his lungs could do nothing except give him agony. He had an instant's lucidity as he realized he was dangling and jerking and twitching, and though he scrabbled at his neck with his hooked fingers he could not loosen the rope's strangling grip. Then, in terror, he pissed himself.

'Yellow bastard,' Sir Simon sneered, and he struck at Thomas's body with his sword, though the blow did little more than slice the flesh at Thomas's waist and swing his body on the rope.

'Leave him be,' one of the men-at-arms said. 'He's a dead 'un,' and they watched until Thomas's movements became spasmodic. Then they mounted and rode on. A group of archers also watched from one of the houses in the square, and their presence scared Sir Simon, who feared they might be friends of Thomas and so, when the Earl's men left the square, he rode with them. His own followers were searching the nearby church of St Michael, and Sir Simon had only come to the square because he had seen the tall stone house and wondered if it contained plunder. Instead he had found Thomas and now Thomas was hanged. It was not the revenge Sir Simon had dreamed of, but there had been pleasure in it and that was a compensation.

Thomas felt nothing now. It was all darkness and no pain. He was dancing the rope to hell, his head to one side, body still swinging slightly, legs twitching, hands curling and feet dripping.

The army stayed five days in Caen. Some three hundred Frenchmen of rank, all of whom could yield ransoms, had been taken prisoner, and they were escorted north to where they could take ship for England. The injured English and Welsh soldiers were carried to the Abbaye aux Dames where they lay in the cloisters, their wounds stinking so high that the Prince and his entourage moved to the Abbaye aux Hommes where the King had his quarters. The bodies of the massacred citizens were cleared from the streets. A priest of the King's household tried to bury the dead decently, as befitted Christians, but when a common grave was dug in the churchyard of St Jean it could hold only five hundred bodies, and no one had time or spades enough to bury the rest, so four and a half thousand corpses were tipped into the rivers. The city's survivors, creeping out of their hiding places when the madness of the sack was over, wandered along the riverbanks to search for their relatives among the corpses that were stranded by the falling tide. Their searches disturbed the wild dogs and the screeching flocks of ravens and gulls that squabbled as they feasted on the bloated dead.

The castle was still in French hands. Its walls were high and thick, and no ladder could scale them. The King sent a herald to demand the garrison's surrender, but the French lords in the great keep politely refused and then invited the English to do their worst, confident that no mangonel or catapult could hurl a stone high enough to breach their lofty walls. The King reckoned they were right, so instead ordered his gunners to break down the castle's stones, and the army's five largest cannon were trundled through the old city on their wagons. Three of the guns were long tubes made from wrought-iron strips bound by steel hoops, while two had been cast in brass by bell-founders and looked like bulbous jars with swollen oval bellies, narrow necks and flaring mouths. All were around five feet long and needed shear-legs to be swung from their wagons onto wooden cradles.

The cradles were set on planks of wood. The ground under the gun carriages had been graded so that the guns could point up towards the castle's gate. Bring down the gate, the King had ordered, and he could release his archers and men-at-arms in an assault. So the gunners, most of them men from Flanders or Italy who were skilled in this work, mixed their gunpowder. It was made from saltpetre, sulphur and charcoal, but the saltpetre was heavier than the other ingredients and

276

always settled to the bottom of the barrels while the charcoal rose to the top so the gunners had to stir the mix thoroughly before they ladled the deadly powder into the bellies of the jars. They placed a shovelful of loam, made from water and clay soil, in the narrow part of each gun's neck before loading the crudely sculpted stone balls that were the missiles. The loam was to seal the firing chamber so that the power of the explosion did not leak away before all the powder had caught the fire. Still more loam was packed about the stone balls to fill the space between the missiles and the barrels, then the gunners had to wait while the loam hardened to make a firmer seal.

The other three guns were quicker to load. Each iron tube was lashed to a massive wooden cradle that ran the length of the gun, then turned in a right angle so that the gun's breech rested against a baulk of solid oak. That breech, a quarter of the gun's length, was separate from the barrel, and was lifted clean out of the cradle and set upright on the ground where it was filled with the precious black powder. Once the three breech chambers were filled they were sealed by willow plugs to contain the explosion, then slotted back into their cradles. The three tube barrels had already been loaded, two with stone balls and the third with a yard-long garro, a giant arrow made of iron.

The three breech chambers had to be worked firmly against the barrels so that the force of the explosion did not escape through the joint between the gun's two parts. The gunners used wooden wedges that they hammered between the breech and the oak at the back of the cradle, and every blow of the mauls sealed the joints imperceptibly tighter. Other gunners were ladling powder into the spare breech chambers that would fire the next shots. It all took time – well over an hour for the loam in the two bulbous guns to set firm enough – and the work attracted a huge crowd of curious onlookers who stood a judicious distance away to be safe from fragments should any of the strange machines explode. The French, just as curious, watched from the castle battlements. Once in a while a defender would shoot a crossbow quarrel, but the range was too long. One bolt came within a dozen yards of the guns, but the rest fell well short and each failure provoked a jeer from the watching archers. Finally the French abandoned the provocation and just watched.

The three tube guns could have been fired first, for they had no loam to set, but the King wanted the first volley to be simultaneous. He envisaged a mighty blow in which the five missiles would shatter the castle gate and, once the gate was down, he would have his gunners gnaw at the gate's arch. The master gunner, a tall and lugubrious Italian, finally declared the weapons ready and so the fuses were fetched. These were short lengths of hollow straw filled with gunpowder, their ends sealed with clay, and the fuses were pushed down through the narrow touchholes. The master gunner pinched the clay seal from each fuse's upper end, then made the sign of the cross. A priest had already blessed the guns, sprinkling them with holy water, and now the master gunner knelt and looked at the King, who was mounted on a tall grey stallion.

The King, yellow-bearded and blue-eyed, looked up at the castle. A new banner had been hung from the ramparts, showing God holding a hand in blessing over a fleur-de-lis. It was time, he thought, to show the

French whose side God was really on. 'You may fire,' he said solemnly.

Five gunners armed themselves with linstocks – long wands that each held a length of glowing linen. They stood well to the side of the guns and, at a signal from the Italian, they touched the fire to the exposed fuses. There was a brief fizzing, a puff of smoke from the touchholes, then the five mouths vanished in a cloud of grey-white smoke in which five monstrous flames stabbed and writhed as the guns themselves, firm-gripped by their cradles, slammed back along their plank bedding to thud against the mounds of earth piled behind each breech. The noise of the weapons hammered louder than the loudest thunder. It was a noise that physically pounded the eardrums and echoed back from the pale castle walls, and when the sound at last faded the smoke still hung in a shabby screen in front of the guns that now lay askew on their carriages with gently smoking muzzles.

The noise had startled a thousand nesting birds up from the old city's roofs and the castle's higher turrets, yet the gate appeared undamaged. The stone balls had shattered themselves against the walls, while the garro had done nothing except gouge a furrow in the approach road. The French, who had ducked behind the battlements when the noise and smoke erupted, now stood and called insults as the gunners stoically began to realign their weapons.

The King, thirty-four years old and not as confident as his bearing suggested, frowned as the smoke cleared. 'Did we use enough powder?' he demanded of the master gunner. The question had to be translated into Italian by a priest.

'Use more powder, sire,' the Italian said, 'and the guns will shatter.' He spoke regretfully. Men always expected his machines to work miracles and he was tired of explaining that even black powder needed time and patience to do its work.

'You know best,' the King said dubiously, 'I'm sure you know best.' He was hiding his disappointment for he had half hoped that the whole castle would shatter like glass when the missiles struck. His entourage, most of them older men, were looking contemptuous for they had little faith in guns and even less in Italian gunners.

'Who,' the King asked a companion, 'is that woman with my son?'

'The Countess of Armorica, sire. She fled from Brittany.'

The King shuddered, not because of Jeanette, but because the rotten smell of the powder smoke was pungent. 'He grows up fast,' he said, with just a touch of jealousy in his voice. He was bedding some peasant girl, who was pleasant enough and knew her business, but she was not as beautiful as the black-haired Countess who accompanied his son.

Jeanette, unaware that the King watched her, gazed at the castle in search of any sign that it had been struck by gunfire. 'So what happened?' she asked the Prince.

'It takes time,' the Prince said, hiding his surprise that the castle gate had not magically vanished in an eruption of splinters. 'But they do say,' he went on, 'that in the future we shall fight with nothing but guns. Myself, I cannot imagine it.'

'They are amusing,' Jeanette said as a gunner carried a bucket of puddled loam to the nearest gun. The grass in front of the guns was burning in a score of places and the air was filled with a stench like rotted eggs that was even more repugnant than the smell of the corpses in the river.

'If it amuses you, my dear, then I am glad we have the machines,' the Prince said, then frowned because a group of his white-and-green-clad archers were jeering the gunners. 'Whatever happened to the man who brought you from Normandy?' he asked. 'I should have thanked him for his services to you.'

Jeanette feared she was blushing, but made her voice careless. 'I have not seen him since we came here.'

The Prince twisted in his saddle. 'Bohun!' he called to the Earl of Northampton. 'Didn't my lady's personal archer join your fellows?'

'He did, sire.'

'So where is he?'

The Earl shrugged. 'Vanished. We think he must have died crossing the river.'

'Poor fellow,' the Prince said, 'poor fellow.'

And Jeanette, to her surprise, felt a pang of sorrow. Then thought it was probably for the best. She was the widow of a count and now the lover of a prince, and Thomas, if he was on the river's bed, could never tell the truth. 'Poor man,' she said lightly, 'and he behaved so gallantly to me.' She was looking away from the Prince in case he saw her flushed face and she found herself staring, to her utter astonishment, at Sir Simon Jekyll, who, with another group of knights, had come for the entertainment of the guns. Sir Simon was laughing, evidently amused that so much noise and smoke had produced so little effect. Jeanette, disbelieving her eyes, just stared at him. She had gone pale. The sight of Sir Simon had brought back the memories of her worst days in La Roche-Derrien, the days of fear, poverty, humiliation and the uncertainty of knowing to whom she could turn for help.

'I fear we never rewarded the fellow,' the Prince said, still speaking of Thomas, then he saw that Jeanette was taking no notice. 'My dear?' the Prince prompted, but she still looked away from him. 'My lady?' The Prince spoke louder, touching her arm.

Sir Simon had noticed there was a woman with the Prince, but he had not realized it was Jeanette. He only saw a slender lady in a pale gold dress, seated side-saddle on an expensive palfrey that was hung with green and white ribbons. The woman wore a tall hat from which a veil stirred in the wind. The veil had concealed her profile, but now she was staring directly at him, indeed she was pointing at him and, to his horror, he recognized the Countess. He also recognized the banner of the young man beside her though at first he could not believe she was with the Prince. Then he saw the grim entourage of mailed men behind the fair-haired youth and he had an impulse to flee, but instead nervelessly dropped to his knees. As the Prince, Jeanette and the horsemen approached him, he fell full length on the ground. His heart was beating wildly, his mind a whirl of panic.

'Your name?' the Prince demanded curtly.

Sir Simon opened his mouth, but no words would come.

'His name,' Jeanette said vengefully, 'is Sir Simon Jekyll. He tried to strip me naked, sire, and then he would have raped me if I had not been rescued. He stole my money, my armour, my horses, my ships and he would have taken my honour with as much delicacy as a wolf stealing a lamb.'

'Is it true?' the Prince demanded.

Sir Simon still could not speak, but the Earl of Northampton intervened. 'The ships, armour and horses, sire, were spoils of war. I granted them to him.'

'And the rest, Bohun?'

'The rest, sire?' The Earl shrugged. 'The rest Sir Simon must explain for himself.'

'But it seems he is speechless,' the Prince said. 'Have you lost your tongue, Jekyll?'

Sir Simon raised his head and caught Jeanette's gaze, and it was so triumphant that he dropped his head again. He knew he should say something, anything, but his tongue seemed too big for his mouth and he feared he would merely stammer nonsense, so he kept silent.

'You tried to smirch a lady's honour,' the Prince accused Sir Simon. Edward of Woodstock had high ideas of chivalry, for his tutors had ever read to him from the romances. He understood that war was not as gentle as the hand-written books liked to suggest, but he believed that those who were in places of honour should display it, whatever the common man might do. The Prince was also in love, another ideal encouraged by the romances. Jeanette had captivated him, and he was determined that her honour would be upheld. He spoke again, but his words were drowned by the sound of a tube gun firing. Everyone turned to stare at the castle, but the stone ball merely shattered against the gate tower, doing no damage.

'Would you fight me for the lady's honour?' the Prince demanded of Sir Simon.

Sir Simon would have been happy to fight the Prince so long as he could have been assured that his victory would bring no reprisals. He knew the boy had a reputation as a warrior, yet the Prince was not full grown and nowhere near as strong or experienced as Sir Simon, but only a fool fought against a prince and expected to win. The King, it was true, entered tournaments, but he did so disguised in plain armour, without a surcoat, so that his opponents had no idea of his identity, but if Sir Simon fought the Prince then he would not dare use his full strength, for any injury done would be repaid a thousandfold by the prince's supporters, and indeed, even as Sir Simon hesitated, the grim men behind the Prince spurred their horses forward as if offering themselves as champions for the fight. Sir Simon, overwhelmed by reality, shook his head.

'If you will not fight,' the Prince said in his high, clear voice, 'then we must assume your guilt and demand recompense. You owe the lady armour and a sword.'

'The armour was fairly taken, sire,' the Earl of Northampton pointed out.

'No man can take armour and weapons from a mere woman fairly,' the Prince snapped. 'Where is the armour now, Jekyll?'

'Lost, sir,' Sir Simon spoke for the first time. He wanted to tell the Prince the whole story, how Jeanette had arranged an ambush, but that tale ended with his own humiliation and he had the sense to keep quiet.

'Then that mail coat will have to suffice,' the Prince declared. 'Take it off. And the sword too.'

Sir Simon gaped at the Prince, but saw he was serious. He unbuckled the sword belt and let it drop, then hauled the mail coat over his head so that he was left in his shirt and breeches.

'What is in the pouch?' the Prince demanded,

pointing at the heavy leather bag suspended about Sir Simon's neck.

Sir Simon sought an answer and found none but the truth, which was that the pouch was the heavy money bag he had taken from Thomas. 'It is money, sire.'

'Then give it to her ladyship.'

Sir Simon lifted the bag over his head and held it out to Jeanette, who smiled sweetly. 'Thank you, Sir Simon,' she said.

'Your horse is forfeit too,' the Prince decreed, 'and you will leave this encampment by midday for you are not welcome in our company. You may go home, Jekyll, but in England you will not have our favour.'

Sir Simon looked into the Prince's eyes for the first time. You damned miserable little pup, he thought, with your mother's milk still sour on your unshaven lips, then he shook as he was struck by the coldness of the Prince's eyes. He bowed, knowing he was being banished, and he knew it was unfair, but there was nothing he could do except appeal to the King, yet the King owed him no favours and no great men of the realm would speak for him, and so he was effectively an outcast. He could go home to England, but there men would soon learn he had incurred royal disfavour and his life would be endless misery. He bowed, he turned and he walked away in his dirty shirt as silent men opened a path for him.

The cannon fired on. They fired four times that day and eight the next, and at the end of the two days there was a splintered rent in the castle gate that might have given entrance to a starved sparrow. The guns had done nothing except hurt the gunners' ears and shatter stone balls against the castle's ramparts. Not a Frenchman had died, though one gunner and an archer had been killed when one of the brass guns exploded into a myriad red-hot scraps of metal. The King, realizing that the attempt was ridiculous, ordered the guns taken away and the siege of the castle abandoned.

And the next day the whole army left Caen. They marched eastwards, going towards Paris, and after them crawled their wagons and their camp followers and their herds of beef cattle, and for a long time afterwards the eastern sky showed white where the dust of their marching hazed the air. But at last the dust settled and the city, ravaged and sacked, was left alone. The folk who had succeeded in escaping from the island crept back to their homes. The splintered door of the castle was pushed open and its garrison came down to see what was left of Caen. For a week the priests carried an image of St Jean about the littered streets and sprinkled holy water to get rid of the lingering stink of the enemy. They said Masses for the souls of the dead, and prayed fervently that the wretched English would meet the King of France and have their own ruin visited on them.

But at least the English were gone, and the violated city, ruined, could stir again.

Light came first. A hazy light, smeared, in which Thomas thought he could see a wide window, but a shadow moved against the window and the light went. He heard voices, then they faded. *In pascuis herbarum adclinavit me*. The words were in his head. He makes me lie down in leafy pastures. A psalm, the same psalm from which his father had quoted his dying words. *Calix meus inebrians*. My cup makes me drunk. Only he was not drunk. Breathing hurt, and his chest felt as though he was being pressed by the torture of the stones. Then there was blessed darkness and oblivion once more.

The light came again. It wavered. The shadow was there, the shadow moved towards him and a cool hand was laid on his forehead.

'I do believe you are going to live,' a man's voice said in a tone of surprise.

Thomas tried to speak, but only managed a strangled, grating sound.

'It astonishes me,' the voice went on, 'what young men can endure. Babies too. Life is marvellously strong. Such a pity we waste it.'

'It's plentiful enough,' another man said.

'The voice of the privileged,' the first man, whose hand was still on Thomas's forehead, answered. 'You take life,' he said, 'so value it as a thief values his victims.'

'And you are a victim?'

'Of course. A learned victim, a wise victim, even a valuable victim, but still a victim. And this young man, what is he?'

'An English archer,' the second voice said sourly, 'and if we had any sense we'd kill him here and now.'

'I think we shall try and feed him instead. Help me raise him.'

Hands pushed Thomas upright in the bed, and a spoonful of warm soup was put into his mouth, but he could not swallow and so spat the soup onto the blankets. Pain seared through him and the darkness came again.

The light came a third time or perhaps a fourth, he

could not tell. Perhaps he dreamed it, but this time an old man stood outlined against the bright window. The man had a long black robe, but he was not a priest or monk, for the robe was not gathered at the waist and he wore a small square black hat over his long white hair.

'God,' Thomas tried to say, though the word came out as a guttural grunt.

The old man turned. He had a long, forked beard and was holding a jordan jar. It had a narrow neck and a round belly, and the bottle was filled with a pale yellow liquid that the man held up to the light. He peered at the liquid, then swilled it about before sniffing the jar's mouth.

'Are you awake?'

'Yes.'

'And you can speak! What a doctor I am! My brilliance astonishes me; if only it would persuade my patients to pay me. But most believe I should be grateful that they don't spit at me. Would you say this urine is clear?'

Thomas nodded and wished he had not for the pain jarred through his neck and down his spine.

'You do not consider it turgid? Not dark? No, indeed not. It smells and tastes healthy too. A good flask of clear yellow urine, and there is no better sign of good health. Alas, it is not yours.' The doctor pushed open the window and poured the urine away. 'Swallow,' he instructed Thomas.

Thomas's mouth was dry, but he obediently tried to swallow and immediately gasped with pain.

'I think,' the doctor said, 'that we had best try a thin gruel. Very thin, with some oil, I believe, or better still, butter. That thing tied about your neck is a strip of cloth which has been soaked in holy water. It was not my doing, but I did not forbid it. You Christians believe in magic – indeed you could have no faith without a trust in magic – so I must indulge your beliefs. Is that a dog's paw about your neck? Don't tell me, I'm sure I don't want to know. However, when you recover, I trust you will understand that it was neither dog paws nor wet cloths that healed you, but my skill. I have bled you, I have applied poultices of dung, moss and clove, and I have sweated you. Eleanor, though, will insist it was her prayers and that tawdry strip of wet cloth that revived you.'

'Eleanor?'

'She cut you down, dear boy. You were half dead. By the time I arrived you were more dead than alive and I advised her to let you expire in peace. I told her you were halfway in what you insist is hell and that I was too old and too tired to enter into a tugging contest with the devil, but Eleanor insisted and I have ever found it difficult to resist her entreaties. Gruel with rancid butter, I think. You are weak, dear boy, very weak. Do you have a name?'

'Thomas.'

'Mine is Mordecai, though you may call me Doctor. You won't, of course. You'll call me a damned Jew, a Christ murderer, a secret worshipper of pigs and a kidnapper of Christian children.' This was all said cheerfully. 'How absurd! Who would want to kidnap children, Christian or otherwise? Vile things. The only mercy of children is that they grow up, as my son has but then, tragically, they beget more children. We do not learn life's lessons.'

'Doctor?' Thomas croaked.

'Thomas?'

'Thank you.'

'An Englishman with manners! The world's wonders never cease. Wait there, Thomas, and do not have the bad manners to die while I'm gone. I shall fetch gruel.'

'Doctor?'

'I am still here.'

'Where am I?'

'In the house of my friend, and quite safe.'

'Your friend?'

'Sir Guillaume d'Evecque, knight of the sea and of the land, and as great a fool as any I know, but a good-hearted fool. He does at least pay me.'

Thomas closed his eyes. He did not really understand what the doctor had said, or perhaps he did not believe it. His head was aching. There was pain all through his body, from his aching head down to his throbbing toes. He thought of his mother, because that was comforting, then he remembered being hauled up the tree and he shivered. He wished he could sleep again, for in sleep there was no pain, but then he was made to sit up and the doctor forced a pungent, oily gruel into his mouth and he managed not to spit it out or throw it up. There must have been mushrooms in the gruel, or else it had been infused with the hemp-like leaves that the Hookton villagers had called angel salad, for after he had eaten he had vivid dreams, but less pain. When he awoke it was dark and he was alone, but he managed to sit up and even stand, though he tottered and had to sit again.

Next morning, when the birds were calling from the oak branches where he had so nearly died, a tall man came into the room. The man was on crutches and his left thigh was swathed in bandages. He turned to look at Thomas and showed a face that was horribly scarred. A blade had cut him from the forehead to the jaw, taking the man's left eye in its savage chop. He had long yellow hair, very shaggy and full, and Thomas guessed the man had been handsome once, though now he looked like a thing of nightmare.

'Mordecai,' the man growled, 'tells me you will live.'

'With God's help,' Thomas said.

'I doubt God's interested in you,' the man said sourly. He looked to be in his thirties and had the bowed legs of a horseman and the deep chest of a man who practises hard with weapons. He swung on the crutches to the window, where he sat on the sill. His beard was streaked with white where the blade had chopped into his jaw and his voice was uncommonly deep and harsh. 'But you might live with Mordecai's help. There isn't a physician to touch him in all Normandy, though Christ alone knows how he does it. He's been squinting at my piss for a week now. I'm crippled, you Jewish halfwit, I tell him, not wounded in the bladder, but he just tells me to shut my mouth and squeeze out more drops. He'll start on you soon.' The man, who wore nothing except a long white shirt, contemplated Thomas moodily. 'I have a notion,' he growled, 'that you are the godforsaken bastard who put an arrow into my thigh. I remember seeing a son of a whore with long hair like yours, then I was hit.'

'You're Sir Guillaume?'

'I am.'

'I meant to kill you,' Thomas said.

'So why shouldn't I kill you?' Sir Guillaume asked.

'You lie in my bed, drink my gruel and breathe my air. English bastard. Worse, you're a Vexille.'

Thomas turned his head to stare at the forbidding Sir Guillaume. He said nothing, for the last three words had mystified him.

'But I choose not to kill you,' Sir Guillaume said, 'because you saved my daughter from rape.'

'Your daughter?'

'Eleanor, you fool. She's a bastard daughter, of course,' Sir Guillaume said. 'Her mother was a servant to my father, but Eleanor is all I've got left and I'm fond of her. She says you were kind to her, which is why she cut you down and why you're lying in my bed. She always was overly sentimental.' He frowned. 'But I still have a mind to slice your damned throat.'

'For four years,' Thomas said, 'I have dreamed of slitting yours.'

Sir Guillaume's one eye gazed at him balefully. 'Of course you have. You're a Vexille.'

'I've never heard of the Vexilles,' Thomas said. 'My name is Thomas of Hookton.'

Thomas half expected Sir Guillaume to frown as he tried to remember Hookton, but his recognition of the name was instant.

'Hookton,' he said, 'Hookton. Good sweet Christ, Hookton.' He was silent for a few heartbeats. 'And of course you're a damned Vexille. You have their badge on your bow.'

'My bow?'

'You gave it to Eleanor to carry! She kept it.'

Thomas closed his eyes. There was pain in his neck and down his back and in his head. 'I think it was my father's badge,' he said, 'but I don't really know because he would never talk of his family. I know he hated his own father. I wasn't very fond of my own, but your men killed him and I swore to avenge him.'

Sir Guillaume turned to gaze out of the window. 'You have truly never heard of the Vexilles?'

'Never.'

'Then you are fortunate.' He stood. 'They are the devil's offspring, and you, I suspect, are one of their pups. I would kill you, boy, with as little conscience as if I stamped on a spider, but you were kind to my bastard daughter and for that I thank you.' He limped from the room.

Leaving Thomas in pain and utterly confused.

Thomas recovered in Sir Guillaume's garden, shaded from the sun by two quince trees under which he waited anxiously for Dr Mordecai's daily verdict on the colour, consistency, taste and smell of his urine. It did not seem to matter to the doctor that Thomas's grotesquely swollen neck was subsiding, nor that he could swallow bread and meat again. All that mattered was the state of his urine. There was, the doctor declared, no finer method of diagnosis. 'The urine betrays all. If it smells rank, or if it is dark, if it tastes of vinegar or should it be cloudy then it is time for vigorous doctoring. But good, pale, sweet-smelling urine like this is the worst news of all.'

'The worst?' Thomas asked, alarmed.

'It means fewer fees for a physician, dear boy.'

The doctor had survived the sack of Caen by hiding in a neighbour's pig shed. 'They slaughtered the pigs, but missed the Jew. Mind you, they broke all my instruments, scattered my medicines, shattered all but three of my bottles and burned my house. Which is why I am forced to live here.' He shuddered, as though living in Sir Guillaume's mansion was a hardship. He smelled Thomas's urine and then, uncertain of his diagnosis, spilled a drop onto a finger and tasted it. 'Very fine,' he said, 'lamentably fine.' He poured the jar's contents onto a bed of lavender where bees were at work. 'So I lost everything,' he said, 'and this after we were assured by our great lords that the city would be safe!' Originally, the doctor had told Thomas, the leaders of the garrison had insisted on defending only the walled city and the castle, but they needed the help of the townsfolk to man the walls and those townsfolk had insisted that the Île St Jean be defended, for that was where the city's wealth lay, and so, at the very last minute, the garrison had streamed across the bridge to disaster. 'Fools,' Mordecai said scornfully, 'fools in steel and glory. Fools.'

Thomas and Mordecai were sharing the house while Sir Guillaume visited his estate in Evecque, some thirty miles south of Caen, where he had gone to raise more men. 'He will fight on,' the doctor said, 'wounded leg or not.'

'What will he do with me?'

'Nothing,' the doctor said confidently. 'He likes you, despite all his bluster. You saved Eleanor, didn't you? He's always been fond of her. His wife wasn't, but he is.'

'What happened to his wife?'

'She died,' Mordecai said, 'she just died.'

Thomas could eat properly now and his strength returned fast so that he could walk about the Île St Jean with Eleanor. The island looked as though a plague had struck, for over half the houses were empty and even those that were occupied were still blighted by the sack. Shutters were missing, doors splintered and the shops had no goods. Some country folk were selling beans, peas and cheeses from wagons, and small boys were offering fresh perch taken from the rivers, but they were still hungry days. They were also nervous days, for the city's survivors feared that the hated English might return and the island was still haunted by the sickly smell of the corpses in the two rivers where the gulls, rats and dogs grew fat.

Eleanor hated walking about the city, preferring to go south into the countryside where blue dragonflies flew above water lilies in the streams that twisted between fields of overripe rye, barley and wheat.

'I love harvest time,' she told Thomas. 'We used to go into the fields and help.' There would be little harvest this year, for there were no folk to cut the grain and so the corn buntings were stripping the heads and pigeons were squabbling over the leavings. 'There should be a feast at harvest's end,' Eleanor said wistfully.

'We had a feast too,' Thomas said, 'and we used to hang corn dollies in the church.'

'Corn dollies?'

He made her a little doll from straw. 'We used to hang thirteen of these above the altar,' he told her, 'one for Christ and one each for the Apostles.' He picked some cornflowers and gave them to Eleanor, who threaded them into her hair. It was very fair hair, like sunlit gold.

They talked incessantly and one day Thomas asked her again about the lance and this time Eleanor nodded.

'I lied to you,' she said, 'because he did have it, but it was stolen.'

'Who stole it?'

She touched her face. 'The man who took his eye.'

'A man called Vexille?'

She nodded solemnly. 'I think so. But it wasn't here, it was in Evecque. That's his real home. He got the Caen house when he married.'

'Tell me about the Vexilles,' Thomas urged her.

'I know nothing of them,' Eleanor said, and he believed her.

They were sitting by a stream where two swans floated and a heron stalked frogs in a reedbed. Thomas had talked earlier of walking away from Caen to find the English army and his words must have been weighing on Eleanor's mind for she frowned at him.

'Will you really go?'

'I don't know.' He wanted to be with the army, for that was where he belonged, though he did not know how he was to find it, nor how he was to survive in a countryside where the English had made themselves hated, but he also wanted to stay. He wanted to learn more about the Vexilles and only Sir Guillaume could satisfy that hunger. And, day by day, he wanted to be with Eleanor. There was a calm gentleness in her that Jeanette had never possessed, a gentleness that made him treat her with tenderness for fear that otherwise he would break her. He never tired of watching her long face with its slightly hollow cheeks and bony nose and big eyes. She was embarrassed by his scrutiny, but did not tell him to stop.

'Sir Guillaume,' she told him, 'tells me I look like my mother, but I don't remember her very well.'

Sir Guillaume came back to Caen with a dozen men-at-arms whom he had hired in northern Alençon. He would lead them to war, he said, along with the half-dozen of his men who had survived the fall of Caen. His leg was still sore, but he could walk without crutches and on the day of his return he summarily ordered Thomas to go with him to the church of St Jean. Eleanor, working in the kitchen, joined them as they left the house and Sir Guillaume did not forbid her to come.

Folk bowed as Sir Guillaume passed and many sought his assurance that the English were truly gone.

'They are marching towards Paris,' he would answer, 'and our king will trap them and kill them.'

'You think so?' Thomas asked after one such assurance.

'I pray so,' Sir Guillaume growled. 'That's what the King is for, isn't it? To protect his people? And God knows, we need protection. I'm told that if you climb that tower,' he nodded towards the church of St Jean that was their destination, 'you can see the smoke from the towns your army has burned. They are conducting a *chevauchée*.'

'*Chevauchée?*' Eleanor asked.

Her father sighed. 'A *chevauchée*, child, is when you march in a great line through your enemy's country and you burn, destroy and break everything in your path. The object of such barbarity is to force your enemy to come out from his fortresses and fight, and I think our king will oblige the English.'

'And the English bows,' Thomas said, 'will cut his army down like hay.'

Sir Guillaume looked angry at that, but then

shrugged. 'A marching army gets worn down,' he said. 'The horses go lame, the boots wear out and the arrows run out. And you haven't seen the might of France, boy. For every knight of yours we have six. You can shoot your arrows till your bows break, but we'll still have enough men left to kill you.' He fished in a pouch hanging at his belt and gave some small coins to the beggars at the churchyard gate, which lay close to the new grave where the five hundred corpses had been buried. It was now a mound of raw earth dotted with dandelions and it stank, for when the English had dug the grave they had struck water not far beneath the surface and so the pit was too shallow and the earth covering was too thin to contain the corruption the grave concealed.

Eleanor clapped a hand to her mouth, then hurried up the steps into the church where the archers had auctioned the town's wives and daughters. The priests had thrice exorcized the church with prayers and holy water, but it still had a sad air, for the statues were broken and the windows shattered. Sir Guillaume genuflected towards the main altar, then led Thomas and Eleanor up a side aisle where a painting on the limewashed wall showed St John escaping from the cauldron of boiling oil that the Emperor Domitian had prepared for him. The saint was shown as an ethereal form, half smoke and half man, floating away in the air while the Roman soldiers looked on in perplexity.

Sir Guillaume approached a side altar where he dropped to his knees beside a great black flagstone and Thomas, to his surprise, saw that the Frenchman was weeping from his one eye. 'I brought you here,' Sir Guillaume said, 'to teach you a lesson about your family.'

Thomas did not contradict him. He did not know that he was a Vexille, but the yale on the silver badge suggested he was.

'Beneath that stone,' Sir Guillaume said, 'lies my wife and my two children. A boy and a girl. He was six, she was eight and their mother was twenty-five years old. The house here belonged to her father. He gave me his daughter as ransom for a boat I captured. It was mere piracy, not war, but I gained a good wife from it.' The tears were flowing now and he closed his eye. Eleanor stood beside him, a hand on his shoulder, while Thomas waited. 'Do you know,' Sir Guillaume asked after a while, 'why we went to Hookton?'

'We thought because the tide took you away from Poole.'

'No, we went to Hookton on purpose. I was paid to go there by a man who called himself the Harlequin.'

'Like hellequin?' Thomas asked.

'It is the same word, only he used the Italian form. A devil's soul, laughing at God, and he even looked like you.' Sir Guillaume crossed himself, then reached out to trace a finger down the edge of the stone. 'We went to fetch a relic from the church. You knew that already, surely?'

Thomas nodded. 'And I have sworn to get it back.'

Sir Guillaume seemed to sneer at that ambition. 'I thought it was all foolishness, but in those days I thought all life was foolishness. Why would some miserable church in an insignificant English village have a precious relic? But the Harlequin insisted he was right, and when we took the village we found the relic.'

'The lance of St George,' Thomas said flatly.

'The lance of St George,' Sir Guillaume agreed. 'I had

a contract with the Harlequin. He paid me a little money, and the balance was kept by a monk in the abbey here. He was a monk that everyone trusted, a scholar, a fierce man whom folk said would become a saint, but when we returned I found that Brother Martin had fled and he had taken the money with him. So I refused to give the lance to the Harlequin. Bring me nine hundred livres in good silver, I told him, and the lance is yours, but he would not pay. So I kept the lance. I kept it in Evecque and the months passed and I heard nothing and I thought the lance had been forgotten. Then, two years ago, in the spring, the Harlequin returned. He came with men-at-arms and he captured the manor. He slaughtered everyone – everyone – and took the lance.'

Thomas stared at the black flagstone. 'You lived?'

'Scarcely,' Sir Guillaume said. He hauled up his black jacket and showed a terrible scar on his belly. 'They gave me three wounds,' he went on. 'One to the head, one to the belly and one to the leg. They told me the one to the head was because I was a fool with no brains, the one in the guts was a reward for my greed and the one to the leg was so I would limp down to hell. Then they left me to watch the corpses of my wife and children while I died. But I lived, thanks to Mordecai.' He stood, wincing as he put his weight onto his left leg. 'I lived,' he said grimly, 'and I swore I would find the man who did that,' he pointed at the flagstone, 'and send his soul screaming into the pit. It took me a year to discover who he was, and you know how I did it? When he came to Evecque he had his men's shields covered with black cloth, but I slashed the cloth of one with my sword and saw the yale. So I asked men about the yale. I asked them in Paris and Anjou, in Burgundy and the Dauphiné, and in the end I found my answer. And where did I find it? After asking the length and breadth of France I found it here, in Caen. A man here knew the badge. The Harlequin is a man called Vexille. I do not know his first name, I do not know his rank, I just know he is a devil called Vexille.'

'So the Vexilles have the lance?'

'They have. And the man who killed my family killed your father.' Sir Guillaume looked ashamed for a brief instant. 'I killed your mother. I think I did, anyway, but she attacked me and I was angry.' He shrugged. 'But I did not kill your father, and in killing your mother I did nothing more than you have done in Brittany.'

'True,' Thomas admitted. He looked into Sir Guillaume's eye and could feel no hatred for his mother's death. 'So we share an enemy,' Thomas said.

'And that enemy,' Sir Guillaume said, 'is the devil.'

He said it grimly, then crossed himself. Thomas suddenly felt cold, for he had found his enemy, and his enemy was Lucifer.

That evening Mordecai rubbed a salve into Thomas's neck. 'It is almost healed, I think,' he said, 'and the pain will go, though perhaps a little will remain to remind you of how close you came to death.' He sniffed the garden scents. 'So Sir Guillaume told you the story of his wife?'

'Yes.'

'And you are related to the man who killed his wife?'

'I don't know,' Thomas said, 'truly I don't, but the yale suggests I am.'

'And Sir Guillaume probably killed your mother, and the man who killed his wife killed your father, and Sir Simon Jekyll tried to kill you.' Mordecai shook his head. 'I nightly lament that I was not born a Christian. I could carry a weapon and join the sport.' He handed Thomas a bottle. 'Perform,' he commanded, 'and what, by the by, is a yale?'

'A heraldic beast,' Thomas explained.

The doctor sniffed. 'God, in His infinite wisdom, made the fishes and the whales on the fifth day, and on the sixth he made the beasts of the land, and He looked at what He had done and saw that it was good. But not good enough for the heralds, who have to add wings, horns, tusks and claws to His inadequate work. Is that all you can do?'

'For the moment.'

'I'd get more juice from squeezing a walnut,' he grumbled, and shuffled away.

Eleanor must have been watching for his departure, for she appeared from under the pear trees that grew at the garden's end and gestured towards the river gate. Thomas followed her down to the bank of the River Orne where they watched an excited trio of small boys trying to spear a pike with English arrows left after the city's capture.

'Will you help my father?' Eleanor asked.

'Help him?'

'You said his enemy was your enemy.'

Thomas sat on the grass and she sat beside him. 'I don't know,' he said. He still did not really believe in any of it. There was a lance, he knew that, and a mystery about his family, but he was reluctant to admit that the lance and the mystery must govern his whole life.

'Does that mean you'll go back to the English army?' Eleanor asked in a small voice.

'I want to stay here,' Thomas said after a pause, 'to be with you.'

She must have known he was going to say something of the sort, but she still blushed and gazed at the swirling water where fish rose to the swarms of insects, and the three boys vainly splashed. 'You must have a woman,' she said softly.

'I did,' Thomas said, and he told her about Jeanette and how she had found the Prince of Wales and so abandoned him without a glance. 'I will never understand her,' he admitted.

'But you love her?' Eleanor asked directly.

'No,' Thomas said.

'You say that because you're with me,' Eleanor declared.

He shook his head. 'My father had a book of St Augustine's sayings and there was one that always puzzled me.' He frowned, trying to remember the Latin. '*Nondum amabam, et amare amabam*. I did not love, but yearned to love.'

Eleanor gave him a sceptical look. 'A very elaborate way of saying you're lonely.'

'Yes,' Thomas agreed.

'So what will you do?' she asked.

Thomas did not speak for a while. He was thinking of the penance he had been given by Father Hobbe. 'I suppose one day I must find the man who killed my father,' he said after a while.

'But what if he is the devil?' she asked seriously.

'Then I shall wear garlic,' Thomas said lightly, 'and pray to St Guinefort.'

303

She looked at the darkening water. 'Did St Augustine really say that thing?'

'*Nondum amabam, et amare amabam*?' Thomas said. 'Yes, he did.'

'I know how he felt,' Eleanor said, and rested her head on his shoulder.

Thomas did not move. He had a choice. Follow the lance or take his black bow back to the army. In truth he did not know what he should do. But Eleanor's body was warm against his and it was comforting and that, for the moment, was enough and so, for the moment, he would stay.

Next morning Sir Guillaume, escorted now by a half-dozen men-at-arms, took Thomas to the Abbaye aux Hommes. A crowd of petitioners stood at the gates, wanting food and clothing that the monks did not have, though the abbey itself had escaped the worst of the plundering because it had been the quarters of the King and of the Prince of Wales. The monks themselves had fled at the approach of the English army. Some had died on the Île St Jean, but most had gone south to a brother house and among those was Brother Germain who, when Sir Guillaume arrived, had just returned from his brief exile.

Brother Germain was tiny, ancient and bent, a wisp of a man with white hair, myopic eyes and delicate hands with which he was trimming a goose quill.

'The English,' the old man said, 'use these feathers for their arrows. We use them for God's word.' Brother Germain, Thomas was told, had been in charge of the monastery's scriptorium for more than thirty years. 'In the course of copying books,' the monk explained, 'one discovers knowledge whether one wishes it or not. Most of it is quite useless, of course. How is Mordecai? He lives?'

'He lives,' Sir Guillaume said, 'and sends you this.' He

305

put a clay pot, sealed with wax, on the sloping surface of the writing desk. The pot slid down until Brother Germain trapped it and pushed it into a pouch. 'A salve,' Sir Guillaume explained to Thomas, 'for Brother Germain's joints.'

'Which ache,' the monk said, 'and only Mordecai can relieve them 'Tis a pity he will burn in hell, but in heaven, I am assured, I shall need no ointments. Who is this?' He peered at Thomas.

'A friend,' Sir Guillaume said, 'who brought me this.' He was carrying Thomas's bow, which he now laid across the desk and tapped the silver plate. Brother Germain stooped to inspect the badge and Thomas heard a sharp intake of breath.

'The yale,' Brother Germain said. He pushed the bow away, then blew the scraps from his sharpened quill off the desk. 'The beast was introduced by the heralds in the last century. Back then, of course, there was real scholarship in the world. Not like today. I get young men from Paris whose heads are stuffed with wool, yet they claim to have doctorates.'

He took a sheet of scrap parchment from a shelf, laid it on the desk and dipped his quill in a pot of vermilion ink. He let a glistening drop fall onto the parchment and then, with the skill gained in a lifetime, drew the ink out of the drop in quick strokes. He hardly seemed to be taking notice of what he was doing, but Thomas, to his amazement, saw a yale taking shape on the parchment.

'The beast is said to be mythical,' Brother Germain said, flicking the quill to make a tusk, 'and maybe it is. Most heraldic beasts seem to be inventions. Who has seen a unicorn?' He put another drop of ink on the parchment, paused a heartbeat, then began on the beast's raised paws. 'There is, however, a notion that the yale exists in Ethiopia. I could not say, not having travelled east of Rouen, nor have I met any traveller who has been there, if indeed Ethiopia even exists.' He frowned. 'The yale is mentioned by Pliny, however, which suggests it was known to the Romans, though God knows they were a credulous race. The beast is said to possess both horns and tusks, which seems extravagant, and is usually depicted as being silver with yellow spots. Alas, our pigments were stolen by the English, but they left us the vermilion which, I suppose, was kind of them. It comes from cinnabar, I'm told. Is that a plant? Father Jacques, rest his soul, always claimed it grows in the Holy Land and perhaps it does. Do I detect that you are limping, Sir Guillaume?'

'A bastard English archer put an arrow in my leg,' Sir Guillaume said, 'and I pray nightly that his soul will roast in hell.'

'You should, instead, give thanks that he was inaccurate. Why do you bring me an English war bow decorated with a yale?'

'Because I thought it would interest you,' Sir Guillaume said, 'and because my young friend here,' he touched Thomas's shoulder, 'wants to know about the Vexilles.'

'He would do much better to forget them,' Brother Germain grumbled.

He was perched on a tall chair and now peered about the room where a dozen young monks tidied the mess left by the monastery's English occupiers. Some of them chattered as they worked, provoking a frown from Brother Germain.

'This is not Caen marketplace!' he snapped. 'If you want to gossip, go to the lavatories. I wish I could. Ask Mordecai if he has an unguent for the bowels, would you?' He glowered about the room for an instant, then struggled to pick up the bow that he had propped against the desk. He looked intently at the yale for an instant, then put the bow down. 'There was always a rumour that a branch of the Vexille family went to England. This seems to confirm it.'

'Who are they?' Thomas asked.

Brother Germain seemed irritated by the direct question, or perhaps the whole subject of the Vexilles made him uncomfortable. 'They were the rulers of Astarac,' he said, 'a county on the borders of Languedoc and the Agenais. That, of course, should tell you all you need to know of them.'

'It tells me nothing,' Thomas confessed.

'Then you probably have a doctorate from Paris!' The old man chuckled at this jest. 'The Counts of Astarac, young man, were Cathars. Southern France was infested by that damned heresy, and Astarac was at the centre of the evil.' He made the sign of the cross with fingers deep-stained by pigments. '*Habere non potest*,' he said solemnly, '*Deum patrem qui ecclesiam non habet matrem.*'

'St Cyprian,' Thomas said. ' "He cannot have God as his father who does not have the Church as his mother." '

'I see you are not from Paris after all,' Brother Germain said. 'The Cathars rejected the Church, looking for salvation within their own dark souls. What would become of the Church if we all did that? If we all pursued our own whims? If God is within us then we need no Church and no Holy Father to lead us to His mercy, and that notion is the most pernicious of heresies, and where did it lead the Cathars? To a life of dissipation, of fleshly lust, of pride and of perversion. They denied the divinity of Christ!' Brother Germain made the sign of the cross again.

'And the Vexilles were Cathars?' Sir Guillaume prompted the old man.

'I suspect they were devil worshippers,' Brother Germain retorted, 'but certainly the Counts of Astarac protected the Cathars, they and a dozen other lords. They were called the dark lords and very few of them were Perfects. The Perfects were the sect leaders, the heresiarchs, and they abstained from wine, intercourse and meat, and no Vexille would willingly abandon those three joys. But the Cathars allowed such sinners to be among their ranks and promised them the joys of heaven if they recanted before their deaths. The dark lords liked such a promise and, when the heresy was assailed by the Church, they fought bitterly.' He shook his head. 'This was a hundred years ago! The Holy Father and the King of France destroyed the Cathars, and Astarac was one of the last fortresses to fall. The fight was dreadful, the dead innumerable, but the heresiarchs and the dark lords were finally scotched.'

'Yet some escaped?' Sir Guillaume suggested gently.

Brother Germain was silent for a while, gazing at the drying vermilion ink. 'There was a story,' he said, 'that some of the Cathar lords did survive, and that they took their riches to countries all across Europe. There is even a rumour that the heresy yet survives, hidden in the lands where Burgundy and the Italian states meet.' He made the sign of the cross. 'I think a part of the Vexille family went to England, to hide there, for it was in England, Sir Guillaume, that you found the lance of St George. Vexille . . .' He said the name thoughtfully. 'It derives, of course, from *vexillaire*, a standard-bearer, and it is said that an early Vexille discovered the lance while on the crusades and thereafter carried it as a standard. It was certainly a symbol of power in those old days. Myself? I am sceptical of these relics. The abbot assures me he has seen three foreskins of the infant Jesus and even I, who hold Him blessed above all things, doubt He was so richly endowed, but I have asked some questions about this lance. There is a legend attached to it. It is said that the man who carries the lance into battle cannot be defeated. Mere legend, of course, but belief in such nonsense inspires the ignorant, and there are few more ignorant than soldiers. What troubles me most, though, is their purpose.'

'Whose purpose?' Thomas asked.

'There is a story,' Brother Germain said, ignoring the question, 'that before the fall of the last heretic fortresses, the surviving dark lords made an oath. They knew the war was lost, they knew their strongholds must fall and that the Inquisition and the forces of God would destroy their people, and so they made an oath to visit vengeance on their enemies. One day, they swore, they would bring down the Throne of France and the Holy Mother Church, and to do it they would use the power of their holiest relics.'

'The lance of St George?' Thomas asked.

'That too,' Brother Germain said.

'That too?' Sir Guillaume repeated the words in a puzzled tone.

Brother Germain dipped his quill and put another

glistening drop of ink on the parchment. Then, deftly, he finished his copy of the badge on Thomas's bow. 'The yale,' he said, 'I have seen before, but the badge you showed me is different. The beast is holding a chalice. But not any chalice, Sir Guillaume. You are right, the bow interests me, and frightens me, for the yale is holding the Grail. The holy, blessed and most precious Grail. It was always rumoured that the Cathars possessed the Grail. There is a tawdry lump of green glass in Genoa Cathedral that is said to be the Grail, but I doubt our dear Lord drank from such a bauble. No, the real Grail exists, and whoever holds it possesses power above all men on earth.' He put down the quill. 'I fear, Sir Guillaume, that the dark lords want their revenge. They gather their strength. But they hide still and the Church has not yet taken notice. Nor will it until the danger is obvious, and by then it will be too late.' Brother Germain lowered his head so that Thomas could only see the bald pink patch among the white hair. 'It is all prophesied,' the monk said; 'it is all in the books.'

'What books?' Sir Guillaume asked.

'*Et confortabitur rex austri et de principibus eius praevalebit super eum,*' Brother Germain said softly.

Sir Guillaume looked quizzically at Thomas. 'And the King from the south will be mighty,' Thomas reluctantly translated, 'but one of his princes will be stronger than him.'

'The Cathars are of the south,' Brother Germain said, 'and the prophet Daniel foresaw it all.' He raised his pigment-stained hands. 'The fight will be terrible, for the soul of the world is at stake, and they will use any weapon, even a woman. *Filiaque regis austri veniet ad regem aquilonis facere amicitiam.*'

'The daughter of the King of the south,' Thomas said, 'shall come to the King of the north and make a treaty.'

Brother Germain heard the distaste in Thomas's voice. 'You don't believe it?' he hissed. 'Why do you think we keep the scriptures from the ignorant? They contain all sorts of prophecies, young man, and each of them given direct to us by God, but such knowledge is confusing to the unlearned. Men go mad when they know too much.' He made the sign of the cross. 'I thank God I shall be dead soon and taken to the bliss above while you must struggle with this darkness.'

Thomas walked to the window and watched two wagons of grain being unloaded by novices. Sir Guillaume's men-at-arms were playing dice in the cloister. That was real, he thought, not some babbling prophet. His father had ever warned him against prophecy. It drives men's minds awry, he had said, and was that why his own mind had gone astray?

'The lance,' Thomas said, trying to cling to fact instead of fancy, 'was taken to England by the Vexille family. My father was one of them, but he fell out with the family and he stole the lance and hid it in his church. He was killed there, and at his death he told me it was his brother's son who did it. I think it is that man, my cousin, who called himself the Harlequin.' He turned to look at Brother Germain. 'My father was a Vexille, but he was no heretic. He was a sinner, yes, but he struggled against his sin, he hated his own father, and he was a loyal son of the Church.'

'He was a priest,' Sir Guillaume explained to the monk.

'And you are his son?' Brother Germain asked in a

disapproving tone. The other monks had abandoned their tidying and were listening avidly.

'I am a priest's son,' Thomas said, 'and a good Christian.'

'So the family discovered where the lance was hidden,' Sir Guillaume took up the story, 'and hired me to retrieve it. But forgot to pay me.'

Brother Germain appeared not to have heard. He was staring at Thomas. 'You are English?'

'The bow is mine,' Thomas acknowledged.

'So you are a Vexille?'

Thomas shrugged. 'It would seem so.'

'Then you are one of the dark lords,' Brother Germain said.

Thomas shook his head. 'I am a Christian,' he said firmly.

'Then you have a God-given duty,' the small man said with surprising force, 'which is to finish the work that was left undone a hundred years ago. Kill them all! Kill them! And kill the woman. You hear me, boy? Kill the daughter of the King of the south before she seduces France to heresy and wickedness.'

'If we can even find the Vexilles,' Sir Guillaume said dubiously, and Thomas noted the word 'we'. 'They don't display their badge. I doubt they use the name Vexille. They hide.'

'But they have the lance now,' Brother Germain said, 'and they will use it for the first of their vengeances. They will destroy France, and in the chaos that ensues, they will attack the Church.' He moaned, as if he was in physical pain. 'You must take away their power, and their power is the Grail.'

So it was not just the lance that Thomas must save.

313

To Father Hobbe's charge had been added all of Christendom. He wanted to laugh. Catharism had died a hundred years before, scourged and burned and dug out of the land like couch grass grubbed from a field! Dark lords, daughters of kings and princes of darkness were figments of the troubadours, not the business of archers. Except that when he looked at Sir Guillaume he saw that the Frenchman was not mocking the task. He was staring at a crucifix hanging on the scriptorium wall and mouthing a silent prayer. God help me, Thomas thought, God help me, but I am being asked to do what all the great knights of Arthur's round table failed to do: to find the Grail.

Philip of Valois, King of France, ordered every Frenchman of military age to gather at Rouen. Demands went to his vassals and appeals were carried to his allies. He had expected the walls of Caen to hold the English for weeks, but the city had fallen in a day and the panicked survivors were spreading across northern France with terrible stories of devils unleashed.

Rouen, nestled in a great loop of the Seine, filled with warriors. Thousands of Genoese crossbowmen came by galley, beaching their ships on the river's bank and thronging the city's taverns, while knights and men-at-arms arrived from Anjou and Picardy, from Alençon and Champagne, from Maine, Touraine and Berry. Every blacksmith's shop became an armoury, every house a barracks and every tavern a brothel. More men arrived, until the city could scarce contain them, and tents had to be set up in the fields south of the city. Wagons crossed the bridge, loaded with hay and newly harvested grain from the rich farmlands north of the river, while from the Seine's southern bank came rumours. The English had taken Evreux, or perhaps it was Bernay? Smoke had been seen at Lisieux, and archers were swarming through the forest of Brotonne. A nun in Louviers had a dream in which the dragon killed St George. King Philip ordered the woman brought to Rouen, but she had a harelip, a hunchback and a stammer, and when she was presented to the King she proved unable to recount the dream, let alone confide God's strategy to His Majesty. She just shuddered and wept and the King dismissed her angrily, but took consolation from the bishop's astrologer who said Mars was in the ascendant and that meant victory was certain.

Rumour said the English were marching on Paris, then another rumour claimed they were going south to protect their territories in Gascony. It was said that every person in Caen had died, that the castle was rubble; then a story went about that the English themselves were dying of a sickness. King Philip, ever a nervous man, became petulant, demanding news, but his advisers persuaded their irritable master that wherever the English were they must eventually starve if they were kept south of the great River Seine that twisted like a snake from Paris to the sea. Edward's men were wasting the land, so needed to keep moving if they were to find food, and if the Seine was blocked then they could not go north towards the harbours on the Channel coast where they might expect supplies from England.

'They use arrows like a woman uses money,' Charles, the Count of Alençon and the King's younger brother, advised Philip, 'but they cannot fetch their arrows from

France. They are brought to them by sea, and the further they go from the sea, the greater their problems.' So if the English were kept south of the Seine then they must eventually fight or make an ignominious retreat to Normandy.

'What of Paris? Paris? What of Paris?' the King demanded.

'Paris will not fall,' the Count assured his brother. The city lay north of the Seine, so the English would need to cross the river and assault the largest ramparts in Christendom, and all the while the garrison would be showering them with crossbow bolts and the missiles from the hundreds of small iron guns that had been mounted on the city walls.

'Maybe they will go south?' Philip worried. 'To Gascony?'

'If they march to Gascony,' the Count said, 'then they will have no boots by the time they arrive, and their arrow store will be gone. Let us pray they do go to Gascony, but above all things pray they do not reach the Seine's northern bank.' For if the English crossed the Seine they would go to the nearest Channel port to receive reinforcements and supplies and, by now, the Count knew, the English would be needing supplies. A marching army tired itself, its men became sick and its horses lame. An army that marched too long would eventually wear out like a tired crossbow.

So the French reinforced the great fortresses that guarded the Seine's crossings and where a bridge could not be guarded, such as the sixteen-arched bridge at Poissy, it was demolished. A hundred men with sledge-hammers broke down the parapets and hammered the stonework of the arches into the river to leave the fifteen stumps of the broken piers studding the Seine like the stepping stones of a giant, while Poissy itself, which lay south of the Seine and was reckoned indefensible, was abandoned and its people evacuated to Paris. The wide river was being turned into an impassable barrier to trap the English in an area where their food must eventually run short. Then, when the devils were weakened, the French would punish them for the terrible damage they had wrought on France. The English were still burning towns and destroying farms so that, in those long summer days, the western and southern horizons were so smeared by smoke plumes that it seemed as if there were permanent clouds on the skylines. At night the world's edge glowed and folk fleeing the fires came to Rouen where, because so many could not be housed or fed, they were ordered across the river and away to wherever they might find shelter.

Sir Simon Jekyll, and Henry Colley, his man-at-arms, were among the fugitives, and they were not refused admittance, for they both rode destriers and were in mail. Colley wore his own mail and rode his own horse, but Sir Simon's mount and gear had been stolen from one of his other men-at-arms before he fled from Caen. Both men carried shields, but they had stripped the leather covers from the willow boards so that the shields bore no device, thus declaring themselves to be masterless men for hire. Scores like them came to the city, seeking a lord who could offer food and pay, but none arrived with the anger that filled Sir Simon.

It was the injustice that galled him. It burned his soul, giving him a lust for revenge. He had come so close to paying all his debts – indeed, when the money from the sale of Jeanette's ships was paid from England he

317

had expected to be free of all encumbrances – but now he was a fugitive. He knew he could have slunk back to England, but any man out of favour with the King or the King's eldest son could expect to be treated as a rebel, and he would be fortunate if he kept an acre of land, let alone his freedom. So he had preferred flight, trusting that his sword would win back the privileges he had lost to the Breton bitch and her puppy lover, and Henry Colley had ridden with him in the belief that any man as skilled in arms as Sir Simon could not fail.

No one questioned their presence in Rouen. Sir Simon's French was tinged with the accent of England's gentry, but so was the French of a score of other men from Normandy. What Sir Simon needed now was a patron, a man who would feed him and give him the chance to fight back against his persecutors, and there were plenty of great men looking for followers. In the fields south of Rouen, where the looping river narrowed the land, a pasture had been set aside as a tourney ground where, in front of a knowing crowd of men-at-arms, anyone could enter the lists to show their prowess. This was not a serious tournament – the swords were blunt and lances were tipped with wooden blocks – but rather it was a chance for masterless men to show their prowess with weapons, and a score of knights, the champions of dukes, counts, viscounts and mere lords, were the judges. Dozens of hopeful men were entering the lists, and any horseman who could last more than a few minutes against the well-mounted and superbly armed champions was sure to find a place in the entourage of a great nobleman.

Sir Simon, on his stolen horse and with his ancient

battered sword, was one of the least impressive men to ride into the pasture. He had no lance, so one of the champions drew a sword and rode to finish him off. At first no one took particular notice of the two men for other combats were taking place, but when the champion was sprawling on the grass and Sir Simon, untouched, rode on, the crowd took notice.

A second champion challenged Sir Simon and was startled by the fury which confronted him. He called out that the combat was not to the death, but merely a demonstration of swordplay, but Sir Simon gritted his teeth and hacked with the sword so savagely that the champion spurred and wheeled his horse away rather than risk injury. Sir Simon turned his horse in the pasture's centre, daring another man to face him, but instead a squire trotted a mare to the field's centre and wordlessly offered the Englishman a lance.

'Who sent it?' Sir Simon demanded.

'My lord.'

'Who is?'

'There,' the squire said, pointing to the pasture's end where a tall man in black armour and riding a black horse waited with his lance.

Sir Simon sheathed his sword and took the lance. It was heavy and not well balanced, and he had no lance rest in his armour that would cradle the long butt to help keep the point raised, but he was a strong man and an angry one, and he reckoned he could manage the cumbersome weapon long enough to break the stranger's confidence.

No other men fought on the field now. They just watched. Wagers were being made and all of them favoured the man in black. Most of the onlookers had seen him fight before, and his horse, his armour and his weapons were all plainly superior. He wore plate mail and his horse stood at least a hand's breadth taller than Sir Simon's sorry mount. His visor was down, so Sir Simon could not see the man's face, while Sir Simon himself had no faceplate, merely an old, cheap helmet like those worn by England's archers. Only Henry Colley laid a bet on Sir Simon, though he had difficulty in doing it for his French was rudimentary, but the money was at last taken.

The stranger's shield was black and decorated with a simple white cross, a device unknown to Sir Simon, while his horse had a black trapper that swept the pasture as the beast began to walk. That was the only signal the stranger gave and Sir Simon responded by lowering the lance and kicking his own horse forward. They were a hundred paces apart and both men moved swiftly into the canter. Sir Simon watched his opponent's lance, judging how firmly it was held. The man was good, for the lance tip scarcely wavered despite the horse's uneven motion. The shield was covering his trunk, as it should be.

If this had been a battle, if the man with the strange shield had not offered Sir Simon a chance of advancement, he might have lowered his own lance to strike his opponent's horse. Or, a more difficult strike, thrust the weapon's tip into the high pommel of his saddle. Sir Simon had seen a lance go clean through the wood and leather of a saddle to gouge into a man's groin, and it was ever a killing blow. But today he was required to show the skill of a knight, to strike clean and hard, and at the same time defend himself from the oncoming lance. The skill of that was to deflect the thrust which, having the weight of a horse behind it, could break a man's back by throwing him against the high cantle. The shock of two heavy horsemen meeting, and with all their weight concentrated into lance points, was like being hit by a cannon's stone.

Sir Simon was not thinking about any of this. He was watching the oncoming lance, glancing at the white cross on the shield where his own lance was aimed, and guiding his horse with pressure from his knees. He had trained to this from the time he could first sit on a pony. He had spent hours tilting at a quintain in his father's yard, and more hours schooling stallions to endure the noise and chaos of battle. He moved his horse slightly to the left like a man wanting to widen the angle at which the lances would strike and so deflect some of their force, and he noted that the stranger did not follow the move to straighten the line, but seemed happy to accept the lesser risk. Then both men rowelled back their spurs and the destriers went into the gallop. Sir Simon touched the horse's right side and straightened the line himself, driving hard at the stranger now, and leaning slightly forward to ready himself for the blow. His opponent was trying to swing towards him, but it was too late. Sir Simon's lance cracked against the black and white shield with a thump that hurled Sir Simon back, but the stranger's lance was not centred and banged against Sir Simon's plain shield and glanced off.

Sir Simon's lance broke into three pieces and he let it fall as he pressed his knee to turn the horse. His opponent's lance was across his body now and was encumbering the black-armoured knight. Sir Simon drew his sword and, while the other man was still trying to rid himself of the lance, gave a backswing that struck his opponent like a hammer blow.

The field was still. Henry Colley held out a hand for his winnings. The man pretended not to understand his crude French, but he understood the knife that the yellow-eyed Englishman suddenly produced and the coins, just as suddenly, appeared.

The knight in the black armour did not continue the fight, but instead curbed his horse and pushed up his visor. 'Who are you?'

'My name is Sir Simon Jekyll.'

'English?'

'I was.'

The two horses stood beside each other. The stranger threw down his lance and hung the shield from his pommel. He had a sallow face with a thin black moustache, clever eyes and a broken nose. He was a young man, not a boy, but a year or two older than Sir Simon.

'What do you want?' he asked Sir Simon.

'A chance to kill the Prince of Wales.'

The man smiled. 'Is that all?'

'Money, food, land, women,' Sir Simon said.

The man gestured to the side of the pasture. 'There are great lords here, Sir Simon, who will offer you pay, food and girls. I can pay you too, but not so well; I can feed you, though it will be common stuff; and the girls you must find for yourself. What I will promise you is that I shall equip you with a better horse, armour and weapons. I lead the best knights in this army and we are sworn to take captives who will make us rich. And none, I think, so rich as the King of England and his whelp. Not kill, mark you, but capture.'

Sir Simon shrugged. 'I'll settle for capturing the bastard,' he said.

'And his father,' the man said, 'I want his father too.'

There was something vengeful in the man's voice that intrigued Sir Simon. 'Why?' he asked.

'My family lived in England,' the man said, 'but when this king took power we supported his mother.'

'So you lost your land?' Sir Simon asked. He was too young to remember the turmoil of those times – when the King's mother had tried to keep power for herself and for her lover and the young Edward had struggled to break free. Young Edward had won and some of his old enemies had not forgotten.

'We lost everything,' the man said, 'but we shall get it back. Will you help?'

Sir Simon hesitated, wondering whether he would not do better with a wealthier lord, but he was intrigued by the man's calmness and by his determination to tear the heart out of England. 'Who are you?' he asked.

'I am sometimes called the Harlequin,' the man said.

The name meant nothing to Sir Simon. 'And you employ only the best?' he asked.

'I told you so.'

'Then you had best employ me,' Sir Simon said, 'with my man.' He nodded towards Henry Colley.

'Good,' the Harlequin said.

So Sir Simon had a new master and the King of France had gathered an army. The great lords: Alençon, John of Hainault, Aumale, the Count of Blois, who was brother to the aspiring Duke of Brittany, the Duke of Lorraine, the Count of Sancerre – all were in Rouen with their vast retinues of heavily armoured men. The army's numbers became so large that men could not count the ranks, but clerks reckoned there were at least eight thousand men-at-arms and five thousand cross-bowmen in Rouen, and that meant that Philip of Valois's army already outnumbered Edward of England's forces, and still more men were coming. John, Count of Luxembourg and King of Bohemia, a friend of Philip of France, was bringing his formidable knights. The King of Majorca came with his famed lances, and the Duke of Normandy was ordered to abandon the siege of an English fortress in the south and bring his army north. The priests blessed the soldiers and promised them that God would recognize the virtue of France's cause and crush the English mercilessly.

The army could not be fed in Rouen, so at last it crossed the bridge to the north bank of the Seine, leaving a formidable garrison behind to guard the river crossing. Once out of the city and on the long roads stretching through the newly harvested fields, men could dimly comprehend just how vast their army was. It stretched for miles in long columns of armed men, troops of horsemen, battalions of crossbowmen and, trailing behind, the innumerable host of infantry armed with axes, billhooks and spears. This was the might of France, and France's friends had rallied to the cause. There was a troop of knights from Scotland – big, savage-looking men who nourished a rare hatred of the English. There were mercenaries from Germany and Italy, and there were knights whose names had become famous in Christendom's tournaments, the elegant killers who had become rich in the sport of war. The French knights spoke not just of defeating Edward of England, but of carrying the war to his kingdom, foreseeing earldoms in Essex and dukedoms in Devonshire.

The Bishop of Meaux encouraged his cook to think of a recipe for archers' fingers, a *daube* perhaps, seasoned with thyme? He would, the bishop insisted, force the dish down Edward of England's throat.

Sir Simon rode a seven-year-old destrier now, a fine grey that must have cost the Harlequin close to a hundred pounds. He wore a hauberk of close-ringed mail covered with a surcoat that bore the white cross. His horse had a chanfron of boiled leather and a black trapper, while at Sir Simon's waist hung a sword made in Poitiers. Henry Colley was almost as well equipped, though in place of a sword he carried a four-foot-long shaft of oak topped with a spiked metal ball.

'They're a solemn bunch,' he complained to Sir Simon about the other men who followed the Harlequin. 'Like bloody monks.'

'They can fight,' Sir Simon said, though he himself was also daunted by the grim dedication of the Harlequin's men.

The men were all confident, but none took the English as lightly as the rest of the army, which had convinced itself that any battle would be won by numbers alone. The Harlequin quizzed Sir Simon and Henry Colley about the English way of fighting, and his questions were shrewd enough to force both men to drop their bombast and think.

'They'll fight on foot,' Sir Simon concluded. He, like all knights, dreamed of a battle conducted on horseback, of swirling men and couched lances, but the English had learned their business in the wars against the Scots and knew that men on foot defended territory much more effectively than horsemen. 'Even the knights will fight on foot,' Sir Simon forecast, 'and for every man-at-arms they'll have two or three archers. Those are the bastards to watch.'

The Harlequin nodded. 'But how do we defeat the archers?'

'Let them run out of arrows,' Sir Simon said. 'They must, eventually. So let every hothead in the army attack, then wait till the arrow bags are empty. Then you'll get your revenge.'

'It is more than revenge I want,' the Harlequin said quietly.

'What?'

The Harlequin, a handsome man, smiled at Sir Simon, though there was no warmth in the smile. 'Power,' he answered very calmly. 'With power, Sir Simon, comes privilege and with privilege, wealth. What are kings,' he asked, 'but men who have risen high? So we shall rise too, and use the defeat of kings as the rungs of our ladder.'

Such talk impressed Sir Simon, though he did not wholly understand it. It seemed to him that the Harlequin was a man of high fancies, but that did not matter because he was also unswervingly dedicated to the defeat of men who were Sir Simon's enemies. Sir Simon daydreamed of the battle; he saw the English prince's frightened face, heard his scream and revelled in the thought of taking the insolent whelp prisoner. Jeanette too. The Harlequin could be as secretive and subtle as he wished so long as he led Sir Simon to those simple desires.

And so the French army marched, and still it grew as men came from the outlying parts of the kingdom and from the vassal states beyond France's frontiers. It marched to seal off the Seine and so trap the English, and its confidence soared when it was learned that the King had made his pilgrimage to the Abbey of St Denis to fetch the oriflamme. It was France's most sacred symbol, a scarlet banner kept by the Benedictines in the abbey where the Kings of France lay entombed, and every man knew that when the oriflamme was unfurled no quarter would be given. It was said to have been carried by Charlemagne himself, and its silk was red as blood, promising carnage to the enemies of France. The English had come to fight, the oriflamme had been released and the dance of the armies had begun.

Sir Guillaume gave Thomas a linen shirt, a good mail coat, a leather-lined helmet and a sword. 'It's old, but good,' he said of the sword, 'a cutter rather than a piercer.' He provided Thomas with a horse, a saddle, a bridle and gave him money. Thomas tried to refuse the last gift, but Sir Guillaume brushed his protest aside. 'You've taken what you wanted from me, I might as well give you the rest.'

'Taken?' Thomas was puzzled, even hurt, by the accusation.

'Eleanor.'

'I've not taken her,' Thomas protested.

Sir Guillaume's ravaged face broke into a grin. 'You will, boy,' he said, 'you will.'

They rode next day, going eastwards in the wake of the English army that was now far off. News had come to Caen of burned towns, but no one knew where the enemy had gone and so Sir Guillaume planned to lead his twelve men-at-arms, his squire and his servant to

Paris. 'Someone will know where the King is,' he said. 'And you, Thomas, what will you do?'

Thomas had been wondering the same ever since he woke to the light in Sir Guillaume's house, but now he must make the decision and, to his surprise, there was no conflict at all. 'I shall go to my king,' he said.

'And what of this Sir Simon? What if he hangs you again?'

'I have the Earl of Northampton's protection,' Thomas said, though he reflected it had not worked before.

'And what of Eleanor?' Sir Guillaume turned to look at his daughter who, to Thomas's surprise, had accompanied them. Her father had given her a small palfrey and, unused to riding, she sat its saddle awkwardly, clutching the high pommel. She did not know why her father had let her come, suggesting to Thomas that perhaps he wanted her to be his cook.

The question made Thomas blush. He knew he could not fight against his own friends, but nor did he want to leave Eleanor. 'I shall come looking for her,' he told Sir Guillaume.

'If you still live,' the Frenchman growled. 'Why don't you fight for me?'

'Because I'm English.'

Sir Guillaume sneered. 'You're Cathar, you're French, you're from Languedoc, who knows what you are? You're a priest's son, a mongrel bastard of heretic stock.'

'I'm English,' Thomas said.

'You're a Christian,' Sir Guillaume retorted, 'and God has given you and me a duty. How are you to fulfil that duty by joining Edward's army?'

Thomas did not answer at once. Had God given him a duty? If so he did not want to accept it, for acceptance

328

meant believing in the legends of the Vexilles. Thomas, in the evening after he had met Brother Germain, had talked with Mordecai in Sir Guillaume's garden, asking the old man if he had ever read the book of Daniel.

Mordecai had sighed, as if he found the question wearisome. 'Years ago,' he'd said, 'many years ago. It is part of the Ketuvim, the writings that all Jewish youths must read. Why?'

'He's a prophet, yes? He tells the future.'

'Dear me,' Mordecai had said, sitting on the bench and dragging his thin fingers through his forked beard. 'You Christians,' he had said, 'insist that prophets tell the future, but that wasn't really what they did at all. They warned Israel. They told us that we would be visited by death, destruction and horror if we did not mend our ways. They were preachers, Thomas, just preachers, though, God knows, they were right about the death, destruction and horror. As for Daniel . . . He is very strange, very strange. He had a head filled with dreams and visions. He was drunk on God, that one.'

'But do you think,' Thomas had asked, 'that Daniel could foretell what is happening now?'

Mordecai had frowned. 'If God wished him to, yes, but why should God wish that? And I assume, Thomas, that you think Daniel might foretell what happens here and now in France, and what possible interest could that hold for the God of Israel? The Ketuvim are full of fancy, vision and mystery, and you Christians see more in them than we ever did. But would I make a decision because Daniel ate a bad oyster and had a vivid dream all those years ago? No, no, no.' He stood and held a jordan bottle high. 'Trust what is before your eyes,

Thomas, what you can smell, hear, taste, touch and see. The rest is dangerous.'

Thomas now looked at Sir Guillaume. He had come to like the Frenchman whose battle-hardened exterior hid a wealth of kindness, and Thomas knew he was in love with the Frenchman's daughter, but, even so, he had a greater loyalty.

'I cannot fight against England,' he said, 'any more than you would carry a lance against King Philip.'

Sir Guillaume dismissed that with a shrug. 'Then fight against the Vexilles.'

But Thomas could not smell, hear, taste, touch or see the Vexilles. He did not believe the king of the south would send his daughter to the north. He did not believe the Holy Grail was hidden in some heretic's fastness. He believed in the strength of a yew bow, the tension of a hemp cord and the power of a white-feathered arrow to kill the King's enemies. To think of dark lords and of heresiarchs was to flirt with the madness that had harrowed his own father.

'If I find the man who killed my father,' he evaded Sir Guillaume's demand, 'then I will kill him.'

'But you will not search for him?'

'Where do I look? Where do you look?' Thomas asked, then offered his own answer. 'If the Vexilles really still exist, if they truly want to destroy France, then where would they begin? In England's army. So I shall look for them there.' That answer was an evasion, but it half convinced Sir Guillaume, who grudgingly conceded that the Vexilles might indeed take their forces to Edward of England.

That night they sheltered in the scorched remains of a farm where they gathered about a small fire on which they roasted the hind legs of a boar that Thomas had shot. The men-at-arms treated Thomas warily. He was, after all, one of the hated English archers whose bows could pierce even plate mail. If he had not been Sir Guillaume's friend they would have wanted to slice off his string fingers in revenge for the pain that the white-fledged arrows had given to the horsemen of France, but instead they treated him with a distant curiosity. After the meal Sir Guillaume gestured to Eleanor and Thomas that they should both accompany him outside. His squire was keeping watch, and Sir Guillaume led them away from the young man, going to the bank of a stream where, with an odd formality, he looked at Thomas. 'So you will leave us,' he said, 'and fight for Edward of England.'

'Yes.'

'But if you see my enemy, if you see the lance, what will you do?'

'Kill him,' Thomas said. Eleanor stood slightly apart, watching and listening.

'He will not be alone,' Sir Guillaume warned, 'but you assure me he is your enemy?'

'I swear it,' Thomas said, puzzled that the question even needed to be asked.

Sir Guillaume took Thomas's right hand. 'You have heard of a brotherhood in arms?'

Thomas nodded. Men of rank frequently made such pacts, swearing to aid each other in battle and share each other's spoils.

'Then I swear a brotherhood to you,' Sir Guillaume said, 'even if we will fight on opposing sides.'

'I swear the same,' Thomas said awkwardly.

Sir Guillaume let Thomas's hand go. 'There,' he said

to Eleanor, 'I'm safe from one damned archer.' He paused, still looking at Eleanor. 'I shall marry again,' he said abruptly, 'and have children again and they will be my heirs. You know what I'm saying, don't you?'

Eleanor's head was lowered, but she looked up at her father briefly, then dropped her gaze again. She said nothing.

'And if I have more children, God willing,' Sir Guillaume said, 'what does that leave for you, Eleanor?'

She gave a very small shrug as if to suggest that the question was not of great interest to her. 'I have never asked you for anything.'

'But what would you have asked for?'

She stared into the ripples of the stream. 'What you gave me,' she said after a while, 'kindness.'

'Nothing else?'

She paused. 'I would have liked to call you Father.'

Sir Guillaume seemed uncomfortable with that answer. He stared northwards. 'You are both bastards,' he said after a while, 'and I envy that.'

'Envy?' Thomas asked.

'A family serves like the banks of a stream. They keep you in your place, but bastards make their own way. They take nothing and they can go anywhere.' He frowned, then flicked a pebble into the water. 'I had always thought, Eleanor, that I would marry you to one of my men-at-arms. Benoit asked me for your hand and so did Fossat. And it's past time you were married. What are you? Fifteen?'

'Fifteen,' she agreed.

'You'll rot away, girl, if you wait any longer,' Sir Guillaume said gruffly, 'so who shall it be? Benoit? Fossat?' He paused. 'Or would you prefer Thomas?'

Eleanor said nothing and Thomas, embarrassed, kept silent.

'You want her?' Sir Guillaume asked him brutally.

'Yes.'

'Eleanor?'

She looked at Thomas, then back to the stream. 'Yes,' she said simply.

'The horse, the mail, the sword and the money,' Sir Guillaume said to Thomas, 'are my bastard daughter's dowry. Look after her, or else become my enemy again.' He turned away.

'Sir Guillaume?' Thomas asked. The Frenchman turned back. 'When you went to Hookton,' Thomas went on, wondering why he asked the question now, 'you took a dark-haired girl prisoner. She was pregnant. Her name was Jane.'

Sir Guillaume nodded. 'She married one of my men. Then died in childbirth. The child too. Why?' He frowned. 'Was the child yours?'

'She was a friend,' Thomas evaded the question.

'She was a pretty friend,' Sir Guillaume said, 'I remember that. And when she died we had twelve Masses said for her English soul.'

'Thank you.'

Sir Guillaume looked from Thomas to Eleanor, then back to Thomas. 'A good night for sleeping under the stars,' he said, 'and we shall leave at dawn.' He walked away.

Thomas and Eleanor sat by the stream. The sky was still not wholly dark, but had a luminous quality like the glow of a candle behind horn. An otter slid down the far side of the stream, its fur glistening where it showed above the water. It raised its head, looked briefly at Thomas, then dived out of sight, to leave a trickle of silver bubbles breaking the dark surface.

Eleanor broke the silence, speaking the only English words she knew. 'I am an archer's woman,' she said.

Thomas smiled. 'Yes,' he said.

And in the morning they rode on and next evening they saw the smear of smoke on the northern horizon and knew it was a sign that the English army was going about its business. They parted in the next dawn.

'How you reach the bastards, I do not know,' Sir Guillaume said, 'but when it is all over, look for me.'

He embraced Thomas, kissed Eleanor, then pulled himself into his saddle. His horse had a long blue trapper decorated with yellow hawks. He settled his right foot into its stirrup, gathered the reins and pushed back his spurs.

A track led north across a heath that was fragrant with thyme and fluttering with blue butterflies. Thomas, his helmet hanging from the saddle's pommel and the sword thumping at his side, rode towards the smoke, and Eleanor, who insisted on carrying his bow because she was an archer's woman, rode with him. They looked back from the low crest of the heath, but Sir Guillaume was already a half-mile westwards, not looking back, hurrying towards the oriflamme.

So Thomas and Eleanor rode on.

The English marched east, ever further from the sea, searching for a place to cross the Seine, but every bridge was broken or else was guarded by a fortress. They still destroyed everything they touched. Their *chevauchée* was a line twenty miles wide and behind it was a charred trail a hundred miles long. Every house was burned and every mill destroyed. The folk of France fled from the army, taking their livestock and the newly gathered harvest with them so that Edward's men had to range ever further to find food. Behind them was desolation while in front lay the formidable walls of Paris. Some men thought the King would assault Paris, others reckoned he would not waste his troops on those great walls, but instead attack one of the strongly fortified bridges that could lead him north of the river. Indeed, the army tried to capture the bridge at Meulan, but the stronghold which guarded its southern end was too massive and its crossbowmen were too many, and the assault failed. The French stood on the ramparts and bared their backsides to insult the defeated English. It was said that the King, confident of crossing the river, had ordered supplies sent to the port of Le Crotoy that lay far to the north, beyond both the Seine and the River Somme, but if the supplies were waiting then they were unreachable because the Seine was a wall behind which the English were penned in a land they had themselves emptied of food. The first horses began to go lame and men, their boots shredded by marching, went barefoot.

The English came closer to Paris, entering the wide lands that were the hunting grounds of the French kings. They took Philip's lodges and stripped them of tapestries and plate, and it was while they hunted his royal deer that the French King sent Edward a formal offer of battle. It was the chivalrous thing to do, and it would, by God's grace, end the harrowing of his farmlands. So Philip of Valois sent a bishop to the English, courteously suggesting that he would wait with his army south of Paris, and the English King graciously accepted the invitation and so the French marched their army through the city and arrayed it among the vine-yards on a hillcrest by Bourg-la-Reine. They would make the English attack them there, forcing the archers and men-at-arms to struggle uphill into massed Genoese crossbows, and the French nobles estimated the value of the ransoms they would fetch for their prisoners.

The French battleline waited, but no sooner had Philip's army settled in its positions than the English treacherously turned about and marched in the other direction, going to the town of Poissy where the bridge across the Seine had been destroyed and the town evacuated. A few French infantrymen, poor soldiers armed with spears and axes, had been left to guard the northern bank, but they could do nothing to stop the swarm of archers, carpenters and masons who used tim-bers ripped from the roofs of Poissy to make a new bridge on the fifteen broken piers of the old. It took two days to repair the bridge and the French were still waiting for their arranged battle among the ripening grapes at Bourg-la-Reine as the English crossed the Seine and started marching northwards. The devils had escaped the trap and were loose again.

It was at Poissy that Thomas, with Eleanor beside him, rejoined the army.

And it was there, by God's Grace, that the hard times began.

Eleanor had been apprehensive about joining the English army. 'They won't like me because I'm French,' she said.

'The army's full of Frenchmen,' Thomas had told her. 'There are Gascons, Bretons, even some Normans, and half the women are French.'

'The archers' women?' she asked, giving him a wry smile. 'But they are not good women?'

'Some are good, some are bad,' Thomas said vaguely, 'but you I shall make into a wife and everyone will know you're special.'

If Eleanor was pleased she showed no sign, but they were now in the broken streets of Poissy, where a rearguard of English archers shouted at them to hurry. The makeshift bridge was about to be destroyed and the army's laggards were being chivvied across its planks. The bridge had no parapets and had been hurriedly made from whatever timbers the army had found in the abandoned town, and the uneven planking swayed, creaked and bent as Thomas and Eleanor led their horses onto the roadway. Eleanor's palfrey became so scared of the uncertain footing that it refused to move until Thomas put a blindfold over its eyes and then, still shaking, it trod slowly and steadily across the planks, which had gaps between them through which Thomas could see the river sliding. They were among the last to cross. Some of the army's wagons had been abandoned in Poissy, their loads distributed onto the hundreds of horses that had been captured south of the Seine.

Once the last stragglers had crossed the bridge the archers began hurling the planks into the river, breaking down the fragile link that had let the English escape across the river. Now, King Edward hoped, they would find new land to waste in the wide plains that lay between the Seine and the Somme and the three battles spread into the twenty-mile-wide line of the *chevauchée* and advanced northwards, camping that night just a short march from the river.

Thomas looked for the Prince of Wales's troops while Eleanor tried to ignore the dirty, tattered and sun-browned archers, who looked more like outlaws than soldiers. They were supposed to be making their shelters for the coming night, but preferred to watch the women and call obscene invitations. 'What are they saying?' Eleanor asked Thomas.

'That you are the most beautiful creature in all France,' he said.

'You lie,' she said, then flinched as a man shouted at her. 'Have they never seen a woman before?'

'Not like you. They probably think you're a princess.'

She scoffed at that, but was not displeased. There were, she saw, women everywhere. They gathered firewood while their men made the shelters and most, Eleanor noted, spoke French. 'There will be many babies next year,' she said.

'True.'

'They will go back to England?' she asked.

'Some, perhaps.' Thomas was not really sure. 'Or they'll go to their garrisons in Gascony.'

'If I marry you,' she asked, 'will I become English?'

'Yes,' Thomas said.

It was getting late and cooking fires were smoking across the stubble fields, though there was precious little to cook. Every pasture held a score of horses and Thomas knew they needed to rest, feed and water their own animals. He had asked many soldiers where the Prince of Wales's men could be found, but one man said west, another east, so in the dusk Thomas simply turned their tired horses towards the nearest village for he did not know where else to go. The place was swarming with troops, but Thomas and Eleanor found a quiet enough spot in the corner of a field where Thomas made a fire while Eleanor, the black bow prominent on her shoulder to demonstrate that she belonged to the army, watered the horses in a stream. They cooked the last of their food and afterwards sat under the hedge and watched the stars brighten above a dark wood. Voices sounded from the village where some women were singing a French song and Eleanor crooned the words softly.

'I remember my mother singing it to me,' she said, plucking strands of grass that she wove into a small bracelet. 'I was not his only bastard,' she said ruefully. 'There were two others I know of. One died when she was very small, and the other is now a soldier.'

'He's your brother.

'Half-brother.' She shrugged. 'I don't know him. He went away.' She put the bracelet on her thin wrist. 'Why do you wear a dog's paw?' she asked.

'Because I'm a fool,' he said, 'and mock God.' That was the truth, he thought ruefully, and he pulled the dry paw hard to break its cord, then tossed it into the field. He did not really believe in St Guinefort; it was an affectation. A dog would not help him recover the lance, and that duty made him grimace, for the penance weighed on his conscience and soul.

'Do you really mock God?' Eleanor asked, worried.

'No. But we jest about the things we fear.'

'And you fear God?'

'Of course,' Thomas said, then stiffened because there had been a rustle in the hedge behind him and a cold blade was suddenly pressed against the back of his neck. The metal felt very sharp.

'What we should do,' a voice said, 'is hang the bastard properly and take his woman. She's pretty.'

'She's pretty,' another man agreed, 'but he ain't good for anything.'

'You bastards!' Thomas said, turning to stare into two grinning faces. It was Jake and Sam. He did not believe it at first, just gazed for a while. 'It is you! What are you doing here?'

Jake slashed at the hedge with his billhook, pushed through and gave Eleanor what he thought was a reassuring grin, though with his scarred face and crossed eyes he looked like something from nightmare. 'Charlie Blois got his face smacked,' Jake said, 'so Will brought us here to give the King of France a bloody nose. She your woman?'

'She's the Queen of bloody Sheba,' Thomas said.

'And the Countess is humping the Prince, I hear,' Jake grinned. 'Will saw you earlier, only you didn't see us. Got your nose in the air. We heard you were dead.'

'I nearly was.'

'Will wants to see you.'

The thought of Will Skeat, of Jake and Sam, came as a vast relief to Thomas, for such men lived in a world far removed from dire prophecies, stolen lances and dark lords. He told Eleanor these men were his friends, his best friends, and that she could trust them, though she looked alarmed at the ironic cheer which greeted Thomas when they ducked into the village tavern. The archers put their hands at their throats and contorted their faces to imitate a hanged man while Will Skeat shook his head in mock despair.

'God's belly,' he said, 'but they can't even hang you properly.' He looked at Eleanor. 'Another countess?'

'The daughter of Sir Guillaume d'Evecque, knight of the sea and of the land,' Thomas said, 'and she's called Eleanor.'

'Yours?' Skeat asked.

'We shall marry.'

'Bloody hellfire,' Skeat said, 'you're still daft as a carrot! You don't marry them, Tom, that's not what they're for. Still, she ain't a bad looker, is she?' He courteously made space for Eleanor on the bench. 'There wasn't much ale,' he went on, 'so we drank it all.' He looked about the tavern. It was so bare there was not even a bunch of herbs hanging from the rafters. 'Bastards cleaned up before they left,' he said sourly, 'and there's about as much plunder here as you'd get hairs off a bald man.'

'What happened in Brittany?' Thomas asked.

Will shrugged. 'Nowt to do with us. Duke Charles led his men into our territory and trapped Tommy Dugdale on a hilltop. Three thousand of them and three hundred with Tommy, and at the end of the day Duke Charles was running like a scalded hare. Arrows, boy, arrows.'

Thomas Dugdale had taken over the Earl of Northampton's responsibilities in Brittany and had been travelling between the English fortresses when the Duke's army caught him, but his archers and men-at-arms, ensconced behind the thick hedge of a hilltop pasture, had cut the enemy into shreds.

'All day they fought,' Skeat said, 'morning to night, and the bastards wouldn't learn their lesson and kept sending men up the hill. They reckoned Tommy had to run out of arrows soon enough, but he was carrying carts of spares to the fortresses, see, so he had enough to last him till doomsday. So Duke Charles lost his best men, the fortresses are safe till he gets some more, and we're up here. The Earl sent for us. Just bring fifty archers, he told me, so I did. And Father Hobbe, of course. We sailed to Caen and joined the army just as it marched out. So what the hell happened to you?'

Thomas told his tale. Skeat shook his head when he heard about the hanging. 'Sir Simon's gone,' he said. 'Probably joined the French.'

'He's done what?'

'Vanished. Your countess caught up with him and pissed all over him from what we hear.' Skeat grinned. 'Luck of the devil, you've got. God knows why I saved you this.' He put a clay jar of ale on the table, then nodded at Thomas's bow that Eleanor was carrying. 'Can you still shoot that thing? I mean you've been bollocking about with the aristocracy for so long that you might have forgotten why God put you on the earth?'

'I can still use it.'

'Then you might as well ride with us,' Skeat said, but confessed he knew little of what the army was doing. 'No one tells me,' he said scornfully, 'but they say there's another river up north and we've got to cross it. Sooner the better, I reckon, as the Frenchies have skimmed this land proper. Couldn't feed a kitten up here.'

It was indeed a bare land. Thomas saw that for himself next day as Will Skeat's men moved slowly north across harvested fields, but the grain, instead of lying in the barns, had already been taken for the French army, just as the livestock had all been driven away. South of the Seine the English had cut grain from abandoned fields and their advance guards had moved swiftly enough to capture thousands of cattle, pigs and goats, but here the land had been scraped bare by an even larger army and so the King ordered haste. He wanted his men to cross the next river, the Somme, to where the French army might not have stripped the land and where, at Le Crotoy, he hoped a fleet would be waiting with supplies, but despite the royal orders the army went painfully slowly. There were fortified towns that promised food and men insisted on trying to assault their walls. They captured some, were repulsed at others, but it all took time that the King did not have, and while he was trying to discipline an army more interested in plunder than progress, the King of France led his army back across the Seine, through Paris and north to the Somme.

A new trap was set, an even deadlier one, for the English were now penned in a land that had been stripped of food. Edward's army at last reached the Somme, but found it was blocked just as the Seine had been barred. Bridges were destroyed or guarded by grim forts with heavy garrisons that would take weeks to dislodge, and the English did not have weeks. They were weakening daily. They had marched from Normandy to the edge of Paris, then they had crossed the Seine and left a path of destruction to the Somme's southern bank and the long journey had abraded the army. Hundreds of men were now barefoot while others hobbled on disintegrating shoes. They had horses enough, but few spare horseshoes or nails, and so men led their animals to save their hooves.

There was grass to feed horses, but little grain for men, and so the foraging parties had to travel long distances to find villages where the peasants might have hidden some of the harvest. The French were becoming bolder now and there were frequent skirmishes at the edges of the army as the French sensed the English vulnerability. Men ate unripe fruit that soured their bellies and loosened their bowels. Some reckoned they had no choice but to march all the way back to Normandy, but others knew the army would fall apart long before they reached the safety of the Norman harbours. The only course was to cross the Somme and march to the English strongholds in Flanders, but the bridges were gone or garrisoned, and when the army crossed desolate marshlands to find fords they discovered the enemy ever waiting on the far bank. They twice tried to force a passage, but both times the French, secure on the higher dry land, were able to cut down the archers in the river by crowding the bank with Genoese crossbows. And so the English retreated and marched westwards, getting ever nearer to the river's mouth, and every step reduced the number of possible crossing places as the river grew wider and deeper. They marched for eight days between the rivers, eight days of increasing hunger and frustration.

'Save your arrows,' a worried Will Skeat warned his men late one afternoon. They were making their camp by a small, deserted village which was as bare as every other place they had found since crossing the Seine. 'We'll need every arrow we've got for a battle,' Skeat went on, 'and Christ knows we've none to waste.'

An hour later, when Thomas was searching a hedgerow for blackberries, a voice called from on high. 'Thomas! Get your evil bones up here!'

Thomas turned to see Will Skeat on the small tower of the village church. He ran to the church, climbed the ladder, past a beam where a bell had hung till the villagers took it away to prevent the English from stealing it, then pulled himself through the hatch and onto the tower's flat roof where a half-dozen men were crowded, among them the Earl of Northampton, who gave Thomas a very wry look.

'I heard you were hanged!'

'I lived, my lord,' Thomas said grimly.

The Earl hesitated, wondering whether to ask if Sir Simon Jekyll had been the hangman, but there was no point in continuing that feud. Sir Simon had fled and the Earl's agreement with him was void. He grimaced instead. 'No one can kill a devil's whelp, eh?' he said, then pointed eastwards, and Thomas stared through the twilight and saw an army on the march.

It was a long way off, on the far northern bank of the river that here flowed between vast reedbeds, but Thomas could still see that the lines of horsemen, wagons, infantry and crossbowmen were filling every lane and track of that distant bank. The army was

345

approaching a walled town, Abbeville, the Earl said, where a bridge crossed the river, and Thomas, gazing at the black lines twisting towards the bridge, felt as though the gates of hell had opened and spewed out a vast horde of lances, swords and crossbows. Then he remembered Sir Guillaume was there and he made the sign of the cross and mouthed a silent prayer that Eleanor's father would survive.

'Sweet Christ,' Will Skeat said, mistaking Thomas's gesture for fear, 'but they want our souls bad.'

'They know we're tired,' the Earl said, 'and they know the arrows must run out in the end, and they know they have more men than we do. Far more.' He turned westwards. 'And we can't run much further.' He pointed again and Thomas saw the flat sheen of the sea. 'They've caught us,' the Earl said. 'They'll cross at Abbeville and attack tomorrow.'

'So we fight,' Will Skeat growled.

'On this ground, Will?' the Earl asked. The land was flat, ideal for cavalry, and with few hedgerows or coppices to protect archers. 'And against so many?' he added. He stared at the distant enemy. 'They outnumber us. Will, they outnumber us. By God, they outnumber us.' He shrugged. 'Time to move on.'

'Move on where?' Skeat asked. 'Why not find our ground and stand?'

'South?' The Earl sounded unsure. 'Maybe we can cross the Seine again and take ships home from Normandy? God knows we can't cross the Somme.' He shaded his eyes as he stared at the river. 'Christ,' he blasphemed, 'but why the hell isn't there a ford? We could have raced the bastards back to our fortresses in Flanders and left Philip stranded like the damned fool he is.'

'Not fight him?' Thomas asked, sounding shocked.

The Earl shook his head. 'We've hurt him. We've robbed him blind. We've marched through his kingdom and left it smouldering, so why fight him? He's spent a fortune on hiring knights and crossbowmen, so why not let him waste that money? Then we come back next year and do it again.' He shrugged. 'Unless we can't escape him.' With those grim words he backed down through the hatch and his entourage followed, leaving Skeat and Thomas alone.

'The real reason they don't want to fight,' Skeat said sourly when the Earl was safe out of earshot, 'is that they're scared of being taken prisoner. A ransom can wipe out a family's fortune in the blink of an eye.' He spat over the tower parapet, then drew Thomas to its northern edge. 'But the real reason I brought you up here, Tom, is because your eyes are better than mine. Can you see a village over there?' He pointed northwards.

It took Thomas a while, but eventually he spotted a group of low roofs amidst the reeds. 'Bloody poor village,' he said sourly.

'But it's still a place we haven't searched for food,' Skeat said, 'and being on a marsh they might have some smoked eels. I like a smoked eel, I do. Better than sour apples and nettle soup. You can go and have a look.'

'Tonight?'

'Why not next week?' Skeat said, going to the roof hatch, 'or next year? Of course I mean tonight, you toad. Hurry yourself.'

Thomas took twenty archers. None of them wanted to go, for it was late in the day and they feared that French patrols might be waiting on the track that twisted endlessly through the dunes and reedbeds that stretched towards the Somme. It was a desolate country. Birds flew from the reeds as the horses picked their way along a track that was so low-lying that in places there were battens of elm to give footing, and all about them the water gurgled and sucked between banks of green-scummed mud.

'Tide's going out,' Jake commented.

Thomas could smell the salt water. They were near enough to the sea for the tides to flow and ebb through this tangle of reeds and marshgrass, though in places the road found a firmer footing on great drifted banks of sand where stiff pale grasses grew. In winter, Thomas thought, this would be a godforsaken place with the cold winds driving the spume across the frozen marsh.

It was very nearly dark when they reached the village, which proved to be a miserable settlement of just a dozen reed-thatched cottages, which were deserted. The folk must have left just before Thomas's archers arrived, for there were still fires in the small rock hearths.

'Look for food,' Thomas said, 'especially smoked eels.'

'Be quicker to catch the bloody eels and smoke them ourselves,' Jake said.

'Get on with it,' Thomas said, then took himself to the end of the village where there was a small wooden church which had been pushed by the wind into a permanently lopsided stance. The church was little more than a shed – maybe it was a shrine to some saint of this misbegotten marshland – but Thomas reckoned the wooden structure would just about bear his weight so he scrambled off the horse onto the moss-thick thatch and then crawled up to the ridge where he clung to the nailed cross that decorated one gable.

He saw no movement in the marshes, though he could see the smear of smoke coming from the French campfires that misted the fading light north of Abbeville. Tomorrow, he thought, the French would cross the bridge and file through the town's gates to confront the English army whose fires burned to the south, and the size of the smoke plumes witnessed how much larger the French army was than the English.

Jake appeared from a nearby cottage with a sack in his hand. 'What is it?' Thomas called.

'Grain!' Jake hefted the sack. 'Bloody damp. Sprouting.'

'No eels?'

'Of course there are no bloody eels,' Jake grumbled. 'Bloody eels got more sense than to live in a hovel like this.'

Thomas grinned and looked off to the sea that lay like a blood-reddened swordblade to the west. There was one distant sail, a speck of white, on the clouded horizon. Gulls wheeled and soared above the river that here was a great wide channel, broken by reeds and banks, sliding towards the sea. It was hard to distinguish between river and marsh, so tangled was the landscape. Then Thomas wondered why the gulls were screaming and diving. He stared at them and saw what at first looked like a dozen cattle on the riverbank. He opened his mouth to call that news to Jake, then he saw that there were men with the cattle. Men and women, perhaps a score of them? He frowned, staring, realizing that the folk must have come from this village. They had presumably seen the English archers approaching and they had fled with their livestock, but to where? The marsh? That was sensible, for the wetlands probably had a score of secret paths where folk could hide, but why had they risked going onto the sand ridge where Thomas could see them? Then he saw that they were not trying to hide, but to escape, for the villagers were now wading across the wide waters towards the northern bank.

Sweet Jesus, he thought, but there was a ford! He stared, not daring to believe his own eyes, but the folk were forging steadily across the river and dragging their cows with them. It was a deep ford, and he guessed it could only be crossed at low tide, but it was there. 'Jake!' he shouted. 'Jake!'

Jake ran across to the church and Thomas leaned far down and hauled him onto the rotting thatch. The building swayed perilously under their weight as Jake scrambled to the ridge, took hold of the sun-bleached wooden cross and looked where Thomas was pointing.

'God's arse,' he said, 'there's a bloody ford!'

'And there are bloody Frenchmen,' Thomas said, for on the river's far bank where firmer land rose from the tangle of marsh and water there were now men in grey mail. They were newly arrived, or else Thomas would have seen them earlier, and their first cooking fires pricked the dark stand of trees where they camped. Their presence showed that the French knew of the ford's existence and wanted to stop the English crossing, but that was none of Thomas's business. His only duty was to let the army know that there was a ford; a possible way out of the trap.

Thomas slid down the church's thatch and jumped to the ground. 'You go back to Will,' he told Jake, 'and tell him there's a ford. And tell him I'll burn the cottages one at a time to serve as a beacon.' It would be dark soon and without a light to guide them no one would be able to find the village.

Jake took six men and rode back to the south. Thomas waited. Every now and then he climbed back to the church roof and stared across the ford and each time he thought he saw more fires among the trees. The French, he reckoned, had placed a formidable force there, and no wonder, for it was the last escape route and they were blocking it. But Thomas still fired the cottages one by one to show the English where that escape might lie.

The flames roared into the night, scattering sparks across the marshes. The archers had found some dried fish concealed in a hut wall and that, with brackish water, was their supper. They were disconsolate, and no wonder.

'We should have stayed in Brittany,' one man said.

'They're going to corner us,' another suggested. He had made a flute from a dried reed and had been playing a melancholy air.

'We've got arrows,' a third man said.

'Enough to kill all those bastards?'

'Have to be enough.'

The flute player blew some faint notes, then became bored and tossed the instrument into the closest fire. Thomas, the night dragging hard on his patience, strolled back to the church, but instead of climbing onto the roof he pushed open the ramshackle door and then opened the one window's shutters to let in the firelight. Then he saw it was not a proper church, but a fishermen's shrine. There was an altar made from sea-whitened planks balanced on two broken barrels, and on the altar was a crude doll-like figure draped with strips of white cloth and crowned with a band of dried seaweed. The fishermen at Hookton had sometimes made such places, especially if a boat was lost at sea, and Thomas's father had always hated them. He had burned one to the ground, calling it a place of idols, but Thomas reckoned fishermen needed the shrines. The sea was a cruel place and the doll, he thought it was female, perhaps represented some saint of the area. Women whose men were long gone to sea could come to pray to the saint, begging that the ship would come home.

The shrine's roof was low and it was more comfortable to kneel. Thomas said a prayer. Let me live, he prayed, let me live, and he found himself thinking of the lance, thinking of Brother Germain and Sir Guillaume and of their fears that a new evil, born of the dark lords, was brewing in the south. It is none of your business, he told himself. It is superstition. The Cathars are dead, burned in the church's fires and gone to hell. Beware of madmen, his father had told him, and who better than his father to know that truth? But was he a Vexille? He bowed his head and prayed that God would keep him from the madness.

'And what are you praying for now?' a voice suddenly asked, startling Thomas, who turned to see Father Hobbe grinning from the low doorway. He had chatted with the priest during the last few days, but he had never been alone with him. Thomas was not even sure he wanted to be, for Father Hobbe's presence was a reminder of his conscience.

'I'm praying for more arrows, father.'

'Please God the prayer's answered,' Father Hobbe said, then settled on the church's earthen floor. 'I had

352

the devil's own task finding my way across the swamp, but I had a mind to talk with you. I have this feeling you've been avoiding me.'

'Father!' Thomas said chidingly.

'So here you are, and with a beautiful girl as well! I tell you, Thomas, if they forced you to lick a leper's arse you'd taste nothing but sweetness. Charmed, you are. They can't even hang you!'

'They can,' Thomas said, 'but not properly.'

'Thank God for that,' the priest said, then smiled. 'So how is the penance going?'

'I haven't found the lance,' Thomas answered curtly.

'But have you even looked for it?' Father Hobbe asked, then drew a piece of bread from his pouch. He broke the small loaf and tossed half to Thomas. 'Don't ask where I got it, but I didn't steal it. Remember, Thomas, you can fail in a penance and still have absolution if you have made a sincere effort.'

Thomas grimaced, not at Father Hobbe's words, but because he had bitten down on a scrap of millstone grit caught in the bread. He spat it out. 'My soul isn't so black as you make it sound, Father.'

'How would you know? All our souls are black.'

'I've made an effort,' Thomas said, then found himself telling the whole tale of how he had gone to Caen and sought out Sir Guillaume's house, and how he had been a guest there, and about Brother Germain and the Cathar Vexilles, and about the prophecy from Daniel and the advice of Mordecai.

Father Hobbe made the sign of the cross when Thomas talked of Mordecai. 'You can't take the word of such a man,' the priest said sternly. 'He may or may not be a good doctor, but the Jews have ever been

Christ's enemy. If he is on anyone's side it must be the devil's.'

'He's a good man,' Thomas insisted.

'Thomas! Thomas!' Father Hobbe said sadly, then frowned for a few heartbeats. 'I have heard,' he said after a while, 'that the Cathar heresy still lives.'

'But it can't challenge France and the Church!'

'You would know?' Father Hobbe asked. 'It reached out across the sea to steal the lance from your father, and you say it reached across France to kill Sir Guillaume's wife. The devil works his business in the dark, Thomas.'

'There's more,' Thomas said, and told the priest the story that the Cathars had the Grail. The light of the burning cottages flickered on the walls and gave the seaweed-crowned image on the altar a sinister cast. 'I don't think I believe any of it,' Thomas concluded.

'And why not?'

'Because if the story is true,' Thomas said, 'then I am not Thomas of Hookton, but Thomas Vexille. I'm not English, but some half-breed Frenchman. I'm not an archer, but noble born.'

'It gets worse,' Father Hobbe said with a smile. 'It means that you have been given a task.'

'They're just stories,' Thomas said scornfully. 'Give me another penance, Father. I'll make a pilgrimage for you, I'll go to Canterbury on my knees if that's what you want.'

'I want nothing of you, Thomas, but God wants a lot from you.'

'Then tell God to choose someone else.'

'I'm not in the habit of giving advice to the Almighty,'

354

Father Hobbe said, 'though I do listen to His. You think there is no Grail?'

'Men have sought it for a thousand years,' Thomas said, 'and no one has found it. Unless the thing in Genoa is real.'

Father Hobbe leaned his head against the wattle wall. 'I have heard,' he said quietly, 'that the real Grail is made of common clay. A simple peasant dish like the one my mother treasured, God rest her soul, for she could only afford the one good dish and then, clumsy fool that I am, I broke it one day. But the Grail, I am told, cannot be broken. You could put it in one of those guns that amused everyone at Caen and it would not break even if you dashed it against a castle wall. And when you place the bread and wine, the blood and flesh, of the Mass in that common piece of clay, Thomas, it turns to gold. Pure, shining gold. That is the Grail and, God help me, it does exist.'

'So you would have me wander the earth looking for a peasant's dish?' Thomas asked.

'God would,' Father Hobbe said, 'and for good reason.' He looked saddened. 'There is heresy everywhere, Thomas. The Church is besieged. The bishops and the cardinals and the abbots are corrupted by wealth, the village priests stew in ignorance and the devil is brewing his evil. Yet there are some of us, a few, who believe that the Church can be refreshed, that it can glow with God's glory again. I think the Grail could do that. I think God has chosen you.'

'Father!'

'And perhaps me,' Father Hobbe said, ignoring Thomas's protest. 'When this is all over,' he waved a hand to encompass the army and its plight, 'I think I may join you. We shall seek your family together.'

'You?' Thomas asked. 'Why?'

'Because God calls,' Father Hobbe said simply, then jerked his head. 'You must go, Thomas, you must go. I shall pray for you.'

Thomas had to go because the night had been disturbed by the sound of horses' hooves and the strident voices of men. Thomas seized his bow and ducked out of the church to find that a score of men-at-arms were now in the village. Their shields carried the lions and stars of the Earl of Northumberland and their commander was demanding to know who was in charge of the archers.

'I am,' Thomas said.

'Where's this ford?'

Thomas made himself a torch from a sheaf of thatch lashed to a pole and, while its flame lasted, he led them across the marsh towards the distant ford. The flames flickered out after a while, but he was close enough to find his way to where he had seen the cattle. The tide had risen again and black water seeped and flooded all about the horsemen, who huddled on a shrinking ridge of sand.

'You can see where the other side is,' Thomas told the men-at-arms, pointing to the fires of the French, which looked to be about a mile away.

'Bastards are waiting for us?'

'Plenty of them too.'

'We're crossing anyway,' the leading man-at-arms said. 'The King's decided it, and we're doing it when the tide falls.' He turned to his men. 'Off your horses. Find the path. Mark it.' He pointed to some pollarded willows. 'Cut staves off them, use them as markers.'

Thomas groped his way back to the village, sometimes wading through water up to his waist. A thin mist was seeping from the flooding tide, and had it not been for the blazing huts in the village he could easily have got lost.

The village, built on the highest piece of land in all the marsh, had attracted a crowd of horsemen by the time Thomas returned. Archers and men-at-arms gathered there and some had already pulled down the shrine to make fires from its timbers.

Will Skeat had come with the rest of his archers. 'The women are with the baggage,' he told Thomas. 'Bloody chaos back there, it is. They're hoping to cross everyone in the morning.'

'Be a fight first,' Thomas said.

'Either that or fight their whole damn army later in the day. Did you find any eels?'

'We ate them.'

Skeat grinned, then turned as a voice hailed him. It was the Earl of Northampton, his horse's trapper spattered with mud almost to the saddle.

'Well done, Will!'

'Weren't me, my lord, it was this clever bastard.' Skeat jerked a thumb at Thomas.

'Hanging did you good, eh?' the Earl said, then watched as a file of men-of-arms climbed onto the village's sand ridge. 'Be ready to move at dawn, Will, and we'll be crossing when the tide falls. I want your boys in front. Leave your horses here; I'll have good men watch them.'

There was small sleep that night, though Thomas did doze as he lay on the sand and waited for the dawn, which brought a pale, misty light. Willow trees loomed

357

in the vapour, while men-at-arms crouched at the tide's edge and stared north to where the mist was thickened by smoke from the enemy's fires. The river ran deceptively quick, hastened by the ebbing tide, but it was still too high to cross.

The sandbank by the ford held Skeat's fifty archers and another fifty under John Armstrong. There were the same number of men-at-arms, all on foot, led by the Earl of Northampton, who had been given the job of leading the crossing. The Prince of Wales had wanted to lead the fight himself, but his father had forbidden it. The Earl, far more experienced, had the responsibility and he was not happy. He would have liked many more men, but the sandbank would hold no more and the paths through the marshland were narrow and treacherous, making it difficult to bring reinforcements.

'You know what to do,' the Earl told Skeat and Armstrong.

'We know.'

'Maybe another two hours?' The Earl was judging the fall of the tide. The two hours crept by and the English could only stare through the thinning mist at the enemy, who formed their battleline at the ford's further side. The receding water let more men come to the sandbank, but the Earl's force was still pitifully small – perhaps two hundred men at most – while the French had double that number of men-at-arms alone. Thomas counted them as best he could, using the method Will Skeat had taught him: to divide the enemy in two, divide again, then count the small unit and multiply it by four, and he wished he had not done it for there were so many, and as well as the men-at-arms there had to be five or six hundred infantry, probably a levy from the country north of Abbeville. They were not a serious threat for, like most infantry, they would be ill-trained and badly armed with ancient weapons and farming tools, but they could still cause trouble if the Earl's men got into difficulties. The only blessing Thomas could find in the misty dawn was that the French seemed to have very few crossbowmen, but why would they need them when they had so many men-at-arms? And the formidable force that now gathered on the river's northern bank would be fighting in the knowledge that if they repelled the English attack then they would have their enemy pinned by the sea where the greater French army could crush them.

Two packhorses brought sheaves of precious arrows that were distributed among the archers. 'Ignore the goddamn peasants,' Skeat told his men. 'Kill the men-at-arms. I want the bastards crying for the goats they call their mothers.'

'There's food on the far side,' John Armstrong told his hungry men. 'Those goddamn bastards will have meat, bread and beer, and it'll be yours if you get through them.'

'And don't waste your arrows,' Skeat growled. 'Shoot proper! Aim, boys, aim. I want to see the bastards bleeding.'

'Watch the wind!' John Armstrong shouted. 'It'll carry arrows to the right.'

Two hundred of the French men-at-arms were on foot at the river's edge, while the other two hundred were mounted and waiting a hundred paces behind. The rabble of infantry was split into two vast lumps, one on each flank. The dismounted men-at-arms were there to stop the English at the water's edge and the mounted men would charge if any did break through, while the infantry was present to give the appearance of numbers and to help in the massacre that would follow the French victory. The French must have been confident for they had stopped every other attempt to ford the Somme.

Except at the other fords the enemy had possessed crossbowmen who had been able to keep the archers in deep water where they could not use their bows properly for fear of soaking the strings and here there were no crossbows.

The Earl of Northampton, on foot like his men, spat towards the river. 'He should have left his foot soldiers behind and brought a thousand Genoese,' he remarked to Will Skeat. 'We'd be in trouble then.'

'They'll have some crossbows,' Skeat said.

'Not enough, Will, not enough.' The Earl was wearing an old helmet, one without any face plate. He was accompanied by a grey-bearded man-at-arms with a deeply lined face, who wore a much-mended coat of mail. 'You know Reginald Cobham, Will?' the Earl asked.

'I've heard of you, Master Cobham,' Will said respectfully.

'And I of you. Master Skeat,' Cobham answered. A whisper went through Skeat's archers that Reginald Cobham was at the ford and men turned to look at the greybeard whose name was celebrated in the army. A common man, like themselves, but old in war and feared by England's enemies.

The Earl looked at a pole which marked one edge of the ford. 'Reckon the water's low enough,' he said, then patted Skeat's shoulder. 'Go and kill some, Will.'

Thomas took one glance behind and saw that every dry spot of the marsh was now crowded with soldiers, horses and women. The English army had come into the lowlands, depending on the Earl to force the crossing.

Off to the east, though none at the ford knew it, the main French army was filing across the bridge at Abbeville, ready to fall on the English rear.

There was a brisk wind coming from the sea, bringing a morning chill and the smell of salt. Gulls called forlorn above the pale reeds. The river's main channel was a half-mile wide and the hundred archers looked a puny force as they spread into a line and waded into the tide. Armstrong's men were on the left, Skeat's on the right, while behind them came the first of the earl's men-at-arms. Those men-at-arms were all on foot and their job was to wait till the arrows had weakened the enemy, then charge into the French with swords, axes and falchions. The enemy had two drummers, who began thumping their goatskins, then a trumpeter startled birds from the trees where the French had camped.

'Note the wind,' Skeat shouted at his men. 'Gusting hard, she is, gusting hard.'

The wind was blowing against the ebbing tide, forcing the river into small waves that whipped white at their tops. The French infantry were shouting. Grey clouds scudded above the green land. The drummers kept up a threatening rhythm. Banners flew above the waiting men-at-arms and Thomas was relieved that none of them showed yellow hawks on a blue field. The water was cold and came to his thighs. He held his bow high, watching the enemy, waiting for the first crossbow bolts to whip across the water.

No bolts came. The archers were within long bowshot

range now, but Will Skeat wanted them closer. A French knight on a black horse caparisoned with a green and blue trapper rode to where his comrades were on foot, then swerved off to one side and splashed into the river.

'Silly bastard wants to make a name,' Skeat said. 'Jake! Dan! Peter! Settle the bastard for me.' The three bows were drawn back and three arrows flew.

The French knight was hurled back in his saddle and his fall provoked the French to fury. They gave their war shout, *'Montjoie St Denis!'* and the men-at-arms came splashing into the river, ready to challenge the archers, who drew back their bows.

'Hold hard!' Skeat shouted. 'Hold hard! Closer, get closer!' The drumbeats were louder. The dead knight was being carried away by his horse as the other French edged back to the dry land. The water only reached to Thomas's knees now and the range was shortening. A hundred paces, no more, and Will Skeat was at last satisfied. 'Start putting them down!' he shouted.

The bowcords were drawn back to men's ears, then loosed. The arrows flew, and while the first flight was still whispering over the wind-flecked water the second flight was released, and as the men put their third arrows on the strings the first whipped home. The sound was of metal striking metal, like a hundred light hammers tapping, and the French ranks were suddenly crouching with shields held high.

'Pick your men!' Skeat shouted. 'Pick your men!' He was using his own bow, shooting it infrequently, always waiting for an enemy to lower a shield before loosing an arrow. Thomas was watching the rabble of infantry to his right. They looked as though they were ready to make a wild charge and he wanted to plant some arrows in their bellies before they reached the water.

A score of French men-at-arms were dead or wounded and their leader was shouting at the others to lock their shields. A dozen of the rearward men-at-arms had dismounted and were hurrying forward to reinforce the riverbank.

'Steady, boys, steady,' John Armstrong called. 'Make the arrows count.'

The enemy shields were quilled with arrows. The French were relying on those shields that were thick enough to slow an arrow, and they were staying low, waiting for the arrows to run out or for the English men-at-arms to come close. Thomas reckoned some of the arrows would have driven clean through the shields to inflict wounds, but they were mostly wasted. He glanced back to the infantry and saw they were not moving yet. The English bows were firing less frequently, waiting for their targets, and the Earl of Northampton must have tired of the delay, or else he feared the turn of the tide for he shouted his men forward. 'St George! St George!'

'Spread wide!' Will Skeat shouted, wanting his men to be on the flanks of the Earl's attack so they could use their arrows when the French stood to receive the charge, but the water rapidly grew deeper as Thomas moved upstream and he could not go as far as he wanted.

'Kill them! Kill them!' The Earl was wading up to the bank now.

'Keep ranks!' Reginald Cobham shouted.

The French men-at-arms gave a cheer, for the proximity of the English charge meant the archers' aim would be blocked, though Thomas did manage to loose two arrows as the defenders stood and before the two groups of men-at-arms met at the river's edge with a clash of steel and shield. Men roared their war cries, St Denis contending with St George.

'Watch right! Watch right!' Thomas shouted, for the peasant infantrymen had started forward and he sent two arrows whistling at them. He was plucking shafts from the arrow bag as fast as he could.

'Take the horsemen!' Will Skeat bellowed, and Thomas changed his aim to send an arrow over the heads of the fighting men at the French horsemen who were advancing down the bank to help their comrades. Some English horsemen had entered the ford now, but they could not ride to meet their French counterparts because the ford's northern exit was blocked by the wild mêlée of men-at-arms.

Men slashed and hacked. Swords met axes, falchions split helmets and skulls. The noise was like the devil's blacksmith shop and blood was swirling down tide in the shallows. A Englishman screamed as he was cut down into the water, then screamed again as two Frenchmen drove axes into his legs and trunk. The Earl was thrusting his sword in short hard lunges, ignoring the hammer blows on his shield.

'Close up! Close up!' Reginald Cobham shouted. A man tripped on a body, opening a gap in the English line, and three howling Frenchmen tried to exploit it, but were met by a man with a double-headed axe who struck down so hard that the heavy blade split a helmet and skull from nape to neck.

'Flank them! Flank them!' Skeat bellowed, and his archers waded closer to the shore to drive their arrows into the sides of the French formation. Two hundred French knights were fighting eighty or ninety English men-at-arms, a brawl of swords and shields and monstrous clangour. Men grunted as they swung. The two front ranks were locked together now, shields against shields, and it was the men behind who did the killing, swinging their blades over the front rank to kill the men beyond. Most of the archers were pouring arrows into the French flanks while a few, led by John Armstrong, had closed up behind the men-at-arms to shoot into the enemy's faces.

The French infantry, thinking the English charge stalled, gave a cheer and began to advance. 'Kill them! Kill them!' Thomas shouted. He had used a whole sheaf of arrows, twenty-four shafts, and had only one sheaf more. He drew the bow back, released, drew again. Some of the French infantry had padded jackets, but they were no protection against the arrows. Sheer numbers was their best defence and they screamed a wild war cry as they pounded down the bank. But then a score of English horsemen came from behind the archers, pushing through them to meet the mad charge. The mailed riders chopped hard into the infantry's front ranks, swords flailing left and right as the peasants hacked back. The horses bit at the enemy, and always kept moving so that no one could slash their hamstrings. A man-at-arms was hauled from his saddle and screamed terribly as he was chopped to death in the shallows. Thomas and his archers drove their arrows into the mob, more horsemen rode to help slaughter them, but still the wild rabble crowded the bank and suddenly Thomas had no arrows left and so he hung the bow round his neck, drew his sword and ran to the river's edge.

A Frenchman lunged at Thomas with a spear. He knocked it aside and brought the sword's tip flashing round to rip the man's gullet. Blood spilled bright as dawn, vanishing into the river. He hacked at a second man. Sam, baby-faced Sam, was beside him with a billhook that he sliced into a skull. It stuck there and Sam kicked the man in frustration, then took an axe from the dying enemy and, leaving his billhook in its victim, swung his new weapon in a great arc to drive the enemy back. Jake still had arrows and was shooting them fast.

A splashing and a cheer announced the arrival of more mounted men-at-arms, who drove into the infantry with heavy lances. The big horses, trained to this carnage, rode over the living and dead while the men-at-arms discarded the spears and started hacking with swords. More archers had come with fresh arrows and were shooting from the river's centre.

Thomas was on the bank now. The front of his mail coat was red with blood, none of it his, and the infantry was retreating. Then Will Skeat gave a great shout that more arrows had come, and Thomas and his archers ran back into the river to find Father Hobbe with a pack mule loaded with two panniers of arrow sheaves.

'Do the Lord's work,' Father Hobbe said, tossing a sheaf to Thomas, who undid its binding and spilled the arrows into his bag. A trumpet sounded from the northern bank and he whirled round to see that the French horsemen were riding to join the fight.

'Put them down!' Skeat shouted. 'Put those bastards down!'

Arrows slashed and sliced at horses. More English men-at-arms were wading the river to thicken the Earl's force and, inch by inch, yard by yard, they were making progress up the bank, but then the enemy horsemen drove into the mêlée with lances and swords. Thomas put an arrow through the mail covering a Frenchman's throat, drove another through a leather chanfron so that the horse reared and screamed and spilled its rider.

'Kill! Kill! Kill!' The Earl of Northampton, bloodied from his helmet to his mailed boots, rammed the sword again and again. He was bone tired and deafened by the crack of steel, but he was climbing the bank and his men were pressed close about him. Cobham was killing with a calm certainty, years of experience behind every blow. English horsemen were in the mêlée now, using their lances over the heads of their compatriots to drive the enemy horses back, but they were also blocking the aim of the archers and Thomas again hung his bow round his neck and drew his sword. 'St George! St George!' The Earl was standing on grass now, out of the reeds, above the high-water mark and behind him the river's edge was a charnel house of dead men, wounded men, blood and screaming.

Father Hobbe, his cassock skirts hitched up to his waist, was fighting with a quarterstaff, ramming the pole into French faces. 'In the name of the Father,' he shouted, and a Frenchmen reeled back with a pulped eye, 'and of the Son,' Father Hobbe snarled as he broke a man's nose, 'and of the Holy Ghost!'

A French knight broke through the English ranks, but a dozen archers swarmed over the horse, hamstrung it and hauled its rider down to the mud where they hacked at him with axe, billhook and sword.

'Archers!' the Earl shouted. 'Archers!' The last of the French horsemen had formed into a charge that threatened to sweep the whole ragged mess of brawling men, both English and French, into the river, but a score of archers, the only ones with arrows now, drove their missiles up the bank to bring the leading rank of horsemen down in a tangle of horses' legs and tumbling weapons.

Another trumpet sounded, this one from the English side, and reinforcements were suddenly streaming over the ford and spurring up onto the higher ground.

'They're breaking! They're breaking.' Thomas did not know who shouted that news, but it was true. The French were shuffling backwards. The infantry, their stomach for battle slaked by the deaths they had suffered, had already retreated, but now the French knights, the men-at-arms, were backing away from the fury of the English assault.

'Just kill them! Kill them! No prisoners! No prisoners!' the Earl of Northampton shouted in French, and his men-at-arms, bloody and wet and tired and angry, shoved up the bank and hacked again at the French, who stepped another pace back.

And then the enemy did break. It was sudden. One moment the two forces were locked in grunting, shoving, hacking battle, and then the French were running and the ford was streaming with mounted men-at-arms who crossed from the southern bank to pursue the broken enemy.

'Jesus,' Will Skeat said, and dropped to his knees and made the sign of the cross. A dying Frenchman groaned nearby, but Skeat ignored him. 'Jesus,' he said again. 'You got any arrows, Tom?'

'Two left.'

'Jesus.' Skeat looked up. There was blood on his

cheeks. 'Those bastards,' he said vengefully. He was speaking of the newly arrived English men-at-arms who crashed past the remnants of the battle to harry the fleeing enemy. 'Those bastards! They get into their camp first, don't they? They'll take all the bloody food!'

But the ford was taken, the trap was broken and the English were across the Somme.

PART THREE

Crécy

The whole English army had crossed before the tide rose again. Horses, wagons, men and women – they all crossed safe so that the French army, marching from Abbeville to trap them, found the corner of land between the river and the sea empty.

All next day the armies faced each other across the ford. The English were drawn up for battle with their four thousand archers lining the river's bank and, behind them, three great blocks of men-at-arms on the higher ground, but the French, strung out on the paths to the ford, were not tempted to force the crossing. A handful of their knights rode into the water and shouted challenges and insults, but the King would not let any English knight respond and the archers, knowing they must conserve their arrows, endured the insults without responding.

'Let the bastards shout,' Will Skeat growled, 'shouting never hurt a man yet.' He grinned at Thomas. 'Depends on the man, of course. Upset Sir Simon, didn't it?'

'He was just a bastard.'

'No, Tom,' Skeat corrected him, 'you're the bastard, and he was a gentleman.' Skeat looked across at the French, who showed no sign of trying to contest the ford. 'Most of them are all right,' he went on, evidently talking of knights and nobles. 'Once they've fought with the archers for a while they learn to look after us on account of us being the mucky bastards what keeps them alive, but there's always a few goddamn idiots. Not our Billy, though.' He turned and looked at the Earl of Northampton, who was pacing up and down by the shallows, itching for the French to come and fight. 'He's a proper gentleman. Knows how to kill the goddamn French.'

Next morning the French were gone, the only sign of them the white cloud of dust hanging over the road which was taking their huge army back to Abbeville. The English went north, slowed by hunger and the lame horses that men were reluctant to abandon. The army climbed from the Somme marshes into a heavily wooded country that yielded no grain, livestock or plunder, while the weather, which had been dry and warm, turned cold and wet during the morning. Rain spat from the east and dripped incessantly from the trees to increase men's misery so that what had seemed like a victorious campaign south of the Seine now felt like an ignominious retreat. Which is what it was, for the English were running from the French and all the men knew it, just as they knew that unless they found food soon their weakness would make them easy pickings for the enemy.

The King had sent a strong force to the mouth of the Somme where, at the small port of Le Crotoy, he expected reinforcements and supplies to be waiting, but instead the small port proved to be held by a garrison of Genoese crossbowmen. The walls were in bad repair, the attackers were hungry and so the Genoese died under a hail of arrows and a storm of men-at-arms.

The English emptied the port's storehouses of food and found a herd of beef cattle collected for the French army's use, but when they climbed the church tower they saw no ships moored in the river's mouth nor any fleet waiting at sea. The arrows, the archers and the grain that should have replenished the army were still in England.

The rain became heavier on the first night that the army camped in the forest. Rumour said that the King and his great men were in a village at the forest's edge, but most of the men were forced to shelter under the dripping trees and eat what little they could scavenge.

'Acorn stew,' Jake grumbled.

'You've eaten worse,' Thomas said.

'And a month ago we ate it off silver plates.' Jake spat out a gritty mouthful. 'So why don't we bloody fight the bastards?'

'Because they're too many,' Thomas said wearily, 'because we've only so many arrows. Because we're worn out.'

The army had marched itself into the ground. Jake, like a dozen other of Will Skeat's archers, had no boots any more. The wounded limped because there were not enough carts and the sick were left behind if they could not walk or crawl. The living stank.

Thomas had made Eleanor and himself a shelter from boughs and turf. It was dry inside the little hut where a small fire spewed a thick smoke.

'What happens to me if you lose?' Eleanor asked him.

'We won't lose,' Thomas said, though there was little conviction in his voice.

'What happens to me?' she asked again.

'You thank the Frenchmen who find you,' he said,

'and tell them you were forced to march with us against your will. Then you send for your father.'

Eleanor thought about those answers for a while, but did not look reassured. She had learned in Caen how men after victory are not amenable to reason, but slaves to their appetites. She shrugged. 'And what happens to you?'

'If I live?' Thomas shook his head. 'I'll be a prisoner. They send us to the galleys in the south, I hear. If they let us live.'

'Why shouldn't they?'

'They don't like archers. They hate archers.' He pushed a pile of wet bracken closer to the fire, trying to dry the fronds before they became their bed. 'Maybe there won't be a battle,' he said, 'because we've stolen a day's march on them.' The French were said to have gone back to Abbeville and to be crossing the river there, which meant that the hunters were coming, but the English were still a day ahead and could, perhaps, reach their fortresses in Flanders. Perhaps.

Eleanor blinked from the smoke. 'Have you seen any knight carrying the lance?'

Thomas shook his head. 'I haven't even looked,' he confessed. The last thing on his mind this night was the mysterious Vexilles. Nor, indeed, did he expect to see the lance. That was Sir Guillaume's fancy and now Father Hobbe's enthusiasm, but it was not Thomas's obsession. Staying alive and finding enough to eat were what consumed him.

'Thomas!' Will Skeat called from outside.

Thomas pushed his head through the hut opening to see a cloaked figure was standing next to Skeat. 'I'm here,' he said.

'You've got company,' Skeat said sourly, turning away.

The cloaked figure stooped to enter the hut and, to Thomas's surprise, it was Jeanette. 'I shouldn't be here,' she greeted him, pushing into the smoky interior where, throwing the hood from her hair, she stared at Eleanor. 'Who's that?'

'My woman,' Thomas spoke in English.

'Tell her to go,' Jeanette said in French.

'Stay here,' Thomas told Eleanor. 'This is the Countess of Armorica.'

Jeanette bridled when Thomas contradicted her, but did not insist that Eleanor left. Instead she pushed a bag at Thomas that proved to contain a leg of ham, a loaf of bread and a stone bottle of wine. The bread, Thomas saw, was the fine white bread that only the rich could afford, while the ham was studded with cloves and sticky with honey.

He handed the bag to Eleanor. 'Food fit for a prince,' he told her.

'I should take it to Will?' Eleanor asked, for the archers had agreed to share all their food.

'Yes, but it can wait,' Thomas said.

'I shall take it now,' Eleanor said, and pulled a cloak over her head before vanishing into the wet darkness.

'She's pretty enough,' Jeanette said in French.

'All my women are pretty,' Thomas said. 'Fit for princes, they are.'

Jeanette looked angry, or perhaps it was just the smoke from the small fire irritating her. She prodded the hut's side. 'This reminds me of our journey.'

'It wasn't cold or wet.' Thomas said. And you were mad, he wanted to add, and I nursed you and you walked away from me without looking back.

Jeanette heard the hostility in his voice. 'He thinks,' she said, 'that I am saying confession.'

'Then tell me your sins,' Thomas responded, 'and you won't have lied to His Highness.'

Jeanette ignored that. 'You know what is going to happen now?'

'We run away, they chase us, and either they catch us or they don't.' He spoke brusquely. 'And if they catch us there'll be a blood-letting.'

'They will catch us,' Jeanette said confidently, 'and there will be a battle.'

'You know that?'

'I listen to what is reported to the Prince,' she said, 'and the French are on the good roads. We are not.'

That made sense. The ford by which the English army had crossed the Seine led only into marshland and forest. It was a link between villages, it lay on no great trading route and so no good roads led from its banks, but the French had crossed the river at Abbeville, a city of merchants, and so the enemy army would have wide roads to hasten their march into Picardy. They were well fed, they were fresh and now they had the good roads to speed them.

'So there'll be a battle,' Thomas said, touching his black bow.

'There is to be a battle,' Jeanette confirmed. 'It's been decided. Probably tomorrow or the next day. The King says there is a hill just outside the forest where we can fight. Better that, he says, than letting the French get ahead and block our road. But either way,' she paused, 'they will win.'

'Maybe,' Thomas allowed.

'They will win,' Jeanette insisted. 'I listen to the conversations, Thomas! They are too many.'

Thomas made the sign of the cross. If Jeanette was right, and he had no reason to think she was deceiving him, then the army's leaders had already given up hope, but that did not mean he had to despair. 'They have to beat us first,' he said stubbornly.

'They will,' Jeanette said brutally, 'and what happens to me then?'

'What happens to you?' Thomas asked in surprise. He leaned cautiously against the fragile wall of his shelter. He sensed that Eleanor had already delivered the food and hurried back to eavesdrop. 'Why should I care,' he asked loudly, 'what happens to you?'

Jeanette shot him a vicious look. 'You once swore to me,' she said, 'that you would help restore my son to me.'

Thomas made the sign of the cross again. 'I did, my lady,' he admitted, reflecting that he made his oaths too easily. One oath was enough for a lifetime and he had made more then he could recall or keep.

'Then help me do that,' Jeanette demanded.

Thomas smiled. 'There's a battle to be won first, my lady.'

Jeanette scowled at the smoke that churned in the small shelter. 'If I am found in the English camp after the battle, Thomas, then I will never see Charles again. Never.'

'Why not?' Thomas demanded. 'It's not as if you'll be in danger, my lady. You're not a common woman. There might not be much chivalry when armies meet, but it just about reaches into the tents of royalty.'

Jeanette shook her head impatiently. 'If the English

win,' she said, 'then I might see Charles again because the Duke will want to curry favour with the King. But if they lose, then he will have no need to make any gesture. And if they lose, Thomas, then I lose everything.'

That, Thomas reckoned, was closer to the nub. If the English lost then Jeanette risked losing whatever wealth she had accumulated in the last weeks, wealth that came from the gifts of a prince. He could see a necklace of what looked like rubies half hidden by her swathing cloak, and doubtless she had dozens of other precious stones set in gold.

'So what do you want of me?' he asked.

She leaned forward and lowered her voice. 'You,' she said, 'and a handful of men. Take me south. I can hire a ship at Le Crotoy and sail to Brittany. I have money now. I can pay my debts in La Roche-Derrien and I can deal with that evil lawyer. No one need know I was even here.'

'The Prince will know,' Thomas said.

She bridled at that. 'You think he will want me for ever?'

'What do I know of him?'

'He will tire of me,' Jeanette said. 'He's a prince. He takes what he wants and when he is tired of it he moves on. But he has been good to me, so I cannot complain.'

Thomas said nothing for a while. She had not been this hard, he reflected, in those lazy summer days when they had lived as vagabonds. 'And your son?' he asked. 'How will you get him back? Pay for him?'

'I will find a way,' she said evasively.

Probably, Thomas thought, she would try to kidnap

the boy, and why not? If she could raise some men then it would be possible. Maybe she would expect Thomas himself to do it and as that thought occurred to him so Jeanette looked into his eyes.

'Help me,' she said, 'please.'

'No,' Thomas said, 'not now.' He held up a hand to ward off her protests. 'One day, God willing,' he went on, 'I'll help find your son, but I'll not leave this army now. If there's to be a battle, my lady, then I'm in it with the rest.'

'I am begging you,' she said.

'No.'

'Then damn you,' she spat, pulled the hood over her black hair and went out into the darkness. There was a short pause, then Eleanor came through the entrance.

'So what did you think?' Thomas asked.

'I think she is pretty,' Eleanor said evasively, then she frowned at him, 'and I think that in battle tomorrow a man could seize you by the hair. I think you should cut it.'

Thomas seemed to flinch. 'You want to go south? Escape battle?'

Eleanor gave him a reproachful look. 'I am an archer's woman,' she said, 'and you will not go south. Will says you are a goddamn fool,' she said the last two words in clumsy English, 'to give up such good food, but thanks you anyway. And Father Hobbe tells you that he is saying Mass tomorrow morning and expects you to be there.'

Thomas drew his knife and gave it to her, then bent his head. She sawed at his pigtail, then at handfuls of black hair that she tossed onto the fire. Thomas said nothing as she cut, but just thought about Father

Hobbe's Mass. A Mass for the dead, he thought, or for those about to die.

For in the wet dark, beyond the forest, the might of France was drawing close. The English had escaped the enemy twice, crossing rivers that were supposed to be impassable, but they could not escape a third time. The French had caught them at last.

The village lay only a short walk north of the forest's edge from which it was separated by a small river that twisted through placid water meadows. The village was an unremarkable place: a duckpond, a small church and a score of cottages with thick thatched roofs, small gardens and high dungheaps. The village, like the forest, was called Crécy.

The fields north of the village rose to a long hill that ran north and south. A country road, rutted by farm carts, ran along the hill's crest, going from Crécy to another village, just as unremarkable, called Wadicourt. If an army had marched from Abbeville and skirted the Forest of Crécy it would come westwards in search of the English and, after a while, they would see the hill between Crécy and Wadicourt rearing in front of them. They would see the stump-like church towers in the two small villages, and between the villages, but much closer to Crécy and high on the ridge top where its sails could catch the winds, a mill. The slope facing the French was long and smooth, untroubled by hedge or ditch, a playground for knights on horseback.

The army was woken before dawn. It was a Saturday, 26 August, and men grumbled at the unseasonable chill. Fires were stirred to life, reflecting flame light from the waiting mail and plate armour. The village of Crécy had been occupied by the King and his great lords, some of whom had slept in the church, and those men were still arming themselves when a chaplain of the royal household came to say a Mass. Candles were lit, a hand-bell sounded and the priest, ignoring the clank of armour that filled the small nave, called on the help of St Zephyrinus, St Gelasinus and both the saints called Genesius, all of whom had their feasts on this day, and the priest also sought aid from Little Sir Hugh of Lincoln, a child who had been murdered by the Jews on this same day nearly two hundred years before. The boy, who was said to have shown a remarkable piety, had been found dead, and no one understood how God could have allowed such a paragon to be snatched from earth so young, but there were Jews in Lincoln and their presence had provided a convenient answer. The priest prayed to them all. St Zephyrinus, he prayed, give us victory. St Gelasinus, he pleaded, be with our men. St Genesius, look after us, and St Genesius, give us strength. Little Sir Hugh, he begged, thou child in God's arms, intercede for us. Dear God, he prayed, in Thy great mercy, spare us. The knights came to the altar in their linen shirts to receive the Sacraments.

In the forest the archers knelt to other priests. They made confession and took the dry, stale bread that was the body of Christ. They made the sign of the cross. No one knew there was to be a battle that day, but they sensed the campaign had come to its end and they must either fight today or the next. Give us enough arrows, the archers prayed, and we shall make the earth red, and they held their yew staves towards the priests who touched the bows and said prayers over them.

Lances were unwrapped. They had been carried on packhorses or wagons and had hardly been used in the campaign, but the knights all dreamed of a proper battle of swirling horsemen punctuated by the shock of lances striking shields. The older and wiser men knew they would fight on foot and that their weapons would mostly be swords or axes or falchions, but still the painted lances were taken from their cloth or leather coverings that protected them from being dried by the sun or warped by rain. 'We can use them as pikes,' the Earl of Northampton suggested.

Squires and pages armed their knights, helping them with the heavy coats of leather, mail and plate. Straps were buckled tight. Destriers were brushed with straw while the smiths dragged sharpening stones down the swords' long blades. The King, who had begun arming himself at four in the morning, knelt and kissed a reliquary which contained a feather from the wing of the angel Gabriel and, when he had crossed himself, told the priest to carry the reliquary to his son. Then, with a golden crown surrounding his helmet, he was helped up onto a grey mare and rode north from the village.

It was dawn and the ridge between the two villages was empty. The mill, its linen sails neatly furled and tethered, creaked in the wind that stirred the long grasses where hares grazed but now cocked their ears and raced away as the horsemen climbed the track to the mill.

The King led, mounted on the mare that was swathed in a trapper bright with the royal arms. The scabbard of his sword was red velvet and encrusted with golden fleur-de-lis, while the hilt was decorated with a dozen great rubies. He carried a long white staff and had brought a dozen companions and a score of knights as escorts, but as his companions were all great lords then they were duly followed by their entourages so that close to three hundred men trailed up the winding track. The higher a man's rank, the closer he rode to the King, while the pages and squires were at the back where they tried to hear the conversation of their betters.

A man-at-arms dismounted and went into the mill. He climbed the ladders, opened the small door that gave access to the sails and there straddled the axle as he peered eastwards.

'See anything?' the King called up cheerfully, but the man was so overcome by being addressed by his king that he could only shake his head dumbly.

The sky was half covered in clouds and the country looked dark. From the mill's height the man-at-arms could see down the long slope to the small fields at its foot, then up another slope to a wood. An empty road ran eastwards beyond the wood. The river, filled with English horses being watered, twisted grey on the right to mark the forest's edge. The King, his visor jammed up against the crown's frontal, stared at the same view. A local man, discovered hiding in the forest, had confirmed that the road from Abbeville came from the east, which meant that the French must cross the small fields at the foot of the slope if they were to make a frontal attack on the hill. The fields had no hedges, merely shallow ditches that would offer no obstacle to a mounted knight.

'If I was Philip,' the Earl of Northampton suggested, 'I'd ride round our north flank, sire.'

'You're not Philip, and I thank God you're not,' Edward of England said. 'He's not clever.'

'And I am?' The Earl sounded surprised.

'You are clever at war, William,' the King said. He stared down the slope for a long time. 'If I was Philip,' he said at last, 'I would be mightily tempted by those fields,' he pointed to the foot of the slope, 'especially if I saw our men waiting on this hill.' The long green slope of the open pastureland was perfect for a cavalry charge. It was an invitation for lances and glory, a place made by God for the lords of France to tear an impudent enemy to ragged shreds.

'The hill's steep, sire,' the Earl of Warwick warned.

'I warrant it won't look so from the foot,' the King said, then turned his horse and spurred northwards along the ridge. The mare trotted easily, revelling in the morning air. 'She's Spanish,' the King told the Earl, 'bought off Grindley. D'you use him?'

'If I can afford his prices.'

'Of course you can, William! A rich man like you? I'll breed her. She might make fine destriers.'

'If she does, sire, I'll buy one from you.'

'If you can't afford Grindley's prices,' the King teased, 'how will you pay mine?'

He spurred the mare into a canter, his plate armour clanking, and the long train of men hurried after him along the track which led north on the ridge's summit. Green shoots of wheat and barley, doomed to die in the winter, grew where the grains had fallen from the carts carrying the harvest to the mill. The King stopped at the ridge's end, just above the village of Wadicourt, and stared northwards. His cousin was right, he thought. Philip should march into that empty countryside and cut him off from Flanders. The French, if they did but know it, were the masters here. Their army was larger, their men fresher and they could dance rings about their tired enemy until the English were forced to a desperate attack or were trapped in a place that offered them no advantage. But Edward knew better than to let every fear prey on his mind. The French were also desperate. They had suffered the humiliation of watching an enemy army wreak havoc across their land and they were in no mood to be clever. They wanted revenge. Offer them a chance, he reckoned, and the odds were good that they would snatch at it, and so the King dismissed his fears and rode down into the village of Wadicourt. A handful of the villagers had dared to stay and those folk, seeing the golden crown encircling the King's helmet and the silver curb chains on his mare, went onto their knees.

'We mean you no harm,' the King called airily, but by morning's end, he knew, their houses would have been ransacked thoroughly.

He turned southwards again, riding along the ground at the foot of the ridge. The valley's turf was soft, but not treacherous. A horse would not flounder here, a charge would be possible and – better still, just as he had reckoned – the hill did not look so steep from this angle. It was deceptive. The long stretch of rising grass looked gentle even, though in truth it would sap the horses' lungs by the time they reached the English men-at-arms. If they ever did reach them.

'How many arrows do we have?' he asked every man in earshot.

'Twelve hundred sheaves,' the Bishop of Durham said.

'Two carts full,' the Earl of Warwick answered.

'Eight hundred and sixty sheaves,' the Earl of North-ampton said.

There was silence for a while. 'The men have some themselves?' the King asked.

'Perhaps a sheaf apiece,' the Earl of Northampton said gloomily.

'It will just have to be enough,' the King said bleakly. He would have liked twice as many arrows, but then he would have liked a lot of things. He could have wished for twice as many men and a hill twice as steep and an enemy led by a man twice as nervous as Philip of Valois who, God knows, was nervous enough any-way, but it was no good wishing. He had to fight and win. He frowned at the southern end of the ridge where it fell away to the village of Crécy. That would be the easiest place for the French to attack, and the closest too, which meant the fight would be hard there. 'Guns, William,' he said to the Earl of Northampton.

'Guns, sire?'

'We'll have the guns on the flanks. Bloody things have to be useful some time!'

'We could roll the things down the hill, sire, perhaps? Maybe crush a man or two?'

The King laughed and rode on. 'Looks like rain.'

'It should hold off a while,' the Earl of Warwick answered. 'And the French may hold off too, sire.'

'You think they won't come, William?'

The Earl shook his head. 'They'll come, sire, but it'll take them time. A lot of time. We might see their van-guard by noon, but their rearguard will still be crossing the bridge in Abbeville. I'll wager they'll wait till tomorrow morning to make a fight.'

'Today or tomorrow,' the King said carelessly, 'it's all the same.'

'We could march on,' the Earl of Warwick suggested.

'And find a better hill?' The King smiled. He was younger and less experienced than many of the earls, but he was also the King and so the decision must rest with him. He was, in truth, filled with doubts, but knew that he must look confident. He would fight here. He said as much and said it firmly.

'We fight here,' the King said again, staring up the slope. He was imagining his army there, seeing it as the French would see it, and he knew his suspicion was right that the lowest part of the ridge, close to Crécy, would be the dangerous ground. That would be his right flank, close under the mill. 'My son will command on the right,' he said, pointing, 'and you, William, will be with him.'

'I will, sire,' the Earl of Northampton agreed.

'And you, my lord, on the left,' the King said to the Earl of Warwick. 'We shall make our line two-thirds of the way up the hill with archers in front and on the flanks.'

'And you, sire?' the Earl of Warwick asked.

'I shall be at the mill,' the King said, then urged his horse up the hill. He dismounted two-thirds of the way up the slope and waited for a squire to take the mare's reins, then he began the morning's real work. He paced along the hill, marking places by prodding the turf with his white staff and instructing the lords who accompanied him that their men would be here, or there, and those lords sent men to summon their commanders so that when the army marched to the long green slope they would know where to go.

'Bring the banners here,' the King ordered, 'and place them where the men are to assemble.'

He kept his army in the three battles that had marched all the way from Normandy. Two, the largest, would make a long, thick line of men-at-arms stretching across the upper reaches of the slope. 'They'll fight on foot,' the King ordered, confirming what every man had expected though one or two of the younger lords still groaned for there was more honour to be gained by fighting from horseback. But Edward cared more about victory than honour. He knew only too well that if his men-at-arms were mounted then the fools would make a charge as soon as the French attacked and his battle would degenerate into a brawl at the hill's foot that the French must win because they had the advantage of numbers. But if his men were on foot then they could not make a crazed charge against horsemen, but must wait behind their shields to be attacked. 'The horses are to be kept at the rear, beyond the ridge,' he commanded. He himself would command the third and smallest battle on the ridge's summit where it would be a reserve.

'You will stay with me, my lord bishop,' the King told the Bishop of Durham.

The bishop, armoured from nape to toes and carrying a massive spiked mace, bridled. 'You'll deny me a chance to break French heads, sire?'

'I shall let you weary God with your prayers instead,' the King said, and his lords laughed. 'And our archers,' the King went on, 'will be here, and here, and here.' He was pacing the turf and ramming the white staff into the grass every few paces. He would cover his line with archers, and mass more at the two flanks. The archers, Edward knew, were his one advantage. Their long, white-fledged arrows would do murder in this place that invited the enemy horsemen into the glorious charge. 'Here,' he stepped on and gouged the turf again, 'and here.'

'You want pits, sire?' the Earl of Northampton asked.

'As many as you like, William,' the King said. The archers, once they were gathered in their groups all along the face of the line, would be told to dig pits in the turf some yards down the slope. The pits did not have to be large, just big enough to break a horse's leg if it did not see the hole. Make enough pits and the charge must be slowed and thrown into disarray. 'And here,' the King had reached the southern end of the ridge, 'we'll park some empty wagons. Put half the guns here, and the other half at the other end. And I want more archers here.'

'If we've any left,' the Earl of Warwick grumbled.

'Wagons?' the Earl of Northampton asked.

'Can't charge a horse across a line of wagons, William,' the King said cheerfully, then beckoned his horse forward and, because his plate armour was so heavy, two pages had to half lift and half push him into the saddle. It meant an undignified scramble, but once he was settled in the saddle he looked back along the ridge that was no longer empty, but was dotted with the first banners showing where men would assemble. In an hour or two, he thought, his whole army would be here to lure the French into the archers' arrows. He wiped the earth from the butt of the staff, then spurred his horse towards Crécy. 'Let's see if there's any food,' he said.

The first flags fluttered on the empty ridge. The sky

pressed grey across distant fields and woods. Rain fell to the north and the wind felt cold. The eastern road, along which the French must come, was deserted still. The priests prayed.

Take pity on us, O Lord, in Thy great mercy, take pity on us.

The man who called himself the Harlequin was in the woods on the hill that lay to the east of the ridge that ran between Crécy and Wadicourt. He had left Abbeville in the middle of the night, forcing the sentries to open the northern gate, and he had led his men through the dark with the help of an Abbeville priest who knew the local roads. Then, hidden by beeches, he had watched the King of England ride and walk the far ridge. Now the King was gone, but the green turf was speckled with banners and the first English troops were straggling up from the village. 'They expect us to fight here,' he remarked.

'It's as good a place as any,' Sir Simon Jekyll observed grumpily. He did not like being roused in the middle of the night. He knew that the strange black-clad man who called himself the Harlequin had offered to be a scout for the French army, but he had not thought that all the Harlequin's followers would be expected to miss their breakfast and grope through a black and empty countryside for six cold hours.

'It is a ridiculous place to fight,' the Harlequin responded. 'They will line that hill with archers and we will have to ride straight into their points. What we should do is go round their flank.' He pointed to the north.

'Tell His Majesty that,' Sir Simon said spitefully.

'I doubt he will listen to me.' The Harlequin heard the scorn, but did not rise to it. 'Not yet. When we have made our name, then he will listen.' He patted his horse's neck. 'I have only faced English arrows once, and then it was merely a single archer, but I saw an arrow go clean through a mail coat.'

'I've seen an arrow go through two inches of oak,' Sir Simon said.

'Three inches,' Henry Colley added. He, like Sir Simon, might have to face those arrows today, but he was still proud of what English weapons could do.

'A dangerous weapon,' the Harlequin acknowledged, though in an unworried voice. He was ever unworried, always confident, perpetually calm, and that self-control irritated Sir Simon, though he was even more annoyed by the Harlequin's faintly hooded eyes which, he realized, reminded him of Thomas of Hookton. He had the same good looks, but at least Thomas of Hookton was dead, and that was one less archer to face this day. 'But archers can be beaten,' the Harlequin added.

Sir Simon reflected that the Frenchman had faced one archer in his whole life, yet had already worked out how to beat them. 'How?'

'You told me how,' the Harlequin reminded Sir Simon. 'You exhaust their arrows, of course. You send them lesser targets, let them kill peasants, fools and mercenaries for an hour or two, then release your main force. What we shall do,' he turned his horse away, 'is charge with the second line. It does not matter what orders we receive, we shall wait till the arrows are running out. Who wants to be killed by some dirty peasant? No glory there, Sir Simon.'

That, Sir Simon acknowledged, was true enough. He followed the Harlequin to the further side of the beech wood where the squires and servants waited with the packhorses. Two messengers were sent back with news of the English dispositions while the rest dismounted and unsaddled their horses. There was time for men and beasts to rest and feed, time to don the battle armour and time for prayer.

The Harlequin prayed frequently, embarrassing Sir Simon, who considered himself a good Christian but one who did not dangle his soul from God's apron strings. He said confession once or twice a year, went to Mass and bared his head when the Sacraments passed by, but otherwise he spared little thought for the pieties. The Harlequin, on the other hand, confided every day to God, though he rarely stepped into a church and had little time for priests. It was as though he had a private relationship with heaven, and that was both annoying and comforting to Sir Simon. It annoyed him because it seemed unmanly, and it comforted him because if God was of any use to a fighting man then it was on a day of battle.

This day, though, seemed special for the Harlequin, for after going down on one knee and praying silently for a while, he stood and ordered his squire to bring him the lance. Sir Simon, wishing they could stop the pious foolery and eat instead, presumed that they were expected to arm themselves and sent Colley to fetch his own lance, but the Harlequin stopped him. 'Wait,' he ordered.

The lances, wrapped in leather, were carried on a packhorse, but the Harlequin's squire fetched a separate lance, one that had travelled on its own horse and was wrapped in linen as well as leather. Sir Simon had assumed it was the Harlequin's personal weapon, but instead, when the linen was pulled from the shaft, he saw it was an ancient and warped spear made from a timber so old and dark that it would surely splinter if it was subjected to the smallest strain. The blade looked to be made of silver, which was foolish, for the metal was too weak to make a killing blade.

Sir Simon grinned. 'You're not fighting with that!'

'We are all fighting with that,' the Harlequin said and, to Sir Simon's surprise, the black-dressed man fell to his knees again. 'Down,' he instructed Sir Simon.

Sir Simon knelt, feeling like a fool.

'You are a good soldier, Sir Simon,' the Harlequin said. 'I have met few men who can handle weapons as you do and I can think of no man I would rather have fighting at my side, but there is more to fighting than swords and lances and arrows. You must think before you fight, and you must always pray, for if God is on your side then no man can beat you.'

Sir Simon, obscurely aware that he was being criticized, made the sign of the cross. 'I pray,' he said defensively.

'Then give thanks to God that we will carry that lance into battle.'

'Why?'

'Because it is the lance of St George, and the man who fights under the protection of that lance will be cradled in God's arms.'

Sir Simon stared at the lance, which had been laid reverently on the grass. There had been a few times in his life, usually when he was half drunk, when he would glimpse something of the mysteries of God. He had once been reduced to tears by a fierce Dominican, though the effect had not lasted beyond his next visit to a tavern, and he had felt shrunken the first time he had stepped into a cathedral and seen the whole vault dimly lit by candles, but such moments were few, infrequent and unwelcome. Yet now, suddenly, the mystery of Christ reached down to touch his heart. He stared at the lance and did not see a tawdry old weapon tricked with an impractical silver blade, but a thing of God-given power. It had been given by Heaven to make men on earth invincible, and Sir Simon was astonished to feel tears prick at his eyes.

'My family brought it from the Holy Land,' the Harlequin said, 'and they claimed that men who fought under the lance's protection could not be defeated, but that was not true. They were beaten, but when all their allies died, when the very fires of hell were lit to burn their followers to death, they lived. They left France and took the lance with them, but my uncle stole it and concealed it from us. Then I found it, and now it will give its blessings to our battle.'

Sir Simon said nothing. He just gazed at the weapon with a look close to awe.

Henry Colley, untouched by the moment's fervour, picked his nose.

'The world,' the Harlequin said, 'is rotting. The Church is corrupt and kings are weak. We have it in our power, Sir Simon, to make a new world, loved by God, but to do it we must destroy the old. We must take power ourselves, then give the power to God. That is why we fight.'

Henry Colley thought the Frenchman was plain crazy, but Sir Simon had an enraptured expression.

'Tell me,' the Harlequin looked at Sir Simon, 'what is the battle flag of the English King?'

'The dragon banner,' Sir Simon said.

The Harlequin offered one his rare smiles. 'Is that not an omen?' he asked, then paused. 'I shall tell you what will happen this day,' he went on. 'The King of France will come and he will be impatient and he will attack. The day will go badly for us. The English will jeer us because we cannot break them, but then we shall carry the lance into battle and you will see God turn the fight. We shall snatch victory from failure. You will take the English King's son as a prisoner and maybe we will even capture Edward himself, and our reward will be Philip of Valois's favour. That is why we fight, Sir Simon – for the King's favour, because that favour means power, riches and land. You will share that wealth, but only so long as you understand that we shall use our power to purge the rot from Christendom. We shall be a scourge against the wicked.'

Mad as a brush, Henry Colley thought. Daft as lights. He watched as the Harlequin stood and went to a pack-horse's pannier from which he took a square of cloth which, unfolded, proved to be a red banner on which a strange beast with horns, tusks and claws reared on its hind legs while clasping a cup in its forepaws.

'This is my family's banner,' the Harlequin said, tying the flag to the lance's long silver head with black ribbons, 'and for many years, Sir Simon, this banner was forbidden in France because its owners had fought against the King and against the Church. Our lands were wasted and our castle is still slighted, but today we shall be heroes and this banner will be back in favour.' He rolled the flag about the lance-head so that the yale was hidden. 'Today,' he said fervently, 'my family is resurrected.'

'What is your family?' Sir Simon asked.

'My name is Guy Vexille,' the Harlequin admitted, 'and I am the Count of Astarac.'

Sir Simon had never heard of Astarac, but he was pleased to learn that his master was a proper nobleman and, to signify his obedience, he held his praying hands towards Guy Vexille in homage. 'I will not disappoint you, my lord,' Sir Simon said with an unaccustomed humility.

'God will not disappoint us today,' Guy Vexille said. He took Sir Simon's hands in his own. 'Today,' he raised his voice to speak to all his knights, 'we shall destroy England.'

For he had the lance.

And the royal army of France was coming.

And the English had offered themselves for slaughter.

'Arrows,' Will Skeat said. He was standing at the wood's edge beside a pile of sheaves unloaded from a wagon, but suddenly paused. 'Good God.' He was staring at Thomas. 'Looks like a rat got your hair.' He frowned. 'Suits you, though. You look grown up at long last. Arrows!' he said again. 'Don't waste them.' He tossed the sheaves one by one to the archers. 'It looks like a lot, but most of you godforsaken lepers have never been in a proper battle and battles swallow arrows like whores swallowing – Good morning, Father Hobbe!'

'You'll spare me a sheaf, Will?'

'Don't waste it on sinners, father,' Will said, throwing

a bundle to the priest. 'Kill some God-fearing Frenchmen.'

'There's no such thing, Will. They're all spawn of Satan.'

Thomas emptied a sheaf into his arrow bag and tucked another into his belt. He had a pair of bowcords in his helmet, safe from the rain that threatened. A smith had come to the archers' encampment and had hammered the nicks from their swords, axes, knives and billhooks, then sharpened the blades with his stones. The smith, who had been wandering the army, said the King had ridden north to look for a battlefield, but he himself reckoned the French would not come that day. 'It's a lot of sweat for nothing,' he had grumbled as he smoothed a stone down Thomas's sword. 'This is French work,' he said, peering at the long blade.

'From Caen.'

'You could sell this for a penny or two,' the praise was grudging, 'good steel. Old, of course, but good.'

Now, with their arrows replenished, the archers placed their belongings into a wagon that would join the rest of the army's baggage and one man, who was sick in his belly, would guard it through the day while a second invalid would stand sentry on the archers' horses. Will Skeat ordered the wagon away, then cast an eye over his assembled archers. 'The bastards are coming,' he growled, 'if not today, then tomorrow, and there are more of them than there are of us, and they ain't hungry and they've all got boots and they think their shit smells of roses because they're bloody French-men, but they die just like anyone else. Shoot their horses and you'll live to see sundown. And remember, they ain't got proper archers so they're going to lose. It ain't difficult to understand. Keep your heads, aim at the horses, don't waste shafts and listen for orders. Let's go, boys.'

They waded the shallow river, one of the many bands of archers who emerged from the trees to file into the village of Crécy where knights were pacing up and down, then stamping their feet and calling on squires or pages to tighten a strap or loosen a buckle to make their armour comfortable. Bunches of horses, tied bridle to bridle, were being led to the back of the hill where, with the army's women, children and baggage, they would stay inside a ring of wagons. The Prince of Wales, armoured from the waist down, was eating a green apple beside the church and he nodded distractedly when Skeat's men respectfully pulled off their helmets. There was no sign of Jeanette, and Thomas wondered if she had fled on her own, then decided he did not care.

Eleanor walked beside him. She touched his arrow bag. 'Do you have enough arrows?'

'Depends how many Frenchmen come,' Thomas said.

'How many Englishmen are there?' Rumour said the army had eight thousand men now, half of them archers, and Thomas reckoned that was probably about right. He gave that figure to Eleanor, who frowned. 'And how many Frenchmen?' she asked.

'The good Lord knows,' Thomas said, but he reckoned it had to be far more than eight thousand, a lot more, but he could do nothing about that now and so he tried to forget the disparity in numbers as the archers climbed towards the windmill.

They crossed the crest to see the long forward slope, and for an instant Thomas had the impression that a great fair was just beginning. Gaudy flags dotted the hill and bands of men wandered between them, and all it needed was some dancing bears and a few jugglers and it would have looked just like the Dorchester fair.

Will Skeat had stopped to search for the Earl of Northampton's banner, then spotted it on the right of the slope, straight down from the mill. He led the men down and a man-at-arms showed them the sticks marking the spot where the archers would fight. 'And the Earl wants horse-pits dug,' the man-at-arms said.

'You heard him!' Will Skeat shouted. 'Get digging!'

Eleanor helped Thomas make the pits. The soil was thick and they used knives to loosen the earth that they scooped out with their hands.

'Why do you dig pits?' Eleanor asked.

'To trip the horses,' Thomas said, kicking the excavated earth away before starting another hole. All along the face of the hill archers were making similar small pits a score of paces in front of their positions. The enemy horsemen might charge at the full gallop, but the pits would check them. They could get through, but only slowly, and the impetus of their charge would be broken and while they tried to thread the treacherous holes they would be under attack from archers.

'There,' Eleanor said, pointing, and Thomas looked up to see a group of horsemen on the far hill crest. The first Frenchmen had arrived and were staring across the valley to where the English army slowly assembled under the banners.

'Be hours yet,' Thomas said. Those Frenchmen, he guessed, were the vanguard who had been sent ahead to find the enemy, while the main French army would still be marching from Abbeville. The crossbowmen, who would surely lead the attack, would all be on foot.

Off to Thomas's right, where the slope fell away to the river and the village, a makeshift fortress of empty wagons was being made. The carts were parked close together to form a barrier against horsemen and between them were guns. These were not the guns that had failed to break Caen Castle, but were much smaller.

'Ribalds,' Will Skeat said to Thomas.

'Ribalds?'

'That's what they're called, ribalds.' He led Thomas and Eleanor along the slope to look at the guns, which were strange bundles of iron tubes. Gunners were stirring the powder, while others were undoing bundles of garros, the long arrow-like iron missiles that were rammed into the tubes. Some of the ribalds had eight barrels, some seven and a few only four. 'Useless bloody things,' Skeat spat, 'but they might frighten the horses.' He nodded a greeting to the archers who were digging pits ahead of the ribalds. The guns were thick here – Thomas counted thirty-four and others were being dragged into place – but they still needed the protection of bowmen.

Skeat leaned on a wagon and stared at the far hill. It was not warm, but he was sweating. 'Are you ill?' Thomas asked.

'Guts are churning a bit,' Skeat admitted, 'but nothing to make a song and dance about.' There were about four hundred French horsemen on the far hill now, and others were appearing from the trees. 'It might not happen,' Skeat said quietly.

'The battle?'

'Philip of France is jumpy,' Skeat said. 'He's got a knack of marching up to battle, then deciding he'd rather be frolicking at home. That's what I hear. Nervous bastard.' He shrugged. 'But if he thinks he's got a chance today, Tom, it's going to be nasty.'

Thomas smiled. 'The pits? The archers?'

'Don't be a bloody fool, boy,' Skeat retorted. 'Not every pit breaks a leg and not every arrow strikes true. We might stop the first charge and maybe the second, but they'll still keep coming and in the end they'll get through. There's just too many of the bastards. They'll be on top of us, Tom, and it'll be up to the men-at-arms to give them a hammering. Just keep your head, boy, and remember it's the men-at-arms who do the close-quarter work. If the bastards get past the pits then take your bow back, wait for a target and stay alive. And if we lose?' He shrugged. 'Leg it for the forest and hide there.'

'What is he saying?' Eleanor asked.

'That it should be easy work today.'

'You are a bad liar, Thomas.'

'Just too many of them,' Skeat said, almost to himself. 'Tommy Dugdale faced worse odds down in Brittany, Tom, but he had plenty of arrows. We're short.'

'We're going to be all right, Will.'

'Aye, well. Maybe.' Skeat pushed himself off the wagon. 'You two go ahead. I need a quiet place for a second.'

Thomas and Eleanor walked back north. The English line was forming now, the scattered flags being swamped by men-at-arms who were forming into blocks. Archers stood ahead of each formation while marshals, armed with white staffs, made sure there were gaps in the line through which the archers could escape if the horsemen came too close. Bundles of lances

403

had been fetched from the village and were being issued to the men-at-arms in the front rank for, if the French did get past the pits and the arrows, the lances would have to be used as pikes.

By mid-morning the whole army was assembled on the hill. It looked far bigger than it really was because so many women had stayed with their men and now sat on the grass or else lay and slept. A fitful sun came and went, racing shadows across the valley. The pits were dug and the guns loaded. Perhaps a thousand Frenchmen watched from the far hill, but none ventured down the slope. 'At least it's better than marching,' Jake said; 'gives us a chance for a rest, eh?'

'Be an easy day,' Sam reckoned. He nodded at the far hill. 'Not many of the bastards, eh?'

'That's only the vanguard, you daft bastard,' Jake said.

'There are more coming?' Sam sounded genuinely surprised.

'Every goddamn bastard in France is coming,' Jake said.

Thomas kept quiet. He was imagining the French army strung along the Abbeville road. They would all know the English had stopped running, that they were waiting, and doubtless the French were hurrying in case they missed the battle. They had to be confident. He made the sign of the cross and Eleanor, sensing his fear, touched his arm.

'You will be all right,' she said.

'You too, my love.'

'You remember your promise to my father?' she asked.

Thomas nodded, but he could not persuade himself

that he would see the lance of St George this day. This day was real, while the lance belonged to some mysterious world of which Thomas really wanted no part. Everyone else, he thought, cared passionately about the relic, and only he, who had as good a reason as any to discover the truth, was indifferent. He wished he had never seen the lance, he wished that the man who had called himself the Harlequin had never come to Hookton, but if the French had not landed, he thought, then he would not be carrying the black bow and would not be on this green hillside and would not have met Eleanor. You cannot turn your back on God, he told himself.

'If I see the lance,' he promised Eleanor, 'I shall fight for it.' That was his penance, though he still hoped he would not have to serve it.

They ate mouldy bread for their midday meal. The French were a dark mass on the far hill, too many to count now, and the first of their infantry had arrived. A spit of rain made those archers who had their strings dangling from a bowtip hurry to coil the cords and shelter them under helmets or hats, but the small rain passed. A wind stirred the grass.

And still the French came to the far hill. They were a horde, they had come to Crécy, and they had come for revenge.

The English waited. Two of Skeat's archers played straw flutes, while the hobelars, who were helping to protect the guns on the army's flanks, sang songs of green woods and running streams. Some men danced the steps they would have used on a village green back home, others slept, many played dice, and all but the sleepers continually looked across the valley to the far hill crest that was thickening with men.

Jake had a linen-wrapped lump of beeswax that he handed round the archers so they could coat their bows. It was not necessary, just something to do. 'Where did you get the wax?' Thomas asked him.

'Stole it, of course, off some daft man-at-arms. Saddle polish, I reckon.'

An argument developed over which wood made the best arrows. It was an old discussion, but it passed the time. Everyone knew ash made the best shafts, but some men liked to claim that birch or hornbeam, even oak, flew just as well. Alder, though heavy, was good for killing deer, but needed a heavy head and did not have the distance for battle.

Sam took one of his new arrows from his bag and showed everyone how warped the shaft was. 'Must be made of bloody blackthorn,' he complained bitterly. 'You could shoot that round a corner.'

'They don't make arrows like they used to,' Will Skeat said, and his archers jeered for it was an old complaint. 'It's true,' Skeat said. 'It's all hurry up and no craftsmanship these days. Who cares? The bastards get paid by the sheaf and the sheaves are sent to London and no one looks at them till they reach us, and what are we going to do? Just look at it!' He took the arrow from Sam and twisted it in his fingers. 'That's not a bloody goose feather! It's a goddamn sparrow feather. No bloody use for anything except scratching your arse.' He tossed the arrow back to Sam. 'No, a proper archer makes his own arrows.'

'I used to,' Thomas said.

'But you're a lazy bastard now, eh, Tom?' Skeat grinned, but the grin faded as he stared across the valley. 'Enough of the goddamn bastards,' he grumbled, looking at the gathering French, then he grimaced as a solitary raindrop splashed on his worn boots. 'I wish it would damn well rain and get it over with. It wants to. If it pisses on us when the bastards are attacking then we might as well run for home because the bows won't shoot.'

Eleanor sat beside Thomas and watched the far hill. There were at least as many men there as were in the English army now, and the French main battle was only just arriving. Mounted men-at-arms were spreading across the hill, organizing themselves into conrois. A conroi was the basic fighting unit for a knight or man-at-arms, and most had between a dozen and twenty men, but those who formed the bodyguards of the great lords were much larger. There were now so many horsemen on the far hilltop that some had to spill down the slope, which was turning into a spread of colour, for the men-at-arms were wearing surcoats embroidered with their lords' badges and the horses had gaudy trappers, while the French banners added more blue and red and yellow and green. Yet, despite the colours, the dull grey of steel and mail still predominated. In front of the horsemen were the first green and red jackets of the Genoese crossbowmen. There was only a handful of those bowmen, but more and more were streaming over the hill to join their comrades.

A cheer sounded from the English centre and Thomas leaned forward to see that archers were scrambling to their feet. His first thought was that the French must have attacked, but there were no enemy horsemen and no arrows flew.

'Up!' Will Skeat shouted suddenly. 'On your feet!'

'What is it?' Jake asked.

Thomas saw the horsemen then. Not Frenchmen, but a dozen Englishmen who rode along the face of the waiting battleline, carefully keeping their horses away from the archers' pits. Three of the horsemen were carrying banners, and one of those flags was a huge standard showing the lilies and the leopards framed in gold. 'It's the King,' a man said, and Skeat's archers began to cheer.

The King stopped and spoke with the men in the centre of the line, then trotted on towards the English right. His escort was mounted on big destriers, but the King rode a grey mare. He wore his bright surcoat, but had hung his crowned helmet from his saddle pommel and so was bare-headed. His royal standard, all red, gold and blue, led the flags, while behind it was the King's personal badge of the flaming sun rising, while the third, which provoked the loudest cheer, was an extravagantly long pennant which showed the fire-spewing dragon of Wessex. It was the flag of England, of the men who had fought the Conqueror, and the Conqueror's descendant now flew it to show that he was of England like the men who cheered him as he rode the grey horse.

He stopped close to Will Skeat's men and raised a white staff to silence the cheers. The archers had pulled off their helmets and some had gone on one knee. The King still looked young, and his hair and beard were as gold as the rising sun on his standard.

'I am grateful,' he began in a voice so hoarse that he paused and started again. 'I am grateful that you are here.' That started the cheering again and Thomas, who was cheering with the others, did not even reflect on what choice they had been given. The King raised the white staff for silence. 'The French, as you see, have decided to join us! Perhaps they are lonely.' It was not a great joke, but it prompted roars of laughter that turned to jeers for the enemy. The King smiled as he waited for the shouts to subside. 'We came here,' he then called, 'only to procure the rights and lands and privileges that are ours by the laws of man and of God. My cousin of France challenges us, and in so doing he defies God.' The men were silent now, listening carefully. The destriers of the King's escort were pawing the ground, but not a man moved. 'God will not endure Philip of France's impudence,' the King went on. 'He will punish France, and you,' he cast a hand to indicate the archers, 'will be His instrument. God is with you, and I promise you, I swear to you before God and on my own life, that I will not leave this field till the last man of my army has marched from here. We stay on this hill together and we fight here together and we shall win together for God, for St George and for England!'

The cheers began again and the King smiled and nodded, then turned as the Earl of Northampton strode from the line. The King leaned down in his saddle and listened to the Earl for a moment, then straightened and smiled again. 'Is there a Master Skeat here?'

Skeat immediately reddened, but did not confess his presence. The Earl was grinning, the King waited, then a score of archers pointed at their leader. 'He's here!'

'Come here!' the King commanded sternly.

Will Skeat looked embarrassed as he threaded through the bowmen and approached the King's horse where he went on one knee. The King drew his ruby-hilted sword and touched it on Skeat's shoulder. 'We are told you are one of our best soldiers, so from henceforth you will be Sir William Skeat.'

The archers shouted even louder. Will Skeat, Sir William now, stayed on his knees as the King spurred on to give the same speech to the last men in the line and to those who manned the guns in the circle of farm carts. The Earl of Northampton, who had plainly been responsible for Skeat's knighthood, raised him up and led him back to his cheering men, and Skeat was still blushing as his archers clapped him on the back.

'Bloody nonsense,' he said to Thomas.

'You deserve it, Will,' Thomas said, then grinned, 'Sir William.'

'Just have to pay more bloody tax, won't I?' Skeat

said, but he looked pleased anyway. Then he frowned as a drop of rain splashed on his bare forehead. 'Bow-strings!' he shouted.

Most of the men were still sheltering their strings, but a handful had to coil the cords as the rain began to fall more heavily. One of the Earl's men-at-arms came to the archers, shouting that the women were to go back beyond the crest. 'You heard him!' Will Skeat called. 'Women to the baggage!'

Some of the women wept, but Eleanor just clung to Thomas for a moment. 'Live,' she said simply, then walked away through the rain, passing the Prince of Wales who, with six other mounted men, was riding to his place among the men-at-arms behind Will Skeat's archers. The Prince had decided to fight on horseback so he could see over the heads of the dismounted men and, to mark his arrival, his banner which was bigger than any other on the right of the field was loosed to the heavy downpour.

Thomas could no longer see across the valley because wide curtains of heavy grey rain were sweeping from the north and obscuring the air. There was nothing to do but sit and wait while the leather backing of his mail became cold and clammy. He hunched miserably, staring into the greyness, knowing that no bow could draw properly till this downpour ended.

'What they should do,' said Father Hobbe, who sat beside Thomas, 'is charge now.'

'They couldn't find their way in this muck, father,' Thomas said. He saw the priest had a bow and an arrow bag, but no other battle equipment. 'You should get some mail,' he said, 'or at least a padded jacket.'

'I'm armoured by the faith, my son.'

'Where's your bowstrings?' Thomas asked, for the priest had neither helmet nor cap.

'I looped them round my . . . well, never mind. It has to be good for something other than pissing, eh? And it's dry down there.' Father Hobbe seemed indecently cheerful. 'I've been walking the lines, Tom, and looking for your lance. It's not here.'

'Hardly goddamn surprising,' Thomas said. 'I never thought it would be.'

Father Hobbe ignored the blasphemy. 'And I had a chat with Father Pryke. Do you know him?'

'No,' Thomas said curtly. The rain was pouring off the front of his helmet onto the broken bridge of his nose. 'How the hell would I know Father Pryke?'

Father Hobbe was not deterred by Thomas's surliness. 'He's confessor to the King and a great man. He'll be a bishop one day soon. I asked him about the Vexilles.' Father Hobbe paused, but Thomas said nothing. 'He remembers the family,' the priest went on. 'He says they had lands in Cheshire, but they supported the Mortimers at the beginning of the King's reign so they were outlawed. He said something else. They were always reckoned pious, but their bishop suspected they had strange ideas. A touch of gnosticism.'

'Cathars,' Thomas said.

'It seems likely, doesn't it?'

'And if it's a pious family,' Thomas said, 'then I probably don't belong. Isn't that good news?'

'You can't escape, Thomas,' Father Hobbe said softly. His usually wild hair was plastered close to his skull by the rain. 'You promised your father. You accepted the penance.'

Thomas shook his head angrily. 'There are a score of

bastards here, father,' he indicated the archers crouching under the rain's lash, 'who've murdered more men than I have. Go and harrow their souls and leave mine alone.'

Father Hobbe shook his head. 'You've been chosen, Thomas, and I'm your conscience. It occurs to me, see, that if the Vexilles supported Mortimer then they can't love our king. If they'll be anywhere today, it'll be over there.' He nodded towards the valley's far side, which was still blotted out by the pelting rain.

'Then they'll live for another day, won't they?' Thomas said.

Father Hobbe frowned. 'You think we're going to lose?' he asked sternly. 'No!'

Thomas shivered. 'It must be getting late in the afternoon, father. If they don't attack now they'll wait till morning. That'll give them a whole day to slaughter us.'

'Ah, Thomas! How God loves you.'

Thomas said nothing to that, but he was thinking that all he wanted was to be an archer, to become Sir Thomas of Hookton as Will had just become Sir William. He was happy serving the King and did not need a heavenly lord to take him into weird battles against dark lords. 'Let me give you some advice, father,' he said.

'It's always welcome, Tom.'

'First bastard that drops, get his helmet and mail. Look after yourself.'

Father Hobbe clapped Thomas's back. 'God is on our side. You heard the King say as much.' He stood and went to talk with other men, and Thomas sat by himself and saw that the rain was lessening at last. He could see the far trees again, see the colours of the French

413

banners and surcoats, and now he could see a mass of red and green crossbowmen at the other side of the valley. They were going nowhere, he reckoned, for a crossbow string was as susceptible to the damp as any other. 'It'll be tomorrow,' he called down to Jake. 'We'll do it all again tomorrow.'

'Let's hope the sun shines,' Jake said.

The wind brought the last drops of rain from the north. It was late. Thomas stood, stretched and stamped his feet. A day wasted, he thought, and a hungry night ahead.

And tomorrow his first real battle.

An excited group of mounted men had gathered about the French King, who was still a half-mile from the hill where the largest part of his army had gathered. There were at least two thousand men-at-arms in the rear-guard who were still marching, but those who had reached the valley hugely outnumbered the waiting English.

'Two to one, sire!' Charles, the Count of Alençon and the King's younger brother, said vehemently. Like the rest of the horsemen his surcoat was soaking and the dye in its badge had run into the white linen. His helmet was beaded with water. 'We must kill them now!' the Count insisted.

But Philip of Valois's instinct was to wait. It would be wise, he thought, to let his whole army gather, to make a proper reconnaissance and then attack next morning, but he was also aware that his companions, especially his brother, thought him cautious. They even believed him to be timid for he had avoided battle with the English before, and even to propose waiting a mere day might make them think he had no stomach for the highest business of kings. He still ventured the proposal, suggesting that the victory would be all the more complete if it was just delayed by one day.

'And if you wait,' Alençon said scathingly, 'Edward will slip away in the night and tomorrow we'll face an empty hill.'

'They're cold, wet, hungry and ready to be slaughtered,' the Duke of Lorraine insisted.

'And if they don't leave, sire,' the Count of Flanders warned, 'they'll have more time to dig trenches and holes.'

'And the signs are good,' John of Hainault, a close companion of the King and the Lord of Beaumont, added.

'The signs?' the King asked.

John of Hainault gestured for a man in a black cloak to step forward. The man, who had a long white beard, bowed low. 'The sun, sire,' he said, 'is in conjunction with Mercury and opposite Saturn. Best of all, noble sire, Mars is in the house of Virgo. It spells victory, and could not be more propitious.'

And how much gold, Philip wondered, had been paid to the astrologer to come up with that prophecy, yet he was also tempted by it. He thought it unwise to do anything without a horoscope and wondered where his own astrologer was. Probably still on the Abbeville road.

'Go now!' Alençon urged his brother.

Guy Vexille, the Count of Astarac, pushed his horse into the throng surrounding the King. He saw a green-and-red-jacketed crossbowman, evidently the commander of the Genoese, and spoke to him in Italian. 'Has the rain affected the strings?'

'Badly,' Carlo Grimaldi, the Genoese leader, admitted. Crossbow strings could not be unstrung like the cords of ordinary bows for the tension in the cords was too great and so the men had simply tried to shelter their weapons under their inadequate coats. 'We should wait till tomorrow,' Grimaldi insisted, 'we can't advance without pavises.'

'What's he saying?' Alençon demanded.

The Count of Astarac translated for His Majesty's benefit, and the King, pale and long-faced, frowned when he heard that the crossbowmen's long shields that protected them from the enemy's arrows while they reloaded their cumbersome weapons had still not arrived. 'How long will they be?' he asked plaintively, but no one knew. 'Why didn't they travel with the bowmen?' he demanded, but again no one had an answer. 'Who are you?' the King finally asked the Count.

'Astarac, sire,' Guy Vexille said.

'Ah.' It was plain the King had no idea who or what Astarac was, nor did he recognize Vexille's shield that bore the simple symbol of the cross, but Vexille's horse and armour were both expensive and so the King did not dispute the man's right to offer advice. 'And you say the bows won't draw?'

'Of course they'll draw!' the Count of Alençon man interrupted. 'The damned Genoese don't want to fight. Bastard Genoese.' He spat. 'The English bows will be just as wet,' he added.

'The crossbows will be weakened, sire,' Vexille explained carefully, ignoring the hostility of the King's younger brother. 'The bows will draw, but they won't have their full range or force.'

'It would be best to wait?' the King asked.

'It would be wise to wait, sire,' Vexille said, 'and it would be especially wise to wait for the pavises.'

'Tomorrow's horoscope?' John of Hainault asked the astrologer.

The man shook his head. 'Neptune approaches the bendings tomorrow, sire. It is not a hopeful conjunction.'

'Attack now! They're wet, tired and hungry,' Alençon urged. 'Attack now!'

The King still looked dubious, but most of the great lords were confident and they hammered him with their arguments. The English were trapped and a delay of even one day might give them a chance to escape. Perhaps their fleet would come to Le Crotoy? Go now, they insisted, even though it was late in the day. Go and kill. Go and win. Show Christendom that God is on the side of the French. Just go, go now. And the King, because he was weak and because he wanted to appear strong, surrendered to their wishes.

So the oriflamme was taken from its leather tube and carried to its place of honour at the front of the men-at-arms. No other flag would be allowed to go ahead of the long plain red banner that flew from its cross-staff and was guarded by thirty picked knights who wore scarlet ribbons on their right arms. The horsemen were given their long lances, then the conrois closed together so the knights and men-at-arms were knee to knee. Drummers took the rain covers from their instruments and Grimaldi, the Genoese commander, was peremptorily told to advance and kill the English archers. The King crossed himself while a score of priests fell to their knees in the wet grass and began to pray.

The lords of France rode to the hill crest where their mailed horsemen waited. By nightfall they would all have wet swords and prisoners enough to break England for ever.

For the oriflamme was going into battle.

'God's teeth!' Will Skeat sounded astonished as he scrambled to his feet. 'The bastards are coming!' His surprise was justified, for it was late in the afternoon, the time when labourers would think of going home from the fields.

The archers stood and stared. The enemy was not yet advancing, but a horde of crossbowmen were spreading across the valley bottom, while above them the French knights and men-at-arms were arming themselves with lances.

Thomas thought it had to be a feint. It would be dark in another three or four hours, yet perhaps the French were confident they could do the business quickly. The crossbowmen were at last starting forward. Thomas took off his helmet to find a bowstring, looped one end over a horn tip, then flexed the shaft to fix the other loop in its nock. He fumbled and had to make three attempts to string the long black weapon. Sweet Jesus, he thought, but they were really coming! Be calm, he told himself, be calm, but he felt as nervous as when he had stood on the slope above Hookton and dared himself to kill a man for the very first time. He pulled open the laces of the arrow bag.

The drums began to beat from the French side of the

valley and a great cheer sounded. There was nothing to explain the cheer; the men-at-arms were not moving and the crossbowmen were still a long way off. English trumpets responded, calling sweet and clear from the windmill where the King and a reserve of men-at-arms waited. Archers were stretching and stamping their feet all along the hill. Four thousand English bows were strung and ready, but there were half as many cross-bowmen again coming towards them, and behind those six thousand Genoese were thousands of mailed horsemen.

'No pavises!' Will Skeat shouted. 'And their strings will be damp.'

'They won't have the reach for us.' Father Hobbe had appeared at Thomas's side again.

Thomas nodded, but was too dry-mouthed to answer. A crossbow in good hands, and there were none better than the Genoese, should outrange a straight bow, but not if it had a damp string. The extra range was no great advantage, for it took so long to rewind a bow that an archer could advance into range and loose six or seven arrows before the enemy was ready to send his second bolt, but even though Thomas understood that imbalance he was still nervous. The enemy looked so numerous and the French drums were great heavy kettles with thick skins that boomed like the devil's own heartbeat in the valley. The enemy horsemen were edging forward, eager to spur their mounts into an English line they expected to be deeply wounded by the crossbows' assault while the English men-at-arms were shuffling together, closing their line to make solid ranks of shields and steel. The mail clinked and jangled.

'God is with you!' a priest shouted.

'Don't waste your arrows,' Will Skeat called. 'Aim true, boys, aim true. They ain't going to stand long.' He repeated the message as he walked along his line. 'You look like you've seen a ghost, Tom.'

'Ten thousand ghosts,' Thomas said.

'There's more of the bastards than that,' Will Skeat said. He turned and gazed at the hill. 'Maybe twelve thousand horsemen?' He grinned. 'So that's twelve thousand arrows, lad.'

There were six thousand crossbowmen and twice as many men-at-arms, who were being reinforced by infantry that was appearing on both French flanks. Thomas doubted that those foot soldiers would take any part in the battle, not unless it turned into a rout, and he understood that the crossbowmen could probably be turned back because they were coming without pavises and would have rain-weakened weapons, but to turn the Genoese back would need arrows, a lot of arrows, and that would mean fewer for the mass of horsemen whose painted lances, held upright, made a thicket along the far hilltop. 'We need more arrows,' he said to Skeat.

'You'll make do with what you've got,' Skeat said, 'we all will. Can't wish for what you ain't got.'

The crossbowmen paused at the foot of the English slope and shook themselves into line before placing their bolts into their bows' troughs. Thomas took out his first arrow and superstitiously kissed its head, which was a wedge of slightly rusted steel with a wicked point and two steep barbs. He laid the arrow over his left hand and slotted its nocked butt onto the centre of the bowstring, which was protected from fraying with a whipping of hemp. He half tensed the bow, taking comfort from the yew's resistance. The arrow lay inside the shaft, to the left of the handgrip. He released the tension, gripped the arrow with his left thumb and flexed the fingers of his right hand.

A sudden blare of trumpets made him jump. Every French drummer and trumpeter was working now, making a cacophony of noise that started the Genoese forward again. They were climbing the English slope, their faces white blurs framed by the grey of their helmets. The French horsemen were coming down the slope, but slowly and in fits and starts, as though they were trying to anticipate the order to charge.

'God is with us!' Father Hobbe called. He was in his archer's stance, left foot far forward, and Thomas saw the priest had no shoes.

'What happened to your boots, father?'

'Some poor boy needed them more than I did. I'll get a French pair.'

Thomas smoothed the feathers of his first arrow.

'Wait!' Will Skeat shouted. 'Wait!' A dog ran out of the English battleline and its owner shouted for it to come back, and in a heartbeat half the archers were calling the dog's name. 'Biter! Biter! Come here, you bastard! Biter!'

'Quiet!' Will Skeat roared as the dog, utterly confused, ran towards the enemy.

Off to Thomas's right the gunners were crouched by the carts, linstocks smoking. Archers stood in the wagons, weapons half braced. The Earl of Northampton had come to stand among the archers.

'You shouldn't be here, my lord,' Will Skeat said.

'The King makes him a knight,' the Earl said, 'and he thinks he can give me orders!' The archers grinned.

'Don't kill all the men-at-arms, Will,' the Earl went on. 'Leave some for us poor swordsmen.'

'You'll get your chance,' Will Skeat said grimly. 'Wait!' he called to the archers. 'Wait!' The Genoese were shouting as they advanced, though their voices were almost drowned by the heavy drumming and the wild trumpet calls. Biter was running back to the English now and a cheer sounded when the dog at last found shelter in the battleline. 'Don't waste your goddamn arrows,' Will Skeat called. 'Take proper aim, like your mothers taught you.'

The Genoese were within bow range now, but not an arrow flew, and the red-and-green-coated crossbowmen still came, bending forward slightly as they trudged up the hill. They were not coming straight at the English, but at a slight angle, which meant that the right of the English line, where Thomas was, would be struck first. It was also the place where the slope was most gradual and Thomas, with a sinking heart, understood he was likely to be in the heart of the fight. Then the Genoese stopped, shuffled into line and began to shout their war cry.

'Too soon,' the Earl muttered.

The crossbows went into the shooting position. They were angled steeply upwards as the Genoese hoped to drop a thick rain of death on the English line.

'Draw!' Skeat said, and Thomas could feel his heart thumping as he pulled the coarse string back to his right ear. He chose a man in the enemy line, placed the arrow tip directly between that man and his right eye, edged the bow to the right because that would compensate for the bias in the weapon's aim, then lifted his left hand and shifted it back to the left because the wind was coming from that direction. Not much wind. He had not thought about aiming the arrow, it was all instinct, but he was still nervous and a muscle was twitching in his right leg. The English line was utterly silent, the crossbowmen were shouting and the French drums and trumpets deafening. The Genoese line looked like green and red statues.

'Let go, you bastards,' a man muttered and the Genoese obeyed him. Six thousand crossbow bolts arced into the sky.

'Now,' Will said, surprisingly softly.

And the arrows flew.

Eleanor crouched by the wagon that held the archers' baggage. Thirty or forty other women were there, many with children, and they all flinched as they heard the trumpets, the drums and the distant shouting. Nearly all the women were French or Breton, though not one was hoping for a French victory, for it was their men who stood on the green hill.

Eleanor prayed for Thomas, for Will Skeat and for her father. The baggage park was beneath the crest of the hill so she could not see what was happening, but she heard the deep, sharp note of the English bowstrings being released, and then the rush of air across feathers that was the sound of thousands of arrows in flight. She shuddered. A dog tethered to the cart, one of the many strays that had been adopted by the archers, whimpered. She patted it. 'There will be meat tonight,' she told the dog. The news had spread that the cattle captured in Le Crotoy would be reaching the army today. If there was an army left to eat them. The bows sounded again, more raggedly. The trumpets still screamed and the drumbeats were constant. She glanced up at the hill crest, half expecting to see arrows in the sky, but there was only grey cloud against which scores of horsemen were outlined. Those horsemen were part of the King's small reserve of troops and Eleanor knew that if she saw them spur forward then the main line would have been breached. The King's royal standard was flying from the topmost vane of the windmill where it stirred in the small breeze to show its gold, crimson and blue.

The vast baggage park was guarded by a mere score of sick or wounded soldiers who would not last a heart-beat if the French broke through the English line. The King's baggage, heaped on three white-painted wagons, had a dozen men-at-arms to guard the royal jewels, but otherwise there was only the host of women and children, and a handful of pageboys who were armed with short swords. The army's thousands of horses were also there, picketed close to the forest and watched by a few crippled men. Eleanor noted that most of the horses were saddled as though the men-at-arms and archers wanted the animals ready in case they had to flee.

A priest had been with the royal baggage, but when the bows sounded he had hurried to the crest and Eleanor was tempted to follow. Better to see what was going on, she thought, than wait here beside the forest and fear what might be happening. She patted the dog and stood, intending to walk to the crest, but just then she saw the woman who had come to Thomas in the damp night in the forest of Crécy. The Countess of Armorica, beautifully dressed in a red gown and with her hair netted in a silver mesh, was riding a small white mare up and down beside the prince's wagons. She paused every now and then to gaze at the crest and then she would stare towards the forest of Crécy-Grange that lay to the west.

A crash startled Eleanor and made her turn to the crest. Nothing explained the terrible noise that had sounded uncannily like a close clap of thunder, but there was no lightning and no rain and the mill stood unharmed. Then a seep of grey-white smoke showed above the mill's furled sails and Eleanor understood that the guns had fired. Ribalds, they were called, she remembered, and she imagined their rusting iron arrows slashing down the slope.

She looked back to the Countess, but Jeanette was gone. She had ridden to the forest, taking her jewels with her. Eleanor saw the red gown flash in the trees, then disappear. So the Countess had fled, fearing the consequences of defeat, and Eleanor, suspecting that the Prince's woman must know more of the English prospects than the archers' women, made the sign of the cross. Then, because she could not bear the waiting any longer, she walked to the crest. If her lover died, she thought, then she wanted to be near him.

Other women followed her. None spoke. They just stood on the hill and watched.

And prayed for their men.

Thomas's second arrow was in the air before his first had reached its greatest height and begun to fall. He reached for a third, then realized he had shot the second in panic and so he paused and stared at the clouded sky that was strangely thick with flickering black shafts that were as dense as starlings and deadlier than hawks. He could see no crossbow bolts, then he laid the third arrow on his left hand and picked a man in the Genoese line. There was an odd pattering noise that startled him and he looked to see it was the hail of Genoese bolts striking the turf around the horse pits.

And a heartbeat later the first English arrow flight slammed home. Scores of crossbowmen were snatched backwards, including the one Thomas had picked out for his third arrow and so he changed his aim to another man, hauled the cord back to his ear and let the shaft fly.

'They're falling short!' the Earl of Northampton shouted exultantly, and some of the archers swore, thinking he spoke of their own arrows, but it was the Genoese bows that had been enfeebled by the rain and not one of their quarrels had reached the English archers who, seeing the chance for slaughter, gave a howling cheer and ran a few paces down the slope.

'Kill them!' Will Skeat shouted.

They killed them. The great bows were drawn again and again, and the white-feathered arrows slashed down the slope to pierce mail and cloth, and to turn the lower hill into a field of death. Some crossbowmen limped away, a few crawled, and the uninjured edged backwards rather than span their weapons.

'Aim well!' the Earl called.

'Don't waste arrows!' Will Skeat shouted.

Thomas shot again, plucked a new arrow from the bag and sought a new target as his previous arrow seared down to strike a man in the thigh. The grass about the Genoese line was thick with arrows that had missed, but more than enough were striking home. The

Genoese line was thinner, much thinner, and it was silent now except for the cries of men being struck and the moans of the wounded. The archers advanced again, right to the edge of their pits, and a new flight of steel poured down the slope.

And the crossbowmen fled.

One moment they had been a ragged line, still thick with men who stood behind the bodies of their comrades, and now they were a rabble who ran as hard as they could to escape the arrows.

'Stop shooting!' Will Skeat bellowed. 'Stop!'

'Hold!' John Armstrong, whose men were to the left of Skeat's band, shouted.

'Well done!' the Earl of Northampton called.

'Back, lads, back!' Will Skeat motioned the archers. 'Sam! David! Go and collect some arrows, quick,' he pointed down the slope to where, amidst the Genoese dying and dead, the white-tipped shafts were thickly stuck in the turf. 'Hurry, lads. John! Peter! Go and help them. Go!'

All along the line archers were running to salvage arrows from the grass, but then a shout of warning came from the men who had remained in their places.

'Get back! Get back!' Will Skeat shouted.

The horsemen were coming.

Sir Guillaume d'Evecque led a conroi of twelve men on the far left of the French second line of horsemen. Ahead of him was a mass of French cavalry belonging to the first battle, to his left was a scatter of infantrymen who sat on the grass, and beyond them the small river twisted through its water meadows beside the forest.

To his right was nothing but horsemen crammed together as they waited for the crossbowmen to weaken the enemy line.

That English line looked pitifully small, perhaps because its men-at-arms were on foot and so took up much less room than mounted knights, yet Sir Guillaume grudgingly acknowledged that the English King had chosen his position well. The French knights could not assault either flank for they were both protected by a village. They could not ride around the English right for that was guarded by the soft lands beside the river, while to circle about Edward's left would mean a long journey around Wadicourt and, by the time the French came in sight of the English again, the archers would surely have been redeployed to meet a French force made ragged by its long detour. Which meant that only a frontal assault could bring a swift victory, and that, in turn, meant riding into the arrows. 'Heads down, shields up and keep close,' he told his men, before clanging down the face-piece of his helmet. Then, knowing he would not charge for some time yet, he pushed the visor back up. His men-at-arms shuffled their horses till they were knee to knee. The wind, it was said, should not be able to blow between the lances of a charging conroi.

'Be a while yet,' Sir Guillaume warned them. The fleeing crossbowmen were running up the French-held hill. Sir Guillaume had watched them advance and mouthed a silent prayer that God would be on the shoulders of the Genoese. Kill some of those damned archers, he had prayed, but spare Thomas. The drummers had been hammering their great kettles, driving down the sticks as if they could defeat the English by noise alone and Sir Guillaume, elated by the moment, had put the butt of his lance on the ground and used it to raise himself in the stirrups so he could see over the heads of the men in front. He had watched the Genoese loose their quarrels, seen the bolts as a quick haze in the sky, and then the English had shot and their arrows were a dark smear against the green slope and grey clouds and Sir Guillaume had watched the Genoese stagger. He had looked to see the English archers falling, but they were coming forward instead, still loosing arrows, and then the two flanks of the small English line had billowed dirty white as the guns added their missiles to the hail of arrows that was whipping down the slope. His horse had twitched uneasily when the crack of the guns rolled over the valley and Sir Guillaume dropped into the saddle and clicked his tongue. He could not pat the horse for the lance was in his right hand and his left arm was strapped into its shield with the three yellow hawks on the blue ground.

The Genoese had broken. At first Sir Guillaume did not credit it, believing that perhaps their commander was trying to trick the English archers into an undisciplined pursuit that would strand them at the bottom of the slope where the crossbows could turn on them. But the English did not move and the fleeing Genoese had not stopped. They ran, leaving a thick line of dead and dying men, and now they climbed in panic towards the French horsemen.

A growl sounded from the French men-at-arms. It was anger, and the sound rose to a great jeer. 'Cowards!' a man near Sir Guillaume called.

The Count of Alençon felt a surge of pure rage. 'They've been paid!' he snarled at a companion. 'Bastards have taken a bribe!'

'Cut them down!' the King called from his place at the edge of the beech wood. 'Cut them down!'

His brother heard him and wanted nothing more than to obey. The Count was in the second line, not the first, but he spurred his horse into a gap between two of the leading conrois and shouted at his men to follow. 'Cut them down!' he called. 'Cut the bastards down!'

The Genoese were between the horsemen and the English line and now they were doomed, for all along the hill the French were spurring forward. Hot-blooded men from the second battle were tangling with the conrois of the first line to form an untidy mass of banners, lances and horses. They should have walked their horses down the hill so that they were still in close order when they reached the climb on the far side, but instead they raked back spurs and, driven by a hatred of their own allies, raced each other to the kill.

'We stay!' Guy Vexille, Count of Astarac, shouted at his men.

'Wait!' Sir Guillaume called. Better to let the first ragged charge spend itself, he reckoned, rather than join the madness.

Perhaps half the French horsemen stayed on the hill. The rest, led by the King's brother, rode down the Genoese. The crossbowmen tried to escape. They ran along the valley in an attempt to reach the northern and southern ends, but the mass of horsemen overlapped them and there was no way out. Some Genoese, sensibly, lay down and curled into balls, others crouched in the shallow ditches, but most were killed or wounded as the horsemen rode over them. The destriers were big beasts with hooves like hammers. They were trained to

430

run men down and the Genoese screamed as they were trampled or slashed.

Some knights used their lances on the crossbowmen and the weight of a horse and armoured man easily drove the wooden spears clean through their victims, but those lances were all lost, left in the mangled torsos of the dead men, and the knights had to draw their swords. For a moment there was chaos in the valley bottom as the horsemen drove a thousand paths through the scattered crossbowmen. Then there were only the mangled remnants of the Genoese mercenaries, their red and green jackets soaked with blood and their weapons lying broken in the mud.

The horsemen, one easy victory under their belt, cheered themselves. '*Montjoie St Denis!*' they shouted. '*Montjoie St Denis!*' Hundreds of flags were being taken forward with the horsemen, threatening to overtake the oriflamme, but the red-ribboned knights guarding the sacred flag spurred ahead of the charge, shouting their challenge as they started up the slope towards the English, and so climbed from a valley floor that was now thick with charging horsemen. The remaining lances were lowered, the spurs went back, but some of the more sensible men, who had waited behind for the next assault, noted that there was no thunder of hoofs coming from the vast charge.

'It's turned to mud,' Sir Guillaume said to no one in particular.

Trappers and surcoats were spattered with the mud churned up by the hoofs from the low ground that had been softened by the rain. For a moment the charge seemed to flounder, then the leading horsemen broke out of the wet valley bottom to find better footing on the English hill. God was with them after all and they screamed their war cry. *'Montjoie St Denis!'* The drums were beating faster than ever and the trumpets screamed to the sky as the horses climbed towards the mill.

'Fools,' Guy Vexille said.

'Poor souls,' Sir Guillaume said.

'What's happening?' the King asked, wondering why his careful ordering of the battlelines had broken even before the fight proper had begun.

But no one answered him. They just watched.

'Jesus, Mary and Joseph,' Father Hobbe said, for it seemed as if half the horsemen of Christendom were coming up the hill.

'Into line!' Will Skeat shouted.

'God be with you!' the Earl of Northampton called, then went back to join his men-at-arms.

'Aim for the horses!' John Armstrong ordered his men.

'Bastards rode down their own bowmen!' Jake said in wonderment.

'So we'll kill the goddamn bastards,' Thomas said vengefully.

The charge was nearing the line of those Genoese who had died in the arrow storm. To Thomas, staring down the hill, the attack was a flurry of garish horse trappers and bright shields, of painted lances and streaming pennants, and now, because the horses had climbed out of the wet ground, every archer could hear the hooves that were louder even than the enemy's kettledrums. The ground was quivering so that Thomas could feel the vibration through the worn soles of his boots that had been a gift from Sir Guillaume. He looked for the three hawks, but could not see them, then forgot Sir Guillaume as his left leg went forward and his right arm hauled back. The arrow's feathers were beside his mouth and he kissed them, then fixed his gaze on a man who carried a black and yellow shield.

'Now!' Will Skeat shouted

The arrows climbed away, hissing as they went. Thomas put a second on the string, hauled and loosed. A third, this time picking out a man with a pig-snout helmet decorated with red ribbons. He was aiming at the horses each time, hoping to drive the wicked-edged blades through the padded trappers and deep into the animals' chests. A fourth arrow. He could see clods of grass and soil being thrown up behind the leading horses. The first arrow was still flying as he hauled back the fourth and looked for another target. He fixed on a man without a surcoat in polished plate armour. He loosed, and just then the man in the plate armour tumbled forward as his horse was struck by another arrow and all along the slope there were screaming horses, flailing hoofs and falling men as the English arrows drove home. A lance cartwheeled up the slope, a cry sounded above the beating hoofbeats, a horse ran into a dying animal and broke its leg and knights were thumping their knees against their horses to make them swerve about the stricken beasts. A fifth arrow, a sixth, and to the men-at-arms behind the line of archers it seemed as though the sky was filled with a never ending stream of arrows that were dark against the darkening clouds, white-tipped, and rising above the slope to plunge into the churning men-at-arms.

Scores of horses had fallen, their riders were trapped in their high saddles and ridden over as they lay helpless, yet still the horsemen came on and the men at the back could see far enough ahead to find gaps between the twitching piles of dead and dying. '*Montjoie St Denis! Montjoie St Denis!*' Spurs raked back to draw blood. To Thomas the slope looked a nightmare of heaving horses with yellow teeth and white eyes, of long lances and arrow-stuck shields, of flying mud, wild banners and grey helmets with slits for eyes and snouts for noses. The banners flew, led by a ribbon-like red streamer. He shot again and again, pouring arrows into the madness, yet for every horse that fell there was another to take its place and another beast behind that. Arrows protruded from trappers, from horses, from men, even from lances, the white feathers bobbing as the charge thundered close.

And then the French front rank was among the pits, and a stallion's leg bone cracked, and the beast's scream soared above the drums, trumpets, clang of mail and the beating of hoofs. Some men rode clean through the pits, but others fell and brought down the horses behind. The French tried to slow the horses and turn them aside, but the charge was committed now and the men behind pressed the ones in front onto the pits and arrows. The bow thumped in Thomas's hand and its arrow seared into a horseman's throat, slitting the mail like linen and hurling the man back so that his lance reared into the sky.

'Back!' Will Skeat was shouting. The charge was too close. Much too close. 'Back! Back! Back! Now! Go!'

The archers ran into the gaps between the men-at-arms, and the French, seeing their tormentors vanish, gave a great cheer. '*Montjoie St Denis*!'

'Shields!' the Earl of Northampton shouted and the English men-at-arms locked their shields together and raised their own lances to make a hedge of points.

'St George!' the Earl screamed. 'St George!'

'*Montjoie St Denis*!' Enough horsemen had got through the arrows and the pits, and still the men-at-arms streamed up the hill.

And now, at last, charged home.

If a plum was thrown at a conroi, the experts said, it should be impaled on a lance. That was how close the horsemen were supposed to be in a charge because that way they stood a chance of living, but if the conroi scattered then each man would end up surrounded by enemies. Your neighbour in a cavalry charge, the experienced men told the younger, should be closer to you than your wife. Closer even than your whore. But the first French charge was a crazed gallop and the men first became scattered when they slaughtered the Genoese and the disarray became worse as they raced uphill to close on the enemy.

The charge was not supposed to be a crazed gallop, but an ordered, dreadful and disciplined assault. The men, lined knee to knee, should have started slowly and stayed close until, and only at the very last minute, they spurred into a gallop to crash their tight-bunched lances home in unison. That was how the men were trained to charge, and their destriers were trained just as hard. A horse's instinct, on facing a packed line of men or cavalry, was to shy away, but the big stallions were ruthlessly schooled to keep running and so crash into the packed enemy and there to keep moving, stamping, biting and rearing. A charge of knights was supposed to be thundering death on hooves, a flail of metal driven by the ponderous weight of men, horses and armour, and properly done it was a mass maker of widows.

But the men of Philip's army who had dreamed of breaking the enemy into ribbons and slaughtering the dazed survivors had reckoned without archers and pits. By the time the undisciplined first French charge reached the English men-at-arms it had broken itself into scraps and then been slowed to a walk because the long, smooth and inviting slope turned out to be an obstacle course of dead horses, unsaddled knights, hissing arrows and leg-cracking pits concealed in the grass. Only a handful of men reached the enemy.

That handful spurred over the last few yards and aimed their lances at the dismounted English men-at-arms, but the horsemen were met by more lances that were braced against the ground and tilted up to pierce their horses' breasts. The stallions ran onto the lances, twisted away and the Frenchmen were falling. The English men-at-arms stepped forward with axes and swords to finish them off.

'Stay in line!' the Earl of Northampton shouted.

More horses were threading through the pits, and there were no archers in front to slow them now. These were the third and fourth ranks of the French charge. They had suffered less damage from arrows and they came to help the men hacking at the English line that still bristled with lances. Men roared their battle cries, hacked with swords and axes, and the dying horses dragged down the English lances so that the French could at last close on the men-at-arms. Steel rang on steel and thumped on wood, but each horseman was faced by two or three men-at-arms, and the French were being dragged from their saddles and butchered on the ground.

'No prisoners!' the Earl of Northampton shouted. 'No prisoners!' Those were the King's orders. To take a man prisoner meant possible wealth, but it also required a moment of courtesy to enquire whether an enemy truly yielded and the English had no time for such civility. They needed only to kill the horsemen who kept streaming up the hill.

The King, watching from beneath the mill's furled sails, which creaked as the wind twitched their tethers, saw that the French had broken through the archers only on the right, where his son fought and where the line lay closest to the French and the slope was gentlest. The great charge had been broken by arrows, but more than enough horsemen had survived and those men were spurring towards the place where the swords rang. When the French charge began it had been spread all across the battlefield, but now it shrank into a wedge shape as the men facing the English left swerved away from the archers there and added their weight to the knights and men-at-arms who hacked at the Prince of Wales's battle. Hundreds of horsemen were still milling about in the valley's muddy bottom, unwilling to face the arrow storm a second time, but French marshals were re-forming those men and sending them up the hill towards the growing mêlée that fought under the banners of Alençon and the Prince of Wales.

'Let me go down there, sire,' the Bishop of Durham, looking ungainly in his heavy mail and holding a massive spiked mace, appealed to the King.

'They're not breaking,' Edward said mildly. His line

of men-at-arms was four ranks deep and only the first two were fighting, and fighting well. A horseman's greatest advantage over infantry was speed, but the French charge had been sapped of all velocity. The horsemen were being forced into a walk to negotiate the corpses and pits, and there was no room beyond to spur into a trot before they were met by a vicious defence of axes, swords, maces and spears. Frenchmen hacked down, but the English held their shields high and stabbed their blades into the horses' guts or else sliced swords across hamstrings. The destriers fell, screaming and kicking, breaking men's legs with their wild thrashing, but every horse down was an added obstacle and, fierce as the French assault was, it was failing to break the line. No English banners had toppled yet, though the King feared for his son's bright flag that was closest to the most violent fighting.

'Have you seen the oriflamme?' he asked his entourage.

'It fell, sire,' a household knight answered. The man pointed down the slope to where a heap of dead horses and broken men were the remnants of the first French attack. 'Somewhere there, sir. Arrows.'

'God bless arrows,' the King said.

A conroi of fourteen Frenchmen managed to negotiate the pits without harm. *'Montjoie St Denis!'* they shouted, and couched their lances as they spurred into the mêlée, where they were met by the Earl of Northampton and a dozen of his men.

The Earl was using a broken lance as a pike and he rammed the splintered shaft into a horse's chest, felt the lance slide off the armour concealed by the trapper, and instinctively lifted his shield. A mace cracked on it, driving one spike clean through the leather and willow, but the Earl had his sword dangling by a strap and he dropped the lance, gripped the sword's hilt and stabbed it into the horse's fetlock, making the beast twist away. He dragged the shield clear of the mace's spikes, swung the sword at the knight, was parried, then a man-at-arms seized the Frenchman's weapon and tugged. The Frenchman pulled back, but the Earl helped and the Frenchman shouted as he was tumbled down to the English feet. A sword ran into the armour gap at his groin and he doubled over, then a mace crushed his helmet and he was left, twitching, as the Earl and his men climbed over his body and hacked at the next horse and man.

The Prince of Wales spurred into the mêlée, made conspicuous by a fillet of gold that circled his black helmet. He was only sixteen, well built, strong, tall and superbly trained. He fended an axe away with his shield and rammed his sword through another horseman's mail.

'Off the bloody horse!' the Earl of Northampton shouted at the Prince. 'Get off the bloody horse!' He ran to the Prince, seized the bridle and tugged the horse away from the fight. A Frenchman spurred in, trying to spear the Prince's back, but a man-at-arms in the Prince's green and white livery slammed his shield into the destrier's mouth and the animal twitched away.

The Earl dragged the Prince back. 'They see a man on horseback, sire,' he shouted up, 'and they think he's French.'

The Prince nodded. His own household knights had reached him now and they helped him down from the saddle. He said nothing. If he had been offended by the Earl, he hid it behind his face-piece as he went back to the mêlée. 'St George! St George!' The Prince's standard-bearer struggled to stay with his master, and the sight of the richly embroidered flag attracted still more screaming Frenchmen.

'In line!' the Earl shouted. 'In line!' but the dead horses and butchered men made obstacles that neither the French nor English could cross and so the men-at-arms, led by the Prince, were scrambling over the bodies to reach more enemies. A disembowelled horse trailed its guts towards the English, then sank onto its forelegs to pitch its rider towards the Prince, who rammed the sword into the man's helmet, mangling the visor and starting blood from the eyeholes. 'St George!' The Prince was exultant and his black armour was streaked with enemy blood. He was fighting with his visor raised, for else he could not see properly, and he was loving the moment. The hours and hours of weapons practice, the sweating days when sergeants had drilled him and beat at his shield and cursed him for not keeping his sword point high, were all proving their worth, and he could have asked for nothing more in this life: a woman in the camp and an enemy coming in their hundreds to be killed.

The French wedge was widening as more men climbed the hill. They had not broken through the line, but they had drawn the two front English ranks across the tideline of dead and wounded, and thus scattered them into groups of men who defended themselves against a welter of horsemen. The Prince was among them. Some Frenchmen, unhorsed but unwounded, were fighting on foot.

'Forward!' the Earl of Northampton shouted at the

441

third rank. It was no longer possible to hold the shield wall tight. Now he had to wade into the horror to protect the Prince, and his men followed him into the maelstrom of horses, blades and carnage. They scrambled over dead horses, tried to avoid the beating hooves of dying horses and drove their blades into living horses to bring the riders down to where they could be savaged.

Each Frenchman had two or three English footmen to contend against, and though the horses snapped their teeth, reared and lashed their hoofs, and though the riders beat left and right with their swords, the unmounted English invariably crippled the destriers in the end, and more French knights were pitched onto the hoof-scarred grass to be bludgeoned or stabbed to death. Some Frenchmen, recognizing the futility, spurred back across the pits to make new conrois among the survivors. Squires brought them spare lances, and the knights, rearmed and wanting revenge, came back to the fight, and always they rode towards the prince's bright flag.

The Earl of Northampton was close to the flag now. He hammered his shield into a horse's face, cut at its legs and stabbed at the rider's thigh. Another conroi came from the right, three of its men still holding lances and the others with swords held far forward. They slammed against the shields of the Prince's bodyguard, driving those men back, but other men in green and white came to their help and the Prince pushed two of them out of the way so he could hack at a destrier's neck. The conroi wheeled away, leaving two of its knights dead.

'Form line!' the Earl shouted. 'Form line!' There was

a lull in the fighting about the Prince's standard, for the French were regrouping.

And just then the second French battle, as large as the first, started down their hill. They came at a walk, knee to booted knee, lances held so close that a wind could not have passed between them.

They were showing how it should be done.

The ponderous drums drove them on. The trumpets seared the sky.

And the French were coming to finish the battle.

'Eight,' Jake said.

Three,' Sam told Will Skeat.

'Seven,' Thomas said. They were counting arrows. Not one archer had died yet, not from Will Skeat's band, but they were perilously low on arrows. Skeat kept looking over the heads of the men-at-arms, fearful that the French would break through, but the line was holding. Once in a while, when no English banner or head was in the way, an archer would loose one of the precious arrows at a horseman, but when a shaft wasted itself by glancing off a helmet Skeat told them to save their supply. A boy had brought a dozen skins of water from the baggage and the men passed the bags around.

Skeat lotted up the arrows and shook his head. No man had more than ten, while Father Hobbe, who admittedly had started with fewer than any of the men, had none.

'Go up the hill, father,' Skeat told the priest, 'and see if they're keeping any shafts back. The King's archers might spare some. Their captain's called Hal Crowley and he knows me. Ask him, anyway.' He did not sound hopeful. 'Right, lads, this way,' he said to the rest and led them towards the southern end of the English line where the French had not closed, then forward of the men-at-arms to reinforce the archers who, as low on arrows as the rest of the army, were keeping up a desultory harassment of any group of horsemen who threatened to approach their position. The guns were still firing intermittently, spewing a noisome stench of powder smoke on the battle's edge, but Thomas could see little evidence that the ribalds were killing any Frenchmen, though their noise, and the whistle of their iron missiles, was keeping the enemy horsemen well away from the flank. 'We'll wait here,' Skeat said, then swore for he had seen the French second line leave the far hill crest. They did not come like the first, in ragged chaos, but steadily and properly. Skeat made the sign of the cross. 'Pray for arrows,' he said.

The King watched his son fight. He had been worried when the Prince had advanced on horseback, but he nodded silent approval when he saw that the boy had possessed the good sense to dismount. The Bishop of Durham pressed to be allowed to go to Prince Edward's help, but the King shook his head. 'He has to learn to win fights.' He paused. 'I did.' The King had no intention of going down into the horror, not because he feared such a fight, but because once entangled with the French horsemen he would not be able to watch the rest of his line. His job was to stay by the mill and trickle reinforcements down to the most threatened parts of his army. Men of his reserve continually pleaded to be allowed into the mêlée, but the King obstinately refused them, even when they complained that their honour would be smirched if they missed the fight. The King dared not let men go, for he was watching the French second battle come down the hill and he knew he must hoard every man in case that great sweep of horsemen battered through his line.

That second French line, almost a mile across and three or four ranks deep, walked down the slope where its horses had to thread the bodies of the slaughtered Genoese. 'Form up!' the conroi leaders shouted when the crossbowmen's bodies were behind them, and the men obediently moved knee to knee again as they rode into the softer ground. The hooves made hardly any sound in the wet soil so the loudest noises of the charge were the clink of mail, the thump of scabbards and the swish of trappers on the long grass. The drummers were still beating on the hill behind, but no trumpets called.

'You see the Prince's banner?' Guy Vexille asked Sir Simon Jekyll, who rode beside him.

'There.' Jekyll pointed his lance tip to where the ragged fight was hottest. All Vexille's conroi had baffles on their lances, placed just back from the tip so that the wooden spears did not bury themselves in their victims' bodies. A lance with a baffle could be dragged free of a dying man and used again. 'The highest flag,' Sir Simon added.

'Follow me!' Vexille shouted, and signalled to Henry Colley, who had been given the job of standard-bearer. Colley was bitter at the assignment, reckoning he should have been allowed to fight with lance and sword, but Sir Simon had told him it was a privilege to carry the lance of St George and Colley was forced to accept the task. He planned to discard the useless lance with its red flag as soon as he entered the mêlée, but for now he carried it high as he wheeled away from the well organized line. Vexille's men followed their banner, and the departure of the conroi left a gap in the French formation and some men called out angrily, even accusing Vexille of cowardice, but the Count of Astarac ignored the jibes as he slanted across the rear of the line to where he judged his horsemen were precisely opposite the Prince's men and there he found a fortuitous gap, forced his horse into the space and let his men follow as best they could.

Thirty paces to Vexille's left a conroi with badges showing yellow hawks on a blue field trotted up the English hill. Vexille did not see Sir Guillaume's banner, nor did Sir Guillaume see his enemy's badge of the yale. Both men were watching the hill ahead, wondering when the archers would shoot and admiring the bravery of the first charge's survivors who repeatedly withdrew a few paces, re-formed and recharged the stubborn English line. Not one man threatened to break the enemy, but they still tried even when they were wounded and their destriers were limping. Then, as the second French charge neared the line of Genoese crossbowmen killed by the English archers, more trumpets sounded from the French hill and the horses pricked back their ears and tried to go into the canter. Men curbed the destriers and twisted awkwardly in their saddles to peer through visor slits to find what the trumpets meant and saw that the last of the French knights, the King and his household warriors, and the blind King of Bohemia and his companions, were trotting forward to add their weight and weapons to the slaughter. The King of France rode beneath his blue banner that was spattered with the golden fleur-de-lis, while the King of Bohemia's flag showed three white feathers on a dark red field. All the horsemen of France were committed now. The drummers sweated, the priests prayed and the royal trumpeters gave a great fanfare to presage the death of the English army.

The Count of Alençon, brother to the King, had begun the crazed charge that had left so many Frenchmen dead on the far slope, but the Count was also dead, his leg broken by his falling horse and his skull crushed by an English axe. The men he had led, those that still lived, were dazed, arrow stung, sweat-blinded and weary, but they fought on, turning their tired horses to thrash swords, maces and axes at men-at-arms, who fended the blows with shields and raked their swords across the horses' legs. Then a new trumpet called much closer to the mêlée. The notes fell in urgent triplets that followed one after the other, and some of the horsemen registered the call and understood they were being ordered to withdraw. Not to retreat, but to make way, for the biggest attack was yet to come.

'God save the King,' Will Skeat said dourly, for he had ten arrows left and half France was coming at him.

Thomas was noticing the strange rhythm of battle, the odd lulls in the violence and the sudden resurrection of horror. Men fought like demons and seemed invincible and then, when the horsemen withdrew to regroup, they would lean on their shields and swords and look like men close to death. The horses would stir again, English voices would shout warnings, and the men-at-arms would straighten and lift their dented blades. The noise on the hill was overwhelming: the occasional crack of the guns that did little except make the battlefield reek with hell's dark stench, the screams of horses, the blacksmiths' clangour of weapons, men panting, shouting and moaning. Dying horses bared their teeth and thrashed the turf. Thomas blinked sweat from his eyes and stared at the long slope that was thick with dead horses, scores of them, hundreds maybe, and beyond them, approaching the bodies of the Genoese who had died under the arrows' lash, even more horsemen were coming beneath a new spread of bright flags. Sir Guillaume? Where was he? Did he live? Then Thomas realized that the terrible opening charge, when the arrows had felled so many horses and men, had been just that, an opening. The real battle was starting now.

'Will! Will!' Father Hobbe's voice called from somewhere behind the men-at-arms. 'Sir William!'

'Here, father!'

The men-at-arms made way for the priest, who was carrying an armload of arrow sheaves and leading a small-frightened boy who carried still more. 'A gift from the royal archers,' Father Hobbe said, and he spilled the sheaves onto the grass. Thomas saw the arrows had the red-dyed feathers of the King's own bowmen. He drew his knife, cut a binding lace, and stuffed the new arrows into his bag.

'Into line! Into line!' the Earl of Northampton shouted hoarsely. His helmet was deeply dented over his right temple and his surcoat was spotted with blood. The Prince of Wales was shouting insults at the French, who were wheeling their horses away, going back through the tangled sprawl of dead and wounded. 'Archers!' The Earl called, then pulled the Prince back into the men-at-arms who were slowly lining themselves into formation. Two men were picking up fallen enemy lances to re-arm the front rank. 'Archers!' the Earl called again.

Will Skeat took his men back into their old position in front of the Earl. 'We're here, my lord.'

'You have arrows?'

'Some.'

'Enough?'

'Some,' Skeat stubbornly answered.

Thomas kicked a broken sword from under his feet. Two or three paces in front of him was a dead horse with flies crawling on its wide white eyes and over the glistening blood on its black nose. Its trapper was white and yellow, and the knight who had ridden the horse was pinned under the body. The man's visor was lifted. Many of the French and nearly all of the English men-at-arms fought with open visors and this dead man's eyes stared straight at Thomas, then suddenly blinked.

'Sweet Jesus,' Thomas swore, as if he had seen a ghost.

'Have pity,' the man whispered in French. 'For Christ's sake, have pity.'

Thomas could not hear him, for the air was filled with the drumbeat of hooves and the bray of trumpets. 'Leave them! They're beat!' Will Skeat bawled, for some of his men were about to draw their bows against those horsemen who had survived the first charge and had withdrawn to realign their ranks well within bowshot range. 'Wait!' Skeat shouted. 'Wait!'

Thomas looked to his left. There were dead men and horses for a mile along the slope, but it seemed the French had only broken through to the English line where he stood. Now they came again and he blinked away sweat and watched the charge come up the slope. They came slowly this time, keeping their discipline. One knight in the French front rank was wearing extravagant white and yellow plumes on his helmet, just as if he were in a tournament. That was a dead man, Thomas thought, for no archer could resist such a flamboyant target.

Thomas looked back at the carnage in front. Were there any English among the dead? It seemed impossible that there should not be, but he could see none. A Frenchman, an arrow deep in his thigh, was staggering in a circle among the corpses, then slumped to his knees. His mail was torn at his waist and his helmet's visor was hanging by a single rivet. For a moment, with his hands clasped over his sword's pommel, he looked just like a man at prayer, then he slowly fell forward. A wounded horse whinnied. A man tried to rise and Thomas saw the red cross of St George on his arm, and the red and yellow quarters of the Earl of Oxford on his jupon. So there were English casualties after all.

'Wait!' Will Skeat shouted, and Thomas looked up to see that the horsemen were closer, much closer. He drew the black bow. He had shot so many arrows that the two calloused string fingers of his right hand were actually sore, while the edge of his left hand had been rubbed raw by the flick of the goose feathers whipping across its skin. The long muscles of his back and arms were sore. He was thirsty. 'Wait!' Skeat shouted again, and Thomas relaxed the string a few inches. The close order of the second charge had been broken by the bodies of the crossbowmen, but the horsemen were re-forming now and were well within bow range. But Will Skeat, knowing how few arrows he had, wanted them all to count. 'Aim true, boys,' he called. 'We've no steel to waste now, so aim true! Kill the damned horses.' The bows stretched to their full extent and the string bit like fire into Thomas's sore fingers.

'Now!' Skeat shouted and a new flight of arrows skimmed the slope, this time with red feathers among the white. Jake's bowstring snapped and he cursed as he fumbled for a replacement. A second flight whipped away, its feathers hissing in the air, and then the third arrows were on the string as the first flight struck. Horses screamed and reared. The riders flinched and then drove back spurs as if they understood that the quickest way to escape the arrows was to ride down the archers. Thomas shot again and again, not thinking now, just looking for a horse, leading it with the steel arrowhead, then releasing. He drew out a white-feathered arrow and saw blood on the quills and knew his bow fingers were bleeding for the first time since he had been a child. He shot again and again until his fingers were raw flesh and he was almost weeping from the pain, but the second charge had lost all its cohesion as the barbed points tortured the horses and the riders encountered the corpses left by the first attack. The French were stalled, unable to ride into the arrow flail, but unwilling to retreat. Horses and men fell, the drums beat on and the rearward horsemen were pushing the front ranks into the bloody ground where the pits waited and the arrows stung. Thomas shot another arrow, watched the red feathers whip into a horse's breast, then fumbled in the arrow bag to find just one shaft left. He swore.

'Arrows?' Sam called, but no one had any to spare.

Thomas shot his last, then turned to find a gap in the

men-at-arms that would let him escape the horsemen who would surely come now the arrows had run out, but there were no gaps.

He felt a heartbeat of pure terror. There was no escape and the French were coming. Then, almost without thinking, he put his right hand under the horn tip of the bow and launched it high over the English men-at-arms so it would fall behind them. The bow was an encumbrance now, so he would be rid of it, and he picked up a fallen shield, hoping to God it showed an English insignia, and pushed his left forearm into the tight loops. He drew his sword and stepped back between two of the lances held by the men-at-arms. Other archers were doing the same.

'Let the archers in!' the Earl of Northampton shouted. 'Let them in!' But the men-at-arms were too fearful of the rapidly approaching French to open their files.

'Ready!' a man shouted. 'Ready!' There was a note of hysteria in his voice. The French horsemen, now that the arrows were exhausted, were streaming up the slope between the corpses and the pits. Their lances were lowered and their spurs raked back as they demanded a last spurt from the horses before they struck the enemy. The trappers were flecked with mud and hung with arrows. Thomas watched a lance, held the unfamiliar shield high and thought how monstrous the enemy's steel faces looked.

'You'll be all right, lad.' A quiet voice spoke behind him. 'Hold the shield high and go for the horse.'

Thomas snatched a look and saw it was the grey-haired Reginald Cobham, the old champion himself, standing in the front rank.

'Brace yourselves!' Cobham shouted.

The horses were on top of them, vast and high, lances reaching, the noise of the hooves and the rattle of mail overwhelming. Frenchmen were shouting victory as they leaned into the lunge.

'Now kill them!' Cobham shouted.

The lances struck the shields and Thomas was hurled back and a hoof thumped his shoulder, but a man behind pushed him upright so he was forced hard against the enemy horse. He had no room to use the sword and the shield was crushed against his side. There was the stench of horse sweat and blood in his nostrils. Something struck his helmet, making his skull ring and vision darken, then miraculously the pressure was gone and he glimpsed a patch of daylight and staggered into it, swinging the sword to where he thought the enemy was. 'Shield up!' a voice screamed and he instinctively obeyed, only to have the shield battered down, but his dazed vision was sharpening and he could see a bright-coloured trapper and a mailed foot in a big leather stirrup close to his left. He rammed his sword through the trapper and into the horse's guts and the beast twisted away. Thomas was dragged along by the trapped blade, but managed to give it a violent tug that jerked it free so sharply that its recoil struck an English shield.

The charge had not broken the line, but had broken against it like a sea wave striking a cliff. The horses recoiled and the English men-at-arms advanced to hack at the horsemen who were relinquishing lances to draw their swords. Thomas was pushed aside by the men-at-arms. He was panting, dazed and sweat-blinded. His head was a blur of pain. An archer was lying dead in front of him, head crushed by a hoof. Why had the man no helmet? Then the men-at-arms were reeling back as more horsemen filed through the dead to thicken the fight, all of them pushing towards the Prince of Wales's high banner. Thomas banged his shield hard into a horse's face, felt a glancing blow on his sword and skewered the blade down the horse's flank. The rider was fighting a man on the other side of his horse and Thomas saw a small gap between the saddle's high pommel and the man's mail skirt, and he shoved the sword up into the Frenchman's belly, heard the man's angry roar turn into a shriek, then saw the horse was falling towards him. He scrambled clear, pushing a man out of his path before the horse collapsed in a crash of armour and beating hooves. English men-at-arms swarmed over the dying beast, going to meet the next enemy. A horse with an iron garro deep in its haunch was rearing and striking with its hooves. Another horse tried to bite Thomas and he struck it with the shield, then flailed at its rider with his sword, but the man wheeled away and Thomas looked desperately for the next enemy.

'No prisoners!' the Earl screamed, seeing a man trying to lead a Frenchman out of the mêlée. The Earl had discarded his shield and was wielding his sword with both hands, hacking it like a woodman's axe and daring any Frenchman to come and challenge him. They dared. More and more horsemen pushed into the horror; there seemed no end of them. The sky was bright with flags and streaked with steel, the grass was gouged by iron and slick with blood. A Frenchman rammed the bottom edge of his shield down onto an Englishman's helmet, wheeled the horse, lunged a sword into an archer's back, wheeled again and struck down at the man still dazed by the shield blow. *'Montjoie St Denis!'* he shouted.

'St George!' The Earl of Northampton, visor up and

face streaked with blood, rammed his sword through a gap in a chanfron to take a horse's eye. The beast reared and its rider fell to be trampled by a horse behind. The Earl looked for the Prince and could not see him, then could not search more, for a fresh conroi with white crosses on black shields was forging through the mêlée, pushing friend and foe alike from their path as they carried their lances towards the Prince's standard.

Thomas saw a baffled lance coming at him and he threw himself to the ground where he curled into a ball and let the heavy horses crash by.

'*Montjoie St Denis!*' the voices yelled above him as the Count of Astarac's conroi struck home.

Sir Guillaume d'Evecque had seen nothing like it. He hoped he never saw it again. He saw a great army breaking itself against a line of men on foot.

It was true that the battle was not lost and Sir Guillaume had convinced himself it could yet be won, but he was also aware of an unnatural sluggishness in himself. He liked war. He loved the release of battle, he relished imposing his will on an enemy and he had ever profited from combat, yet he suddenly knew he did not want to charge up the hill. There was a doom in this place, and he pushed that thought away and kicked his spurs back. '*Montjoie St Denis!*' he shouted, but knew he was just pretending the enthusiasm. No one else in the charge seemed afflicted by doubts. The knights were beginning to jostle each other as they strove to aim their lances at the English line. Very few arrows were flying now, and none at all were coming from the chaos ahead where the Prince of Wales's banner flew so high.

Horsemen were now charging home all along the line, hacking at the English ranks with swords and axe, but more and more men were angling across the slope to join the fury on the English right. It was there, Sir Guillaume told himself, that the battle would be won and the English broken. It would be hard work, of course, and bloody work, hacking through the prince's troops, but once the French horsemen were in the rear of the English line it would collapse like rotted wood, and no amount of reinforcements from the top of the hill could stop that panicked rout. So fight, he told himself, fight, but there was still the nagging fear that he was riding into disaster. He had never felt anything like it and he hated it, cursing himself for being a coward!

A dismounted French knight, his helmet's face-piece torn away and blood dripping from a hand holding a broken sword, while his other hand gripped the remnants of a shield that had been split into two, staggered down the hill, then dropped to his knees and vomited. A riderless horse, stirrups flapping, galloped white-eyed across the line of the charge with its torn trapper trailing in the grass. The turf here was flecked by the white feathers of fallen arrows that looked like a field of flowers.

'Go! Go! Go!' Sir Guillaume shouted at his men, and knew he was shouting at himself. He would never tell men to go on a battlefield, but to come, to follow, and he cursed himself for using the word and stared ahead, looking for a victim for his lance, and he watched for the pits and tried to ignore the mêlée that was just to his right. He planned to widen the mêlée by boring into the English line where it was still lightly engaged. Die a hero, he told himself, carry the damned lance right up the hill and let no man ever say that Sir Guillaume d'Evecque was a coward.

Then a great cheer sounded from his right and he dared look there, away from the pits. He saw the Prince of Wales's great banner was toppling into the struggling men. The French were cheering and Sir Guillaume's gloom lifted magically for it was a French banner that pressed ahead, going over the place where the Prince's flag had flown, and then Sir Guillaume saw the banner. He saw it and stared at it. He saw a yale holding a cup and he pressed his knee to turn his horse and shouted at his men to follow him. 'To war!' he shouted. To kill. And there was no more sluggishness and no more doubts. For Sir Guillaume had found his enemy.

The King saw the enemy knights with the white-crossed shields pierce his son's battle and then he watched his son's banner fall. He could not see his son's black armour. Nothing showed on his face.

'Let me go!' the Bishop of Durham demanded.

The King brushed a horsefly from his horse's neck. 'Pray for him,' he instructed the bishop.

'What the hell use will prayer be?' the bishop demanded, and hefted his fearful mace. 'Let me go, sire!'

'I need you here,' the King said mildly, 'and the boy must learn as I did.' I have other sons, Edward of England told himself, though none like that one. That son will be a great king one day, a warrior king, a scourge of our enemies. If he lives. And he must learn to live in the chaos and terror of battle. 'You will stay,' he told the bishop firmly, then beckoned a herald. 'That badge,' he said, pointing to the red banner with the yale, 'whose is it?'

The herald stared at the banner for a long time, then frowned as if uncertain of his opinion.

'Well?' the King prompted him.

'I haven't seen it in sixteen years,' the herald said, sounding dubious of his own judgement, 'but I do believe it's the badge of the Vexille family, sire.'

'The Vexilles?' the King asked.

'Vexilles?' the bishop roared. 'Vexilles! Damned traitors. They fled from France in your great-grandfather's reign, sire, and he gave them land in Cheshire. Then they sided with Mortimer.'

'Ah,' the King said, half smiling. So the Vexilles had supported his mother and her lover, Mortimer, who together had tried to keep him from the throne. No wonder they fought well. They were trying to avenge the loss of their Cheshire estates.

'The eldest son never left England,' the bishop said, staring down at the widening struggle on the slope. He had to raise his voice to be heard above the din of steel. 'He was a strange fellow. Became a priest! Can you credit it? An eldest son! Didn't like his father, he claimed, but we locked him up all the same.'

'On my orders?' the King asked.

'You were very young, sire, so one of your council made sure the Vexille priest couldn't cause trouble. Sealed him up in a monastery, then beat and starved him till he was convinced he was holy. After that he was harmless so they put him into a country parish to rot. He must be dead by now.' The bishop frowned because the English line was bending backwards, pushed by the conroi of Vexille knights. 'Let me go

458

down, sire,' he pleaded, 'I pray you, let me take my men down.'

'I asked you to pray to God rather than to me.'

'I have a score of priests praying,' the bishop said, 'and so do the French. We're deafening God with our prayers. Please, sire, I beg you!'

The King relented. 'Go on foot,' he told the bishop, 'and with only one conroi.'

The bishop howled in triumph, then slid awkwardly off his destrier's back. 'Barratt!' he shouted to one of his men-at-arms. 'Bring your fellows! Come on!' The bishop hefted his wickedly spiked mace, then ran down the hill, bellowing at the French that the time of their death had come.

The herald counted the conroi that followed the bishop down the slope. 'Can twenty men make a difference, sire?' he asked the King.

'It will make small difference to my son,' the King said, hoping his son yet lived, 'but a great difference to the bishop. I think I would have had an enemy in the Church for ever if I'd not released him to his passion.' He watched as the bishop thrust the rear English ranks aside and, still bellowing, waded into the mêlée. There was still no sign of the prince's black armour, nor of his standard.

The herald backed his palfrey away from the King, who made the sign of the cross, then twitched his ruby-hilted sword to make certain the day's earlier rain had not rusted the blade into the scabbard's metal throat. The weapon moved easily enough and he knew he might need it yet, but for now he crossed his mailed hands on his saddle's pommel and just watched the battle.

He would let his son win it, he decided. Or else lose his son.

The herald stole a look at his king and saw that Edward of England's eyes were closed. The King was at prayer.

The battle had spread along the hill. Every part of the English line was engaged now, though in most places the fighting was light. The arrows had taken their toll, but there was none left and so the French could ride right up to the dismounted men-at-arms. Some Frenchmen tried to break through, but most were content to shout insults in the hope of drawing a handful of the dismounted English out of the shield wall. But the English discipline held. They returned insult for insult, inviting the French to come and die on their blades.

Only where the Prince of Wales's banner had flown was the fighting ferocious, and there, and for a hundred paces on either side, the two armies had become inextricably tangled. The English line had been torn, but it had not been pierced. Its rear ranks still defended the hill while the front ranks had been scattered into the enemy where they fought against the surrounding horsemen. The Earls of Northampton and Warwick had tried to keep the line steady, but the Prince of Wales had broken the formation by his eagerness to carry the fight to the enemy and the Prince's bodyguards were now down the slope near to the pits where so many horses lay with broken legs. It was there that Guy Vexille had lanced the Prince's standard-bearer so that the great flag, with its lilies and leopards and gilded fringe, was being trampled by the iron-shod hoofs of his conroi.

Thomas was twenty yards away, curled into the bloody belly of a dead horse and flinching every time another destrier trod near him. Noise overwhelmed him, but through the shrieks and hammering he could hear English voices still shouting defiance and he lifted his head to see Will Skeat with Father Hobbe, a handful of archers and two men-at-arms defending themselves against French horsemen. Thomas was tempted to stay in his blood-reeking haven, but he forced himself to scramble over the horse's body and run to Skeat's side. A French sword glanced off his helmet, he bounced off the rump of a horse, then stumbled into the small group.

'Still alive, lad?' Skeat said.

'Jesus,' Thomas swore.

'He ain't interested. Come on, you bastard! Come on!' Skeat was calling to a Frenchman, but the enemy preferred to carry his unbroken lance towards the battle raging about the fallen standard. 'They're still coming,' Skeat said in tones of wonderment. 'No end to the goddamn bastards.'

An archer in the prince's green and white livery, without a helmet and bleeding from a deep shoulder wound, lurched towards Skeat's group. A Frenchman saw him, casually wheeled his horse and chopped down with a battle-axe.

'The bastard!' Sam said, and, before Skeat could stop him, he ran from the group and leaped up onto the back of the Frenchman's horse. He put an arm round the knight's neck then simply fell backwards, dragging the man from the high saddle. Two enemy men-at-arms tried to intervene, but the victim's horse was in their way.

'Protect him!' Skeat shouted, and led his group to

461

where Sam was beating fists at the Frenchman's armour. Skeat pushed Sam away, lifted the Frenchman's breastplate just enough to let a sword enter, then slid his blade into the man's chest. 'Bastard,' Skeat said. 'Got no right to kill archers. Bastard.' He twisted the sword, rammed it in further, then yanked it free.

Sam lifted the battle-axe and grinned. 'Proper weapon,' he said, then turned as the two would-be rescuers came riding in. 'Bastards, bastards,' Sam shouted as he chopped the axe at the nearer horse. Skeat and one of the men-at-arms were flailing swords at the other beast. Thomas tried to protect them with his shield as he stabbed up at the Frenchman and felt his sword deflected by shield or armour, then the two horses, both bleeding, wheeled away.

'Stay together,' Skeat said, 'stay together. Watch our backs, Tom.'

Thomas did not answer.

'Tom!' Skeat shouted.

But Thomas had seen the lance. There were thousands of lances on the field, but most of them were painted in spiralling colours, and this one was black, warped and feeble. It was the lance of St George that had hung in the cobwebs of his childhood nave and now it was being used as the pole of a standard and the flag that hung from the silver blade was red as blood and embroidered with a silver yale. His heart lurched. The lance was here! All the mysteries he had tried so hard to avoid were on this battlefield. The Vexilles were here. His father's killer was probably here.

'Tom!' Skeat shouted again.

Thomas just pointed at the flag. 'I have to kill them.'

'Don't be a fool, Tom,' Skeat said, then whipped back

as a horseman crashed in from the lower slope. The man tried to veer away from the group of infantry, but Father Hobbe, the only man still carrying a bow, thrust the weapon into the horse's front legs, tangling them and snapping the bow. The horse collapsed with a crash by their side and Sam whacked the axe into the screaming knight's spine.

'Vexille!' Thomas shouted as loud as he could. 'Vexille!'

'Lost his bloody head,' Skeat said to Father Hobbe.

'He hasn't,' the priest said. He was without a weapon now, but when Sam had finished chopping his new axe through mail and leather, the priest took the dead Frenchman's falchion that he hefted appreciatively.

'Vexille! Vexille!' Thomas screamed.

One of the knights about the yale standard heard the shout and turned his pig-snouted helmet. It seemed to Thomas that the man stared at him through the snout's eye-slits for a long time, though it could only have been for a heartbeat or two because the man was assailed by footmen. He was defending himself skilfully, his horse dancing the battle steps to keep itself from being hamstrung, but the rider beat down one Englishman's sword and slashed his left spur across the face of the other before turning the quick horse and killing the first man with a lunge of his sword. The second man reeled away and the pig-snouted knight turned and trotted straight at Thomas.

'Asking for bloody trouble,' Skeat growled, but went to Thomas's side. The knight swerved at the last moment and beat down with his sword. Thomas parried and was shocked by the force of the man's blow that stung his shield arm to his shoulder. The horse was gone, turned, came back and the knight beat at him again. Skeat lunged at the horse, but the destrier had a mail coat under its trapper and the sword slid away. Thomas parried again and was half beaten to his knees. Then the horseman was three paces away, the destrier was swivelling fast and the knight raised his sword hand and pushed up his pig-snout, and Thomas saw it was Sir Simon Jekyll.

Anger rose in Thomas like bile and, ignoring Skeat's warning shout, he ran forward, sword swinging. Sir Simon parried the blow with contemptuous ease, the trained horse sidestepped delicately and Sir Simon's blade was coming back fast. Thomas had to twist aside and even so, fast as he was, the blade clanged against his helmet with stunning force.

'This time you'll die,' Sir Simon said, and he lunged with the blade, thrusting with killing force on Thomas's mail-clad chest, but Thomas had tripped on a corpse and was already falling backwards. The lunge pushed him down faster and he sprawled on his back, his head spinning from the blow to his helmet. There was no one to help him any more, for he had dashed away from Skeat's group that was defending itself against a new rush of horsemen. Thomas tried to stand, but a pain ripped at his head and he was winded by the blow to his chest. Then Sir Simon was leaning down from his saddle and his long sword was seeking Thomas's unprotected face. 'Goddamn bastard,' Sir Simon said, then opened his mouth wide as though he was yawning. He stared at Thomas, then spewed a stream of blood that spattered Thomas's face. A lance had gone clean through Sir Simon's side and Thomas, shaking the blood from his eyes, saw that a Frenchman had thrust the blue and yellow lance. A horseman? Only the French were mounted, but Thomas had seen the horseman let go of the lance that was hanging from Sir Simon's side and now the Englishman, eyes rolling, was swaying in his saddle, choking and dying. Then Thomas saw the trappers of the horsemen who had swept past him. They showed yellow hawks on a blue field.

Thomas staggered to his feet. Sweet Christ, he thought, but he had to learn how to fight with a sword. A bow was not enough. Sir Guillaume's men were past him now, cutting into the Vexille conroi. Will Skeat shouted at Thomas to come back, but he stubbornly followed Sir Guillaume's men. Frenchman was fighting Frenchman! The Vexilles had almost broken the English line, but now they had to defend their backs while English men-at-arms tried to haul them from their saddles.

'Vexille! Vexille!' Sir Guillaume shouted, not knowing which visored man was his enemy. He beat again and again on a man's shield, bending him back in his saddle, then he chopped the sword down on the horse's neck and the beast dropped, and an Englishman, a priest, was slashing the fallen knight's head with a falchion.

A flash of rearing colour made Sir Guillaume look to his right. The Prince of Wales's banner had been rescued and raised. He looked back to find Vexille, but saw only a half-dozen horsemen with white crosses on their black shields. He spurred towards them, raised his own shield to fend off an axe blow and lunged his sword into a man's thigh, twisted it clear, felt a blow on his back, turned the horse with his knee and parried a high sword blow. Men were shouting at him, demanding to know why he fought his own side, then the Vexille's standard-bearer began to topple as his horse was hamstrung. Two archers were slashing at the beast's legs and the silver yale fell into the mêlée as Henry Colley let go of the old lance to draw his sword.

'Bastards!' he shouted at the men who had hamstrung his horse. 'Bastards!' He slashed the blade down, hacking into a man's mailed shoulder, then a great roar made him turn to see a heavy man in plate and mail and with a crucifix about his neck, wielding a mace. Colley, still on his collapsing horse, swung at the bishop, who hammered the sword away with his shield and then slammed the mace down onto Colley's helmet. 'In the name of God!' the bishop roared as he dragged the spikes free of the mangled helmet. Colley was dead, his skull crushed, and the bishop swung the bloody mace at a horse with a yellow and blue trapper, but the rider swerved at the last instant.

Sir Guillaume never saw the bishop with his mace. Instead he had seen that one of the Vexille conroi had finer armour than the others and he raked back his spurs to reach that man, but felt his own horse faltering and he looked behind to glimpse, through the constricting slits in his visor, that Englishmen were hacking at his horse's rear legs. He beat the swords back, but the animal was sinking down and a huge voice was shouting, 'Clear my way! I want to kill the bastard. In the name of Christ, out of the way!' Sir Guillaume did not understand the words, but suddenly an arm was around his neck and he was being hauled out of the saddle. He shouted in anger, then had the breath driven from him as he thumped onto the ground. A man was holding him down and Sir Guillaume tried to hit him with his sword, but his wounded horse was thrashing

466

beside him, threatening to roll on him and Sir Guillaume's assailant dragged him free, then twisted the Frenchman's sword away. 'Just lie there!' A voice shouted at Sir Guillaume.

'Is the goddamned bastard dead?' the bishop roared.

'He's dead!' Thomas shouted.

'Praise God! On! On! Kill!'

'Thomas?' Sir Guillaume squirmed.

'Don't move!' Thomas said.

'I want Vexille!'

'They've gone!' Thomas shouted. 'They've gone! Lie still!'

Guy Vexille, assailed from two sides and with his red banner fallen, had pulled his three remaining men back, but only to join the last of the French horsemen. The King himself, with his friend the King of Bohemia, was entering the mêlée. Although John of Bohemia was blind, he had insisted on fighting and so his bodyguard had tied their horses' reins together and put the King's destrier in their centre so that he could not lose them. 'Prague!' They shouted their war cry. 'Prague!' The King's son, Prince Charles, was also tied into the group. 'Prague!' he shouted as the Bohemian knights led the last charge, except it was not a charge, but a blundering advance through a tangle of corpses and thrashing bodies and terrified horses.

The Prince of Wales still lived. The gold fillet had been half cut from his helmet and the top edge of his shield had been split in a half-dozen places, but now he led the countercharge and a hundred men went with him, snarling and screaming, wanting nothing else but to maul this last enemy who came in the dying light to the killing place where so many Frenchmen had died.

467

The Earl of Northampton, who had been mustering the rearward ranks of the prince's battle to keep them in line, sensed that the battle had turned. The vast pressure against the English men-at-arms had weakened and though the French were trying again their best men were bloodied or dead, and the new ones were coming too slowly and so he shouted at his footmen to follow him.

'Just kill them!' he shouted. 'Just kill them!'

Archers, men-at-arms, and even hobelars, who had come from their place inside the wagon circles that protected the guns on the flanks of the line, swarmed at the French. To Thomas, crouching beside Sir Guillaume, it was like the mindless rage at the bridge of Caen all over again. This was madness released, a blood-crazed madness, but the French would suffer for it. The English had endured deep into the long summer evening and they wanted revenge for the terror of watching the big horses come at them, and so they clawed and beat and slashed at the royal horsemen. The Prince of Wales led them, fighting beside archers and men-at-arms, hacking down horses and butchering their riders in a frenzy of blood. The King of Majorca died and the Count of St Pol and the Duke of Lorraine and the Count of Flanders. Then Bohemia's flag with its three white feathers fell, and the blind King was dragged down to be butchered by axes, maces and swords. A king's ransom died with the King, and his son bled to death on his father's body, as his bodyguard, hampered by the dead horses that were still tied to the living beasts, were slaughtered one after the other by Englishmen no longer shouting a war cry but screaming in a howling frenzy like lost souls. They were streaked with blood, stained and spattered and soaked in it, but the blood was French. The Prince of Wales cursed the dying Bohemians, blaming them for barring his approach to the French King, whose blue and gold banner still flew. Two English men-at-arms were hacking at the King's horse, the royal bodyguard was spurring to kill them, more men in English livery were running to bring Philip down and the Prince wanted to be there, to be the man who took the enemy King captive, but one of the Bohemian horses, dying, lurched on its side and the Prince was still wearing his spurs and one of them became caught in the dying horse's trapper. The Prince lurched, was trapped, and it was then that Guy Vexille saw the black armour and the royal surcoat and the broken fillet of gold and saw, too, that the Prince was unbalanced amidst the dying horses.

So Guy Vexille turned and charged.

Thomas saw Vexille turn. He could not reach the charging horseman with his sword, for that would mean clambering over the same horses where the Prince was trapped, but under his right hand was a black ash shaft tipped with silver, and he snatched up the lance and ran at the charging man. Skeat was there too, scrambling over the Bohemian horses with his old sword.

The lance of St George struck Guy Vexille on the chest. The silver blade crumpled and tangled with the crimson banner, but the old ash shaft had just enough strength to knock the horseman back and keep his sword from the Prince, who was being pulled free by two of his men-at-arms. Vexille hacked again, reaching far from his saddle and Will Skeat bellowed at him and thrust his sword hard up at Vexille's waist, but the black shield deflected the lunge and Vexille's trained horse instinctively turned into the attack and the rider slashed down hard.

'No!' Thomas shouted. He thrust the lance again, but it was a feeble weapon and the dry ash splintered against Vexille's shield. Will Skeat was sinking, blood showing at the ragged gash in his helmet. Vexille raised his sword to strike at Skeat a second time as Thomas stumbled forward. The sword fell, slicing into Skeat's head, then the blank mask of Vexille's dark visor swung towards Thomas. Will Skeat was on the ground, not moving. Vexille's horse turned to bring its master to where he could kill most efficiently and Thomas saw death in the Frenchman's bright sword, but then, in panicked desperation, he rammed the broken end of the black lance into the destrier's open mouth and gouged the ragged wood deep into the animal's tongue. The stallion sheered away, screaming and rearing and Vexille was thrown hard against his saddle's cantle.

The horse, eyes white behind its chanfron and mouth dripping blood, turned back to Thomas, but the Prince of Wales had been freed from the dying horse and he brought two men-at-arms to attack Vexille's other flank and the horseman parried the Prince's sword blow, then saw he must be overwhelmed and so drove back his spurs to take his horse through the mêlée and away from danger.

'*Calix meus inebrians!*' Thomas shouted. He did not know why. The words just came to him, his father's dying words, but they made Vexille look back. He stared through the eye slits, saw the dark-haired man who was holding his own banner, then a new surge of vengeful Englishmen spilled down the slope and he pricked his

470

horse through the carnage and the dying men and the broken dreams of France.

A cheer sounded from the English hilltop. The King had ordered his mounted reserve of knights to charge the French and as those men lowered their lances still more horses were being hurried from the baggage park so that more men could mount and pursue the beaten enemy.

John of Hainault, Lord of Beaumont, took the French King's reins and dragged Philip away from the mêlée. The horse was a remount, for one royal horse had already been killed, while the King himself had taken a wound in the face because he had insisted on fighting with his visor up so that his men would know he was on the field.

'It is time go, sire,' the Lord of Beaumont said gently.

'Is it over?' Philip asked. There were tears in his eyes and incredulity in his voice.

'It's over, sire,' the Lord of Beaumont said. The English were howling like dogs and the chivalry of France was twitching and bleeding on a hillside. John of Hainault did not know how it had happened, only that the battle, the oriflamme and the pride of France were all lost. 'Come, sire,' he said, and dragged the King's horse away. Groups of French knights, their horses' trappers rattling with arrows, were crossing the valley to the far woods that were dark with the coming night.

'That astrologer, John,' the French King said.

'Sire?'

'Have him put to death. Bloodily. You hear me? Bloodily!' The King was weeping as, with the handful of his bodyguard that was left, he rode away.

More and more Frenchmen were fleeing to seek

safety in the gathering dark and their retreat turned into a gallop as the first English horsemen of the battle burst through the remnants of their battered line to begin the pursuit.

The English slope seemed to twitch as the men at arms wandered among the wounded and dead. The twitching was the jerking of the dying men and horses. The valley floor was scattered with the Genoese who had been killed by their own paymasters. It was suddenly very quiet. There was no clang of steel, no hoarse shouts and no drums. There were moans and weeping and sometimes a gasp, but it seemed quiet. The wind stirred the fallen banners and flickered the white feathers of the fallen arrows that had reminded Sir Guillaume of a spread of flowers.

And it was over.

Sir William Skeat lived. He could not speak, there was no life in his eyes and he seemed deaf. He could not walk, though he seemed to try when Thomas lifted him, but then his legs crumpled and he sagged to the bloody ground.

Father Hobbe lifted Skeat's helmet away, doing it with an extraordinary gentleness. Blood poured from Skeat's grey hair and Thomas gagged when he saw the sword cut in the scalp. There were scraps of skull, strands of hair and Skeat's brain all open to the air.

'Will?' Thomas knelt in front of him. 'Will?'

Skeat looked at him, but did not seem to see him. He had a half smile and empty eyes.

'Will!' Thomas said.

'He's going to die, Thomas,' Father Hobbe said softly.

'He is not! Goddamn it, he is not! You hear me? He will live. You bloody pray for him!'

'I will pray, God knows how I will pray,' Father Hobbe soothed Thomas, 'but first we must doctor him.'

Eleanor helped. She washed Will Skeat's scalp, then she and Father Hobbe laid scraps of broken skull like pieces of shattered tile. Afterwards Eleanor tore a strip of cloth from her blue dress and gently bound the strip about Will Skeat's skull, tying it beneath his chin so that when it was done he looked like an old woman in a scarf. He had said nothing as Eleanor and the priest bandaged him, and if he had felt any pain it did not show on his face.

'Drink, Will,' Thomas said, and held out a water bottle taken from a dead Frenchman, but Skeat ignored the offer. Eleanor took the bottle and held it to his mouth, but the water just spilled down his chin. It was dark by then. Sam and Jake had made a fire, using a battle-axe to chop French lances for fuel. Will Skeat just sat by the flames. He breathed, but nothing else.

'I have seen it before,' Sir Guillaume told Thomas. He had hardly spoken since the battle, but now sat beside Thomas. He had watched his daughter tend Skeat and he had accepted food and drink from her, but he had shrugged away her conversation.

'Will he recover?' Thomas asked.

Sir Guillaume shrugged. 'I saw a man cut through the skull. He lived another four years, but only because the sisters in the abbaye looked after him.'

'He will live!' Thomas said.

Sir Guillaume lifted one of Skeat's hands, held it for a few seconds, then let it drop. 'Maybe,' he sounded sceptical. 'You were fond of him?'

'He's like a father,' Thomas said.

'Fathers die,' Sir Guillaume said bleakly. He looked drained, like a man who had turned his sword against his own king and failed in his duty.

'He will live,' Thomas said stubbornly.

'Sleep,' Sir Guillaume said, 'I will watch him.'

Thomas slept among the dead, in the battle line where the wounded moaned and the night wind stirred the white feathers flecking the valley. Will Skeat was no different in the morning. He just sat, eyes vacant, gazing at nothing and stinking because he had fouled himself.

'I shall find the Earl,' Father Hobbe said, 'and have him send Will back to England.'

The army stirred itself sluggishly. Forty English men-at-arms and as many archers were buried in Crécy's church yard, but the hundreds of French corpses, all but for the great princes and noblest lords, were left on the hill. The folk of Crécy could bury them if they wished, Edward of England did not care.

Father Hobbe looked for the Earl of Northampton, but two thousand French infantry had arrived just after dawn, coming to reinforce an army that had already been broken, and in the misty light they had thought the mounted men who greeted them were friends and then the horsemen dropped their visors, couched their lances and put back their spurs. The Earl led them.

Most of the English knights had been denied a chance to fight on horseback in the previous day's battle, but now, this Sunday morning, they'd been given their moment and the great destriers had torn bloody gaps in the marching ranks, then wheeled to cut the survivors into ragged terror. The French had fled, pursued by the implacable horsemen, who had cut and thrust until their arms were weary with the killing.

Back on the hill between Crécy and Wadicourt a pile of enemy banners was gathered. The flags were torn and some were still damp with blood. The oriflamme was carried to Edward who folded it and ordered the priests to give thanks. His son lived, the battle was won and all Christendom would know how God favoured the English cause. He declared he would spend this one day on the field to mark the victory, then march on. His army was still tired, but it had boots now and it would be fed. Cattle were roaring as archers slaughtered them and more archers were bringing food from the hill where the French army had abandoned its supplies. Other men were plucking arrows from the field and tying them into sheaves while their women plundered the dead.

The Earl of Northampton came back to Crécy's hill roaring and grinning. 'Like slaughtering sheep!' he exulted, then roamed up and down the line trying to relive the excitements of the last two days. He stopped by Thomas and grinned at the archers and their women.

'You look different, young Thomas!' he said happily, but then looked down and saw Will Skeat sitting like a child with his head bound by the blue scarf. 'Will?' the Earl said in puzzlement. 'Sir William?'

Skeat just sat.

'He was cut through the skull, my lord,' Thomas said.

The Earl's bombast fled like air from a pricked bladder. He slumped in his saddle, shaking his head. 'No,' he protested, 'no. Not Will!' He still had a bloody sword in his hand, but now he wiped the blade through the mane of his horse and pushed it into the scabbard. 'I was going to send him back to Brittany,' he said. 'Will he live?'

No one answered.

'Will?' the Earl called, then clumsily dismounted from the clinging saddle. He crouched by the Yorkshireman. 'Will? Talk to me, Will!'

'He must go to England, my lord,' Father Hobbe said.

'Of course,' the Earl said.

'No,' Thomas said.

The Earl frowned at him. 'No?'

'There is a doctor in Caen, my lord,' Thomas spoke in French now, 'and I would take him there. This doctor works miracles, my lord.'

The Earl smiled sadly. 'Caen is in French hands again, Thomas,' he said, 'and I doubt they'll welcome you.'

'He will be welcome,' Sir Guillaume said, and the Earl noticed the Frenchman and his unfamiliar livery for the first time.

'He is a prisoner, my lord,' Thomas explained, 'but also a friend. We serve you, so his ransom is yours, but he alone can take Will to Caen.'

'Is it a large ransom?' the Earl asked.

'Vast,' Thomas said.

'Then your ransom, sir,' the Earl spoke to Sir Guillaume, 'is Will Skeat's life.' He stood and took his horse's reins from an archer, then turned back to Thomas. The boy looked different, he thought, looked like a man. He had cut his hair, that was it. Chopped it, anyway. And he looked like a soldier now, like a man who could lead archers into battle. 'I want you in the spring, Thomas,' he said. 'There'll be archers to lead, and if Will can't do it, then you must. Look after him now, but in the spring you'll serve me again, you hear?'

476

'Yes, my lord.'

'I hope your doctor can work miracles,' the Earl said, then he walked on.

Sir Guillaume had understood the things that had been said in French, but not the rest and now he looked at Thomas. 'We go to Caen?' he asked.

'We take Will to Doctor Mordecai,' Thomas said.

'And after that?'

'I go to the Earl,' Thomas said curtly.

Sir Guillaume flinched. 'And Vexille, what of him?'

'What of him?' Thomas asked brutally. 'He's lost his damned lance.' He looked at Father Hobbe and spoke in English. 'Is my penance done, father?'

Father Hobbe nodded. He had taken the broken lance from Thomas and entrusted it to the King's confessor who had promised that the relic would be taken to Westminster. 'You have done your penance,' the priest said.

Sir Guillaume spoke no English, but he must have understood Father Hobbe's tone for he gave Thomas a hurt look. 'Vexille still lives,' he said. 'He killed your father and my family. Even God wants him dead!' There were tears in Sir Guillaume's eye. 'Would you leave me as broken as the lance?' he asked Thomas.

'What would you have me do?' Thomas demanded.

'Find Vexille. Kill him.' He spoke fiercely, but Thomas said nothing. 'He has the Grail!' the Frenchman insisted.

'We don't know that,' Thomas said angrily. God and Christ, he thought, but spare me! I can be an archers' leader. I can go to Caen and let Mordecai work his miracle and then lead Skeat's men into battle. We can win for God, for Will, for the King and for England. He turned on the Frenchman. 'I am an English archer,'

477

he said harshly, 'not a knight of the round table.'

Sir Guillaume smiled. 'Tell me, Thomas,' he said gently, 'was your father the eldest or a younger son?'

Thomas opened his mouth. He was about to say that of course Father Ralph had been a younger son, then realized he did not know. His father had never said, and that meant that perhaps his father had hidden the truth as he had hidden so many things.

'Think hard, my lord,' Sir Guillaume said pointedly, 'think hard. And remember, the Harlequin maimed your friend and the Harlequin lives.'

I am an English archer, Thomas thought, and I want nothing more.

But God wants more, he thought, but he did not want that burden.

It was enough that the sun shone on summer fields, on white feathers and dead men.

And that Hookton was avenged.

Historical Note

Only two actions in the book are pure invention: the initial attack on Hookton (though the French did make many such landings on the English coast) and the fight between Sir Simon Jekyll's knights and the men-at-arms under Sir Geoffrey de Pont Blanc outside La Roche-Derrien. Other than those all the sieges, battles and skirmishes are lifted from history, as was Sir Geoffrey's death in Lannion. La Roche-Derrien fell to escalade, rather than an attack from its riverside, but I wanted to give Thomas something to do, so took liberties with the Earl of Northampton's achievement. The Earl did all that he is credited with in the novel: the capture of La Roche-Derrien, the successful crossing of the Somme at Blanchetaque ford, as well as his exploits in the battle of Crécy. The capture and sack of Caen happened very much as described in the novel, as did the famous battle of Crécy. It was, in brief, an horrific and terrifying period of history which is now recognized as the beginning of the Hundred Years War.

I thought, when I began reading for and researching the novel, that I would be much concerned with chivalry, courtesy and knightly gallantry. Those things must have existed, but not on these battlefields, which were brutal, unforgiving and vicious. The book's epigraph, quoted from King Jean II of France, serves as a corrective; 'many deadly battles have been fought, people slaughtered, churches robbed, souls destroyed, young women and virgins deflowered, respectable wives and widows dishonoured; towns, manors and buildings burned, and robberies, cruelties and ambushes committed on the highways.' Those words, written some fourteen years after the battle of Crécy, justified the reasons why King Jean was surrendering almost a third of French territory to the English; the humiliation was preferable to a continuation of such ghastly and horrid warfare.

Set-piece battles like Crécy were comparatively rare in the long Anglo-French wars, perhaps because they were so utterly destructive, though the casualty figures for Crécy show that it was the French who suffered and not the English. Losses are hard to compute, but at a minimum the French lost two thousand men and the figure was probably nearer four thousand, most of them knights and men-at-arms. The Genoese losses were very high, and at least half of them were killed by their own side. The English losses were paltry, perhaps fewer than a hundred. Most of the credit must go to the English archers, but even when the French did break through the screen of arrows, they lost heavily. A horseman who had lost the momentum of the charge and was unsupported by other horsemen was easy prey to footmen, and so the cavalry of France was butchered in the mêlée. After the battle, when the French were seeking explanations for their loss, they blamed the Genoese, and there were massacres of Genoese mercenaries in many French towns, but the real French mistake was to attack in a hurry late on the Saturday afternoon instead of waiting until Sunday when they could have arranged their army more carefully. And, having made the decision to attack, they then lost discipline and so threw away their first wave of horsemen, and the remnants of that charge obstructed the better conducted second wave.

There has been a great deal of discussion about the English dispositions in the battle, most of it centring on where the archers were placed. Most historians place them on the English wings, but I have followed Robert Hardy's suggestion that they were arrayed all along the line, as well as on the wings. When it comes to matters about bows, archers and their exploits, Mr Hardy is a good man to heed.

Battles were rare, but the *chevauchée*, an expedition that set out deliberately to waste the enemy's territory, was common. It was, of course, economic warfare – the fourteenth-century equivalent of carpet bombing. Contemporaries, describing the French countryside after the passage of an English *chevauchée*, recorded that France was 'overwhelmed and trampled under foot', that it was on 'the verge of utter ruin' or 'tormented and war-ravaged'. No chivalry there, little gallantry and less courtesy. France would eventually recover and expel the English from France, but only after she had learned to cope with the *chevauchée* and, more importantly, the English (and Welsh) archers.

The word longbow does not appear in the novel, for that word was not used in the fourteenth century (it is for the same reason that Edward of Woodstock, the Prince of Wales, is not called the Black Prince – a later coinage). The bow was simply that, the bow, or perhaps the great bow or the war bow. Much ink has been wasted discussing the origins of the longbow, whether it is Welsh or English, a medieval invention or stretching back to the neolithic, but the salient fact is that it had emerged in the years leading up to the Hundred Years War as a battle-winning weapon. What made it so effective was the number of bowmen who could be assembled in an army. One or two longbows might do damage, but thousands would destroy an army and the English, alone in Europe, were capable of assembling those numbers. Why? The technology could not be simpler, yet still other countries did not produce archers. Part of the answer is surely in the great difficulty it took to become an expert archer. It needed hours and years of practice, and the habit of such practice took hold in only some English and Welsh regions. There had probably been such experts in Britain since the neolithic (yew bows as long as the ones used at Crécy have been found in neolithic graves), but equally probably there were only a few experts, but for some reason or another the Middle Ages saw a popular enthusiasm for the pursuit of archery in parts of England and Wales that led to the rise of the longbow as a mass weapon of war, and certainly once that enthusiasm waned then the bow quickly disappeared from the English arsenal. Common wisdom has it that the longbow was replaced by the gun, but it is more true to say that the longbow withered despite the gun. Benjamin Franklin, no fool, reckoned the American rebels would have won their war much more swiftly had they been practised longbowmen and it is quite certain that a battalion of archers could have outshot and beaten, easily, a battalion of Wellington's veterans armed with smoothbore muskets. But a gun (or crossbow) was much easier to master than a longbow. The longbow, in brief, was a phenomenon, probably fed by a popular craze for archery that translated into a battle-winning weapon for England's kings. It also raised the status of the infantryman, as even the dullest English nobleman came to realize that his life depended on archers, and it is no wonder that archers outnumbered men-at-arms in the English armies of the period.

I have to record an enormous debt to Jonathan Sumption, author of *Trial by Battle, the Hundred Years War, Volume 1*. It is a rank offence to full-time authors like myself that a man who successfully practices as a lawyer can write such superb books in what is, presumably, his 'spare' time, but I am grateful he did so and recommend his history to anyone who wishes to learn more of the period. Any mistakes that remain are entirely my own.

VAGABOND

VAGABOND

is for

June and Eddie Bell

in friendship and gratitude

CONTENTS

PART ONE

England, October 1346

Arrows on the Hill

It was October, the time of the year's dying when cattle were being slaughtered before winter and when the northern winds brought a promise of ice. The chestnut leaves had turned golden, the beeches were trees of flame and the oaks were made from bronze. Thomas of Hookton, with his woman, Eleanor, and his friend, Father Hobbe, came to the upland farm at dusk and the farmer refused to open his door, but shouted through the wood that the travellers could sleep in the byre. Rain rattled on the mouldering thatch. Thomas led their one horse under the roof that they shared with a wood-pile, six pigs in a stout timber pen and a scattering of feathers where a hen had been plucked. The feathers reminded Father Hobbe that it was St Gallus's day and he told Eleanor how the blessed saint, coming home in a winter's night, had found a bear stealing his dinner. 'He told the animal off!' Father Hobbe said. 'He gave it a right talking-to, he did, and then he made it fetch his firewood.'

'I've seen a picture of that,' Eleanor said. 'Didn't the bear become his servant?'

'That's because Gallus was a holy man,' Father Hobbe explained. 'Bears wouldn't fetch firewood for just any-one! Only for a holy man.'

'A holy man,' Thomas put in, 'who is the patron saint of hens.' Thomas knew all about the saints, more indeed than Father Hobbe. 'Why would a chicken want a saint?' he enquired sarcastically.

'Gallus is the patron of hens?' Eleanor asked, confused by Thomas's tone. 'Not bears?'

'Of hens,' Father Hobbe confirmed. 'Indeed of all poultry.'

'But why?' Eleanor wanted to know.

'Because he once expelled a wicked demon from a young girl.' Father Hobbe, broad-faced, hair like a stickleback's spines, peasant-born, stocky, young and eager, liked to tell stories of the blessed saints. 'A whole bundle of bishops had tried to drive the demon out,' he went on, 'and they had all failed, but the blessed Gallus came along and he cursed the demon. He cursed it! And it screeched in terror' – Father Hobbe waved his hands in the air to imitate the evil spirit's panic – 'and then it fled from her body, it did, and it looked just like a black hen – a pullet. A black pullet.'

'I've never seen a picture of that,' Eleanor remarked in her accented English, then, gazing out through the byre door, 'but I'd like to see a real bear carrying firewood,' she added wistfully.

Thomas sat beside her and stared into the wet dusk, which was hazed by a small mist. He was not sure it really was St Gallus's day for he had lost his reckoning while they travelled. Perhaps it was already St Audrey's day? It was October, he knew that, and he knew that one thousand, three hundred and forty-six years had passed since Christ had been born, but he was not sure which day it was. It was easy to lose count. His father had once recited all the Sunday services on a Saturday

4

and he had had to do them again the next day. Thomas surreptitiously made the sign of the cross. He was a priest's bastard and that was said to bring bad luck. He shivered. There was a heaviness in the air that owed nothing to the setting sun nor to the rain clouds nor to the mist. God help us, he thought, but there was an evil in this dusk and he made the sign of the cross again and said a silent prayer to St Gallus and his obedient bear. There had been a dancing bear in London, its teeth nothing but rotted yellow stumps and its brown flanks matted with blood from its owner's goad. The street dogs had snarled at it, slunk about it and shrank back when the bear swung on them.

'How far to Durham?' Eleanor asked, this time speaking French, her native language.

'Tomorrow, I think,' Thomas answered, still gazing north to where the heavy dark was shrouding the land. 'She asked,' he explained in English to Father Hobbe, 'when we would reach Durham.'

'Tomorrow, pray God,' the priest said.

'Tomorrow you can rest,' Thomas promised Eleanor in French. She was pregnant with a child that, God willing, would be born in the springtime. Thomas was not sure how he felt about being a father. It seemed too early for him to become responsible, but Eleanor was happy and he liked to please her and so he told her he was happy as well. Some of the time, that was even true.

'And tomorrow,' Father Hobbe said, 'we shall fetch our answers.'

'Tomorrow,' Thomas corrected him, 'we shall ask our questions.'

'God will not let us come this far to be disappointed,'

Father Hobbe said, and then, to keep Thomas from arguing, he laid out their meagre supper. 'That's all that's left of the bread,' he said, 'and we should save some of the cheese and an apple for breakfast.' He made the sign of the cross over the food, blessing it, then broke the hard bread into three pieces. 'We should eat before nightfall.'

Darkness brought a brittle cold. A brief shower passed and after it the wind dropped. Thomas slept closest to the byre door and sometime after the wind died he woke because there was a light in the northern sky.

He rolled over, sat up and he forgot that he was cold, forgot his hunger, forgot all the small nagging discomforts of life, for he could see the Grail. The Holy Grail, the most precious of all Christ's bequests to man, lost these thousand years and more, and he could see it glowing in the sky like shining blood and about it, bright as the glittering crown of a saint, rays of dazzling shimmer filled the heaven.

Thomas wanted to believe. He wanted the Grail to exist. He thought that if the Grail were to be found then all the world's evil would be drained into its depths. He so wanted to believe and that October night he saw the Grail like a great burning cup in the north and his eyes filled with tears so that the image blurred, yet he could see it still, and it seemed to him that a vapour boiled from the holy vessel. Beyond it, in ranks rising to the heights of the air, were rows of angels, their wings touched by fire. All the northern sky was smoke and gold and scarlet, glowing in the night as a sign to doubting Thomas. 'Oh, Lord,' he said aloud and he threw off his blanket and knelt in the byre's cold doorway, 'oh, Lord.'

'Thomas?' Eleanor, beside him had awoken. She sat up and stared into the night. 'Fire,' she said in French, '*c'est un grand incendie*.' Her voice was awed.

'*C'est un incendie?*' Thomas asked, then came fully awake and saw there was indeed a great fire on the horizon from where the flames boiled up to light a cup-shaped chasm in the clouds.

'There is an army there,' Eleanor whispered in French. 'Look!' She pointed to another glow, farther off. They had seen such lights in the sky in France, flamelight reflected from cloud where England's army blazed its way across Normandy and Picardy.

Thomas still gazed north, but now in disappointment. It was an army? Not the Grail?

'Thomas?' Eleanor was worried.

'It's just rumour,' he said. He was a priest's bastard and he had been raised on the sacred scriptures and in Matthew's Gospel it had been promised that at the end of time there would be battles and rumours of battles. The scriptures promised that the world would come to its finish in a welter of war and blood, and in the last village, where the folk had watched them suspiciously, a sullen priest had accused them of being Scottish spies. Father Hobbe had bridled at that, threatening to box his fellow priest's ears, but Thomas had calmed both men down, and then spoken with a shepherd who said he had seen smoke in the northern hills. The Scots, the shepherd said, were marching south, though the priest's woman scoffed at the tale, claiming that the Scottish troops were nothing but cattle raiders. 'Bar your door at night,' she advised, 'and they'll leave you alone.'

The far light subsided. It was not the Grail.

'Thomas?' Eleanor frowned at him.

'I had a dream,' he said, 'just a dream.'

'I felt the child move,' she said, and she touched his shoulder. 'Will you and I be married?'

'In Durham,' he promised her. He was a bastard and he wanted no child of his to carry the same taint. 'We shall reach the city tomorrow,' he reassured Eleanor, 'and you and I will marry in a church and then we shall ask our questions.' And, he prayed, let one of the answers be that the Grail did not exist. Let it be a dream, a mere trick of fire and cloud in a night sky, for else Thomas feared it would lead to madness. He wanted to abandon this search; he wanted to give up the Grail and return to being what he was and what he wanted to be: an archer of England.

Bernard de Taillebourg, Frenchman, Dominican friar and Inquisitor, spent the autumn night in a pig pen and when dawn came thick and white with fog, he went to his knees and thanked God for the privilege of sleeping in fouled straw. Then, mindful of his high task, he said a prayer to St Dominic, begging the saint to intercede with God to make this day's work good. 'As the flame in thy mouth lights us to truth' – he spoke aloud – 'so let it light our path to success.' He rocked forward in the intensity of his emotion and his head struck against a rough stone pillar that supported one corner of the pen. Pain jabbed through his skull and he invited more by forcing his forehead back against the stone, grinding the skin until he felt the blood trickle down to his nose. 'Blessed Dominic,' he cried, 'blessed Dominic! God be thanked for thy glory! Light our way!' The blood was on his lips now and he licked it and reflected on all the pain that the saints and martyrs had endured for the Church. His hands were clasped and there was a smile on his haggard face.

Soldiers who, the night before, had burned much of the village to ash and raped the women who failed to escape and killed the men who tried to protect the women, now watched the priest drive his head repeatedly against the blood-spattered stone. 'Dominic,' Bernard de Taillebourg gasped, 'oh, Dominic!' Some of the soldiers made the sign of the cross for they recognized a holy man when they saw one. One or two even knelt, though it was awkward in their mail coats, but most just watched the priest warily, or else watched his servant who, sitting outside the sty, returned their gaze.

The servant, like Bernard de Taillebourg, was a Frenchman, but something in the younger man's appearance suggested a more exotic birth. His skin was sallow, almost as dark as a Moor's, and his long hair was sleekly black which, with his narrow face, gave him a feral look. He wore mail and a sword and, though he was nothing but a priest's servant, he carried himself with confidence and dignity. His dress was elegant, something strange in this ragged army. No one knew his name. No one even wanted to ask, just as no one wanted to ask why he never ate or chatted with the other servants, but kept himself fastidiously apart. Now the mysterious servant watched the soldiers and in his left hand he held a knife with a very long and thin blade, and once he knew enough men were looking at him, he balanced the knife on an outstretched finger. The knife was poised on its sharp tip, which was prevented from piercing the servant's skin by the cut-off finger of a mail glove that he wore like a sheath.

9

Then he jerked the finger and the knife span in the air, blade glittering, to come down, tip first, to balance on his finger again. The servant had not looked at the knife once, but kept his dark-eyed gaze fixed on the soldiers. The priest, oblivious to the display, was howling prayers, his thin cheeks laced with blood. 'Dominic! Dominic! Light our path!' The knife span again, its wicked blade catching the foggy morning's small light. 'Dominic! Guide us! Guide us!'

'On your horses! Mount up! Move yourselves!' A grey-haired man, a big shield slung from his left shoulder, pushed through the onlookers. 'We've not got all day! What in the name of the devil are you all gawking at? Jesus Christ on His goddamn cross, what is this, Eskdale bloody fair? For Christ's sake, move! Move!' The shield on his shoulder was blazoned with the badge of a red heart, but the paint was so faded and the shield's leather cover so scarred that the badge was hard to distinguish. 'Oh, suffering Christ!' The man had spotted the Dominican and his servant. 'Father! We're going now. Right now! And I don't wait for prayers.' He turned back to his men. 'Mount up! Move your bones! There's devil's work to be done!'

'Douglas!' the Dominican snapped.

The grey-haired man turned back fast. 'My name, priest, is Sir William, and you'll do well to remember it.'

The priest blinked. He seemed to be suffering a momentary confusion, still caught up in the ecstasy of his pain-driven prayer, then he gave a perfunctory bow as if acknowledging his fault in using Sir William's surname. 'I was talking to the blessed Dominic,' he explained.

'Aye, well, I hope you asked him to shift this damn fog?'

'And he will lead us today! He will guide us!'

'Then he'd best get his damn boots on,' Sir William Douglas, Knight of Liddesdale, growled at the priest, 'for we're leaving whether your saint is ready or not.' Sir William's chain mail was battle-torn and patched with newer rings. Rust showed at the hem and at the elbows. His faded shield, like his weather-beaten face, was scarred. He was forty-six now and he reckoned he had a sword, arrow or spear scar for each of those years that had turned his hair and short beard white. Now he pulled open the sty's heavy gate. 'On your trotters, father. I've a horse for you.'

'I shall walk,' Bernard de Taillebourg said, picking up a stout staff with a leather thong threaded through its tip, 'as our Lord walked.'

'Then you'll not get wet crossing the streams, eh, is that it?' Sir William chuckled. 'You'll walk on water will you, father? You and your servant?' Alone among his men he did not seem impressed by the French priest or wary of the priest's well-armed servant, but Sir William Douglas was famously unafraid of any man. He was a border chieftain who employed murder, fire, sword and lance to protect his land and some fierce priest from Paris was hardly likely to impress him. Sir William, indeed, was not overfond of priests, but his King had ordered him to take Bernard de Taillebourg on this morning's raid and Sir William had grudgingly consented.

All around him soldiers pulled themselves into their saddles. They were lightly armed for they expected to meet no enemies. A few, like Sir William, carried

11

shields, but most were content with just a sword. Bernard de Taillebourg, his friar's robes mud-spattered and damp, hurried alongside Sir William. 'Will you go into the city?'

'Of course I'll not go into the bloody city. There's a truce, remember?'

'But if there's a truce . . .'

'If there's a bloody truce then we leave them be.'

The French priest's English was good, but it took him a few moments to work out what Sir William's last three words had meant. 'There'll be no fighting?'

'Not between us and the city, no. And there's no goddamned English army within a hundred miles so there'll be no fighting. All we're doing is looking for food and forage, father, food and forage. Feed your men and feed your animals and that's the way to win your wars.' Sir William, as he spoke, climbed onto his horse, which was held by a squire. He pushed his boots into the stirrups, plucked the skirts of his mail coat from under his thighs and gathered the reins. 'I'll get you close to the city, father, but after that you'll have to shift for yourself.'

'Shift?' Bernard de Taillebourg asked, but Sir William had already turned away and spurred his horse down a muddy lane that ran between low stone walls. Two hundred mounted men-at-arms, grim and grey on this foggy morning, streamed after him and the priest, buffeted by their big dirty horses, struggled to keep up. The servant followed with apparent unconcern. He was evidently accustomed to being among soldiers and showed no apprehension, indeed his demeanour suggested he might be better with his weapons than most of the men who rode behind Sir William.

The Dominican and his servant had travelled to Scotland with a dozen other messengers sent to King David II by Philip of Valois, King of France. The embassy had been a cry for help. The English had burned their way across Normandy and Picardy, they had slaughtered the French King's army near a village called Crécy and their archers now held a dozen fastnesses in Brittany while their savage horsemen rode from Edward of England's ancestral possessions in Gascony. All that was bad, but even worse, and as if to show all Europe that France could be dismembered with impunity, the English King was now laying siege to the great fortress harbour of Calais. Philip of Valois was doing his best to raise the siege, but winter was coming, his nobles grumbled that their King was no warrior, and so he had appealed for aid to Scotland's King David, son of Robert the Bruce. Invade England, the French King had pleaded, and thus force Edward to abandon the siege of Calais to protect his homeland. The Scots had pondered the invitation, then were persuaded by the French King's embassy that England lay defenceless. How could it be otherwise? Edward of England's army was all at Calais or else in Brittany or Gascony, and there was no one left to defend England, and that meant the old enemy was helpless, it was asking to be raped and all the riches of England were just waiting to fall into Scottish hands.

And so the Scots had come south.

It was the largest army that Scotland had ever sent across the border. The great lords were all there, the sons and grandsons of the warriors who had humbled England in the bloody slaughter about the Bannockburn, and those lords had brought their men-at-arms who had grown hard with incessant frontier battles, but this time, smelling plunder, they were accompanied by the clan chiefs from the mountains and islands: chiefs leading wild tribesmen who spoke a language of their own and fought like devils unleashed. They had come in their thousands to make themselves rich and the French messengers, their duty done, had sailed home to tell Philip of Valois that Edward of England would surely raise his siege of Calais when he learned that the Scots were ravaging his northern lands.

The French embassy had sailed for home, but Bernard de Taillebourg had stayed. He had business in northern England, but in the first days of the invasion he had experienced nothing except frustration. The Scottish army was twelve thousand strong, larger than the army with which Edward of England had defeated the French at Crécy, yet once across the frontier the great army had stopped to besiege a lonely fortress garrisoned by a mere thirty-eight men, and though the thirty-eight had all died, it had wasted four days. More time was spent negotiating with the citizens of Carlisle who had paid gold to have their city spared, and then the young Scottish King frittered away three more days pillaging the great priory of the Black Canons at Hexham. Now, ten days after they had crossed the frontier, and after wandering across the northern English moors, the Scottish army had at last reached Durham. The city had offered a thousand golden pounds if they could be spared and King David had given them two days to raise the money. Which meant that Bernard de Taillebourg had two days to find a way to enter the city, to which end, slipping in the mud and half blinded by the fog, he followed Sir William Douglas into a valley, across a

14

stream and up a steep hill. 'Which way is the city?' he demanded of Sir William.

'When the fog lifts, father, I'll tell you.'

'They'll respect the truce?'

'They're holy men in Durham, father,' Sir William answered wryly, 'but better still, they're frightened men.' It had been the monks of the city who had negotiated the ransom and Sir William had advised against acceptance. If monks offered a thousand pounds, he reckoned, then it would have been better to have killed the monks and taken two thousand, but King David had overruled him. David the Bruce had spent much of his youth in France and so considered himself cultured, but Sir William was not thus hampered by scruples. 'You'll be safe if you can talk your way into the city,' Sir William reassured the priest.

The horsemen had reached the hilltop and Sir William turned south along the ridge, still following a track that was edged with stone walls and which led, after a mile or so, to a deserted hamlet where four cottages, so low that their shaggy thatched roofs seemed to swell out of the straggling turf, clustered by a crossroads. In the centre of the crossroads, where the muddy ruts surrounded a patch of nettles and grass, a stone cross leaned southwards. Sir William curbed his horse beside the monument and stared at the carved dragon encircling the shaft. The cross was missing one arm. A dozen of his men dismounted and ducked into the low cottages, but they found no one and nothing, though in one cottage the embers of a fire still glowed and so they used the smouldering wood to fire the four thatched roofs. The thatch was reluctant to catch the fire for it was so damp that mushrooms grew on the mossy straw.

Sir William took his foot from the stirrup and tried to kick the broken cross over, but it would not shift. He grunted with the effort, saw Bernard de Taillebourg's disapproving expression and scowled. 'It's not holy ground, father. It's only bloody England.' He peered at the carved dragon, its mouth agape as it stretched up the stone shaft. 'Ugly bastard thing, isn't it?'

'Dragons are creatures of sin, things of the devil,' Bernard de Taillebourg said, 'so of course it is ugly.'

'A thing of the devil, eh?' Sir William kicked the cross again. 'My mother,' he explained as he gave the cross a third futile kick, 'always told me that the bloody English buried their stolen gold beneath dragons' crosses.'

Two minutes later the cross had been heaved aside and a half-dozen men were peering disappointedly into the hole it had left. Smoke from the burning roofs thickened the fog, swirled over the road and vanished into the greyness of the morning air. 'No gold,' Sir William grunted, then he summoned his men and led them southwards out of the choking smoke. He was looking for any livestock that could be driven back to the Scottish army, but the fields were empty. The fire of the burning cottages was a hazed gold and red in the fog behind the raiders, a glow that slowly faded until only the smell of the fire was left and then, suddenly, hugely, filling the whole world with the alarm of its noise, a peal of bells clanged about the sky. Sir William, presuming the sound came from the east, turned through a gap in the wall into a pasture where he checked his horse and stood in the stirrups. He was listening to the sound, but in the fog it was impossible to tell where the bells were or how far away they were being tolled and then the sound stopped as suddenly as it had began.

The fog was thinning now, shredding away through the orange leaves of a stand of elms. White mushrooms dotted the empty pasture where Bernard de Taillebourg dropped to his knees and began to pray aloud. 'Quiet, father!' Sir William snapped.

The priest made the sign of the cross as though imploring heaven to forgive Sir William's impiety in interrupting a prayer. 'You said there was no enemy,' he complained.

'I'm not listening for any bloody enemy,' Sir William said, 'but for animals. I'm listening for cattle bells or sheep bells.' Yet Sir William seemed strangely nervous for a man who sought only livestock. He kept twisting in his saddle, peering into the fog and scowling at the small noises of curb chains or hooves stamping on damp earth. He snarled at the men-at-arms closest to him to be silent. He had been a soldier before some of these men had even been born and he had not stayed alive by ignoring his instincts and now, in this damp fog, he smelt danger. Sense told him there was nothing to fear, that the English army was far away across the sea, but he smelt death all the same and, quite unaware of what he was doing, he pulled the shield off his shoulder and pushed his left arm through its carrying loops. It was a big shield, one made before men began adding plates of armour to their mail, a shield wide enough to screen a man's whole body.

A soldier called out from the pasture's edge and Sir William grasped his sword's hilt, then he saw that the man had only exclaimed at the sudden appearance of towers in the fog which was now little more than a mist on the ridge's top, though in the deep valleys either side the fog flowed like a white river. And across the

17

eastern river, way off to the north where they emerged from the spectral whiteness of another hill crest, was a great cathedral and a castle. They towered through the mist, vast and dark, like buildings from some doom-laden wizard's imagination, and Bernard de Taillebourg's servant, who felt he had not seen civilization in weeks, stared entranced at the two buildings. Black-robed monks crowded the tallest of the cathedral's two towers and the servant saw them pointing at the Scottish horsemen.

'Durham,' Sir William grunted. The bells, he reckoned, must have been summoning the faithful to their morning prayers.

'I have to go there!' The Dominican climbed from his knees and, seizing his staff, set off towards the mist-shrouded city.

Sir William spurred his horse in front of the Frenchman. 'What's your hurry, father?' he demanded, and de Taillebourg tried to dodge past the Scotsman, but there was a scraping sound and suddenly a blade, cold and heavy and grey, was in the Dominican's face. 'I asked you, father, what the hurry was?' Sir William's voice was as cold as his sword; then, alerted by one of his men, he glanced over and saw that the priest's servant had half drawn his own weapon. 'If your bastard man doesn't sheathe his blade, father' – Sir William spoke softly, but there was a terrible menace in his voice – 'I'll have his collops for my supper.'

De Taillebourg said something in French and the servant reluctantly pushed the blade fully home. The priest looked up at Sir William. 'Have you no fear for your mortal soul?' he asked.

Sir William smiled, paused and looked about the hilltop, but he saw nothing untoward in the shredding fog and decided his earlier nervousness had been the result of imagination. The result, perhaps, of too much beef, pork and wine the previous night. The Scots had feasted in the captured home of Durham's prior and the prior lived well, judging by his larder and cellar, but rich suppers gave men premonitions. 'I keep my own priest to worry about my soul,' Sir William said, then raised the tip of his sword to force de Taillebourg's face upwards. 'Why does a Frenchman have business with our enemies in Durham?' he demanded.

'It is Church business,' de Taillebourg said firmly.

'I don't give a damn whose business it is,' Sir William said, 'I still wish to know.'

'Obstruct me,' de Taillebourg said, pushing the sword blade away, 'and I shall have the King punish you and the Church condemn you and the Holy Father send your soul to eternal perdition. I shall summon —'

'Shut your goddamned bloody face!' Sir William said. 'Do you think, priest, that you can frighten me? Our King is a puppy and the Church does what its pay-masters tell it to do.' He moved the blade back, this time resting it against the Dominican's neck. 'Now tell me your business. Tell me why a Frenchman stays with us instead of going home with his countrymen. Tell me what you want in Durham.'

Bernard de Taillebourg clutched the crucifix that hung about his neck and held it towards Sir William. In another man the gesture might have been taken as a display of fear, but in the Dominican it looked rather as though he threatened Sir William's soul with the powers of heaven. Sir William merely gave the crucifix a hungry glance as if appraising its value, but the cross was of plain wood while the little figure of Christ, twisted in death's agony, was only made of yellowed bone. If the figure had been made of gold then Sir William might have taken the bauble, but instead he spat in derision. A few of his men, fearing God more than their master, made the sign of the cross, but most did not care. They watched the servant closely, for he looked dangerous, but a middle-aged cleric from Paris, however fierce and gaunt he might be, did not scare them. 'So what will you do?' de Taillebourg asked Sir William scornfully. 'Kill me?'

'If I must,' Sir William said implacably. The presence of the priest with the French embassy had been a puzzle, and his staying on when the others left only compounded the mystery, but a garrulous man-at-arms, one of the Frenchmen who had brought two hundred suits of plate armour as a gift to the Scots, had told Sir William that the priest was pursuing a great treasure and if that treasure was in Durham then Sir William wanted to know. He wanted a share. 'I've killed priests before,' he told de Taillebourg, 'and another priest sold me an indulgence for the killings, so don't think I fear you or your Church. There's no sin that can't be bought off, no pardon that can't be purchased.'

The Dominican shrugged. Two of Sir William's men were behind him, their swords drawn, and he understood that these Scotsmen would indeed kill him and his servant. These men who followed the red heart of Douglas were border ruffians, bred to battle as a hound was raised to the chase and the Dominican knew there was no point in continuing to threaten their souls for they gave no thought to such things. 'I am going into Durham,' de Taillebourg said, 'to find a man.'

'What man?' Sir William asked, his sword still at the priest's neck.

'He is a monk,' de Taillebourg explained patiently, 'and an old man now, so old that he may not even be alive. He is a Frenchman, a Benedictine, and he fled Paris many years ago.'

'Why did he run?'

'Because the King wanted his head.'

'A monk's head?' Sir William sounded sceptical.

'He was not always a Benedictine,' de Taillebourg said, 'but was once a Templar.'

'Ah.' Sir William began to understand.

'And he knows,' de Taillebourg continued, 'where a great treasure is hidden.'

'The Templar treasure?'

'It is said to be hidden in Paris,' de Taillebourg said, 'hidden for all these years, but it was only last year that we discovered the Frenchman was alive and in England. The Benedictine, you see, was once the sacrist of the Templars. You know what that is?'

'Don't patronize me, father,' Sir William said coldly.

De Taillebourg inclined his head to acknowledge the justice of the reproof. 'If any man knows where the Templar treasure is,' he went on humbly, 'it is the man who was their sacrist, and now, we hear, that man lives in Durham.'

Sir William took the sword away. Everything the priest said made sense. The Knights Templar, an order of monkish soldiers who were sworn to protect the pilgrims' roads between Christendom and Jerusalem, had become rich beyond the dreams of kings, and that was foolish for it made kings jealous and jealous kings make bad enemies. The King of France was just such an enemy and he had ordered the Templars destroyed: to which end a heresy had been cooked up, lawyers had effortlessly distorted truths and the Templars had been suppressed. Their leaders had been burned and their lands confiscated, but their treasures, the fabled treasures of the Templars, had never been found and the order's sacrist, the man responsible for keeping those treasures safe, would surely know their fate, 'When were the Templars disbanded?' Sir William asked.

'Twenty-nine years ago,' de Taillebourg answered.

So the sacrist could yet be alive, Sir William thought. He would be an old man, but alive. Sir William sheathed his sword, utterly convinced by de Taillebourg's tale, yet none of it was true except that there was an old monk in Durham, but he was not French and he had never been a Templar and, in all probability, knew nothing of any Templar treasure. But Bernard de Taillebourg had spoken persuasively, and the story of the missing hoard was one that echoed through Europe, spoken of whenever men gathered to exchange tales of marvels. Sir William wanted the story to be true and that, more than anything, persuaded him it was. 'If you find this man,' he said to de Taillebourg, 'and if he lives, and if you then find the treasure, then it will be because we made it possible. It will be because we brought you here, and because we protected you on your journey to Durham.'

'True, Sir William,' de Taillebourg said.

Sir William was surprised by the priest's ready agreement. He frowned, shifted in his saddle and stared down at the Dominican as if gauging the priest's trustworthiness. 'So we must share in the treasure,' he demanded.

'Of course,' de Taillebourg said instantly.

22

Sir William was no fool. Let the priest go into Durham and he would never see the man again. Sir William twisted in his saddle and stared north towards the cathedral. The Templar treasure was said to be the gold from Jerusalem, more gold than men could dream of, and Sir William was honest enough to know that he did not possess the resources to divert some of that golden trove to Liddesdale. The King must be used. David II might be a weak lad, scarce breeched and too softened by having lived in France, but kings had resources denied to knights and David of Scotland could talk to Philip of France as a near equal, while any message from William Douglas would be ignored in Paris. 'Jamie!' he snapped at his nephew who was one of the two men guarding de Taillebourg. 'You and Dougal will take this priest back to the King.'

'You must let me go!' Bernard de Taillebourg protested.

Sir William leaned from his saddle. 'You want me to cut off your priestly balls to make myself a purse?' He smiled at the Dominican, then looked back to his nephew. 'Tell the King this French priest has news that concerns us and tell him to hold him safe till I return.' Sir William had decided that if there was an ancient French monk in Durham then he should be questioned by the King of Scotland's servants and the monk's information, if he had any, could then be sold to the French King. 'Take him, Jamie,' he commanded, 'and watch that damned servant! Take his sword.'

James Douglas grinned at the thought of a mere priest and his servant giving him trouble, but he still obeyed his uncle. He demanded that the servant yield his sword and, when the man bridled at the order, Jamie half drew his own blade. De Taillebourg sharply instructed his servant to obey and the sword was sullenly handed over. Jamie Douglas grinned as he hung the sword from his own belt. 'They'll not bother me, uncle.'

'Away with you,' Sir William said and watched as his nephew and his companion, both well mounted on fine stallions captured from the Percy lands in Northumberland, escorted the priest and his servant back towards the King's encampment. Doubtless the priest would complain to the King and David, so much weaker than his great father, would worry about the displeasure of God and the French, but David would worry a great deal more about Sir William's displeasure. Sir William smiled at that thought, then saw that some of his men on the far side of the field had dismounted. 'Who the devil told you to unhorse?' he shouted angrily, then he saw they were not his men at all, but strangers revealed by the shredding mist, and he remembered his instincts and cursed himself for wasting time on the priest.

And as he cursed so the first arrow flickered from the south. The sound it made was a hiss, feather in air, then it struck home and the noise was like a pole-axe cleaving flesh. It was a heavy thump edged with the tearing of steel in muscle and ending with the harsh scrape of blade on bone, and then a grunt from the victim and a heartbeat of silence.

And after that the scream.

Thomas of Hookton heard the bells, deep-toned and sonorous, not the sound of bells hung in some village church, but bells of thunderous power. Durham, he thought, and he felt a great weariness for the journey had been so long.

It had begun in Picardy, on a field stinking of dead men and horses, a place of fallen banners, broken weapons and spent arrows. It had been a great victory and Thomas had wondered why it left him dulled and nervous. The English had marched north to besiege Calais, but Thomas, duty bound to serve the Earl of Northampton, had received the Earl's permission to take a wounded comrade to Caen where there was a doctor of extraordinary skill. Then, however, it was decreed that no man could leave the army without the King's permission and so the Earl approached the King and thus Edward Plantagenet heard of Thomas of Hookton and how his father had been a priest who had been born to a family of French exiles called Vexille, and how it was rumoured that the Vexille family had once possessed the Grail. It was only a rumour, of course, a wisp of a story in a hard world, yet the story was of the Holy Grail and that was the most precious thing that had ever existed, if indeed it had existed; and the King had questioned Thomas of Hookton and Thomas had tried to scorn the truth of the Grail story, but then the Bishop of Durham, who had fought in the shield wall that broke the French assaults, told how Thomas's father had once been imprisoned in Durham. 'He was mad,' the bishop explained to the King, 'wits flown to the winds! So they locked him up for his own good.'

'Did he talk of the Grail?' the King asked, and the Bishop of Durham had answered that there was one man left in his diocese who might know, an old monk called Hugh Collimore who had nursed the mad Ralph Vexille, Thomas's father. The King might have dismissed the tales as so much churchly gossip had not Thomas recovered his father's heritage, the lance of St George, in the battle that had left so many dead on the green slope above the village of Crécy. The battle had also left Thomas's friend and commander Sir William Skeat wounded and he wanted to take Skeat to the doctor in Normandy, but the King had insisted that Thomas go to Durham and speak with Brother Collimore. So Eleanor's father had taken Sir William Skeat to Caen and Thomas, Eleanor and Father Hobbe had accompanied a royal chaplain and a knight of King Edward's household to England, but in London the chaplain and the knight had both fallen sick with an early winter fever and so Thomas and his companions had travelled north alone and now they were close to Durham, on a foggy morning, listening to the cathedral's bells. Eleanor, like Father Hobbe, was excited for she believed that discovering the Grail would bring peace and justice to a world that stank of burned cottages. There would be no more sorrow, Eleanor thought, and no more war, and perhaps even no more sickness.

Thomas wanted to believe it. He wanted his night vision to be real, not flame and smoke, yet if the Grail existed at all he thought that it would be in some great cathedral, guarded by angels. Or else it was gone from this world, and if there was no Grail on earth then Thomas's faith was in a war bow made of Italian yew, painted black, strung with hemp, that drove an arrow made of ash, fledged with goose feathers and tipped with steel. On the bow's belly, where his left hand gripped the yew, there was a silver plate engraved with a yale, a fabulous beast of claws and horns and tusks and scales that was the badge of his father's family, the

Vexilles. The yale held a cup and Thomas had been told it was the Grail. Always the Grail. It beckoned him, mocked him, bent his life, changed all, yet never appeared except in a dream of fire. It was mystery, just as Thomas's family was a mystery, but perhaps Brother Collimore could cast light on that mystery and so Thomas had come north. He might not learn of the Grail, but he expected to discover more about his family and that, at least, made the journey worthwhile.

'Which way?' Father Hobbe asked.

'God knows,' Thomas said. Fog shrouded the land.

'The bells sounded that way.' Father Hobbe pointed north and east. He was energetic, full of enthusiasm, and naïvely trusting in Thomas's sense of direction, though in truth Thomas did not know where he was. Earlier they had come to a fork in the road and he had randomly taken the left-hand track that now faded to a mere scar on the grass as it climbed. Mushrooms grew in the pasture, which was wet and heavy with dew so that their horse slipped as it climbed. The horse was Thomas's mare and it was carrying their small baggage and in one of the sacks hanging from the saddle's pommel was a letter from the Bishop of Durham to John Fossor, the Prior of Durham. 'Most beloved brother in Christ,' the letter began, and went on to instruct Fossor to allow Thomas of Hookton and his companions to question Brother Collimore concerning Father Ralph Vexille, 'whom you will not remember for he was kept closed up in your house before you came to Durham, indeed before I came to the See, but there will be some who know of him and Brother Collimore, if it pleases God that he yet lives, will have certain knowledge of him and of the great treasure that he concealed. We

27

request this in the name of the King and in the service of Almighty God who has blessed our arms in this present endeavour.'

'*Qu'est-ce que c'est?*' Eleanor asked, pointing up the hill where a dull reddish glow discoloured the fog.

'What?' Father Hobbe, the only one who did not speak French, asked.

'Quiet,' Thomas warned him, holding up his hand. He could smell burning and see the flicker of flames, but there were no voices. He took his bow from where it hung from the saddle and he strung it, bending the huge stave to loop the hemp string over the piece of nocked horn. He pulled an arrow from the bag and then, motioning Eleanor and Father Hobbe to stay where they were, he edged up the track to the shelter of a deep hedge where larks and finches flitted through the dying leaves. The fires were roaring, suggesting they were newly set. He crept closer, the bow half drawn, until he could see there had been three or four cottages about a crossroads and their rafters and thatch were well ablaze and sending sparks whirling up into the damp grey. The fires looked recent, but there was no one in sight: no enemy, no men in mail, so he beckoned Eleanor and Father Hobbe forward and then, over the sound of the fire, he heard a scream. It was far off, or perhaps it was close but muffled by fog, and Thomas stared through the smoke and the fog and past the seething flames and suddenly two men in mail, both mounted on black stallions, cantered into view. The horsemen had black hats, black boots and black scab-barded swords and they were escorting two other men who were on foot. One was a priest, a Dominican judging by his black and white garb, and he had a bloodied

28

face, while the other man was tall, dressed in mail, and had long black hair and a narrow, intelligent face. The two followed the horsemen through the smoky fog, then paused at the crossroads where the priest dropped to his knees and made the sign of the cross.

The leading horseman seemed irritated by the priest's prayer for he turned his horse back and, drawing his sword, prodded the blade at the kneeling man. The priest looked up and, to Thomas's astonishment, suddenly rammed his staff up into the stallion's throat. The beast twitched away and the priest slammed the staff hard at the rider's sword arm. The horseman, unbalanced by his stallion's jerking motion, tried to cut down across his body with his long blade. The second horseman was already unsaddled, though Thomas had not seen him fall, and the black-haired man in mail was astride his body with a long knife drawn. Thomas just stared in puzzlement for he was convinced that neither the two horsemen nor the priest nor the black-haired man had uttered the scream, yet no other folk were in sight. One of the two horsemen was already dead and the other now fought the priest in silence and Thomas had a sense that the conflict was unreal, that he was dreaming, that in truth this was a morality play in dumb show: the black-clad horseman was the devil and the priest was God's will and Thomas's doubts about the Grail were about to be resolved by whoever won and then Father Hobbe seized the great bow from Thomas. 'We must help!'

Yet the priest hardly needed help. He used the staff like a sword, parrying his opponent's cut, lunging hard to bruise the rider's ribs, then the man with the long black hair rammed a sword up into the horseman's back and the man arched, shivered, and his own sword dropped. He stared down at the priest for a moment, then he fell backwards from his saddle. His feet were momentarily trapped in the stirrups and the horse, panicking, galloped uphill. The killer wiped the blade of his sword, then took a scabbard from one of the dead men.

The priest had run to secure the other horse and now, sensing he was being watched, he turned to see two men and a woman in the fog. One of the men was a priest who had an arrow on a bowstring. 'They were going to kill me!' Bernard de Taillebourg protested in French. The black-haired man turned fast, the sword rising in threat.

'It's all right,' Thomas said to Father Hobbe and he took the black bow away from his friend and hung it on his shoulder. God had spoken, the priest had won the fight and Thomas was reminded of his night vision when the Grail had loomed in the clouds like a cup of fire. Then he saw that under the bruises and blood the strange priest's face was hard and lean, a martyr's face, with the look of a man who had hungered for God and achieved an evident saintliness and Thomas almost fell to his knees. 'Who are you?' he called to the Dominican.

'I am a messenger.' Bernard de Taillebourg snatched at any explanation to cover his confusion. He had escaped from his Scottish escort and now he wondered how he was to escape from the tall young man with the long black bow, but then a flight of arrows hissed from the south and one thumped into a nearby elm trunk while a second skidded along the wet grass, and a horse shrieked nearby and men were shouting in disorder. Father de Taillebourg called to his servant to catch the second horse, which was trotting uphill and, by the time it was caught, de Taillebourg saw that the stranger with the bow had forgotten him and was staring south to where the arrows flew.

So he turned towards the city, called his servant to follow him and kicked back his heels.

For God, for France, for St Denis and for the Grail.

Sir William Douglas cursed. Arrows were hissing all about him. Horses were screaming and men were lying dead or injured on the grass. For a heartbeat he felt bewildered, then he realized that his forage party had blundered into an English force, but what kind of force? There was no English army nearby! The whole English army was in France, not here! Which meant, surely, that the citizens of Durham had broken their truce and that thought filled Sir William with a terrible anger. Christ, he thought, but there would not be one stone left on another when he had finished with the city, and he tugged the big shield to cover his body and spurred south towards the bowmen who were lining a low hedge. He reckoned there were not so many of them, maybe only fifty, and he still had nearly two hundred men mounted and so he roared the order to charge. Swords scraped from scabbards. 'Kill the bastards!' Sir William shouted. 'Kill them!' He was savaging his horse with his spurs and thrusting other confused horsemen aside in his eagerness to reach the hedge. He knew the charge would be ragged, knew some of his men must die, but once they were over the blackthorn and in among the bastards they would kill them all.

Bloody archers, he thought. He hated archers. He

especially hated English archers and he detested traitor-ous, truce-breaking Durham archers above all others. 'On! On!' he shouted. 'Douglas! Douglas!' He liked to let his enemies know who was killing them, and who would be raping their wives when they were dead. If the city had broken the truce, then God help that city for he would sack, rape and burn the whole of it. He would fire the houses, plough the ashes and leave the bones of its citizens to the winter blight, and for years men would see the bare stones of the ruined cathedral and watch the birds nesting in the castle's empty towers and they would know that the Knight of Liddesdale had worked his revenge.

'Douglas!' he shouted, 'Douglas!' and he felt the thump of arrows smacking into his shield and then his horse screamed and he knew more arrows must have driven deep into its chest for he could feel the beast stumbling. He kicked his feet from the stirrups as the horse slewed sideways. Men charged past him, scream-ing defiance, then Sir William threw himself out of the saddle and onto his shield that slid along the wet grass like a sledge, and he heard his horse screaming in pain, but he himself was unhurt, hardly even bruised and he pushed himself up, found his sword that he had dropped when he fell and ran on with his horsemen. A rider had an arrow sticking from his knee. A horse went down, eyes white, teeth bared, blood flecking from the arrow wounds. The first horsemen were at the hedge and some had found a gap and were spurring through and Sir William saw that the damned English bowmen were running away. Bastards, he thought, cowardly bloody English rotten whoreson bastards, then more bows sounded harsh to his left and he saw a man fall from a horse with an arrow through his head and the fog lifted enough to show that the enemy archers had not run away, but had merely joined a solid mass of dismounted men-at-arms. The bowstrings sounded again. A horse reared in pain and an arrow sliced into its belly. A man staggered, was struck again and fell back with a crash of mail.

Sweet Christ, Sir William thought, but there was a damned army here! A whole damned army! 'Back! Back!' he bellowed. 'Haul off! Back!' He yelled till he was hoarse. Another arrow drove into his shield, its point whipping through the leather-covered willow and, in his rage, he slapped at it, breaking the ash shaft.

'Uncle! Uncle!' a man shouted and Sir William saw it was Robbie Douglas, one of his eight nephews who rode with the Scottish army, bringing him a horse, but a pair of English arrows struck the beast's quarter and, enraged by pain, it broke away from Robbie's grasp.

'Go north!' Sir William shouted at his nephew. 'Go on, Robbie!'

Instead Robbie rode to his uncle. An arrow struck his saddle, another glanced off his helmet, but he leaned down, took Sir William's hand and dragged him northwards. Arrows followed them, but the fog swirled thick and hid them. Sir William shook off his nephew's grip and stumbled north, made clumsy by his shield stuck with arrows and by his heavy mail. God damn it, God damn it!

'Mind left! Mind left!' a Scottish voice cried and Sir William saw some English horsemen coming from the hedgerow. One saw Sir William and thought he would be easy pickings. The English had been no more ready for battle than the Scotsmen. A few wore mail, but none was properly armoured and none had lances. But Sir William reckoned they must have detected his presence long before they loosed their first arrows, and the anger at being so ambushed made him step towards the horseman who was holding his sword out like a spear. Sir William did not even bother to try and parry. He just thrust his heavy shield up, punching it into the horse's mouth, and he heard the animal whinny in pain as he swept his sword at its legs and the beast twisted away and the rider was flailing for balance and was still trying to calm his horse when Sir William's sword tore up under his mail and into his guts. 'Bastard,' Sir William snarled and the man was whimpering as Sir William twisted the blade, and then Robbie rode up on the man's far side and chopped his sword down onto his neck so that the Englishman's head was all but severed as he fell from the saddle. The other horsemen had mysteriously shied away, but then arrows flew again and Sir William knew the fickle fog was thinning. He dragged his sword free of the corpse, scabbarded the wet blade and hauled himself into the dead man's saddle. 'Away!' he shouted at Robbie who seemed inclined to take on the whole English force single-handed. 'Away, boy! Come on!'

By God, he thought, but it hurt to run from an enemy, yet there was no shame in two hundred men fleeing six or seven hundred. And when the fog lifted there could be a proper battle, a murderous clash of men and steel, and Sir William would teach these bastard English how to fight. He kicked his borrowed horse on, intent on carrying news of the English to the rest of the Scottish army, but then saw an archer lurking in a hedge. A woman and a priest were with the man and Sir William put a hand to his sword hilt and thought about swerving aside to take some revenge for the arrows that had ripped into his forage party, but behind him the other Englishmen were shouting their war cry: 'St George! St George!' and so Sir William left the isolated archer alone. He rode on, leaving good men on the autumn grass. They were dead and dying, wounded and frightened. But he was a Douglas. He would come back and he would have his revenge.

A rush of panicked horsemen galloped past the hedge where Thomas, Eleanor and Father Hobbe crouched. Half a dozen horses were riderless while at least a score of others were bleeding from wounds out of which the arrows jutted with their white goose feathers spattered red. The riders were followed by thirty or forty men on foot, some limping, some with arrows stuck in their clothes and a few carrying saddles. They hurried past the burning cottages as a new volley of arrows hastened their retreat, then the thump of hooves made them look back in panic and some of the fugitives broke into a clumsy run as a score of mail-clad horsemen thundered from the mist. Great clods of wet earth spewed up from the horses' hooves. The stallions were being curbed, forced to take brief steps as their riders took aim at their victims, then the spurs went back as the horses were released to the kill and Eleanor cried aloud in anticipation of the carnage. The heavy swords chopped down. One or two of the fugitives dropped to their knees and held their hands up in surrender, but most tried to escape. One dodged behind a galloping horseman and fled towards the hedge, saw Thomas and his bow and turned straight back into the path of another rider who drove the edge of his heavy sword into the man's face.

The Scotsman went onto his knees, mouth open as though he would scream, but no sound came, only blood seeping between the fingers that were clasped over his nose and eyes. The horseman, who had no shield or helmet, turned his stallion and then leaned out of the saddle to chop his sword into his victim's neck, killing the man as if he were a cow being pole-axed and that was oddly appropriate because Thomas saw that the mounted killer was wearing the badge of a brown cow on his jupon, which was a short jerkin-like coat half covering his mail hauberk. The jupon was torn, bloodstained and the cow badge had faded so that at first Thomas thought it was a bull. Then the horseman swerved towards Thomas, raised his bloody sword in threat and then noticed the bow and checked his horse. 'English?'

'And proud of it!' Father Hobbe answered for Thomas.

A second horseman, this one with three black ravens embroidered on his white jupon, reined in beside the first. Three prisoners were being pushed towards the two horsemen. 'How the devil did you get this far in front?' the newly arrived man asked Thomas.

'In front?' Thomas asked.

'Of the rest of us.'

'We walked,' Thomas said, 'from France. Or at least from London.'

'From Southampton!' Father Hobbe corrected Thomas with a pedantry that was utterly out of place on this smoke-stinking hilltop where a Scotsman writhed in his death agonies.

'France?' The first man, tangle-haired, brown-faced, and with a northern accent so thick that Thomas found it hard to understand, sounded as if he had never heard of France. 'You were in France?' he asked.

'With the King.'

'You're with us now,' the second man said threateningly, then looked Eleanor up and down. 'Did you bring the doxie back from France?'

'Yes,' Thomas replied curtly.

'He lies, he lies,' a new voice said and a third horseman pushed himself forward. He was a lanky man, maybe thirty years old, with a face so red and raw that it looked as though he had scraped his skin off with the bristles when he shaved his sunken cheeks and long jaw. His dark hair was worn long and tied at the nape of his neck with a leather lace. His horse, a scarred roan, was as thin as the rider and had white nervous eyes. 'I hate goddamn liars,' the man said, staring at Thomas, then he turned and gave a baleful glance at the prisoners, one of whom wore the red heart badge of the Knight of Liddesdale on his jupon. 'Almost as much as I hate goddamn Douglases.'

The newcomer wore a padded gambeson in place of a hauberk or haubergeon. It was the kind of protection an archer might wear if he could afford nothing better, yet this man plainly outranked archers for he wore a gold chain about his neck, a mark of distinction reserved for the gentry and above. A battered pig-snouted helmet, as scarred as the horse, hung from his saddle's pommel, a sword, plainly scabbarded in leather was at his hip, while a shield, painted white with a black axe, hung from his left shoulder. He also had a coiled whip hanging at his belt. 'The Scots have archers,' the man said, looking at Thomas, then his unfriendly gaze moved on to Eleanor, 'and they have women.'

'I'm English,' Thomas insisted.

38

'We're all English,' Father Hobbe said firmly, forgetting that Eleanor was a Norman.

'A Scotsman would say he was English if it stopped him from being gutted,' the raw-faced man said caustically. The other two horsemen had fallen back, evidently wary of the thin man who now uncoiled the leather whip and, with a casual skill, flicked it so that the tip snaked out and cracked the air an inch or so from Eleanor's face. 'Is she English?'

'She's French,' Thomas said.

The horseman did not answer straightaway, but just stared at Eleanor. The whip rippled as his hand trembled. He saw a fair, slight girl with golden hair and large, frightened eyes. Her pregnancy did not show yet and there was a delicacy to her that spoke of luxury and rare delight. 'Scot, Welsh, French, what does it matter?' the man asked. 'She's a woman. Do you care where a horse was born before you ride it?' His own scarred and thin horse became frightened just then because the veering wind blew a sour gust of smoke to its nostrils. It stepped sideways in a series of small, nervous steps until the man drove his spurs back so savagely that he pierced the padded trapper and made the destrier stand shivering in fear. 'What she is' – the man spoke to Thomas and pointed his whip handle at Eleanor – 'don't matter, but you're a Scot.'

'I'm English,' Thomas said again. A dozen other men wearing the badge of the black axe had come to gaze at Thomas and his companions. The men surrounded the three Scottish prisoners who seemed to know who the horseman with the whip was and did not like the knowledge. More bowmen and men-at-arms watched the cottages burning and laughed at the panicked rats that scrambled from what was left of the collapsed mossy thatch.

Thomas took an arrow from his bag and immediately four or five archers wearing the black-axe livery put arrows on their own strings. The other men in the axe livery grinned expectantly as if they knew this game and enjoyed it, but before it could be played out the horseman was distracted by one of the Scottish prisoners, the man wearing Sir William Douglas's badge who, taking advantage of his captors' interest in Thomas and Eleanor, had broken free and run northwards. He had not gone twenty paces before he was ridden down by one of the English men-at-arms and the thin man, amused by the Scotsman's desperate bid for freedom, pointed at one of the burning cottages. 'Warm the bastard up,' he ordered. 'Dickon! Beggar!' He spoke to two dismounted men-at-arms. 'Look after those three.' He nodded towards Thomas. 'Watch 'em close!'

Dickon, the younger of the two, was round-faced and grinning, but Beggar was an enormous man, a shambling giant with a face so bearded that his nose and eyes alone could be seen through the tangled, crusted hair beneath the brim of the rusted iron cap that served as a helmet. Thomas was six feet in height, the length of a bow, but he was dwarfed by Beggar whose vast chest strained at a leather jerkin studded with metal plates. At the giant's waist, suspended by two lengths of rope, were a sword and a morningstar. The sword had no scabbard and its edge was chipped, while one of the spikes on the big metal ball of the morningstar was bent and smeared with blood and hair. The weapon's three-foot haft banged against the giant's bare legs as he lurched towards Eleanor. 'Pretty,' he said, 'pretty.'

40

'Beggar! Down, boy! Down!' Dickon ordered cheerfully and Beggar dutifully twitched away from Eleanor, though he still gazed at her and made a low growling noise in his throat. Then a scream made him look towards the nearest burning cottage where the Scotsman, stripped naked now, had been thrust in and out of the fire. The prisoner's long hair was alight and he frantically beat at the flames as he ran in panicked circles to the amusement of his English captors. Two other Scottish prisoners were squatting nearby, held on the ground by drawn swords.

The thin horseman watched as an archer swathed the prisoner's hair in a piece of sacking to extinguish the flames. 'How many of you are there?' the thin man asked.

'Thousands!' the Scotsman answered defiantly.

The horseman leaned on his saddle's pommel. 'How many thousands, cully?'

The Scotsman, his beard and hair smoking and his naked skin blackened by embers and lacerated by cuts, did his best to look defiant. 'More than enough to take you back home in a cage.'

'He shouldn't say that to Scarecrow!' Dickon said, amused. 'He shouldn't say that!'

'Scarecrow?' Thomas asked. It seemed an appropriate nickname for the horseman with the black axe badge was lean, poor and frightening.

'He be Sir Geoffrey Carr to you, cully,' Dickon said, watching the Scarecrow admiringly.

'And who is Sir Geoffrey Carr?' Thomas asked.

'He be Scarecrow and he be Lord of Lackby,' Dickon said in a tone which suggested everyone knew who Sir Geoffrey Carr was, 'and he be having his Scarecrow games now!' Dickon grinned because Sir Geoffrey, the whip coiled at his waist again, had dropped down from his horse and with a drawn knife, approached the Scottish prisoner.

'Hold him down,' Sir Geoffrey ordered the archers, 'hold him down and spread his legs.'

'*Non!*' Eleanor cried in protest.

'Pretty,' Beggar said in his voice that rumbled deep inside his huge chest.

The Scotsman screamed and tried to pull himself away, but he was tripped, then held down by three archers while the man evidently known throughout the north as the Scarecrow knelt between his legs. Somewhere in the clearing fog a raven cawed. A handful of archers was staring north in case the Scots returned, but most were watching the Scarecrow and his knife. 'You want to keep your shrivelled collops?' Sir Geoffrey asked the Scotsman. 'Then tell me how many there are of you.'

'Fifteen thousand? Sixteen?' The Scotsman was suddenly eager to talk.

'He means ten or eleven thousand,' Sir Geoffrey announced to the listening archers, 'which is more than enough for our few arrows. And is your bastard King here?'

The Scotsman bridled at that, but a touch of the knife blade to his groin reminded him of his predicament. 'David Bruce is here, aye.'

'Who else?'

The desperate Scotsman named his army's other leaders. The King's nephew and heir to his throne, Lord Robert Stewart, was with the invading army, as were the Earls of Moray, of March, of Wigtown, Fife and Menteith. He named others, clan chiefs and wild men from the wastelands of the far north, but Carr was more interested in two of the earls. 'Fife and Menteith?' he asked. 'They're here?'

'Aye, sir, they are.'

'But they swore fealty to King Edward,' Sir Geoffrey said, evidently disbelieving the man.

'They march with us now,' the Scotsman insisted, 'as does Douglas of Liddesdale.'

'That ripe bastard,' Sir Geoffrey said, 'that shit of hell.' He stared northwards through the fog shredding from the ridge, which was being revealed as a narrow and rocky plateau running north and south. The pasture on the plateau was thin and the ridge's weathered stone protruded through the grass like the ribs of a starving man. Off to the north-east, beyond the valley of mist, the cathedral and castle of Durham reared up on their river-lapped crag, while to the west were hills and woods and stone-walled fields cut with small streams. Two buzzards sailed above the ridge, going towards the Scottish army that was still concealed by the fog which lingered to the north, but Thomas was thinking that it would not be long before troops came to find the men who had run their fellow Scots away from the crossroads.

Sir Geoffrey leaned back and went to return his knife to its scabbard, then seemed to remember something and grinned at the prisoner. 'You were going to take me back to Scotland in a cage, is that right?'

'No!'

'But you were! And why would I want to see Scotland? I can peer down a jakes whenever I want.' He spat at the prisoner then nodded at the archers. 'Hold him.'

43

'No!' the Scotsman shouted, then the shout turned to a terrible scream as Sir Geoffrey leaned forward with the knife again. The prisoner twitched and heaved as the Scarecrow, the front of his padded gambeson now sheeted with blood, stood up. The prisoner was still screaming, hands clutched to his bloody groin, and the sight brought a smile to the Scarecrow's lips. 'Throw the rest of him into the fire,' he said, then turned to look at the other two Scottish prisoners. 'Who is your master?' he demanded of them.

They hesitated, then one licked his lips. 'We serve Douglas,' he said proudly.

'I hate Douglas. I hate every Douglas that ever dropped out of the devil's backside.' Sir Geoffrey shuddered, then turned to his horse. 'Burn them both,' he ordered.

Thomas, looking away from the sudden blood, had seen a stone cross fallen at the crossroad's centre. He stared at it, not seeing the carved dragon, but hearing the echoes of the noise and then the new screams as the prisoners were hurled into the flames. Eleanor ran to him and held his arm tight.

'Pretty,' Beggar said.

'Here, Beggar, here!' Sir Geoffrey called. 'Hoist me!' The giant made a step with his hands and Sir Geoffrey used it to climb into his saddle, then he kicked the horse towards Thomas and Eleanor. 'I'm always hungry,' Sir Geoffrey said, 'after a gelding.' He turned to watch the fire where one of the Scotsmen, hair flaming, tried to escape, but was prodded back into the inferno by a dozen bowstaves. The man's howl was abruptly cut short as he collapsed. 'I'm in the mood to geld and burn Scotsmen today,' Sir Geoffrey said, 'and you look like a Scot to me, boy.'

44

'I'm not a boy,' Thomas said, the anger rising in him.

'You look like a bloody boy to me, boy. A Scots boy, maybe?' Sir Geoffrey, plainly amused by Thomas's temper, grinned at his newest victim who did indeed look young, though Thomas was twenty-two summers old and had fought for the last four of them in Brittany, Normandy and Picardy. 'You look Scots, boy,' the Scarecrow said, daring Thomas to defy him again. 'All the Scots are black!' he appealed to the crowd to judge Thomas's complexion, and it was true that Thomas had a sun-darkened skin and black hair, but so did a score or more of the Scarecrow's own archers. And though Thomas looked young he also looked hard. His hair was cropped close to his skull and four years of war had hollowed his cheeks, but there was still something distinctive in his looks, a handsomeness that attracted the eye and served to spur Sir Geoffrey Carr's jealousy. 'What's on your horse?' Sir Geoffrey jerked his head towards Thomas's mare.

'Nothing of yours,' Thomas said.

'What's mine is mine, boy, and what's yours is mine if I want it. Mine to take or mine to give. Beggar! You want that girl?'

Beggar grinned behind his beard and jerked his head up and down. 'Pretty,' he said. He scratched at the lice in his beard. 'Beggar likes pretty.'

'I reckon you can have the pretty when I'm through with her,' Sir Geoffrey said with a grin and he took the whip from where it hung at his waist and cracked it in the air. Thomas saw that the long leather thong had a small iron claw at its end. Sir Geoffrey grinned at Thomas again, then drew back the whip as a threat. 'Strip her, Beggar,' he said, 'let's give the boys a bit of pleasure,' and he was still grinning as Thomas swung his heavy bowstave hard into the teeth of Sir Geoffrey's horse and the animal reared up, screaming, as Thomas knew it would, and the Scarecrow, unready for the motion, fell backwards, flailing for balance, and his men, who should have protected him, were so intent on the burning Scottish prisoners that not one drew a bow or a blade before Thomas had dragged Sir Geoffrey down from the saddle and had him on the ground with a knife at his throat.

'I've been killing men for four years,' Thomas said, 'and not all of them were Frenchmen.'

'Thomas!' Eleanor screamed.

'Take her, Beggar! Take her!' Sir Geoffrey shouted. He heaved up, but Thomas was an archer and years of drawing his big black bow had given him extraordinary strength in the arms and chest and Sir Geoffrey could not budge him, so he spat at Thomas instead. 'Take her, Beggar!' he yelled again.

The Scarecrow's men ran towards their master, but checked when they saw that Thomas had a knife at his captive's throat.

'Strip her, Beggar! Strip the pretty! We'll all have her!' Sir Geoffrey bawled, apparently oblivious of the blade at his gullet.

'Who reads here? Who reads?' Father Hobbe bellowed. The odd question checked everyone, even Beggar who had already snatched off Eleanor's hat and now had his huge left arm around her neck while his right hand gripped the neckline of her frock. 'Who in this company can read?' Father Hobbe demanded again as he brandished the parchment he had taken from one of the sacks on the back of Thomas's horse. 'This

46

is a letter from my lord the Bishop of Durham who is with our lord the King in France and it is sent to John Fossor, Prior of Durham, and only Englishmen who have fought with our King would carry such a letter. We have brought it from France.'

'It proves nothing!' Sir Geoffrey shouted, then spat at Thomas again as the blade was pressed hard into his throat.

'And in what language is this letter written?' A new horseman had spurred through the Scarecrow's men. He wore no surcoat or jupon, but the badge on his battered shield was a scallop shell on a cross and it proclaimed that he was not one of Sir Geoffrey's followers. 'What language?' he asked once more.

'Latin,' Thomas said, his knife still pressing hard into Sir Geoffrey's neck.

'Let Sir Geoffrey up,' the newcomer commanded Thomas, 'and I shall read the letter.'

'Tell him to let my woman go,' Thomas snarled.

The horseman looked surprised at being given an order by a mere archer, but he did not protest. Instead he urged his horse towards Beggar. 'Let her go,' he said and, when the big man did not obey, he half drew his sword. 'You want me to crop your ears, Beggar? Is that it? Two ears gone? Then your nose, then your cock, is that what you want, Beggar? You want to be shorn like a summer ewe? Trimmed down like an elf?'

'Let her go, Beggar,' Sir Geoffrey said sullenly.

Beggar obeyed and stepped back and the horseman leaned down from his saddle to take the letter from Father Hobbe. 'Let Sir Geoffrey go,' the newcomer ordered Thomas, 'for we shall have peace between Englishmen today, at least for a day.'

The horseman was an old man, at least fifty years old, with a great shock of white hair that looked as though it had never been close to a brush or comb. He was a large man, tall and big-bellied, on a sturdy horse that had no trapper, but only a tattered saddle cloth. The man's full-length mail coat was sadly rusted in places and torn in others, while over the coat he had a breastplate that had lost two of its straps. A long sword hung at his right thigh. He looked to Thomas like a yeoman farmer who had ridden to war with whatever equipment his neighbours could lend him, but he had been recognized by Sir Geoffrey's archers who had snatched off their hats and helmets when he appeared and who now treated him with deference. Even Sir Geoffrey seemed cowed by the white-haired man who frowned as he read the letter. '*Thesaurus*, eh?' He was speaking to himself. 'And a fine kettle of fish that is! A *thesaurus* indeed!' *Thesaurus* was Latin, but the rest of his words were spoken in Norman French and he was evidently confident that no archer would understand him.

'Mention of treasure' – Thomas used the same language, which had been taught to him by his father – 'makes men excited. Over-excited.'

'Good Lord above, good Lord indeed, you speak French! Miracles never cease. *Thesaurus*, it does mean treasure, doesn't it? My Latin is not what it was when I was young. I had it flogged into me by a priest and it seems to have mostly leaked out since. A treasure, eh? And you speak French!' The horseman showed genial surprise that Thomas spoke the language of aristocrats, though Sir Geoffrey, who did not speak French, looked alarmed for it suggested Thomas might be a good deal

48

better born than he had thought. The horseman gave the letter back to Father Hobbe, then spurred to Sir Geoffrey. 'You were picking a squabble with an Englishman, Sir Geoffrey, a messenger, no less, from our lord the King. How do you explain that?'

'I don't have to explain anything,' Sir Geoffrey said, 'my lord.' The last two words were added reluctantly.

'I should fillet you now,' his lordship said mildly, 'then have you stuffed and mounted on a pole to scare the crows away from my newly born lambs. I could show you at Skipton Fair, Sir Geoffrey, as an example to other sinners.' He seemed to consider that idea for a few heartbeats, then shook his head. 'Just get on your horse,' he said, 'and fight the Scots today instead of quarrelling with your fellow Englishman.' He turned in his saddle and raised his voice so all the archers and men-at-arms could hear him. 'All of you, back down the ridge! And quick, before the Scots come and drive you off! You want to join those rascals in the fire?' He pointed to the three Scottish prisoners who were now nothing but dark shrivelled shapes in the bright flames, then he beckoned Thomas and changed his language to French. 'You've really come from France?'

'Yes, my lord.'

'Then do me the courtesy, my dear fellow, of speaking with me.'

They went south, leaving a broken stone cross, burned men and arrow-struck corpses in a thinning mist, where the army of Scotland had come to Durham.

Bernard de Taillebourg took the crucifix from about his neck and kissed the writhing figure of Christ that was pinned to the small wooden cross. 'God be with you, my brother,' he murmured to the old man lying on the stone bench cushioned by a palliasse of straw and a folded blanket. A second blanket, just as thin, covered the old man whose hair was white and wispy.

'It is cold,' Brother Hugh Collimore said feebly, 'so cold.' He spoke in French, though to de Taillebourg the old monk's accent was barbarous for it was the French of Normandy and of England's Norman rulers.

'Winter comes,' de Taillebourg said. 'You can smell it on the wind.'

'I am dying' – Brother Collimore turned his red-rimmed eyes on his visitor – 'and can smell nothing. Who are you?'

'Take this,' de Taillebourg said and gave his crucifix to the old monk, then he stoked up the wood fire, put two more logs on the revived blaze and sniffed a jug of mulled wine that sat in the hearth. It was not too rank and so he poured some into a horn cup. 'At least you have a fire,' he said, stooping to peer through the small window, no bigger than an arrow slit, that faced west across the encircling Wear. The monk's hospital was on the slope of Durham's hill, beneath the cathedral, and de Taillebourg could see the Scottish men-at-arms carrying their lances through the straggling remnants of mist on the skyline. Few of the mail-clad men had horses, he noticed, suggesting that the Scots planned to fight on foot.

Brother Collimore, his face pale and his voice frail, gripped the small cross. 'The dying are allowed a fire,' he said, as though he had been accused of indulging himself in luxury. 'Who are you?'

'I come from Cardinal Bessières,' de Taillebourg said,

'in Paris, and he sends you his greetings. Drink this, it will warm you.' He held the mulled wine towards the old man.

Collimore refused the wine. His eyes were cautious. 'Cardinal Bessières?' he asked, his tone implying that the name was new to him.

'The Pope's legate in France.' De Taillebourg was surprised that the monk did not recognize the name, but thought perhaps the dying man's ignorance would be useful. 'And the Cardinal is a man,' the Dominican went on, 'who loves the Church as fiercely as he loves God.'

'If he loves the Church,' Collimore said with a surprising force, 'then he will use his influence to persuade the Holy Father to take the papacy back to Rome.' The statement exhausted him and he closed his eyes. He had never been a big man, but now, beneath his lice-ridden blanket, he seemed to have shrunk to the size of a ten-year-old and his white hair was thin and fine like a small infant's. 'Let him move the papacy to Rome,' he said again, though feebly, 'for all our troubles have worsened since it was moved to Avignon.'

'Cardinal Bessières wants nothing more than to move the Holy Father back to Rome,' de Taillebourg lied, 'and perhaps you, brother, can help us achieve that.'

Brother Collimore appeared not to hear the words. He had opened his eyes again, but just lay gazing up at the whitewashed stones of the arched ceiling. The room was low, chill and white. Sometimes, when the summer sun was high, he could see the flicker of reflected water on the white stones. In heaven, he thought, he would be forever within sight of crystal rivers and under a warm sun. 'I was in Rome once,' he said wistfully. 'I remember going down some steps into a church where a choir sang. So beautiful.'

'The Cardinal wants your help,' de Taillebourg said.

'There was a saint there.' Collimore was frowning, trying to remember. 'Her bones were yellow.'

'So the Cardinal sent me to see you, brother,' de Taillebourg said softly. His servant, dark-eyed and elegant, watched from the door.

'Cardinal Bessières,' Brother Collimore said in a whisper.

'He sends you his greetings in Christ, brother.'

'What Bessières wants,' Collimore said, still in a whisper, 'he takes with whips and scorpions.'

De Taillebourg half smiled. So Collimore did know of Cardinal Bessières after all, and no wonder, but perhaps fear of Bessières would be sufficient to elicit the truth. The monk had closed his eyes again and his lips were moving silently, suggesting he was praying. De Taillebourg did not disturb the prayers, but just gazed through the small window to where the Scots were making their battle line on the far hill. The invaders faced southwards so that the left end of their line was nearest to the city and de Taillebourg could see men jostling for position as they tried to take the places of honour closest to their lords. The Scots had evidently decided to fight on foot so that the English archers could not destroy their men-at-arms by cutting down their horses. There was no sign of those English yet, though from all de Taillebourg had heard they could not have assembled a great force. Their army was in France, outside Calais, not here, so perhaps it was merely a local lord leading his retainers? Yet plainly there were enough men to persuade the Scots to form a battle line, and de Taillebourg did not expect

52

David's army to be delayed for long. Which meant that if he wanted to hear the old man's story and be away from Durham before the Scots entered the city then he had best make haste. He looked back at the monk, 'Cardinal Bessières wants only the glory of the Church and of God. And he wants to know about Father Ralph Vexille.'

'Dear God,' Collimore said, and his fingers traced the bone figure on the small crucifix as he opened his eyes and turned his head to stare at the priest. The monk's expression suggested it was the first time he had really noticed de Taillebourg and he shuddered, recognizing in his visitor a man who believed suffering gave merit. A man, Collimore reflected, who would be as implacable as his master in Paris. 'Vexille!' Collimore said, as though he had almost forgotten the name, and then he sighed. 'It is a long tale,' he said tiredly.

'Then I will tell you what I know of it,' de Taillebourg said. The gaunt Dominican was pacing the room now, turning and turning again in the small space under the highest part of the arched ceiling. 'You have heard,' he demanded, 'that a battle was fought in Picardy in the summer? Edward of England fought his cousin of France and a man came from the south to fight for France and on his banner was the device of a yale holding a cup.' Collimore blinked, but said nothing. His eyes were fixed on de Taillebourg who, in turn, stopped his pacing to look at the priest. 'A yale holding a cup,' he repeated.

'I know the beast,' Collimore said sadly. A yale was an heraldic animal, unknown in nature, clawed like a lion, horned like a goat and scaled like a dragon.

'He came from the south,' de Taillebourg said, 'and

he thought that by fighting for France he would wash from his family's crest the ancient stains of heresy and of treason.' Brother Collimore was far too sick to see that the priest's servant was now listening intently, almost fiercely, or to notice that the Dominican had raised his voice slightly to make it easier for the servant, who still stood in the doorway, to overhear. 'This man came from the south, riding in pride, believing his soul to be beyond reproof, but no man is beyond God's reach. He thought he would ride in victory into the King's affections, but instead he shared France's defeat. God will sometimes humble us, brother, before raising us to glory.' De Taillebourg spoke to the old monk, but his words were for his servant's ears. 'And after the battle, brother, when France wept, I found this man and he talked of you.'

Brother Collimore looked startled, but said nothing.

'He talked of you,' Father de Taillebourg said, 'to me. And I am an Inquisitor.'

Brother Collimore's fingers fluttered in an attempt to make the sign of the cross. 'The Inquisition,' he said feebly, 'has no authority in England.'

'The Inquisition has authority in heaven and in hell, and you think little England can stand against us?' The fury in de Taillebourg's voice echoed in the hospital cell. 'To root out heresy, brother, we will ride to the ends of the earth.'

The Inquisition, like the Dominican order of friars, was dedicated to the eradication of heresy, and to do it they employed fire and pain. They could not shed blood, for that was against the law of the Church, but any pain inflicted without blood-letting was permitted, and the Inquisition knew well that fire cauterized bleeding and that the rack did not pierce a heretic's skin and that great weights pressed on a man's chest burst no veins. In cellars reeking of fire, fear, urine and smoke, in a darkness shot through with flamelight and the screams of heretics, the Inquisition hunted down the enemies of God and, by the application of bloodless pain, brought their souls into a blessed unity with Christ.

'A man came from the south,' de Taillebourg said to Collimore again, 'and the crest on his shield was a yale holding a cup.'

'A Vexille,' Collimore said.

'A Vexille,' de Taillebourg said, 'who knew your name. Now why, brother, would a heretic from the southern lands know the name of an English monk in Durham?'

Brother Collimore sighed. 'They all knew,' he said tiredly, 'the whole family knew. They knew because Ralph Vexille was sent to me. The bishop thought I could cure him of madness, but his family feared he would tell me secrets instead. They wanted him dead, but we locked him away in a cell where no one but I could reach him.'

'And what secrets did he tell you?' de Taillebourg asked.

'Madness,' Brother Collimore said, 'just madness.' The servant stood in the doorway and watched him.

'Tell me of the madness,' the Dominican ordered.

'The mad speak of a thousand things,' Brother Collimore said, 'they speak of spirits and phantoms, of snow in summer and darkness in the daylight.'

'But Father Ralph spoke to you of the Grail,' de Taillebourg said flatly.

'He spoke of the Grail,' Brother Collimore confirmed.

The Dominican let out a sigh of relief. 'What did he tell you of the Grail?'

Hugh Collimore said nothing for a while. His chest rose and fell so feebly that the motion was scarcely visible, then he shook his head. 'He told me that his family had owned the Grail and that he had stolen and hidden it! But he spoke of a hundred such things. A hundred such things.'

'Where would he have hidden it?' de Taillebourg enquired.

'He was mad. Mad. It was my job, you know, to look after the mad? We starved or beat them to drive the devils out, but it did not always work. In winter we would plunge them into the river, through the ice, and that worked. Devils hate the cold. It worked with Ralph Vexille, or mostly it worked. We released him after a while. The demons were gone, you see.'

'Where did he hide the Grail?' De Taillebourg's voice was harder and louder.

Brother Collimore stared at the flicker of reflected water light on the ceiling. 'He was mad,' he whispered, 'but he was harmless. Harmless. And when he left here he was sent to a parish in the south. In the far south.'

'At Hookton in Dorset?'

'At Hookton in Dorset,' Brother Collimore agreed, 'where he had a son. He was a great sinner, you see, even though he was a priest. He had a son.'

Father de Taillebourg stared at the monk who had, at last, given him some news. A son? 'What do you know of the son?'

'Nothing.' Brother Collimore sounded surprised that he should be asked.

'And what do you know of the Grail?' de Taillebourg probed.

'I know that Ralph Vexille was mad,' Collimore said in a whisper.

De Taillebourg sat on the hard bed. 'How mad?'

Collimore's voice became even softer. 'He said that even if you found the Grail then you would not know it, not unless you were worthy.' He paused and a look of puzzlement, almost amazement, showed briefly on his face. 'You had to be worthy, he said, to know what the Grail was, but if you were worthy then it would shine like the very sun. It would dazzle you.'

De Taillebourg leaned close to the monk. 'You believed him?'

'I believe Ralph Vexille was mad,' Brother Collimore said.

'The mad sometimes speak truth,' de Taillebourg said.

'I think,' Brother Collimore went on as though the Inquisitor had not spoken, 'that God gave Ralph Vexille a burden too great for him to bear.'

'The Grail?' de Taillebourg asked.

'Could you bear it? I could not.'

'So where is it?' de Taillebourg persisted. 'Where is it?'

Brother Collimore looked puzzled again. 'How would I know?'

'It was not at Hookton,' de Taillebourg said, 'Guy Vexille searched for it.'

'Guy Vexille?' Brother Collimore asked.

'The man who came from the south, brother, to fight for France and ended in my custody.'

'Poor man,' the monk said.

Father de Taillebourg shook his head. 'I merely

showed him the rack, let him feel the pincers and smell the smoke. Then I offered him life and he told me all he knew and he told me the Grail was not at Hookton.'

The old monk's face twitched in a smile. 'You did not hear me, father. If a man is unworthy then the Grail would not reveal itself. Guy Vexille could not have been worthy.'

'But Father Ralph did possess it?' De Taillebourg sought reassurance. 'You think he really possessed it?'

'I did not say as much,' the monk said.

'But you believe he did?' de Taillebourg asked and, when Brother Collimore said nothing, he nodded to himself. 'You do believe he did.' He slipped off the bed, going to his knees and a look of awe came to his face as his linked hands clawed at each other. 'The Grail,' he said in a tone of utter wonder.

'He was mad,' Brother Collimore warned him.

De Taillebourg was not listening. 'The grail,' he said again, '*le Graal*!' He was clutching himself now, rocking back and forth in ecstasy. '*Le Graal*!'

'The mad say things,' Brother Collimore said, 'and they do not know what they say.'

'Or God speaks through them,' de Taillebourg said fiercely.

'Then God sometimes has a terrible tongue,' the old monk replied.

'You must tell me,' de Taillebourg insisted, 'all that Father Ralph told you.'

'But it was so long ago!'

'It is *le Graal*!' de Taillebourg shouted and, in his frustration, he shook the old man. 'It is *le Graal*! Don't tell me you have forgotten.' He glanced through the window and saw, raised on the far ridge, the red saltire on the yellow banner of the Scottish King and beneath it a mass of grey-mailed men with their thicket of lances, pikes and spears. No English foe was in sight, but de Taillebourg would not have cared if all the armies of Christendom were come to Durham for he had found his vision, it was the Grail, and though the world should tremble with armies all about him, he would pursue it.

And an old monk talked.

The horseman with the rusted mail, broken-strapped breastplate and scallop-decorated shield named himself as Lord Outhwaite of Witcar. 'Do you know the place?' he asked Thomas.

'Witcar, my lord? I've not heard of it.'

'Not heard of Witcar! Dear me. And it's such a pleasant place, very pleasant. Good soil, sweet water, fine hunting. Ah, there you are!' This last was to a small boy mounted on a large horse and leading a second destrier by the reins. The boy wore a jupon that had the scalloped cross emblazoned in yellow and red and, tugging the warhorse behind him, he spurred towards his master.

'Sorry, my lord,' the boy said, 'but Hereward do haul away, he do.' Hereward was evidently the destrier he led. 'And he hauled me clean away from you!'

'Give him to this young man here,' Lord Outhwaite said. 'You can ride?' he added earnestly to Thomas.

'Yes, my lord.'

'Hereward is a handful though, a rare handful. Kick him hard to let him know who's master.'

A score of men appeared in Lord Outhwaite's livery, all mounted and all with armour in better repair than their master's. Lord Outhwaite turned them back south. 'We were marching on Durham,' he told Thomas, 'just minding our own affairs as good Christians should, and the wretched Scots appeared! We won't make Durham now. I was married there, you know? In the cathedral. Thirty-two years ago, can you credit it?' He beamed happily at Thomas. 'And my dear Margaret still lives, God be praised. She'd like to hear your tale. You really were at Wadicourt?'

'I was, my lord.'

'Fortunate you, fortunate you!' Lord Outhwaite said, then hailed yet more of his men to turn them about before they blundered into the Scots. Thomas was rapidly coming to realize that Lord Outhwaite, despite his ragged mail and dishevelled appearance, was a great lord, one of the magnates of the north country, and his lordship confirmed this opinion by grumbling that he had been forbidden by the King to fight in France because he and his men might be needed to fend off an invasion by the Scots. 'And he was quite right!' Lord Outhwaite sounded surprised. 'The wretches have come south! Did I tell you my eldest boy was in Picardy? That's why I'm wearing this.' He plucked at a rent in the old mail coat. 'I gave him the best armour we had because I thought we wouldn't need it here! Young David of Scotland always seemed peaceable enough to me, but now England's overrun by his fellows. Is it true that the slaughter at Wadicourt was vast?'

'It was a field of dead, my lord.'

'Theirs, not ours, God and His saints be thanked.' His lordship looked across at some archers straggling southwards. 'Don't dawdle!' he called in English. 'The Scots will be looking for you soon enough.' He looked back to Thomas and grinned. 'So what would you have done if I hadn't come along?' he asked, still using English. 'Cut the Scarecrow's throat?'

'If I had to.'

'And had your own slit by his men,' Lord Outhwaite observed cheerfully. 'He's a poisonous tosspot. God only knows why his mother didn't drown him at birth, but then she was a goddamned turd-hearted witch if ever there was one.' Like many lords who had grown up speaking French, Lord Outhwaite had learned his English from his parents' servants and so spoke it coarsely. 'He deserves a slit throat, the Scarecrow does, but he's a bad enemy to have. He holds a grudge better than any man alive, but he has so many grudges that maybe he don't have room for one more. He hates Sir William Douglas most of all.'

'Why?'

'Because Willie had him prisoner. Mind you, Willie Douglas has held most of us prisoner at one time or another and one or two of us have even held him in return, but the ransom near killed Sir Geoffrey. He's down to his last score of retainers and I'd be surprised if he's got more than three halfpennies in a pot. The Scarecrow's a poor man, very poor, but he's proud, and that makes him a bad enemy to have.' Lord Outhwaite paused to raise a genial hand to a group of archers wearing his livery. 'Wonderful fellows, wonderful. So tell me about the battle at Wadicourt. Is it true that the French rode down their own archers?'

'They did, my lord. Genoese crossbowmen.'

'So tell me all that happened.'

Lord Outhwaite had received a letter from his eldest son that told of the battle in Picardy, but he was

61

desperate to hear of the fight from someone who had stood on that long green slope between the villages of Wadicourt and Crécy, and Thomas now told how the enemy had attacked late in the afternoon and how the arrows had flown down the hill to cut the King of France's great army into heaps of screaming men and horses, and how some of the enemy had still come through the line of newly dug pits and past the arrows to hack at the English men-at-arms, and how, by the battle's end, there were no arrows left, just archers with bleeding fingers and a long hill of dying men and animals. The very sky had seemed rinsed with blood.

The telling of the tale took Thomas down off the ridge and out of sight of Durham. Eleanor and Father Hobbe walked behind, leading the mare and sometimes interjecting with their own comments, while a score of Lord Outhwaite's retainers rode on either side to listen to the battle's tale. Thomas told it well and it was plain Lord Outhwaite liked him; Thomas of Hookton had always possessed a charm that had protected and recommended him, even though it sometimes made men like Sir Geoffrey Carr jealous. Sir Geoffrey had ridden ahead and, when Thomas reached the water meadows where the English force gathered, the knight pointed at him as if he were launching a curse and Thomas countered by making the sign of the cross. Sir Geoffrey spat.

Lord Outhwaite scowled at the Scarecrow. 'I have not forgotten the letter your priest showed me' – he spoke to Thomas in French now – 'but I trust you will not leave us to deliver it to Durham yourself? Not while we have enemies to fight?'

'Can I stand with your lordship's archers?' Thomas asked.

Eleanor hissed her disapproval, but both men ignored her. Lord Outhwaite nodded his acceptance of Thomas's offer, then gestured that the younger man should climb down from the horse. 'One thing does puzzle me, though,' he went on, 'and that is why our lord the King should entrust such an errand to one so young.'

'And so base born?' Thomas asked with a smile, knowing that was the real question Lord Outhwaite had been too fastidious to ask.

His lordship laughed to be found out. 'You speak French, young man, but carry a bow. What are you? Base or well born?'

'Well enough, my lord, but out of wedlock.'

'Ah!'

'And the answer to your question, my lord, is that our lord the King sent me with one of his chaplains and a household knight, but both caught a sickness in London and that is where they remain. I came on with my companions.'

'Because you were eager to speak with this old monk?'

'If he lives, yes, because he can tell me about my father's family. My family.'

'And he can tell you about this treasure, this *thesaurus*. You know of it?'

'I know something of it, my lord,' Thomas said cautiously.

'Which is why the King sent you, eh?' Lord Outhwaite queried, but did not give Thomas time to answer the question. He gathered his reins. 'Fight with my archers, young man, but take care to stay alive, eh? I would like to know more of your *thesaurus*. Is the treasure really as great as the letter says?'

Thomas turned away from the ragged-haired Lord Outhwaite and stared up the ridge where there was nothing to be seen now except the bright-leaved trees and a thinning plume of smoke from the burned-out hovels. 'If it exists, my lord' – he spoke in French – 'then it is the kind of treasure that is guarded by angels and sought by demons.'

'And you seek it?' Lord Outhwaite asked with a smile.

Thomas returned the smile. 'I merely seek the Prior of Durham, my lord, to give him the bishop's letter.'

'You want Prior Fossor, eh?' Lord Outhwaite nodded towards a group of monks. 'That's him over there. The one in the saddle.' He had indicated a tall, white-haired monk who was astride a grey mare and surrounded by a score of other monks, all on foot, one of whom carried a strange banner that was nothing but a white scrap of cloth hanging from a painted pole. 'Talk to him,' Lord Outhwaite said, 'then seek my flag. God be with you!' He said the last four words in English.

'And with your lordship,' Thomas and Father Hobbe answered together.

Thomas walked towards the Prior, threading his way through archers who clustered about three wagons to receive spare sheaves of arrows. The small English army had been marching towards Durham on two separate roads and now the men straggled across fields to come together in case the Scots descended from the high ground. Men-at-arms hauled mail coats over their heads and the richer among them buckled on whatever pieces of plate armour they owned. The army's leaders must have had a swift conference for the first standards were being carried northwards, showing that the English wanted to confront the Scots on the higher ground of the ridge rather than be attacked in the water meadows or try to reach Durham by a circuitous route. Thomas had become accustomed to the English banners in Brittany, Normandy and Picardy, but these flags were all strange to him: a silver crescent, a brown cow, a blue lion, the Scarecrow's black axe, a red boar's head, Lord Outhwaite's scallop-emblazoned cross and, gaudiest of all, a great scarlet flag showing a pair of crossed keys thickly embroidered in gold and silver threads. The prior's flag looked shabby and cheap compared to all those other banners for it was nothing but a small square of frayed cloth beneath which the prior was working himself into a frenzy. 'Go and do God's work,' he shouted at some nearby archers, 'for the Scots are animals! Animals! Cut them down! Kill them all! God will reward each death! Go and smite them! Kill them!' He saw Thomas approaching. 'You want a blessing, my son? Then God give strength to your bow and add bite to your arrows! May your arm never tire and your eye never dim. God and the saints bless you while you kill!'

Thomas crossed himself then held out the letter. 'I came to give you this, sir,' he said.

The prior seemed astonished that an archer should address him so familiarly, let alone have a letter for him and at first he did not take the parchment, but one of his monks snatched it from Thomas and, seeing the broken seal, raised his eyebrows. 'My lord the bishop writes to you,' he said.

'They are animals!' the prior repeated, still caught up in his peroration, then he realized what the monk had said. 'My lord bishop writes?'

'To you, brother,' the monk said.

The prior seized the painted pole and dragged the makeshift banner down so it hung near to Thomas's face. 'You may kiss it,' he said grandly.

'Kiss it?' Thomas was quite taken aback. The ragged cloth, now it was close by his nose, smelt musty.

'It is St Cuthbert's corporax cloth,' the prior said excitedly, 'taken from his tomb, my son! The blessed St Cuthbert will fight for us! The very angels of heaven will follow him into the battle.'

Thomas, faced with the saint's relic, went to his knees and drew the cloth to his lips. It was linen, he thought, and now he could see it was embroidered about its edge with an intricate pattern in faded blue thread. In the centre of the cloth, which was used during Mass to hold the wafers, was an elaborate cross, embroidered in silver threads that scarcely showed against the frayed white linen. 'It is really St Cuthbert's cloth?' he asked.

'His alone!' the prior exclaimed. 'We opened his tomb in the cathedral this very morning, and we prayed to him and he will fight for us today!' The prior jerked the flag up and waved it towards some men-at-arms who spurred their horses northwards. 'Perform God's work! Kill them all! Dung the fields with their noxious flesh, water it with their treacherous blood!'

'The bishop wants this young man to speak with Brother Hugh Collimore,' the monk who had read the letter now told the prior, 'and the King wishes it too. His lordship says there is a treasure to be found.'

'The King wishes it?' the prior looked in astonishment at Thomas. 'The King wishes it?' he asked again and then he came to his senses and realized there was great advantage in royal patronage and so he snatched the letter and read it himself, only to find even more advantage than he had anticipated. 'You come in search of a great *thesaurus*?' he asked Thomas suspiciously.

'So the bishop believes, sir,' Thomas responded.

'What treasure?' the prior snapped and all the monks gaped at him as the notion of a treasure momentarily made them forget the proximity of the Scottish army.

'The treasure, sir' – Thomas avoided giving a truthful answer – 'is known to Brother Collimore.'

'But why send you?' the prior asked, and it was a fair question for Thomas looked young and possessed no apparent rank.

'Because I have some knowledge of the matter too,' Thomas said, wondering if he had said too much.

The prior folded the letter, inadvertently tearing off the seal as he did so, and thrust it into a pouch that hung from his knotted belt. 'We shall talk after the battle,' he said, 'and then, and only then, I shall decide whether you may see Brother Collimore. He is sick, you know? Ailing, poor soul. Maybe he is dying. It may not be seemly for you to disturb him. We shall see, we shall see.' He plainly wanted to talk to the old monk himself and so be the sole possessor of whatever knowledge Collimore might have. 'God bless you, my son,' the prior dismissed Thomas, then hoisted his sacred banner and hurried north. Most of the English army was already climbing the ridge, leaving only their wagons and a crowd of women, children and those men too sick to walk. The monks, making a procession behind their corporax cloth, began to sing as they followed the soldiers.

Thomas ran to a cart and took a sheaf of arrows, which he thrust into his belt. He could see that Lord

Outhwaite's men-at-arms were riding towards the ridge, followed by a large group of archers. 'Maybe the two of you should stay here,' he said to Father Hobbe.

'No!' Eleanor said. 'And you should not be fighting.'

'Not fight?' Thomas asked.

'It is not your battle!' Eleanor insisted. 'We should go to the city! We should find the monk.'

Thomas paused. He was thinking of the priest who, in the swirl of fog and smoke, had killed the Scotsman and then spoken to him in French. I am a messenger, the priest had said. '*Je suis un avant-coureur,*' had been his exact words and an *avant-coureur* was more than a mere messenger. A herald, perhaps? An angel even? Thomas could not drive away the image of that silent fight, the men so ill matched, a soldier against a priest, yet the priest had won and then had turned his gaunt, bloodied face on Thomas and announced himself: '*Je suis un avant-coureur.*' It was a sign, Thomas thought, and he did not want to believe in signs and visions, he wanted to believe in his bow. He thought perhaps Eleanor was right and that the conflict with its unexpected victor was a sign from heaven that he should follow the *avant-coureur* into the city, but there were also enemies up on the hill and he was an archer and archers did not walk away from a battle. 'We'll go to the city,' he said, 'after the fight.'

'Why?' she demanded fiercely.

But Thomas would not explain. He just started walking, climbing a hill where larks and finches flitted through the hedges and fieldfares, brown and grey, called from the empty pastures. The fog was all gone and a drying wind blew across the Wear.

And then, from where the Scots waited on the higher ground, the drums began to beat.

Sir William Douglas, Knight of Liddesdale, prepared himself for battle. He pulled on leather breeches thick enough to thwart a sword cut and over his linen shirt he hung a crucifix that had been blessed by a priest in Santiago de Compostela where St James was buried. Sir William Douglas was not a particularly religious man, but he paid a priest to look after his soul and the priest had assured Sir William that wearing the crucifix of St James, the son of thunder, would ensure he received the last rites safe in his own bed. About his waist he tied a strip of red silk that had been torn from one of the banners captured from the English at Bannockburn. The silk had been dipped in the holy water of the font in the chapel of Sir William's castle at Hermitage and Sir William had been persuaded that the scrap of silk would ensure victory over the old and much hated enemy.

He wore a haubergeon taken from an Englishman killed in one of Sir William's many raids south of the border. Sir William remembered that killing well. He had seen the quality of the Englishman's haubergeon at the very beginning of the fight and he had bellowed at his men to leave the fellow alone, then he had cut the man down by striking at his ankles and the Englishman, on his knees, had made a mewing sound that had made Sir William's men laugh. The man had surrendered, but Sir William had cut his throat anyway because he thought any man who made a mewing sound was not a real warrior. It had taken the servants at Hermitage two weeks to wash the blood out of the fine mesh of the mail. Most of the Scottish leaders were dressed in hauberks, which covered a man's body from neck to calves, while the haubergeon was much shorter and left the legs unprotected, but Sir William intended to fight on foot and he knew that a hauberk's weight wearied a man quickly and tired men were easily killed. Over the haubergeon he wore a full-length surcoat that showed his badge of the red heart. His helmet was a sallet, lacking any visor or face protection, but in battle Sir William liked to see what his enemies to the left and right were doing. A man in a full helm or in one of the fashionable pig-snouted visors could see nothing except what the slit right in front of his eyes let him see, which was why men in visored helmets spent the battle jerking their heads left and right, left and right, like a chicken among foxes, and they twitched until their necks were sore and even then they rarely saw the blow that crushed their skulls. Sir William, in battle, looked for men whose heads were jerking like hens, back and forth, for he knew they were nervous men who could afford a fine helmet and thus pay a finer ransom. He carried his big shield. It was really too heavy for a man on foot, but he expected the English to loose their archery storm and the shield was thick enough to absorb the crashing impact of yard-long, steel-pointed arrows. He could rest the foot of the shield on the ground and crouch safe behind it and, when the English ran out of arrows, he could always discard it. He carried a spear in case the English horsemen charged, and a sword, which was his favourite killing weapon. The sword's hilt encased a scrap of hair cut from the corpse of St Andrew, or at least that was what the pardoner who had sold Sir William the scrap had claimed.

Robbie Douglas, Sir William's nephew, wore mail and a sallet, and carried a sword and shield. It had been Robbie who had brought Sir William the news that Jamie Douglas, Robbie's older brother, had been killed, presumably by the Dominican priest's servant. Or perhaps Father de Taillebourg had done the killing? Certainly he must have ordered it. Robbie Douglas, twenty years old, had wept for his brother. 'How could a priest do it?' Robbie had demanded of his uncle.

'You have a strange idea of priests, Robbie,' Sir William had said. 'Most priests are weak men given God's authority and that makes them dangerous. I thank God no Douglas has ever put on a priest's robe. We're all too honest.'

'When this day's done, uncle,' Robbie Douglas said, 'you'll let me go after that priest.'

Sir William smiled. He might not be an overtly religious man, but he did hold one creed sacred and that was that any family member's murder must be avenged and Robbie, he reckoned, would do vengeance well. He was a good young man, hard and handsome, tall and straightforward, and Sir William was proud of his youngest sister's son. 'We'll talk at day's end,' Sir William promised him, 'but till then, Robbie, stay close to me.'

'I will, uncle.'

'We'll kill a good few Englishmen, God willing,' Sir William said, then led his nephew to meet the King and to receive the blessing of the royal chaplains.

Sir William, like most of the Scottish knights and chieftains, was in mail, but the King wore French-made plate, a thing so rare north of the border that men from the wild tribes came to stare at this sun-reflecting creature made of moving metal. The young King seemed just as impressed for he took off his surcoat and walked up and down admiring himself and being admired as his lords came for a blessing and to offer advice. The Earl of Moray, whom Sir William believed was a fool, wanted to fight on horseback and the King was tempted to agree. His father, the great Robert the Bruce, had beaten the English at the Bannockburn on horseback, and not just beaten them, but humiliated them. The flower of Scotland had ridden down the nobility of England and David, King now of his father's country, wanted to do the same. He wanted blood beneath his hooves and glory attached to his name; he wanted his reputation to spread through Christendom and so he turned and gazed longingly at his red and yellow painted lance propped against the bough of an elm.

Sir William Douglas saw where the King was looking. 'Archers,' he said laconically.

'There were archers at the Bannockburn,' the Earl of Moray insisted.

'Aye, and the fools didn't know how to use them,' Sir William said, 'but you can't depend on the English being fools for ever.'

'And how many archers can they have?' the Earl asked. 'There are said to be thousands of bowmen in France, hundreds more in Brittany and as many again in Gascony, so how many can they have here?'

'They have enough,' Sir William growled curtly, not bothering to hide the contempt he felt for John Randolph, third Earl of Moray. The Earl was just as experienced in war as Sir William, but he had spent too long as a prisoner of the English and the consequent hatred made him impetuous.

The King, young and inexperienced, wanted to side with the Earl whose friend he was, but he saw that his other lords were agreeing with Sir William who, though he held no great title nor position of state, was more battle-hardened than any man in Scotland. The Earl of Moray sensed that he was losing the argument and he urged haste. 'Charge now, sir,' he suggested, 'before they can make a battle line.' He pointed southwards to where the first English troops were appearing in the pastures. 'Cut the bastards down before they're ready.'

'That,' the Earl of Menteith put in quietly, 'was the advice given to Philip of Valois in Picardy. It didn't serve there and it won't serve here.'

'Besides which,' Sir William Douglas remarked caustically, 'we have to contend with stone walls.' He pointed to the walls which bounded the pastures where the English were beginning to form their line. 'Maybe Moray can tell us how armoured knights get past stone walls?' he suggested.

The Earl of Moray bridled. 'You take me for a fool, Douglas?'

'I take you as you show yourself, John Randolph,' Sir William answered.

'Gentlemen!' the King snapped. He had not noticed the stone walls when he formed his battle line beside the burning cottages and the fallen cross. He had only seen the empty green pastures and the wide road and his even wider dream of glory. Now he watched the enemy straggle from the far trees. There were plenty of archers coming, and he had heard how those bowmen could fill the sky with their arrows and how their steel arrow heads drove deep into horses and how the horses then went mad with pain. And he dared not lose this battle. He had promised his nobles that they would celebrate the feast of Christmas in the hall of the English King in London and if he lost then he would lose their respect and encourage some to rebellion. He had to win and, being impatient, he wanted to win quickly. 'If we charge fast enough,' he suggested tentatively, 'before they all reach their lines —'

'Then, you'll break your horse's legs on the stone walls,' Sir William said with scant respect for his royal master. 'If your majesty's horse even gets that far. You can't protect a horse from arrows, sir, but you can weather the storm on foot. Put your pikes up front, but mix them with men-at-arms who can use their shields to protect the pike-holders. Shields up, heads down and hold hard, that's how we win this.'

The King tugged at the espalier which covered his right shoulder and had an annoying habit of riding up on the top edge of the breastplate. Traditionally the defence of Scottish armies was in the hands of pikemen who used their monstrously long weapons to hold off the enemy knights, but pikemen needed both hands to hold their unwieldy blades and so became easy targets for English bowmen who liked to boast that they carried the lives of Scottish pikemen in their arrow bags. So protect the pikemen with the shields of the men-at-arms and let the enemy waste their arrows. It made sense, but it still irked David Bruce that he could not lead his horsemen in an earth-shaking assault while the trumpets screamed at the heavens.

Sir William saw his King's hesitation and pressed his

argument. 'We have to stand, sir, and we have to wait, and we have to let our shields take the arrows, but in the end, sir, they'll tire of wasting shafts and they'll come to the attack and that's when we'll chop them down like dogs.'

A growl of assent greeted this. The Scottish lords, hard men all, armed and armoured, bearded and grim, were confident that they could win this fight because they so outnumbered the enemy, but they also knew there was no short cut to victory, not when archers opposed them, and so they would have to do what Sir William said: endure the arrows, goad the enemy, then give them slaughter.

The King heard his lords agree with Sir William and so, reluctantly, he abandoned his dream of breaking the enemy with mounted knights. That was a disappointment, but he looked about his lords and thought that with such men beside him he could not possibly lose. 'We shall fight on foot,' he decreed, 'and chop them down like dogs. We shall slaughter them like whipped puppies!' And afterwards, he thought, when the survivors were fleeing southwards, the Scottish cavalry could finish the slaughter.

But for now it would be footman against footman and so the war banners of Scotland were carried forward and planted across the ridge. The burning cottages were mere embers now that cradled three shrunken bodies, black and small as children, and the King planted his flags close to those dead. He had his own standard, red saltire on yellow field, and the banner of Scotland's saint, white saltire on blue, in the line's centre and to left and right the flags of the lesser lords flew. The lion of Stewart brandished its blade, the Randolph falcon spread its wings while to east and west the stars and axes and crosses snapped in the wind. The army was arrayed in three divisions, called sheltrons, and the three sheltrons were so large that the men on the far flanks jostled in towards the centre to keep themselves on the flatter ground of the ridge's summit.

The rearmost ranks of the sheltrons were composed of the tribesmen from the islands and the north, men who fought bare-legged, without metal armour, wielding vast swords that could club a man to death as easily as cut him down. They were fearsome fighters, but their lack of armour made them horribly vulnerable to arrows and so they were placed at the rear and the leading ranks of the three sheltrons were filled by men-at-arms and pikemen. The men-at-arms carried swords, axes, maces or war-hammers and, most important, the shields that could protect the pikemen whose weapons were tipped with a spike, a hook and an axehead. The spike could hold an enemy at bay, the hook could haul an armoured man out of the saddle or off his feet, and the axe could smash through his mail or plate. The line bristled with the pikes that made a steel hedge to greet the English and priests walked along the hedge consecrating the weapons and the men who held them. Soldiers knelt to receive their blessings. A few of the lords, like the King himself, were mounted, but only so that they could see over the heads of their army, and those men stared south to see the last of the English troops come into view. So few of them! Such a small army to beat! To the left of the Scots was Durham, its towers and ramparts thick with folk watching the battle, and in front was this small army of Englishmen who did not possess the sense to retreat south towards York. They would fight on the ridge instead and the Scots had the advantage of position and numbers. 'If you hate them!' Sir William Douglas shouted at his men on the right of the Scottish battle line, 'then let them hear you!'

The Scots bellowed their hatred. They clashed swords and spears against their shields, they shrieked to the sky and, in the line's centre, where the King's sheltron waited under the banners of the cross, a troop of drummers began to beat huge goatskin drums. Each drum was a big ring of oak over which was stretched two goat skins that were tightened with ropes until an acorn, dropped onto a skin, would bounce as high as the hand that had let it go and the drums, beaten with withies, made a sharp, almost metallic sound that filled the sky. They made an assault of pure noise.

'If you hate the English, let them know!' the Earl of March shouted from the left of the Scottish line that lay closest to the city. 'If you hate the English, let them know!' and the roar became louder, the clash of spear stave on shield was stronger, and the noise of Scotland's hate spread across the ridge so that nine thousand men were howling at the three thousand who were foolish enough to confront them.

'We shall cut them down like stalks of barley,' a priest promised, 'we shall soak the fields with their stinking blood and fill all hell with their English souls.'

'Their women are yours!' Sir William told his men. 'Their wives and their daughters will be your toys tonight!' He grinned at his nephew Robbie. 'You'll have your pick of Durham's women, Robbie.'

'And London's women,' Robbie said, 'before Christmas.'

'Aye, them too,' Sir William promised.

'In the name of the Father, and of the Son, and of the Holy Ghost,' the King's senior chaplain shouted, 'send them all to hell! Each and every foul one of them to hell! For every Englishman you kill today means a thousand less weeks in purgatory!'

'If you hate the English,' Lord Robert Stewart, Steward of Scotland and heir to the throne, called, 'let them hear!' And the noise of that hate was like a thunder that filled the deep valley of the Wear, and the thunder reverberated from the crag where Durham stood and still the noise swelled to tell the whole north country that the Scots had come south.

And David, King of those Scots, was glad that he had come to this place where the dragon cross had fallen and the burning houses smoked and the English waited to be killed. For this day he would bring glory to St Andrew, to the great house of Bruce, and to Scotland.

Thomas, Father Hobbe and Eleanor followed the prior and his monks who were still chanting, though the brothers' voices were now ragged for they were breathless from hurrying. St Cuthbert's corporax cloth swayed to and fro and the banner attracted a straggling procession of women and children who, not wanting to wait out of sight of their men, carried spare sheaves of arrows up the hill. Thomas wanted to go faster, to get past the monks and find Lord Outhwaite's men, but Eleanor deliberately hung back until he turned on her angrily. 'You can walk faster,' he protested in French.

'I can walk faster,' she said, 'and you can ignore a battle!' Father Hobbe, leading the horse, understood the tone even though he did not comprehend the words. He sighed, thus earning himself a savage look from Eleanor. 'You do not need to fight!' she went on.

'I'm an archer,' Thomas said stubbornly, 'and there's an enemy up there.'

'Your King sent you to find the Grail!' Eleanor insisted. 'Not to die! Not to leave me alone! Me and a baby!' She had stopped now, hands clutching her belly and with tears in her eyes. 'I am to be alone here? In England?'

'I won't die here,' Thomas said scathingly.

'You know that?' Eleanor was even more scathing. 'God spoke to you, perhaps? You know what other men do not? You know the day of your dying?'

Thomas was taken aback by the outburst. Eleanor was a strong girl, not given to tantrums, but she was distraught and weeping now. 'Those men,' Thomas said, 'the Scarecrow and Beggar, they won't touch you. I'll be here.'

'It isn't them!' Eleanor wailed. 'I had a dream last night. A dream.'

Thomas put his hands on her shoulders. His hands were huge and strengthened by hauling on the hempen string of the big bow. 'I dreamed of the Grail last night,' he said, knowing that was not quite true. He had not dreamed of the Grail, rather he had woken to a vision which had turned out to be a deception, but he could not tell Eleanor that. 'It was golden and beautiful,' he said, 'like a cup of fire.'

'In my dream,' Eleanor said, gazing up at him, 'you were dead and your body was all black and swollen.'

'What is she saying?' Father Hobbe asked.

'She had a bad dream,' Thomas said in English, 'a nightmare.'

'The devil sends us nightmares,' the priest asserted. 'It is well known. Tell her that.'

Thomas translated that for her, then he stroked a wisp of golden hair away from her forehead and tucked it under her knitted cap. He loved her face, so earnest and narrow, so cat-like, but with big eyes and an expressive mouth. 'It was just a nightmare,' he reassured her, '*un cauchemar.*'

'The Scarecrow,' Eleanor said with a shudder, 'he is the *cauchemar.*'

Thomas drew her into an embrace. 'He won't come near you,' he promised her. He could hear a distant chanting, but nothing like the monks' solemn prayers. This was a jeering, insistent chant, heavy as the drumbeat that gave it rhythm. He could not hear the words, but he did not need to. 'The enemy,' he said to Eleanor, 'are waiting for us.'

'They are not my enemy,' she said fiercely.

'If they get into Durham,' Thomas retorted, 'then they will not know that. They will take you anyway.'

'Everyone hates the English. Do you know that? The French hate you, the Bretons hate you, the Scots hate you, every man in Christendom hates you! And why? Because you love fighting! You do! Everyone knows that about the English. And you? You have no need to fight today, it is not your quarrel, but you can't wait to be there, to kill again!'

Thomas did not know what to say, for there was truth in what Eleanor had said. He shrugged and picked up his heavy bow. 'I fight for my King, and there's an army of enemies on the hill here. They outnumber us. Do you know what will happen if they get into Durham?'

'I know,' Eleanor said firmly, and she did know for she had been in Caen when the English archers, disobeying their King, had swarmed across the bridge and laid the town waste.

'If we don't fight them and stop them here,' Thomas said, 'then their horsemen will hunt us all down. One after the other.'

'You said you would marry me,' Eleanor declared, crying again. 'I don't want my baby to be fatherless, I don't want it to be like me.' She meant illegitimate.

'I will marry you, I promise. When the battle is done

we shall be married in Durham. In the cathedral, yes?'
He smiled at her. 'We can be married in the cathedral.'

Eleanor was pleased with the promise, but too furious
to show her pleasure. 'We should go to the cathedral
now,' she snapped. 'We would be safe there. We should
pray at the high altar.'

'You can go to the city,' Thomas said. 'Let me fight
my King's enemies and you go to the city, you and
Father Hobbe, and you find the old monk and you can
both talk to him, and afterwards you can go to the
cathedral and wait for me there.' He unstrapped one
of the big sacks on the mare's back and took out his
haubergeon, which he hauled over his head. The leather
lining felt stiff and cold, and smelt of mould. He forced
his hands down the sleeves, then strapped the sword
belt about his waist and hung the weapon on his right
side. 'Go to the city,' he told Eleanor, 'and talk to the
monk.'

Eleanor was crying. 'You are going to die,' she said,
'I dreamed it.'

'I can't go to the city,' Father Hobbe protested.

'You're a priest,' Thomas barked, 'not a soldier! Take
Eleanor to Durham. Find Brother Collimore and talk
to him.' The prior had insisted that Thomas wait and
suddenly it seemed very sensible to send Father Hobbe
to talk to the old monk before the prior poisoned his
memories. 'Both of you,' Thomas insisted, 'talk to
Brother Collimore. You know what to ask him. And I
shall see you there this evening, in the cathedral.' He
took his sallet, with its broad rim to deflect the down-
ward stroke of a blade, and tied it onto his head. He
was angry with Eleanor because he sensed she was
right. The imminent battle was not his concern except

82

that fighting was his trade and England his country. 'I will not die,' he told Eleanor with an obstinate irrationality, 'and you will see me tonight.' He tossed the horse's reins to Father Hobbe. 'Keep Eleanor safe,' he told the priest. 'The Scarecrow won't risk anything inside the monastery or in the cathedral.'

He wanted to kiss Eleanor goodbye, but she was angry with him and he was angry with her and so he took his bow and his arrow bag and walked away. She said nothing for, like Thomas, she was too proud to back away from the quarrel. Besides, she knew she was right. This clash with the Scots was not Thomas's fight, whereas the Grail was his duty. Father Hobbe, caught between their obstinacy, walked in silence, but did note that Eleanor turned more than once, evidently hoping to catch Thomas looking back, but all she saw was her lover climbing the path with the great bow across his shoulder.

It was a huge bow, taller than most men and as thick about its belly as an archer's wrist. It was made from yew; Thomas was fairly sure it was Italian yew though he could never be certain because the raw stave had drifted ashore from a wrecked ship. He had shaped the stave, leaving the centre thick, and he had steamed the tips to curve them against the way the bow would bend when it was drawn. He had painted the bow black, using wax, oil and soot, then tipped the two ends of the stave with pieces of nocked antler horn to hold the cord. The stave had been cut so that at the belly of the bow, where it faced Thomas when he drew the hempen string, there was hard heartwood which was compressed when the arrow was hauled back while the outer belly was springy sapwood and when he released

83

the cord the heartwood snapped out of its compression and the sapwood pulled it back into shape and between them they sent the arrow hissing with savage force. The belly of the bow, where his left hand gripped the yew, was whipped with hemp and above the hemp, which had been stiffened with hoof glue, he had nailed a scrap of silver cut from a crushed Mass vessel that his father had used in Hookton church, and the piece of silver cup showed the yale with the Grail in its clawed grip. The yale came from Thomas's family's coat of arms, though he had not known that when he grew up for his father had never told him the tale. He had never told Thomas he was a Vexille from a family that had been lords of the Cathar heretics, a family that had been burned out of their home in southern France and which had fled to hide themselves in the darkest corners of Christendom.

Thomas knew little of the Cathar heresy. He knew his bow and he knew how to select an arrow of slender ash or birch or hornbeam, and he knew how to fledge the shaft with goose feathers and how to tip it with steel. He knew all that, yet he did not know how to drive that arrow through shield, mail and flesh. That was instinct, something he had practised since childhood; practised till his string fingers were bleeding; practised until he no longer thought when he drew the string back to his ear; practised until, like all archers, he was broad across the chest and hugely muscled in his arms. He did not need to know how to use a bow, it was just an instinct like breathing or waking or fighting.

He turned when he reached a stand of hornbeams that guarded the upper path like a rampart. Eleanor was walking stubbornly away and Thomas had an urge to shout to her, but knew she was already too far off and would not hear him. He had quarrelled with her before; men and women, it seemed to Thomas, spent half their lives fighting and half loving and the intensity of the first fed the passion of the second, and he almost smiled for he recognized Eleanor's stubbornness and he even liked it; and then he turned and walked through the trampled drifts of fallen hornbeam leaves along the path between stone-walled pastures where hundreds of saddled stallions were grazing. These were the war-horses of the English knights and men-at-arms and their presence in the pastures told Thomas that the English expected the Scots to attack because a knight was far better able to defend himself on foot. The horses were kept saddled so that the mailed men-at-arms could either retreat swiftly or else mount up and pursue a beaten enemy.

Thomas could still not see the Scottish army, but he could hear their chanting, which was given force by the hellish beat of the big drums. The sound was making some of the pastured stallions nervous and three of them, pursued by pageboys, galloped beside the stone wall with their eyes showing white. More pages were exercising destriers just behind the English line, which was divided into three battles. Each battle had a knot of horsemen at the centre of its rear rank, the mounted men being the commanders beneath their bright banners, while in front of them were four or five rows of men-at-arms carrying swords, axes, spears and shields, and ahead of the men-at-arms, and crowded thick in the spaces between the three battles, were the archers.

The Scots, two arrow shots away from the English, were on slightly higher ground and also divided into three divisions which, like the English battles, were arrayed beneath their clusters of commanders' banners. The tallest flag, the red and yellow royal standard, was in the centre. The Scottish knights and men-at-arms, like the English, were on foot, but each of their sheltrons was much larger than its opposing English battle, three or four times larger, but Thomas, tall enough to look over the English line, could see there were not many archers in the enemy ranks. Here and there along the Scottish line he could see some long bowstaves and there were a few crossbows visible among the thicket of pikes, but there were not nearly so many bowmen as were in the English array, though the English, in turn, were hugely outnumbered by the Scottish army. So the battle, if it ever started, would be between arrows and Scottish pikes and men-at-arms, and if there were not enough arrows then the ridge must become an English graveyard.

Lord Outhwaite's banner of the cross and scallop shell was in the left-hand battle and Thomas crossed to it. The prior, dismounted now, was in the space between the left and centre divisions where one of his monks swung a censer and another brandished the Mass cloth on its painted pole. The prior himself was shouting, though Thomas could not tell whether he called insults at the enemy or prayers to God for the Scottish chanting was so loud. Thomas could not distinguish the enemy's words either, but the sentiment was plain enough and it was sped on its way by the massive drums.

Thomas could see the huge drums now and observe the passion with which the drummers beat the great skins to make a noise as sharp as snapping bone. Loud, rhythmic and reverberating, an assault of ear-piercing thunder, and in front of the drums at the centre of the enemy line some bearded men whirled in a wild dance. They came darting from the rear of the Scottish line and they wore no mail or iron, but were draped in thick folds of cloth and brandished long-bladed swords about their heads and had small round leather shields, scarce larger than serving platters, strapped to their left forearms. Behind them the Scottish men-at-arms beat the flats of their sword blades against their shields while the pikemen thumped the ground with the butts of their long weapons to add to the noise of the huge drums. The sound was so great that the prior's monks had abandoned their chanting and now just gazed at the enemy.

'What they do' – Lord Outhwaite, on foot like his men, had to raise his voice to make himself heard – 'is try to scare us with noise before they kill us.' His lordship limped, whether through age or some old wound, Thomas did not like to ask; it was plain he wanted somewhere he could pace about and kick the turf and so he had come to talk with the monks, though now he turned his friendly face on Thomas. 'And you want to be most careful of those scoundrels,' he said, pointing at the dancing men, 'because they're wilder than scalded cats. It's said they skin their captives alive.' Lord Outhwaite made the sign of the cross. 'You don't often see them this far south.'

'Them?' Thomas asked.

'They're tribesmen from the farthest north,' one of the monks explained. He was a tall man with a fringe of grey hair, a scarred face and only one eye. 'Scoundrels, they are,' the monk went on, 'scoundrels! They bow down to idols!' He shook his head sadly. 'I've never

87

journeyed that far north, but I hear their land is shrouded in perpetual fog and that if a man dies with a wound to his back then his woman eats her own young and throws herself off the cliffs for the shame of it.'

'Truly?' Thomas asked.

'It's what I've heard,' the monk said, making the sign of the cross.

'They live on birds' nests, seaweed and raw fish.' Lord Outhwaite took up the tale, then smiled. 'Mind you, some of my people in Witcar do that, but at least they pray to God as well. At least I think they do.'

'But your folk don't have cloven hooves,' the monk said, staring at the enemy.

'The Scots do?' a much younger monk with a face left horribly scarred by smallpox asked anxiously.

'The clansmen do,' Lord Outhwaite said. 'They're scarcely human!' He shook his head then held out a hand to the older monk. 'It's Brother Michael, isn't it?'

'Your lordship flatters to remember me,' the monk answered, pleased.

'He was once a man-at-arms to my Lord Percy,' Lord Outhwaite explained to Thomas, 'and a good one!'

'Before I lost this to the Scots,' Brother Michael said, raising his right arm so that the sleeve of his robe fell to reveal a stump at his wrist, 'and this,' he pointed to his empty eye socket, 'so now I pray instead of fight.' He turned and gazed at the Scottish line. 'They are noisy today,' he grumbled.

'They're confident,' Lord Outhwaite said placidly, 'and so they should be. When was the last time a Scottish army outnumbered us?'

'They might outnumber us,' Brother Michael said,

'but they've picked a strange place to do it. They should have gone to the southern end of the ridge.'

'And so they should, brother,' Lord Outhwaite agreed, 'but let us be grateful for small mercies.' What Brother Michael meant was the Scots were sacrificing their advantage of numbers by fighting on the narrow ridge top where the English line, though thinner and with far fewer men, could not be overlapped. If the Scots had gone further south, where the ridge widened as it fell away to the water meadows, they could have outflanked their enemy. Their choice of ground might have been a mistake that helped the English, but that was small consolation when Thomas tried to estimate the size of the enemy army. Other men were doing the same and their guesses ranged from six to sixteen thousand, though Lord Outhwaite reckoned there were no more than eight thousand Scots. 'Which is only three or four times our number,' he said cheerfully, 'and not enough of them are archers. God be thanked for English archers.'

'Amen,' Brother Michael said.

The smallpox-scarred younger monk was staring in fascination at the thick Scottish line. 'I've heard that the Scots paint their faces blue. I can't see any though.'

Lord Outhwaite looked astonished. 'You heard what?'

'That they paint their faces blue, my lord,' the monk said, embarrassed now, 'or maybe they only paint half the face. To scare us.'

'To scare us?' His lordship was amused. 'To make us laugh, more like. I've never seen it.'

'Nor I,' Brother Michael put in.

'It's just what I've heard,' the young monk said.

'They're frightening enough without paint,' Lord Outhwaite pointed to a banner opposite his own part of the line. 'I see Sir William's here.'

'Sir William?' Thomas asked.

'Willie Douglas,' Lord Outhwaite said. 'I was a prisoner of his for two years and I'm still paying the bankers because of it.' He meant that his family had borrowed money to pay the ransom. 'I liked him, though. He's a rogue. And he's fighting with Moray?'

'Moray?' Brother Michael asked.

'John Randolph, Earl of Moray.' Lord Outhwaite nodded at another banner close to the red-heart flag of Douglas. 'They hate each other. God knows why they're together in the line.' He stared again at the Scottish drummers who leaned far back to balance the big instruments against their bellies. 'I hate those drums,' he said mildly. 'Paint their faces blue! I never heard such nonsense!' he chuckled.

The prior was haranguing the nearest troops now, telling them that the Scots had destroyed the great religious house at Hexham. 'They defiled God's holy church! They killed the brethren! They have stolen from Christ Himself and put tears onto the cheeks of God! Wreak His vengeance! Show no mercy!' The nearest archers flexed their fingers, licked lips and stared at the enemy who were showing no sign of advancing. 'You will kill them,' the prior shrieked, 'and God will bless you for it! He will shower blessings on you!'

'They want us to attack them,' Brother Michael remarked drily. He seemed embarrassed by his prior's passion.

'Aye,' Lord Outhwaite said, 'and they think we'll attack on horseback. See the pikes?'

'They're good against men on foot too, my lord,' Brother Michael said.

'That they are, that they are,' Lord Outhwaite agreed. 'Nasty things, pikes.' He fidgeted with some of the loose rings of his mail coat and looked surprised when one of them came away in his fingers. 'I do like Willie Douglas,' he said. 'We used to hunt together when I was his prisoner. We caught some very fine boar in Liddesdale, I remember.' He frowned. 'Such noisy drums.'

'Will we attack them?' the young monk summoned up the courage to enquire.

'Dear me no, I do hope not,' Lord Outhwaite said. 'We're outnumbered! Much better to hold our ground and let them come to us.'

'And if they don't come?' Thomas asked.

'Then they'll slink off home with empty pockets,' Lord Outhwaite said, 'and they won't like that, they won't like it at all. They're only here for plunder! That's why they dislike us so much.'

'Dislike us? Because they're here for plunder?' Thomas had not understood his lordship's thinking.

'They're envious, young man! Plain envious. We have riches, they don't, and there are few things more calculated to provoke hatred than such an imbalance. I had a neighbour in Witcar who seemed a reasonable fellow, but then he and his men tried to take advantage of my absence when I was Douglas's prisoner. They tried to ambush the coin for my ransom, if you can believe it! It was just envy, it seems, for he was poor.'

'And now he's dead, my lord?' Thomas asked, amused.

'Dear me, no,' his lordship said reprovingly, 'he's in a very deep hole in the bottom of my keep. Deep down with the rats. I throw him coins every now and then to remind him why he's there.' He stood on tiptoe and gazed westwards where the hills were higher. He was looking for Scottish men-at-arms riding to make an assault from the south, but he saw none. 'His father,' he said, meaning Robert the Bruce, 'wouldn't be waiting there. He'd have men riding around our flanks to put the fear of God up our arses, but this young pup doesn't know his trade, does he? He's in the wrong place altogether!'

'He's put his faith in numbers,' Brother Michael said.

'And perhaps their numbers will suffice,' Lord Outhwaite replied gloomily and made the sign of the cross.

Thomas, now that he had a chance to see the ground between the armies, could understand why Lord Outhwaite was so scornful of the Scottish King who had drawn up his army just south of the burned cottages where the dragon cross had fallen. It was not just that the narrowness of the ridge confined the Scots, denying them a chance to outflank the numerically inferior English, but that the ill-chosen battlefield was obstructed by thick blackthorn hedges and at least one stone wall. No army could advance across those obstacles and hope to hold its line intact, but the Scottish King seemed confident that the English would attack him for he did not move. His men shouted insults in the hope of provoking an attack, but the English stayed stubbornly in their ranks.

The Scots jeered even louder when a tall man on a great horse rode out from the centre of the English line. His stallion had purple ribbons twisted into its black mane and a purple trapper embroidered with golden keys that was so long that it swept the ground behind the horse's rear hooves. The stallion's head was protected by a leather face plate on which was mounted a silver horn, twisted like a unicorn's weapon. The rider wore plate armour that was polished bright and had a sleeveless surcoat of purple and gold, the same colours displayed by his page, standard-bearer and the dozen knights who followed him. The tall rider had no sword, but instead was armed with a great spiked morningstar like the one Beggar carried. The Scottish drummers redoubled their efforts, the Scots soldiers shouted insults and the English cheered until the tall man raised a mailed hand for silence.

'We're to get a homily from his grace,' Lord Outhwaite said gloomily. 'Very fond of the sound of his own voice is his grace.'

The tall man was evidently the Archbishop of York and, when the English ranks were silent, he again raised his mailed right hand high above his purple plumed helmet and made an extravagant sign of the cross. '*Dominus vobiscum*,' he called. '*Dominus vobiscum*.' He rode down the line, repeating the invocation. 'You will kill God's enemy today,' he called after each promise that God would be with the English. He had to shout to make himself heard over the din of the enemy. 'God is with you, and you will do His work by making many widows and orphans. You will fill Scotland with grief as a just punishment for their godless impiety. The Lord of Hosts is with you; God's vengeance is your task!' The Archbishop's horse stepped high, its head tossing up and down as his grace carried his encouragement out to the flanks of his army. The last wisps of mist had long burned away and, though there was still a chill in the air, the sun had warmth and its light glinted off thousands of Scottish blades. A pair of one-horse wagons had come from the city and a dozen women were distributing dried herrings, bread and skins of ale.

Lord Outhwaite's squire brought an empty herring barrel so his lordship could sit. A man played a reed pipe nearby and Brother Michael sang an old country song about the badger and the pardoner and Lord Outhwaite laughed at the words, then nodded his head towards the ground between the armies where two horsemen, one from each army, were meeting. 'I see we're being courteous today,' he remarked. An English herald in a gaudy tabard had ridden towards the Scots and a priest, hastily appointed as Scotland's herald, had come to greet him. The two men bowed from their saddles, talked a while, then returned to their respective armies. The Englishman, coming near the line, spread his hands in a gesture that said the Scots were being stubborn.

'They come this far south and won't fight?' the prior demanded angrily.

'They want us to start the battle,' Lord Outhwaite said mildly, 'and we want them to do the same.' The heralds had met to discuss how the battle should be fought and each had plainly demanded that the other side begin by making an assault, and both sides had refused the invitation, so now the Scots tried again to provoke the English by insult. Some of the enemy advanced to within bowshot and shouted that the English were pigs and their mothers were sows, and when an archer raised his bow to reward the insults an English captain shouted at him. 'Don't waste arrows on words,' he called.

'Cowards!' A Scotsman dared to come even closer to the English line, well within half a bowshot. 'You bastard cowards! Your mothers are whores who suckled you on goat piss! Your wives are sows! Whores and sows! You hear me? You bastards! English bastards! You're the devil's turds!' The fury of his hatred made him shake. He had a bristling beard, a ragged jupon and a coat of mail with a great rent in its backside so that when he turned round and bent over he presented his naked arse to the English. It was meant as an insult, but was greeted by a roar of laughter.

'They'll have to attack us sooner or later,' Lord Outhwaite stated calmly. 'Either that or go home with nothing, and I can't see them doing that. You don't raise an army of that size without hope of profit.'

'They sacked Hexham,' the prior observed gloomily.

'And got nothing but baubles,' Lord Outhwaite said dismissively. 'The real treasures of Hexham were taken away for safekeeping long ago. I hear Carlisle paid them well enough to be left alone, but well enough to make eight or nine thousand men rich?' He shook his head. 'Those soldiers don't get paid,' he told Thomas, 'they're not like our men. The King of Scotland doesn't have the cash to pay his soldiers. No, they want to take some rich prisoners today, then sack Durham and York, and if they're not to go home poor and empty-handed then they'd best hitch up their shields and come at us.'

But still the Scots would not move and the English were too few to make an attack, though a straggle of men were constantly arriving to reinforce the Archbishop's army. They were mostly local men and few had any armour or any weapons other than farm implements like axes and mattocks. It was close to midday now and the sun had chased the chill off the land so that Thomas was sweating under his leather and mail. Two of the prior's lay servants had arrived with a horse-drawn cart loaded with casks of small beer, sacks of bread, a box of apples and a great cheese, and a dozen of the younger monks carried the provisions along the English line. Most of the army was sitting now, some were even sleeping and many of the Scots were doing the same. Even their drummers had given up, laying their great instruments on the pasture. A dozen ravens circled overhead and Thomas, thinking their presence presaged death, made the sign of the cross, then was relieved when the dark birds flew north across the Scottish troops.

A group of archers had come from the city and were cramming arrows into their quivers, a sure sign that they had never fought with the bow for a quiver was a poor instrument in battle. Quivers were likely to spill arrows when a man ran, and few held more than a score of points. Archers like Thomas preferred a big bag made of linen stretched about a withy frame in which the arrows stood upright, their feathers kept from being crushed by the frame and their steel heads projecting through the bag's neck, which was secured by a lace. Thomas had selected his arrows carefully, rejecting any with warped shafts or kinked feathers. In France, where many of the enemy knights possessed expensive plate armour, the English would use bodkin arrows with long, narrow and heavy heads that lacked barbs and so were more likely to pierce breastplates or helmets, but here they were still using the hunting arrows with their wicked barbs that made them impossible to pull out of a wound. They were called flesh arrows, but even a flesh arrow could pierce mail at two hundred paces.

Thomas slept for a time in the early afternoon, only waking when Lord Outhwaite's horse almost stepped on him. His lordship, along with the other English commanders, had been summoned to the Archbishop and so he had called for his horse and, accompanied by his squire, rode to the army's centre. One of the Archbishop's chaplains carried a silver crucifix along the line. The crucifix had a leather bag hanging just below the feet of Christ and in the bag, the chaplain claimed, were the knuckle bones of the martyred St Oswald. 'Kiss the bag and God will preserve you,' the chaplain promised, and archers and men-at-arms jostled for a chance to obey. Thomas could not get close enough to kiss the bag, but he did manage to reach out and touch it. Many men had amulets or strips of cloth given them by their wives, lovers or daughters when they left their farms or houses to march against the invaders. They touched those talismans now as the Scots, sensing that something was about to happen at last, climbed to their feet. One of their great drums began its awful noise.

Thomas glanced to his right where he could just see the tops of the cathedral's twin towers and the banner flying from the castle's ramparts. Eleanor and Father Hobbe should be in the city by now and Thomas felt a pang of regret that he had parted from his woman in such anger, then he gripped his bow so that the touch of its wood might keep her from evil. He consoled himself with the knowledge that Eleanor would be safe in the city and tonight, when the battle was won, they could make up their quarrel. Then, he supposed, they would marry. He was not sure he really wanted to marry, it seemed too early in his life to have a wife even if it was Eleanor, whom he was sure he loved, but he was equally sure she would want him to abandon the yew bow and settle in a house and that was the very last thing Thomas wanted. What he wanted was to be a leader of archers, to be a man like Will Skeat. He wanted to have his own band of bowmen that he could hire out to great lords. There was no shortage of opportunity. Rumour said that the Italian states would pay a fortune for English archers and Thomas wanted a part of it, but Eleanor must be looked after and he did not want their child to be a bastard. There were enough bastards in the world without adding another.

The English lords talked for a while. There were a dozen of them and they glanced constantly at the enemy and Thomas was close enough to see the anxiety on their faces. Was it worry that the enemy was too many? Or that the Scots were refusing battle and, in the next morning's mist, might vanish northwards?

Brother Michael came and rested his old bones on the herring barrel that had served Lord Outhwaite as a seat. 'They'll send you archers forward. That's what I'd do. Send you archers forward to provoke the bastards. Either that or drive them off, but you don't drive Scotsmen off that easily. They're brave bastards.'

'Brave? Then why aren't they attacking?'

'Because they're not fools. They can see these.' Brother Michael touched the black stave of Thomas's bow. 'They've learned what archers can do. You've heard of Halidon Hill?' He raised his eyebrows in surprise when Thomas shook his head. 'Of course, you're from the south. Christ could come again in the north and you southerners would never hear about it, or believe it if you did. But it was thirteen years ago now and they attacked us by Berwick and we cut them down in droves. Or our archers did, and they won't be enthusiastic about suffering the same fate here.' Brother Michael frowned as a small click sounded. 'What was that?'

Something had touched Thomas's helmet and he turned to see the Scarecrow, Sir Geoffrey Carr, who had cracked his whip, just glancing the metal claw at its tip off the crest of Thomas's sallet. Sir Geoffrey coiled his whip as he jeered at Thomas. 'Sheltering behind monks' skirts, are we?'

Brother Michael restrained Thomas. 'Go, Sir Geoffrey,' the monk ordered, 'before I call down a curse onto your black soul.'

Sir Geoffrey put a finger into a nostril and pulled out something slimy that he flicked towards the monk. 'You think you frighten me, you one-eyed bastard? You who lost your balls when your hand was chopped off?' He laughed, then looked back to Thomas. 'You picked a fight with me, boy, and you didn't give me a chance to finish it.'

'Not now!' Brother Michael snapped.

Sir Geoffrey ignored the monk. 'Fighting your betters, boy? You can hang for that. No' – he shuddered, then pointed a long bony finger at Thomas – 'you *will* hang for that! You hear me? You will hang for it.' He spat at Thomas, then turned his roan horse and spurred it back down the line.

'How come you know the Scarecrow?' Brother Michael asked.

'We just met.'

'An evil creature,' Brother Michael said, making the sign of the cross, 'born under a waning moon when a storm was blowing.' He was still watching the Scarecrow. 'Men say that Sir Geoffrey owes money to the devil himself. He had to pay a ransom to Douglas of Liddesdale and he borrowed deep from the bankers to do it. His manor, his fields, everything he owns is in danger if he can't pay, and even if he makes a fortune today he'll just throw it away at dice. The Scarecrow's a fool, but a dangerous one.' He turned his one eye on Thomas. 'Did you really pick a fight with him?'

'He wanted to rape my woman.'

'Aye, that's our Scarecrow. So be careful, young man, because he doesn't forget slights and he never forgives them.'

The English lords must have come to some agreement for they reached out their mailed fists and touched metal knuckle on metal knuckle, then Lord Outhwaite turned his horse back towards his men. 'John! John!' he called to the captain of his archers. 'We'll not wait for them to make up their minds,' he said as he dismounted, 'but be provocative.' It seemed Brother Michael's prognostication was right; the archers would be sent forward to annoy the Scots. The plan was to enrage them with arrows and so spur them into a hasty attack.

A squire rode Lord Outhwaite's horse back to the walled pasture as the Archbishop of York rode his destrier out in front of the army. 'God will help you!' he called to the men of the central division that he commanded. 'The Scots fear us!' he shouted. 'They know that with God's help we will make many children fatherless in their blighted land! They stand and watch us because they fear us. So we must go to them.' That sentiment brought a cheer. The Archbishop raised a hand to silence his men. 'I want the archers to go forward,' he called, 'only the archers! Sting them! Kill them! And God bless you all. God bless you mightily!'

So the archers would begin the battle. The Scots were stubbornly refusing to move in hope that the English would make the attack, for it was much easier to defend ground than assault a formed enemy, but now the English archers would go forward to goad, sting and harass the enemy until they either ran away or, more likely, advanced to take revenge.

Thomas had already selected his best arrow. It was new, so new that the green-tinted glue that was pasted about the thread holding the feathers in place was still tacky, but it had a breasted shaft, one that was slightly wider behind the head and then tapered away towards the feathers. Such a shaft would hit hard and it was a lovely straight piece of ash, a third as long again as Thomas's arm, and Thomas would not waste it even though his opening shot would be at very long range.

It would be a long shot for the Scottish King was at the rear of the big central sheltron of his army, but it would not be an impossible shot for the black bow was huge and Thomas was young, strong and accurate.

'God be with you,' Brother Michael said.

'Aim true!' Lord Outhwaite called.

'God speed your arrows!' the Archbishop of York shouted.

The drummers beat louder, the Scots jeered and the archers of England advanced.

Bernard de Taillebourg already knew much of what the old monk told him, but now that the story was flowing he did not interrupt. It was the tale of a family that had been lords of an obscure county in southern France. The county was called Astarac and it lay close to the Cathar lands and, in time, became infected with the heresy. 'The false teaching spread,' Brother Collimore had said, 'like a murrain. From the inland sea to the ocean, and northwards into Burgundy.' Father de Taillebourg knew all this, but he had said nothing, just let the old man go on describing how, when the Cathars were burned out of the land and the fires of their deaths had sent the smoke pouring to heaven to tell God and His angels that the true religion had been restored to the lands between France and Aragon, the Vexilles, among the last of the nobility to be contaminated by the Cathar evil, had fled to the farthest corners of Christendom. 'But before they left,' Brother Collimore said, gazing up at the white painted arch of the ceiling, 'they took the treasures of the heretics for safekeeping.'

'And the Grail was among them?'

'So they said, but who knows?' Brother Collimore turned his head and frowned at the Dominican. 'If they possessed the Grail, why did it not help them? I have never understood that.' He closed his eyes. Sometimes, when the old man was pausing to draw breath and almost seemed asleep, de Taillebourg would look through the window to see the two armies on the far hill. They did not move, though the noise they made was like the crackling and roaring of a great fire. The roaring was the noise of men's voices and the crackling was the drums and the twin sounds rose and fell with the vagaries of the wind gusting in the rocky defile above the River Wear. Father de Taillebourg's servant still stood in the doorway where he was half hidden by one of many piles of undressed stone that were stacked in the open space between the castle and the cathedral. Scaffolding hid the cathedral's nearest tower and small boys, eager to get a glimpse of the fighting, were scrambling up the web of lashed poles. The masons had abandoned their work to watch the two armies.

Now, after questioning why the Grail had not helped the Vexilles, Brother Collimore did fall into a brief sleep and de Taillebourg crossed to his black-dressed servant. 'Do you believe him?'

The servant shrugged and said nothing.

'Has anything surprised you?' de Taillebourg asked.

'That Father Ralph has a son,' the servant answered. 'That was new to me.'

'We must speak with that son,' the Dominican said grimly, then turned back because the old monk had woken.

'Where was I?' Brother Collimore asked. A small trickle of spittle ran from a corner of his lips.

'You were wondering why the Grail did not help the Vexilles,' Bernard de Taillebourg reminded him.

'It should have done,' the old monk said. 'If they possessed the Grail why did they not become powerful?'

Father de Taillebourg smiled. 'Suppose,' he said to the old monk, 'that the infidel Muslims were to gain possession of the Grail, do you think God would grant them its power? The Grail is a great treasure, brother, the greatest of all the treasures upon the earth, but it is not greater than God.'

'No,' Brother Collimore agreed.

'And if God does not approve of the Grail-keeper then the Grail will be powerless.'

'Yes,' Brother Collimore acknowledged.

'You say the Vexilles fled?'

'They fled the Inquisitors,' Brother Collimore said with a sly glance at de Taillebourg, 'and one branch of the family came here to England where they did some service to the King. Not our present King, of course,' the old monk made clear, 'but his great-grandfather, the last Henry.'

'What service?' de Taillebourg asked.

'They gave the King a hoof from St George's horse.' The monk spoke as though such things were commonplace. 'A hoof set in gold and capable of working miracles. At least the King believed it did for his son was cured of a fever by being touched with the hoof. I am told the hoof is still in Westminster Abbey.'

The family had been rewarded with land in Cheshire, Collimore went on, and if they were heretics they did not show it, but lived like any other noble family. Their downfall, he said, had come at the beginning of the present reign when the young King's mother, aided by the Mortimer family, had tried to keep her son from taking power. The Vexilles had sided with the Queen and when she lost they had fled back to the continent. 'All of them except one son,' Brother Collimore said, 'the eldest son, and that was Ralph, of course. Poor Ralph.'

'But if his family had fled back to France, why did you treat him?' de Taillebourg asked, puzzlement marring the face that had blood scabs on the abrasions where he had beaten himself against the stone that morning. 'Why not just execute him as a traitor?'

'He had taken holy orders,' Collimore protested, 'he could not be executed! Besides, it was known he hated his father and he had declared himself for the King.'

'So he was not all mad,' de Taillebourg put in drily.

'He also possessed money,' Collimore went on, 'he was noble and he claimed to know the secret of the Vexilles.'

'The Cathar treasures?'

'But the demon was in him even then! He declared himself a bishop and preached wild sermons in the London streets. He said he would lead a new crusade to drive the infidel from Jerusalem and promised that the Grail would ensure success.'

'So you locked him up?'

'He was sent to me,' Brother Collimore said reprovingly, 'because it was known that I could defeat the demons.' He paused, remembering. 'In my time I scourged hundreds of them! Hundreds!'

'But you did not fully cure Ralph Vexille?'

The monk shook his head. 'He was like a man spurred and whipped by God so that he wept and screamed and beat himself till the blood ran.' Brother Collimore, unaware that he could have been describing de Taillebourg, shuddered. 'And he was haunted by women too. I think we never cured him of that, but if we did not drive the demons clean out of him we did manage to make them hide so deep that they rarely dared show themselves.'

'Was the Grail a dream given to him by demons?' the Dominican asked.

'That was what we wanted to know,' Brother Collimore replied.

'And what answer did you find?'

'I told my masters that Father Ralph lied. That he had invented the Grail. That there was no truth in his madness. And then, when his demons no longer made him a nuisance, he was sent to a parish in the far south where he could preach to the gulls and to the seals. He no longer called himself a lord, he was simply Father Ralph, and we sent him away to be forgotten.'

'To be forgotten?' de Taillebourg repeated. 'Yet you had news of him. You discovered he had a son.'

The old monk nodded. 'We had a brother house near Dorchester and they sent me news. They told me that Father Ralph had found himself a woman, a house-keeper, but what country priest doesn't? And he had a son and he hung an old spear in his church and said it was St George's lance.'

De Taillebourg peered at the western hill for the noise had become much louder. It looked as though the English, who were by far the smaller army, were advancing and that meant they would lose the battle and that meant Father de Taillebourg had to be out of this monastery, indeed out of this city, before Sir William Douglas arrived seeking vengeance. 'You told your masters that Father Ralph lied. Did he?'

The old monk paused and to de Taillebourg it seemed as if the firmament itself held its breath. 'I don't think he lied,' Collimore whispered.

'So why did you tell them he did?'

'Because I liked him,' Brother Collimore said, 'and I did not think we could whip the truth out of him, or starve it from him, or pull it out by trying to drown him in cold water. I thought he was harmless and should be left to God.'

De Taillebourg gazed through the window. The Grail, he thought, the Grail. The hounds of God were on the scent. He would find it! 'One of the family came back

106

from France,' the Dominican said, 'and stole the lance and killed Father Ralph.'

'I heard.'

'But they did not find the Grail.'

'God be thanked for that,' Brother Collimore said faintly.

De Taillebourg heard a movement and saw that his servant, who had been listening intently, was now watching the courtyard. The servant must have heard someone approaching and de Taillebourg, leaning closer to Brother Collimore, lowered his voice so he would not be overheard. 'How many people know of Father Ralph and the Grail?'

Brother Collimore thought for a few heartbeats. 'No one has spoken of it for years,' he said, 'until the new bishop came. He must have heard rumours for he asked me about it. I told him that Ralph Vexille was mad.'

'He believed you?'

'He was disappointed. He wanted the Grail for the cathedral.'

Of course he did, de Taillebourg thought, for any cathedral that possessed the Grail would become the richest church in Christendom. Even Genoa, which had its gaudy piece of green glass that they claimed was the Grail, took money from thousands of pilgrims. But put the real Grail in a church and folk would come to it in their hundreds of thousands and they would bring coins and jewels by the wagonload. Kings, queens, princes and dukes would throng the aisle and compete to offer their wealth.

The servant had vanished, slipping soundlessly behind one of the piles of building stone, and de Taillebourg waited, watching the door and wondering what trouble would show there. Then, instead of trouble, a young priest appeared. He wore a rough cloth gown, had unruly hair and a broad, guileless, sunburned face. A young woman, pale and frail, was with him. She seemed nervous, but the priest greeted de Taillebourg cheerfully. 'A good day to you, father.'

'And to you, father,' de Taillebourg responded politely. His servant had reappeared behind the strangers, preventing them from leaving unless de Taillebourg gave his permission. 'I am taking Brother Collimore's confession,' de Taillebourg said.

'A good one, I hope,' Father Hobbe said, then smiled. 'You don't sound English, father?'

'I am French,' de Taillebourg said.

'As am I,' Eleanor said in that language, 'and we have come to talk with Brother Collimore.'

'Talk with him?' de Taillebourg asked pleasantly.

'The bishop sent us,' Eleanor said proudly, 'and the King did too.'

'Which King, child?'

'Edouard d'Angleterre,' Eleanor boasted. Father Hobbe, who spoke no French, was looking from Eleanor to the Dominican.

'Why would Edward send you?' de Taillebourg asked and, when Eleanor looked flustered, he repeated the question. 'Why would Edward send you?'

'I don't know, father,' Eleanor said.

'I think you do, my child, I think you do.' He stood and Father Hobbe, sensing trouble, took Eleanor's wrist and tried to pull her from the room, but de Taillebourg nodded at his servant and gestured towards Father Hobbe and the English priest was still trying to understand why he was suspicious of the Dominican when the knife slid between his ribs. He made a choking noise, then coughed and the breath rattled in his throat as he slid down to the flagstones. Eleanor tried to run, but she was not nearly fast enough and de Taillebourg caught her by the wrist and jerked her roughly back. She screamed and the Dominican silenced her by clapping a hand over her mouth.

'What's happening?' Brother Collimore asked.

'We are doing God's work,' de Taillebourg said soothingly, 'God's work.'

And on the ridge the arrows flew.

Thomas advanced with the archers of the left-hand battle and they had not gone more than twenty yards when, just beyond a ditch, a bank and some newly planted blackthorn saplings, they were forced to their right because a great scoop had been taken out of the ridge's flank to leave a hollow of ground with sides too steep for the plough. The hollow was filled with bracken that had turned yellow and at its far side was a lichen-covered stone wall and Thomas's arrow bag caught and tore on a rough piece of the coping as he clambered across. Only one arrow fell out, but it dropped into a mushroom fairy ring and he tried to work out whether that was a good or a bad omen, but the noise of the Scottish drums distracted him. He picked up the arrow and hurried on. All the enemy drummers were working now, rattling their skins in a frenzy so that the air itself seemed to vibrate. The Scottish men-at-arms were hefting their shields, making sure they protected the pikemen, and a crossbowman was working the ratchet that dragged back his cord and lodged it on the trigger's hook. The man glanced up anxiously at the advancing English bowmen, then discarded the ratchet handles and laid a metal quarrel in the crossbow's firing trough. The enemy had begun to shout and Thomas could distinguish some words now. 'If you hate the English,' he heard, then a crossbow bolt hummed past him and he forgot about the enemy chant. Hundreds of English archers were advancing through the fields, most of them running. The Scots only had a few crossbows, but those weapons outranged the longer war bows of the English who were hurrying to close that range. An arrow slithered across the grass in front of Thomas. Not a crossbow bolt, but an arrow from one of the few Scottish yew bows and the sight of the arrow told him he was almost in range. The first of the English archers had stopped and drawn back their cords and then their arrows flickered into the sky. A bowman in a padded leather jerkin fell backwards with a crossbow bolt embedded in his forehead. Blood spurted skywards where his last arrow, shot almost vertically, soared uselessly.

'Aim at the archers!' a man in a rusted breastplate bellowed. 'Kill their archers first!'

Thomas stopped and looked for the royal standard. It was off to his right, a long way off, but he had shot at further targets in his time and so he turned and braced himself and then, in the name of God and St George, he put his chosen arrow onto the string and drew the white goose feathers back to his ear. He was staring at King David II of Scotland, saw the sun glint gold off the royal helmet, saw too that the King's visor was open and he aimed for the chest, nudged the bow right to compensate for the wind, and loosed. The arrow went true, not vibrating as a badly made arrow would, and

Thomas watched it climb and saw it fall and saw the King jerk backwards and then the courtiers closed about him and Thomas laid his second arrow across his left hand and sought another target. A Scottish archer was limping from the line, an arrow in his leg. The men-at-arms closed about the wounded man, sealing their line with heavy shields. Thomas could hear hounds baying deep among the enemy formation, or perhaps he was hearing the war howl of the tribesmen. The King had turned away and men were leaning towards him. The sky was filled with the whisper of flying arrows and the noise of the bows was a steady, deep music. The French called it the devil's harp music. There were no Scottish archers left that Thomas could see. They had all been made targets by the English bowmen and the arrows had ripped the enemy archers into bloody misery, so now the English turned their missiles on the men with pikes, swords, axes and spears. The tribesmen, all hair and beard and fury, were beyond the men-at-arms who were arrayed six or eight men deep, so the arrows rattled and clanged on armour and shields. The Scottish knights and men-at-arms and pike-carriers were sheltering as best they could, crouching under the bitter steel rain, but some arrows always found the gaps between the shields while others drove clean through the leather-covered willow boards. The thudding sound of the arrows hitting shields was rivalling the sharper noise of the drums.

'Forward, boys! Forward!' One of the archers' leaders encouraged his men to go twenty paces nearer the enemy so that their arrows could bite harder into the Scottish ranks. 'Kill them, lads!' Two of his men were lying on the grass, proof that the Scottish archers had

111

done some damage before they were overwhelmed with English arrows. Another Englishman was staggering as though he were drunk, weaving back towards his own side and clutching his belly from which blood trickled down his leggings. A bow's cord broke, squirting the arrow sideways as the archer swore and reached under his tunic to find a spare.

The Scots could do nothing now. They had no archers left and the English edged closer and closer until they were driving their arrows in a flat trajectory that whipped the steel heads through shields, mail and even the rare suit of plate armour. Thomas was scarce seventy yards from the enemy line and choosing his targets with cold deliberation. He could see a man's leg showing under a shield and he put an arrow through the thigh. The drummers had fled and two of their instruments, their skins split like rotten fruit, lay discarded on the turf. A nobleman's horse was close behind the dismounted ranks and Thomas put a missile deep into the destrier's chest and, when he next looked, the animal was down and there was a flurry of panicking men trying to escape its thrashing hooves and all of those men, exposing themselves by letting their shields waver, went down under the sting of the arrows and then a moment later a pack of a dozen hunting dogs, long-haired, yellow-fanged and howling, burst out of the cowering ranks and were tumbled down by the slicing arrows.

'Is it always this easy?' a boy, evidently at his first battle, asked a nearby archer.

'If the other side don't have archers,' the older man answered, 'and so long as our arrows last, then it's easy. After that it's shit hard.'

Thomas drew and released, shooting at an angle across the Scottish front to whip a long shaft behind a shield and into a bearded man's face. The Scottish King was still on his horse, but protected now by four shields that were all bristling with arrows and Thomas remembered the French horses labouring up the Picardy slope with the feather-tipped shafts sticking from their necks, legs and bodies. He rummaged in his torn arrow bag, found another missile and shot it at the King's horse. The enemy was under the flail now and they would either run from the arrow storm or else, enraged, charge the smaller English army and, judging by the shouts coming from the men behind the arrow-stuck shields, Thomas suspected they would attack.

He was right. He had time to shoot one last arrow and then there was a sudden terrifying roar and the whole Scottish line, seemingly without anyone giving an order, charged. They ran howling and screaming, stung into the attack by the arrows, and the English archers fled. Thousands of enraged Scotsmen were charging and the archers, even if they shot every arrow they possessed into the advancing horde, would be overwhelmed in a heartbeat and so they ran to find shelter behind their own men-at-arms. Thomas tripped as he climbed the stone wall, but he picked himself up and ran on, then saw that other archers had stopped and were shooting at their pursuers. The stone wall was holding up the Scots and he turned round himself and put two arrows into defenceless men before the enemy surged across the barrier and forced him back again. He was running towards the small gap in the English line where St Cuthbert's Mass cloth waved, but the space was choked with archers trying to get behind the armoured line and so Thomas went to his right, aiming for the sliver of open ground that lay between the army's flank and the ridge's steep side.

'Shields forward!' a grizzled warrior, his helmet visor pushed up, shouted at the English men-at-arms. 'Brace hard! Brace hard!' The English line, only four or five ranks deep, steadied to meet the wild attack with their shields thrust forward and right legs braced back. 'St George! St George!' a man called. 'Hold hard now! Thrust hard and hold hard!'

Thomas was on the flank of the army now and he turned to see that the Scots, in their precipitate charge, had widened their line. They had been arrayed shoulder to shoulder in their first position, but now, running, they had spread out and that meant their westernmost sheltron had been pushed down the ridge's slope and into the deep hollow that so unexpectedly narrowed the battle ground. They were down in the hollow's bottom, staring up at the skyline, doomed.

'Archers!' Thomas shouted, thinking himself back in France and responsible for a troop of Will Skeat's bowmen. 'Archers!' he bellowed, advancing to the hollow's lip. 'Now kill them!' Men came to his side, yelped in triumph and drew back their cords.

Now was the killing time, the archers' time. The Scottish right wing was down in the sunken ground and the archers were above them and could not miss. Two monks were bringing spare sheaves of arrows, each sheaf holding twenty-four shafts evenly spaced about two leather discs that kept the arrows apart and so protected their feathers from being crushed. The monks cut the twine holding the arrows and spilt the missiles on the ground beside the archers who drew again and again and killed again and again as they shot down into the pit of death. Thomas heard the deafening crash as the men-at-arms collided in the field's centre, but here, on the English left, the Scots would never come to their enemy's shields because they had spilled into the low yellow bracken of death's kingdom.

Thomas's childhood had been spent in Hookton, a village on England's south coast where a stream, coming to the sea, had carved a deep channel in the shingle beach. The channel curved to leave a hook of land that protected the fishing boats and once a year, when the rats became too thick in the holds and bilges of the boats, the fishermen would strand their craft at the bottom of the stream, fill their bilges with stones and let the incoming tide flood the stinking hulls. It was a holiday for the village children who, standing on the top of the Hook, waited for the rats to flee the boats and then, with cheers and screams of delight, they would stone the animals. The rats would panic and that would only increase the children's glee as the adults stood around and laughed, applauded and encouraged.

It was like that now. The Scots were in the low ground, the archers were on the lip of the hill and death was their dominion. The arrows were flashing straight down the slope, scarce any arc in their flight, and striking home with the sound of cleavers hitting flesh. The Scots writhed and died in the hollow and the yellow autumn bracken turned red. Some of the enemy tried to climb towards their tormentors, but they became the easiest targets. Some attempted to escape up the far side and were struck in the back, while some fled down the hill in ragged disarray. Sir Thomas Rokeby, Sheriff of Yorkshire and commander of the English left, saw their escape and ordered two score of his men to mount their horses and scour the valley. The mailed riders swung their swords and morningstars to finish the archers' bloody work.

The base of the hollow was a writhing, bloody mass. A man in plate armour, a plumed helmet on his head, tried to climb out of the carnage and two arrows whipped through his breastplate and a third found a slit in his visor and he fell back, twitching. A thicket of arrows jutted from the falcon on his shield. The arrows became fewer now, for there were not many Scotsmen left to kill and then the first archers scrambled down the slope with drawn knives to pillage the dead and kill the wounded.

'Who hates the English now?' one of the archers jeered. 'Come on, you bastards, let's hear you? Who hates the English now?'

Then a shout sounded from the centre. 'Archers! To the right! To the right!' The voice had a note of sheer panic. 'To the right! For God's sake, now!'

The men-at-arms of the English left were scarcely engaged in the fight because the archers were slaughtering the Scots in the low bracken. The English centre was holding firm for the Archbishop's men were arrayed behind a stone wall which, though only waist high, was a more than adequate barrier against the Scottish assault. The invaders could stab, lunge and hack over the wall's coping, and they could try to climb it and they could even try to pull it down stone by stone, but they could not push it over and so they were checked by it and the English, though far fewer, were able to hold even though the Scots were lunging at them with their heavy pikes. Some English knights called for their horses and, once mounted and armed with lances, pressed up close behind their beleaguered comrades and rammed the lances at Scottish eyes. Other men-at-arms ducked under the unwieldy pikes and hacked with swords and axes at the enemy and all the while the long arrows drove in from the left. The noise in the centre was the shouting of men in the rearward ranks, the screaming of the wounded, the clangour of blade on blade, the crack of blade on shield and the clatter of lance on pike, but the wall meant that neither side could press the other back and so, crammed against the stones and encumbered by the dead, they just lunged, hacked, suffered, bled and died.

But on the English right, where Lord Neville and Lord Percy commanded, the wall was unfinished, nothing more than a pile of stones that offered no obstacle to the assault of the Scottish left wing that was commanded by the Earl of March and by the King's nephew, Lord Robert Stewart. Their sheltron, closest to the city, was the largest of the three Scottish divisions and it came at the English like a pack of wolves who had not fed in a month. The attackers wanted blood and the archers fled from their howling charge like sheep scattering before fangs and then the Scots struck the English right and the sheer momentum of their assault drove the defenders back twenty paces before, somehow, the men-at-arms managed to hold the Scots who were now stumbling over the bodies of the men they had wounded or killed. The English, cramming themselves shoulder to shoulder, crouched behind their shields and shoved back, stabbing swords at ankles and faces, and grunting with the effort of holding the vast pressure of the Scottish horde.

It was hard to fight in the front ranks. Men shoved from behind so that Englishmen and Scotsmen were close as lovers, too close to wield a sword in anything except a rudimentary stab. The ranks behind had more room and a Scotsman chopped down with a pike that he wielded like a giant axe, its blade crunching down into an enemy's head to split helmet, leather liner, scalp and skull as easily as an unboiled egg. Blood fountained across a dozen men as the dead soldier fell and other Scots pushed into the gap his death had caused, and a clansman tripped on the body and screamed as an Englishman sawed at his exposed neck with a blunt knife. The pike dropped again, killing a second man, and this time, when it was lifted up, the dead man's crumpled visor was caught on the pike's bloody spike.

The drums, those that were still whole, had begun their noise again, and the Scots heaved to their rhythm. 'The Bruce! The Bruce!' some chanted while others called on their patron, 'St Andrew! St Andrew!' Lord Robert Stewart, gaudy in his blue and yellow colours and with a thin fillet of gold about the brow of his helmet, used a two-handed sword to chop at the English men-at-arms who cowered from the rampant Scots. Lord Robert, safe from arrows at last, had lifted his visor so he could see the enemy. 'Come on!' he screamed at his men. 'Come on! Hard into them! Kill them! Kill them!' The King had promised that the Christmas feast would be in London and there seemed only a small screen of frightened men to break before that promise could come true. The riches of Durham, York and London were just a few sword strokes away; all the wealth of Norwich and Oxford, of Bristol and South-ampton was only a handful of deaths from Scottish purses. 'Scotland! Scotland! Scotland!' Lord Robert called. 'Scotland!' And the pikeman, because the trapped visor was obstructing his blade, was beating on a man's helmet with the hook side of his weapon's head, not chopping through the metal, but smashing it, hammering the broken helmet into the dying man's brain so that blood and jelly oozed from the visor's slits. An Englishman screamed as a Scottish pike struck through his mail into his groin. A boy, perhaps a page, reeled back with his eyes bloodied from a sword slash. 'Scotland!' Lord Robert could smell the victory now. So close! He shoved on, felt the English line jar and move back, saw how thin it was, fended off a lunge with his shield, stabbed with his sword to kill a fallen and wounded enemy, shouted at his squires to keep a watch for any rich English nobleman whose ransom could enrich the house of Stewart. Men grunted as they stabbed and hacked. A tribesman reeled from the fight, gasping for breath, trying to hold his guts inside his slashed belly. A drummer was beating the Scots on. 'Bring my horse!' Lord Robert called to a squire. He knew that the beaten English line had to break in a moment and then he would mount, take his lance, and pursue the beaten enemy. 'On! On!' he shouted. 'On!' And the man wielding the long-hafted pike, the huge Scotsman who had driven a gap into the English front rank and who seemed to be carving a bloody path south all by himself, suddenly made a mewing noise. His pike, high in the air where it was still fouled with the bent visor, faltered. The man jerked and his mouth opened and closed, opened and closed again, but he could not speak because an arrow, its white feathers bloodied, jutted from his head.

An arrow, Lord Robert saw, and suddenly the air was thick with them and he pulled down the visor of his helmet so that the day went dark.

The damned English archers were back.

Sir William Douglas had not realized how deep and steep-sided was the bracken-covered saddle in the ridge's flank until he reached its base and there, under the flail of the archers, found he could neither go forward nor back. The front two ranks of Scottish men-at-arms were all either dead or wounded and their bodies made a heap over which he could not climb in his heavy mail. Robbie was screaming defiance and trying to scramble over that heap, but Sir William unceremoniously dragged his nephew back and thrust him down into the bracken. 'This isn't a place to die, Robbie!'

'Bastards!'

'They may be bastards, but we're the fools!' Sir William crouched beside his nephew, covering them both with his huge shield. To go back was unthinkable, for that would be running from the enemy, yet he could not advance and so he just marvelled at the force of the arrows as they thumped into the shield's face. A rush of bearded tribesmen, more nimble than the men-at-arms because they refused to wear metal armour, seethed past him, howling their wild defiance as they scrambled bare-legged across the heap of dying Scots, but then the English arrows began to strike and hurl the clansmen back. The arrows made sounds like bladders rupturing as they struck and the clansmen mewed and groaned, twitching as more arrows thumped home. Each missile provoked a spurt of blood so that Sir William and Robbie Douglas, unscathed beneath their heavy shield, were spattered with gore.

A sudden tumult among the nearby men-at-arms provoked more arrows and Sir William bellowed angrily at the soldiers to lie down, hoping that stillness would persuade the English archers that no Scotsmen lived, but the men-at-arms called back that the Earl of Moray had been hit. 'Not before time,' Sir William growled to Robbie. He hated the Earl more than he hated the English, and he grinned when a man shouted that his lordship was not just hit, but dead, and then another hail of arrows silenced the Earl's retainers and Sir William heard the missiles clanging on metal, thumping into flesh and striking the willow boards of shields, and when the rattle of arrows was done there was just the moaning and weeping, the hissing of breath, and the creak of leather as men died or tried to extricate themselves from under the piles of dying.

'What happened?' Robbie asked.

'We didn't scout the land properly,' Sir William answered. 'We outnumber the bastards and that made us confident.' Ominously, in the arrowless quiet, he heard laughter and the thump of boots. A scream sounded and Sir William, who was old in war, knew that the English troops were coming down into the bowl to finish off the injured. 'We're going to run back soon,' he told Robbie, 'there's no choice in it. Cover your arse with your shield and run like the devil.'

'We're running away?' Robbie asked, appalled.

Sir William sighed. 'Robbie, you damned fool, you can run forward and you can die and I'll tell your mother you died like a brave man and a halfwit, or you can get the hell back up the hill with me and try to win this battle.'

Robbie did not argue, but just looked back up the Scottish side of the hollow where the bracken was flecked with white-feathered arrows. 'Tell me when to run,' he said.

A dozen archers and as many English men-at-arms were using knives to cut Scottish throats. They would pause before finishing off a man-at-arms to discover whether he had any value as a source of ransom, but few men had such value and the clansmen had none. The latter, hated above all the Scots because they were so different, were treated as vermin. Sir William cautiously raised his head and decided this was the moment to retreat. It was better to scramble out of this bloody trap than be captured and so, ignoring the indignant shouts of the English, he and his nephew scrambled back up the slope. To Sir William's surprise no arrows came. He had expected the grass and bracken to be thrashed with arrows as he clambered out of the hollow, but he and Robbie were left alone. He turned halfway up the slope and saw that the English bowmen had vanished, leaving only men-at-arms on this flank of the field. At their head, watching him from the hollow's farther lip, was Lord Outhwaite, who had once been Sir William's prisoner. Outhwaite, who was lame, was using a spear as a stave and, seeing Sir William, he raised the weapon in greeting.

'Get yourself some proper armour, Willie!' Sir William shouted. Lord Outhwaite, like the Knight of

Liddesdale, had been christened William. 'We're not done with you yet.'

'I fear not, Sir William, I do indeed fear not,' Lord Outhwaite called back. He steadied himself with his spear. 'I trust you're well?'

'Of course I'm not well, you bloody fool! Half my men are down there.'

'My dear fellow,' Outhwaite said with a grimace, and then waved genially as Sir William pushed Robbie on up the hill and followed him to safety.

Sir William, once back on the high ground, took stock. He could see that the Scots had been beaten here on their right, but that had been their own fault for charging headlong into the low ground where the archers had been able to kill with impunity. Those archers had mysteriously vanished, but Sir William guessed they had been pulled clear across the field to the Scottish left flank that had advanced a long way ahead of the centre. He could tell that because Lord Robert Stewart's blue and yellow banner of the lion was so far ahead of the King's red and yellow flag. So the battle was going well on the left, but Sir William could see it was going nowhere in the centre because of the stone wall that obstructed the Scottish advance.

'We'll achieve nothing here,' he told Robbie, 'so let's be useful.' He turned and raised his bloody sword. 'Douglas!' he shouted. 'Douglas!' His standard-bearer had disappeared and Sir William supposed that the man, with his red-hearted flag, was dead in the low ground. 'Douglas!' he called again and, when sufficient of his men had come to him, he led them to the embattled central sheltron. 'We fight here,' he told them, then pushed his way to the King who was on horseback in the second or third rank, fighting beneath his banner that was thick stuck with arrows. He was also fighting with his visor raised and Sir William saw that the King's face was half obscured with blood. 'Put your visor down!' he roared.

The King was trying to stab a long lance across the stone wall, but the press of men made his efforts futile. His blue and yellow surcoat had been torn to reveal the bright plate metal beneath. An arrow thudded into his right espalier that had again ridden up on the breast-plate and he tugged it down just as another arrow ripped open the left ear of his stallion. He saw Sir William and grinned as though this was fine sport. 'Pull your visor down!' Sir William bellowed and he saw that the King was not grinning, but rather a whole flap of his cheek had been torn away and the blood was still welling from the wound and spilling from the helmet's lower rim to soak the torn surcoat. 'Have your cheek bandaged!' Sir William shouted over the din of fighting.

The King let his frightened horse back away from the wall. 'What happened on the right?' His voice was made indistinct by his wound.

'They killed us,' Sir William said curtly, inadvertently jerking his long sword so that drops of blood sprayed from its tip. 'No, they murdered us,' he growled. 'There was a break in the ground and it snared us.'

'Our left is winning! We'll break them there!' The King's mouth kept filling with blood, which he spat out, but despite the copious bleeding he did not seem over-concerned with the wound. It had been inflicted at the very beginning of the battle when an arrow had hissed over the heads of his army to rip a gouge in his cheek before spending itself in his helmet's liner. 'We'll hold them here,' he told Sir William.

'John Randolph's dead,' Sir William told him. 'The Earl of Moray,' he added when he saw that the King had not understood his first words.

'Dead?' King David blinked, then spat more blood. 'He's dead? Not a prisoner?' Another arrow slapped at his flag, but the King was oblivious of the danger. He turned and stared at his enemy's flags. 'We'll have the Archbishop say a prayer over his grave, then the bastard can say grace over our supper.' He saw a gap in the front Scottish rank and spurred his horse to fill it, then lunged with his lance at an English defender. The King's blow broke the man's shoulder, mangling the bloody wound with the debris of torn mail. 'Bastards!' the King spat. 'We're winning!' he called to his men, then a rush of Douglas's followers pushed between him and the wall. The newcomers struck the stone wall like a great wave, but the wall proved stronger and the wave broke on its stones. Swords and axes clashed over the coping and men from both sides dragged the dead out of their paths to clear a passage to the slaughter. 'We'll hold the bastards here,' the King assured Sir William, 'and turn their right.'

But Sir William, his ears ever attuned to the noise of battle, had heard something new. For the last few minutes he had been listening to shouts, clangour, screams and drums, but one sound had been missing and that was the devil's harp music, the deep-toned pluck of bowstrings, but he heard it again now and he knew that though scores of the enemy might have been killed, few of those dead were archers. And now the bows of England had begun their awful work again. 'You want advice, sire?'

'Of course.' The King looked bright-eyed. His destrier, wounded by several arrows, took small nervous steps away from the thickest fighting that raged just paces away.

'Put your visor down,' Sir William said, 'and then pull back.'

'Pull back?' The King wondered if he had misheard.

'Pull back!' Sir William said again, and he sounded hard and sure, yet he was not certain why he had given the advice. It was another damn premonition like the one he had experienced in the fog at dawn, yet he knew the advice was good. Pull back now, pull all the way back to Scotland where there were great castles that could withstand a storm of arrows, yet he knew he could not explain the advice. He could find no reason for it. A dread had seized his heart and filled him with foreboding. From any other man the advice would have been reckoned cowardice, but no one would ever accuse Sir William Douglas, the Knight of Liddesdale, of cowardice.

The King thought the advice was a bad jest and he gave a snorting laugh. 'We're winning!' he told Sir William as more blood spilt from his helmet and slopped down to his saddle. 'Is there any danger on the right?' he asked.

'None,' Sir William said. The hollow in the ground would be as effective at stopping an English advance as it had been at foiling the Scottish attack.

'Then we'll win this battle on our left,' the King declared, then hauled on his reins to turn away. 'Pull back indeed!' The King laughed, then took a piece of linen from one of his chaplains and pushed it between his cheek and his helmet. 'We're winning!' he said to

Sir William again, then spurred to the east. He was riding to bring Scotland victory and to show that he was a worthy son of the great Bruce. 'St Andrew!' he shouted through thick blood. 'St Andrew!'

'You think we should pull back, uncle?' Robbie Douglas asked. He was as confused as the King. 'But we're winning!'

'Are we?' Sir William listened to the music of the bows. 'Best say your prayers, Robbie,' he said, 'best say your bloody prayers and ask God to let the devil take the bloody archers.'

And pray that God or the devil was listening.

Sir Geoffrey Carr was stationed on the English left where the Scots had been so decisively rebuffed by the terrain and his few men-at-arms were now down in the blood-reeking hollow in search of prisoners. The Scarecrow had watched the Scots trapped in the low ground and he had grinned with feral delight as the arrows had slashed down into the attackers. One enraged tribesman, his thick folds of swathing plaid stuck with arrows as thick as a hedgehog's spines, had tried to fight up the slope. He had been swearing and cursing, repeatedly struck by arrows, one was even sticking from his skull, which was smothered in tangled hair, and another was caught in the thicket of his beard, yet still he had come, bleeding and ranting, so filled with hate that he did not even know he should be dead, and he managed to struggle within five paces of the bowmen before Sir Geoffrey had flicked his whip to take the man's left eye from its socket clean as a hazel from its shell and then an archer had stepped forward

128

and casually split the man's arrow-spitted skull with an axe. The Scarecrow coiled the whip and fingered the damp on the tip's iron claw. 'I do enjoy a battle,' he had said to no one in particular. Once the attack was stalled he had seen that one of the Scottish lords, all gaudy in blue and silver, was lying dead among the heap of corpses and that was a pity. That was a real pity. There was a fortune gone with that death and Sir Geoffrey, remembering his debts, had ordered his men down into the pit to cut throats, pillage corpses and find any prisoner worth a half-decent ransom. His archers had been taken off to the other side of the field, but his men-at-arms were left to find some cash. 'Hurry, Beggar!' Sir Geoffrey shouted, 'Hurry! Prisoners and plunder! Look for gentlemen and lords! Not that there are any gentlemen in Scotland!' This last observation, made only to himself, amused the Scarecrow so that he laughed aloud. The joke seemed to improve as he thought about it and he almost doubled over in merriment. 'Gentlemen in Scotland!' he repeated and then he saw a young monk staring worriedly at him.

The monk was one of the prior's men, distributing food and ale to the troops, but he had been alarmed by Sir Geoffrey's wild cackle. The Scarecrow, going abruptly silent, stared wide-eyed at the monk and then, silently, let the coils of the whip fall from his hand. The soft leather made no sound as it rippled down, then Sir Geoffrey moved his right arm at lightning speed and the whip struck to loop itself about the young monk's neck. Sir Geoffrey jerked the lash. 'Come here, boy,' he ordered.

The jerk made the monk stumble so that he dropped the bread and apples he had been carrying, then he was standing close beside Sir Geoffrey's horse and the Scarecrow was leaning down from the saddle so that the monk could smell his fetid breath. 'Listen, you pious little turd,' Sir Geoffrey hissed, 'if you don't tell me the truth I'll cut off what you don't need and what you don't use except to piss through and feed it to my swine, do you understand me, boy?'

The monk, terrified, just nodded.

Sir Geoffrey looped the whip one more time round the young man's neck and gave it a good tug just to let the monk know who was in charge. 'An archer, fellow with a black bow, had a letter for your prior.'

'He did, sir, yes, sir.'

'And did the prior read it?'

'Yes, sir, he did, sir.'

'And did he tell you what was in it?'

The monk instinctively shook his head, then saw the rage in the Scarecrow's eye and in his panic he blurted out the word he had first overheard when the letter was opened. '*Thesaurus*, sir, that's what's in it, *thesaurus*.'

'*Thesaurus*?' Sir Geoffrey said, stumbling over the foreign word. 'And what, you gelded piece of weasel shit, what, in the name of a thousand virgins, is a *thesaurus*?'

'Treasure, sir, treasure. Latin, sir. *Thesaurus*, sir, is Latin for . . .' the monk's voice trailed away. '. . . treasure,' he finished lamely.

'Treasure.' Sir Geoffrey repeated the word flatly.

The monk, half choking, was suddenly eager to repeat the gossip that had circulated amongst the brethren since Thomas of Hookton had encountered the prior. 'The King sent him, sir, his majesty himself, and my

130

lord the bishop too, sir, from France, and they're looking for a treasure, sir, but no one knows what it is.'

'The King?'

'Or where it is, sir, yes, sir, the King himself, sir. He sent him, sir.'

Sir Geoffrey looked into the monk's eyes, saw no guile and so unlooped the whip. 'You dropped some apples, boy.'

'I did, sir, I did, sir, yes.'

'Feed one to my horse.' He watched the monk retrieve an apple, then his face suddenly contorted with anger. 'Wipe the mud off it first, you toadspawn! Clean it!' He shuddered, then stared northwards, but he was not seeing the surviving Scots of the enemy's right wing scramble out of the low ground and he did not even notice the escape of his hated enemy, Sir William Douglas, who had impoverished him. He saw none of these things because the Scarecrow was thinking of treasure. Of gold. Of heaps of gold. Of his heart's desire. Of money and jewels and coins and plate and women and everything a heart could ever want.

The sheltron on the Scottish left, rampant and savage, forced the English right so far back that a great gap appeared between the English centre, behind its stone wall, and the retreating division on its right. That retreat meant that the right flank of the central division was now exposed to Scottish attack, indeed the rear of the Archbishop's battle was exposed to the Scots, but then, from all across the ridge, the archers came to the rescue.

They came to make a new line that protected the Archbishop's flank, a line that faced sideways onto the triumphant Scottish assault and the swarm of archers drove their arrows into Lord Robert Stewart's sheltron. They could not miss. These were bowmen who started their archery practice at a hundred paces and finished over two hundred paces from the straw-filled targets, and now they were shooting at twenty paces and the arrows flew with such force that some pierced through mail, body and mail again. Men in armour were being spitted by the arrows and the right-hand side of the Scottish advance crumpled in blood and pain, and every man who fell exposed another victim to the bowmen who were shooting as fast as they could lay their arrows on the cords. The Scots were dying by the score. They were dying and they were screaming. Some men instinctively tried to charge the archers, but were immediately cut down; no troops could stand that assault of feathered steel and suddenly the Scots were pulling back, tripping over the dead left by their charge, stumbling back across the pasture to where they had begun their charge and they were pursued every step of the way by the hissing arrows until, at last, an English voice ordered the archers to rest their bows. 'But stay here!' the man ordered, wanting the archers who had come from the left wing to stay on the beleaguered right.

Thomas was among the archers. He counted his arrows, finding only seven left in his bag and so he began hunting in the grass for shot arrows that were not badly damaged, but then a man nudged him and pointed to a cart that was trundling across the field with spare sheaves. Thomas was astonished. 'In France we were ever running out of arrows.'

'Not here.' The man had a hare lip, which made him hard to understand. 'They keep 'em in Durham. In the

132

castle. Three counties send 'em here.' He scooped up two new sheaves.

The arrows were made all across England and Wales. Some folk cut and trimmed the shafts, others collected the feathers, women span the cords and men boiled the hide, hoof and verdigris glue while smiths forged the heads, and then the separate parts were carried to towns where the arrows were assembled, bundled and sent on to London, York, Chester or Durham where they awaited an emergency. Thomas broke the twine on two sheaves and put the new arrows in a bag he had taken from a dead archer. He had found the man lying behind the Archbishop's troops and Thomas had left his old torn bag beside the man's body and now had a new bag filled with fresh arrows. He flexed the fingers of his right hand. They were sore, proof he had not shot enough arrows since the battle in Picardy. His back ached as it always did after he had shot the bow twenty or more times. Each draw was the equivalent of lifting a man one-handed and the effort of it dug the ache deep into his spine, but the arrows had driven the Scottish left wing clean back to where it had started and where, like their English enemies, they now drew breath. The ground between the two armies was littered with spent arrows, dead men and wounded, some of whom moved slowly as they tried to drag themselves back to their comrades. Two dogs sniffed at a corpse, but skittered away when a monk shied a stone at them.

Thomas unlooped the string of his bow so that the stave straightened. Some archers liked to leave their weapons permanently strung until the stave had taken on the curve of a tensioned bow, and were said to have followed the string; the curve was supposed to show that the bow was well used and thus that its owner was an experienced soldier, but Thomas reckoned a bow that had followed the string was weakened and so he unstrung his as often as he could. That also helped to preserve the cord. It was difficult to fashion a cord of exactly the right length, and inevitably it stretched, but a good hempen string, soaked with glue, could last the best part of a year if it was kept dry and not subjected to constant tension. Like many archers, Thomas liked to reinforce his bowcords with women's hair because that was meant to protect the strings from snapping in a fight. That and praying to St Sebastian. Thomas let the string hang from the top of the bow, then squatted in the grass where he took the arrows from his bag one by one and span them between his fingers to detect any warping in their shafts.

'The bastards will be back!' A man with a silver crescent on his surcoat strode down the line. 'They'll be back for more! But you've done well!' The silver crescent was half obscured by blood. An archer spat and another impulsively stroked his unstrung bow. Thomas thought that if he lay down he would probably sleep, but he was assailed by the ridiculous fear that the other archers would retreat and leave him there, sleeping, and the Scots would find and kill him. The Scots, though, were resting like the English. Some men were bent over as if they caught their breath, others were sitting on the grass while a few clustered round a barrel of water or ale. The big drums were silent, but Thomas could hear the scrape of stone on steel as men sharpened blades blunted by the battle's first clash. No insults were being shouted on either side now, men just eyed each other warily. Priests knelt beside dying men, praying their souls into heaven, while women shrieked because their husbands, lovers or sons were dead. The English right wing, its numbers thinned by the ferocity of the Scottish attack, had moved back to its original place and behind them were scores of dead and dying men. The Scottish casualties left behind by the precipitate retreat were being stripped and searched and a fight broke out between two men squabbling over a handful of tarnished coins. Two monks carried water to the wounded. A small child played with broken rings from a mail coat while his mother attempted to prise a broken visor off a pike that she reckoned would make a good axe. A Scotsman, thought dead, suddenly groaned and turned over and a man-at-arms stepped to him and stabbed down with his sword. The enemy stiffened, relaxed and did not move again. 'Ain't resurrection day yet, you bastard,' the man-at-arms said as he dragged his sword free. 'Goddamn son of a whore,' he grumbled, wiping his sword on the dead man's ragged surcoat, 'waking up like that! Gave me a turn!' He was not speaking to anyone in particular, but just crouched beside the man he had killed and began searching his clothes.

The cathedral towers and castle walls were thick with spectators. A heron flew beneath the ramparts, following the looping river that sparkled prettily under the autumn sun. Thomas could hear corncrakes down the slope. Butterflies, surely the last of the year, flew above the blood-slicked grass. The Scots were standing, stretching, pulling on helmets, pushing their forearms into their shield loops and hefting newly sharpened swords, pikes and spears. Some glanced over to the city and imagined the treasures stored in the cathedral crypt and castle cellars. They dreamed of chests crammed with

135

gold, vats overflowing with coin, rooms heaped with silver, taverns running with ale and streets filled with women. 'In the name of the Father and of the Son,' a priest called, 'and of the Holy Ghost. St Andrew is with you. You fight for your King! The enemy are godless imps of Satan! God is with us!'

'Up, boys, up!' an archer called on the English side. Men stood, strung their bows and took the first arrow from the bag. Some crossed themselves, oblivious that the Scots did the same.

Lord Robert Stewart, mounted on a fresh grey stallion, pushed his way towards the front of the Scottish left wing. 'They'll have few arrows left,' he promised his men, 'few arrows. We can break them!' His men had so nearly broken the damned English last time. So nearly, and surely another howling rush would obliterate the small defiant army and open the road to the opulent riches of the south.

'For St Andrew!' Lord Robert called and the drummers began their beating, 'for our King! For Scotland!'

And the howling began again.

Bernard de Taillebourg went to the cathedral when his business in the monastery's small hospital was finished. His servant was readying the horses as the Dominican strode down the great nave between the vast pillars painted in jagged stripes of red, yellow, green and blue. He went to the tomb of St Cuthbert to say a prayer. He was not certain that Cuthbert was an important saint – he was certainly not one of the blessed souls who commanded the ear of God in heaven – but he was much revered locally, and his tomb, thickly decorated with jewels, gold and silver, testified to that devotion.

At least a hundred women were gathered about the grave, most of them crying, and de Taillebourg pushed some out of his way so he could get close enough to touch the embroidered pall that shrouded the tomb. One woman snarled at him, then realized he was a priest and, seeing his bloodied, bruised face, begged his forgiveness. Bernard de Taillebourg ignored her, stooping instead to the tomb. The pall was tasselled and the women had tied little shreds of cloth to the tassels, each scrap a prayer. Most prayers were for health, for the restoration of a limb, for the gift of sight, or to save a child's life, but today they were begging Cuthbert to bring their menfolk safely down from the hill.

Bernard de Taillebourg added his own prayer. Go to St Denis, he beseeched Cuthbert, and ask him to speak to God. Cuthbert, even if he could not hold God's attention, could certainly find St Denis who, being French, was bound to be closer to God than Cuthbert. Beg Denis to pray that God's speed attend my errand and that God's blessing be upon the search and that God's grace give it success. And pray God to forgive us our sins, but know that our sins, grievous though they be, are committed only in God's service. He moaned at the thought of this day's sins, then he kissed the pall and took a coin from the purse under his robe. He dropped the coin in the great metal jar where pilgrims gave what they could to the shrine and then he hurried back down the cathedral's nave. A crude building, he thought, its coloured pillars so fat and gross and its carvings as clumsy as a child's scratchings, so unlike the new and graceful abbeys and churches that were rising in France. He dipped his fingers in the holy water, made the sign of the cross and went out into the sunlight where his servant was waiting with their mounts.

'You could have left without me,' he said to the servant.

'It would be easier,' the servant said, 'to kill you on the road and then go on without you.'

'But you won't do that,' de Taillebourg said, 'because the grace of God has come into your soul.'

'Thanks be to God,' the servant said.

The man was not a servant by birth, but a knight and gently born. Now, at de Taillebourg's pleasure, he was being punished for his sins and for the sins of his family. There were those, and Cardinal Bessières was among them, who thought the man should have been stretched on the rack, that he should have been pressed by great weights, that the burning irons should have seared into his flesh so that his back arched as he screamed repentance at the ceiling, but de Taillebourg had persuaded the Cardinal to do nothing except show this man the instruments of the Inquisition's torture. 'Then give him to me,' de Taillebourg had said, 'and let him lead me to the Grail.'

'Kill him afterwards,' the Cardinal had instructed the Inquisitor.

'All will be different when we have the Grail,' de Taillebourg had said evasively. He still did not know whether he would have to kill this thin young man with the sun-dark skin and the black eyes and the narrow face who had once called himself the Harlequin. He had adopted the name out of pride because harlequins were lost souls, but de Taillebourg believed he might well have saved this harlequin's soul. The Harlequin's real name was Guy Vexille, Count of Astarac, and it had been Guy Vexille whom de Taillebourg had been describing when he spoke to Brother Collimore about the man who had come from the south to fight for France in Picardy. Vexille had been seized after the battle when the French King had been looking for scapegoats and a man who dared display the crest of a family declared heretic and rebel had made a good scapegoat.

Vexille had been given to the Inquisition in the expectation that they would torture the heresy out of him, but de Taillebourg had liked the Harlequin. He had recognized a fellow soul, a hard man, a dedicated man, a man who knew that this life meant nothing because all that counted was the next, and so de Taillebourg had spared Vexille the agonies. He had merely shown him the chamber where men and women screamed their apologies to God, and then he had questioned him gently and Vexille had revealed how he had once sailed to England to find the Grail and, though he had killed his uncle, Thomas's father, he had not found it. Now, with de Taillebourg, he had listened to Eleanor tell Thomas's story. 'Did you believe her?' the Dominican now asked.

'I believed her,' Vexille said.

'But was she deceived?' The Inquisitor wondered. Eleanor had told them that Thomas had been charged to seek the Grail, but that his faith was weak and his search half-hearted. 'We shall still have to kill him,' de Taillebourg added.

'Of course.'

De Taillebourg frowned. 'You do not mind?'

'Killing?' Guy Vexille sounded surprised that de Taillebourg should even ask. 'Killing is my job, father,' the

Harlequin said. Cardinal Bessières had decreed that everyone who sought the Grail should be killed, all except those who sought it on the Cardinal's own behalf, and Guy Vexille had willingly become God's murderer. He certainly had no qualms about slitting his cousin Thomas's throat. 'You want to wait here for him?' he asked the Inquisitor. 'The girl said he would be in the cathedral after the battle.'

De Taillebourg looked across to the hill. The Scots would win, he was sure, and that made it doubtful that Thomas of Hookton would come to the city. More likely he would flee southwards in panic. 'We shall go to Hookton.'

'I searched Hookton once,' Guy Vexille said.

'Then you will search it again,' de Taillebourg snapped.

'Yes, father.' Guy Vexille humbly lowered his head. He was a sinner; it was required of him that he show penitence and so he did not argue. He just did de Taillebourg's bidding and his reward, he had been promised, would be reinstatement. He would be given back his pride, allowed to lead men to war again and forgiven by the Church.

'We shall leave now,' de Taillebourg said. He wanted to go before William Douglas came in search of them and, even more urgently, before anyone discovered the three bodies in the hospital cell. The Dominican had closed the door on the corpses and doubtless the monks would believe Collimore was sleeping and so would not disturb him, but de Taillebourg still wanted to be free of the city when the bodies were found and so he pulled himself into the saddle of one of the horses they had stolen from Jamie Douglas that morning. It seemed a

140

long time ago now. He pushed his shoes into the stir-rups, then kicked a beggar away. The man had been clawing at de Taillebourg's leg, whining that he was hungry, but now reeled away from the priest's savage thrust.

The noise of battle swelled. The Dominican looked at the ridge again, but the fight was none of his business. If the English and the Scots wished to maul each other then let them. He had greater matters on his mind, matters of God and the Grail and of heaven and hell. He had sins on his conscience too, but they would be shriven by the Holy Father and even heaven would understand those sins once he had found the Grail.

The gates of the city, though strongly guarded, were open so that the wounded could be brought inside and food and drink carried to the ridge. The guards were older men and had been ordered to make certain that no Scottish raiders tried to enter the city, but they had not been charged to stop anyone leaving and so they took no notice of the haggard priest with the bruised face mounted on a warhorse, nor of his elegant servant. So de Taillebourg and the Harlequin rode out of Durham, turned towards the York road, put back their heels and, as the sound of battle echoed from the city's crag, rode away southwards.

It was mid-afternoon when the Scots attacked a second time, but this assault, unlike the first, did not come hard on the heels of fleeing archers. Instead the archers were drawn up ready to receive the charge and this time the arrows flew thick as starlings. Those on the Scottish left who had so nearly broken the English line were now faced by twice as many archers, and their charge, which had begun so confidently, slowed to a crawl and then stopped altogether as men crouched behind shields. The Scottish right never advanced at all, while the King's central sheltron was checked fifty paces from the stone wall behind which a crowd of archers sent an incessant shower of arrows. The Scots would not retreat, they could not advance, and for a time the long-shafted arrows thumped onto shields and into carelessly exposed bodies, then Lord Robert Stewart's men edged back out of range and the King's sheltron followed and so another pause came over the red-earthed battlefield. The drums were silent and no more insults were being shouted across the littered pastureland. The Scottish lords, those who still lived, gathered under their King's saltire banner and the Archbishop of York, seeing his enemies in council, called his own lords together. The Englishmen were gloomy. The enemy, they reasoned, would never expose themselves to what the Archbishop described as a third baptism of arrows. 'The bastards will slink off northwards,' the Archbishop predicted, 'God damn their bloody souls.'

'Then we follow them,' Lord Percy said.

'They move faster than us,' the Archbishop said. He had taken off his helmet and its leather liner had left an indentation in his hair, circling his skull.

'We'll slaughter their foot,' another lord said wolfishly.

'Damn their infantry,' the Archbishop snapped, impatient with such foolery. He wanted to capture the Scottish lords, the men mounted on the swiftest and most expensive horses, for it was their ransoms that would make him rich, and he especially wanted to capture those Scottish nobles like the Earl of Menteith who had sworn fealty to Edward of England and whose presence in the enemy army proved their treachery. Such men would not be ransomed, but would be executed as an example to other men who broke their oaths, but if the Archbishop was victorious today then he could lead this small army into Scotland and take the traitors' estates. He would take everything from them: the timber from their parks, the sheets from their beds, the beds themselves, the slates off their roofs, their pots, their pans, their cattle, even the rushes from their streambeds. 'But they won't attack again,' the Archbishop said.

'Then we shall have to be clever,' Lord Outhwaite put in cheerfully.

The other lords looked suspiciously at Outhwaite. Cleverness was not a quality they prized for it hunted no boars, killed no stags, enjoyed no women and took no prisoners. Churchmen could be clever, and doubtless there were clever fools at Oxford, and even women could be clever so long as they did not flaunt it, but on a battlefield? Cleverness?

'Clever?' Lord Neville asked pointedly.

'They fear our archers,' Lord Outhwaite said, 'but if our archers are seen to have few arrows, then that fear will go and they might well attack again.'

'Indeed, indeed . . .' the Archbishop began and then stopped, for he was quite as clever as Lord Outhwaite, clever enough, indeed, to hide how clever he was. 'But how would we convince them?' he asked.

Lord Outhwaite obliged the Archbishop by explaining what he suspected the Archbishop had already grasped. 'I think, your grace, that if our archers are seen scavenging the field for arrows then the enemy will draw the correct conclusion.'

'Or, in this case,' the Archbishop laid it on broadly for the benefit of the other lords, 'the incorrect conclusion.'

'Oh, that's good,' one of those other lords said warmly.

'It could be made even better, your grace,' Lord Outhwaite suggested diffidently, 'if our horses were brought forward? The enemy might then assume we were readying ourselves to flee?'

The Archbishop did not hesitate. 'Bring all the horses up,' he said.

'But . . .' A lord was frowning.

'Archers to scavenge for arrows, squires and pages to bring up the horses for the men-at-arms,' the Archbishop snapped, understanding completely what Lord Outhwaite had in mind and eager to put it into effect before the enemy decided to withdraw northwards.

Lord Outhwaite gave the orders to the bowmen himself and, within a few moments, scores of archers were out in the space between the armies where they gathered spent arrows. Some of the archers grumbled, calling it tomfoolery because they felt exposed to the Scottish troops who once again began to jeer them. One archer, farther forward than most, was struck in the chest by a crossbow quarrel and he fell to his knees, a look of astonishment on his face, and choked up blood into his cupped palm. Then he began weeping and that only made the choking worse and then a second man, going to help the first, was hit in the thigh by the same crossbow. The Scots were howling their derision at the wounded men, then cowered as a dozen English archers loosed arrows at the lone crossbowman. 'Save your arrows! Save your arrows!' Lord Outhwaite, mounted on his horse, roared at the bowmen. He galloped closer to them. 'Save your arrows! For God's sake! Save them!' He was bellowing loud enough for the enemy to hear him, then a group of Scotsmen, tired of sheltering from the archers, ran forward in an evident attempt to cut off Lord Outhwaite's retreat and all the English scampered for their own line. Lord Outhwaite put back his spurs and easily evaded the rush of men who contented themselves with butchering the two wounded archers. The rest of the Scots, seeing the English run, laughed and jeered. Lord Outhwaite turned and gazed at the two dead bowmen. 'We should have brought those lads in,' he chided himself.

No one answered. Some of the archers were looking resentfully at the men-at-arms, supposing that their horses had been brought up to aid their flight, but then Lord Outhwaite barked at groups of archers to get behind the men-at-arms. 'Line up at the back! Not all of you. We're trying to make them believe we're short of arrows and if you didn't have arrows you wouldn't be standing out in front, now would you? Hold the horses where they are!' He shouted this last order to the squires, pages and servants who had brought up the destriers. The men-at-arms were not to mount yet, the horses were simply being held at the back of the line, just behind the place where half the archers now formed. The enemy, seeing the horses, must conclude that the English, short of arrows, were contemplating flight.

And so the simple trap was baited.

A silence fell on the battlefield, except that the wounded were moaning, ravens calling and some women crying. The monks began to chant again, but they were still on the English left and to Thomas, now on the right, the sound was faint. A bell rang in the city. 'I do fear we're being too clever,' Outhwaite remarked to Thomas. His lordship was not a man who could keep silent and there was no one else in the right-hand division convenient for conversation and so he selected Thomas. He sighed. 'It doesn't always work, being clever.'

'It worked for us in Brittany, my lord.'

'You were in Brittany as well as Picardy?' Lord Outhwaite asked. He was still mounted and was gazing over the men-at-arms towards the Scots.

'I served a clever man there, my lord.'

'And who was that?' Lord Outhwaite was pretending to be interested, perhaps regretting that he had even begun the conversation.

'Will Skeat, my lord, only he's Sir William now. The King knighted him at the battle.'

'Will Skeat?' Lord Outhwaite was engaged now. 'You served Will? By the good Lord, you did? Dear William. I haven't heard that name in many a year. How is he?'

'Not well, my lord,' Thomas said, and he told how Will Skeat, a commoner who had become the leader of a band of archers and men-at-arms who were feared wherever men spoke French, had been grievously wounded at the battle in Picardy. 'He was taken to Caen, my lord.'

Lord Outhwaite frowned. 'That's back in French hands, surely?'

'A Frenchman took him there, my lord,' Thomas explained, 'a friend, because there's a doctor in the city who can work miracles.' At the end of the battle, when

146

men could at last think they had lived through the horror, Skeat's skull had been opened to the sky and when Thomas had last seen him Skeat had been dumb, blind and powerless.

'I don't know why the French make better physicians,' Lord Outhwaite said in mild annoyance, 'but it seems they do. My father always said they did, and he had much trouble with his phlegm.'

'This man's Jewish, my lord.'

'And with his shoulders. Jewish! Did you say Jewish?' Lord Outhwaite sounded alarmed. 'I have nothing against Jews,' he went on, though without conviction, 'but I can think of a dozen good reasons why one should never resort to a Jewish physician.'

'Truly, my lord?'

'My dear fellow, how can they harness the power of the saints? Or the healing properties of relics? Or the efficacy of holy water? Even prayer is a mystery to them. My mother, rest her soul, had great pain in her knees. Too much praying, I always thought, but her physician ordered her to wrap her legs in cloths that had been placed on the grave of St Cuthbert and to pray thrice a day to St Gregory of Nazianzus and it worked! It worked! But no Jew could prescribe such a cure, could he? And if he did it would be blasphemous and bound to fail. I must say I think it most ill advised to have placed poor Will into a Jew's hands. He deserves better, indeed he does.' He shook his head reprovingly. 'Will served my father for a time, but was too smart a fellow to stay cooped up on the Scottish border. Not enough plunder, you see? Went off on his own, he did. Poor Will.'

'The Jewish doctor,' Thomas said stubbornly, 'cured me.'

147

'We can only pray.' Lord Outhwaite ignored Thomas's claim and spoke in a tone which suggested that prayer, though needful, would almost certainly prove useless. Then he cheered up suddenly. 'Ah! I think our friends are stirring!' The Scottish drums had begun to beat and all along the enemy's line men were hitching up shields, dropping visors or hefting swords. They could see that the English had brought their horses closer, presumably to aid their retreat, and that the enemy line was apparently stripped of half its archers, so they must have believed that those bowmen were perilously short of missiles, yet the Scots still chose to advance on foot, knowing that even a handful of arrows could madden their horses and throw a mounted charge into chaos. They shouted as they advanced, as much to hearten themselves as put fear in the English, but they became more confident when they reached the place where the bodies lay from their last charge and still no arrows flew.

'Not yet, lads, not yet.' Lord Outhwaite had taken command of the archers on the right wing. The Lords Percy and Neville commanded here, yet both were content to allow the older man give orders to the bowmen while they waited with their men-at-arms. Lord Outhwaite glanced constantly across the field to where the Scots advanced on the English left wing, where his own men were, but he was satisfied that the hollow of ground would go on protecting them just as the stone wall shielded the centre. It was here on the side of the ridge closest to Durham where the Scots were strongest and the English most vulnerable. 'Let them get closer,' he warned the archers. 'We want to finish them off once and for all, poor fellows.' He began tapping his fingers on his saddle's pommel, keeping time with the few remaining big Scottish drums and waiting until the front rank of Scots was only a hundred paces away. 'Foremost archers,' he called when he judged the enemy was close enough, 'that's you fellows in front of the line! Start shooting!'

About half the archers were in plain sight in the army's front and they now drew their bows, cocked the arrows up into the air and loosed. The Scots, seeing the volley coming, began to run, hoping to close the range quickly so that only a handful of the arrows would hurt.

'All archers!' Lord Outhwaite boomed, fearing he had waited too long, and the archers who had been concealed behind the men-at-arms began to shoot over the heads of the troops in front. The Scots were close now, close enough so that even the worst archer could not fail to hit his mark, so close that the arrows were again piercing through mail and bodies, and strewing the ground with more wounded and dying men. Thomas could hear the arrows striking home. Some clanged off armour, some thumped into shields, but many made a sound like a butcher's axe when it slaughtered cattle at winter's coming. He aimed at a big man whose visor was raised and sent an arrow down his throat. Another arrow into a tribesman whose face was contorted with hate. Then an arrow's nock split on him, spinning the broken missile away when he released the string. He plucked the feathered scraps from the string, took a new arrow and drove it into another bearded tribesman who was all fury and hair. A mounted Scotsman was encouraging his men forward and then he was flailing in the saddle, struck by three arrows and Thomas loosed another shaft, striking a man-at-arms clean in the chest so that the point ripped through mail, leather, bone and flesh. His next arrow sank into a shield. The Scots were floundering, trying to force themselves into the rain of death. 'Steady, boys, steady!' an archer called to his fellows, fearing they were snatching at the strings and thus not using the full force of their bows.

'Keep shooting!' Lord Outhwaite called. His fingers still tapped the pommel of his saddle, though the Scottish drums were faltering. 'Lovely work! Lovely work!'

'Horses!' Lord Percy ordered. He could see that the Scots were on the edge of despair for the English archers were not after all short of arrows. 'Horses!' he bellowed again, and his men-at-arms ran back to haul themselves into saddles. Pages and squires handed up the big heavy lances as men fiddled armoured feet into stirrups, glanced at the suffering enemy and then snapped down their visors.

'Shoot! Shoot!' Lord Outhwaite called. 'That's the way, lads!' The arrows were pitiless. The Scottish wounded cried to God, called for their mothers and still the feathered death hammered home. One man, wearing the lion of Stewart, spewed a pink mist of blood and spittle. He was on his knees, but managed to stand, took a step, fell to his knees again, shuffled forward, blew more blood-stained bubbles and then an arrow buried itself in his eye and went through his brain to scrape against the back of his skull and he went backwards as though hit by a thunderbolt.

Then the great horses came.

'For England, Edward and St George!' Lord Percy called and a trumpeter took up the challenge as the great destriers charged. They unceremoniously thrust the archers aside as the lances dropped.

The turf shook. Only a few horsemen were attacking, but the shock of their charge struck the enemy with stunning force and the Scots reeled back. Lances were relinquished in men's bodies as the knights drew swords and hacked down at frightened, cowering men who could not run because the press of bodies was too great. More horsemen were mounting up and those men-at-arms who did not want to wait for their stallions were running forward to join the carnage. The archers joined them, drawing swords or swinging axes. The drums were at last silent and the slaughter had begun.

Thomas had seen it happen before. He had seen how, in an eyeblink, a battle could change. The Scots had been pressing all day, they had so nearly shattered the English, they were rampant and winning, yet now they were beaten and the men of the Scottish left, who had come so close to giving their King his victory, were the ones who broke. The English warhorses galloped into their ranks to make bloody lanes and the riders swung swords, axes, clubs and morningstars at panicked men. The English archers joined in, mobbing the slower Scots like packs of hounds leaping onto deer. 'Prisoners!' Lord Percy shouted at his retainers. 'I want prisoners!' A Scotsman swung an axe at his horse, missed and was chopped down by his lordship's sword, an archer finished the job with a knife and then slit the man's padded jerkin to search for coins. Two carpenters from Durham hacked with woodworker's adzes at a struggling man-at-arms, bludgeoning his skull, killing him slowly. An archer reeled back, gasping, his belly cut open and a Scot followed him, screaming in rage, but then was tripped by a bowstave and went down under a swarm of men. The trappers of the English horses were dripping with blood as their riders turned to cut their way back through the Scottish host. They had ridden clean through and now spurred back to meet the next wave of English men-at-arms who fought with visors open for the panicking enemy was not offering any real resistance.

Yet the Scottish right and centre were intact.

The right had again been pushed into the low ground, but now, instead of archers fighting them from the rim, they faced the English men-at-arms who were foolish enough to go down into the hollow to meet the Scottish charge. Mailed men clashed over the bodies of the Scottish dead, clambering awkwardly in their metal suits to swing swords and axes against shields and skulls. Men grunted as they killed. They snarled, attacked and died in the muddy bracken, yet the fight was futile for if either side gained an advantage they only pressed their enemy back up the slope and immediately the losing side had the ground as their ally and they would press back downhill and more dead joined the corpses in the hollow's bottom and so the fight surged forward and back, each great swing leaving men weeping and dying, calling on Jesus, cursing their enemy, bleeding.

Beggar was there, a great rock of a man who stood astride the corpse of the Earl of Moray, mocking the Scots and inviting them to fight, and half a dozen came and were killed before a pack of Highland clansmen came screaming to kill him and he roared at them, swinging his huge spiked mace, and to the Scarecrow, watching from above, he looked like a great shaggy bear assailed by mastiffs. Sir William Douglas, too canny to be caught a second time in the low ground, also watched from the opposing rim and was amazed that men would go willingly down to the slaughter. Then, knowing that the battle would neither be won nor lost in that pit of death, he turned back to the centre where the King's sheltron still had a chance of gaining a great victory despite the disaster on the Scottish left.

For the King's men had got past the stone wall. In places they had pulled it down and in others it had at last collapsed before the press of men, and though the fallen stones still presented a formidable obstacle to soldiers cumbered by heavy shields and coats of mail they were clambering across and thrusting back the English centre. The Scots had charged into the arrows, endured them and even trapped a score of archers whom they slaughtered gleefully and now they hacked and stabbed their way towards the Archbishop's great banner. The King, his visor sticky with blood from his wounded cheek, was in the forefront of the sheltron. The King's chaplain was beside his master, wielding a spiked club, and Sir William and his nephew joined the attack. Sir William was suddenly ashamed of the premonition that had made him advise a retreat. This was how Scotsmen fought! With passion and savagery. The English centre was reeling back, scarce holding its ranks. Sir William saw that the enemy had fetched their horses close up to the battle line and he surmised they were readying themselves to flee and so he redoubled his efforts. 'Kill them!' he roared. If the Scots could break the line then the English would be in chaos, unable to reach their horses, and mere meat for the butchers.

'Kill! Kill!' the King, conspicuous on horseback, shouted at his men.

'Prisoners!' the Earl of Menteith, more sensible, called. 'Take prisoners!'

'Break them! Break them now!' Sir William roared. He slammed his shield forward to receive a sword stroke, stabbed beneath it and felt his blade pierce a mail coat. He turned the sword and jerked it free before the flesh could grip the steel. He pushed with his shield, unable to see over its top rim, felt the enemy stagger back, lowered the shield in anticipation of a lunge underneath, then rammed it forward again, throwing the enemy back. He stumbled forward, almost losing his footing by tripping on the man he had wounded, but he caught his weight by dropping the bottom edge of the shield on the ground, pushed himself upright and thrust the sword into a bearded face. The blade glanced off the cheekbone, taking an eye, and that man fell backwards, mouth agape, abandoning the fight. Sir William half ducked to avoid an axe blow, caught another sword on his shield and stabbed wildly towards the two men attacking him. Robbie, swearing and cursing, killed the axeman, then kicked a fallen man-at-arms in the face. Sir William lunged underhand and felt his sword scrape on broken mail and he twisted to stop the blade being trapped and yanked it back so that a gush of blood spilled through the metal rings of the wounded man's armour. That man fell, gasping and twitching, and more Englishmen came from the right, desperate to stop the Scottish attack that threatened to pierce clean through the Archbishop's line. 'Douglas!' Sir William roared. 'Douglas!' He was calling on his followers to come and support him, to shove and to gouge and to hack the last enemy down. He and his nephew had carved a bloody path deep into the Archbishop's ranks and it would take only a moment's fierce fighting to break the English centre and then the real slaughter could begin.

Sir William ducked as another axe flailed at him. Robbie killed that man, driving his sword through the axeman's throat, but Robbie immediately had to parry a spear thrust and in doing it he staggered back against his uncle. Sir William shoved his nephew upright and hammered his shield into an enemy's face. Where the hell were his men? 'Douglas!' Sir William thundered again. 'Douglas!'

And just then a sword or spear tangled his feet and he fell and instinctively he covered himself with the shield. Men pounded past him and he prayed that they were his followers who were breaking the last English resistance and he waited for the enemy's screaming to begin, but instead there was an insistent tap on his helmet. The tapping stopped, then started again. 'Sir William?' a gentle voice enquired.

The screaming had begun so Sir William could scarcely hear, but the gentle tapping on the crown of his helmet persuaded him it was safe to lower his shield. It took him a moment to see what was happening for his helmet had been wrenched askew when he fell and he had to pull it round. 'God's teeth,' he said when the world came into view.

'Dear Sir William,' the kindly voice said, 'I assume you yield? Of course you do. And is that young Robbie? My, how you've grown, young man! I remember you as a pup.'

'Oh, God's teeth,' Sir William said again, looking up at Lord Outhwaite.

'Can I give you a hand?' Lord Outhwaite asked solicitously, reaching down from his saddle. 'And then we can talk ransoms.'

'Jesus,' Sir William said, 'God damn it!' for he understood now that the feet pounding past had been English feet and that the screaming was coming from the Scots.

The English centre had held after all, and for the Scots the battle had turned to utter disaster.

It was the archers again. The Scots had lost men all day and still they outnumbered their enemy, but they had no answer to the arrows and when the Scottish centre broke down the wall and surged across its remains, so the Scottish left had retreated and exposed the flank of the King's sheltron to the English arrows.

It took a few moments for the bowmen to realize their advantage. They had joined the pursuit of the broken Scottish left and were unaware how close to victory was the Scottish centre, but then one of Lord Neville's men understood the danger. 'Archers!' His roar could be heard clear across the Wear in Durham. *'Archers!'* Men broke off their plundering and pulled arrows from the bags.

The bows began sounding again, each deep harp note driving an arrow into the flank of the rampaging Scots. David's sheltron had forced the central English battle back across a pasture, they had stretched it thin and they were closing on the Archbishop's great banner, and then the arrows began to bite and after the arrows came the men-at-arms from the English right wing, the retainers of Lord Percy and of Lord Neville, and some were already mounted on their big horses that were trained to bite, rear and kick with their iron-shod hooves. The archers, discarding their bows yet again, followed the horsemen with axes and swords, and this time their women came as well with knives unsheathed.

The Scottish King hacked at an Englishman, saw him

156

fall, then heard his standard-bearer shout in terror and he turned to see the great banner falling. The standard-bearer's horse had been hamstrung; it screamed as it collapsed and a rabble of archers and men-at-arms clawed at man and beast, snatched at the banner and hauled the standard-bearer down to a ghastly death, but then the royal chaplain seized the reins of the King's horse and dragged David Bruce out of the mêlée. More Scotsmen gathered about their King, escorting him away, and behind them the English were hacking down from saddles, chopping with their swords, cursing as they killed, and the King tried to turn back and continue the fight, but the chaplain forced his horse away. 'Ride, sir! Ride!' the chaplain shouted. Frightened men blundered into the King's horse that trampled on a clansman then stumbled on a corpse. There were Englishmen in the Scottish rear now and the King, seeing his danger, put back his spurs. An enemy knight took a swing at him, but the King parried the blow and galloped past the danger. His army had disintegrated into groups of desperate fugitives. He saw the Earl of Menteith try to mount a horse, but an archer seized his lordship's leg and hauled him back, then sat on him and put a knife to his throat. The Earl shouted that he yielded. The Earl of Fife was a prisoner, the Earl of Strathearn was dead, the Earl of Wigtown was being assailed by two English knights whose swords rang on his plate armour like blacksmiths' hammers. One of the big Scottish drums, its skins split and tattered, rolled down the hill, going faster and faster as the slope steepened, thumping hollow on the rocks until at last it fell sideways and slid to a halt.

The King's great banner was in English hands now as were the standards of a dozen Scottish lords. A few

Scots galloped north. Lord Robert Stewart, who had so nearly won the day, was free and clear on the eastern side of the ridge while the King plunged down the western side, going into shadow because the sun was now lower than the hills towards which he rode in desperate need of refuge. He thought of his wife. Was she pregnant? He had been told that Lord Robert had hired a witch to lay a spell on her womb so that the throne would pass from Bruce to Stewart. 'Sir! Sir!' One of his men was screaming at him and the King came out of his reverie to see a group of English archers already down in the valley. How had they headed him off? He pulled on the reins, leaned right to help the horse round and felt the arrow thump into the stallion's chest. Another of his men was down, tumbling along the stony ground that was tearing his mail into bright shreds. A horse screamed, blood fanned across the dusk and another arrow slammed into the King's shield that was slung on his back. A third arrow was caught in his horse's mane and the stallion was slowing, plunging up and down as it laboured for breath.

The King struck back with his spurs, but the horse could not go faster. He grimaced and the gesture opened the crusted wound on his cheek so that blood spilled from his open visor down his ripped surcoat. The horse stumbled again. There was a stream ahead and a small stone bridge and the King marvelled that anyone should make a masonry bridge over so slight a watercourse, and then the horse's front legs just collapsed and the King was rolling on the ground, miraculously free of his dying mount and without any broken bones and he scrambled up and ran to the bridge where three of his men waited on horseback, one with a riderless stallion.

But even before the King could reach the three men the arrows flickered and hammered home, each one making the horses stagger sideways from the shock of its impact. The stallion screamed, tore itself free of the man's grasp and galloped eastwards with blood dripping from its belly. Another horse collapsed with an arrow deep in its rump, two in its belly and another in its jugular. 'Under the bridge!' the King shouted. There would be shelter under the arch, a place to hide, and when he had a dozen men he would make a break for it. Dusk could not be far off and if they waited for nightfall and then walked all night they might be in Scotland by dawn.

So four Scotsmen, one of them a King, huddled under the stone bridge and caught their breath. The arrows had stopped flying, their horses were all dead and the King dared to hope that the English archers had gone in search of other prey. 'We wait here,' he whispered. He could hear screams from the high ground, he could hear hooves on the slope, but none sounded close to the little low bridge. He shuddered, realizing the magnitude of the disaster. His army was gone, his great hopes were nothing, the Christmas feast would not be in London and Scotland lay open to its enemies. He peered northwards. A group of clansmen splashed through the stream and suddenly six English horsemen appeared and drove their destriers off the high bank and the big swords hacked down and there was blood swirling downstream to run around the King's mailed feet and he shrank back into the shadows as the men-at-arms spurred westwards to find more fugitives. Horses clattered over the bridge and the four Scotsmen said nothing, dared not even look at each other until the sound of the hooves had faded. A trumpet was calling from the ridge and its note was hateful: triumphant and scornful. The King closed his eyes because he feared he would shed tears.

'You must see a physician, sir,' a man said and the King opened his eyes to see it was one of his servants who had spoken.

'This can't be cured,' the King said, meaning Scotland.

'The cheek will mend, sir,' the servant said reassuringly.

The King stared at his retainer as though the man had spoken in some strange foreign tongue and then, terribly and suddenly, his badly wounded cheek began to hurt. There had been no pain all day, but now it was agony and the King felt tears well from his eyes. Not from pain, but shame, and then, as he tried to blink the tears away there were shouts, falling shadows and the splash of boots as men jumped from the bridge. The attackers had swords and spears and they plunged under the bridge's arch like otter-hunters come to the kill and the King roared his defiance and leaped at the man who was in front and his rage was such that he forgot to draw his sword and instead punched the man with his armoured fist and he felt the Englishman's teeth crunch under the blow, saw the blood spurt and he drove the man down into the stream, hammering him, and then he could not move because other men were pinioning him. The man beneath him, half drowned with broken teeth and bloodied lips, began to laugh.

For he had taken a prisoner. And he would be rich.

He had captured the King.

PART TWO

England and Normandy, 1346–7

The Winter Siege

It was dark in the cathedral. So dark that the bright colours painted on the pillars and walls had faded into blackness. The only light came from the candles on the side altars and from beyond the rood screen where flames shivered in the choir and black-robed monks chanted. Their voices wove a spell in the dark, twining and falling, surging and rising, a sound that would have brought tears to Thomas's eyes if he had possessed any tears left to shed. *'Libera me, Domine, de morte aeterna,'* the monks intoned as the candle smoke twisted up to the cathedral's roof. Deliver me, Lord, from everlasting death, and on the flagstones of the choir lay the coffin in which Brother Hugh Collimore lay undelivered, his hands crossed on his tunic, his eyes closed and, unknown to the prior, a pagan coin placed beneath his tongue by one of the other monks who feared the devil would take Collimore's soul if the ferryman who carried the souls of the departed across the river of the afterworld was not paid.

'Requiem aeternam dona eis, Domine,' the monks chanted, requesting the Lord to give Brother Collimore eternal rest, and in the city beneath the cathedral, in the small houses that clung to the side of the rock, there was weeping for so many Durham men had been killed

in the battle, but the weeping was as nothing to the tears that would be shed when the news of the disaster returned to Scotland. The King was taken prisoner, and so was Sir William Douglas and the Earls of Fife and of Menteith and of Wigtown, and the Earl of Moray was dead as was the Constable of Scotland and the King's Marshal and the King's Chamberlain, all of them butchered, their bodies stripped naked and mocked by their enemies, and with them were hundreds of their countrymen, their white flesh laced bloody and food now for foxes and wolves and dogs and ravens. The gorestained Scottish standards were on the altar of Durham's cathedral and the remnants of David's great army were fleeing through the night and on their heels were the vengeful English going to ravage and plunder the lowlands, to take back what had been stolen and then to steal some more. '*Et lux perpetua luceat eis,*' the monks chanted, praying that eternal light would shine upon the dead monk, while on the ridge the other dead lay beneath the dark where the white owls shrieked.

'You must confide in me,' the prior hissed at Thomas at the back of the cathedral. Small candles flickered on the scores of side altars where priests, many of them refugees from nearby villages sacked by the Scots, said Masses for the dead. The Latin of those rural priests was often execrable, a source of amusement to the cathedral's own clergy and to the prior who sat beside Thomas on a stone ledge. 'I am your superior in God,' the prior insisted, but still Thomas stayed silent and the prior became angry. 'The King has commanded you! The bishop's letter says so! So tell me what you seek.'

'I want my woman back,' Thomas said, and he was glad it was dark in the cathedral for his eyes were red from crying. Eleanor was dead and Father Hobbe was dead and Brother Collimore was dead, all of them knifed and no one knew by whom, though one of the monks spoke of a dark man, a servant who had come with the foreign priest, and Thomas was remembering the messenger he had seen in the dawn, and Eleanor had been alive then and they had not quarrelled and now she was dead and it was his fault. His fault. The sorrow came to him, overwhelmed him and he howled his misery at the cathedral's nave.

'Be quiet!' said the prior, shocked at the noise.

'I loved her!'

'There are other women, hundreds of them.' Disgusted, he made the sign of the cross. 'What did the King send you to find? I order you to tell me.'

'She was pregnant,' Thomas said, gazing up into the roof, 'and I was going to marry her.' His soul felt as empty and dark as the space above him.

'I order you to tell me!' the prior repeated. 'In the name of God, I order you!'

'If the King wishes you to know what I seek,' Thomas spoke in French though the prior had been using English, 'then the King will be pleased to tell you.'

The prior stared angrily towards the rood screen. The French language, tongue of aristocrats, had silenced him, making him wonder who this archer was. Two men-at-arms, their mail clinking slightly, walked across the flagstones on their way to thank St Cuthbert for their survival. Most of the English army was far to the north, resting through the dark hours before resuming their pursuit of the beaten enemy, but some knights and men-at-arms had come to the city where they guarded the valuable prisoners who had been placed in the bishop's residence in the castle. Perhaps, the prior thought, the treasure that Thomas of Hookton sought was no longer important; after all, a king had been captured along with half the earls of Scotland and their ransoms would wring that wretched country dry, yet he could not rid himself of the word *thesaurus*. A treasure, and the Church was ever in need of money. He stood. 'You forget,' he said coldly, 'that you are my guest.'

'I do not forget,' Thomas said. He had been given space in the monks' guest quarters, or rather in their stables for there were greater men who needed the warmer rooms. 'I do not forget,' he said again, tiredly.

The prior now gazed up into the roof's high darkness. 'Perhaps,' he suggested, 'you know more of Brother Collimore's murder than you pretend?' Thomas did not answer; the prior's words were nonsense and the prior knew it, for he and Thomas had both been on the battlefield when the old monk had been killed, and Thomas's grief over Eleanor's murder was heartfelt, but the prior was angry and frustrated and he spoke unthinkingly. Hopes of treasure did that to a man. 'You will stay in Durham,' the prior commanded, 'until I give you permission to leave. I have given instructions that your horse is to be kept in my stables. You understand me?'

'I understand you,' Thomas said tiredly, then he watched the prior walk away. More men-at-arms were entering the cathedral, their heavy swords clattering against pillars and tombs. In the shadows, behind one of the side altars, the Scarecrow, Beggar and Dickon watched Thomas. They had been shadowing him since the battle's end. Sir Geoffrey was wearing a fine coat of mail now, which he had taken from a dead Scotsman, and he had debated whether to join the pursuit, but instead had sent a sergeant and a half-dozen men with orders to take whatever they could when the pillage of Scotland began. Sir Geoffrey himself was gambling that Thomas's treasure, because it had interested a king, would be worthy of his own interest and so he had decided to follow the archer.

Thomas, oblivious of the Scarecrow's gaze, bent forward, eyes tight shut, thinking he would never be whole again. His back and arm muscles burned from a day of drawing a bow and the fingers of his right hand were scraped raw by the cord. If he closed his eyes he saw nothing but Scotsmen coming towards him and the bow making a dark line down memory's picture and the white of the arrows' feathers dwindling in their flight, and then that picture would vanish and he would see Eleanor writhing under the knife that had tortured her. They had made her speak. Yet what did she know? That Thomas had doubted the Grail, that he was a reluctant searcher, that he only wanted to be a leader of archers, and that he had let his woman and his friend go to their deaths.

A hand touched the back of his head and Thomas almost hurled himself aside in the expectation of something worse, a blade, perhaps, but then a voice spoke and it was Lord Outhwaite. 'Come outside, young man,' he ordered Thomas, 'somewhere that the Scarecrow can't overhear us.' He said that loudly and in English, then softened his tone and used French. 'I've been looking for you.' He touched Thomas's arm, encouraging him. 'I heard about your girl and I was sorry. She was a pretty thing.'

'She was, my lord.'

'Her voice suggested she was well born,' Lord Outhwaite said, 'so her family will doubtless help you exact revenge?'

'Her father is titled, my lord, but she was his bastard.'

'Ah!' Lord Outhwaite stumped along, helping his limping gait with the spear he had carried for most of the day. 'Then he probably won't help, will he? But you can do it on your own. You seem capable enough.' His lordship had taken Thomas into a cold, fresh night. A high moon flirted with silver-edged clouds while on the western ridge great fires burned to plume a veil of red-touched smoke above the city. The fires lit the battlefield for the men and women of Durham who searched the dead for plunder and knifed the Scottish wounded to make them dead so they could also be plundered. 'I'm too old to join a pursuit,' Lord Outhwaite said, staring at the distant fires, 'too old and too stiff in the joints. It's a young man's hunt, and they'll pursue them all the way to Edinburgh. Have you ever seen Edinburgh Castle?'

'No, my lord.' Thomas spoke dully, not caring if he ever saw Edinburgh or its castle.

'Oh, it's fine! Very fine!' Lord Outhwaite said enthusiastically. 'Sir William Douglas captured it from us. He smuggled men past the gate inside barrels. Great big barrels. A clever man, eh? And now he's my prisoner.' Lord Outhwaite peered at the castle as though he expected to see Sir William Douglas and the other highborn Scottish captives shinning down from the battlements. Two torches in slanting metal cressets lit the entrance where a dozen men-at-arms stood guard. 'A rogue, our William, a rogue. Why is the Scarecrow following you?'

'I've no idea, my lord.'

'I think you do.' His lordship rested against a pile of stone. The area by the cathedral was heaped with stone and timber for the builders were repairing one of the great towers. 'He knows you seek a treasure so he now seeks it too.'

Thomas paid attention to that, looking sharply at his lordship, then looking back at the cathedral. Sir Geoffrey and his two men had come to the door, but they evidently dared not venture any closer for fear of Lord Outhwaite's displeasure. 'How can he know?' Thomas asked.

'How can he not know?' Lord Outhwaite asked. 'The monks know about it, and that's as good as asking a herald to announce it. Monks gossip like market wives! So the Scarecrow knows you might be the source of great wealth and he wants it. What is this treasure?'

'Just treasure, my lord, though I doubt it has great intrinsic worth.'

Lord Outhwaite smiled. He said nothing for a while, but just stared across the dark gulf above the river. 'You told me, did you not,' he said finally, 'that the King sent you in the company of a household knight and a chaplain from the royal household?'

'Yes, my lord.'

'And they fell ill in London?'

'They did.'

'A sickly place. I was there twice, and twice is more than enough! Noxious! My pigs live in cleaner conditions! But a royal chaplain, eh? No doubt a clever fellow, not a country priest, eh? Not some ignorant peasant tricked out with a phrase or two of Latin, but a rising man, a fellow who'll be a bishop before long if

169

he survives his fever. Now why would the King send such a man?'

'You must ask him, my lord.'

'A royal chaplain, no less,' Lord Outhwaite went on as though Thomas had not spoken, then he fell silent. A scatter of stars showed between the clouds and he gazed up at them, then sighed. 'Once,' he said, 'a long time ago, I saw a crystal vial of our Lord's blood. It was in Flanders and it liquefied in answer to prayer! There's another vial in Gloucestershire, I'm told, but I've not seen that one. I did once stroke the beard of St Jerome in Nantes; I've held a hair from the tail of Balaam's ass; I've kissed a feather from the wing of St Gabriel and brandished the very jawbone with which Samson slew so many Philistines! I have seen a sandal of St Paul, a fingernail from Mary Magdalene and six fragments of the true cross, one of them stained by the very same holy blood that I saw in Flanders. I have glimpsed the bones of the fishes with which our Lord fed the five thousand, I have felt the sharpness of one of the arrow heads that felled St Sebastian and smelt a leaf from the apple tree of the Garden of Eden. In my own chapel, young man, I have a knuckle bone of St Thomas and a hinge from the box in which the frankincense was given to the Christ child. That hinge cost me a great deal of money, a great deal. So tell me, Thomas, what relic is more precious than all those I have seen and all those I hope to see in the great churches of Christendom?'

Thomas stared at the fires on the ridge where so many dead lay. Was Eleanor in heaven already? Or was she doomed to spend thousands of years in purgatory? That thought reminded him that he had to pay for Masses to be said for her soul.

'You stay silent,' Lord Outhwaite observed. 'But tell me, young man, do you think I really possess a hinge from the Christ child's toy box of frankincense?'

'I wouldn't know, my lord.'

'I sometimes doubt it,' Lord Outhwaite said genially, 'but my wife believes! And that's what matters: belief. If you believe a thing possesses God's power then it will work its power for you.' He paused, his great shaggy head raised to the darkness as if he smelt for enemies. 'I think you search for a thing of God's power, a great thing, and I believe that the devil is trying to stop you. Satan himself is stirring his creatures to thwart you.' Lord Outhwaite turned an anxious face on Thomas. 'This strange priest and his dark servant are the devil's minions and so is Sir Geoffrey! He is an imp of Satan if ever there was one.' He threw a glance towards the cathedral's porch where the Scarecrow and his two henchmen had retreated into the shadows as a procession of cowled monks came into the night. 'Satan is working mischief,' Lord Outhwaite said, 'and you must fight it. Do you have sufficient funds?'

After the talk of the devil the commonplace question about funds surprised Thomas. 'Do I have funds, my lord?'

'If the devil fights you, young man, then I would help you and few things in this world are more helpful than money. You have a search to make, you have journeys to finish and you will need funds. So, do you have enough?'

'No, my lord,' Thomas said.

'Then permit me to help you.' Lord Outhwaite placed a bag of coins on the pile of stones. 'And perhaps you would take a companion on your search?'

'A companion?' Thomas asked, still bemused.

'Not me! Not me! I'm much too old.' Lord Outhwaite chuckled. 'No, but I confess I am fond of Willie Douglas. The priest who I think killed your woman also killed Douglas's nephew, and Douglas wants revenge. He asks, no, he begs that the dead man's brother be permitted to travel with you.'

'He's a prisoner, surely?'

'I suppose he is, but young Robbie's hardly worth ransoming. I suppose I might fetch a few pounds for him, but nothing like the fortune I intend to exact for his uncle. No, I'd rather Robbie travelled with you. He wants to find the priest and his servant and I think he could help you.' Lord Outhwaite paused and when Thomas did not answer, he pressed his request. 'He's a good young man, Robbie. I know him, I like him, and he's capable. A good soldier too, I'm told.'

Thomas shrugged. At this moment he did not care if half Scotland travelled with him. 'He can come with me, my lord,' he said, 'if I'm allowed to go anywhere.'

'What do you mean? Allowed?'

'I'm not permitted to travel.' Thomas sounded bitter. 'The prior has forbidden me to leave the city and he's taken my horse.' Thomas had found the horse, brought into Durham by Father Hobbe, tied at the monastery's gate.

Lord Outhwaite laughed. 'And you will obey the prior?'

'I can't afford to lose a good horse, my lord,' Thomas said.

'I have horses,' Lord Outhwaite said dismissively, 'including two good Scottish horses that I took today, and at dawn tomorrow the Archbishop's messengers

172

will ride south to take news of this day to London and three of my men will accompany them. I suggest you and Robbie go with them. That will get the two of you safe to London and after that? Where will you go after that?'

'I'm going home, my lord,' Thomas said, 'to Hookton, to the village where my father lived.'

'And will that murderous priest expect you to go there?'

'I can't say.'

'He will search for you. Doubtless he considered waiting for you here, but that was too dangerous. Yet he'll want your knowledge, Thomas, and he'll torment you to find it. Sir Geoffrey will do the same. That wretched Scarecrow will do anything for money, but I suspect the priest is the more dangerous.'

'So I keep my eyes open and my arrows sharp?'

'I would be cleverer than that,' Lord Outhwaite said. 'I have always found that if a man is hunting you then it's best that he finds you in a place of your own choosing. Don't be ambushed, but be ready to ambush him.'

Thomas accepted the wisdom of the advice, but sounded dubious all the same. 'And how will they know where I go?'

'Because I will tell them,' Lord Outhwaite said, 'or rather, when the prior complains that you have disobeyed him by leaving the city, I shall tell him and his monks will then inform anyone whose ears they can reach. Monks are garrulous creatures. So where would you like to face your enemies, young man? At your home?'

'No, my lord,' Thomas said hastily, then thought for a few heartbeats. 'At La Roche-Derrien,' he went on.

'In Brittany?' Lord Outhwaite sounded surprised. 'Is what you seek in Brittany?'

'I don't know where it is, my lord, but I have friends in Brittany.'

'Ah, and I trust you will also see me as a friend.' He pushed the bag of coins towards Thomas. 'Take it.'

'I shall repay you, my lord.'

'You will repay me,' his lordship said, standing, 'by bringing me the treasure and letting me touch it just once before it goes to the King.' He glanced at the cathedral where Sir Geoffrey lurked. 'I think you had better sleep in the castle tonight. I have men there who can keep that wretched Scarecrow at bay. Come.'

Sir Geoffrey Carr watched the two men go. He could not attack Thomas while Lord Outhwaite was with him, for Lord Outhwaite was too powerful; but power, the Scarecrow knew, came from money and it seemed there was treasure adrift in the world, treasure that interested the King and now interested Lord Outhwaite too.

So the Scarecrow, come hell or the devil to oppose him, intended to find it first.

Thomas was not going to La Roche-Derrien. He had lied, naming the town because he knew it and because he did not mind if his pursuers went there, but he planned to be elsewhere. He would go to Hookton to see if his father had hidden the Grail there and afterwards, for he did not expect to find it, he would go to France for it was there that the English army laid siege to Calais and it was there that his friends were, and there that an archer could find proper employment. Will Skeat's men were in the siege lines and Will's archers had wanted Thomas to be their leader and he knew he could do the job. He could lead his own band of men, be as feared as Will Skeat was feared. He thought about it as he rode southwards, though he did not think consistently or well. He was too obsessed with the deaths of Eleanor and Father Hobbe, and torturing himself with the memory of his last look back at Eleanor and his remembrance of that glance meant that he saw the country through which he rode distorted by tears.

Thomas was supposed to ride south with the men carrying the news of the English victory to London, but he got no further than York. He was supposed to leave York at dawn, but Robbie Douglas had vanished. The Scotsman's horse was still in the Archbishop's stables and his baggage was where he had dropped it in the yard, but Robbie was gone. For a moment Thomas was tempted to leave the Scot behind, but some vague sense of resented duty made him stay. Or perhaps it was that he did not much care for the company of the men-at-arms who rode with their triumphant news and so he let them go and went to look for his companion.

He found the Scot gaping up at the gilded bosses of the Minster's ceiling. 'We're supposed to be riding south,' Thomas said.

'Aye,' Robbie answered curtly, otherwise ignoring Thomas.

Thomas waited. After a short while: 'I said that we're supposed to be riding south.'

'So we are,' Robbie agreed, 'and I'm not stopping you.' He waved a magnanimous arm. 'Ride on!'

'You're giving up the hunt for de Taillebourg?' Thomas asked. He had learned the priest's name from Robbie.

'No.' Robbie still had his head back as he stared at the magnificence of the transept's ceiling. 'I'll find him and then I'll gralloch the bastard.'

Thomas did not know what gralloch meant, but decided the word was bad news for de Taillebourg. 'So why the hell are you here?'

Robbie frowned. He had a shock of curling brown hair and a snub face that, at first glance, made him look boyish, though a second look would detect the strength in his jawline and the hardness of his eyes. He at last turned those eyes on Thomas. 'What I can't stand,' he said, 'are those damned laddies! Those bastards!'

It took a couple of heartbeats before Thomas realized he meant the men-at-arms who had been their companions on the ride from Durham to York, the men who were now two hours south on the road to London. 'What was wrong with them?'

'Did you hear them last night? Did you?' Robbie's indignation flared, attracting the attention of two men who were on a high trestle where they were painting the feeding of the five thousand on the nave's wall. 'And the night before?' Robbie went on.

'They got drunk,' Thomas said, 'but so did we.'

'Telling how they fought the battle!' Robbie said. 'And to hear the bastards you'd think we ran away!'

'You did,' Thomas said.

Robbie had not heard him. 'You'd think we didn't fight at all! Boasting, they were, and we nearly won. You hear that?' He poked an aggressive finger into Thomas's chest. 'We damn nearly won, and those bastards made us sound like cowards!'

'You lost,' Thomas said.

Robbie stared at Thomas as though he could not

believe his ears. 'We drove you back halfway to bloody London! Had you running, we did! Pissing in your breeks! We damn nearly won, we did, and those bastards are gloating. Just gloating! I wanted to murder the pack of them!' A score of folk were listening. Two pilgrims, making their way on their knees to the shrine behind the high altar, were staring open-mouthed at Robbie. A priest was frowning nervously, while a child sucked its thumb and gazed aghast at the shock-headed man who was shouting so loudly. 'You hear me?' Robbie yelled. 'We damn nearly won!'

Thomas walked away.

'Where are you off to?' Robbie demanded.

'South,' Thomas said. He understood Robbie's embarrassment. The messengers, carrying news of the battle, could not resist embellishing the story of the fight when they were entertained in castle or monastery and so a hard-fought, savage piece of carnage had become an easy victory. No wonder Robbie was offended, but Thomas had small sympathy. He turned and pointed at the Scotsman. 'You should have stayed at home.'

Robbie spat in disgust, then became aware of his audience. 'Had you running,' he said hotly, then leaped over to catch up with Thomas. He grinned and there was a sudden and appealing charm in his face. 'I didn't mean to shout at you,' he said, 'I was just angry.'

'Me too,' Thomas said, but his anger was at himself and it was mingled with guilt and grief that did not lessen as the two rode south. They took to the road in mornings heavy with dew, rode through autumn mists, hunched under the lash of rain, and for almost every step of the journey Thomas thought of Eleanor. Lord

Outhwaite had promised to bury her and have Masses said for her soul and Thomas sometimes wished he was sharing her grave.

'So why is de Taillebourg chasing you?' Robbie asked on the day they rode away from York. They spoke in English for, though Robbie was from the noble house of Douglas, he spoke no French.

For a time Thomas said nothing, and just when Robbie thought he would not answer at all he gave a snort of derision. 'Because,' he said, 'the bastard believes that my father possessed the Grail.'

'The Grail!' Robbie crossed himself. 'I heard it was in Scotland.'

'In Scotland?' Thomas asked, astonished. 'I know Genoa claims to have it, but Scotland?'

'And why not?' Robbie bristled. 'Mind you,' he relented, 'I've heard there's one in Spain, too.'

'Spain?'

'And if the Spanish have one,' Robbie said, 'then the French will have to have one as well, and for all I know the Portuguese too.' He shrugged, then looked back to Thomas. 'So did your father have another?'

Thomas did not know what to answer. His father had been wayward, mad, brilliant, difficult and tortured. He had been a great sinner and, for all that, he might well have been a saint as well. Father Ralph had laughed at the wider reaches of superstition, he had mocked the pig bones sold by pardoners as relics of the saints, yet he had hung an old, blackened and bent spear in his church's rafters and claimed it was the lance of St George. He had never mentioned the Grail to Thomas, but since his death Thomas had learned that the history of his family was entwined with the Grail.

In the end he elected to tell Robbie the truth. 'I don't know,' he said, 'I simply don't know.'

Robbie ducked under a branch that grew low across the road. 'Are you telling me this is the real Grail?'

'If it exists,' Thomas said and he wondered again if it did. He supposed it was possible, but wished it was not. Yet he had been charged with the duty of finding out and so he would seek his father's one friend and he would ask that man about the Grail and when he received the expected answer he would go back to France and join Skeat's archers. Will Skeat himself, his one-time commander and friend, was stranded in Caen, and Thomas had no knowledge whether Will still lived or, if he did, whether he could speak or understand or even walk. He could find out by sending a letter to Sir Guillaume d'Evecque, Eleanor's father, and Will could be given safe passage in return for the release of some minor French nobleman. Thomas would repay Lord Outhwaite with money plundered from the enemy and then, he told himself, he would find his consolation in the practice of his skill, in archery, in the killing of the King's enemies. Perhaps de Taillebourg would come and find him and Thomas would kill him like he would put down a rat. As for Robbie? Thomas had decided he liked the Scotsman, but he did not care whether he stayed or went.

Robbie only understood that de Taillebourg would seek Thomas and so he would stay at the archer's side until he could kill the Dominican. He had no other ambition, just to avenge his brother: that was a family duty. 'You touch a Douglas,' he told Thomas, 'and we'll fillet you. We'll skin you alive. It's a blood feud, see?'

'Even if the killer is the priest?'

'It's either him or his servant,' Robbie said, 'and the servant obeys the master: either way the priest's responsible, so he dies. I'll slit his bloody throat.' He rode for a while in silence, then grinned. 'And then I'll go to hell, but at least there'll be plenty of Douglases keeping the devil company.' He laughed.

It took ten days to reach London and, once there, Robbie pretended to be unimpressed, as though Scotland had cities of this size in every other valley, but after a while he dropped the pretence and just stared in awe at the great buildings, crowded streets and serried market stalls. Thomas used Lord Outhwaite's coins so they could lodge in a tavern just outside the city walls beside the horse pond in Smithfield and close to the green where more than three hundred traders had their stalls. 'And it's not even market day?' Robbie exclaimed, then snatched at Thomas's sleeve. 'Look!' A juggler was spinning half a dozen balls in the air – that was nothing unusual for any county fair would show the same – but this man was standing on two swords, using them as stilts, with his bare feet poised on the swords' points. 'How does he do it?' Robbie asked. 'And look!' A dancing bear was shuffling to the tune of a flute just beneath the gibbet where two bodies hung. This was the place where London's felons were brought to be sent on their swift way to hell. Both corpses were encased in chains to hold the rotting flesh to their bones and the stench of the decaying corpses mingled with the smell of smoke and the reek of the frightened cattle who were bought and sold on the green, which stretched between London's wall and the Priory of St Bartholomew where Thomas paid a priest to say Masses for the souls of Eleanor and Father Hobbe.

Thomas, pretending to Robbie that he was far more familiar with London than was the truth, had chosen the tavern in Smithfield for no other reason than its sign was two crossed arrows. This was only his second visit to the city and he was as impressed, confused, dazzled and surprised as Robbie. They wandered the streets, gaping at churches and noblemen's houses, and Thomas used Lord Outhwaite's money to buy himself some new boots, calfskin leggings, an oxhide coat and a fine woollen cloak. He was tempted by a sleek French razor in an ivory case, but, not knowing the razor's value, feared he was being cheated; he reckoned he could steal himself a razor from a Frenchman's corpse when he reached Calais. Instead he paid a barber to shave him and then, dressed in his new finery, spent the cost of the unbought razor on one of the tavern's women and afterwards lay with tears in his eyes because he was thinking of Eleanor.

'Is there a reason we're in London?' Robbie asked him that night.

Thomas drained his ale and beckoned the girl to bring more. 'It's on our way to Dorset.'

'That's as good a reason as any.'

London was not really on the way from Durham to Dorchester, but the roads to the capital were so much better than those that wandered across the country and so it was quicker to travel through the great city. However, after three days, Thomas knew they must move on and so he and Robbie rode westwards. They skirted Westminster and Thomas thought for an idle heartbeat of visiting John Pryke, the royal chaplain sent to accompany him to Durham who had fallen ill in London and now either lived or died in the abbey's hospital, but

Thomas had no stomach to talk of the Grail and so he rode on.

The air became cleaner as they went deeper into the country. It was not reckoned safe to travel these roads, but Thomas's face was so grim that other travellers reckoned he was the danger rather than the prey. He was unshaven and he dressed, as he always had, in black, and the misery of the last days had put deep lines on his thin face. With Robbie's mass of unkempt hair, the two of them looked like any other vagabonds who wandered the roads, except these two were fearsomely armed. Thomas carried his sword, bow and arrow bag, while Robbie had his uncle's sword with the scrap of St Andrew's hair encased in its hilt. Sir William had reckoned he would have small use for the sword in the next few years while his family attempted to find the vast ransom, and so he had lent it to Robbie with the encouragement to use it well.

'You think de Taillebourg will be in Dorset?' Robbie asked Thomas as they rode through a stinging rain shower.

'I doubt it.'

'So why are we going?'

'Because he may go there eventually,' Thomas said, 'him and his damn servant.' He knew nothing about the servant except what Robbie had told him: that the man was fastidious, elegant, dark in looks and mysterious, but Robbie had never heard his name. Thomas, finding it hard to believe that a priest would have killed Eleanor, had persuaded himself that the servant was the killer and so planned to make the man suffer in agony.

It was late afternoon when they ducked under the

arch of Dorchester's east gate. A guard there, alarmed by their weapons, challenged them, but backed down when Thomas answered in French. It suggested he was an aristocrat and the guard sullenly let the two horsemen pass, then watched as they climbed East Street past All Saints' church and the county jail. The houses grew more prosperous as they neared the town's centre and, close to St Peter's church, the wool-merchants' homes might not have been out of place in London. Thomas could smell the shambles behind the houses where the butchers worked their trade, then he led Robbie into Cornhill, past the shop of the pewterer who had a stammer and a wall eye, then past the blacksmith where he had once bought some arrow heads. He knew most of these folk. The Dogman, a legless beggar who had come by his nickname because he lapped water from the River Cerne like a dog, was heaving down South Street on the wooden bricks strapped to his hands. Dick Adyn, brother of the town's jailer, was driving three sheep up the hill and paused to deliver a genial insult to Willie Palmer who was closing up his hosiery shop. A young priest hurried into an alley with a book wrapped in his arms and averted his eyes from a woman squatting in the gutter. A gust of wind blew woodsmoke low into the street. Dorcas Galton, brown hair drawn up into a bun, shook a rug out of an upstairs window and laughed aloud at something Dick Adyn said. They all spoke in the local accent, soft and broad and buzzing like Thomas's own, and he almost curbed the horse to speak with them, but Dick Adyn glanced at him and then looked swiftly away and Dorcas slammed the window shut. Robbie looked formidable, but Thomas's gaunt looks were even more frightening and none of the townsfolk recognized him as the bastard son of Hookton's last priest. They would know him if he introduced himself, but war had changed Thomas. It had given him a hardness that repelled strangers. He had left Dorset a boy, but come back as one of Edward of England's prized killers and when he left the town by the south gate a constable gave both him and Robbie good riddance and told them to stay away. 'Be lucky the pair of you ain't in jail!' the man called, emboldened by his municipal coat of mail and ancient spear. Thomas stopped his horse, turned in the saddle and just stared at the man who suddenly found reason to duck back into the alley beside the gate. Thomas spat and rode on.

'Your home town?' Robbie asked caustically.

'Not now,' Thomas said and he wondered where home was these days, and for some odd reason La Roche-Derrien came unbidden to his thoughts and he found himself remembering Jeanette Chenier in her great house beside the River Jaudy, and that recollection of an old love made him feel guilty yet again for Eleanor. 'Where's your home town?' he asked Robbie rather than dwell on memories.

'I grew up close to Langholm.'

'Where's that?'

'On the River Esk,' Robbie said, 'not far north of the border. It's a hard country, so it is. Not like this.'

'This is a good countryside,' Thomas said mildly. He looked up at the high green walls of Maiden Castle where the devil played on All Hallow's Eve and where the corncrakes now made their harsh song. There were ripe blackberries in the hedgerows and, as the shadows lengthened, fox cubs skittering at the edge of the fields. A few miles on and the evening had almost shaded to night, but he could smell the sea now and he imagined that he could hear it, sucking and surging on the Dorset shingle. This was the ghost time of day when the souls of the dead flickered at the edges of men's sight and when good folk hurried home to their fire and to their thatch and to their bolted doors. A dog howled in one of the villages.

Thomas had thought to ride to Down Mapperley where Sir Giles Marriott, the squire of Hookton among other villages, had his hall, but it was late and he did not think it wise to arrive at the hall after dark. Besides, Thomas wanted to see Hookton before he spoke with Sir Giles and so he turned his tired horse towards the sea and led Robbie under the high dark loom of Lipp Hill. 'I killed my first men up on that hill,' he boasted.

'With the bow?'

'Four of them,' Thomas said, 'with four arrows.' That was not entirely true for he must have shot seven or eight arrows, maybe more, but he had still killed four of the raiders who had come across the Channel to pillage Hookton. And now he was deep in the twilight shadow of Hookton's sea valley and he could see the fret of breaking waves flashing white in the late dusk as he rode down beside the stream to the place where his father had preached and died.

No one lived there now. The raiders had left the village dead. The houses had been burned, the church roof had fallen and the villagers were buried in a grave-yard choked by nettles, thorn and thistles. It was four and a half years since that raiding party had landed at Hookton led by Thomas's cousin, Guy Vexille, the Count of Astarac, and by Eleanor's father, Sir Guillaume d'Evecque. Thomas had killed four of the crossbowmen and that had been the beginning of his life as an archer. He had abandoned his studies at Oxford and, until this moment, had never returned to Hookton. 'This was home,' he told Robbie.

'What happened?'

'The French happened,' Thomas said and gestured at the darkling sea. 'They sailed from Normandy.'

'Jesus.' Robbie, for some reason, was surprised. He knew that the borderlands of England and Scotland were places where buildings were burned, cattle stolen, women raped and men killed, but he had never thought it happened this far south. He slid down from his horse and walked to a heap of nettles that had been a cottage. 'There was a village here?'

'A fishing village,' Thomas said and he strode down what was once the street to where the nets had been mended and the women had smoked fish. His father's house was a heap of burned-out timbers, choked with bindweed now. The other cottages were the same, their thatch and wattle reduced to ash and soil. Only the church to the west of the stream was recognizable, its gaunt walls open to the sky. Thomas and Robbie tied their horses to hazel saplings in the graveyard, then took their baggage into the ruined church. It was already too dark to explore, yet Thomas could not sleep and so he went down to the beach and he remembered that Easter morning when the Norman ships had grounded on the shingle and the men had come shrieking in the dawn with swords and crossbows, axes and fire. They had come for the Grail. Guy Vexille believed it to be in his uncle's possession and so the Harlequin had put the village of Hookton to the sword. He had burned it, destroyed it and gone from it without the Grail.

The stream made its little noise as it twisted inside the shingle Hook on its way to meet the great sound of the sea. Thomas sat down on the Hook, swathed in his new cloak, with the great black bow beside him. The chaplain, John Pryke, had talked of the Grail in the same awed tones that Father Hobbe had used when he spoke of the relic. The Grail, Father Pryke said, was not just the cup from which Christ had drunk wine at the Last Supper, but the vessel into which Christ's dying blood had poured from the cross. 'Longinus,' Father Pryke had said in his excitable manner, 'was the centurion beneath the cross and, when the spear struck the dolorous blow, he raised the dish to catch the blood!'

How, Thomas wondered, did the cup go from the upper room where Christ had eaten his last meal into the possession of a Roman centurion? And, stranger still, how had it reached Ralph Vexille? He closed his eyes, swaying back and forwards, ashamed of his disbelief. Father Hobbe had always called him Doubting Thomas. 'You mustn't seek explanations,' Father Hobbe had said again and again, 'because the Grail is a miracle. It transcends explanations.'

'*C'est une tasse magique*,' Eleanor had added, implicitly adding her reproof to Father Hobbe's.

Thomas so wanted to believe it was a magic cup. He wanted to believe that the Grail existed just beyond human sight, behind a veil of disbelief, a thing half visible, shimmering, wonderful, poised in light and glowing like pale fire. He wanted to believe that one day it would take on substance and that from its bowl, which had held the wine and the blood of Christ, would flow peace and healing. Yet if God wanted the world to be at peace and if He wanted sickness defeated, why

187

did He hide the Grail? Father Hobbe's answer had been that mankind was not worthy to hold the cup, and Thomas wondered if that was true. Was anyone worthy? And perhaps, Thomas thought, if the Grail had any magic then it was to exaggerate the faults and virtues of those who sought it. Father Hobbe had become more saintlike in his pursuit and the strange priest and his dark servant more malevolent. It was like one of those crystal lenses that jewellers used to magnify their work, only the Grail was a crystal that magnified character. What, Thomas wondered, did it reveal of his own? He remembered his unease at the thought of marrying Eleanor, and suddenly he began to weep, to heave with sobs, to cry more than he had already cried since her murder. He rocked to and fro, his grief as deep as the sea that beat on the shingle, and it was made worse by the knowledge that he was a sinner, unshriven, his soul doomed to hell.

He missed his woman, he hated himself, he felt empty, alone and doomed, and so, in his father's dead village, he wept.

It began to rain later, a steady rain that soaked through the new cloak and chilled Thomas and Robbie to the bone. They had lit a fire that flickered feebly in the old church, hissing under the rain and giving them a small illusion of warmth. 'Are there wolves here?' Robbie asked.

'Supposed to be,' Thomas said, 'though I never saw one.'

'We have wolves in Eskdale,' Robbie said, 'and at night their eyes glow red. Like fire.'

'There are monsters in the sea here,' Thomas said. 'Their bodies wash ashore sometimes and you can find their bones in the cliffs. Sometimes, even on calm days, men wouldn't come back from fishing and you'd know the monsters had taken them.' He shivered and crossed himself.

'When my grandfather died,' Robbie said, 'the wolves circled the house and howled.'

'Is it a big house?'

Robbie seemed surprised by the question. He considered it for a moment, then nodded. 'Aye,' he said. 'My father's a laird.'

'A lord?'

'Like a lord,' Robbie said.

'He wasn't at the battle?'

'He lost a leg and an arm at Berwick. So we boys have to fight for him.' He said he was the youngest of four sons. 'Three now,' he said, crossing himself and thinking of Jamie.

They half slept, woke, shivered, and in the dawn Thomas walked back to the Hook to watch the new day seep grey along the sea's ragged edge. The rain had stopped, though a cold wind shredded the wave-tops. The grey turned a leprous white, then silvery as the gulls called over the long shingle where, at the top of the Hook's bank, he found the weathered remnants of four posts. They had not been there when he left, but beneath one of them, half buried in stones, was a yellowish scrap of skull and he guessed this was one of the crossbowmen he had killed with his tall black bow on that Easter day. Four posts, four dead men and Thomas supposed that the four heads had been placed on the poles to gaze out to sea till the gulls pecked out their eyes and flensed the flesh back to the bare skulls.

He stared into the ruined village, but could see no one. Robbie was still inside the church from which a tiny wisp of smoke drifted, but otherwise Thomas was alone with the gulls. There were not even sheep, cattle or goats on Lipp Hill. He walked back inland, his feet crunching on the shingle, then realized he still held the broken curve of skull and he hurled it into the stream where the fishing boats had been flooded to rid them of rats and then, feeling hungry, he went and took the piece of hard cheese and dark bread from the saddlebag that he had dumped beside the church door. The walls of the church, now he could see them properly in the daylight, appeared lower than he remembered, probably because local folk had come with carts and taken the stones away for barns or sties or house walls. Inside the church there was only a tangle of thorns, nettles and a few gnarled lengths of charred timber that had long been overgrown by grass. 'I was almost killed in here,' he told Robbie, and he described how the raiders had beaten on the church door as he had kicked out the horn panes of the east window and jumped down into the graveyard. He remembered how his foot had crushed the silver Mass cup as he scrambled over the altar.

Had that silver cup been the Grail? He laughed aloud at the thought. The Mass cup had been a silver goblet on which was incised the badge of the Vexilles, and that badge, cut from the crushed cup, was now pinned to Thomas's bow. It was all that was left of the old goblet, but it had not been the Grail. The Grail was much older, much more mysterious and much more frightening.

The altar was long gone, but there was a shallow clay

bowl in the nettles where it had stood. Thomas kicked the plants aside and picked up the bowl, remembering how his father would fill it with wafers before the Mass and cover it with a piece of linen cloth and then hurry it to the church, getting angry if any of the villagers did not take off their hats and bow to the sacrament as he passed. Thomas had kicked the bowl as he climbed onto the altar to escape the Frenchmen, and here it still was. He smiled ruefully, thought about keeping the bowl, but tossed it back into the nettles. Archers should travel light.

'Someone's coming,' Robbie warned him, running to fetch his uncle's sword. Thomas picked up the bow and took an arrow from his bag, and just then he heard the thump of hooves and the baying of hounds. He went to the ruins of the door and saw a dozen great deerhounds splashing through the stream with tongues lolling between their fangs; he had no time to run from them, only to flatten himself against the wall as the hounds streaked for him.

'Argos! Maera! Back off now! Mind your goddamn manners!' the horseman bellowed at his hounds, reinforcing his commands with the crack of a whip over their heads, but the beasts surrounded Thomas and leaped up at him. Yet it was not in threat: they were licking his face and wagging their tails. 'Orthos!' the huntsman snapped at one dog, then he stared hard at Thomas. He did not recognize him, but the hounds obviously knew him and that gave the huntsman pause.

'Jake,' Thomas said.

'Sweet Jesus Christ!' Jake said. 'Sweet Jesus! Look what the tide brought in. Orthos! Argos! Off and away, you bastards, off and away!' The whip cracked loud and the hounds, still excited, backed away. Jake shook his head. 'It's Thomas, isn't it?'

'How are you, Jake?'

'Older,' Jake Churchill said gruffly, then climbed down from the saddle, pushed through the hounds and greeted Thomas with an embrace. 'It was your damned father who named these dogs. He thought it was a joke. It's good to see you, boy.' Jake was grey-bearded, his face dark as a nut from the weather and his skin scarred from countless brushes with thorns. He was Sir Giles Marriott's chief huntsman and he had taught Thomas how to shoot a bow and how to stalk a deer and how to go hidden and silent through country. 'Good Christ Almighty, boy,' he said, 'but you've fair grown up. Look at the size of you!'

'Boys do grow up, Jake,' Thomas said, then gestured at Robbie. 'He's a friend.'

Jake nodded at the Scotsman, then hauled two of the hounds away from Thomas. The dogs, named for hounds from Greek and Latin myth, whined excitedly. 'And what the hell are you two doing down here?' Jake wanted to know. 'You should have come up to the hall like Christians!'

'We got here late,' Thomas explained, 'and I wanted to see the place.'

'Nothing to see here,' Jake said scornfully. 'Nothing but hares here now.'

'You're hunting hare now?'

'I don't bring ten brace of hounds to snaffle hares, boy. No, Lally Gooden's boy saw the pair of you sneaking in here last night and so Sir Giles sent me down to see what evil was brewing. We had a pair of vagabonds trying to set up home here in the spring and they had to be whipped on their way. And last week there was a pair of foreigners creeping about.'

'Foreigners?' Thomas asked, knowing that Jake could well mean nothing more than that the strangers had come from the next parish.

'A priest and his man,' Jake said, 'and if he hadn't been a priest I'd have loosed the dogs on him. I don't like foreigners, don't see no point to them. Those horses of yours looks hungry. So do the two of you. You want breakfast? Or are you going to stand there and spoil those damned hounds by patting them half to death?'

They rode back to Down Mapperley, following the hounds through the tiny village. Thomas remembered the place as big, twice the size of Hookton, and as a child he had thought it almost a town, but now he saw how small it was. Small and low, so that on horseback he towered above the thatched cottages that had seemed so palatial when he was a child. The dung-heaps beside each cottage were as high as the thatch. Sir Giles Marriott's hall, just beyond the village, was also thatched, the moss-thick roof sweeping almost to the ground. 'He'll be pleased to see you,' Jake promised.

And so Sir Giles was. He was an old man now, a widower who had once been wary of Thomas's wildness, but now greeted him like a lost son. 'You're thin, boy, too thin. Ain't good for a man to be thin. You'll have breakfast, the two of you? Pease pudding and small ale is what we've got. There was bread yesterday, but not today. When do we bake more bread, Gooden?' This was demanded of a servant.

'Today's Wednesday, sir,' the servant said reprovingly.

'Tomorrow then,' Sir Giles told Thomas. 'Bread

tomorrow, no bread today. It's bad luck to bake bread on Wednesday. It poisons you, Wednesday's bread. I must have eaten Monday's. You say you're Scottish?' This was to Robbie.

'I am, sir.'

'I thought all Scotsmen had beards,' Sir Giles said. 'There was a Scotsman in Dorchester, wasn't there Gooden? You remember him? He had a beard. He played the gittern and danced well. You must remember him.'

'He was from the Scilly Isles,' the servant said.

'That's what I just said. But he had a beard, didn't he?'

'He did, Sir Giles. A big one.'

'There you are then,' Sir Giles spooned some pease pudding into a mouth that only had two teeth left. He was fat, white-haired and red-faced and at least fifty years old. 'Can't ride a horse these days, Thomas,' he admitted. 'Ain't good for anything now except sitting about the place and watching the weather. Did Jake tell you there be foreigners scuttling about?'

'He did, sir.'

'A priest! Black and white robes like a magpie. He wanted to talk about your father and I said there was nothing to talk about. Father Ralph's dead, I said, and God rest his poor soul.'

'Did the priest ask for me, sir?' Thomas asked.

Sir Giles grinned. 'I said I hadn't seen you in years and hoped never to see you again, and then his servant asked me where he might look for you and I told him not to talk to his betters without permission. He didn't like that!' he chuckled. 'So then the magpie asked about your father and I said I hardly knew him. That was a lie, of course, but he believed me and took himself off.

Put some logs on that fire, Gooden. A man could freeze to death in his own hall if it was left to you.'

'So the priest left, sir?' Robbie asked. It seemed unlike de Taillebourg just to accept a denial and meekly go away.

'He was frightened of dogs,' Sir Giles said, still amused. 'I had some of the hounds in here and if he hadn't been dressed like a magpie I'd have let them loose, but it don't do to kill priests. There's always trouble afterwards. The devil comes and plays his games if you kill a priest. But I didn't like him and I told him I wasn't sure how long I could keep the dogs heeled. There's some ham in the kitchen. Would you like some ham, Thomas?'

'No, sir.'

'I do hate winter.' Sir Giles stared into the fire, which now blazed huge in his wide hearth. The hall had smoke blackened beams supporting the huge expanse of thatch. At one end a carved timber screen hid the kitchens while the private rooms were at the other end, though since his wife had died Sir Giles no longer used the small chambers, but lived, ate and slept beside the hall fire. 'I reckon this'll be my last winter, Thomas.'

'I hope not, sir.'

'Hope what you damned well like, but I won't last it through. Not when the ice comes. A man can't keep warm these days, Thomas. It bites into you, the cold does, bites into your marrow and I don't like it. Your father never liked it either.' He was staring at Thomas now. 'Your father always said you'd go away. Not to Oxford. He knew you didn't like that. Like whipping a destrier between the shafts, he used to say. He knew you'd run off and be a soldier. He always said you had wild blood in you.' Sir Giles smiled, remembering. 'But he also said you'd come home one day. He said you'd come back to show him what a fine fellow you'd become.'

Thomas blinked back tears. Had his father really said that? 'I came back this time,' he said, 'to ask you a question, sir. The same question, I think, that the French priest wanted to ask you.'

'Questions!' Sir Giles grumbled. 'I never did like questions. They need answers, see? Of course you want some ham! What do you mean, no? Gooden? Ask your daughter to unwrap that ham, will you?'

Sir Giles heaved himself to his feet and shuffled across the hall to a great chest of dark, polished oak. He raised the lid and, groaning with the effort of bending over, began to rummage through the clothes and boots that were jumbled inside. 'I find now, Thomas,' he went on, 'that I don't need questions. I sit in the manor court every second week and I know whether they're guilty or innocent the moment they're fetched into the hall! Mind you, we have to pretend otherwise, don't we? Now, where is it? Ah!' He found whatever he sought and brought it back to the table. 'There, Thomas, damn your question and that's your answer.' He pushed the bundle across the table.

It was a small object wrapped in ancient sacking. Thomas had an absurd premonition that this was the Grail itself and was ridiculously disappointed when he discovered the bundle contained a book. The book's front cover was a soft leather flap, four or five times larger than the pages, which could be used to wrap the volume that, when Thomas opened it, proved to be written in his father's hand. However, being by his father, nothing in it was straightforward. Thomas leafed through the pages swiftly, discovering notes written in Latin, Greek and a strange script which he thought must be Hebrew. He turned back to the first page where only three words were written and, reading them, felt his blood run cold. *'Calix meus inebrians.'*

'Is it your answer?' Sir Giles asked.

'Yes, sir.'

Sir Giles peered at the first page. 'It's Latin that, isn't it?'

'Yes, sir.'

'Thought it was. I looked, of course, but couldn't make head nor tail of it and I didn't like to ask Sir John,' – Sir John was the priest of St Peter's in Dorchester – 'or that lawyer fellow, what's his name? The one who dribbles when he gets excited. He speaks Latin, or he says he does. What does it mean?'

'"My cup makes me drunk",' Thomas said.

'"My cup makes me drunk"!' Sir Giles thought that was splendidly funny. 'Aye, your father's wits were well off the wind. A good man, a good man, but dear me! "My cup makes me drunk"!'

'It's from one of the psalms,' Thomas said, turning to the second page, which was written in the script he thought was Hebrew, though there was something odd about it. One of the recurrent symbols looked like a human eye and Thomas had never seen that in a Hebrew script before though, in all honesty, he had seen little Hebrew. 'It's from the psalm, sir,' he went on, 'that begins by saying God is our shepherd.'

'He's not my shepherd,' Sir Giles grumbled. 'I'm not some damned sheep.'

'Nor me, sir,' Robbie declared.

'I did hear' – Sir Giles looked at Robbie – 'that the King of Scotland was taken prisoner.'

'He was, sir?' Robbie asked innocently.

'Probably nonsense,' Sir Giles replied, then he began telling a long tale about meeting a bearded Scotsman in London, and Thomas ignored the story to look through the pages of his father's book. He felt a kind of strange disappointment because the book suggested that the search for the Grail was justified. He wanted someone to tell him it was nonsense, to release him from the cup's thrall, but his father had taken it seriously enough to write this book. But his father, Thomas reminded himself, had been mad.

Mary, Gooden's daughter, brought in the ham. Thomas had known Mary since they were both children playing in puddles and he smiled a greeting at her, then saw that Robbie was gazing at her as though she was an apparition from heaven. She had dark long hair and a full mouth and Thomas was sure Robbie would be discovering more than a few rivals in Down Mapperley. He waited until Mary had gone, then held up the book. 'Did my father ever talk to you about this, sir?'

'He talked of everything,' Sir Giles said. 'Talked like a woman, he did. Never stopped! I was your father's friend, Thomas, but I was never much of a man for religion. If he talked of it too much, I fell asleep. He liked that.' Sir Giles paused to cut a slice of ham. 'But your father was mad.'

'You think this is madness, sir?' Thomas held up the book again.

'Your father was mad for God, but he was no fool. I never knew a man with so much common sense and I miss it. I miss the advice.'

'Does that girl work here?' Robbie asked, gesturing at the screen behind which Mary had disappeared.

'All her life,' Sir Giles said. 'You remember Mary, Thomas?'

'I tried to drown her when we were both children,' Thomas said. He turned the pages of his father's book again though he had no time now to tease any meanings from the tangled words. 'You do know what this is, sir, don't you?'

Sir Giles paused, then nodded. 'I know, Thomas, that many men want what your father claims to have possessed.'

'So he did make that claim?'

Another pause. 'He hinted at it,' Sir Giles said heavily, 'and I don't envy you.'

'Me?'

'Because he gave me that book, Thomas, and he said that if anything happened to him I was to keep it until you were old enough and man enough to take up the task. That's what he said.' Sir Giles stared at Thomas and saw his old friend's son flinch. 'But if the two of you want to stay for a while,' he said, 'then you'd be welcome. Jake Churchill needs help. He tells me he's never seen so many fox cubs and if we don't kill some of the bastards then there'll be some rare massacres among the lambs next year.'

Thomas glanced at Robbie. Their task was to find de Taillebourg and avenge the deaths of Eleanor, Father Hobbe and Robbie's brother, but it was unlikely, he thought, that the Dominican would come back here. Robbie, however, plainly wanted to stay: Mary Gooden had seen to that. And Thomas was tired. He did not know where to seek the priest and so the chance to stay in this hall was welcome. It would be an opportunity to study the book and thus follow his father down the long, tortuous path of the Grail.

'We'll stay, sir,' Thomas said.

For a while.

It was the first time that Thomas had ever lived like a lord. Not a great lord, perhaps, not as an earl or a duke with scores of men to command, but still in privilege, ensconced in the manor – even if the manor was a thatched timber hall with a beaten earth floor – the days his to wile away as other people did life's hard work of cutting firewood, drawing water, milking cows, churning butter, pounding dough and washing clothes. Robbie was more used to it, but reckoned life was much easier in Dorset. 'Back home,' he said, 'there's always some damn English raiders coming over the hill to steal your cattle or take your grain.'

'Whereas you,' Thomas said, 'would never dream of riding south and stealing from the English.'

'Why would I even think of such a thing?' Robbie asked, grinning.

So, as winter closed down on the land, they hunted Sir Giles Marriott's acres to make the fields safe for the lambing season and to bring back venison to Sir Giles's table; they drank in the Dorchester taverns and laughed at the mummers who came for the winter fair. Thomas found old friends and told them stories of Brittany, Normandy and Picardy, some of which were true, and he won the golden arrow at the fair's archery competition and he presented it to Sir Giles who hung it in the hall and declared it the finest trophy he had ever seen. 'My son could shoot a good arrow. A very good arrow. I'd like to think he could have won this trophy himself.'

Sir Giles's only son had died of a fever and his only daughter was married to a knight who held land in Devon and Sir Giles liked neither son-in-law nor daughter. 'They'll inherit the property when I die,' he told Thomas, 'so you and Robbie may as well enjoy it now.'

Thomas persuaded himself that he was not ignoring the search for the Grail because of the hours he spent poring over his father's book. The pages were thick vellum, expensive and rare, which showed how important these notes had been to Father Ralph, but even so they made small sense to Thomas. Much of the book was stories. One told how a blind man, caressing the cup, had received his sight but then, disappointed in the Grail's appearance, lost it again. Another told how a Moorish warrior had tried to steal the Grail and been turned into a serpent for his impiety. The longest tale in the book was about Perceval, a knight of antiquity who went on crusade and discovered the Grail in Christ's tomb. This time the Latin word used to describe the grail was *crater*, meaning bowl, whereas on other pages it was *calix*, a cup, and Thomas wondered if there was any significance in the distinction. If his father had possessed the Grail, would he not have known whether it was a cup or a bowl? Or perhaps there was no real difference. Whatever, the long tale told how the bowl had sat on a shelf of Christ's tomb in plain view of all who entered the sepulchre, both Christian pilgrims and their pagan enemies, yet not till Sir Perceval entered the grotto on his knees was the Grail actually seen by anyone, for Sir Perceval was a man of righteousness and thus worthy of having his eyes opened. Sir Perceval removed the bowl, bringing it back to Christendom where he planned to build a shrine worthy of the treasure, but, the tale laconically recorded, 'he died'. Thomas's father had written beneath this abrupt conclusion: 'Sir Perceval was Count of Astarac and was known by another name. He married a Vexille.'

'Sir Perceval!' Sir Giles was impressed. 'He was a member of your family, eh? Your father never mentioned that to me. At least I don't think he did. I did sleep through a lot of his tales.'

'He usually scoffed at stories like this,' Thomas said.

'We often mock what we fear,' Sir Giles observed sententiously. Suddenly he grinned. 'Jake tells me you caught that old dog fox by the Five Marys.' The Five Marys were ancient grave mounds that the locals claimed were dug by giants and Thomas had never understood why there were six of them.

'It wasn't there,' Thomas said, 'but back of the White Nothe.'

'Back of White Nothe? Up on the cliffs?' Sir Giles stared at Thomas, then laughed. 'You were on Holgate's land! You rascals!' Sir Giles, who had always complained mightily when Thomas had poached from his land, now found this predation on a neighbour hugely amusing. 'He's an old woman, Holgate. So are you making head or tail of that book?'

'I wish I knew,' Thomas said, staring at the name Astarac. All he knew was that Astarac was a fief or county in southern France and the home of the Vexille family before they were declared rebel and heretic. He had also learned that Astarac was close to the Cathar heartlands, close enough for the contagion to catch the Vexilles, and when, a hundred years before, the French King and the true Church had burned the heretics out of the land they had also forced the Vexilles to flee. Now it seemed that the legendary Sir Perceval was a Vexille? It seemed to Thomas that the further he penetrated the mystery the greater the entanglement. 'Did my father ever talk to you of Astarac, sir?' He asked Sir Giles.

'Astarac? What's that?'

'Where his family came from.'

'No, no, he grew up in Cheshire. That's what he always said.'

But Cheshire had merely been a refuge, a place to hide from the Inquisition: was that where the Grail was now hidden? Thomas turned a page to find a long passage describing how a raiding column had tried to attack the tower of Astarac and had been repulsed by the sight of the Grail. 'It dazzled them,' Father Ralph had written, 'so that 364 of them were cut down.' Another page recorded that it was impossible for a man to tell a lie while he held his hand on the Grail, 'or else he will be stricken dead'. A barren woman would be granted the gift of children by stroking the Grail and if a man were to drink from it on Good Friday he would be vouchsafed a glimpse of 'she whom he will take to wife in heaven'. Another story related how a knight, carrying the Grail across a wilderness, was pursued by heathens and, when it seemed he must be caught, God sent a vast eagle that caught him, his horse and the precious Grail up into the sky, leaving the pagan warriors howling in frustrated rage.

One phrase was copied over and over in the pages of

the book: '*Transfer calicem istem a me*', and Thomas could feel his father's misery and frustration reaching through the repeated phrase. 'Take this cup from me,' the words meant and they were the same words Christ had spoken in the Garden of Gethsemane as he pleaded with God the Father to spare him the pain of hanging on the tree. The phrase was sometimes written in Greek, a language Thomas had studied but never mastered fully; he managed to decipher most of the Greek text, but the Hebrew remained a mystery.

Sir John, the ancient vicar of St Peter's, agreed that it was a strange kind of Hebrew. 'I've forgotten all the Hebrew I ever learned,' he told Thomas, 'but I don't remember seeing a letter like that!' He pointed to the symbol that looked like a human eye. 'Very odd, Thomas, very odd. It's almost Hebrew.' He paused a while, then said plaintively, 'If only poor Nathan was still here.'

'Nathan?'

'He was before your time, Thomas. Nathan collected leeches and sent them to London. Physicians there prized Dorset leeches, did you know that? But, of course, Nathan was a Jew and he left with the others.' The Jews had been expelled from England almost fifty years before, an event still green in the priest's memory. 'No one has ever discovered where he found his leeches,' Sir John went on, 'and I sometimes wonder if he put a curse on them.' He frowned at the book. 'This belonged to your father?'

'It did.'

'Poor Father Ralph,' Sir John said, intimating that the book must have been the product of madness. He closed the volume and carefully wrapped the soft leather cover about the pages.

There was no sign of de Taillebourg, nor any news of Thomas's friends in Normandy. He wrote a difficult letter to Sir Guillaume which told how his daughter had died and begging for any news of Will Skeat whom Sir Guillaume had taken to Caen to be treated by Mordecai, the Jewish doctor. The letter went to Southampton and from there to Guernsey and Thomas was assured it would be sent on to Normandy, but no reply had come by Christmas and Thomas assumed the letter was lost. Thomas also wrote to Lord Outhwaite, assuring his lordship that he was being assiduous in his search and recounting some of the stories from his father's book.

Lord Outhwaite sent a reply that congratulated Thomas on what he had discovered, then revealed that Sir Geoffrey Carr had left for Brittany with half a dozen men. Rumour, Lord Outhwaite reported, claimed that the Scarecrow's debts were larger than ever, 'which, perhaps, is why he has gone to Brittany'. It would not just be hope of plunder that had taken the Scarecrow to La Roche-Derrien, but the law which said a debtor was not required to make repayments while he served the King abroad. 'Will you follow the Scarecrow?' Lord Outhwaite enquired, and Thomas sent an answer saying he would be in La Roche-Derrien by the time Lord Outhwaite read these words, and then did nothing about leaving Dorset. It was Christmas, he told himself, and he had always enjoyed Christmas.

Sir Giles celebrated the twelve days of the feast in high style. He ate no meat from Advent Sunday, which was not a particular hardship for he loved eels and fish, but on Christmas Eve he ate nothing but bread, readying himself for the first feast of the season. Twelve empty hives were brought into the hall and decorated with sprigs of ivy and holly; a great candle, big enough to burn through the whole season, was placed on the high table and a vast log set to burn in the hearth, and Sir Giles's neighbours were invited to drink wine and ale, and eat beef, wild boar, venison, goose and brawn. The wassail cup, filled with mulled and spiced claret, was passed about the hall and Sir Giles, as he did every night of Christmas, wept for his dead wife and was drunkenly asleep by the time the candles burned out. On the fourth night of Christmas, Thomas and Robbie joined the hogglers as, disguised as ghosts and green men and wild men, they pranced about the parish extorting funds for the Church. They went as far as Dorchester, encroaching on two other parishes as they did, and got into a fight with the hogglers from All Saints' and they ended the night in the Dorchester jail from which they were released by an amused George Adyn who brought them a morning pot of ale and one of his wife's famous hog's puddings. The Twelfth Night feast was a boar that Robbie had speared, and after it was eaten, and when the guests were lying half drunk and satiated on the hall rushes, it began to snow. Thomas stood in the doorway and watched the flakes whirling in the light of a flickering torch.

'We must be away soon,' Robbie had come to join him.

'Away?'

'We have work to do,' the Scot said.

Thomas knew that was true, but he did not want to leave. 'I thought you were happy enough here?'

'So I am,' Robbie said, 'and Sir Giles is more generous than I deserve.'

'So?'

'It's Mary,' Robbie said. He was embarrassed and did not finish.

'Pregnant?' Thomas guessed.

Robbie crossed himself. 'It seems so.'

Thomas stared at the snow. 'If you give her enough money to make a dowry,' he said, 'she'll thrive.'

'I've only got three pounds left,' Robbie said. He had been given a purse by his uncle, Sir William, supposedly with enough money to last a year.

'That should be enough,' Thomas said. The snow whirled in a gust of wind.

'It'll leave me with nothing!' Robbie protested.

'You should have thought of that before you ploughed the field,' Thomas said, remembering how he had been in just this predicament with a girl in Hookton. He turned back to the hall where a harpist and flautist made music to the drunks. 'We should go,' he said, 'but I don't know where.'

'You said you wanted to go to Calais?'

Thomas shrugged. 'You think de Taillebourg will seek us there?'

'I think,' Robbie said, 'that once he knows you have that book he'll follow you into hell itself.'

Thomas knew Robbie was right, but the book was not proving to be of any great help. It never specifically said that Father Ralph had possessed the Grail, nor described a place where a searcher might look for it. Thomas and Robbie had been looking. They had combed the sea caves in the cliffs near Hookton where they had found driftwood, limpets and seaweed. There had been no golden cup half hidden in the shingle. So where to go now? Where to look? If Thomas went to

Calais then he could join the army, but he doubted de Taillebourg would seek him out in the heart of England's soldiery. Maybe, Thomas thought, he should go back to Brittany and he knew that it was not the Grail or the necessity to face de Taillebourg that attracted him to La Roche-Derrien, but the thought that Jeanette Chenier might have returned home. He thought of her often, thought of her black hair, of her fierce spirit and defiance, and every time he thought of her he suffered guilt because of Eleanor.

The snow did not last. It thawed and a hard rain came from the west to lash the Dorset coast. A big English ship was wrecked on the Chesil shingle and Thomas and Robbie took one of Sir Giles's wagons down to the beach and with the aid of Jake Churchill and two of his sons fought off a score of other men to rescue six packs of wool that they carried back to Down Mapperley and presented to Sir Giles who thereby made a year's income in one day.

And next morning the French priest came to Dorchester.

The news was brought by George Adyn. 'I know as you said we should be watching for foreigners,' he told Thomas, 'and this one be real foreign. Dressed like a priest, he is, but who knows? Looks like a vagabond, he does. You say the word' – he winked at Thomas – 'and we'll give the bugger a proper whipping and send him on up to Shaftesbury.'

'What will they do with him there?' Robbie asked.

'Give him another whipping and send him back,' George said.

'Is he a Dominican?' Thomas asked.

'How would I know? He's talking gibberish, he is. He don't talk proper, not like a Christian.'

'What colour is his gown?'

'Black, of course.'

'I'll come and talk to him,' Thomas said.

'He only jabbers away, he does. Your honour!' This was in greeting to Sir Giles, and Thomas then had to wait while the two men discussed the health of various cousins and nephews and other relatives, and it was close to midday by the time he and Robbie rode into Dorchester and Thomas thought, for the thousandth time, what a good town this was and how it would be a pleasure to live here.

The priest was brought out into the small jail yard. It was a fine day. Two blackbirds hopped along the top wall and an aconite was blooming in the yard corner. The priest proved to be a young man, very short, with a squashed nose, protuberant eyes and bristling black hair. He wore a gown so shabby, torn and stained that it was little wonder the constables had thought the man a vagrant; a misconception that made the little priest indignant. 'Is this how the English treat God's servants? Hell is too good for you English! I shall tell the bishop and he will tell the Archbishop and he will inform the Holy Father and you will all be declared anathema! You will all be excommunicated!'

'See what I mean?' George Adyn asked. 'Yaps away like a dog fox, but he don't make sense.'

'He's speaking French,' Thomas told him, then turned to the priest. 'What's your name?'

'I want to see the bishop now. Here!'

'What's your name?'

'Bring me the local priest!'

'I'll punch your bloody ears out first,' Thomas said. 'Now what's your name?'

He was called Father Pascal, and he had just endured a journey of exquisite discomfort, crossing the winter seas from Normandy, from a place south of Caen. He had travelled first to Guernsey and then on to Southampton from where he had walked, and he had done it all without any knowledge of English. It was a miracle to Thomas that Father Pascal had come this far. And it seemed even more of a miracle because Father Pascal had been sent to Hookton from Evecque, with a message for Thomas.

Sir Guillaume d'Evecque had sent him, or rather Father Pascal had volunteered to make the journey, and it was urgent for he was bringing a plea for help. Evecque was under siege. 'It is terrible!' Father Pascal said. By now, calmed and placated, he was by the fire in the Three Cocks where he was eating goose and drinking bragget, a mixture of warmed mead and dark ale. 'It is the Count of Coutances who is besieging him. The Count!'

'Why is that terrible?' Thomas enquired.

'Because the Count is his liege lord!' the priest exclaimed, and Thomas understood why Father Pascal said it was terrible. Sir Guillaume held his lands in fief to the Count and by making war on his own tenant the Count was declaring Sir Guillaume an outlaw.

'But why?' Thomas asked.

Father Pascal shrugged. 'The Count says it is because of what happened at the battle. Do you know what happened at the battle?'

'I know,' Thomas said, and because he was translating

for Robbie he had to explain anyway. The priest referred to the battle that had been fought the previous summer by the forest at Crécy. Sir Guillaume had been in the French army, but in the middle of the fight he had seen his enemy, Guy Vexille, and had turned his men-at-arms against Vexille's troops.

'The Count says that is treason,' the priest explained, 'and the King has given his blessing.'

Thomas said nothing for a while. 'How did you know I was here?' he finally asked.

'You sent a letter to Sir Guillaume.'

'I didn't think it reached him.'

'Of course it did. Last year. Before this trouble started.'

Sir Guillaume was in trouble, but his manor of Evecque, Father Pascal said, was built of stone and blessed with a moat and so far the Count of Coutances had found it impossible to break the wall or cross the moat, but the Count had scores of men while Sir Guillaume had a garrison of only nine. 'There are some women too' – Father Pascal tore at a goose leg with his teeth – 'but they don't count.'

'Does he have food?'

'Plenty, and the well is good.'

'So he can hold for a time?'

The priest shrugged. 'Maybe? Maybe not? He thinks so, but what do I know? And the Count has a machine, a . . .' He frowned, trying to find the word.

'A trebuchet?'

'No, no, a springald!' A springald was like a massive crossbow that shot a huge dart. Father Pascal stripped the last morsel off the bone. 'It is very slow and it broke once. But they mended it. It batters at the wall. Oh, and your friend is there,' he mumbled, his mouth full.

'My friend?'

'Skeat, is that the name? He's there with the doctor. He can talk now, and he walks. He is much better, yes? But he cannot recognize people, not unless they speak.'

'Unless they speak?' Thomas asked, puzzled.

'If he sees you,' the priest explained, 'he does not know you. Then you speak and he knows you.' He shrugged again. 'Strange, eh?' He drained his pot. 'So what will you do, monsieur?'

'What does Sir Guillaume want me to do?'

'He wants you close by in case he needs to escape, but he's written a letter to the King explaining what happened in the battle. I sent the letter to Paris. Sir Guillaume thinks the King may relent so he waits for an answer, but me? I think Sir Guillaume is like this goose. Plucked and cooked.'

'Did he say anything about his daughter?'

'His daughter?' Father Pascal was puzzled. 'Oh! The bastard daughter? He said you would kill whoever killed her.'

'I will, too.'

'And that he wants your help.'

'He can have it,' Thomas said, 'and we'll leave tomorrow.' He looked at Robbie. 'We're going back to war.'

'Who am I fighting for?'

Thomas grinned. 'Me.'

Thomas, Robbie and the priest left next morning. Thomas took a change of clothes, a full arrow bag, his bow, sword and mail coat and, wrapped in a piece of deerskin, his father's book that seemed like a heavy

213

piece of baggage. In truth it was lighter than a sheaf of arrows, yet the duty its possession implied weighed on Thomas's conscience. He told himself he was merely riding to help Sir Guillaume, yet he knew he was continuing the quest for his father's secret.

Two of Sir Giles's tenants rode with them to bring back the mare that Father Pascal rode and the two stallions which Sir Giles had purchased from Thomas and Robbie. 'You don't want to take them on a boat,' Sir Giles said, 'horses and boats don't mix.'

'He paid us too much,' Robbie remarked as they rode away.

'He doesn't want his son-in-law to get it,' Thomas said. 'Besides, he's a generous man. He gave Mary Gooden another three pounds as well. For her dowry. He's a lucky man.'

Something in Thomas's tone caught Robbie's attention. '"He" is? You mean she's found a husband?'

'A nice fellow. A thatcher in Tolpuddle. They'll be wed next week.'

'Next week!' Robbie sounded aggrieved that his girl was marrying. It did not matter that he was abandoning her, it still cut his pride. 'But why would he marry her?' he asked after a while. 'Or doesn't he know she's pregnant?'

'He thinks the child is his,' Thomas said, keeping a straight face, 'and well it might be, I hear.'

'Jesus!' Robbie swore when that made sense, then he turned to look back along the road and he smiled, remembering the good times. 'He's a kind man,' he said of Sir Giles.

'A lonely one,' Thomas said. Sir Giles had not wanted them to leave, but accepted they could not stay.

Robbie sniffed the air. 'There's more snow coming.'

'Never!' It was a morning of gentle sunlight. Crocus and aconite were showing in sheltered spots and the hedgerows were noisy with chaffinches and robins. But Robbie had indeed smelt snow. As the day wore on, the skies became low and grey, the wind went into the east and hit their faces with a new bite and the snow followed. They found shelter in a verderer's house in the woods, crowding in with the man, his wife, five daughters and three sons. Two cows had a byre at one end of the house and four goats were tethered at the other. Father Pascal confided to Thomas that this was very like the house in which he had grown up, but he wondered if conventions in England were the same as in the Limousin. 'Conventions?' Thomas asked.

'In our house,' Father Pascal said, blushing, 'the women pissed with the cows and the men with the goats. I would not want to do the wrong thing.'

'It's the same here,' Thomas assured him.

Father Pascal had proved a good companion. He had a fine singing voice and once they had shared their food with the verderer and his family the priest sang some French songs. Afterwards, as the snow still fell and the smoke from the fire swirled thick under the thatch, he sat and talked with Thomas. He had been the village priest at Evecque and, when the Count of Coutances attacked, he had found refuge in the manor. 'But I do not like being cooped up,' he said, and so he had offered to carry Sir Guillaume's message to England. He had escaped from Evecque, he said, by first throwing his clothes across the moat and then swimming after them. 'It was cold,' he said, 'I have never been so cold! I told myself it is better to be cold than to be in hell, but I don't know. It was terrible.'

'What does Sir Guillaume want us to do?' Thomas asked him.

'He did not say. Perhaps, if the besiegers can be discouraged . . . ?' He shrugged. 'The winter is not a good time for a siege, I think. Inside Evecque they are comfortable, they are warm, they have the harvest stored, and the besiegers? They are wet and cold. If you can make them more uncomfortable, who knows? Perhaps they will abandon the siege?'

'And you? What will you do?'

'I have no work left at Evecque,' the priest said. Sir Guillaume had been declared a traitor and his goods pronounced forfeited so his serfs had been taken off to the Count of Coutances's estates, while his tenants, pillaged and raped by the besiegers, had mostly fled. 'So perhaps I go to Paris? I cannot go to the Bishop of Caen.'

'Why not?'

'Because he has sent men to help the Count of Coutances.' Father Pascal shook his head in sad wonderment. 'The bishop was impoverished by the English in the summer,' he explained, 'so he needs money, land and goods, and he hopes to get some from Evecque. Greed is a great provoker of war.'

'Yet you're on Sir Guillaume's side?'

Father Pascal shrugged. 'He is a good man. But now? Now I must look to Paris for preferment. Or maybe Dijon. I have a cousin there.'

They struggled east for the next two days, riding across the dead heaths of the New Forest, which lay under a soft whiteness. At night the small lights of the forest villages glittered hard in the cold. Thomas feared if they would reach Normandy too late to help Sir Guillaume, but that doubt was not reason enough to abandon the effort and so they struggled on. Their last few miles to Southampton were through a melting slush of mud and snow, and Thomas wondered how they were to reach Normandy, which was an enemy province. He doubted that any shipping would go there from Southampton because any English boat going close to the Normandy coast was liable to be snapped up by pirates. He knew plenty of boats would be going to Brittany, but that was a long walk from Caen. 'We go through the islands, of course,' Father Pascal said.

They spent one night in a tavern and next morning found space on the *Ursula*, a cog bound for Guernsey and carrying barrels of salt pork, kegs of nails, barrel staves, iron ingots, pots packed in sawdust, bolts of wool, sheaves of arrows and three crates of cattle horns. It was also carrying a dozen bowmen who were travelling to the garrison of the castle which guarded the anchorage at St Peter Port. Come a bad west wind, the *Ursula*'s captain told them, and dozens of ships carrying wine from Gascony to England could be blown up-channel and St Peter Port was one of their last harbours of refuge, though the French sailors knew it too and in bad weather their ships would swarm off the island trying to pick up a prize or two. 'Does that mean they'll be waiting for us?' Thomas asked. The Isle of Wight was slipping astern and the ship was plunging into a winter-grey sea.

'Not waiting for us, they won't be, not us. They know the *Ursula*, they do,' the captain, a toothless man with a face horribly scarred from the pox, grinned, 'they do know her and they do love her.' Which meant, presumably, that he had paid his dues to the men of Cherbourg and Carteret. However, he had paid no dues to Neptune or whatever spirit governed the winter sea for, though he claimed some special foreknowledge of winds and waves and asserted that both would be calm, the *Ursula* rolled like a bell swung on a beam: up and down, pitching hard over so that the cargo slid in the hold with a noise like thunder; and the evening sky was grey as death and then sleet began to seethe on the torn water. The captain, clinging to the steering oar with a grin, said it was nothing but a little blow that should not worry any good Christian, but others in his crew either touched the crucifix nailed to the single mast or else bowed their heads to a small shrine on the afterdeck where a crude wooden image was wrapped in bright ribbons. The image was supposed to be St Ursula, the patron of ships, and Thomas said a prayer to her himself as he crouched in a small space under the foredeck, ostensibly sheltering there with the other passengers, but the overhead deck seams gaped and a mixture of rainwater and seawater continually slopped through. Three of the archers were sick and even Thomas, who had crossed the channel twice before and had been raised among fishermen and spent days aboard their small boats, was feeling ill. Robbie, who had never been to sea, looked cheerful and interested in everything that was happening aboard.

'It's these round ships,' he yelled over the noise, 'they roll!'

'You know about ships, do you?' Thomas asked.

'It seems obvious,' Robbie said.

Thomas tried to sleep. He wrapped himself in his

damp cloak, curled up and lay as still as the pitching boat would let him and, astonishingly, he did fall asleep. He woke a dozen times that night and each time he wondered where he was and when he remembered he wondered whether the night would ever end or whether he would ever be warm again.

Dawn was sickly grey and the cold bit into Thomas's bones, but the crew was altogether more cheerful for the wind had dropped and the sea was merely sullen, the long foam-streaked waves rising and falling sluggishly about a wicked group of rocks that appeared to be home for a myriad seabirds. It was the only land in sight.

The captain stumped across the deck to stand beside Thomas. 'The Casquets,' he said, nodding at the rocks. 'A lot of widows have been made on those old stones.' He made the sign of the cross, spat over the gunwales for luck and then looked up to a widening rift in the clouds. 'We're making good time,' he said, 'thanks be to God and to Ursula.' He looked askance at Thomas. 'So what takes you to the islands?'

Thomas thought of inventing some excuse, family perhaps, then thought the truth might elicit something more interesting. 'We want to go on to Normandy,' he said.

'They don't like Englishmen much in Normandy, not since our King paid them a visit last year.'

'I was there.'

'Then you'll know why they don't like us.'

Thomas knew the captain was right. The English had killed thousands in Caen, then burned farms, mills and villages in a great swathe east and north. It was a cruel way to wage war, but it could persuade the enemy to come out of his strongholds and give battle. Doubtless that was why the Count of Coutances was laying Evecque's lands waste, in hope that Sir Guillaume would be enticed out of his stone walls to defend them. Except Sir Guillaume had only nine men and could not hope to face the Count in open battle. 'We've business in Caen,' Thomas admitted, 'if we can ever reach the place.'

The captain picked at a nostril, then flicked something into the sea. 'Look for the troy frairs,' he said.

'The what?'

'*Troy Frairs*,' he said again. 'It's a boat and that's her name. It's French. She ain't big, no larger than that little tub.' He pointed to a small fishing boat, her hull tarred black, from which two men cast weighted nets into the broken sea about the Casquets. 'A man called Ugly Peter runs the *Troy Frairs*. He might carry you to Caen, or maybe to Carteret or Cherbourg. Not that I told you that.'

'Of course not,' Thomas said. He supposed the captain meant that Ugly Peter commanded a boat called *Les Trois Frères*. He stared at the fishing boat and wondered what kind of life it was to drag sustenance from this hard sea. It was easier, no doubt, to smuggle wool into Normandy and wine back to the islands.

All morning they ran southwards until at last they made landfall. A small island lay off to the east and a larger, Guernsey, to the west, and from both rose pillars of smoke from cooking fires that promised shelter and warm food, but though that promise fluttered in the sky, the wind backed and the tide turned and it took the rest of the day for the *Ursula* to beat down to the harbour where she anchored under the loom of the castle built on its rocky island. Thomas, Robbie and Father Pascal were rowed ashore and found respite from the cold wind in a tavern with a fire burning in a wide hearth beside which they ate fish stew and black bread washed down with a watery ale. They slept on straw-filled sacks that were home to lice.

It was four days before Ugly Peter, whose real name was Pierre Savon, put into the harbour, and another two before he was ready to leave again with a cargo of wool on which no duty would be paid. He was happy to take passengers, though only at a price which left Robbie and Thomas feeling robbed. Father Pascal was carried free on the grounds that he was a Norman and a priest which meant, according to Pierre the Ugly, that God loved him twice over and so was unlikely to sink *Les Trois Frères* so long as Father Pascal was aboard.

God must have loved the priest for he sent a gentle west wind, clear skies and calm seas so that *Les Trois Frères* seemed to fly her way to the River Orne. They went up to Caen on the tide, arriving in the morning, and once they were ashore Father Pascal offered Thomas and Robbie a blessing, then hitched up his shabby robe and began walking east to Paris. Thomas and Robbie, carrying heavy bundles of mail, weapons, arrows and spare clothing, went south through the city.

Caen looked no better than when Thomas had left it the previous year after it had been laid waste by English archers who, disregarding their King's orders to discontinue their attack, had swarmed over the river and hacked to death hundreds of men and women inside the city. Robbie stared in awe at the destruction on Île St Jean, the newest part of Caen, which had suffered most from the English sack. Few of the burned houses had been rebuilt and there were ribs, skulls and long bones showing in the rivers' mud at the falling tide's margin. The shops were half bare, though a few countryfolk were in town selling food from carts and Thomas bought dried fish, bread and rock-hard cheese. Some looked askance at his bowstave, but he assured them he was a Scotsman and thus an ally of France. 'They do have proper bows in Scotland, don't they?' he asked Robbie.

'Of course we do.'

'Then why didn't you use them at Durham?'

'We just don't have enough,' Robbie said, 'and besides, we'd rather kill you bastards up close. Make sure you're dead, see?' He stared open-mouthed at a girl carrying a pail of milk. 'I'm in love.'

'If it's got tits you fall in love,' Thomas said. 'Now come on.' He led Robbie to Sir Guillaume's town house, the place where he had met Eleanor, and though Sir Guillaume's crest of three hawks was still carved in stone above the door there was now a new banner flying over the house: a flag showing a hump-backed boar with great tusks. 'Whose flag is that?' Thomas had crossed the small square to talk with a cooper who was hammering an iron ring down the flanks of a new barrel.

'It's the Count of Coutances,' the cooper said, 'and the bastard's already raised our rents. And I don't care if you do serve him.' He straightened and frowned at the bowstave. 'Are you English?'

'*Écossais*,' Thomas said.

'Ah!' The cooper was intrigued and leaned closer to Thomas. 'Is it true, monsieur,' he asked, 'that you paint your faces blue in battle?'

222

'Always,' Thomas said, 'and our arses.'

'*Formidable*!' the cooper said, impressed.

'What's he saying?' Robbie asked.

'Nothing.' Thomas pointed at the oak which grew at the centre of the small square. A few shrivelled leaves still clung to the twigs. 'I was hanged from that tree,' he told Robbie.

'Aye, and I'm the Pope of Avignon.' Robbie heaved up his bundle. 'Did you ask him where we could buy horses?'

'Expensive things, horses,' Thomas said, 'and I thought we might save ourselves the bother of buying.'

'We're footpads now?'

'Indeed,' Thomas said. He led Robbie off the island across the bridge where so many archers had died in the frenzied attack, and then through the old city. That had been less damaged than the Île St Jean because no one had tried to defend the narrow streets, while the castle, which had never fallen to the English, had only suffered from cannon balls that had done little except chip the stones about the gate. A red and yellow banner flew from the castle rampart and men-at-arms, wearing the same coloured livery, challenged Thomas and Robbie as they were leaving the old city. Thomas answered by saying they were Scottish soldiers seeking employment from the Count of Coutances. 'I thought he'd be here,' Thomas lied, 'but we hear he's at Evecque.'

'And getting nowhere,' the guard commander said. He was a bearded man whose helmet had a great split that suggested he had taken it from a corpse. 'He's been pissing at those walls for two months now and got nowhere, but if you want to die at Evecque, boys, then good luck to you.'

They walked past the walls of the Abbaye aux Dames and Thomas had a sudden vision of Jeanette again. She had been his lover, but then had met Edward Woodstock, the Prince of Wales, and what chance did Thomas have after that? It had been here, in the Abbaye aux Dames, that Jeanette and the Prince had lived during the brief siege of Caen. Where was Jeanette now? Thomas wondered. Back in Brittany? Still seeking her infant son? Did she ever think of him? Or did she regret fleeing from the Prince of Wales in the belief that the Picardy battle would be lost? Perhaps, by now, she would be married again. Thomas suspected she had taken a small fortune in jewels when she had fled the English army, and a rich widow, scarce more than twenty years old, made an attractive bride.

'What happens' – Robbie interrupted his thoughts – 'if they find out you're not Scottish?'

Thomas held up the two fingers of his right hand that drew the bowcord. 'They cut those off.'

'Is that all?'

'Those are the first things they cut off.'

They walked on south through a country of small steep hills, tight fields, thick woods and deep lanes. Thomas had never been to Evecque and, though it was not far from Caen, some of the peasants they asked had never heard of it, but when Thomas asked which way the soldiers had been going during the winter they pointed on southwards. They spent their first night in a roofless hovel, a place that had evidently been abandoned when the English came in the summer and swept through Normandy.

They woke at dawn and Thomas put two arrows into a tree, just to keep in practice. He was cutting the steel heads out of the trunk when Robbie picked up the bow. 'Can you teach me to use it?' he asked.

'What I can teach you,' Thomas said, 'will take ten minutes. But the rest will need a lifetime. I began shooting arrows when I was seven and after ten years I was beginning to get good at it.'

'It can't be that difficult,' Robbie protested, 'I've killed a stag with a bow.'

'That was a hunting bow,' Thomas said. He gave Robbie one of the arrows and pointed to a willow that had stubbornly kept its leaves. 'Hit the trunk.'

Robbie laughed. 'I can't miss!' The willow was scarcely thirty paces away.

'Go on, then.'

Robbie drew the bow, glancing once at Thomas as he realized just how much strength was needed to bend the great yew stave. It was twice as stiff as the shorter hunting bows he had used in Scotland. 'Jesus,' he said softly as he hauled the string back to his nose and realized his left arm was trembling slightly with the tension of the weapon, but he peered down the arrow to check his aim and was about to loose when Thomas held up a hand. 'You're not ready yet.'

'I damn well am,' Robbie said, though the words came out as grunts for the bow needed immense force to hold in the drawn position.

'You're not ready,' Thomas said, 'because there's four inches of the arrow sticking out in front of the bow. You have to pull it back until the arrow head touches your left hand.'

'Oh, sweet Jesus,' Robbie said and took a breath, nerved himself and pulled until the string was past his nose, past his eye and close by his right ear. The steel arrow head touched his left hand, but now he could no longer aim by looking down the arrow's shaft. He frowned as he realized the difficulty that implied, then compensated by edging the bow to the right. His left arm was shaking with the tension and, unable to keep the arrow drawn, he released, then twitched as the hemp string whipped along his inner left forearm. The arrow's feathers flashed white as they passed a foot from the willow's trunk. Robbie swore in amazement, then handed the bow to Thomas. 'So the trick of it,' he said, 'is learning how to aim it?'

'The trick,' Thomas said, 'is not aiming at all. It's something that just happens. You look at the target and you let the arrow fly.' Some archers, the lazy ones, only drew to the eye and that made them accurate, but their arrows lacked force. The good archers, the archers who drove down armies or brought down kings in shining armour, pulled the string all the way back. 'I taught a woman to shoot last summer,' Thomas said, taking back the bow, 'and she became good. Really good. She hit a hare at seventy paces.'

'A woman!'

'I let her use a longer string,' Thomas said, 'so the bow didn't need as much strength, but she was still good.' He remembered Jeanette's delight when the hare tumbled in the grass, squealing, the arrow pinned through its haunches. Jeanette. Why was he thinking of her so much?

They walked on through a world edged white with frost. The puddles had frozen and the leafless hedgerows were outlined with a sharp white rime that faded as the sun climbed. They crossed two streams, then climbed through beechwoods towards a plateau which, when they reached it, proved to be a wild place of thin turf that had never been cut with a plough. A few gorse bushes broke the grass, but otherwise the road ran across a featureless plain beneath an empty sky. Thomas had thought that the heathland would be nothing but a narrow belt of high country and that they must soon drop into the wooded valleys again, but the road stretched on and he felt ever more like a hare on a chalk upland under the gaze of a buzzard. Robbie felt the same and the two of them left the road to walk where the gorse provided some intermittent cover.

Thomas kept looking ahead and behind. This was horse country, a firm-turfed upland where riders could go full gallop and where there were no woods or gullies in which two men on foot could hide. And the high ground seemed to extend for ever.

At midday they reached a circle of standing stones, each about the height of a man and heavily encrusted with lichen. The circle was twenty yards across and one of the stones had fallen and they rested their backs against it while they took a meal of bread and cheese. 'The devil's wedding party, eh?' Robbie said.

'The stones, you mean?'

'We have them in Scotland.' Robbie twisted round and brushed fragments of snail shell from the fallen stone. 'They're people who were turned into rocks by the devil.'

'In Dorset,' Thomas said, 'folk say that God turned them into stone.'

Robbie wrinkled his face at that idea. 'Why would God do that?'

'For dancing on the sabbath.'

'They'd just go to hell for that,' Robbie said, then idly

scratched at the turf with his heel. 'We dig the stones up when we have the time. Look for gold, see?'

'You ever find any?'

'We do in the mounds sometimes. Pots anyway, and beads. Rubbish really. We throw it away as often as not. And we find elf stones, of course.' He meant the mysterious stone arrow heads that were supposedly shot from elfin bowstrings. He stretched out, enjoying the feeble warmth of the sun that was now as high as it would climb in the midwinter sky. 'I miss Scotland.'

'I've never been.'

'God's own country,' Robbie said forcefully, and he was still talking about Scotland's wonders when Thomas fell gently asleep. He dozed, then was woken because Robbie had kicked him.

The Scot was standing on the fallen stone. 'What is it?' Thomas asked.

'Company.'

Thomas stood beside him and saw four horsemen a mile or more to the north. He dropped back to the turf, pulled upon his bundle and took out a single sheaf of arrows, then hooked the bowstring over the nocked tips of the stave. 'Maybe they haven't seen us,' he said optimistically.

'They have,' Robbie commented, and Thomas climbed onto the stone again to see that the horsemen had left the road; they had stopped now and one of them stood in his stirrups to get a better look at the two strangers at the stone circle. Thomas could see they were wearing mail coats under their cloaks. 'I can take three of them,' he said, patting the bow, 'if you manage the fourth.'

'Ah, be kind to a poor Scotsman,' Robbie said, drawing his uncle's sword, 'leave me two. I have to make money, remember.' He might have been facing a fight with four horsemen in Normandy, but he was still a prisoner of Lord Outhwaite and so bound to pay his ransom that had been set at a mere two hundred pounds. His uncle's was ten thousand and in Scotland the Douglas clan would be worrying how to raise it.

The horsemen still watched Thomas and Robbie, doubtless wondering who and what they were. The riders would not be fearful; after all they were mailed and armed and the two strangers were on foot and men on foot were almost certainly peasants and peasants were no threat to horsemen in armour. 'A patrol from Evecque?' Robbie wondered aloud.

'Probably.' The Count of Coutances would have men roaming the country looking for food. Or perhaps the horsemen were reinforcements riding to the Count's aid, but whoever they were they would regard any stranger in this countryside as prey for their weapons.

'They're coming,' Robbie said as the four men spread into a line. The riders must have assumed the two strangers would try to escape and so were making the line to snare them. 'The four horsemen, eh?' Robbie said. 'I can never remember what the fourth one is.'

'Death, war, pestilence and famine,' Thomas said, putting the first arrow on the string.

'It's famine I always forget,' Robbie said. The four riders were a half-mile away, swords drawn, cantering on the fine solid turf. Thomas was holding the bow low so they would not be ready for the arrows. He could hear the hoofbeats now and he thought of the four horsemen of the apocalypse, the dreadful quartet of riders whose appearance would presage the end of time and the last great struggle between heaven and hell.

War would appear on a horse the colour of blood, famine would be on a black stallion, pestilence would ravage the world on a white mount while death would ride the pale horse. Thomas had a sudden memory of his father sitting bolt upright, head back, intoning the Latin: '*et ecce equus pallidus*'. Father Ralph used to say the words to annoy his housekeeper and lover, Thomas's mother, who, though she knew no Latin, understood that the words were about death and hell and she thought, rightly as it turned out, that her priest lover was inviting hell and death to Hookton.

'Behold a pale horse,' Thomas said. Robbie gave him a puzzled look. '"I saw a pale horse,"' Thomas quoted, '"and the name of its rider was Death, and Hell followed him."'

'Is hell another of the riders?' Robbie asked.

'Hell is what these bastards are about to get,' Thomas said and he brought up the bow and dragged back the cord and felt a sudden anger and hate in his heart for the four men, and then the bow sounded, the cord's note hard and deep, and before the sound had died he was already plucking a second arrow from where he had stuck a dozen point-down in the turf. He hauled the cord back and the four horsemen were still riding straight for them as Thomas aimed at the left-hand rider. He loosed, took a third arrow, and now the sound of the hooves on the frost-hardened turf was as loud as the Scottish drums at Durham and the second man from the right was thrashing left and right, falling back, an arrow jutting from his chest and the rider on the left was lying back on his saddle's cantle, and the other two, at last understanding their danger, were swerving to throw off Thomas's aim. Gobbets of earth and grass were thrown up from the horses' hooves as they slewed away. If the two unwounded riders had any sense, Thomas thought, they would ride away as though Hell and Death were on their heels, ride back the way they had come in a desperate bid to escape the arrows, but instead, with the rage of men who had been challenged by what they believed to be an inferior enemy, they curved back towards their prey and Thomas let the third arrow fly. The first two men were both out of it, one fallen from his saddle and the other lolling on his horse that just cropped the winter-pale turf; and the third arrow flew hard and straight at its victim, but his galloping horse tossed up its head and the arrow slid down the side of its skull, blood bright on the black hide: the horse twisted away from the pain and the rider, unready for the turn, was flailing for balance, but Thomas had no time to watch him for the fourth rider was inside the stone circle and closing on him. The man had a vast black cloak that billowed behind as he turned the pale grey horse and he shouted his defiance as he stretched out the sword to whip the point like a lance head into Thomas's chest, but Thomas had his fourth arrow on the cord and the man suddenly understood that he was a split second too late. '*Non!*' he shouted, and Thomas did not even draw the bow fully back, but let it fly off the half-string and the arrow still had enough force to bury itself in the man's head, splitting the bridge of his nose and driving deep into his skull. He twitched, his sword arm dropped, Thomas felt the wind as the man's horse thundered past him and then the rider fell back over the stallion's rump.

The third man, the one unseated from the black horse, had fallen in the stone circle's centre and now approached Robbie. Thomas plucked an arrow from the turf. 'No!' Robbie called. 'He's mine.'

Thomas relaxed the string.

'*Chien bâtard*,' the man said to Robbie. He was much older than the Scotsman and must have taken Robbie for a mere boy for he half smiled as he came fast forward to lunge his sword and Robbie stepped back, parried, and the blades rang like bells in the clear air. '*Bâtard*!' the man spat and attacked again.

Robbie stepped back once more, yielding ground until he had almost reached the stone ring, and his retreat worried Thomas who had stretched his string again, but then Robbie parried so fast and riposted so quickly that the Frenchman was going backwards in a sudden and desperate hurry. 'You English bastard,' Robbie said. He swung his blade low and the man dropped his own blade to parry and Robbie just kicked it aside and lunged so that his uncle's blade sank into the man's neck. 'Bastard English bastard,' Robbie snarled, ripping the blade free in a spray of bright blood. 'Bloody English pig!' He freed the sword and swung it back to bury its edge in what was left of the man's neck.

Thomas watched the man fall. Blood was bright on the grass. 'He wasn't English,' Thomas said.

'It's just a habit when I fight,' Robbie said. 'It's the way my uncle trained me.' He stepped towards his victim. 'Is he dead?'

'You half cut off his head,' Thomas said, 'what do you think?'

'I think I'll take his money,' Robbie said and knelt beside the dead man.

One of the first two men to be struck by Thomas's arrows was still alive. The breath bubbled in his throat and showed pink and frothy at his lips. He was the man lolling in his saddle and he moaned as Thomas spilled him down to the ground.

'Is he going to live?' Robbie had crossed to see what Thomas was doing.

'Christ, no,' Thomas said and took out his knife.

'Jesus!' Robbie stepped back as the man's throat was cut. 'Did you have to?'

'I don't want the Count of Coutances to know there are only two of us,' Thomas said. 'I want the Count of Coutances to be as scared as hell of us. I want him to think the devil's own horsemen are hunting his men.'

They searched the four corpses and, after a lumbering chase, managed to collect the four horses. From the bodies and the saddlebags they took close to eighteen pounds of bad French silver coinage, two rings, three good daggers, four swords, a fine mail coat that Robbie claimed to replace his own, and a gold chain that they hacked in half with one of the captured swords. Then Thomas used the two worst swords to picket a pair of the horses beside the road and on the horses' backs he tied two of the corpses so that they hung in the saddle, bending sideways with vacant eyes and white skin laced with blood. The other two corpses, stripped of their mail, were placed on the road and in each of their dead mouths Thomas put sprigs of gorse. That gesture meant nothing, but to whoever found the bodies it would suggest something strange, even Satanic. 'It'll worry the bastards,' Thomas explained.

'Four dead men should give them a twitch,' Robbie said.

'They'll be scared to hell if they think the devil's loose,' Thomas said. The Count of Coutances would scoff if he knew there were only two young men come as reinforcements for Sir Guillaume d'Evecque, but he could not ignore four corpses and hints of weird ritual. And he could not ignore death.

To which end, when the corpses were arranged, Thomas took the big black cloak, the money and the weapons, the best of the stallions and the pale horse.

For the pale horse belonged to Death.

And with it Thomas could make nightmares.

A single short burst of thunder sounded as Thomas and Robbie neared Evecque. They did not know how close they were, but they were riding through country where all the farms and cottages had been destroyed which told Thomas that they must be within the manor's boundaries. Robbie, on hearing the rumble, looked puzzled for the sky immediately above them was clear, although there were dark clouds to the south. 'It's too cold for thunder,' he said.

'Maybe it's different in France?'

They left the road and followed a farm track that twisted through woods and petered out beside a burned building that still smoked gently. It made little sense to burn such steadings and Thomas doubted that the Count of Coutances had initially ordered the destruction, but Sir Guillaume's long defiance and the bloody-mindedness of most soldiers would ensure that the pillage and burning would happen anyway. Thomas had done the same in Brittany. He had listened to the screams and protests of families who had to watch their home being burned and then he had touched the fire to the thatch. It was war. The Scots did it to the English, the English to the Scots, and here the Count of Coutances was doing it to his own tenant.

A second clap of thunder sounded and just after its echo had died Thomas saw a great veil of smoke in the eastern sky. He pointed to it and Robbie, recognizing the smear of campfires and realizing the need for silence, just nodded. They left their horses in a thicket of hazel saplings and then climbed a long wooded hill. The setting sun was behind them, throwing their shadows long on the dead leaves. A woodpecker, red-headed and wings barred white, whirred loud and low above their heads as they crossed the ridge line to see the village and manor of Evecque beneath them.

Thomas had never seen Sir Guillaume's manor before. He had imagined it would be like Sir Giles Marriott's hall with one great barn-like room and a few thatched outbuildings, but Evecque was much more like a small castle. At the corner closest to Thomas it even had a tower: a square and not very tall tower, but properly crenellated and flying its banner of three stooping hawks to show that Sir Guillaume was not yet beaten. The manor's saving feature, though, was its moat, which was wide and thickly covered with a vivid green scum. The manor's high walls rose sheer from the water and had few windows, and those were nothing but arrow slits. The roof was thatched and sloped inwards to a small courtyard. The besiegers, whose tents and shelters lay in the village to the north of the manor, had succeeded in setting fire to the roof at some point, but Sir Guillaume's few defenders must have managed to extinguish the flames for only one small portion of the thatch was missing or blackened. None of those defenders was visible now, though some of them must have been peering though the arrow slits that showed as small black specks against the grey stone. The only visible damage to the manor was some broken stones at one corner of the tower where it looked as though a giant beast had nibbled at the masonry, and that was probably the work of the springald that Father Pascal had mentioned, but the oversized crossbow had obviously broken again and irremediably for Thomas could see it lying in two gigantic pieces in the field beside the tiny stone village church. It had done very little damage before its main beam broke and Thomas wondered if the eastern, hidden, side of the building had been hurt more. The manor's entrance must be on that far side and Thomas suspected the main siege works would also be there.

Only a score of besiegers were in sight, most doing nothing more threatening than sitting outside the village houses, though a half-dozen men were gathered around what looked like a small table in the churchyard. None of the Count's men was closer to the manor than a hundred and fifty paces, which suggested that the defenders had succeeded in killing some of their enemies with crossbows and the rest had learned to give the garrison a wide berth. The village itself was small, not much bigger than Down Mapperley, and, like the Dorset village, had a watermill. There were a dozen tents to the south of the houses and twice as many little turf shelters and Thomas tried to work out how many men could be sheltered in the village, tents and turf huts and decided the Count must now have about 120 men.

'What do we do?' Robbie asked.

'Nothing for now. Just watch.'

It was a tedious vigil for there was little activity beneath them. Some women carried pails of water from the watermill's race, others were cooking on open fires or collecting clothes that had been spread out to dry over some bushes at the edge of the fields. The Count of Coutances's banner, showing the black boar on a white field spangled with blue flowers, flew on a make-shift staff outside the largest house in the village. Six other banners hung above the thatched rooftops, show-ing that other lords had come to share the plunder. A half-dozen squires or pages exercised some warhorses in the meadow behind the encampment, but otherwise Evecque's attackers were doing little except wait. Siege work was boring work. Thomas remembered the idle days outside La Roche-Derrien, though those long hours had been broken by the terror and excitement of the occasional assault. These men, unable to assault Evecque's walls because of the moat, could only wait and hope to starve the garrison into surrender or else tempt it into a sally by burning farms. Or perhaps they were waiting for a long piece of seasoned wood to repair the broken arm of the abandoned springald.

Then, just as Thomas was deciding that he had seen enough, the group of men who had been gathered about what he had thought was a low table beside the churchyard hedge suddenly ran back towards the church.

'What in God's name is that?' Robbie asked, and Thomas saw that it had not been a table they were crowding round, but a vast pot cradled in a heavy wooden frame.

'It's a cannon,' Thomas said, unable to hide his awe, and just then the gun fired and the great metal pot and its huge wooden cradle both vanished inside a swelling burst of dirty smoke and, out of the corner of his eye, he saw a piece of stone fly away from the damaged corner of the manor. A thousand birds flew up from hedgerows, thatch and trees as the gun's booming thunder rolled up the hill and washed past him. That vast clap of sound was the thunder they had heard earlier in the afternoon. The Count of Coutances had managed to find a gun and was using it to nibble away at the manor. The English had used guns at Caen last summer, though not all the guns in their army, nor all the best efforts of the Italian gunners, had hurt Caen's castle. Indeed, as the smoke slowly cleared from the encampment, Thomas saw that this shot had made little impact on the manor. The noise seemed more violent than the missile itself, yet he supposed that if the Count's gunners could fire enough stones then eventually the masonry must give way and the tower collapse into the moat to make a rubble causeway across the water. Stone by stone, fragment by fragment, maybe three or four shots a day, and thus the besiegers would undermine the tower and make their rough path into Evecque.

A man rolled a small barrel out of the church, but another man waved him back and the barrel was taken back inside. The church had to be their powder store, Thomas thought, and the man had been sent back because the gunners had shot their last missile for the day and would not reload until morning. And that suggested an idea, but he pushed it away as impractical and stupid.

'Have you seen enough?' he asked Robbie.

'I've never seen a gun before,' Robbie said, staring down at the distant pot as if hoping that it would be fired again, but Thomas knew it was unlikely that the gunners would discharge it again this evening. It took a long time to charge a cannon and, once the black powder was packed into its belly and the missile put into the neck, the gun had to be sealed with damp loam. The loam would confine the explosion that propelled the missile and it needed time to dry before the gun was fired, so it was unlikely that there would be another shot before morning. 'It sounds more trouble than it's worth,' Robbie said sourly when Thomas had explained it. 'So you reckon they'll not fire again?'

'They'll wait till morning.'

'I've seen enough then,' Robbie said and they crawled back through the beeches until they were over the ridge, then went down to their picketed horses and rode into the falling night. There was a half-moon, cold and high, and the night was bitter, so bitter they decided they must risk a fire, though they did their best to hide it by taking refuge in a deep gully with rock walls where they made a crude roof of boughs covered in hastily cut turfs. The fire flickered through the holes in the roof to light the rock walls red, but Thomas doubted that any of the besiegers would patrol the woods in the dark. No one willingly went into deep trees at night for all kinds of beasts and monsters and ghosts stalked the woodlands, and that thought reminded Thomas of the summer journey he had made with Jeanette when they had slept night after night in the woods. It had been a happy time and the remembrance of it made him feel sorry for himself and then, as ever, guilty for Eleanor's sake and he held his hands to the small fire. 'Are there green men in Scotland?' he asked Robbie.

'In the woods, you mean? There are goblins. Evil little bastards, they are.' Robbie made the sign of the cross and, in case that was not sufficient, leaned over and touched the iron hilt of his uncle's sword.

Thomas was thinking of goblins and other creatures, things that waited in the night woods. Did he really want to go back to Evecque tonight? 'Did you notice,' he said to Robbie, 'that no one in Coutances's camp seemed very disturbed that four of their horsemen hadn't returned? We didn't see anyone going looking for them, did we?'

Robbie thought about it, then shrugged. 'Maybe the horsemen didn't come from the camp?'

'They did,' Thomas said with a confidence he did not entirely feel and for a moment he guiltily wondered if the four horsemen had nothing to do with Evecque, then reminded himself that the riders had initiated the fight. 'They must have come from Evecque,' he said, 'and they'll be worried there by now.'

'So?'

'So will they have put more sentries on their camp tonight?'

Robbie shrugged. 'Does it matter?'

'I'm thinking,' Thomas said, 'that I have to tell Sir Guillaume that we're here, and I don't know how to do that except by making a big noise.'

'You could write a message,' Robbie suggested, 'and put it round an arrow?'

Thomas stared at him. 'I don't have parchment,' he said patiently, 'and I don't have ink, and have you ever tried shooting an arrow wrapped up in parchment? It would probably fly like a dead bird. I'd have to stand by the moat and it would be easier to throw the arrow from there.'

Robbie shrugged. 'So what do we do?'

'Make a noise. Announce ourselves.' Thomas paused. 'And I'm thinking that the cannon will break the tower down eventually if we don't do something.'

'The cannon?' Robbie asked, then stared at Thomas. 'Sweet Jesus,' he said after a while as he thought of the difficulties. 'Tonight?'

'Once Coutances and his men know we're here,' Thomas said, 'they'll double their sentries, but I'll bet the bastards are half asleep tonight.'

'Aye, and wrapped up warm if they've any damn sense,' Robbie said. He frowned. 'But that gun looked like a rare great pot. How the hell do you break it?'

'I was thinking of the black powder in the church,' Thomas said.

'Set fire to it?'

'There're plenty of campfires in the village,' Thomas said and he wondered what would happen if they were captured in the enemy encampment, but it was pointless to worry about that. If the gun was to be made useless then it was best to strike before the Count of Coutances knew an enemy had come to harass him, and that made this night the ideal opportunity. 'You don't have to come,' Thomas told Robbie. 'It's not as if your friends are inside the manor.'

'Hold your breath,' Robbie said scornfully. He frowned again. 'What's going to happen afterwards?'

'Afterwards?' Thomas thought. 'It depends on Sir Guillaume. If he gets no answer from the King then he'll want to break out. So he has to know we're here.'

'Why?'

'In case he needs our help. He did send for us, didn't he? Sent for me, anyway. So we go on making a noise.

242

We make ourselves a nuisance. We give the Count of Coutances some nightmares.'

'The two of us?'

'You and me,' Thomas said, and the saying of it made him realize that Robbie had become a friend. 'I think you and I can make trouble,' he added with a smile. And they would begin this night. In this bitter and cold night, beneath a hard-edged moon, they would conjure the first of their nightmares.

They went on foot and despite the bright half-moon it was dark under the trees and Thomas began to worry about whatever demons, goblins and spectres haunted these Norman woods. Jeanette had told him that in Brittany there were *nains* and *gorics* that stalked the dark, while in Dorset it was the Green Man who stamped and growled in the trees behind Lipp Hill, and the fishermen spoke of the souls of the drowned men who would sometimes drag themselves on shore and moan for the wives they had left behind. On All Soul's Eve the devil and the dead danced on Maiden Castle, and on other nights there were lesser ghosts in and about the village and up on the hill and in the church tower and wherever a man looked, which was why no one left his house at night without a scrap of iron or a piece of mistletoe or, at the very least, a piece of cloth that had been touched by a holy wafer. Thomas's father had hated that superstition, but when his people had lifted their hands for the sacrament and he saw a scrap of cloth tied about their palms he had not refused them.

And Thomas had his own superstitions. He would only ever pick up the bow with his left hand; the first arrow to be shot from a newly strung bow had to be tapped three times against the stave, once for the Father, once for the Son and a third time for the Holy Spirit; he would not wear white clothes and he put his left boot on before his right. For a long time he had worn a dog's paw about his neck, then had thrown it away in the conviction it brought ill luck, but now, after Eleanor's death, he wondered if he should have kept it. Thinking of Eleanor, his mind slid back to the darker beauty of Jeanette. Did she remember him? Then he tried not to think of her, because thinking of an old love might bring ill luck and he touched the bole of a tree as he passed to cleanse away the thought.

Thomas was looking for the red glow of dying camp-fires beyond the trees that would tell him that they were close to Evecque, but the only light was the silver of the moon tangled in the high branches. *Nains* and *gorics*: what were they? Jeanette had never told him, except to say they were spirits that haunted the country. They must have something similar here in Normandy. Or perhaps they had witches? He touched another tree. His mother had firmly believed in witches and his father had instructed Thomas to say his paternoster if he ever got lost. Witches, Father Ralph had believed, preyed upon lost children, and later, much later, Thomas's father had told him that witches began their invocation of the devil by saying the paternoster backwards and Thomas, of course, had tried it though he had never dared finish the whole prayer. *Olam a son arebil des*, the backward Paternoster began, and he could say it still, even managing the difficult reversals of *temptationem* and *supersubstantialem*, though he was careful never to finish the whole prayer in case there was a stench of brimstone, a crack of flame and the terror of the devil descending on black wings with eyes of fire.

'What are you muttering?' Robbie asked.

'I'm trying to say *supersubstantialem* backwards,' Thomas said.

Robbie chuckled. 'You're a strange one, Thomas.'

'*Melait nats bus repus*,' Thomas said.

'Is that French?' Robbie said. 'Because I have to learn it.'

'You will,' Thomas promised him, then at last he glimpsed fires between the trees and they both went silent as they climbed the long slope to the crest among the beeches that overlooked Evecque.

No lights showed from the manor. A clean and cold moonlight glistened on the green-scummed moat that looked smooth as ice – perhaps it was ice? – and the white moon threw a black shadow into the damaged corner of the tower, while a glow of firelight showed on the manor's farther side, confirming Thomas's suspicion that there was a siege work opposite the building's entrance. He guessed that the Count's men had dug trenches from which they could douse the gateway with crossbow bolts as other men tried to bridge the moat where the draw-bridge would be missing. Thomas remembered the cross-bow bolts spitting from the walls of La Roche-Derrien and he shivered. It was bitter cold. Soon, Thomas thought, the dew would turn to frost, silvering the world. Like Robbie he was wearing a wool shirt beneath a leather jerkin and a coat of mail over which he had a cloak, yet still he was shivering and he wished he was back in the shelter of their gully where the fire burned.

'I can't see anyone,' Robbie said.

Nor could Thomas, but he went on looking for the

sentries. Maybe the cold was keeping everyone under a roof? He searched the shadows near the guttering campfires, watched for any movement in the darkness about the church and still saw no one. Doubtless there were sentinels in the siege works opposite the manor entrance, but surely they would be watching for any defender trying to sneak out of the back of the manor? Except who would swim a moat on a night this cold? And the besiegers were surely bored by now and their watchfulness would be low. He saw a silver-edged cloud sailing closer to the moon. 'When the cloud covers the moon,' he told Robbie, 'we go.'

'And God bless us both,' Robbie said fervently, making the sign of the cross. The cloud seemed to move so slowly, then at last it veiled the moon and the glimmering landscape faded into grey and black. There was still a wan, faint light, but Thomas doubted the night would get any blacker and so he stood, brushed the twigs off his cloak and started towards the village along a track that had been beaten across the eastern slope of the ridge. He guessed the path had been made by pigs being taken to get fat on the beechmast in the woods and he remembered how Hookton's pigs had roamed the shingle eating fish heads and how his mother had always claimed it tainted the taste of their bacon. Fishy bacon, she had called it, and compared it unfavourably with the bacon of her native Weald in Kent. That, she had always said, had been proper bacon, nourished on beechmast and acorn, the best. Thomas stumbled on a tussock of grass. It was difficult to follow the track because the night suddenly seemed much darker, perhaps because they were on lower ground.

He was thinking of bacon and all the time they were

getting closer to the village and Thomas was suddenly scared. He had seen no sentries, but what about dogs? One barking bitch in the night and he and Robbie could be dead men. He had not brought the bow, but suddenly wished he had – though what could he do with it? Shoot a dog? At least the path was easily visible now for it was lit by the campfires and the two of them walked confidently as though they belonged in the village. 'You must do this all the time,' Thomas said to Robbie softly.

'This?'

'When you raid across the border.'

'Hell, we stay in the open country. Go after cattle and horses.'

They were among the shelters now and stopped talking. A sound of deep snoring came from one small turf hut and an unseen dog whined, but did not bark. A man was sitting in a chair outside a tent, presumably guarding whoever slept inside, but the guard himself was asleep. A small wind stirred the branches in an orchard by the church and the stream made a splashing noise as it plunged over the little weir beside the mill. A woman laughed softly in one of the houses where some men began to sing. The tune was new to Thomas and the deep voices smothered the sound of the churchyard gate, which squealed as he pushed it open. The church had a small wooden belfry and Thomas could hear the wind sighing on the bell. 'Is that you, Georges?' a man called from the porch.

'*Non.*' Thomas spoke more curtly than he intended, and the tone brought the man out from the black shadows of the porch's arch and Thomas, thinking he had initiated trouble, put his hand behind his back to grasp the hilt of his dagger.

'Sorry, sir.' The man had mistaken Thomas for an officer, maybe even a lord. 'I've been expecting a relief, sir.'

'He's probably still sleeping,' Thomas said.

The man stretched, yawning hugely. 'The bastard never wakes up.' The sentry was little more than a shadow in the dark, but Thomas sensed he was a big man. 'And it's cold here,' the man went on, 'God, but it's cold. Did Guy and his men come back?'

'One of their horses threw a shoe,' Thomas said.

'That's what it was! And I thought they'd found that ale shop in Saint-Germain. Christ and his angels, but that girl with the one eye! Have you seen her?'

'Not yet,' Thomas said. He was still holding his dagger, one of the weapons that the archers called a misericord because it was used to put unhorsed and wounded men-at-arms out of their misery. The blade was slender and sufficiently flexible to slide between the joints of armour and seek out the life beneath, but he was reluctant to draw it. This sentry suspected nothing and his only offence was to want a long conversation. 'Is the church open?' Thomas asked the sentry.

'Of course. Why not?'

'We have to pray,' Thomas said.

'Must be a guilty conscience that makes men pray at night, eh?' The sentry was affable.

'Too many one-eyed girls,' Thomas said. Robbie, not speaking French, stood to one side and stared at the great black shadow of the gun.

'A sin worth repenting,' the man chuckled, then he drew himself up. 'Would you wait here while I wake Georges? It won't take a moment.'

'Take as long as you like,' Thomas said grandly, 'we

248

shall be here till dawn. You can let Georges sleep if you want. The two of us will keep watch.'

'You're a living saint,' the man said, then he fetched his blanket from the porch before walking away with a cheerful goodnight. Thomas, when the man was gone, walked into the porch where he immediately kicked an empty barrel that rolled over with a great clatter. He swore and went still, but no one called from the village to demand an explanation for the noise.

Robbie crouched beside him. The dark was impenetrable in the porch, but they groped with their hands to discover a half-dozen empty barrels. They stank of rotten eggs and Thomas guessed they had once held black powder. He whispered to Robbie the gist of the conversation he had held with the sentry. 'But what I don't know,' he went on, 'is whether he's going to wake Georges or not. I don't think so, but I couldn't tell.'

'Who does he think we are?'

'Two men-at-arms probably,' Thomas said. He pushed the empty barrels aside, then stood and groped for the rope that lifted the latch of the church door. He found it, then winced as the hinges squealed. Thomas could still see nothing, but the church had the same sour stench as the empty barrels. 'We need some light,' he whispered. His eyes slowly became accustomed to the gloom and he saw the faintest glimmer of light showing from the big eastern window over the altar. There was not even a small flame burning above the sanctuary where the wafers were kept, presumably because it was too dangerous with the gunpowder being stored in the nave. Thomas found the powder easily enough by bumping into the stack of barrels that were just inside the door. There were at least two score of them each about the size of a water pail, and Thomas guessed the cannon used one or maybe two barrels for each shot. Say three or four shots a day? So maybe there was two weeks' supply of powder here. 'We need some light,' he said again, turning, but Robbie made no response. 'Where are you?' Thomas hissed the question, but again there was no answer and then he heard a boot thump hollow against one of the empty barrels in the porch and he saw Robbie's shadow flicker in the clouded moonlight of the graveyard.

Thomas waited. A campfire smouldered not far beyond the thorn hedge that kept cattle out of the village's graves and he saw a shadow crouch beside the dying flames and then there was a sudden flare of brightness, like summer lightning, and Robbie reeled back and then Thomas, dazzled and alarmed by the flare, could see nothing. He had gone to the church door and he expected to hear a shout from one of the men in the village, but instead he heard only the squeal of the gate and the Scotsman's footsteps. 'I used an empty barrel,' Robbie said, 'except it wasn't as empty as I thought. Or else the powder gets into the wood.'

He was standing in the porch and the barrel was in his hands; he had used it to scoop up some embers. The powder residue had flared, burning his eyebrows, and now fire leaped up the barrel's inside. 'What do I do with it?' he asked.

'Christ!' Thomas imagined the church exploding. 'Give it to me,' he said, and he took the barrel, which was hot to the touch, and he ran with it into the church, his way lit by the flames, and he thrust the burning wood deep between two stacks of full barrels. 'Now we get out,' he said to Robbie.

'Did you look for the poor box?' Robbie said. 'Only if we're going to smash the church, we might as well take the poor box.'

'Come on!' Thomas snatched Robbie's arm and dragged him through the porch.

'It's a waste to leave it,' Robbie said.

'There's no bloody poor box,' Thomas said, 'the village is full of soldiers, you idiot!'

They ran, dodging between graves and pounding past the bulbous cannon, which lay in its wooden firing cradle. They climbed a fence that filled a gap in the thorn hedge, then sprinted past the gaunt shape of the broken springald and the turf-roofed shelters, not caring if they made a noise, and two dogs began to bark, then a third howled at them and a man jumped up from beside the entrance of one of the big tents. '*Qui va là?*' he called, and began to wind his crossbow, but Thomas and Robbie were already past him and out in the open field where they stumbled on the uneven turf. The moon came from behind the cloud and Thomas could see his breath like a mist.

'*Halte!*' the man shouted.

Thomas and Robbie stopped. Not because the man had given them the order, but because a red light was filling the world. They turned and stared, and the sentry who had challenged them now forgot them as the night became scarlet.

Thomas was not sure what he had expected. A lance of flame to pierce the heavens? A great noise like thunder? Instead the noise was almost soft, like a giant's inrush of breath, and a soft blossoming flame spilled from the church windows as though the gates of hell had just been opened and the fires of death were filling the nave, but that great red glow only lasted an instant before the roof of the church lifted off and Thomas distinctly saw the black rafters splaying apart like butchered ribs. 'Sweet Jesus Christ,' he blasphemed.

'God in His heaven,' Robbie said, wide-eyed.

Now the flames and smoke and air were boiling above the cauldron of the unroofed church, and still new barrels exploded, one after the other, each one pulsing a wave of fire and fumes into the sky. Neither Thomas nor Robbie knew it, but the powder had needed stirring because the heavier saltpetre found its way to the bottom of the barrels and the lighter charcoal was left at the top and that meant much of the powder was slow to catch the fire, but the explosions were serving to mix the remaining powder that pulsed bright and scarlet to spew a red cloud over the village.

Every dog in Evecque was barking or howling, and men, women and children were crawling from their beds to stare at the hellish glow. The noise of the explosions rolled across the meadows and echoed from the manor walls and startled hundreds of birds up from their roosts in the woodlands. Debris splashed in the moat, throwing up sharp-edged shards of thin ice that mirrored the fire so it seemed the manor was surrounded by a lake of sparkling flame.

'Jesus,' Robbie said in awe, then the two of them ran on towards the beech trees at the high eastern side of the pastureland.

Thomas began to laugh as he stumbled up the path to the trees. 'I'll go to hell for that,' he said, stopping among the beeches and making the sign of the cross.

'For burning a church?' Robbie was grinning, his eyes reflecting the brightness of the fires. 'You should see what we did to the Black Canons at Hexham! Christ, half Scotland will be in hell for that one.'

They watched the fire for a few moments, then turned into the darkness of the woods. Dawn was not far off. There was a lightness in the east where a wan grey, pale as death, edged the sky. 'We have to go deeper into the forest,' Thomas said, 'we have to hide.'

Because the hunt for the saboteurs was about to start and in the first light, as the smoke still made a great pall above Evecques, the Count of Coutances sent twenty horsemen and a pack of hounds to find the men who had destroyed his store of powder, but the day was cold, the ground hard with frost and the quarry's small scent faded early. Next day, in his petulance, the Count ordered his forces to make an attack. They had been readying gabions – great basketwork tubes woven from willow that were filled with earth and stones – and the plan was to fill the moat with the gabions and then swarm over the resultant bridge to assault the gatehouse. The gateway lacked its drawbridge which had been taken down early in the siege to leave an open and inviting archway which was blocked by nothing more than a low stone barricade.

The Count's advisers told him there were not enough gabions, that the moat was deeper than he thought, that the time was not propitious, that Venus was in the ascendant and Mars in the decline, and that he should, in brief, wait until the stars smiled on him and the garrison was hungrier and more desperate, but the Count had lost face and he ordered the assault anyway and his men did their best. They were protected so long as they held the gabions, for the earth-filled baskets were proof against any crossbow bolt, but once the gabions were thrown into the moat the attackers were exposed to Sir Guillaume's six crossbowmen who were sheltering behind the low stone wall that had been built across the manor's entrance arch where the drawbridge had once been. The Count had crossbowmen of his own and they were protected by pavises, full-length shields carried by a second man to protect the archer while he laboriously wound the cord of the crossbow, but the men throwing the gabions had no protection once their burdens were thrown and eight of them died before the rest realized that the moat really was too deep and that there were not nearly enough gabions. Two pavise-holders and a crossbowman were badly wounded before the Count accepted he was wasting his time and called the attackers back. Then he cursed Sir Guillaume on the fourteen hump-backed devils of St Candace before getting drunk.

Thomas and Robbie survived. On the day after they had burned the Count's powder Thomas shot a deer, and next day Robbie discovered a rotting hare in a gap in a hedge and when he pulled the body out discovered a snare that must have been set by one of Sir Guillaume's tenants who had either been killed or chased off by the Count's men. Robbie washed the snare in a stream and set it in another hedge and next morning found a hare choking in the tightening noose.

They dared not sleep in the same place two nights running, but there was plenty of shelter in the deserted and burned-out farms. They spent most of the next weeks in the country south of Evecque where the valleys were deeper, the hills steeper and the woods thicker. Here there were plenty of hiding places and it was in that tangled landscape that they made the

Count's nightmare worse. Tales began to be told in the besiegers' encampment of a tall man in black on a pale horse and whenever the man on the pale horse appeared, someone would die. The death would be caused by a long arrow, an English arrow, yet the man on the horse had no bow, only a staff topped by a deer's skull, and everyone knew what creature rode the pale horse and what a skull on a pole denoted. The men who had seen the apparition told their womenfolk in the Count's encampment and the womenfolk cried to the Count's chaplain and the Count said they were dreaming, but the corpses were real enough. Four brothers, come from distant Lyons to earn money by serving in the siege, packed their belongings and went. Others threatened to follow. Death stalked Evecque.

The Count's chaplain said folk were touched by the moon and he rode into the dangerous south country, loudly chanting prayers and scattering holy water, and when the chaplain survived unscathed the Count told his men they had been fools, that there was no Death riding a pale horse, and next day two men died only this time they were in the east. The tales grew in the telling. The horseman was now accompanied by giant hounds whose eyes glowed, and the horseman did not even need to appear to explain any misfortune. If a horse tripped, if a man broke a bone, if a woman spilled food, if a crossbow string snapped, then it was blamed on the mysterious man who rode the pale horse.

The confidence of the besiegers plunged. There were mutterings of doom and six men-at-arms went south to seek employment in Gascony. Those who remained grumbled that they did the devil's work and nothing the Count of Coutances did seemed to restore his men's spirits. He tried cutting back trees to stop the mysterious archer shooting into the camp, but there were too many trees and not enough axes, and the arrows still came. He sent to the Bishop of Caen who wrote a blessing on a piece of vellum and sent it back, but that had no effect on the black-cloaked rider whose appearance presaged death, and so the Count, who fervently believed he did God's work and feared to fail in case he incurred God's wrath, now appealed to God for help.

He wrote to Paris.

Louis Bessières, Cardinal Archbishop of Livorno, a city he had only seen once when he travelled to Rome (on his return, he had made a detour so he would not be forced to see Livorno a second time), walked slowly down the Quai des Orfèvres on the Île de la Cité in Paris. Two servants went ahead of him, using staves to clear the way for the Cardinal who appeared not to be paying attention to the lean, hollow-cheeked priest who spoke to him so urgently. The Cardinal, instead, examined the wares on offer in the goldsmiths' shops lining the quai that was named for their trade: Goldsmith's Quay. He admired a necklace of rubies and even considered buying it, but then discovered a flaw in one of the stones. 'So sad,' he murmured, then moved to the next shop. 'Exquisite!' he exclaimed of a salt cellar made in silver and emblazoned with four panels on which pictures of country life were enamelled in blue, red, yellow and black. A man ploughed on one panel and broadcast seed on the next, a woman cut the harvest on the third while on the last panel the two sat at table admiring a glowing loaf of bread. 'Quite exquisite,' the Cardinal enthused, 'don't you think it beautiful?'

Bernard de Taillebourg scarcely gave the salt cellar a glance. 'The devil is at work against us, your eminence,' he said angrily.

'The devil is always at work against us, Bernard,' the Cardinal said reprovingly, 'that is the devil's job. There would be something desperately amiss in the world if the devil were not at work against us.' He caressed the salt cellar, running his fingers over the delicate curves of the panels, then decided the shape of the base was not quite right. Something crude there, he thought, a clumsiness in the design and, with a smile for the shopkeeper, he put it back on the table and strolled on. The sun shone; there was even some warmth in the winter air and a sparkle on the Seine. A legless man with wooden blocks on his stumps swung on short crutches across the road and held out a dirty hand towards the Cardinal whose servants rushed at the man with their staves. 'No, no!' the Cardinal called and felt in his purse for some coins. 'God's blessing on you, my son,' he said. Cardinal Bessières liked giving alms, he liked the melting gratitude on the faces of the poor, and he especially liked their look of relief when he called off his servants a heartbeat before they used their staves. Sometimes the Cardinal paused just a fraction too long and he liked that too. But today was a warm, sunlit day stolen from a grey winter and so he was in a kindly mood.

Once past the Sabot d'Or, a tavern for scriveners, he turned away from the river into the tangle of alleys that twisted about the labyrinthine buildings of the royal palace. Parliament, such as it was, met here, and the lawyers scuttled the dark passages like rats, yet here and

257

there, piercing the gloom, gorgeous buildings reared up to the sun. The Cardinal loved these alleys and had a fancy that shops magically disappeared overnight to be replaced by others. Had that laundry always been there? And why had he never noticed the bakery? And surely there had been a lute-makers' business beside the public privy? A furrier hung bear coats from a rack and the Cardinal paused to feel the pelts. De Taillebourg still yapped at him, but he scarcely listened.

Just past the furrier's was an archway guarded by men in blue and gold livery. They wore polished breast-plates, plumed helmets and carried pikes with brightly polished blades. Few folk got past them, but the guards hastily stepped back and bowed as the Cardinal passed. He gave them a benevolent wave suggestive of a blessing, then followed a damp passage into a courtyard. This was all royal land now and the courtiers offered the Cardinal respectful bows for he was more than a cardinal, he was also Papal Legate to the throne of France. He was God's ambassador and Bessières looked the part for he was a tall man, strongly built and burly enough to overawe most men without his scarlet robes. He was good-looking and knew it, and vain, which he pretended he did not know, and he was ambitious, which he hid from the world but not from himself. After all, a cardinal archbishop had only one more throne to mount before he came to the crystal steps of the greatest throne of all and Bernard de Taillebourg seemed the unlikely instrument that might give Louis Bessières the triple crown for which he yearned.

And so the Cardinal wearily turned his attention to the Dominican as the two left the courtyard and climbed the stairs into the Sainte-Chapelle. 'Tell me' – Bessières broke into whatever de Taillebourg had been saying – 'about your servant. Did he obey you?'

De Taillebourg, so rudely interrupted, took a few seconds to adjust his thoughts, then he nodded. 'He obeyed me in all things.'

'He showed humility?'

'He did his best to show humility.'

'Ah! So he still has pride?'

'It is ingrained in him,' de Taillebourg said, 'but he fought it.'

'And he did not desert you?'

'No, your eminence.'

'So he is back here in Paris?'

'Of course,' de Taillebourg said curtly, then realized what tone he had used. 'He is at the friary, your eminence,' he added humbly.

'I wonder whether we should show him the undercroft again?' the Cardinal suggested as he walked slowly towards the altar. He loved the Sainte-Chapelle, loved the light that flooded between the high slender pillars. This was, he thought, as close to heaven as man came on earth: a place of supple beauty, overwhelming brightness and enchanting grace. He wished he had thought to order some singing, for the sound of eunuchs' voices piercing the high fanwork of the chapel's stones could take a man very close to ecstasy. Priests were running to the high altar, knowing what it was that the Cardinal had come to see. 'I do find,' he went on, 'that a few moments in the undercroft compel a man to seek God's grace.'

De Taillebourg shook his head. 'He has been there already, your eminence.'

'Take him again.' There was a hardness in the Cardinal's voice now. 'Show him the instruments. Show him a soul on the rack or under the fire. Let him know that hell is not confined to Satan's realm. But do it today. We may have to send you both away.'

'Send us away?' De Taillebourg sounded surprised.

The Cardinal did not enlighten him. Instead he knelt before the high altar and took off his scarlet hat. He rarely, and only reluctantly, removed the hat in public for he was uncomfortably aware that he was going bald, but it was necessary now. Necessary and awe-inspiring, for one of the priests had opened the reliquary beneath the altar and brought out the purple cushion with its lace fringe and golden tassels, which he now presented to the Cardinal. And on the cushion lay the crown. It was so old, so fragile, so black and so very brittle that the Cardinal held his breath as he reached for it. The very earth seemed to stop in its motion, all sounds went silent, even heaven was still as he reached and then touched and then lifted the crown that was so light it seemed to have scarce any weight at all.

It was the crown of thorns.

It was the very crown that had been crammed onto Christ's head where it became imbued with his sweat and blood, and the Cardinal's eyes filled with tears as he raised it to his lips and kissed it gently. The twigs, woven into the spiky circlet, were spindly. They were frail as a wren's leg bones, yet the thorns were sharp still, as sharp as the day when they had been raked over the Saviour's head to pour blood down His precious face, and the Cardinal lifted the crown high, using two hands, and he marvelled at its lightness as he lowered it onto his thinning scalp to let it rest there. Then, hands clasped, he stared up at the golden cross on the altar.

He knew the clergy of Sainte-Chapelle disliked his

coming here and wearing the crown of thorns. They had complained of it to the Archbishop of Paris and the Archbishop had whined to the King, but Bessières still came because he had the power to come. He had the Pope's delegated power and France needed the Pope's support. England was besieging Calais and Flanders was warring in the north and all of Gascony was now again swearing allegiance to Edward of England and Brittany was in revolt against its rightful French Duke and seethed with English bowmen. France was assailed and only the Pope could persuade the powers of Christendom to come to its aid.

And the Pope would probably do that for the Holy Father was himself French. Clement had been born in the Limousin and had been Chancellor of France before being elected to the throne of St Peter and installed in the great papal palace at Avignon. And there, in Avignon, Clement listened to the Romans who tried to persuade him to move the papacy back to their eternal city. They whispered and plotted, bribed and whispered again, and Bessières feared that Clement might one day give in to those wheedling voices.

But if Louis Bessières became Pope then there would be no more talk of Rome. Rome was a ruin, a pestilent sewer surrounded by petty states forever at war with each other, and God's Vicar on earth could never be safe there. But while Avignon was a good refuge for the papacy, it was not perfect because the city and its county of Venaissin both belonged to the kingdom of Naples and the Pope, in Louis Bessières's view, should not be a tenant.

Nor should the Pope live in some provincial city. Rome had once ruled the world so the Pope had belonged in Rome, but in Avignon? The Cardinal, the thorns resting so lightly on his brow, stared up at the great blue and scarlet of the passion window above the altar; he knew which city deserved the papacy. Only one. And Louis Bessières was certain that, once he was Pope, he could persuade the King of France to yield the Île de la Cité to the Holy Father and so Cardinal Bessières would bring the papacy north and give it a new and glorious refuge. The palace would be his home, the Cathedral of Notre Dame would be his new St Peter's and this glorious Sainte-Chapelle his private shrine where the crown of thorns would be his own relic. Perhaps, he thought, the thorns should be incorporated into the Pope's triple crown. He liked that idea, and he imagined praying here on his private island. The goldsmiths and the beggars, the lawyers and the whores, the laundries and the lute-makers would be sent across the bridges to the rest of Paris and the Île de la Cité would become a holy place. And then the Vicar of Christ would have the power of France always at his side and so the kingdom of God would spread and the infidel would be slain and there would be peace on earth.

But how to become Pope? There were a dozen men who wanted to succeed Clement, yet Bessières alone of those rivals knew of the Vexilles, and he alone knew that they had once owned the Holy Grail and might, perhaps, own it still.

Which was why Bessières had sent de Taillebourg to Scotland. The Dominican had returned empty-handed, but he had learned some things. 'So you do not think the Grail is in England?' Bessières now asked him, keeping his voice low so that Sainte-Chapelle's priests could not overhear their conversation.

'It may be hidden there,' de Taillebourg sounded gloomy, 'but it is not in Hookton. Guy Vexille searched the place when he raided it. We looked again and it is nothing but ruin.'

'You still think Sir Guillaume took it to Evecque?'

'I think it possible, your eminence,' de Taillebourg said. Then: 'Not likely,' he qualified the answer, 'but possible.'

'The siege goes badly. I was wrong about Coutances. I offered him a thousand fewer years in purgatory if he captured Evecque by St Timothy's Day, but he does not have the vigour to press a siege. Tell me about this bastard son.'

De Taillebourg made a dismissive gesture. 'He is nothing. He doubts the Grail even exists. All he wants is to be a soldier.'

'An archer, you tell me?'

'An archer,' de Taillebourg confirmed.

'I think you are wrong about him. Coutances writes to say that their work is being impeded by an archer. One archer who shoots long arrows of the English type.'

De Taillebourg said nothing.

'One archer,' the Cardinal pressed on, 'who probably destroyed Coutances's whole stock of black powder. It was the only supply in Normandy! If we want more it will have to be brought from Paris.'

The Cardinal lifted the crown from his head and placed it on the cushion. Then, slowly, reverently, he pressed his forefinger against one of the thorns and the watching priests leaned forward. They feared he was trying to steal one of the thorns, but the Cardinal was only drawing blood. He winced as the thorn broke his skin, then he lifted his finger to his mouth and sucked.

There was a heavy gold ring on the finger and hidden beneath the ruby, which was cunningly hinged, was a thorn he had stolen eight months before. Sometimes, in the privacy of his bed chamber, he scratched his forehead with the thorn and imagined being God's deputy on earth. And Guy Vexille was the key to that ambition. 'What you will do,' he ordered de Taillebourg when the taste of the blood was gone, 'is show Guy Vexille the undercroft again to remind him what hell awaits him if he fails us. Then go with him to Evecque.'

'You'd send Vexille to Evecque?' De Taillebourg could not hide his surprise.

'He is ruthless and he is cruel,' the Cardinal said as he stood and put on his hat, 'and you tell me he is ours. So we shall spend money and we shall give him black powder and enough men to crush Evecque and bring Sir Guillaume to the undercroft.' He watched as the crown of thorns was taken back to its reliquary. And soon, he thought, in this chapel, in this place of light and glory, he would have a greater prize. He would have a treasure to bring all Christendom and its riches to his throne of gold. He would have the Grail.

Thomas and Robbie were both filthy; their clothes were caked with dirt; their mail coats were snagged with twigs, dead leaves and earth; and their hair was uncut, greasy and matted. At night they shivered, the cold seeping into the marrow of their souls, but by day they had never felt so alive for they played a game of life and death in the small valleys and tangled woods about Evecque. Robbie, clad in a swathing black cloak and carrying the skull on its pole, rode the white horse to lead Coutances's men into ambush where Thomas killed. Sometimes Thomas merely wounded, but he rarely missed for he was shooting at close range, forced to it by the thickness of the woods, and the game reminded him of the songs the archers liked to sing and the tales their women told about the army's campfires. They were the songs and tales of the common folk, ones never sung by the troubadours, and they told of an outlaw called Robin Hood. It was either Hood or Hude, Thomas was not sure for he had never seen it written down, but he knew Hood was an English hero who had lived a couple of hundred years before and his enemies had been England's French-speaking nobility. Hood had fought them with an English weapon, the war bow, and today's nobility doubtless thought the stories were subversive which was why no troubadour sung them in the great halls. Thomas had sometimes thought he might write them down himself, except no one ever wrote in English. Every book Thomas had ever seen was in Latin or French. But why should the Hood songs not be put between covers? Some nights he told the Hood tales to Robbie as the two of them shivered in whatever poor shelter they had found, but the Scotsman thought the stories dull things. 'I prefer the tales of King Arthur,' he said.

'You have those in Scotland?' Thomas asked, surprised.

'Of course we do!' Robbie said. 'Arthur was Scots.'

'Don't be so bloody daft!' Thomas said, offended.

'He was a Scotsman,' Robbie insisted, 'and he killed the bloody English.'

'He was English,' Thomas said, 'and he'd probably never heard of the bloody Scots.'

'Go to hell,' Robbie snarled.

'I'll see you there first,' Thomas spat and thought that if he ever did write the Hood tales he would have the legendary bowman go north and spit a few Scots on some honest English arrows.

They were both ashamed of their tempers next morning. 'It's because I'm hungry,' Robbie said, 'I'm always short-tempered when I'm hungry.'

'And you're always hungry,' Thomas said.

Robbie laughed, then heaved the saddle onto his white horse. The beast shivered. Neither horse had eaten well and they were both weak so Thomas and Robbie were being cautious, not wanting to be trapped in open country where the Count's better horses could outrun their two tired destriers. At least the weather had turned less cold, but then great bands of rain swept in from the western ocean and for a week it poured down and no English bow could be drawn in such weather. The Count of Coutances would doubtless be beginning to believe that his chaplain's holy water had driven the pale horse from Evecque and so spared his men, but his enemies were also spared for no more powder had come for the cannon and now the meadows about the moated house were so waterlogged that trenches flooded and the besiegers were wading through mud. Horses developed hoof rot and men stayed in their shelters shivering with fever.

At every dawn Thomas and Robbie rode first to the woods south of Evecque and there, on the side of the manor where the Count had no entrenchments and only a small sentry post, they stood at the edge of the trees and waved. They had received an answering wave on the third morning that they signalled the garrison, but after that there was nothing until the week of the rain. Then, on the morning after they had argued about King Arthur, Thomas and Robbie waved to the manor and this time they saw a man appear on the roof. He raised a crossbow and shot high into the air. The quarrel was not aimed at the sentry post and if the men on guard there even saw its flight they did nothing, but Thomas watched it fall into the pasture where it splashed in a puddle and skidded through the wet grass.

They did not ride out that day. Instead they waited until evening, until the darkness had fallen, and then Thomas and Robbie crept to the pasture and, on hands and knees, searched the thick wet grass and old cow-dung. It seemed to take them hours, but at last Robbie found the bolt and discovered there was a waxed packet wrapped about the short shaft. 'You see?' Robbie said when they were back in their shelter and shivering beside a feeble fire. 'It can be done.' He gestured at the message wrapped about the quarrel. To make the bolt fly the message had been whipped to the shaft with cotton cord that had shrunk and Thomas had to cut it free, then he unwrapped the waxed parchment and held it close to the fire so he could read the message, which had been written with charcoal. 'It's from Sir Guillaume,' Thomas said, 'and he wants us to go to Caen.'

'Caen?'

'And we're to find a' – Thomas frowned and held the letter with its crabbed handwriting even closer to the flames – 'we're to find a shipmaster called Pierre Villeroy.'

'I wonder if that's Ugly Peter,' Robbie put in.

'No,' Thomas said, peering close at the parchment, 'this man's ship is called the *Pentecost*, and if he's not there we're to look for Jean Lapoullier or Guy Vergon.' Thomas was holding the message so close to the fire that it began to brown and curl as he read the last words aloud. 'Tell Villeroy I want the *Pentecost* ready by St Clement's Day and he must provision for ten passengers going to Dunkirk. Wait with him, and we shall meet you in Caen. Set a fire in the woods tonight to show you have received this.'

That night they did set a fire in the woods. It blazed briefly, then rain came and the fire died, but Thomas was sure the garrison would have seen the flames.

And by dawn, wet, tired and filthy, they were back in Caen.

Thomas and Robbie searched the city's quays but there was no sign of Pierre Villeroy or of his ship, the *Pentecost*, but a tavern-keeper reckoned Villeroy was not far away. 'He carried a cargo of stone to Cabourg,' the man told Thomas, 'and he reckoned he should be back today or tomorrow, and the weather won't have held him up.' He looked askance at the bowstave. 'Is that a goddamn bow?' He meant an English bow.

'Hunting bow from Argentan,' Thomas said carelessly and the lie satisfied the tavern-keeper for there were some men in every French community who could use the long hunting bow, but they were very few and never enough to coalesce into the kind of army that turned hillsides red with noble blood.

'If Villeroy's back today,' the man said, 'he'll be drinking in my tavern tonight.'

'You'll point him out to me?' Thomas asked.

'You can't miss Pierre,' the man laughed, 'he's a giant! A giant with a bald head, a beard you could breed mice in and a poxed skin. You'll recognize Pierre without me.'

Thomas reckoned that Sir Guillaume would be in a hurry when he reached Caen and would not want to waste time coaxing horses onto the *Pentecost*, therefore he spent the day haggling about prices for the two stallions and that night, flush with money, he and Robbie returned to the tavern. There was no sign of a big-bearded giant with a bald head, but it was raining, they were both chilled and reckoned they might as well wait and so they ordered eel stew, bread and mulled wine. A blind man played a harp in the tavern's corner, then began singing about sailors and seals and the strange sea beasts that rose from the ocean floor to howl at the waning moon. Then the food arrived and just as Thomas was about to taste it a stocky man with a broken nose crossed the tavern floor and planted himself belligerently in front of Thomas. He pointed at the bow. 'That's an English bow,' the man said flatly.

'It's a hunting bow from Argentan,' Thomas said. He knew it was dangerous to carry such a distinctive weapon and last summer, when he and Jeanette had walked from Brittany to Normandy, he had disguised the bowstave as a pilgrim's staff, but he had been more careless on this visit. 'It's just a hunting bow,' he repeated casually, then flinched because the eel stew was so hot.

'What does the bastard want?' Robbie asked.

The man heard him. 'You're English.'

'Do I sound English?' Thomas asked.

'So how does he sound?' The man pointed to Robbie. 'Or has he lost his tongue now?'

'He's Scottish.'

'Oh, I'm sure, and I'm the goddamn Duke of Normandy.'

'What you are,' Thomas said mildly, 'is a goddamn nuisance,' and he heaved the bowl of soup into the man's face and kicked the table into his groin. 'Get out!' he told Robbie.

'Christ, I love a fight!' Robbie said. A half-dozen of the scalded man's friends were charging across the floor and Thomas hurled a bench at their legs, tripping two, and Robbie swung his sword at another man.

'They're English!' the scalded man shouted from the floor. 'They're Goddamns!' The English were hated in Caen.

'He's calling you English,' Thomas told Robbie.

'I'll piss down his throat,' Robbie snarled, kicking the scalded man in the head, then he punched another man with the hilt of his sword and was screaming his Scottish war cry as he advanced on the survivors.

Thomas had snatched up their baggage and his bow-stave and pulled open a door. 'Come on!' he shouted.

'Call me English, you tosspots!' Robbie challenged. His sword was holding the attackers at bay, but Thomas knew they would summon their courage and charge home and Robbie would almost certainly have to kill one to escape and then there would be a hue and cry and they would be lucky not to end dangling at rope ends from the castle battlements, so he just dragged Robbie backwards through the tavern door. 'Run!'

'I was enjoying that,' Robbie insisted and tried to head back into the tavern, but Thomas pulled him hard away and then shoulder-charged a man coming into the alley.

'Run!' Thomas shouted again and pushed Robbie towards the Île's centre. They dodged into an alley, sprinted across a small square and finally went to ground in the shadows of the porch of St Jean's church. Their pursuers searched for a few minutes, but the night was cold and the patience of the hunters limited.

'There were six of them,' Thomas said.

'We were winning!' Robbie said truculently.

'And tomorrow,' Thomas said, 'when we're supposed to be finding Pierre Villeroy or one of the others, you'd rather be in Caen's jail?'

'I haven't punched a man since the fight at Durham,' Robbie said, 'not properly.'

'What about the hoggling fight in Dorchester?'

'We were too drunk. Doesn't count.' He started to laugh. 'Anyway, you started it.'

'I did?'

'Aye,' Robbie said, 'you chucked the eel stew right in his face! All that stew.'

'I was only trying to save your life,' Thomas pointed out. 'Christ! You were talking English in Caen! They hate the English!'

'So they should,' Robbie said, 'so they should, but what am I supposed to do here? Keep my mouth shut? Hell! It's my language too. God knows why it's called English.'

'Because it is English,' Thomas said, 'and King Arthur spoke it.'

'Sweet Jesus!' Robbie said, then laughed again. 'Hell, I hit that one fellow so hard he won't know what day it is when he wakes up.'

They found shelter in one of the many houses that were still abandoned after the savagery of the English assault in the summer. The house's owners were either far away, or more likely their bones were in the big common grave in the churchyard or mired in the river's bed.

Next morning they went down to the quays again. Thomas remembered wading through the strong current as the crossbowmen fired from the moored ships. The quarrels had spat up small fountains of water and, because he dared not get his bowstring wet, he had not been able to shoot back. Now he and Robbie walked down the quays to discover the *Pentecost* had magically appeared in the night. She was as big a ship as any that made it upriver, a ship capable of crossing to England with a score of men and horses aboard, but she was high and dry now as the falling tide stranded her on the mud. Thomas and Robbie gingerly crossed the narrow gangplank to hear a monstrous snoring coming from a small fetid cabin in the stern. Thomas fancied the deck itself vibrated every time the man drew breath and he wondered how any creature who made such a sound would react to being woken, but just then a waif of a girl, pale as a dawn mist and thin as an arrow, climbed from the cabin hatch and put some clothes on the deck and a finger to her lips. She looked very fragile and, as she pulled up her robe to tug on stockings, showed legs like twigs. Thomas doubted she could have been more than thirteen years old.

'He's sleeping,' she whispered.

'So I hear,' Thomas said.

'Sh!' She touched her finger to her lips again then hauled a thick woollen shirt over her night-gown, put her thin feet into huge boots and wrapped herself in a big leather coat. She pulled a greasy woollen hat over her fair hair and picked up a bag that appeared to be made of ancient frayed sailcloth. 'I'm going to buy food,' she said quietly, 'and there's a fire to be made in the forepeak. You'll find a flint and steel on the shelf. Don't wake him!'

With that warning she tiptoed off the ship, swathed in her great coat and boots, and Thomas, appalled at the depth and loudness of the snoring, decided discretion was the best course. He went to the forepeak where he found an iron brazier standing on a stone slab. A fire was already laid in the brazier and, after opening the hatch above to serve as a chimney, he struck sparks from the flint. The kindling was damp, but after a while the fire caught and he fed it scraps of wood so that by the time the girl came back there was a respectable blaze. 'I'm Yvette,' she said, apparently incurious as to who Thomas and Robbie were, 'Pierre's wife,' she explained, then fetched out a huge blackened pan onto which she broke twelve eggs. 'Do you want to eat too?' she asked Thomas.

'We'd like to.'

'You can buy some eggs from me,' she said, nodding at her sailcloth bag, 'and there's some ham and bread in there. He likes his ham.'

Thomas looked at the eggs whitening on the fire. 'Those are all for Pierre?'

'He's hungry in the morning,' she explained, 'so why don't you cut the ham? He likes it thick.' The ship suddenly creaked and rolled slightly on the mud. 'He's awake,' Yvette said, taking a pewter plate from the shelf. There was a groan from the deck, then footsteps and

Thomas backed out of the forepeak and turned to find the biggest man he had ever seen.

Pierre Villeroy was a foot taller than Thomas's bow. He had a chest like a hogshead, a smoothly bald pate, a face terribly scarred by the childhood pox and a beard in which a hare could have become lost. He blinked at Thomas. 'You've come to work,' he grunted.

'No, I brought you a message.'

'Only we've got to start soon,' Villeroy said in a voice that seemed to rumble from some deep cavern.

'A message from Sir Guillaume d'Evecque,' Thomas explained.

'Have to use the low tide, see?' Villeroy said. 'I've three tubs of moss in the hold. I've always used moss. My father did. Others use shredded hemp, but I don't like it, don't like it at all. Nothing works half as well as fresh moss. It holds, see? And mixes better with the pitch.' His ferocious face suddenly creased into a gap-toothed smile. '*Mon caneton*!' he declared as Yvette brought out his plate heaped with food.

Yvette, his duckling, provided Thomas and Robbie with two eggs apiece, then produced two hammers and a pair of strange iron instruments that looked like blunt chisels. 'We're caulking the seams,' Villeroy explained, 'so I'll heat the pitch and you two can ram moss between the planks.' He scooped a mess of egg yolk into his mouth with his fingers. 'Have to do it while the ship's high and dry between tides.'

'But we've brought you a message,' Thomas insisted.

'I know you have. From Sir Guillaume. Which means he wants the *Pentecost* for a voyage and what Sir Guillaume wants he gets because he's been good to me, he has, but the *Pentecost* ain't no good to him if she sinks,

274

is she? Ain't no good down on the seabed with all the drowned mariners, is she? She has to be caulked. My darling and I almost drowned ourselves yesterday, didn't we, my duckling?'

'She was taking on water,' Yvette agreed.

'Gurgling away, it was,' Villeroy declared loudly, 'all the way from Cabourg to here, so if Sir Guillaume wants to go somewhere then you two had better start work!' He beamed at them above his vast beard, which was now streaked with egg yolk.

'He wants to go to Dunkirk,' Thomas said.

'Planning on making a run for it, is he?' Villeroy mused aloud. 'He'll be over that moat and on his horses and up and away before the Count of Coutances knows what year it is.'

'Why Dunkirk?' Yvette wondered.

'He's joining the English, of course,' Villeroy said without a trace of any resentment for that presumed betrayal by Sir Guillaume. 'His lord has turned against him, the bishops is pissing down his gullet and they do say the King has a finger in the pie, so he might as well change sides now. Dunkirk? He'll be joining the siege of Calais.' He scooped more eggs and ham into his mouth. 'So when does Sir Guillaume want to sail?'

'St Clement's Day,' Thomas said.

'When's that?'

None of them knew. Thomas knew which day of the month was the feast of St Clement, but he did not know how many days away that was, and that ignorance gave him an excuse to avoid what he was certain would be a disgustingly messy, cold and wet job. 'I'll find out,' he said, 'and be back to help you.'

'I'll come with you,' Robbie volunteered.

'You stay here,' Thomas said sternly, 'Monsieur Villeroy has a job for you.'

'A job?' Robbie had not understood the earlier conversation.

'It's nothing much,' Thomas reassured him, 'you'll enjoy it!'

Robbie was suspicious. 'So where are you going?'

'To church, Robbie Douglas,' Thomas said, 'I'm going to church.'

The English had captured Caen the previous summer, then occupied the city just long enough to rape its women and plunder its wealth. They had left Caen battered, bleeding and shocked, but Thomas had stayed when the army marched away. He had been sick and Dr Mordecai had treated him in Sir Guillaume's house and later, when Thomas had been well enough to walk, Sir Guillaume had taken him to the Abbaye aux Hommes to meet Brother Germain, the head of the monastery's scriptorium and as wise a man as any Thomas had ever met. Brother Germain would certainly know when St Clement's Day was, but that was not the only reason Thomas was going to the abbey. He had realized that if any man could understand the strange script in his father's notebook it was the old monk, and the thought that perhaps this morning he would find an answer to the Grail's mystery gave Thomas a pang of excitement. That surprised him. He often doubted the Grail's existence and even more frequently wished the cup would pass from him, but now, suddenly, he felt the thrill of the hunt. More, he was suddenly overwhelmed with the solemnity of the quest, so much so that he stopped walking and stared into the shimmering light reflected from the river and tried to recall his vision

277

of fire and gold in the northern English night. How stupid to doubt, he thought suddenly. Of course the Grail existed! It was just waiting to be found and so bring happiness to a broken world.

'Mind out!' Thomas was startled from his reverie by a man pushing a barrow of oyster shells who barged past him. A small dog was tied to the barrow and it lunged at Thomas, snapping ineffectually at his ankles before yelping as the rope dragged it onwards. Thomas was hardly aware of man or dog. Instead he was thinking that the Grail must hide itself from the unworthy by giving them doubts. To find it, then, all he had to do was believe in it and, perhaps, to request a little help from Brother Germain.

A porter accosted Thomas in the abbey's gateway, then immediately suffered a coughing fit. The man doubled over, gasped for breath, then straightened slowly and blew his nose onto his fingers, 'I've caught my death,' he wheezed, 'that's what it is, I've caught my death.' He hawked up a gob of mucus and spat it towards the beggars by the gate. 'The scriptorium's that way,' he said, 'past the cloister.'

Thomas made his way to the sunlit room where a score of monks stood at tall, sloping desks. A small fire burned in a central hearth, ostensibly to keep the ink from freezing, but the high room was still cold enough for the monks' breath to mist above their parchments. They were all copying books and the stone chamber clicked and scratched with the sound of the quills. Two novice monks were pounding powder for paints at a side table, another was scraping a lambskin and a fourth was sharpening goose quills, all of them nervous of Brother Germain who sat on a dais where he worked at his own manuscript. Germain was old and small, fragile and bent, with wispy white hair, milky myopic eyes and a bad-tempered expression. His face had been just three inches from his work until he heard Thomas's footsteps, then he abruptly looked up and, though he could not see well, he did at least observe that his unannounced visitor had a sword at his side. 'What business does a soldier have in God's house?' Brother Germain snarled. 'Come to finish what the English started last summer?'

'I have business with you, brother,' Thomas said. The scratching of the quills had abruptly ceased as the monks tried to overhear the conversation.

'Work!' Brother Germain snapped at the monks. 'Work! You are not translated to heaven yet! You have duties, attend to them!' Quills rattled in ink pots and the scratching and pounding and scraping began again. Brother Germain looked alarmed as Thomas stepped up onto the dais. 'Do I know you?' he snarled.

'We met last summer. Sir Guillaume brought me to see you.'

'Sir Guillaume!' Brother Germain, startled, laid his quill down. 'Sir Guillaume? I doubt we'll see him again! Ha! Mewed up by Coutances, that's what I hear, and a good thing. You know what he did?'

'Coutances?'

'Sir Guillaume, you fool! He turned against the King in Picardy! Turned against the King. He made himself a traitor. He was always a fool, always risking his neck, but now he'll be lucky to keep his head. What's that?'

Thomas had unwrapped the book and now placed it on the desk. 'I was hoping, brother,' he said humbly, 'that you could make some sense of —'

'You want me to read it, eh? Never learned yourself and now you think I have nothing better to do than read some nonsense so you can determine its value?' Folk who could not read sometimes came into possession of books and brought them to the monastery to have them valued, hoping against hope that some collection of pious advice might turn out to be a rare book of theology, astrology or philosophy. 'What did you say your name was?' Brother Germain demanded.

'I didn't,' Thomas said, 'but I'm called Thomas.'

The name held no apparent memories for Brother Germain, but nor was he interested any longer for he was immersed in the book, mouthing words under his breath, turning pages with long white fingers, lost in wonder, and then he leafed back to the first page and read the Latin aloud. '"*Calix meus inebrians*".' He breathed the words as if they were sacred, then made the sign of the cross and turned to the next page which was in the strange Hebrew script and he became even more excited. '"To my son,"' he said aloud, evidently translating, '"who is the son of the Tirshatha and the grandson of Hachaliah."' He turned his short-sighted eyes on Thomas. 'Is that you?'

'Me?'

'Are you the grandson of Hachaliah?' Germain asked and, despite his bad eyesight, he must have detected the puzzlement on Thomas's face. 'Oh, never mind!' he said impatiently. 'Do you know what this is?'

'Stories,' Thomas said. 'Stories of the Grail.'

'Stories! Stories! You're like children, you soldiers. Mindless, cruel, uneducated and greedy for stories. You know what this script is?' He poked a long finger at the strange letters which were dotted with the eye-like symbols. 'You know what it is?'

'It's Hebrew, isn't it?'

'"It's Hebrew, isn't it?"' Brother Germain mocked Thomas with mimicry. 'Of course it's Hebrew, even a fool educated at the university in Paris would know that, but it's their magical script. It's the lettering the Jews use to work their charms, their dark magic.' He peered close at one of the pages. 'There, you see? The devil's name, Abracadabra!' He frowned for a few seconds. 'The writer claims Abracadabra can be raised to this world by invoking his name above the Grail. That seems plausible.' Brother Germain made the sign of the cross again to ward off evil, then peered up at Thomas. 'Where did you get this?' He asked the question sharply, but did not wait for an answer. 'You're him, aren't you?'

'Him?'

'The Vexille that Sir Guillaume brought to me,' Brother Germain said accusingly and made the sign of the cross again. 'You're English!' He made that sound even worse. 'Who will you take this book to?'

'I want to understand it first,' Thomas said, confused by the question.

'Understand it! You?' Brother Germain scoffed. 'No, no. You must leave it with me, young man, so I can make a copy of it and then the book itself must go to Paris, to the Dominicans there. They sent a man to ask about you.'

'About me?' Thomas was even more confused now.

'About the Vexille family. It seems one of your foul brood fought at the King's side this summer, and now he has submitted to the Church. The Inquisition have had . . .' Brother German paused, evidently seeking the right word, '. . . conversations with him.'

'With Guy?' Thomas asked. He knew Guy was his cousin, knew Guy had fought on the French side in Picardy and he knew Guy had killed his father in search of the Grail, but he knew little more.

'Who else? And now, they do say, Guy Vexille is reconciled to the Church,' Brother Germain said as he turned the pages. 'Reconciled to the Church indeed! Can a wolf lay down with lambs? Who wrote this?'

'My father.'

'So you are Hachaliah's grandson,' Brother Germain said with reverence, then he closed his thin hands over the book. 'Thank you for bringing it to me,' he said.

'Can you tell me what the Hebrew passages say?' Thomas asked, baffled by Brother Germain's last words.

'Tell you? Of course I can tell you, but it will mean nothing. You know who Hachaliah was? You are familiar with the Tirshatha? Of course not. The answers would be wasted on you! But I thank you for bringing me the book.' He drew a scrap of parchment towards him, took up his quill and dipped it in the ink. 'If you take this note to the sacristan he will give you a reward. Now I have work.' He signed the note and held it towards Thomas.

Thomas reached for the book. 'I can't leave it here,' he said.

'Can't leave it here! Of course you can! Such a thing belongs to the Church. Besides, I must make a copy.' Brother Germain folded his hands over the book and hunched over it. 'You will leave it,' he hissed.

Thomas had thought of Brother Germain as a friend, or at least not as an enemy, and even the old monk's harsh words about Sir Guillaume's treachery had not altered that opinion, Germain had said that the book must go to Paris, to the Dominicans, but Thomas now understood that Germain was allied with those men of the Inquisition who, in turn, had Guy Vexille on their side. And Thomas understood too that those formidable men were seeking the Grail with an avidity he had not appreciated until this moment, and their path to the Grail lay through him and this book. Those men were his enemies, and that meant that Brother Germain was also his foe and it had been a terrible mistake to bring the book to the abbey. He felt a sudden fear as he reached for the book. 'I have to leave,' he insisted.

Brother Germain tried to hold onto the book, but his twig-like arms could not compete with Thomas's bow-given strength. He nevertheless clutched it stubbornly, threatening to tear its soft leather cover. 'Where will you go?' Brother Germain demanded, then tried to trick Thomas with a false promise. 'If you leave it,' he said, 'I shall make a copy and send the book to you when it is finished.'

Thomas was going north to Dunkirk so he named a place in the other direction. 'I'm going to La Roche-Derrien,' he lied.

'An English garrison?' Brother Germain still tried to pull the book away, then yelped as Thomas slapped his hands. 'You can't take that to the English!'

'I am taking it to La Roche-Derrien,' Thomas said, finally retrieving the book. He folded the soft leather cover over the pages, then half drew his sword because several of the younger monks had slipped from their high stools and looked as though they wanted to stop him, but the sight of the blade dissuaded them from any violence. They just watched as he walked away.

The porter was coughing still, then leaned against the arch and fought for breath while tears streamed from his eyes. 'At least it ain't leprosy,' he managed to say to Thomas, 'I know it ain't leprosy. My brother had leprosy and he didn't cough. Not much anyway.'

'When is St Clement's Day?' Thomas remembered to ask.

'Day after tomorrow, and God love me if I live to see it.'

No one followed Thomas, but that afternoon, while he and Robbie were standing up to their crotches in flooding cold river water and pounding thick moss into the *Pentecost*'s planking, a patrol of soldiers in red and yellow livery asked Pierre Villeroy if he had seen an Englishman dressed in mail and a black cloak.

'That's him down there,' Villeroy said, pointing to Thomas, then laughed. 'If I see an Englishman,' he went on, 'I'll piss down the bastard's throat till he drowns.'

'Bring him to the castle instead,' the patrol's leader said, then led his men to question the crew on the next boat.

Villeroy waited till the soldiers were out of earshot. 'For that,' he said to Thomas, 'you owe me two more rows of caulking.'

'Jesus Christ!' Thomas swore.

'Now *He* was a properly skilled carpenter,' Villeroy observed through a mouthful of Yvette's apple pie, 'but He was also the Son of God, wasn't he? So he didn't have to do menial jobs like caulking, so it's no damn good asking for His help. Just bang the moss in hard, boy, bang it in hard.'

*   *   *

Sir Guillaume had held the manor from its attackers for close on three months and did not doubt he could hold it indefinitely so long as the Count of Coutances did not bring more gunpowder to the village, but Sir Guillaume knew that his time in Normandy was ended. The Count of Coutances was his liege lord, Sir Guillaume held land of him as the Count held land of the King, and if a man was declared a traitor by his liege lord, and if the King supported the declaration, then a man had no future unless he was to find another lord who owed fealty to a different King. Sir Guillaume had written to the King and he had appealed to friends who had influence at court, but no reply had come. The siege had continued, and so Sir Guillaume must leave the manor. That saddened him for Evecque was his home. He knew every inch of its pastures, knew where to find the shed deer antlers, knew where the young hares lay trembling in the long grass, and knew where the pike brooded like demons in the deeper streams. It was home, but a man declared a traitor had no home and so, on the eve of St Clement's, when his besiegers were sunk in a damp winter gloom, he made his escape.

He had never doubted his ability to escape. The Count of Coutances was a dull, unimaginative, middle-aged man whose experience of war had always been in the service of greater lords. The Count was averse to risk and given to a blustery temper whenever the world escaped his understanding, which happened frequently. The Count certainly did not understand why great men in Paris were encouraging him to besiege Evecque, but he saw the chance of enriching himself and so he obeyed them, even though he was wary of Sir Guillaume. Sir Guillaume was in his thirties and had spent half his life fighting, usually on his own account, and in Normandy he was called the lord of the sea and of the land because he fought on both with enthusiasm and effectiveness. He had been handsome once, hard-faced and golden-haired, but Guy Vexille, Count of Astarac, had taken one eye and had left scars that made Sir Guillaume's face even harder. He was a formidable man, a fighter, but in the hierarchy of kings, princes, dukes and counts he was a lesser being and his lands made it tempting to declare him a traitor.

There were twelve men, three women and eight horses inside the manor, which meant every horse but one had to carry two riders. After nightfall, when rain was softly falling across Evecque's waterlogged fields, Sir Guillaume ordered planks, put across the gap where the drawbridge should have been, and then the horses, blindfolded, were led one by one across the perilous bridge. The besiegers, huddled from the cold and rain, saw and heard nothing, even though the sentries in the forwardmost works had been placed to guard against just such an attempt to escape.

The horses' blindfolds were taken off, the fugitives mounted and then rode northwards. They were challenged just once by a sentry who demanded to know who they were. 'Who the hell do you think we are?' Sir Guillaume retorted, and the savagery in his voice persuaded the sentry not to ask any more questions. By dawn they were in Caen and the Count of Coutances was still none the wiser. It was only when one of the sentries saw the planks spanning the moat that the besiegers realized their enemy was gone, and even then the Count wasted time by searching the manor. He found furniture, straw and cooking pots, but no treasures.

An hour later a hundred black-cloaked men arrived at Evecque. Their leader carried no banner and their shields had no badges. They looked battle-hardened, like men who earned their living by renting their lances and swords to whoever paid the most, and they curbed their horses beside the makeshift bridge over Evecque's moat and two of them, one a priest, crossed into the courtyard. 'What's been taken?' the priest demanded curtly.

The Count of Coutances turned angrily on the man who wore Dominican robes. 'Who are you?'

'What have your men plundered here?' the priest, gaunt and angry, asked again.

'Nothing,' the Count assured him.

'Then where's the garrison?'

'The garrison? Escaped.'

Bernard de Taillebourg spat in his rage. Guy Vexille, next to him, gazed up at the tower which now flew the Count's banner. 'When did they escape?' he asked. 'And where did they go?'

The Count bridled at the tone. 'Who are you?' he demanded, for Vexille wore no badge on his black surcoat.

'Your equal,' Vexille said coldly, 'and my lord the King will want to know where they have gone.'

No one knew, though a few questions eventually elicited that some of the besiegers had been aware of horsemen going northwards in the cold night and that surely meant that Sir Guillaume and his men had ridden to Caen. And if the Grail had been hidden in Evecque then that would have gone north as well and so de Taillebourg ordered his men to remount their tired horses.

They reached Caen in the early afternoon, but by then the *Pentecost* was halfway down the river to the sea, blown northwards by a fitful wind that barely gave headway against the last of the flooding tide. Pierre Villeroy grumbled at the futility of trying to stem the tide, but Sir Guillaume insisted for he expected his enemies to appear at any moment. He had only two men-at-arms with him now, for the rest had not wanted to follow their lord to a new allegiance. Even Sir Guillaume had little enthusiasm for that enforced loyalty. 'You think I want to fight for Edward of England?' he grumbled to Thomas. 'But what choice do I have? My own lord turned against me. So I'll swear fealty to your Edward and at least I'll live.' That was why he was going to Dunkirk, so that he could make the small journey to the English siege lines about Calais and make his obeisance to King Edward.

The horses had to be abandoned on the quay, so all Sir Guillaume brought aboard the *Pentecost* was his armour, some clothes and three leather bags of money that he dumped on the deck before offering Thomas an embrace. And then Thomas had turned to his old friend, Will Skeat, who had glanced at him without recognition and then looked away. Thomas, about to speak, checked himself. Skeat was wearing a sallet and his hair, white as snow now, hung lank beneath its battered metal brim. His face was thinner than ever, deep-lined, and with a vague look as though he had just woken and did not know where he was. He also looked old. He could not have been more than forty-five, yet he looked sixty, though at least he was alive. When Thomas had last seen him he had been dreadfully wounded with a sword cut through the scalp which had laid his brain open and it had been a miracle he had lived long enough to reach Normandy and the skilled attentions of Mordecai, the Jewish doctor who was now being helped across the precarious gangplank.

Thomas took another step towards his old friend who again glanced at him without recognition. 'Will?' Thomas said, puzzled. 'Will?'

And at the sound of Thomas's voice light came into Skeat's eyes. 'Thomas!' he exclaimed. 'By God, it is you!' He stepped towards Thomas, stumbling slightly, and the two men embraced. 'By God, Thomas, it's grand to hear an English voice. I've heard nowt but foreign jabber all winter. Good God, boy, you look older.'

'I am older,' Thomas said. 'But how are you, Will?'

'I'm alive, Tom, I'm alive, though I sometimes wonder if it wouldn't have been better to die. Weak as a kitten, I am.' His speech was slightly slurred, as if he had drunk too much, but he was plainly sober.

'I shouldn't call you plain Will now, should I,' Thomas asked, 'for you're Sir William now.'

'Sir William! Me?' Skeat laughed. 'You're full of crap, boy, just like you always were. Always too clever for your own good, eh, Tom?' Skeat did not remember the battle in Picardy, did not remember the King knighting him before the first French charge. Thomas had sometimes wondered whether that act had been pure desperation to raise the archers' spirits for the King had surely seen how hugely his little, sick army was outnumbered and he could not have believed his men would survive. But survive they did, and win, though the cost to Skeat had been terrible. He took off his sallet to scratch his pate and one side of his scalp was revealed as a wrinkled horror of lumpy scar, pink and white. 'Weak as a kitten,'

Skeat said again, 'and I haven't pulled a bow in weeks.'

Mordecai insisted that Skeat had to rest. Then he greeted Thomas as Villeroy let go the mooring lines and used a sweep to shove the *Pentecost* into the river's current. Mordecai grumbled about the cold, about the privations of the siege and about the horrors of being aboard a ship, then he smiled his wise old smile. 'You look good, Thomas. For a man who was once hanged you look indecently good. How's your urine?'

'Clear and sweet.'

'Your friend Sir William, now —' Mordecai jerked his head towards the forecabin where Skeat had been bedded down in a pile of skeepskins – 'his urine is very murky. I fear you did me no favours by sending him to me.'

'He's alive.'

'I don't know why.'

'And I sent him to you because you're the best.'

'You flatter me.' Mordecai staggered slightly because the ship had rocked in a small river wave that no one else had noticed, yet he looked alarmed; had he been a Christian he would doubtless have warded off imminent danger by the sign of the cross. Instead he looked worriedly at the ragged sail as though he feared it might collapse and smother him. 'I do detest ships,' he said plaintively. 'Unnatural things. Poor Skeat. He seems to be recovering, I admit, but I cannot boast that I did anything except wash the wound and stop people putting charms of mouldy bread and holy water on his scalp. I find religion and medicine mix uneasily. Skeat lives, I think, because poor Eleanor did the right thing when he was wounded.' Eleanor had put the broken piece of skull on the exposed brain, made a poultice of

290

moss and spider web, then bandaged the wound. 'I was sorry about Eleanor.'

'Me too,' Thomas said. 'She was pregnant. We were going to marry.'

'She was a dear thing, a dear thing.'

'Sir Guillaume must be angry?'

Mordecai rocked his head from side to side. 'When he received your letter? That was before the siege, of course.' He frowned, trying to remember. 'Angry? I don't think so. He grunted, that was all. He was fond of Eleanor, of course, but she was a servant's child, not . . .' He paused. 'Well, it's sad. But as you say, your friend Sir William lived. The brain is a strange thing, Thomas. He understands, I think, though he cannot remember. His speech is slurred, and that might have been expected, but strangest of all is that he does not recognize anyone with his eyes. I will walk into a room and he'll ignore me, then I speak and he knows me. We have all got into the habit of speaking as we get near him. You'll get used to it.' Mordecai smiled. 'But it is good to see you.'

'So you travel to Calais with us?' Thomas asked.

'Dear me, no! Calais?' He shuddered. 'But I couldn't stay in Normandy. I suspect that the Count of Coutances, cheated of Sir Guillaume, would love to make an example of a Jew, so from Dunkirk I shall travel south again. To Montpellier first, I think. My son is studying medicine there. And from Montpellier? I might go to Avignon.'

'Avignon?'

'The Pope is very hospitable to Jews,' Mordecai said, reaching out for the gunwale as the *Pentecost* shivered under a small wind gust, 'and we need hospitality.'

Mordecai had intimated that Sir Guillaume's reaction to Eleanor's death was callous, but that was not evident when Sir Guillaume spoke of his lost daughter with Thomas as the *Pentecost* cleared the river's mouth and the cold waves stretched to the grey horizon. Sir Guillaume, his ravaged face hard and grim, looked close to tears as he heard how Eleanor had died. 'Do you know anything more about the men who killed her?' he asked when Thomas had finished his tale. Thomas could only repeat what Lord Outhwaite had told him after the battle, about the French priest called de Taillebourg and his strange servant.

'De Taillebourg,' Sir Guillaume said flatly, 'another man to kill, eh?' He made the sign of the cross. 'She was illegitimate' – he spoke of Eleanor, not to Thomas, but to the wind, instead – 'but she was a sweet girl. All of my children are dead now.' He gazed at the ocean, his dirty long yellow hair stirring in the breeze. 'We have so many men to kill, you and I' – he spoke to Thomas now – 'and the Grail to find.'

'Others are looking for it,' Thomas said.

'Then we must find it before them,' Sir Guillaume growled. 'But we go to Calais first, I make my allegiance to Edward and then we fight. By God, Thomas, we fight.' He turned and scowled at his two men-at-arms as if reflecting on how his fortunes and following had been shrunk by fate, then he saw Robbie and grinned. 'I like your Scotsman.'

'He can fight,' Thomas said.

'That's why I like him. And he wants to kill de Taillebourg too?'

'Three of us want to kill him.'

'Then God help the bastard because we'll serve his

tripes to the dogs,' Sir Guillaume growled. 'But he'll have to be told you're in the Calais siege lines, eh? If he's to come looking for us he has to know where you are.'

To reach Calais the *Pentecost* needed to go east and north, but once clear of the land she merely wallowed instead of sailing. A small south-west wind had taken her clear of the river mouth, but then, long before she was out of sight of the Norman shore, the breeze faded and the big ragged sail flapped and slatted and banged on the yard. The ship rolled like a barrel in a long dull swell that came from the west where dark clouds heaped like some gloom-laden range of hills. The winter day faded early, the last of its cold light a sullen glint beneath the clouds. A few spots of fire showed on the darkening land. 'The tide will take us up the sleeve,' Villeroy said gloomily, 'then float us down again. Then up and down and up and down till God or St Nicholas sends us wind.'

The tide took them up the English Channel as Villeroy had predicted, then drifted them down again. Thomas, Robbie and Sir Guillaume's two men-at-arms took it in turns to go down into the stone-filled bilge and hand up pails of water. 'Of course she leaks,' Villeroy told a worried Mordecai, 'all ships leak. She'd leak like a sieve if I didn't caulk her every few months. Bang in the moss and pray to St Nick. It keeps us all from drowning.'

The night was black. The few lights ashore flickered in a damp haze. The sea broke feebly against the hull, and the sail hung uselessly. For a time a fishing boat lay close, a lantern burning on its deck, and Thomas listened to the low chant as the men hauled a net, then they unshipped oars and rowed eastwards until their tiny glimmering light vanished in the haze. 'A west wind will come,' Villeroy said, 'it always does. West from the lost lands.'

'The lost lands?' Thomas asked.

'Out there,' Villeroy said, pointing into the black west. 'If you go as far as a man can sail you'll find the lost lands and you'll see a mountain taller than the sky where Arthur sleeps with his knights.' Villeroy made the sign of the cross. 'And on the clifftops under the mountain you can see the souls of the drowned sailors calling for their womenfolk. It's cold there, always cold, cold and fog-smothered.'

'My father saw those lands once,' Yvette put in.

'He said he did,' Villeroy commented, 'but he was a rare drinker.'

'He said the sea was full of fish,' Yvette went on as if her husband had not spoken, 'and the trees were very small.'

'Cider, he drank,' Villeroy offered. 'Whole orchards went down his gullet, but he could sail a boat, your father. Drunk or sober, he was a seaman.'

Thomas was staring into the western darkness, imagining a voyage to the land where King Arthur and his knights slept under the fog and where the souls of the drowned called for their lost lovers. 'Time to bail ship,' Villeroy said to him, and Thomas went down into the bilge and scooped the water into buckets until his arms were aching with tiredness, and then he went to the forepeak and slept in the cocoon of sheepskins that Villeroy kept there because, he said, it was colder at sea than on land and a man should drown warm.

Dawn came slow, seeping into the east like a grey stain. The steering oar creaked in its ropes, doing nothing as the ship rocked on the windless swell. The Norman coast was still in sight, a grey-green slash to the south, and as the winter light grew Thomas saw three small ships rowing out from the coast. The three headed up channel until they were east of the *Pentecost*; Thomas assumed they were fishermen and he wished that Villeroy's boat had oars and so could make some progress in this frustrating stillness. There was a pair of great sweeps lashed to the deck, but Yvette said they were only useful in port. 'She's too heavy to row for long,' she said, 'especially when she's full.'

'Full?'

'We carry cargo,' Yvette said. Her man was sleeping in the stern cabin, his snores seeming to vibrate the whole ship. 'Up and down the coast we go,' Yvette said, 'with wool and wine, bronze and iron, building stone and hides.'

'You like it?'

'I love it.' She smiled at him and her young face, which was strangely wedgelike, took on a beauty as she did so. 'My mother now,' she went on, 'she was going to have me put into the bishop's service. Cleaning and washing, cooking and cleaning till your hands are fair worn away by work, but Pierre told me I could live free as a bird on his boat and so we do, so we do.'

'Just the two of you?' The *Pentecost* seemed a large ship for just two, even if one of them was a giant.

'No one else will sail with us,' Yvette said. 'It's bad luck to have a woman on a boat. My father always said that.'

'He was a fisherman?'

'A good one,' Yvette said, 'but he drowned all the same. He was caught on the Casquets on a bad night.'

She looked up at Thomas earnestly. 'He did see the lost lands, you know.'

'I believe you.'

'He sailed ever so far north and then west, and he said the men from the north lands know the fishing grounds of the lost lands well and there's fish as far as you can see. He said you could walk on the sea it was so thick with fish, and one day he was creeping through the fog and he saw the land and he saw the trees like bushes and he saw the dead souls on shore. They were dark, he said, like they'd been scorched by hell's fires, and he took fright and he turned and sailed away. It took him two months to get there and a month and a half to come home and all his fish had gone bad because he wouldn't go ashore and smoke them.'

'I believe you,' Thomas said again, though he was not really sure that he did.

'And I think if I drown,' Yvette said, 'then me and Pierre will go to the lost lands together and he won't have to sit on the cliffs and call for me.' She spoke very matter-of-factly, then went to ready some breakfast for her man whose snoring had just ceased.

Sir Guillaume emerged from the forecabin. He blinked at the winter daylight, then strolled aft and pissed across the stern rail while he stared at the three boats which had rowed out from the river and were now a mile or so east of the *Pentecost*. 'So you saw Brother Germain?' he asked Thomas.

'I wish I hadn't.'

'He's a scholar,' Sir Guillaume said, pulling up his trews and tying the waist knot, 'which means he doesn't have balls. Doesn't need to. He's clever, mind you, clever, but he was never on our side, Thomas.'

'I thought he was your friend.'

'When I had power and money, Thomas,' Sir Guillaume said, 'I had many friends, but Brother Germain was never one of them. He's always been a good son of the Church and I should never have introduced you to him.'

'Why not?'

'Once he learned you were a Vexille he reported our conversation to the bishop and the bishop told the Archbishop and the Archbishop told the Cardinal and the Cardinal spoke to whoever gives him his crumbs, and suddenly the Church got excited about the Vexilles and the fact that your family had once owned the Grail. And it was just about then that Guy Vexille reappeared so the Inquisition took hold of him.' He paused, gazing at the horizon, then made the sign of the cross. 'That's who your de Taillebourg is, I'd wager my life on it. He's a Dominican and most Inquisitors are hounds of God.' He turned his one eye on Thomas. 'Why do they call them the hounds of God?'

'It's a joke,' Thomas said, 'from the Latin. *Domini canis*: the hound of God.'

'Doesn't make me laugh,' Sir Guillaume said gloomily. 'If one of those bastards gets hold of you it's red-hot pokers in the eyes and screams in the night. And I hear they got hold of Guy Vexille and I hope they hurt him.'

'So Guy Vexille is a prisoner?' Thomas was surprised. Brother Germain had said his cousin was reconciled with the Church.

'That's what I heard. I heard he was singing psalms on the Inquisition's rack. And doubtless he told them that your father had possessed the Grail, and how he sailed to Hookton to find it and how he failed. But who else went to Hookton? Me, that's who, so I think Coutances was told to find me, arrest me and haul me to Paris. And meanwhile they sent men to England to find out what they could.'

'And to kill Eleanor,' Thomas said bleakly.

'Which they'll pay for,' Sir Guillaume said.

'And now,' Thomas said, 'they've sent men here.'

'What?' Sir Guillaume asked, startled.

Thomas pointed at the three fishing boats which now were rowing directly towards the *Pentecost*. They were too far away for him to see who or what was on board, but something about their deliberate approach alarmed him. Yvette, coming aft with bread, ham and cheese, saw Thomas and Sir Guillaume staring and she joined them, then uttered a curse that only a fisherman's daughter would ever have learned and ran to the stern cabin and shouted for her man to get on deck.

Yvette's eyes were accustomed to the sea and she knew these were no fishing boats. They had too many men aboard for a start and after a while Thomas could see those men for himself and his eyes, which were more used to looking for enemies among the green leaves, saw that some of them wore mail and he knew that no man went to sea in mail unless he was intent on killing.

'They'll have crossbows.' Villeroy was on deck now, tying the neck cords of a swathing leather cloak and looking from the approaching boats up to the clouds as if he might see a breath of wind coming from the heavens. The sea was still heaving in great swells, but the water was smooth as beaten brass and there were no wind-driven ripples streaking the swells' long flanks. 'Crossbows,' Villeroy repeated gloomily.

'You want me to surrender?' Sir Guillaume asked Villeroy. His voice was sour, suggesting the question was nothing but sarcasm.

'Ain't for me to tell your lordship what to do' – Villeroy sounded just as sarcastic – 'but your men could fetch some of the bigger stones out of the bilge.'

'What will that achieve?' Sir Guillaume asked.

'I'll drop 'em on the bastards when they try to board. Those little boats? A stone'll go straight through their bottoms and then yon bastards will be trying to swim with mail strapped to their chests.' Villeroy grinned. 'Hard to swim when you're wrapped in iron.'

The stones were fetched, and Thomas readied his arrows and bow. Robbie had donned his mail coat and had his uncle's sword at his side. Sir Guillaume's two men-at-arms were with him in the waist of the boat, the place where any boarding attempt would be made for there the gunwale was closest to the sea. Thomas went to the higher stern where Will Skeat joined him and though he did not recognize Thomas he did see the bow and held out a hand.

'It's me, Will,' Thomas said.

'I know it's you,' Skeat said. He lied and was embarrassed. 'Let me try the bow, boy.'

Thomas gave him the great black stave and watched in sadness as Skeat failed to draw it even halfway. Skeat thrust the weapon back to Thomas with a look of embarrassment. 'I'm not what I was,' he muttered.

'You'll be back, Will.'

Skeat spat over the gunwale. 'Did the King really knight me?'

'He did.'

'Sometimes I think I can remember the battle, Tom,

then it fades. Like a fog.' Skeat stared at the three approaching boats, which had spread into a line. Their oarsmen were pulling hard and Thomas could see crossbowmen standing in the bows and stern of each craft. 'Have you ever shot an arrow from a boat?' Skeat asked.

'Never.'

'You're moving and they're moving. It makes it hard. But take it slow, lad, take it slow.'

A man shouted from the closest boat, but the pursuers were still too far away and whatever the man said was lost in the air. 'St Nicholas, St Ursula,' Villeroy prayed, 'send us wind, and send us plenty of it.'

'He's having a go at us,' Skeat said because a crossbowman in the bows of the central boat had raised his weapon. He seemed to cock it high in the air, then he shot and the bolt banged with astonishing force low into the *Pentecost*'s stern. Sir Guillaume, ignoring the threat, climbed onto the rail and took hold of the backstay to keep his balance. 'They're Coutances's men,' he told Thomas, and Thomas saw that some of the men in the nearest boat were wearing the green and black livery that had been the uniform of Evecque's besiegers. More crossbows twanged and two of the bolts thudded into the stern planks and two others whipped past Sir Guillaume to slap into the impotent sail, but most splashed into the sea. It might have been calm, but the crossbowmen were still having a hard time aiming their weapons from the small boats.

And the three attacking boats were small. Each held eight or ten oarsmen and about the same number of archers or men-at-arms. The three craft had plainly been chosen for their speed under oars, but they were dwarfed by the *Pentecost* which would make any attempt

300

to board the bigger vessel very perilous, though one of the three boats seemed determined to come alongside Villeroy's ship. 'What they're going to do,' Sir Guillaume said, 'is let those two boats shower us with quarrels while this bastard' – he gestured at the boat that was pulling hard to close on the *Pentecost* – 'puts her men on board.'

More crossbow bolts thumped into the hull. Two more quarrels pierced the sail and another hit the mast just above a weathered crucifix that was nailed to the tarred timber. The figure of Christ, white as bone, had lost its left arm and Thomas wondered if that was a bad omen, then tried to forget it as he drew the big bow and shot off an arrow. He only had thirty-four shafts left, but this was not the time to stint on them and so, while the first was still in the air, he loosed a second and the crossbowmen had not finished winding their cords back as the first arrow slashed a rower's arm and the second drove a splinter up from the boat's bow, then a third arrow hissed above the oarsmen's heads to splash into the sea. The rowers ducked, then one gasped and fell forward with an arrow in his back, and the next instant a man-at-arms was struck in the thigh and fell onto two of the oarsmen and there was sudden chaos aboard the boat which slewed sharply away with its oars clattering against each other. Thomas lowered the big bow.

'Taught you well,' Will Skeat said fervently. 'Ah, Tom, you always were a lethal bastard.'

The boat pulled away. Thomas's arrows had been far more accurate than the crossbow bolts for he had been shooting from a much larger and more stable ship than the narrow and overburdened rowboats. Only one of the men aboard those smaller ships had been killed, but the frequency of Thomas's first arrows had put the fear of God into the rowers who could not see where the missiles came from, but only hear the hiss of feathers and the cries of the wounded. Now the other two boats overtook the third and the crossbowmen levelled their weapons.

Thomas took an arrow from the bag and worried what would happen when he had no more shafts, but just then a swirl of ripples showed that a wind was coming across the water. An east wind, of all things, the most unlikely of all winds in this sea, but it came from the east nonetheless and the *Pentecost*'s big brown sail filled and slackened, then filled again, and suddenly she was turning away from her pursuers and the water was gurgling down her flanks. Coutances's men pulled hard on their oars. 'Down!' Sir Guillaume shouted and Thomas dropped behind the rail as a volley of crossbow bolts punched into the *Pentecost*'s hull or flew high to tear the ragged sail. Villeroy shouted at Yvette to man the steering oar, then he sheeted down the mainsail before diving into the stern cabin to fetch a huge and evidently ancient crossbow that he cocked with a long iron lever. He loaded a rusty bolt into the groove, then shot it at the nearest pursuer. 'Bastards,' he roared. 'Your mothers were goats! They were whoring goats! Poxed whoring goats! Bastards!' He cocked the weapon again, loaded another corroded missile and shot it away, but the bolt plunged into the sea. The *Pentecost* was gathering speed and already out of crossbow range.

The wind filled and the *Pentecost* drew further away from her pursuers. The three rowboats had first gone up channel in the expectation that the flooding tide and

302

a possible western wind would bring the *Pentecost* to them, but with the wind coming from the east the oarsmen could not keep up with their quarry and so the three boats fell astern and finally abandoned the chase. But just as they gave up, so two new pursuers appeared in the mouth of the River Orne. Two ships, both of them large and equipped with big square sails like the *Pentecost*'s mainsail, were coming out to sea. 'The one in front is the *Saint-Esprit*,' Villeroy said. Even at this distance from the river mouth he could distinguish the two boats, 'and the other is the *Marie*. She sails like a pregnant pig, but the *Saint-Esprit* will catch us.'

'The *Saint-Esprit*?' Sir Guillaume sounded appalled. 'Jean Lapoullier?'

'Who else?'

'I thought he was a friend!'

'He was your friend,' Villeroy said, 'so long as you had land and money, but what do you have now?'

Sir Guillaume brooded on the truth of that question for a while. 'So why are you helping me?'

'Because I'm a fool,' Villeroy said cheerfully, 'and because you'll pay me damn well.'

Sir Guillaume grunted at that truism. 'Not if we sail in the wrong direction,' he added after a while.

'The right direction,' Villeroy pointed out, 'is away from the *Saint-Esprit* and downwind, so we'll stand on west.'

They stood on westwards all day. They made good speed, but still the big *Saint-Esprit* slowly closed the gap. In the morning she had been a blur on the horizon; by midday Thomas could see the little platform at her masthead where, Villeroy told him, crossbowmen would be stationed; and by mid-afternoon he could see

the black and white eyes painted on her bows. The east
wind had increased all through the day until it was
blowing strong and cold, whipping the wavetops into
white streamers. Sir Guillaume suggested going north,
maybe as far as the English shore, but Villeroy claimed
not to know that coastline and said he was unsure
where he could find shelter there if the weather turned
bad. 'And this time of year it can turn fast as a woman's
temper,' Villeroy added, and as if to prove him right
they ran into violent sleet squalls that hissed on the sea
and buffeted the ship and cut visibility down to a few
yards. Sir Guillaume again urged a northward course,
suggesting they turn while the ship was hidden inside
the squall, but Villeroy stubbornly refused and Thomas
guessed that the huge man feared being accosted by
English ships that loved nothing better than capturing
French vessels.

Another squall crashed past them, the rain bouncing
up a hand's breadth from the deck and the sleet making
a slushy white coating on the eastern flank of every
halyard and sheet. Villeroy feared that his sail would
split, but dared not shorten the canvas because whenever the squalls passed, leaving the sea white and frantic, the *Saint-Esprit* was always in sight and always a
little closer. 'She's a quick one,' Villeroy said grudgingly,
'and Lapoullier knows how to sail her.'

Yet the short winter day was passing and night would
offer a chance for the *Pentecost* to escape. The pursuers
knew that and they must have been praying that their
ship would be given a little extra speed; as dusk fell,
she was closing the gap inch by inch, yet still the *Pentecost* kept her lead. They were out of sight of land now,
two ships on a seething and darkening ocean, and then,

when the night was almost complete, the first flame arrow streaked out from the *Saint-Esprit*'s bow.

It was shot from a crossbow. The flames seared the night, arcing up and then plunging to fall in the *Pentecost*'s wake. 'Send him an arrow back,' Sir Guillaume growled.

'Too far,' Thomas said. A good crossbow would always outrange a yew stave, though in the time it took to reload the crossbow the English archer would have run within range and loosed half a dozen arrows. But Thomas could not do that in this gathering darkness, nor did he dare waste arrows. He could only wait and watch as a second fire bolt slashed up against the clouds. It too fell behind.

'They don't fly as well,' Will Skeat said.

'What's that, Will?' Thomas had not heard clearly.

'They wrap the shaft in cloth and it slows them down. You ever shot a fire arrow, Tom?'

'Never.'

'Takes fifty paces off the range,' Skeat said, watching a third arrow plunge into the sea, 'and plays hell with accuracy.'

'That one was closer,' Sir Guillaume said.

Villeroy had put a barrel on the deck and he was filling it with seawater. Yvette, meanwhile, had nimbly climbed the rigging to perch herself on the crosstrees where the one yard hung from the masthead and now she hauled up canvas pails of water which she used to soak the sail.

'Can we use fire arrows?' Sir Guillaume asked. 'That thing must have the range.' He nodded at Villeroy's monstrous crossbow. Thomas translated the question for Will Skeat whose French was still rudimentary.

'Fire arrows?' Skeat's face wrinkled as he thought. 'You have to have pitch, Tom,' he said dubiously, 'and you must soak it into the wool and then bind the woollen cloth onto the arrow real hard, but fray the edges a little to get the fire burning nicely. Fire has to be deep in the cloth, not just on the edge because that won't last, and when it's burning hard and deep you send the arrow off before it eats through the shaft.'

'No,' Thomas translated for Sir Guillaume, 'we can't.'

Sir Guillaume cursed, then turned away as the first fire arrow thumped into the *Pentecost*, but the bolt struck low on the stern, so low that the next heave of a wave extinguished the flames with an audible hiss. 'We must be able to do something!' Sir Guillaume raged.

'We can be patient,' Villeroy said. He was standing at the stern oar.

'I can use your bow?' Sir Guillaume asked the big sailor and, when Villeroy nodded, Sir Guillaume cocked the huge crossbow and sent a quarrel back towards the *Saint-Esprit*. He grunted as he pulled on the lever to cock the weapon again, astonished at the strength needed. A crossbow drawn by a lever was usually much weaker than the bows armed with a wormscrew and ratchet, but Villeroy's bow was massive. Sir Guillaume's bolts must have struck the pursuing ship, but it was too dark to tell if any damage had been done. Thomas doubted it for the *Saint-Esprit*'s bows were high and her gunwales stout. Sir Guillaume was merely driving metal into planks, but the *Saint-Esprit*'s fiery missiles were beginning to threaten the *Pentecost*. Three or four enemy crossbows were firing now and Thomas and Robbie were busy dousing the burning bolts with water, then a flaming quarrel hit the sail and creeping fire began to glow on the canvas, but Yvette succeeded in extinguishing it just as Villeroy pushed the steering oar hard over. Thomas heard the oar's long shank creak under the strain and felt the ship lurch as she turned southwards. 'The *Saint-Esprit* was never quite as quick off the wind,' Villeroy said, 'and she wallows in a cross sea.'

'And we're quicker?' Thomas asked.

'We'll find out,' Villeroy said.

'Why didn't we try to find out earlier?' Sir Guillaume snarled the question.

'Because we didn't have sea room,' Villeroy answered placidly as a flaming bolt seared over the stern deck like a meteor. 'But we're well clear of the cape now.' He meant they were safely to the west of the Norman peninsula and south of them now were the rock-studded sea reaches between Normandy and Brittany. The turn meant that the range suddenly shortened as the *Saint-Esprit* held on westwards and Thomas shot a clutch of arrows at the dim figures of armoured men in the pursuing ship's waist. Yvette had come down to the deck and was hauling on ropes and, when she was satisfied with the new set of the sail, she clambered back up to her eyrie just as two more fire bolts thumped into the canvas and Thomas saw the flames leap up the sail as Yvette dragged up buckets. Thomas sent another arrow high into the night so that it plunged down onto the enemy deck and Sir Guillaume was shooting the heavier crossbow bolts as fast as he could, but neither man was rewarded with a cry of pain. Then the range opened again and Thomas unstrung his bow. The *Saint-Esprit* was turning to follow the *Pentecost* south and, for a few heartbeats, she seemed to disappear in the dark, but then another fire arrow climbed from her deck and in its sudden light Thomas saw she had made the turn and was again in the *Pentecost*'s wake. Villeroy's sail was still burning, giving the *Saint-Esprit* a mark she could not fail to follow and the pursuing bowmen sent three arrows together, their flames flickering hungrily in the night, and Yvette heaved desperately on the buckets, but the sail was ablaze now and the ship was slowing as the canvas lost its force and then, blessedly, there was a seething hiss and a squall came lashing in from the east.

The sleet pelted down with an extraordinary violence, rattling on the charred sail and drumming on the deck, and Thomas thought it would last forever, but it stopped as suddenly as it had begun and all on board the *Pentecost* stared astern, waiting for the next fire bolt to climb from the *Saint-Esprit*'s deck, but when the flame finally seared into the sky it was a long way off, much too far away for its light to illuminate the *Pentecost* and Villeroy grunted. 'They reckoned we'd turn back west in that squall,' he said with amusement, 'but they were being too clever for their own good.' The *Saint-Esprit* had tried to head off the *Pentecost*, thinking Villeroy would put his ship straight downwind again, but the pursuers had made the wrong guess and they were now a long way to the north and west of their quarry.

More fire arrows burned in the dark, but now they were being shot in all directions in hope that the small light of one would glint a dull reflection from the *Pentecost*'s hull, but Villeroy's ship was drawing ever farther away, pulled by the remnants of her scorched sail. If it had not been for the squall, Thomas thought, they would surely have been overhauled and captured, and he wondered whether the hand of God was somehow sheltering him because he possessed the book of the Grail. Then guilt assailed him; the guilt of doubting the Grail's existence; of wasting Lord Outhwaite's money instead of spending it on the pursuit of the Grail; then the greater guilt and pity of Eleanor and Father Hobbe's wasteful deaths, and so he dropped to his knees on the deck and stared up at the one-armed crucifix. Forgive me, Lord, he prayed, forgive me.

'Sails cost money,' Villeroy said.

'You shall have a new sail, Pierre,' Sir Guillaume promised.

'And let's pray that what's left of this one will get us somewhere,' Villeroy said sourly. Off to the north a last fire arrow etched red across the black, and then there was no more light, just the endless dark of a broken sea in which the *Pentecost* survived under her tattered sail.

Dawn found them in a mist and with a fitful breeze that fluttered a sail so weakened that Villeroy and Yvette doubled it on itself so that the wind would have more than charred holes to blow upon, and when they reset it the *Pentecost* limped south and west and everyone on board thanked God for the mist because it hid them from the pirates that haunted the gulf between Normandy and Brittany. Villeroy was not sure where they were, though he was certain enough that the Norman coast was to the east and that all the land in that direction was in fealty to the Count of Coutances and so they held on south and west with Yvette perched in the bows to keep a lookout for the frequent reefs. 'They breed rocks, these waters,' Villeroy grumbled.

'Then go into deeper water,' Sir Guillaume suggested.

The big man spat overboard. 'Deeper water breeds English pirates out of the isles.'

They pushed on south, the wind dying and the sea calming. It was still cold, but there was no more sleet and, when a feeble sun began to burn off the shredding mists, Thomas sat beside Mordecai in the bow. 'I have a question for you,' he said.

'My father told me never to get on board a ship,' Mordecai responded. His long face was pale and his beard, which he usually brushed so carefully, was tangled. He was shivering despite a makeshift cloak of sheepskins. 'Did you know,' he went on, 'that Flemish sailors claim that you can calm a storm by throwing a Jew overboard?'

'Do they really?'

'So I'm told,' Mordecai said, 'and if I was on board a Flemish ship I might welcome drowning as an alternative to this existence. What is that?'

Thomas had unwrapped the book that his father had bequeathed him. 'My question,' he said, ignoring Mordecai's question, 'is who is Hachaliah.'

'Hachaliah?' Mordecai repeated the name, then shook his head. 'Do you think the Flemings carry Jews aboard their ships as a precaution? It would seem a sensible, if cruel, thing to do. Why die when a Jew can die?'

Thomas opened the book to the first page of Hebrew script where Brother Germain had deciphered the name Hachaliah. 'There,' he said, giving the book to the doctor, 'Hachaliah.'

Mordecai peered at the page. 'Grandson of Hachaliah,' he translated aloud, 'and son of the Tirshatha. Of course! It's a confusion about Jonah and the great fish.'

'Hachaliah is?' Thomas asked, staring at the page of strange script.

'No, dear boy!' Mordecai said. 'The superstition about

310

Jews and storms is a confusion about Jonah, a mere ignorant confusion.' He looked back at the page. 'Are you the son of the Tirshatha?'

'I'm the bastard son of a priest,' Thomas said.

'And did your father write this?'

'Yes.'

'For you?'

Thomas nodded. 'I think so.'

'Then you are the son of the Tirshatha and the grandson of Hachaliah,' Mordecai said, then smiled. 'Ah! Of course! Nehemiah. My memory is almost as bad as poor Skeat's, eh? Fancy forgetting that Hachaliah was the father of Nehemiah.'

Thomas was still none the wiser. 'Nehemiah?'

'And he was the Tirshatha, of course he was. Extraordinary, isn't it, how we Jews prosper in foreign states and then they tire of us and we get blamed for every little accident. Then time passes and we are restored to our offices. The Tirshatha, Thomas, was the Governor of Judaea under the Persians. Nehemiah was the Tirshatha, not the King, of course, just Governor for a time under the rule of Artaxerxes.' Mordecai's erudition was impressive, but hardly enlightening. Why would Father Ralph identify himself with Nehemiah who must have lived hundreds of years before Christ, before the Grail? The only answer that Thomas could conjure up was the usual one of his father's madness. Mordecai was turning the parchment pages and winced when one cracked. 'How people do yearn,' he said, 'for miracles.' He prodded a page with a finger stained by all the medicines he had pounded and stirred. '"A golden cup in the Lord's hand that made all the earth drunk", now what on earth does that mean?'

'He's talking about the Grail,' Thomas said.

'I had understood that, Thomas,' Mordecai chided him gently, 'but those words were not written about the Grail. It refers to Babylon. Part of the lamentations of Jeremiah.' He turned another page. 'People like mystery. They want nothing explained, because when things are explained then there is no hope left. I have seen folk dying and known there is nothing to be done, and I am asked to go because the priest will soon arrive with his dish covered by a cloth, and everyone prays for a miracle. It never happens. And the person dies and I get blamed, not God or the priest, but I!' He let the book fall on his lap where the pages stirred in the small wind. 'These are just stories of the Grail, and some odd scriptures that might refer to it. A book, really, of meditations.' He frowned. 'Did your father truly believe the Grail existed?'

Thomas was about to give a vigorous affirmative, but paused, remembering. For much of the time his father had been a wry, amused and clever man, but there had been other times when he had been a wild, shrieking creature, struggling with God and desperate to make sense of the sacred mysteries. 'I think,' Thomas said carefully, 'that he did believe in the Grail.'

'Of course he did,' Mordecai said suddenly, 'how stupid of me! Of course your father believed in the Grail because he believed that he possessed it!'

'He did?' Thomas asked. He was utterly confused now.

'Nehemiah was more than the Tirshatha of Judaea,' the doctor said, 'he was cupbearer to Artaxerxes. He says so at the beginning of his writings. "I was the King's cupbearer." There.' He pointed to a line of Hebrew script. '"I was the King's cupbearer." Your father's words, Thomas, taken from Nehemiah's story.'

Thomas stared at the writing and knew that Mordecai was right. That was his father's testimony. He had been cupbearer to the greatest King of all, to God Himself, to Christ, and the phrase confirmed Thomas's dreams. Father Ralph had been the cupbearer. He had possessed the Grail. It did exist. Thomas shivered.

'I think' – Mordecai spoke gently – 'that your father believed he possessed the Grail, but it seems unlikely.'

'Unlikely!' Thomas protested.

'I am merely a Jew,' Mordecai said blandly, 'so what can I know of the saviour of mankind? And there are those who say I should not even speak of such things, but so far as I understand Jesus was not rich. Am I right?'

'He was poor,' Thomas said.

'So I am right, he was not a rich man, and at the end of his life he attends a *seder*.'

'A *seder*?'

'The Passover feast, Thomas. And at the *seder* he eats bread and drinks wine, and the Grail, tell me if I am wrong, was either the bread dish or the wine goblet, yes?'

'Yes.'

'Yes,' Mordecai echoed and glanced off to his left where a small fishing boat rode the broken swell. There had been no sign of the *Saint-Esprit* all morning, and none of the smaller boats they passed showed any interest in the *Pentecost*. 'Yet if Jesus was poor,' Mordecai said, 'what kind of *seder* dish would he use? One made of gold? One ringed with jewels? Or a piece of common pottery?'

'Whatever he used,' Thomas said, 'God could transform.'

'Ah yes, of course, I was forgetting,' Mordecai said. He sounded disappointed, but then he smiled and gave Thomas the book. 'When we reach wherever we are going,' he said, 'I can write down translations of the Hebrew for you and I hope it helps.'

'Thomas!' Sir Guillaume bellowed from the stern. 'We need fresh arms to bail water!'

The caulking had not been finished and the *Pentecost* was taking water at an alarming rate and so Thomas went down into the bilge and handed up the pails to Robbie who jettisoned the water over the side. Sir Guillaume had been pressing Villeroy to go north and east again in an attempt to run past Caen and make Dunkirk, but Villeroy was unhappy with his small sail and even more unhappy with the leaking hull. 'I have to put in somewhere soon,' he growled, 'and you have to buy me a sail.'

They dared not call into Normandy. It was well known throughout the province that Sir Guillaume had been declared a traitor and if the *Pentecost* was searched – and it was probable on this smuggling coast that she would be – then Sir Guillaume would be discovered. That left Brittany and Sir Guillaume was eager to make Saint-Malo or Saint-Brieuc, but Thomas protested from the bilge that he and Will Skeat would be considered enemies by the Breton authorities who, in those towns, held allegiance to Duke Charles who was struggling against the English-backed rebels who reckoned Duke Jean was Brittany's true ruler. 'So where would you go?' Sir Guillaume demanded. 'England?'

'We'll never make England,' Villeroy said unhappily, looking at his sail.

'The islands?' Thomas suggested, thinking of Guernsey or Jersey.

'The islands!' Sir Guillaume liked that idea.

This time it was Villeroy who objected. 'Can't do it,' he said bluntly and explained that the *Pentecost* was a Guernsey boat and he had been one of the men who helped capture her. 'I take her into the isles,' he said, 'and they'll take her back and me with her.'

'For God's sake!' Sir Guillaume snarled. 'Then where do we go?'

'Can you make Tréguier?' Will Skeat asked and everyone was so astonished he had spoken that for a few heartbeats no one responded.

'Tréguier?' Villeroy asked after a while, then nodded. 'Like as not,' he said.

'Why Tréguier?' Sir Guillaume demanded.

'It was in English hands last I heard,' Skeat said.

'Still is,' Villeroy put in.

'And we've got friends there,' Skeat went on.

And enemies, Thomas thought. Tréguier was not just the closest Breton port in English hands, but also the harbour closest to La Roche-Derrien where Sir Geoffrey Carr, the Scarecrow, had gone. And Thomas had told Brother Germain that he was headed for the same small town, and that would surely mean de Taillebourg would hear of it and follow. And perhaps Jeanette was there too, and suddenly, though Thomas had been saying for weeks that he would not go back, he desperately wanted to reach La Roche-Derrien.

For it was there in Brittany, he possessed friends, old lovers and enemies he wanted to kill.

PART THREE

Brittany, Spring 1347

The King's Cupbearer

Jeanette Chenier, Comtesse d'Armorique, had lost her husband, her parents, her fortune, her house, her son and her royal lover, and all before she was twenty years old.

Her husband had been lost to an English arrow and had died in agony, weeping like a child.

Her parents had died of the bloody flux and their bedclothes had been burned before they were buried near the altar of St Renan's church. They had left Jeanette, their only remaining child, a small fortune in gold, a wine-shipping business and the great merchant's house on the river in La Roche-Derrien.

Jeanette had spent much of the fortune on equipping ships and men to fight the hated English who had killed her husband, but the English won and thus the fortune vanished.

Jeanette had begged help from Charles of Blois, Duke of Brittany and her dead husband's kinsman, and that was how she had lost her son. The three-year-old Charles, named for the duke, had been snatched from her. She was called a whore because she was a merchant's daughter and thus unworthy to be an aristocrat and Charles of Blois, to show Jeanette how much he despised her, had raped her. Her son, now the Count

319

of Armorica, was being raised by one of Charles of Blois's loyal supporters to ensure that the boy's extensive lands stayed sworn to the house of Blois. So Jeanette, who had lost her fortune in the attempt to make Duke Charles the undisputed ruler of Brittany, learned a new hatred and found a new lover, Thomas of Hookton. She fled north with him to the English army in Normandy and there she had caught the eye of Edward of Woodstock, Prince of Wales, and so Jeanette had abandoned Thomas. But then, fearing that the English would be crushed by the French in Picardy and that the victorious French would punish her for her choice of lover, she had fled again. She had been wrong about the battle, the English had won, but she could not go back. Kings, and the sons of Kings, did not reward fickleness and so Jeanette Chenier, dowager Countess of Armorica, had gone back to La Roche-Derrien to find she had lost her house.

When she had left La Roche-Derrien she had been deeply in debt and Monsieur Belas, a lawyer, had taken the house to pay those debts. Jeanette, on her return, possessed money enough to pay all she owed, for the Prince of Wales had been generous with jewels, but Belas would not move from the house. The law was on his side. Some of the English who occupied La Roche-Derrien showed sympathy for Jeanette, but they did not interfere with the decision of the court and it would not have mattered overmuch if they had, for everyone knew the English could not stay in the small town for long. Duke Charles was gathering a new army in Rennes and La Roche-Derrien was the most isolated and remote of all the English strongholds in Brittany, and when Duke Charles snapped up the town he would reward

Monsieur Belas, his agent, and scorn Jeanette Chenier whom he called a whore because she was not nobly born.

So Jeanette, unable to claim back her house, found another, much smaller, close to La Roche-Derrien's southern gate and she confessed her sins to the priest at St Renan's church, who said she had been wicked beyond man's measure and perhaps beyond God's measure as well; the priest promised her absolution if she would sin with him and he hoisted up his robes and reached for her, then cried aloud as Jeanette kicked him. She continued to take mass at St Renan's, for it was her childhood church and her parents were buried beneath the painting of Christ emerging from the tomb with a golden light about His head, and the priest dared not refuse her the sacrament and dared not meet her eyes.

Jeanette had lost her servants when she fled north with Thomas, but she hired a fourteen-year-old girl to be her kitchen maid and the girl's idiot brother to draw water and collect firewood. The Prince's jewels, Jeanette reckoned, would last her a year and something would turn up by then. She was young, she was truly beautiful, she was filled with anger, her child was still a hostage and she was inspired by hatred. Some in the town feared she was mad because she was much thinner than when she had left La Roche-Derrien, but her hair was still raven-black, her skin as smooth as the rare silk that only the wealthiest could afford and her eyes were big and bright. Men came and begged her favours, but were told they could not speak to her again unless they brought her the shrivelled heart of Belas the lawyer and the shrivelled prick of Charles of Blois. 'Bring them both to me in reliquaries,' she told them, 'but bring me my son alive.' Her anger repelled men and some of them spread the tale that she was moon-touched, perhaps a witch. The priest of St Renan's confided to the other clergy in the town that Jeanette had tried to tempt him and he spoke darkly of bringing in the Inquisition, but the English would not permit it for the King of England refused to let the torturers of God work their dark arts in his possessions. 'There's enough grumbling,' Dick Totesham, commander of the English garrison in La Roche-Derrien said, 'without bringing in damned friars to stir up trouble.'

Totesham and his garrison knew that Charles of Blois was raising an army that would attack La Roche-Derrien before marching on to besiege the other English strongholds in Brittany, and so they worked hard to make the town's walls higher and to build new ramparts outside the old. Local farm labourers were whipped to the work. They were forced to push barrowloads of clay and rock, they drove timbers into the soil to make palisades and they dug ditches. They hated the English for forcing them to work without pay, but the English did not care for they had to defend themselves and Totesham pleaded with Westminster to send him more men and on the feast of St Felix, in the middle of January, a troop of Welsh archers landed at Tréguier, which was the small harbour an hour and a half's walk upriver from La Roche-Derrien, but the garrison's only other reinforcements were a few knights and men-at-arms who were down on their luck and came to the small town in hope of plunder and prisoners. Some of those knights came from as far away as Flanders, lured by false rumours of the riches to be had in Brittany, and another six men-at-arms arrived from northern England, led by a malevolent, raw-faced man who carried a whip and a heavy load of grudges, and they were La Roche-Derrien's last reinforcements before the *Pentecost* came to the river.

La Roche-Derrien's garrison was small, but Duke Charles's army was large and grew even larger. Spies in English pay told of Genoese crossbowmen arriving at Rennes in companies a hundred strong, and of men-at-arms riding from France to swear fealty to Charles of Blois. His army swelled and the King of England, apparently careless of his garrisons in Brittany, sent them no help. Which meant that La Roche-Derrien, smallest of all the English fortress towns in Brittany and the one closest to the enemy, was doomed.

Thomas felt strangely unsettled as the *Pentecost* slipped between the low rocky outcrops that marked the mouth of the River Jaudy. Was it a failure, he wondered, to be coming back to this small town? Or had God sent him because it was here that the enemies of the Grail would be seeking him? That was how Thomas thought of the mysterious de Taillebourg and his servant. Or perhaps, he told himself, he was merely nervous of seeing Jeanette again. Their history was too tangled, there was too much hate mixed with the love, yet he did want to see her and he was worried she would not want to see him. He tried and failed to conjure a picture of her face as the incoming tide carried the *Pentecost* into the river's mouth, where guillemots spread their ragged black wings to dry above rocks fretted with white foam. A seal raised its glistening head, stared indignantly at

Thomas and then went back to the depths. The river-banks came closer, bringing the smell of land. There were boulders and pale grass and small wind-bent trees, while in the shallows there were sinuous fish traps made from woven willow stakes. A small girl, scarce more than six years old, used a stone to knock limpets from the rocks. 'It's a poor supper, that,' Will Skeat remarked.

'It is, Will, it is.'

'Ah, Tom!' Skeat smiled, recognizing the voice. 'You never had limpets for supper!'

'I did!' Thomas protested. 'And for breakfast too.'

'A man who speaks Latin and French? Eating limpets?' Skeat grinned. 'You can write, ain't that so, Tom?'

'Good as a priest, Will.'

'I reckon we should send a letter to his lordship,' Skeat said, meaning the Earl of Northampton, 'and ask for my men to be shipped here, only he won't do that without money, will he?'

'He owes you money,' Thomas said.

Skeat frowned at Thomas. 'He does?'

'Your men have been serving him these last months. He has to pay for that.'

Skeat shook his head. 'The Earl was never slow to pay for good soldiers. He'll be keeping their purses full, I'll be bound, and if I want them here I'll have to per-suade him to let them go and I'll have to pay their passages too.' Skeat's men were contracted to fight for the Earl of Northampton who, after campaigning in Brittany, had joined the King in Normandy and now served him near Calais. 'I'll have to pay passage for men and horses, Thomas,' Skeat went on, 'and unless things have changed since I got slapped about the head that won't be cheap. Won't be cheap. And why would the Earl want them to leave Calais? They'll have a bellyful of fighting come springtime.'

The question was a good one, Thomas thought, for there surely would be some vicious fighting near Calais when the winter ended. So far as Thomas knew the town had not fallen, but the English had surrounded it and the French King was said to be raising a great army that would attack the besiegers in springtime.

'There'll be plenty of fighting here come spring,' Thomas said, nodding at the riverbank, which was very close now. The fields beyond the banks were fallow, but at least the barns and farmhouses still stood for these lands fed La Roche-Derrien's garrison and so they had been spared the pillage, rape and fire that had crackled across the rest of the dukedom.

'There'll be fighting here,' Skeat agreed, 'but more in Calais. Maybe you and I should go there, Tom?'

Thomas said nothing. He feared Skeat could no longer command a band of men-at-arms and archers. His old friend was too prone to forgetfulness or to sudden bouts of vagueness and melancholy, and those attacks were made worse by the times when Skeat seemed like his old self – except he never was *quite* like the old Will Skeat who had been so swift in war, savage in decision and clever in battle. Now he repeated himself, became confused and was too frequently puzzled – as he was now by a guardboat flying England's red cross on its white field that pulled downstream towards the *Pentecost*. Skeat frowned at the small craft. 'Is he an enemy?'

'Flying our flag, Will.'

'He is?'

A mail-clad man stood up in the rowboat's bows and hailed the *Pentecost*. 'Who are you?'

'Sir William Skeat!' Thomas shouted back, using the name that would be most welcome in Brittany.

There was a pause, maybe of incredulity. 'Sir William Skeat?' the man called back. 'Will Skeat, you mean?'

'The King knighted him,' Thomas told the man.

'I keep forgetting that myself,' Skeat said.

The portside oarsmen backed water so that the guard boat turned in the tide alongside the *Pentecost*. 'What are you carrying?' the man asked.

'Empty!' Thomas shouted.

The man stared up at the ragged, scorched, doubled sail. 'You had trouble?'

'Off Normandy.'

'Time those bastards were killed once and for all,' the man grumbled, then gestured upriver to where Tréguier's houses smeared the sky with their woodsmoke. 'Tie up outboard of the *Edward*,' he ordered them. 'There's a harbour fee you'll have to pay. Six shillings.'

'Six shillings?' Villeroy exploded when he was told. 'Six bloody shillings! Do they think we pull money off the seabed in nets?'

Thus Thomas and Will Skeat came back to Tréguier where the cathedral had lost its tower after Bretons who supported Charles of Blois had fired crossbows at the English from its summit. In retaliation the English had pulled the tower down and shipped the stone to London. The little harbour town was scantily populated now for it had no walls and Charles of Blois's men sometimes raided the warehouses behind the quay. Small ships could go all the way upriver to La Roche-

Derrien, but the *Pentecost* drew too much water and so she tied herself alongside the English cog and then a dozen men in red-crossed jupons came aboard to take the harbour fee and look for contraband or else a healthy bribe to persuade them to ignore whatever they might discover, but they found neither goods nor bribe. Their commander, a fat man with a weeping ulcer on his forehead, confirmed that Richard Totesham still commanded at La Roche-Derrien. 'He be there,' the fat man said, 'and Sir Thomas Dagworth commands in Brest.'

'Dagworth!' Skeat sounded pleased. 'He's a good one, he is. So's Dick Totesham,' he added to Thomas, then looked puzzled as Sir Guillaume emerged from the forecabin.

'It's Sir Guillaume,' Thomas said in a low voice.

''Course it is,' Skeat said.

Sir Guillaume dropped the saddlebags on the deck and the chink of coins drew an expectant gaze from the fat man. Sir Guillaume met his gaze and half drew his sword.

'Reckon I be going,' the fat man said.

'Reckon you do,' Skeat said with a chuckle.

Robbie heaved his baggage onto the deck, then stared across the waist of the *Edward* to where four girls were gutting herrings and chucking the offal into the air where gulls snatched it in mid flight. The girls strung the gutted fish on long poles that would be placed in the smokers at the quay's end. 'Are they all as pretty as that?' Robbie asked.

'Prettier,' Thomas said, wondering how the Scot could see the girl's faces under their bonnets.

'I'm going to like Brittany,' Robbie said.

There were debts to be paid before they could leave. Sir Guillaume paid off Villeroy and added enough cash to buy a new sail. 'You might do well,' he advised the big man, 'to avoid Caen for a while.'

'We'll go on down to Gascony,' Villeroy said. 'There's always trade in Gascony. Maybe we'll even poke on down to Portugal?'

'Perhaps,' Mordecai spoke shyly, 'you would let me come?'

'You?' Sir Guillaume turned on the doctor. 'You hate goddamn ships.'

'I have to go south,' Mordecai said wearily, 'to Montpellier first of all. The further south a man is, the friendlier the people. I would rather suffer a month of sea and cold than meet Duke Charles's men.'

'Passage to Gascony' – Sir Guillaume offered Villeroy a gold coin – 'for a friend of mine.'

Villeroy glanced at Yvette, who shrugged, and that persuaded the big man to agree. 'You're welcome, doctor,' he said.

So they said farewell to Mordecai and then Thomas and Robbie, Will Skeat and Sir Guillaume and his two men-at-arms went ashore. A boat was going upstream to La Roche-Derrien, but not till later in the day and so the two men-at-arms were left with the baggage and Thomas led the others along the narrow track that followed the river's western bank. They wore mail and carried weapons for the local peasantry were not friendly to the English, but the only men they passed were a dozen drab labourers pitch-forking dung from two carts. The men paused to watch the soldiers pass, but said nothing. 'And by this time tomorrow,' Thomas commented, 'Charles of Blois will know we've arrived.'

'He'll be quaking in his boots,' Skeat said with a grin.

It began to rain as they reached the bridge which led into La Roche-Derrien. Thomas stopped under the arch of the protective barbican on the bank opposite the town and pointed upstream to the ramshackle quay where he and Skeat's other archers had sneaked into La Roche-Derrien on the night it first fell to the English. 'Remember that place, Will?' he asked.

' 'Course I remember,' Skeat said, though he looked vague and Thomas did not say more.

They crossed the stone bridge and hurried down the street to the house by the tavern that had always been Richard Totesham's headquarters and Totesham himself was just sliding out of his saddle as they arrived. He turned and scowled at the newcomers, then recognized Will Skeat and stared at his old friend as though he had seen a ghost. Skeat looked blankly back and his lack of recognition troubled Totesham. 'Will?' the garrison commander asked. 'Will? Is it you, Will?'

A look of astonished delight animated Skeat's face. 'Dick Totesham! Of all the folk to meet!'

Totesham was puzzled that Skeat should be surprised to meet him in a garrison he commanded, but then he saw the emptiness in his old friend's eyes and frowned. 'Are you well, Will?'

'I had a bash on the head,' Skeat said, 'but a doctor cobbled me together again. Things get blurred here and there, just blurred.'

The two clasped hands. They were both men who had been born penniless and become soldiers, then earned the trust of their masters and gained the profits of prisoners ransomed and property plundered until they were wealthy enough to raise their own bands of men, which they hired to the King or to a noble and so became richer still as they ravaged more enemy lands. When the troubadours sang of battle they named the King as the fighting hero, and extolled the exploits of dukes, earls, barons and knights, but it was men like Totesham and Skeat who did most of England's fighting.

Totesham clapped Skeat good-naturedly on the shoulder. 'Tell me you've brought your men, Will.'

'God knows where they are,' Skeat said. 'I haven't laid eyes on them in months.'

'They're outside Calais,' Thomas put in.

'Dear God.' Totesham made the sign of the cross. He was a squat man, grey-haired and broad-faced, who held La Roche-Derrien's garrison together by sheer force of character, but he knew he had too few men. Far too few men. 'I've a hundred and thirty-two men under orders,' he told Skeat, 'and half of those are sick. Then there's fifty or sixty mercenaries who might or might not stay till Charles of Blois arrives. Of course the townsfolk will fight for us, or most of them will.'

'They will?' Thomas interrupted, astonished at the claim. When the English had captured the town the previous year the town's people had fought bitterly to defend their walls, and when they had lost they had been subjected to rape and plunder, yet now they supported the garrison?

'Trade's good,' Totesham explained. 'They've never been so rich! Ships to Gascony, to Portugal, to Flanders and to England. Making money, they are. They don't want us to leave, so yes, some will fight for us and it'll help, but it's not like having trained men.'

The other English troops in Brittany were a long way to the west so when Charles of Blois came with his army, Totesham would have to hold the small town for two or three weeks before he could expect any relief and, even with the inhabitants' help, he doubted he could do it. He had sent a petition to the King at Calais begging that more men be sent to La Roche-Derrien. 'We are far from help,' his clerk had written to Totesham's dictation, 'and our enemies gather close about.' Totesham, seeing Will Skeat, had assumed that Skeat's men had arrived in answer to his petition and he could not hide his disappointment. 'You'll write to the King yourself?' Totesham asked Will.

'Tom here can write for me.'

'Ask for your men to be sent,' Totesham urged. 'I need three or four hundred more archers, but your fifty or sixty would help.'

'Tommy Dagworth can't send you any?' Skeat asked.

'He's as hard pressed as I am. Too much land to hold, too few men and the King won't hear of us surrendering a single acre to Charles of Blois.'

'So why doesn't he send reinforcements?' Sir Guillaume asked.

'Because he ain't got men to spare,' Totesham said, 'which is no reason for us not to ask.'

Totesham took them inside his house where a fire blazed in a big hearth and his servants brought jugs of mulled wine and plates of bread and cold pork. A baby lay in a wooden cradle by the fire and Totesham blushed when he admitted it was his. 'Newly married,' he told Skeat, then ordered a maid to take the baby away before it began crying. He flinched when Skeat took off his hat to reveal his scarred, thick-ridged scalp, then he insisted on hearing Will's story, and when it was told he thanked Sir Guillaume for the help the Frenchman had given his friend. Thomas and Robbie got a cooler welcome, the latter because he was Scottish and the former because Totesham remembered Thomas from the previous year. 'You were a bloody nuisance,' Totesham said bluntly, 'you and the Countess of Armorica.'

'Is she here?' Thomas asked.

'She came back, aye.' Totesham sounded guarded.

'We can go back to her house, Will,' Thomas said to Skeat.

'No you can't,' Totesham said firmly. 'She lost the house. It was sold to pay her debts and she's been screaming about it ever since, but it was sold fair and square. And the lawyer who bought it has paid us a quittance to be left in peace and I don't want him disturbed, so the two of you can find yourself space at the Two Foxes. Then come and have supper.' This invitation was to Will Skeat and to Sir Guillaume and pointedly not to Thomas or Robbie.

Thomas did not mind. He and Robbie found a room to share in the tavern called the Two Foxes and afterwards, as Robbie had his first taste of Breton ale, Thomas went to St Renan's church, which was one of the smallest in La Roche-Derrien, but also one of the wealthiest because Jeanette's father had endowed it. He had built a bell tower and paid to have fine pictures painted on its walls, though by the time Thomas reached St Renan's it was too dark to see the Saviour walking on Galilee's water or the souls tumbling down to their fiery hell. The only light in the church came from some candles burning on the altar where a silver reliquary held St Renan's tongue, but Thomas knew there was another treasure beneath the altar, something almost as rare as a saint's silent tongue, and he wanted to consult it. It

332

was a book, a gift from Jeanette's father, and Thomas had been astonished to find it there, not just because the book had survived the fall of the town – though in truth not many soldiers would seek books for plunder – but because there was any book in a small church in a Breton town. Books were rare and that was St Renan's treasure: a bible. Most of the New Testament was missing, evidently because some soldiers had taken those pages to use in the latrines, but all of the Old Testament remained. Thomas threaded his way through the black-dressed old ladies who knelt and prayed in the nave and he found the book beneath the altar and blew off the dust and cobwebs, then put it beside the candles. One of the women hissed that he was being impious, but Thomas ignored her.

He turned the stiff pages, sometimes stopping to admire a painted capital. There was a bible in St Peter's church in Dorchester and his father had possessed one, and Thomas must have seen a dozen in Oxford, but he had seen few others and, as he searched the pages, he marvelled at the time it must take to copy such a vast book. More women protested his annexation of the altar and so, to placate them, he went a few steps away and sat cross-legged with the heavy book on his lap. He was now too far from the candles and found it hard to read the script, which was mostly ill done. The capitals were pretty, suggesting they had been done by a skilled hand, but most of the writing was cramped and his task was made no easier by his ignorance of where to look in the huge book. He began at the end of the Old Testament, but did not find what he wanted and so he leafed back, the huge pages crackling as he turned them. He knew what he sought was not in the Psalms so he turned those pages fast, then slowed again, seeking words out of the ill-written script and then, suddenly, the names jumped from the page. '*Neemias Athersatha filius Achelai*', 'Nehemiah the Governor, son of Hachaliah'. He read the whole passage, but did not find what he sought, and so he leafed still further back, page by stiff page, knowing he was close, and there, at last, it was.

'*Ego enim eram pincerna regis.*'

He stared at the phrase, read it aloud. '"*Ego enim eram pincerna regis.*"'

'For I was the King's cupbearer.'

Mordecai had thought Father Ralph's book was a plea to God to make the Grail true, but Thomas did not agree. His father did not want to be the cupbearer. No, the notebook was a way of confessing and of hiding the truth. His father had left a trail for him to follow. Go from Hachaliah to the Tirshatha and realize that the Governor was also the cupbearer: *ego enim eram pincerna regis*. 'Was', Thomas thought. Did that mean his father had lost the Grail? It was more likely that he knew Thomas would only read the book after his death. But Thomas was certain of one thing: the words confirmed that the Grail did exist and his father had been its reluctant keeper. I was the King's cupbearer; let this cup pass from me; the cup makes me drunk. The cup existed and Thomas felt a shiver go though his body. He stared at the candles on the altar and his eyes blurred with tears. Eleanor had been right. The Grail existed and it was waiting to be found and to put the world right and to bring God to man and man to God and peace on earth. It existed. It was the Grail.

'My father,' a woman said, 'gave that book to the church.'

'I know he did,' Thomas said, then he closed the bible and he turned to look at Jeanette and he was almost frightened to see her in case she was less beautiful than he remembered, or perhaps he feared the sight of her would engender hatred because she had abandoned him, but instead he felt tears in his eyes when he saw her face. *'Merle,'* he said softly, using her nickname. It meant Blackbird.

'Thomas.' Her voice was toneless, then she flicked her head towards an old woman dressed and veiled in black. 'Madame Verlon,' Jeanette said, 'who is nervous of life, told me that an English soldier was stealing the bible.'

'So you came to fight the soldier?' Thomas asked. A candle guttered to his right, its flame flickering as fast as a small bird's heart.

Jeanette shrugged. 'The priest here is a coward and would not challenge an English archer, so who else would come?'

'Madame Verlon can rest safe,' Thomas said as he put the bible back under the altar.

'She also said' – Jeanette's voice had a quaver in it – 'that the man stealing the bible had a big black bow.' Which was why, she implied, she had come herself instead of sending for help. She had guessed it was Thomas.

'At least you did not have to come far,' Thomas said, gesturing to the side door which led into the yard of Jeanette's father's house. He was pretending not to know that she had lost the house.

Her head jerked back. 'I do not live there,' she said curtly, 'not now.'

A dozen women were listening and they stepped

nervously back as Thomas came towards them. 'Then perhaps, madame,' he said to Jeanette, 'you will let me escort you home?'

She nodded abruptly. Her eyes seemed very bright and big in the candlelight. She was thinner, Thomas thought, or perhaps that was the darkness in the church shadowing her cheeks. She had a bonnet tied under her chin and a great black cloak that swept on the flagstones as she followed him to the western door. 'You remember Belas?' she asked him.

'I remember the name,' Thomas said. 'Wasn't he a lawyer?'

'He is a lawyer,' Jeanette said, 'and a thing of bile, a creature of slime, a cheat. What was that English word you taught me? A tosspot. He is a tosspot. When I came home he had bought the house, claiming it was sold to pay my debts. But he had bought the debts! He promised to look after my business, waited till I was gone, then took my house. And now I am back he won't let me pay what I owed. He says it is paid. I said I would buy the house from him for more than he paid, but he just laughs at me.'

Thomas held the door for her. Rain was spitting in the street. 'You don't want the house,' he told her, 'not if Charles of Blois comes back. You should be gone by then.'

'You're still telling me what to do, Thomas?' she asked and then, as if to soften the harshness of her words, she took his arm. Or perhaps she put her hand through his elbow because the street was steep and slippery. 'I will stay here, I think.'

'If you hadn't escaped from him,' Thomas said, 'Charles was going to marry you to one of his men-at-arms. If he finds you here he'll do that. Or worse.'

'He already has my child. He has already raped me. What more can he do? No' – she clutched Thomas's arm fiercely – 'I shall stay in my little house by the south gate and when he rides into the town I will sink a crossbow quarrel in his belly.'

'I'm surprised you haven't put a quarrel into Belas's belly.'

'You think I would hang for a lawyer's death?' Jeanette asked and gave a short, hard laugh. 'No, I shall save my death for the life of Charles of Blois and all Brittany and France will know he was killed by a woman.'

'Unless he returns your child?'

'He won't!' she said fiercely. 'He answered no appeals.' She meant, Thomas was sure, that the Prince of Wales, maybe the King as well, had written to Charles of Blois, but the appeals had achieved nothing, and why should they? England was Charles's most bitter enemy. 'It's all about land, Thomas,' she said wearily, 'land and money.' She meant that her son, who at three years old was the Count of Armorica, was the rightful heir to great swathes of western Brittany that were presently under English occupation. If the child were to give fealty to Duke Jean, who was Edward of England's candidate to rule Brittany, then the claim of Charles of Blois to sovereignty of the duchy would be seriously weakened and so Charles had taken the child and would keep him till he was of an age to swear fealty.

'Where is Charles?' Thomas asked. It was one of the ironies of Jeanette's life that her son had been named after his great-uncle in an attempt to win his favour.

'He is in the Tower of Roncelets,' Jeanette said, 'which is south of Rennes. He is being raised by the Lord of Roncelets.' She turned on Thomas. 'It's almost a year since I've seen him!'

'The Tower of Roncelets,' Thomas said, 'it's a castle?'

'I've not seen it. A tower, I suppose. Yes, a castle.'

'You're sure he's there?'

'I'm sure of nothing,' Jeanette said wearily, 'but I received a letter which said Charles was there and I have no reason to doubt it.'

'Who wrote the letter?'

'I don't know. It was not signed.' She walked in silence for a few paces, her hand warm on his arm. 'It was Belas,' she said finally. 'I don't know that for sure, but it must be. He was goading me, tormenting me. It is not enough that he has my house and Charles of Blois has my child, Belas wants me to suffer. Or else he wants me to go to Roncelets knowing that I would be given back to Charles of Blois. I'm sure it was Belas. He hates me.'

'Why?'

'Why do you think?' she asked scornfully. 'I have something he wants, something all men want, but I won't give it to him.'

They walked on through dark streets. Singing sounded from some taverns, and somewhere a woman screamed at her man. A dog barked and was silenced. The rain pattered on thatch, dripped from the eaves and made the muddy street slippery. A red glow slowly appeared ahead, growing as they came closer until Thomas saw the flames of two braziers warming the guards on the south gate and he remembered how he and Jake and Sam had opened that gate to let in the

English army. 'I promised you once,' he said to Jeanette, 'that I would fetch Charles back.'

'You and I, Thomas,' Jeanette said, 'made too many promises.' She still sounded weary.

'I should start keeping some of mine,' Thomas said. 'But to reach Roncelets I need horses.'

'I can afford horses,' Jeanette said, stopping by a dark doorway. 'I live here,' she went on, then looked into his face. He was tall, but she was very nearly the same height. 'The Count of Roncelets is famous as a warrior. You mustn't die to keep a promise you should never have made.'

'It was made, though,' Thomas said.

She nodded. 'That is true.'

There was a long pause. Thomas could hear a sentry's footsteps on the wall. 'I —' he began.

'No,' she said hastily.

'I didn't . . .'

'Another time. I must get used to your being here. I'm tired of men, Thomas. Since Picardy . . .' She paused and Thomas thought she would say no more, but then she shrugged. 'Since Picardy I have lived like a nun.'

He kissed her forehead. 'I love you,' he said, meaning it, but surprised all the same that he had spoken the thought aloud.

For a heartbeat she did not speak. The reflected light from the two braziers glinted red in her eyes. 'What happened to that girl?' she asked. 'That little pale thing who was so protective of you?'

'I failed to protect her,' Thomas said, 'and she died.'

'Men are such bastards,' she said, then turned and pulled the rope that lifted the latch of the door. She paused for a moment. 'But I'm glad you're here,' she said without looking back, and then the door was shut, the bolt slid home and she was gone.

Sir Geoffrey Carr had begun to think his foray to Brittany was a mistake. For a long time there had been no sign of Thomas of Hookton and once the archer arrived he had made little effort to discover any treasure. It was mysterious and all the time Sir Geoffrey's debts were growing. But then, at last, the Scarecrow discovered what plans Thomas of Hookton was hatching. That new knowledge took Sir Geoffrey to Maître Belas's house.

Rain poured on La Roche-Derrien. It was one of the wettest winters in memory. The ditch beyond the strengthened town wall was flooded so it looked like a moat, and many of the River Jaudy's water meadows resembled lakes. The streets of the town were sticky with mud, men's boots were thick with it and women went to market wearing awkward wooden pattens that slipped treacherously on the steeper streets and still thick mud was smeared on the hems of their dresses and cloaks. The only good things about such rain was the protection it offered against fire and, for the English, the knowledge that it would make any siege of the town difficult. Siege engines, whether catapults, trebuchets or guns, needed a solid base, not a quagmire, and men could not assault through a marsh. Richard Totesham was said to be praying for more rain and giving thanks every morning that dawned grey, heavy and damp.

'A wet winter, Sir Geoffrey,' Belas greeted the Scarecrow, then gave his visitor a covert inspection. A raw and ugly face, he thought, and while Sir Geoffrey's clothes were of a fine quality, they had also been made for a fatter man which suggested that either the English-man had recently lost weight or, more likely, the clothes had been taken from a man he had killed in battle. A coiled whip hung at his belt, which seemed a strange accoutrement, but the lawyer never presumed to understand soldiers. 'A very wet winter,' Belas went on, waving the Scarecrow into a chair.

'It's a pissing wet winter,' Sir Geoffrey snarled to cover his nervousness, 'nothing but rain, cold and chilblains.' He was nervous because he was not certain that this thin and watchful lawyer was as sympathetic to Charles of Blois as tavern rumour suggested, and he had been forced to leave Beggar and Dickon in the courtyard below and he felt vulnerable without their protective company, especially as the lawyer had a great hulking attendant who was dressed in a leather jerkin and had a long sword at his side.

'Pierre protects me,' Belas said. He had seen Sir Geoffrey glancing at the big man. 'He protects me from the enemies all honest lawyers make. Please, Sir Geoffrey, sit yourself.' He gestured again at a chair. A small fire burned in the hearth, the smoke vanishing up a newly made chimney. The lawyer had a face as hungry as a stoat and pale as a grass-snake's belly. He was wearing a black gown and a black cloak edged with black fur and a black hat with flaps that covered his ears, though he now pushed one flap up so he could hear the Scarecrow's voice. '*Parlez-vous français*?' he asked.

'No.'

'*Brezoneg a ouzit*?' the lawyer enquired and, when he saw the dumb incomprehension on the Scarecrow's face, shrugged. 'You don't speak Breton?'

'I just told you, didn't I? I don't talk French.'

'French and Breton are not the same language, Sir Geoffrey.'

'They're not bloody English,' Sir Geoffrey said belligerently.

'Indeed they are not. Alas, I do not speak English well, but I learn fast. It is, after all, the language of our new masters.'

'Masters?' the Scarecrow asked. 'Or enemies?'

Belas shrugged. 'I am a man of, how do you say? Of affairs. A man of affairs. It is not possible, I think, to be such and not to make enemies.' He shrugged again, as if he spoke of trivialities, then he leaned back in his chair. 'But you come on business, Sir Geoffrey? You have property to convey, perhaps? A contract to make?'

'Jeanette Chenier, Countess of Armorica,' Sir Geoffrey said bluntly.

Belas was surprised, but did not show it. He was alert, though. He knew well enough that Jeanette wanted revenge and he was ever watchful for her machinations, but now he pretended indifference. 'I know of the lady,' he admitted.

'She knows you. And she don't like you, *Monsieur* Belas,' Sir Geoffrey said, making his pronunciation of the name sound like a sneer. 'She don't like you one small bit. She'd like to have your collops in a skillet and kindle a fierce fire under them.'

Belas turned to the papers on his desk as though his visitor was being tedious. 'I told you, Sir Geoffrey, that a lawyer inevitably makes enemies. It is nothing to worry about. The law protects me.'

'Piss on the law, Belas.' Sir Geoffrey spoke flatly. His eyes, curiously pale, watched the lawyer, who pretended to be busy sharpening a quill. 'Suppose the lady got her son back?' the Scarecrow went on. 'Suppose the lady takes her son to Edward of England and has the boy swear fealty to Duke Jean? The law won't stop them chopping off your collops then, will it? One, two, snip, snip and stoke the fire, lawyer.'

'Such an eventuality,' Belas said in apparent boredom, 'could have no possible repercussions for me.'

'So your English ain't bad, eh?' Sir Geoffrey sneered. 'I don't pretend to know the law, monsieur, but I know folk. If the Countess gets her son then she'll go to Calais and see the King.'

'So?' Belas asked, still pretending carelessness.

'Three months' – Sir Geoffrey held up three fingers – 'four, maybe, before your Charles of Blois can get here. And she might be in Calais in four weeks' time and back here with the King's piece of parchment inside eight weeks, and by then she'll be valuable. Her son has what the King wants and he'll give her what she wants, and what she wants is your collops. She'll bite them off with her little white teeth and then she'll skin you alive, monsieur, and the law won't help you. Not against the King, it won't.'

Belas had been pretending to read a parchment, which he now released so that it rolled up with a snap. He stared at the Scarecrow, then shrugged. 'I doubt, Sir Geoffrey, that what you describe is likely to happen. The Countess's son is not here.'

'But suppose, monsieur, just suppose, that a party of men is readying themselves to go to Roncelets and fetch the little tosspot?'

Belas paused. He had heard a rumour that just such a raid was being planned, but he had doubted the rumour's truth for such tales had been told a score

343

of times and come to nothing. Yet something in Sir Geoffrey's tone suggested that this time there might be some meat on the bone. 'A party of men,' Belas responded flatly.

'A party of men,' the Scarecrow confirmed, 'that plans to ride to Roncelets and watch until the little darling is taken out for his morning piddle and then they'll snatch him, bring him back here and put your collops in the frying pan.'

Belas unrolled the parchment and pretended to read it again. 'It is hardly surprising, Sir Geoffrey,' he said carelessly, 'that Madame Chenier conspires for the return of her son. It is to be expected. But why should you bother me with it? What harm can it do me?' He dipped the newly sharpened quill in his ink pot. 'And how do you know about this planned raid?'

'Because I ask the right questions, don't I?' the Scarecrow answered.

In truth the Scarecrow had heard rumours that Thomas planned a raid on Rostrenen, but other men in the town had sworn that Rostrenen had been picked over so often that a sparrow would die of starvation there now. So what, the Scarecrow had wondered, was Thomas really doing? Sir Geoffrey was certain that Thomas was riding to find the treasure, the same treasure that had taken him to Durham, but why would it be at Rostrenen? What was there? Sir Geoffrey had accosted one of Richard Totesham's deputies in a tavern and bought the man ale and asked about Rostrenen and the man had laughed and shaken his head. 'You don't want to ride on that nonsense,' he told Sir Geoffrey.

'Nonsense?'

'They ain't going to Rostrenen. They're going to

Roncelets. Well, we don't know that for certain,' the man had continued, 'but the Countess of Armorica is up to her pretty neck in the whole business, so that means it must be Roncelets. And you want my advice, Sir Geoffrey? Stay out of it. They don't call Roncelets the wasp's nest for nothing.'

Sir Geoffrey, more confused than ever, asked more questions and slowly he came to understand that the *thesaurus* Thomas sought was not thick golden coins, nor leather bags filled with jewels, but instead was land: the Breton estates of the Count of Armorica, and if Jeanette's little son swore allegiance to Duke Jean, then the English cause in Brittany was advanced. It was a treasure in its way, a political treasure: not so satisfying as gold, but it was still valuable. Quite what the land had to do with Durham the Scarecrow did not know. Perhaps Thomas had gone there to find some deeds? Or a grant made by a previous duke? Some lawyer's nonsense, and it did not matter; what mattered was that Thomas was riding to seize a boy who could bring political muscle to the King of England, and Sir Geoffrey had then wondered how he could benefit from the child and for a time he had toyed with the wild idea of kidnapping the boy and taking him to Calais himself, but then he had realized there was a far safer profit to be made by simply betraying Thomas. Which was why he was here, and Belas, he suspected, was interested, but the lawyer was also pretending that the raid on Roncelets was none of his business and so the Scarecrow decided it was time to force the lawyer's hand. He stood and pulled down his rain-soaked jerkin. 'You ain't interested, monsieur?' he asked. 'So be it. You know your business better than I do, but I know how many are going to Roncelets and I know who leads them and I can tell you when they're going.' The quill was no longer moving and drips of ink were falling from its tip to blot the parchment, but Belas did not notice as the Scarecrow's harsh voice ground on. 'Of course they ain't told Mr Totesham what they're doing, on account that officially he'd disapprove, which he might or he might not, I wouldn't know, so he thinks they're going to burn some farms near Rostrenen, which maybe they will and maybe they won't, but whatever they say and whatever Master Totesham might believe, I know they're going to Roncelets.'

'How do you know?' Belas asked quietly.

'I know!' Sir Geoffrey said harshly.

Belas put down the pen. 'Sit,' he ordered the Scarecrow, 'and tell me what you want.'

'Two things,' Sir Geoffrey said as he sat again. 'I came to this damned town to make money, but we're having thin pickings, monsieur, thin pickings.' Very thin, for English troops had been pillaging Brittany for months and there were no farms within a day's ride that had not been burned and robbed, while to ride further afield was to risk strong enemy patrols. Beyond the walls of its fortresses Brittany was a wilderness of ambush, danger and ruin and the Scarecrow had quickly discovered that it would be a hard landscape in which to make a fortune.

'So money is the first thing you want,' Belas said acidly. 'And the second?'

'Refuge,' Sir Geoffrey said.

'Refuge?'

'When Charles of Blois takes the town,' the Scarecrow said, 'then I want to be in your courtyard.'

'I cannot think why,' Belas said drily, 'but of course you will be welcome. And as for money?' He licked his lips. 'Let us first see how good your information is.'

'And if it is good?' the Scarecrow asked.

Belas considered for a moment. 'Seventy *écus*?' he suggested. 'Eighty, perhaps?'

'Seventy *écus*?' The Scarecrow paused to convert it into pounds, then spat. 'Just ten pounds! No! I want a hundred pounds and I want them in English-struck coin.'

They settled on sixty English pounds, to be paid when Belas had proof that Sir Geoffrey was telling him the truth, and that truth was that Thomas of Hookton was leading men to Roncelets and they were leaving on the eve of Valentine's Feast which was just over two weeks away.

'Why so long?' Belas wanted to know.

'He wants more men. He's only got half a dozen now and he's trying to persuade others to go with him. He's telling them there's gold to be had at Roncelets.'

'If you want money,' Belas asked acidly, 'why don't you ride with him?'

'Because I'm seeing you instead,' Sir Geoffrey answered.

Belas leaned back in his chair and steepled his pale, long fingers. 'And that is all you want?' he asked the Englishman. 'Some money and refuge?'

The Scarecrow stood, bending his head under the room's low beams. 'You pay me once,' he said, 'and you'll pay me again.'

'Perhaps,' Belas said evasively.

'I give you what you want,' Sir Geoffrey said, 'and you'll pay me.' He went to the door, then stopped because Belas had called him back.

'Did you say Thomas of Hookton?' Belas asked and there was an undeniable interest in his voice.

'Thomas of Hookton,' the Scarecrow confirmed.

'Thank you,' Belas said, and he looked down at a scroll he had just unrolled and it seemed he found Thomas's name written there for his finger checked and he smiled. 'Thank you,' he said again and, to Sir Geoffrey's astonishment, the lawyer took a small purse from a chest beside his desk and pushed it towards the Scarecrow. 'For that news, Sir Geoffrey, I do thank you.'

Sir Geoffrey, back down in the courtyard, found he had been given ten pounds of English gold. Ten pounds for just mentioning Thomas's name? He suspected there was much more to learn about Thomas's plans, but at least he had gold in his pocket now, so the visit to the lawyer had been profitable and there was the promise of more lawyer's gold to come.

But it was still bloody raining.

Thomas persuaded Richard Totesham that instead of writing another plea to the King they should appeal to the Earl of Northampton who was now among the leaders of the army besieging Calais. The letter reminded his lordship of his great victory in capturing La Roche-Derrien and stressed that achievement might all be for naught if the garrison was not reinforced. Richard Totesham dictated most of the words and Will Skeat put a cross beside his name at the foot of the letter which claimed, truthfully enough, that Charles of Blois was assembling a new and mighty army in Rennes.

'Master Totesham,' Thomas wrote, 'who sends your lordship humble greetings, reckons that Charles's army

348

already numbers a thousand men-at-arms, two times that number in crossbowmen and other men besides, while in our garrison we have scarce a hundred healthy men, while your kinsman, Sir Thomas Dagworth, who is a week's march away, can raise no more than six or seven hundred men.'

Sir Thomas Dagworth, the English commander in Brittany, was married to the Earl of Northampton's sister and Totesham was hoping that family pride alone would persuade the Earl to avoid a defeat in Brittany, and if Northampton were to send Skeat's archers, just the archers and not the men-at-arms, it would double the number of bowmen on La Roche-Derrien's walls and give Totesham a chance to resist a siege. Send the archers, the letter pleaded, with their bows, their arrows, but without their horses and Totesham would send them back to Calais when Charles of Blois was repulsed. 'He won't believe that,' Totesham grumbled, 'he'll know I'll want to keep them, so make sure he knows it's a solemn promise. Tell him I swear on Our Lady and on St George that the archers will go back.'

The description of Charles of Blois's army was real enough. Spies in English pay sent the news which, in truth, Charles was eager for his enemies to learn for the more La Roche-Derrien's garrison was out-numbered the lower its hopes would be. Charles already had close to four thousand men, more were coming every week, and his engineers had hired nine great siege engines to hurl boulders at the walls of the English towns and fortresses in his duchy. La Roche-Derrien would be attacked first and few men gave it a hope of lasting longer than a month.

'It is not true, I trust,' Totesham said sourly to Thomas

when the letter was written, 'that you have designs on Roncelets?'

'On Roncelets?' Thomas pretended not to have heard of the place. 'Not Roncelets, sir, but Rostrenen.'

Totesham gazed at Thomas with dislike. 'There's nothing at Rostrenen,' the garrison commander said icily.

'I hear there's food there, sir,' Thomas said.

'Whereas' – Totesham continued as if Thomas had not spoken – 'the Countess of Armorica's son is said to be held at Roncelets.'

'Is he, sir?' Thomas asked disingenuously.

'And if it's a swiving you want,' – Totesham ignored Thomas's lies – 'then I can recommend the brothel behind St Brieuc's chantry.'

'We're riding to Rostrenen,' Thomas insisted.

'And none of my men will ride with you,' Totesham said, meaning none that took his wages, though that still left the mercenaries.

Sir Guillaume had agreed to ride with Thomas, though he was uncomfortable about the prospects for success. He had bought horses for himself and his two men but he reckoned they were of poor quality. 'If it comes to a chase out of Roncelets,' he said, 'we'll be trounced. So take a lot of men to put up a decent fight.'

Thomas's first instinct had been to ride with just a handful of others, but a few men on bad horses would be easy bait. More men made the expedition safer.

'And why are you going anyway?' Sir Guillaume demanded. 'Just to get into the widow's skirts?'

'Because I made a promise to her,' Thomas said, and it was true, though Sir Guillaume's reason had the more truth. 'And because,' Thomas went on, 'I need to let our enemies know that I'm here.'

'You mean de Taillebourg?' Sir Guillaume asked. 'He knows already.'

'You think so?'

'Brother Germain will have told him,' Sir Guillaume said confidently, 'in which case I reckon your Dominican is already in Rennes. He'll come for you in good time.'

'If I raid Roncelets,' Thomas said, 'they'll hear of me. Then, I can be sure they'll come.'

By Candlemas he knew he could rely on Robbie, on Sir Guillaume and his two men-at-arms and he had found seven other men who had been lured by the rumours of Roncelets' wealth or by the prospect of Jeanette's good opinion. Robbie wanted to leave straightaway, but Will Skeat, like Sir Guillaume, advised Thomas to take a larger party. 'This ain't like northern England,' Skeat said, 'you can't run for the border. You get caught, Tom, and you'll need a dozen good men to lock shields and break heads. Reckon I ought to come with you.'

'No,' Thomas said hastily. Skeat had his lucid moments, but too often was vague and forgetful, though now he tried to help Thomas by recommending other men to go on the raid. Most turned the invitation down: the Tower of Roncelets was too far off, they claimed, or the Lord of Roncelets was too powerful and the odds against the raiders too great. Some were frightened of offending Totesham who, fearing to lose any of his garrison, had decreed that no raids should go farther than a day's ride from the town. His caution meant there was little plunder to be had and it was only the poorest mercenaries who, desperate for anything they could turn into cash, offered to ride with Thomas.

'Twelve men is enough,' Robbie insisted. 'Sweet Christ, but I've been on enough raids into England. My brother and I once took a herd of cattle from Lord Percy with just three other men and Percy had half the county searching for us. Go in fast and come out quicker. Twelve men is enough.'

Thomas was almost convinced by Robbie's fervent words, but he worried that the odds were still too uneven and the horses too badly conditioned to allow them to go swiftly in and come out quicker. 'I want more men,' he told Robbie.

'If you go on dithering,' Robbie told him, 'the enemy will hear about you. They'll be waiting for us.'

'They won't know where to wait,' Thomas said, 'or what to think.' He had spread a score of rumours about the raid's purpose and hoped that the enemy would be thoroughly confused. 'But we'll go soon,' he promised Robbie.

'Sweet God, but who's left to ask?' Robbie demanded. 'Let's ride now!'

But that same day a ship came to Tréguier and three more Flemish men-at-arms rode into the garrison. Thomas found them that night in a tavern by the river's edge. The three complained how they had been in the English lines at Calais, but there was too little fighting there and thus few prospects of wealthy prisoners. They wanted to try their luck in Brittany and so they had come to La Roche-Derrien. Thomas spoke to their leader, a gaunt man with a twisted mouth and with two fingers missing from his right hand, who listened, grunted an acknowledgement and said he would think about it. Next morning all three Flemings came to the Two Foxes tavern and said they were willing to ride. 'We came here to fight,' their leader, who was called Lodewijk, said, 'so we go.'

'So let's leave!' Robbie urged Thomas.

Thomas would have liked to recruit still more men, but he knew he had waited long enough. 'We'll go,' he told Robbie, then he went to find Will Skeat and made the older man promise to keep an eye on Jeanette. She liked and trusted Skeat and Thomas was confident enough to leave his father's notebook in her keeping. 'We shall be back,' he told her, 'in six or seven days.'

'God be with you,' Jeanette said. She clung to Thomas for an instant. 'God be with you,' she said again, 'and bring me my son.'

And next dawn, in a mist that pearled their long mail coats, the fifteen horsemen rode.

Lodewijk – he insisted it was Sir Lodewijk though his two companions sniggered whenever he did – refused to speak French, claiming that the language made his tongue sour. 'It is a people of filth,' Lodewijk maintained, 'the French. Filth. The word is good, *ja*? Filth?'

'The word is good,' Thomas agreed.

Jan and Pieter, Sir Lodewijk's companions, spoke only in guttural Flemish spiced with a handful of English curses they must have learned near Calais.

'What's happening in Calais?' Thomas asked Sir Lodewijk as they rode south.

'Nothing. The town is . . . what you say?' Sir Lodewijk made a circling motion with his hand.

'Surrounded.'

'*Ja*, the town is goddamn surrounded. By the English, *ja*? And by . . .' He paused, uncertain of the word he wanted, then pointed to a stretch of waterlogged ground that lay east of the road. 'By that.'

'Marshes.'

'*Ja*! By bloody marshes. And the goddamn bloody French, they are on . . .' Again he was lost for words, so jabbed his mailed finger at the lowering sky.

'Higher ground?' Thomas guessed.

'*Ja*! Bloody high ground. Not so bloody high, I think, but higher. And they . . .' He put a hand over his eyes, as if shading them.

'Stare?'

'*Ja*! They stare at each other. So nothing is happens but they and we gets bloody wet. Pissing wet, *ja*?'

They got wet later that morning when the rains swept in from the ocean. Great curtains of grey lashed the deserted farmlands and upland heaths where the trees were permanently bent towards the east. When Thomas had first come to Brittany this had been a productive land of farms, orchards, mills and grazing, but now it was blasted naked. The fruit trees, untended, were thick with bullfinches, the fields were choked with weeds and the pastures tangled with couch grass. Here and there a few folk still tried to scratch a living, but they were constantly being forced to La Roche-Derrien to work on the ramparts and their harvests and livestock were forever being stolen by English patrols. If any such Bretons were aware of the fifteen horsemen they took care to hide themselves and so it seemed as though Thomas and his companions rode through a deserted country.

They rode with one spare horse. They should have had more because only the three Flemings were mounted on good stallions. Sea voyages usually had a bad effect on horses, but Sir Lodewijk made it plain their journey had been unusually quick. 'Bloody winds, *ja*?' He whirled his hand and made a whooshing noise to suggest the strength of the winds which had brought the destriers through in such fine fettle. 'Quick! Bloody quick!'

The Flemings were not only well mounted, but well

equipped. Jan and Pieter had fine mail hauberks while Sir Lodewijk had his chest, both thighs and one arm protected by good plate that was strapped over a leather-backed mail haubergeon. The three wore black surcoats with a broad white stripe running down front and back, and all had undecorated shields, though Sir Lodewijk's horse's trapper displayed a badge showing a knife dripping blood. He tried to explain the device, but his English could not cope and Thomas was left with the vague impression that it was the mark of a trading guild in Bruges. 'The butchers?' he suggested to Robbie. 'Is that what he said? Butchers?'

'Bloody butchers don't make war. Except on pigs,' Robbie said. He was in a fine mood. Raiding was in his blood and he had heard stories in La Roche-Derrien's taverns of the plunder that could be stolen if a man was willing to break Richard Totesham's rule and ride further than a day's journey from the town. 'The trouble in the north of England,' he told Thomas, 'is that if it's worth stealing then it's behind big bloody walls. We scratch up some cattle now and then, and a year ago I stole a fine horse off my Lord Percy, but there's not any gold and silver to be had. Nothing that you'd call real plunder. The Mass vessels are all wood or pewter or clay, and the poor boxes are poorer than the poor. And ride too far south and the bastards will be waiting for you on the way home. I hate bloody English archers.'

'I'm a bloody English archer.'

'You're different,' Robbie said, and he meant it for he was puzzled by Thomas. Most archers were country born, the sons of yeomen or smiths or bailiffs, while a few were the sons of labourers, but none in Robbie's experience was well born, which Thomas plainly was for he spoke French and Latin, he was confident in the company of lords and other archers deferred to him. Robbie might look like a wild Scottish fighter, but he was the son of a gentleman and nephew to the Knight of Liddesdale, and thus he regarded archers as inferior beings who, in a properly arranged universe, could be ridden down and slaughtered like game, but he liked Thomas. 'You're just bloody different,' he said. 'Mind you, when my ransom's paid and I'm safe home, I'll come back and kill you.'

Thomas laughed, but it was forced laughter. He was nervous. He put the nervousness down to being in the unfamiliar position of leading a raid. This was his idea, and it had been his promises that brought most of these men on the long ride. He had claimed that Roncelets, being so far from any English stronghold, lay in unplundered country. Snatch the child, he had promised them, and they could then pillage as much as they wished or at least until the enemy woke up and organized a pursuit, and that promise had persuaded men to follow him and the responsibility of it weighed on Thomas. He also resented worrying. His ambition, after all, was to be the leader of a war band like Will Skeat had been before his injury, and what hope did he have of being a good leader if he fretted over a little raid like this? Yet fret he did, and he worried most of all that he might not have anticipated everything that could go wrong; and the men who had joined him gave him small consolation for, except for his friends and the newly arrived Flemings, they were the poorest and least well equipped of all the adventurers who had come to La Roche-Derrien in search of wealth. One of them, a quarrelsome man-at-arms from western Brittany, became drunk on the first day and Thomas discovered he had two water skins filled with a fierce apple spirit. He broke both skins, whereupon the enraged Breton drew his sword and attacked Thomas, but he was too drunk to see properly and a knee to his groin and a thump over the head put him down hard. Thomas took the man's horse and left him groaning in the mud, which meant he was down to fourteen men. 'That will have helped,' Sir Guillaume said cheerfully.

Thomas said nothing. He deserved to be mocked, he thought.

'No, I mean it! You knock a man down one day and you might do it again. You know why some men are bad leaders?'

'Why?'

'They want to be liked.'

'That's bad?' Thomas asked.

'Men want to admire their leaders, they want to fear them, and above all they want them to be successful. What does being liked have to do with any of that? If the leader is a good man he will be liked and if he's not, he won't, and if he is a good man and a bad leader then he is better off dead. You see? I am full of wisdom.' Sir Guillaume laughed. He might be down on his luck, his manor lost and fortune gone, but he was riding to a fight and that cheered him. 'The good thing about this rain,' he said, 'is that the enemy won't expect you to be riding in it. It's stay-at-home weather.'

'They'll know we've left La Roche-Derrien,' Thomas said. He was certain that Charles of Blois had as many spies in the town as the English had in Rennes.

'He won't know yet,' Sir Guillaume said. 'We're travelling faster than any message can go. Anyway, while they know we've left La Roche-Derrien, they don't know where we're going.'

They rode south in hope that the enemy would think they were planning to scavenge the farms near Guingamp, then late in the first day they turned eastwards and climbed into a high, empty country. The hazels were in blossom and rooks were calling from the bare elm tops, signs that the year was turning away from winter. They camped in a deserted farm, sheltered by low scorched stone walls, and before the last glimmer of dusk faded they had a good augury when Robbie, rooting about in the ruins of the barn, discovered a leather bag half buried beside the broken wall. The exorbitant rain had washed the earth away above the bag which held a small silver plate and three handfuls of coins. Whoever had buried the money must have thought the coins too heavy to carry or else had feared being robbed during their exile from the house.

'We, how do you say?' Sir Lodewijk made a chopping motion with his hand as if he cut up a pie.

'Share?'

'*Ja*! We share?'

'No,' Thomas said. That had not been the agreement. He would have preferred to have shared, for that was how Will Skeat had treated spoils, but the men who rode with him wanted to keep whatever they found.

Sir Lodewijk bridled. 'It is how we do it, *ja*? We share.'

'We don't share,' Sir Guillaume said harshly, 'it's been agreed.' He spoke in French and Sir Lodewijk reacted as though he had been struck, but he understood well enough and just turned and walked away.

'Tell your Scottish friend to watch his back,' Sir Guillaume said to Thomas.

'Lodewijk's not so bad,' Thomas said, 'you just don't like him because he's Flemish.'

'I hate the Flemish,' Sir Guillaume agreed, 'they're dull, stupid porkwits. Like the English.'

The small argument with the Flemings did not fester. Next morning Sir Lodewijk and his companions were cheerful and, because their horses were much fresher and fitter than any others, they volunteered, with much broken English and elaborate hand signals, to ride ahead as scouts and all day their black and white surcoats appeared and reappeared far ahead and each time they waved the main party on, signalling that there was no danger. The deeper they went into enemy territory the greater the risk, but the Flemings' watchfulness meant that they made good progress. They were weaving a path either side of the main highway that ran east and west along Brittany's spine, a road flanked by deep woods, which hid the raiders from the few people who travelled on the road. They saw only two drovers with their skinny cattle and a priest leading a band of pilgrims who walked barefoot, waved tattered branches and sang a dirge. No pickings there.

Next day they went south again. They were now entering a country where the farms had escaped English raiders and so the people were unafraid of horsemen and the pastures were filled with ewes and their new-born lambs, many of which had been torn to bloody scraps because the men of Brittany were too busy hunting each other and so the foxes thrived and the lambs died. Shepherds' dogs barked at the grey-mailed men, and now Thomas no longer had the Flemings ride ahead, but instead he and Sir Guillaume led the horsemen and, if challenged, they answered in French, claiming to be supporters of Charles of Blois. 'Where's Roncelets?' they constantly asked and at first found no one who knew, but as the morning wore on they discovered a man who had at least heard of the place, then another who said his father had once been there and he thought it was beyond the ridge, the forest and the river, and then a third who gave them precise directions. The tower, he said, was no more than a half-day's journey away at the far end of a long wooded ridge that ran between two rivers. He showed them where to ford the nearer river, told them to follow the ridge crest southwards and then bowed his head in thanks for the coin Thomas gave him.

They crossed the river, climbed the ridge and rode south. Thomas knew they must be close to Roncelets when they stopped for the third night, but he did not press on for he reckoned it would be better to come to the tower in the dawn and so they camped under beech trees, shivering because they dared not light a fire, and Thomas slept badly because he was listening to the strange things crackle and rustle deep in the woods and he feared those noises might be made by patrols sent out by the Lord of Roncelets. Yet no patrols found them. Thomas doubted there were any patrols except in his imagination, yet still he could not sleep and so, very early, while the others snored, he blundered through the trees to where the ridge's flank fell steeply away and he stared into the night in hope of seeing a glimmer of light cast from the battlements of the Tower of Roncelets. He saw nothing, but he heard sheep bleating piteously further down the slope and he guessed that a fox had got among the lambs and was slaughtering them.

'The shepherd's not doing his job.' Someone spoke

in French and Thomas turned, thinking it was one of Sir Guillaume's men-at-arms, but saw, in the small moonlight, that it was Sir Lodewijk.

'I thought you wouldn't use French?' Thomas said.

'There are times when I do,' Sir Lodewijk said and he strolled to stand beside Thomas and then, smiling, he rammed a makeshift club into Thomas's belly and when Thomas gasped and bent over the Fleming slammed the broken branch over his head and then kicked him in the chest. The attack was sudden, unexpected and overwhelming. Thomas was fighting for breath, half doubled over, staggering, and he tried to straighten and claw at Sir Lodewijk's eyes, but the club hit him a resounding blow on the side of the head and Thomas was down.

The Flemings' three horses had been tied to trees a small way from the others. No one had thought that strange and no one had remarked that the beasts had been left saddled and no one woke as the horses were untethered and led away. Sir Guillaume alone stirred when Sir Lodewijk collected his pieces of plate armour. 'Is it dawn?' he asked.

'Not yet,' Sir Lodewijk answered in soft French, then carried his armour and weapons out to the wood's edge where Jan and Pieter were lashing Thomas's wrists and ankles. They slung him belly down on a horse's back, tied him to the beast's girth strap and then took him eastwards.

Sir Guillaume woke properly twenty minutes later. The birds were filling the trees with song and the sun was a hint of light in the misted east.

Thomas had vanished. His mail coat, his arrow bag, his sword, his helmet, his cloak, his saddle and his big black bow were all still there, but Thomas and the three Flemings were gone.

Thomas was taken to the Tower of Roncelets, a four-square, unadorned fortress that reared from an outcrop of rock high above a river bend. A bridge, made of the same grey stone as the tower, carried the high road to Nantes across the river and no merchant could move his goods across the bridge without paying dues to the Lord of Roncelets whose banner of two black chevrons on a yellow field flew from the tower's high ramparts. His men wore the black and yellow stripes as a livery and were inevitably called *guêpes*, wasps. This far east in Brittany the folk spoke French rather than Breton and their tower was nicknamed the Guêpier, the wasp's nest, though on this late winter's morning most of the soldiers in the village wore plain black liveries rather than the waspish stripes of the Lord of Roncelets. The newcomers were quartered in the little cottages that lay between the Guêpier and the bridge and it was in one of those cottages that Sir Lodewijk and his two companions rejoined their comrades. 'He's up in the castle' – Sir Lodewijk jerked his head towards the tower – 'and God help him.'

'No trouble?' a man asked.

'No trouble at all,' Sir Lodewijk said. He had drawn a knife and was cutting off the white stripes that had been sewn onto his surcoat. 'He made it easy for us. A stupid bloody Englishman, eh?'

'So why do they want him?'

'God knows and who cares? All that matters is that they've got him and the devil will have him soon.' Sir

Lodewijk yawned hugely. 'And there's a dozen more of them out in the woods so we're riding out to find them.'

Fifty horsemen rode westwards from the village. The sound of their hooves and their curb chains and creaking leather armour was loud, but quickly faded when they rode into the ridge's thick woods. A pair of kingfishers, startling blue, whipped up the river and vanished in shadows. Long weeds waved in the current where a flash of silver showed that the salmon were returning. A girl carried a pail of milk down the village street and wept because in the night she had been raped by one of the black-liveried soldiers and she knew it was futile to complain for no one would protect her or even make a protest on her behalf. The village priest saw her, understood why she was weeping, and reversed his course so he would not have to face her. The black and yellow flag on the Guêpier's ramparts flapped in a small gust of wind, then hung limp. Two young men with hooded falcons perched on their arms rode out of the tower and turned south. The great door grated shut behind them and the sound of the heavy locking bar dropping into its brackets could be heard throughout the village.

Thomas heard it too. The sound shuddered through the rock on which the Guêpier was built and reverberated up the winding stair to the long, bare room where he had been taken. Two windows lit the chamber, but the wall was so thick and the embrasures so deep that Thomas, who was chained between the windows, could not see through either of them. An empty hearth stood on the opposite wall, the stones of its chimney hood stained black. The floor's wide wooden boards were scarred and worn by too many nail-studded boots and

Thomas guessed this had been a barrack room. It probably still was, but now it was needed as his prison and so the men-at-arms had been ordered out and Thomas carried in and manacled to the iron ring set into the wall between the two windows. The manacles encircled his wrists and held them behind his back and were connected to the iron ring in the wall by three feet of chain. He had tested the ring, seeing if he could shift it or perhaps snap a link of the chain, but all he did was hurt his wrists. A woman laughed somewhere in the tower. Feet sounded on the circular stairs beyond the door, but no one came into the room and the footsteps faded.

Thomas wondered why the iron ring should have been cemented into the wall. It seemed an odd thing to have so high up the tower where no horse would ever need to be tied. Maybe it had been placed there when the castle had been built. He had watched once as men hauled stones to the top of a church tower and they had used a pulley attached to a ring like this one. It was better to think of the ring and of stones and of masons making the tower than to reflect on his idiocy in being so easily captured, or to wonder what was about to happen to him, though of course he did wonder about that and nowhere in his imagination was the answer comforting. He tugged on the ring again, hoping that it had been there a long time and that the mortar that bedded it would have been weakened, but all he did was break the skin of his wrists on the manacles' sharp edges. The woman laughed again and a child's voice sounded.

A bird flew in one of the windows, fluttered for a few heartbeats and then vanished again, evidently rejecting the room as a nesting site. Thomas closed his eyes and softly recited the prayer of the Grail, the same prayer that Christ had uttered in Gethsemane: *'Pater, si vis, transfer calicem istum a me.'* Father, if you're willing, take this cup from me. Thomas repeated the prayer over and over, suspecting it was a waste of breath. God had not spared his own son the agony of Golgotha so why would He spare Thomas? Yet what hope did he have without prayer? He wanted to weep for his own naïveté in thinking he could ride here and somehow snatch the child from this stronghold that stank of woodsmoke, horse dung and rancid fat. It had all been so stupid and he knew he had not done it for the Grail, but to impress Jeanette. He was a fool, such a damned fool, and like a fool he had walked into his enemy's trap and he knew he would not be ransomed. What value did he have? So why was he even alive? Because they wanted something from him and just then the door to the room opened and Thomas opened his eyes.

A man in a monk's black robe carried two trestles into the room. He had untonsured hair, suggesting he was a lay servant to a monastery. 'Who are you?' Thomas asked.

The man, who was short and had a slight limp, gave no answer, but just placed the two trestles in the centre of the floor and, a moment later, brought in five planks that he laid across the trestles to make a table. A second untonsured man, similarly robed in black, entered the room and stared at Thomas. 'Who are you?' Thomas asked again, but the second man was as silent as the first. He was a big man with bony ridges over his eyes and sunken cheeks and he inspected Thomas as if he were appraising a bullock at slaughter time.

'Are you going to make the fire?' the first man asked.

'In a minute,' the second man said and he pulled a short-bladed knife from a sheath at his belt and walked towards Thomas. 'Stay still,' he growled, 'and you don't get hurt.'

'Who are you?'

'No one you know and no one you'll ever know,' the man said, then he seized the neck of Thomas's woollen jerkin and, with one savage cut, slit it down the front. The blade touched, but did not break Thomas's skin. Thomas pulled back, but the man simply followed him, slashing and tugging at the torn cloth until Thomas's chest was naked, then he slit down the sleeves and pulled the jerkin away so that Thomas was naked from the waist up. Then the man pointed at Thomas's right foot, 'lift it,' he ordered. Thomas hesitated and the man sighed. 'I can make you do it,' he said, 'and that will hurt, or you can do it yourself and it won't hurt.'

He pulled off both of Thomas's boots, then cut the waist of his breeches.

'No!' Thomas protested.

'Don't waste your breath,' the man said, and he sawed and tugged and ripped with the blade until he had cut through the breeches and could pull them away to leave Thomas shivering and naked. Then the man scooped up the boots and torn clothes and carried them out of the room.

The other man was carrying things into the room and placing them on the table. There was a book and a pot, presumably of ink, because the man placed two goose feathers beside the book and a small ivory-handled knife to trim the quills. Then he put a crucifix on the table, two large candles like those that would grace the altar of a church, three pokers, a pair of pincers and a curious instrument that Thomas could not see properly. Last of all he put two chairs behind the table and a wooden bucket within Thomas's reach. 'You know what that's for, don't you?' he asked, knocking the bucket with his foot.

'Who are you? Please!'

'Don't want you to make a mess on the floor, do we?'

The bigger man came back into the room carrying some kindling and a basket of logs. 'At least you'll be warm,' he said to Thomas with evident amusement. He had a small clay pot filled with glowing embers that he used to light the kindling, then he piled on the smaller logs and held his hands to the growing flames. 'Nice and warm,' he said, 'and that's a blessing in winter. Never known a winter like it! Rain! We should be building an ark.'

A long way off a bell tolled twice. The fire began to crackle and some of the smoke seeped out into the room, perhaps because the chimney was cold. 'What he really likes,' the big man who had laid the fire said, 'is a brazier.'

'Who?' Thomas asked.

'He always likes a brazier, he does, but not on a wooden floor. I told him.'

'Who?' Thomas demanded.

'Don't want to burn the place down! Not a brazier, I told him, not on a wooden floor, so we had to use the hearth.' The big man watched the fire for a while. 'That seems to be burning proper, don't it?' He heaped a half-dozen larger logs on the fire and then backed away. He gave Thomas a casual look, shook his head as if the prisoner was beyond help and then both men left the room.

The firewood was dry and so the flames blazed high, fast and fierce. More smoke billowed into the room and gusted out of the windows. Thomas, in a sudden spurt of rage, dragged at the manacles, heaving with all his archer's strength to pull the iron ring from the wall, but all he achieved was to cut the iron gyves further into his bleeding wrists. He stared up at the ceiling, which was simply planks over beams, presumably the floor of the chamber above. He had heard no footsteps up there, but then there came the sound of feet just beyond the door and he stepped back to the wall.

A woman and a small child came in. Thomas crouched to hide his nakedness and the woman laughed at his modesty. The child laughed too and it took Thomas a few seconds to realize that the boy was Jeanette's son, Charles, who was gazing at him with interest, curiosity, but no recognition. The woman was tall, fair-haired, very pretty and very pregnant. She wore a pale blue dress that was belted above her swollen belly and was trimmed with white lace and little loops of pearls. Her hat was a blue spire with a brief veil that she pushed away from her eyes to see Thomas better. Thomas drew up his knees to hide himself, but the woman brazenly crossed the room to stare down at him. 'Such a pity,' she said.

'A pity?' Thomas asked.

She did not elaborate. 'Are you really English?' she demanded and looked peeved when Thomas did not answer. 'They're making a rack downstairs, Englishman. Windlasses and ropes to stretch you. Have you ever seen a man after he's been racked? He flops. It's amusing, but not, I think, for the man himself.'

Thomas still ignored her, looking instead at the small

boy who had a round face, black hair and the fierce dark eyes of Jeanette, his mother. 'You remember me, Charles?' Thomas asked, but the boy just stared at him blankly. 'Your mother sends you greetings,' Thomas said and saw the surprise on the boy's face.

'Mama?' Charles, who was almost four, asked.

The woman snatched at Charles's hand and dragged him away as though Thomas carried a contagion. 'Who are you?' she asked angrily.

'Your mother loves you, Charles,' Thomas told the wide-eyed boy.

'Who are you?' the woman insisted, and then turned as the door was pushed open.

A Dominican priest came in. He was gaunt, thin and tall with short grey hair and a fierce face. He frowned when he saw the woman and child. 'You should not be here, my lady,' he said harshly.

'You forget, priest, who rules here,' the pregnant woman retorted.

'Your husband,' the priest said firmly, 'and he will not want you here, so you will leave.' The priest held the door open and the woman, whom Thomas assumed to be the Lady of Roncelets, hesitated for a heartbeat and stalked out. Charles looked back once, then was dragged out of the room just before another Dominican entered, this one a younger man, small and bald, with a towel folded over one arm and a bowl of water in his hands. He was followed by the two robed servants who walked with folded hands and downcast eyes to stand beside the fire. The first priest, the gaunt one, closed the door, then he and his fellow priest walked to the table.

'Who are you?' Thomas asked the gaunt priest,

though he suspected he knew the answer. He was trying to remember that misted morning in Durham when he had seen de Taillebourg fight Robbie's brother. He thought it was the same man, the priest who had murdered Eleanor or else ordered her death, but he could not be certain.

The two priests ignored him. The smaller man put the water and towel on the table, then both men knelt. 'In the name of the Father and of the Son and of the Holy Ghost,' the older priest said, making the sign of the cross, 'amen.' He stood, opened his eyes and looked down at Thomas who was still crouching on the pitted floorboards. 'You are Thomas of Hookton,' he said formally, 'bastard son of Father Ralph, priest of that place?'

'Who are you?'

'Answer me, please,' the Dominican said.

Thomas stared up into the man's eyes and recognized the terrible strength in the priest and knew that he dared not give in to that strength. He had to resist from the very first and so he said nothing.

The priest sighed at this display of petty obstinacy. 'You are Thomas of Hookton,' he declared, 'Lodewijk says so. In which case, greetings, Thomas. My name is Bernard de Taillebourg and I am a friar of the Dominican order and, by the grace of God and at the pleasure of the Holy Father, an Inquisitor of the faith. My brother in Christ' – here de Taillebourg gestured at the younger priest, who had settled at the table where he opened the book and picked up one of the quills – 'is Father Cailloux, who is also an Inquisitor of the faith.'

'You are a bastard,' Thomas said, staring at de Taillebourg, 'you're a murdering bastard.'

He might have spared his breath for de Taillebourg

showed no reaction. 'You will stand, please,' the priest demanded.

'A motherless murdering bastard,' Thomas said, making no move.

De Taillebourg made a small gesture and the two servants ran forward and took Thomas by his arms and dragged him upright and, when he threatened to collapse, the bigger one slapped him hard in the face, stinging the bruise left by the blow Sir Lodewijk had given him before dawn. De Taillebourg waited till the men were back beside the fire. 'I am charged by Cardinal Bessières,' he said tonelessly, 'to discover the whereabouts of a relic and we are informed that you can assist us in this matter, which is deemed to be of such importance that we are empowered by the Church and by Almighty God to ensure that you tell us the truth. Do you understand what that means, Thomas?'

'You killed my woman,' Thomas said, 'and one day, priest, you're going to roast in hell and the devils will dance on your shrivelled arse.'

De Taillebourg again showed no reaction. He was not using his chair, but standing tall and arrow-thin behind the table on which he rested the tips of his long, pale fingers. 'We know,' he said, 'that your father might have possessed the Grail, and we know that he gave you a book in which he wrote his account of that most precious thing. I tell you that we know of these matters so that you do not waste our time or your pain by denying them. Yet we shall need to know more and that is why we are here. You understand me, Thomas?'

'The devil will piss in your mouth, priest, and shit in your nostrils.'

De Taillebourg looked faintly pained as if Thomas's

372

crudity was tiresome. 'The Church grants us the authority to question you, Thomas,' he continued in a mild voice, 'but in her infinite mercy she also commands that we do not shed blood. We may use pain, indeed it is our duty to employ pain, but it must be pain without bloodshed. This means we may employ fire' – his long pale fingers touched one of the pokers on the table – 'and we may crush you and we may stretch you and God will forgive us for it will be done in His name and in His most holy service.'

'Amen,' Brother Cailloux said and, like the two servants, made the sign of the cross. De Taillebourg pushed all three of the pokers to the edge of the table and the smaller servant ran across the room, took the irons and plunged them into the fire.

'We do not employ pain lightly,' de Taillebourg said, 'or wantonly, but with prayerful regret and with pity and with a tearful concern for your immortal soul.'

'You're a murderer,' Thomas said, 'and your soul will sear in hell.'

'Now,' de Taillebourg continued, apparently oblivious to Thomas's insults, 'let us start with the book. You told Brother Germain in Caen that your father wrote it. Is that true?'

And so it began. A gentle questioning at first to which Thomas gave no answers for he was consumed by a hatred for de Taillebourg, a hatred fed by the memory of Eleanor's pale and blood-laced body, yet the questioning was insistent and unceasing, and the threat of an awful pain was in the three pokers that heated in the fire, and so Thomas persuaded himself that de Taillebourg knew some things and there could be very little harm in telling him others. Besides, the Dominican was so very reasonable and so very patient. He endured Thomas's anger, he ignored the abuse, he expressed again and again an unwillingness to employ torture and said he only wanted the truth, however inadequate and so, after an hour, Thomas began to answer the questions. Why suffer, he asked himself, when he did not possess what the Dominican wanted? He did not know where the Grail was, he was not even certain that the Grail existed and so, hesitantly at first, and then more willingly, he talked.

There was a book, yes, and much of it was in strange languages and scripts and Thomas claimed to have no idea what those mysterious passages meant. As for the rest he admitted a knowledge of Latin and agreed he had read those parts of the book, but he dismissed them as vague, repetitive and unhelpful. 'They were just stories,' he said.

'What kind of stories?'

'A man received his sight after looking at the Grail and then, when he was disappointed in its appearance, he lost his sight again.'

'God be praised for that,' Father Cailloux interjected, then dipped the quill in ink and wrote down the miracle.

'What else?' de Taillebourg asked.

'Stories of soldiers winning battles because of the Grail, stories of healings,' Thomas said.

'Do you believe them?'

'The stories?' Thomas pretended to think, then nodded. 'If God has given us the Grail, father,' he said, 'then it will surely work miracles.'

'Did your father possess the Grail?'

'I don't know.'

So de Taillebourg asked him about Father Ralph and Thomas told how his father had walked the stony beach at Hookton wailing for his sins and sometimes preaching to the wild things of the sea and the sky.

'Are you saying he was mad?' de Taillebourg asked.

'He was mad with God,' Thomas said.

'Mad with God,' de Taillebourg repeated, as though the words intrigued him. 'Are you suggesting he was a saint?'

'I think many saints must have been like him,' Thomas replied cautiously, 'but he was also a great mocker of superstitions.'

'What do you mean?'

'He was very fond of St Guinefort,' Thomas said, 'and called on him whenever some minor problem occurred.'

'Is it mockery to do that?' de Taillebourg asked.

'St Guinefort was a dog,' Thomas said.

'I know what St Guinefort was,' de Taillebourg said testily, 'but are you saying God could not use a dog to effect His sacred purposes?'

'I am saying that my father did not believe a dog could be a saint, and so he mocked.'

'Did he mock the Grail?'

'Never,' Thomas answered truthfully, 'not once.'

'And in his book' – de Taillebourg suddenly reverted to the earlier subject – 'did he say how the Grail came to be in his possession?'

For the last few moments Thomas had been aware that there was someone standing on the other side of the door. De Taillebourg had closed it, but the latch had been silently lifted and the door pushed gently ajar. Someone was there, listening, and Thomas assumed it was the Lady of Roncelets. 'He never claimed that the

Grail was in his possession,' he countered, 'but he did say that it was once owned by his family.'

'Once owned,' de Taillebourg said flatly, 'by the Vexilles.'

'Yes,' Thomas replied and he was sure the door moved a fraction.

Father Cailloux's pen scratched on the parchment. Everything Thomas said was being written down and he remembered a wandering Franciscan preacher at a fair in Dorchester shouting at the people that every sin they ever committed was being recorded in a great book in heaven and when they died and went to the judgement before God the book would be opened and their sins read out, and George Adyn had made the crowd laugh by calling out that there was not enough ink in Christendom to record what his brother was doing with Dorcas Churchill in Puddletown. The sins, the Franciscan had angrily retorted, were recorded in letters of fire, the same fire that would roast adulterers in the depths of hell.

'And who is Hachaliah?' de Taillebourg asked.

Thomas was surprised by the question and hesitated. Then he tried to look puzzled. 'Who?'

'Hachaliah,' de Taillebourg repeated patiently.

'I don't know,' Thomas said.

'I think you do,' de Taillebourg declared softly.

Thomas stared at the priest's strong, bony face. It reminded him of his father's face for it had the same grim determination, a hard-jawed inwardness which hinted that this man would not care what others thought of his behaviour because he justified himself only to God. 'Brother Germain mentioned the name,' Thomas said cautiously, 'but what it means I don't know.'

'I don't believe you,' de Taillebourg insisted.

'Father,' Thomas said firmly, 'I do not know what it means. I asked Brother Germain and he refused to tell me. He said it was beyond someone of my wits to understand.'

De Taillebourg stared at Thomas in silence. The fire roared hollow in the chimney and the big servant shifted the pokers as one of the logs collapsed. 'The prisoner says he doesn't know,' de Taillebourg dictated to Father Cailloux without taking his gaze from Thomas. The servants put more logs on the fire and de Taillebourg let Thomas stare at the pokers and worry about them for a moment before he resumed his questioning. 'So,' the Dominican asked, 'where is the book now?'

'In La Roche-Derrien,' Thomas said promptly.

'Where in La Roche-Derrien?'

'With my baggage,' Thomas said, 'which I left with an old friend, Will Skeat.' That was not true. He had left the book in Jeanette's keeping, but he did not want to expose her to danger. Will Skeat, even with a damaged memory, could look after himself better than the Blackbird. 'Sir William Skeat,' Thomas added.

'Does Sir William know what the book is?' de Taillebourg asked.

'He can't even read! No, he doesn't know.'

There were other questions then, scores of them. De Taillebourg wanted to know the story of Thomas's life, why he had abandoned Oxford, why he had become an archer, when he had last made confession, what had he been doing in Durham? What did the King of England know of the Grail? What did the Bishop of Durham know? The questions went on and on until Thomas was faint from hunger and from standing, yet de Taillebourg seemed indefatigable. As evening came on and the light from the two windows paled and darkened he still persisted. The two servants had long looked rebellious while Father Cailloux kept frowning and glancing at the windows as if to suggest that the time for a meal was long past, but de Taillebourg did not know hunger. He just pressed and pressed. With whom had Thomas travelled to London? What had he done in Dorset? Had he searched for the Grail in Hookton? Brother Cailloux filled page after page with Thomas's answers and, as the evening wore on, he had to light the candles so he could see to write. The flames of the fire cast shadows from the table legs and Thomas was swaying with fatigue when at last de Taillebourg nodded. 'I shall think and pray about all your answers tonight, Thomas,' he said, 'and in the morning we shall continue.'

'Water,' Thomas croaked, 'I need water.'

'You shall be given food and drink,' de Taillebourg said.

One of the servants removed the pokers from the fire. Father Cailloux closed the book and gave Thomas a glance which seemed to have some sympathy. A blanket was fetched and with it came a meal of smoked fish, beans, bread and water, and one of Thomas's hands was unmanacled so he could eat it. Two guards, both in plain black surcoats, watched him eat, and when he was done they snapped the manacles back about his wrist and he sensed a pin being pushed through the clasp to secure it. That gave him hope and when he was left alone he tried to reach the pin with his fingers, but both the gyves were deep bracelets and he could not reach the clasp. He was trapped.

He lay back against the wall, huddled in the blanket

and watching the dying fire. No heat crossed the room and Thomas shivered uncontrollably. He contorted his fingers as he tried to reach the clasp of the manacles, but it was impossible and he suddenly moaned involuntarily as he anticipated the pain. He had been spared torture this day, but did that mean he had escaped it altogether? He deserved to, he thought, for he had mostly told the truth. He had told de Taillebourg that he did not know where the Grail was, that he was not even certain it existed, that he had rarely heard his father speak of it and that he would rather be an archer in the King of England's army than a seeker of the Grail. Again he felt a terrible shame that he had been captured so easily. He should have been on his way back to La Roche-Derrien by now, riding home to the taverns and the laughter and the ale and the easy company of soldiers. There were tears in his eyes and he was ashamed of that too. Laughter sounded from deep in the castle and he thought he could hear the sound of a harp playing.

Then the door opened.

He could only see that a man had come into the room. The visitor was wearing a swathing black cloak that made him appear a sinister shadow as he crossed to the table where he stopped and stared down at Thomas. The fire's dying timbers were behind the man, edging his tall cloaked figure with red, but illuminating Thomas. 'I am told,' the man said, 'that he did not burn you today?'

Thomas said nothing, just huddled under the blanket.

'He likes burning people,' the visitor said. 'He does like it. I have watched him. He shudders as the flesh bubbles.' He went to the fire, picked up one of the pokers and thrust it into the smouldering embers before piling new logs over the dying flames. The dry wood burned quickly and, in the flaring light, Thomas could see the man for the first time. He had a narrow, sallow face, a long nose, a strong jaw and black hair swept back from a high forehead. It was a good face, intelligent and hard, then it was shadowed as the man turned away from the fire. 'I am your cousin,' he said.

A stab of hatred coursed through Thomas. 'You're Guy Vexille?'

'I am the Count of Astarac,' Vexille said. He walked slowly towards Thomas. 'Were you at the battle by the forest of Crécy?'

'Yes.'

'An archer?'

'Yes.'

'And at the battle's end,' Guy Vexille said, 'you shouted three words in Latin.'

'*Calix meus inebrians,*' Thomas said.

Guy Vexille perched on the edge of the table and gazed at Thomas for a long time. His face was in shadow so Thomas could see no expression, only the faint glimmer of his eyes. '"*Calix meus inebrians*",' Vexille said at last. 'It is the secret motto of our family. Not the one we show on our crest. You know what that is?'

'No.'

'"*Pie repone te*",' Guy Vexille said.

'"In pious trust",' Thomas translated.

'You're strangely well educated for an archer,' Vexille said. He stood and paced up and down as he spoke. 'We display "*pie repone te*", but our real motto is "*calix meus inebrians*''. We are the secret guardians of the Grail. Our family has held it for generations, we were entrusted with it by God, and your father stole it.'

'You killed him,' Thomas said.

'And I am proud of that,' Guy Vexille said, then suddenly stopped and turned to Thomas. 'Were you the archer on the hill that day?'

'Yes.'

'You shoot well, Thomas.'

'That was the first day I ever killed a man,' Thomas said, 'and it was a mistake.'

'A mistake?'

'I killed the wrong one.'

Guy Vexille smiled, then went back to the fire and pulled out the poker to see its tip was a dull red. He pushed it back into the heat. 'I killed your father,' he said, 'and I killed your woman in Durham and I killed the priest who was evidently your friend.'

'You were de Taillebourg's servant?' Thomas asked, astonished. He had hated Guy Vexille because of his father's death. Now he had two more deaths to add to that hatred.

'I was indeed his servant,' Vexille confirmed. 'It was the penance put on me by de Taillebourg, the punishment of humility. But now I am a soldier again and charged with recovering the Grail.'

Thomas hugged his knees under the blanket. 'If the Grail has so much power,' he asked, 'then why is our family so powerless?'

Guy Vexille thought about the question for a moment, then shrugged. 'Because we squabbled,' he said, 'because we were sinners, because we were not worthy. But we shall change that, Thomas. We shall recover our strength and our virtue.' Guy Vexille stooped to the fire and took the poker from the flames and swept it like a sword so that it made a hissing sound and its red-hot tip seared an arc of light in the dim room. 'Have you thought, Thomas,' he asked, 'of helping me?'

'Helping you?'

Vexille paced close to Thomas. He still swung the poker in great scything cuts so that the light trailed like a falling star to leave wispy lines of smoke in the dark room. 'Your father,' he went on, 'was the elder brother. Did you know that? If you were legitimate, you would be Count of Astarac.' He dropped the poker's tip so that it was close to Thomas's face, so close that Thomas could feel the scorching heat. 'Join me,' Guy Vexille said intensely, 'tell me what you know, help me retrieve the book and go with me on the quest for the Grail.' He crouched so that his face was at the same height as Thomas's. 'Bring glory to our family, Thomas,' he said softly, 'such glory that you and I could rule all Christendom and, with the power of the Grail, lead a crusade against the infidel that will leave them writhing in agony. You and I, Thomas! We are the Lord's anointed, the Grail guardians, and if we join hands then for generations men will talk of us as the greatest warrior saints that the Church ever knew.' His voice was deep, even, almost musical. 'Will you help me, Thomas?'

'No,' Thomas said.

The poker came close to Thomas's right eye, so close that it loomed like a great sullen sun, but Thomas did not twitch away. He did not think his cousin would plunge the poker into his eye, but he did think Guy Vexille wanted him to flinch and so he stayed still.

'Your friends got away today,' Vexille said. 'Fifty of

us rode to catch them and somehow they avoided us. They went deep into the trees.'

'Good.'

'But all they can do is retreat to La Roche-Derrien and they'll be trapped there. Come the spring, Thomas, we shall close that trap.' Thomas said nothing. The poker cooled and went dark, and Thomas at last dared to blink. 'Like all the Vexilles,' Guy said, taking the poker away and standing, 'you are as brave as you are foolish. Do you know where the Grail is?'

'No.'

Guy Vexille stared at him, judging that answer, then shrugged. 'Do you think the Grail exists, Thomas?'

Thomas paused, then gave the answer he had denied to de Taillebourg through all the long day. 'Yes.'

'You're right,' Vexille said, 'you're right. It does exist. We had it and your father stole it and you are the key to finding it.'

'I know nothing of it!' Thomas protested.

'But de Taillebourg won't believe that,' Vexille said, dropping the poker onto the table. 'De Taillebourg wants the Grail as a starving man wants bread. He dreams of it. He moans in his sleep and he weeps for it.' Vexille paused, then smiled. 'When the pain becomes too much to bear, Thomas, and it will, and when you are wishing that you were dead, and you will, then tell de Taillebourg that you repent and that you will become my liege man. The pain will stop then, and you will live.'

It had been Vexille, Thomas realized, who had been listening outside the door. And tomorrow he would listen again. Thomas closed his eyes. *Pater*, he prayed, *si vis, transfer calicem istem a me*. He opened his eyes again. 'Why did you kill Eleanor?' he asked.

'Why not?'

'That is a ridiculous answer,' Thomas snarled.

Vexille's head snapped back as if he had been struck. 'Because she knew we existed,' he said, 'that's why.'

'Existed?'

'She knew we were in England, she knew what we wanted,' Guy Vexille said. 'She knew we had spoken to Brother Collimore. If the King of England had learned that we were searching for the Grail in his kingdom then he would have stopped us. He would have imprisoned us. He would have done to us what we are doing to you.'

'You think Eleanor could have betrayed you to the King?' Thomas asked, incredulous.

'I think it was better that no one knew why we were there,' Guy Vexille said. 'But do you know what, Thomas? That old monk could tell us nothing except that you existed. All that effort, that long journey, the killings, the Scottish weather, just to learn about you! He didn't know where the Grail was, couldn't imagine where your father might have hidden it, but he did know about you and we have been seeking you ever since. Father de Taillebourg wants to question you, Thomas, he wants to make you cry with pain until you tell him what I suspect you cannot tell him, but I don't want your pain. I want your friendship.'

'And I want you dead,' Thomas said.

Vexille shook his head sadly, then stooped so that he was near to Thomas. 'Cousin,' he said quietly, 'one day you will kneel to me. One day you will place your hands between my hands and you will pledge your allegiance and we shall exchange the kiss of lord and man, and thus you will become my liege man and we shall ride

384

together, beneath the cross, to glory. We shall be as brothers, I promise it.' He kissed his fingers then laid the tips on Thomas's cheek and the touch of them was almost like a caress. 'I promise it, brother,' Vexille whispered, 'now goodnight.'

'God damn you, Guy Vexille,' Thomas snarled.

'*Calix meus inebrians*,' Guy Vexille said, and went.

Thomas lay shivering in the dawn. Every footstep in the castle made him cringe. Beyond the deep windows cockerels crowed and birds sang and he had an impression, for what reason he did not know, that there were thick woods outside the Tower of Roncelets and he wondered if he would ever see green leaves again. A sullen servant brought him a breakfast of bread, hard cheese and water and, while he ate, the manacles were unpinned and a wasp-liveried guard watched him, but the gyves were again fixed onto his wrists as soon as he had finished. The bucket was carried away to be emptied and another put in its place.

Bernard de Taillebourg arrived shortly after and, while his servants revived the fire and Father Cailloux settled himself at the makeshift table, the tall Dominican greeted Thomas politely. 'Did you sleep well? Was your breakfast adequate? It's colder today, isn't it? I've never known a winter as wet. The river flooded in Rennes for the first time in years! All those cellars under water.'

Thomas, cold and frightened, did not respond and de Taillebourg did not take offence. Instead he waited as Father Cailloux dipped a quill in the ink, then ordered the taller servant to take Thomas's blanket away. 'Now,' he said when his prisoner was naked, 'to business. Let us talk about your father's notebook. Who else is aware of the book's existence?'

'No one,' Thomas said, 'except Brother Germain and you know about him.'

De Taillebourg frowned. 'But, Thomas, someone must have given it to you! And that person is surely aware of it! Who gave it to you?'

'A lawyer in Dorchester,' Thomas lied glibly.

'A name, please, give me a name.'

'John Rowley,' Thomas said, making the name up.

'Spell it, please,' de Taillebourg said and after Thomas had obeyed the Inquisitor paced up and down in apparent frustration. 'This Rowley must have known what the book was, surely?'

'It was wrapped in a cloak of my father's and in a bundle of other old clothes. He didn't look.'

'He might have done.'

'John Rowley,' Thomas said, spinning his invention, 'is old and fat. He won't go searching for the Grail. Besides, he thought my father was mad, so why would he be interested in a book of his? All Rowley's interested in is ale, mead and mutton pies.'

The three pokers were heating in the fire again. It had started to rain and gusts of cold wind sometimes blew drops through the open windows. Thomas remembered his cousin's warning in the night that de Taillebourg liked to inflict pain, yet the Dominican's voice was mild and reasonable and Thomas sensed he had survived the worst. He had endured a day of de Taillebourg's questioning and his answers seemed to have satisfied the stern Dominican who was now reduced to filling in the gaps of Thomas's story. He wanted to know about the lance of St George and

Thomas told how the weapon had hung in Hookton's church and how it had been stolen and how he had taken it back at the battle outside the forest of Crécy. Did Thomas believe it was the real lance? de Taillebourg asked and Thomas shook his head. 'I don't know,' he said, 'but my father believed it was.'

'And your cousin stole the lance from Hookton's church?'

'Yes.'

'Presumably,' de Taillebourg mused, 'so that no one would realize he sailed to England to search for the Grail. The lance was a disguise.' He thought about that and Thomas, not feeling the need to comment, said nothing. 'Did the lance have a blade?' de Taillebourg asked.

'A long one.'

'Yet, surely, if this was the lance that killed the dragon,' de Taillebourg observed, 'the blade would have melted in the beast's blood?'

'Would it?' Thomas asked.

'Of course it would!' de Taillebourg insisted, staring at Thomas as though he were mad. 'Dragon's blood is molten! Molten and fiery.' He shrugged as if to acknowledge that the lance was irrelevant to his quest. Father Cailloux's pen scratched as he tried to keep up with the interrogation and the two servants stood by the fire, scarcely bothering to hide their boredom as de Taillebourg looked for a new subject to explore. He chose Will Skeat for some reason and asked about his wound and about his memory lapses. Was Thomas really sure Skeat could not read?

'He can't read!' Thomas said. He sounded now as though he were reassuring de Taillebourg and that was a measure of his confidence. He had begun the previous day with insults and hate, but now he was eagerly helping the Dominican towards the end of the interrogation. He had survived.

'Skeat can't read,' de Taillebourg said as he paced up and down 'I suppose that's not surprising. So he won't be looking at the notebook you left in his keeping?'

'I'll be lucky if he doesn't use its pages to wipe his arse. That's the only use Will Skeat has for paper or parchment.'

De Taillebourg gave a dutiful smile then stared up at the ceiling. He was silent for a long time, but at last shot Thomas a puzzled look. 'Who is Hachaliah?'

The question took Thomas by surprise and he must have shown it. 'I don't know,' he managed to say after a pause.

De Taillebourg watched Thomas. The room was suddenly tense; the servants were fully awake and Father Cailloux was no longer writing, but gazing at Thomas. De Taillebourg smiled. 'I'm going to give you one last chance, Thomas,' he said in his deep voice. 'Who is Hachaliah?'

Thomas knew he must brazen it out. Get past this, he thought, and the interrogation would be done. 'I'd never heard of him,' he said, doing his best to sound guileless, 'before Brother Germain mentioned his name.'

Why de Taillebourg seized on Hachaliah as the weak point of Thomas's defences was a mystery, but it was a shrewd seizure for if the Dominican could prove that Thomas knew who Hachaliah was then he could prove that Thomas had translated at least one of the Hebrew passages in the book. He could prove that Thomas had lied through the whole interrogation and he would open whole new areas of revelation. So de Taillebourg pressed hard and when Thomas continued with his denials the priest beckoned to the servants. Father Cailloux flinched.

'I told you,' Thomas said nervously, 'I really don't know who Hachaliah is.'

'But my duty to God,' de Taillebourg said, taking the first of the red-hot pokers from the tall servant, 'is to make sure you are not telling lies.' He looked at Thomas with what appeared to be sympathy, 'I don't want to hurt you, Thomas. I just want the truth. So tell me, who is Hachaliah?'

Thomas swallowed. 'I don't know,' he said, then repeated it in a louder voice, 'I don't know!'

'I think you do,' de Taillebourg said, and so the pain began.

'In the name of the Father,' de Taillebourg prayed as he placed the iron against the bare flesh of Thomas's leg, 'and of the Son and of the Holy Ghost.' The two servants held Thomas down and the pain was worse than he could have believed and he tried to twist away from it, but he could not move and his nostrils were filled with the stench of burning flesh and still he would not answer the question for he thought that by revealing his lies he would open himself to more punishment. Somewhere in his shrieking head he believed that if he persisted in the lie then de Taillebourg must believe him and he would cease to use the fire, but in a competition of patience between torturer and prisoner the prisoner has no chance. A second poker was heated and its tip traced down Thomas's ribs. 'Who is Hachaliah?' de Taillebourg asked.

'I've told you —'

The red-hot iron was put to his chest and drawn down to his belly to leave a line of burning, puckered, raw flesh and the wound was instantly cauterized so it left no blood and Thomas's scream echoed from the high ceiling. The third poker was waiting and the first was being reheated so that the pain did not need to stop, and then Thomas was turned onto his burned belly and the strange device which he had not been able to recognize when it was first put on the table was placed over a knuckle of his left hand and he knew it was an iron vice, screw-driven, and de Taillebourg tightened the screw and the pain made Thomas jerk and scream again. He lost consciousness, but Father Cailloux brought him back to his senses with the towel and cold water.

'Who is Hachaliah?' de Taillebourg asked.

Such a stupid question, Thomas thought. As if the answer was important! 'I don't know!' He moaned the words and prayed that de Taillebourg would believe him, but the pain came again and the best moments, other than pure oblivion, were when Thomas drifted in and out of consciousness and it seemed that the pain was a dream – a bad dream, but still only a dream – and the worst moments were when he realized it was not a dream and that his world was reduced to agony, pure agony, and then de Taillebourg would apply more pain, either tightening a screw to shatter a finger or else placing the hot iron on his flesh.

'Tell me, Thomas,' the Dominican said gently, 'just tell me and the pain will end. It will end if you just tell me. Please, Thomas, you think I enjoy this? In the name of God, I hate it so tell me, please, tell me.'

So Thomas did. Hachaliah was the father of the

Tirshatha, and the Tirshatha was the father of Nehemiah.

'And Nehemiah,' de Taillebourg asked, 'was what?'

'Was the cup bearer to the King,' Thomas sobbed.

'Why do men lie to God?' de Taillebourg asked. He had put the finger-vice back on the table and the three pokers were all in the fire. 'Why?' he asked again. 'The truth is always discovered, God ensures that. So, Thomas, after all, you did know more than you claimed and we shall have to discover your other lies, but let us talk first, though, about Hachaliah. Do you think this citation from the book of Esdras is your father's way of proclaiming his possession of the Grail?'

'Yes,' Thomas said, 'yes, yes, yes.' He was hunched against the wall, his broken hands manacled behind him, his body a mass of pain, but perhaps the hurt would end if he confessed all.

'But Brother Germain tells me that the Hachaliah entry in your father's book,' de Taillebourg said, 'was written in Hebrew. Do you know Hebrew, Thomas?'

'No.'

'So who translated the passage for you.'

'Brother Germain.'

'And Brother Germain told you who Hachaliah was?' de Taillebourg asked.

'No,' Thomas whimpered. There was no point in lying for the Dominican would doubtless check with the old monk, but the answer opened a new question that, in turn, would reveal other areas where Thomas had lied. Thomas knew that, but it was too late to resist now.

'So who did tell you?' de Taillebourg asked.

'A doctor,' Thomas said softly.

'A doctor,' de Taillebourg repeated. 'That doesn't help me, Thomas. You want me to use the fire again? What doctor? A doctor of theology? A physician? And if you asked this mysterious doctor to explain the significance of the passage, was he not curious why you wished to know?'

So Thomas confessed it was Mordecai, and admitted that Mordecai had looked at the notebook and de Taillebourg thumped the table in the first display of temper he had shown in all the long hours of questioning. 'You showed the book to a Jew?' He hissed the question, his voice incredulous. 'To a Jew? In the name of God and of all the precious saints, what were you thinking? To a Jew! To a man of the race that killed our dear Saviour! If the Jews find the Grail, you fool, they will raise the Antichrist! You will suffer for that betrayal! You must suffer!' He crossed the room, snatched a poker from the fire, and brought it back to where Thomas huddled against the wall. 'To a Jew!' de Taillebourg shouted and he scored the poker's glowing tip down Thomas's leg. 'You foul thing!' he snarled over Thomas's screams. 'You are a traitor to God, a traitor to Christ, a traitor to the Church! You are no better than Judas Iscariot!'

The pain went on. The hours went on. It seemed to Thomas that there was nothing left but pain. He had lied when there had been no pain and so now all his previous answers were being checked against the measure of agony he could endure without losing consciousness.

'So where is the Grail?' de Taillebourg demanded.

'I don't know,' Thomas said and then, louder, 'I don't know!' He watched the red-hot iron come to his skin and by now he was shrieking before it even touched.

The screaming did no good because the torture went on. And on. And Thomas talked, telling all he knew, and he was even tempted to do as Guy Vexille had suggested and beg de Taillebourg to let him swear allegiance to his cousin, but then, somewhere in the red horror of his torment, he thought of Eleanor and kept silent.

On the fourth day, when he was quivering, when even a twitch of de Taillebourg's hand was enough to make him whimper and beg for mercy, the Lord of Roncelets came into the room. He was a tall man with short bristling black hair and a broken nose and two missing front teeth. He was wearing his own waspish livery, the two black chevrons on yellow, and he sneered at Thomas's scarred and broken body. 'You didn't bring the rack upstairs, father.' He sounded disappointed.

'It wasn't necessary,' de Taillebourg said.

The Lord of Roncelets prodded Thomas with a mailed foot. 'You say the bastard's an English archer?'

'He is.'

'Then cut off his bow fingers,' Roncelets said savagely.

'I cannot shed blood,' de Taillebourg said.

'By God, I can.' Roncelets pulled a knife from his belt.

'He is my charge!' de Taillebourg snapped. 'He is in God's hands and you will not touch him. You will not shed his blood!'

'This is my castle, priest,' Roncelets growled.

'And your soul is in my hands,' de Taillebourg retorted.

'He's an archer! An English archer! He came here to snatch the Chenier boy! That's my business!'

'His fingers have been shattered by the vice,' de Taillebourg said, 'so he's an archer no longer.'

Roncelets was placated by that news. He prodded

Thomas again. 'He's a piece of piss, priest, that's what he is. A piece of feeble piss.' He spat on Thomas, not because he hated Thomas in particular, but because he detested all archers who had dethroned the knight from his rightful place as king of the battlefield. 'What will you do with him?' he asked.

'Pray for his soul,' de Taillebourg said curtly and when the Lord of Roncelets was gone he did exactly that. It was evident he had finished his questioning for he produced a small vial of holy oil and he gave Thomas the final rites of the church, touching the oil to his brow and to his burned breast and then he said the prayers for the dying. *'Sana me, Domine,'* de Taillebourg intoned, his fingers gentle on Thomas's brow, *'quoniam conturbata sunt ossa mea.'* Heal me, Lord, for my bones are twisted with pain. And when that was said and done Thomas was carried down the castle stairs into a dungeon sunk into a pit in the rock crag on which the Guêpier was built. The floor was the bare black stone, as damp as it was cold. His manacles were removed as he was locked in the cell and he thought he must go mad for his body was all pain and his fingers were shattered and he was no longer an archer for how could he draw a bow with broken hands? Then the fever came and he wept as he shivered and sweated and at night, when he was half sleeping, he gibbered in his nightmares; and he wept again when he woke for he had not endured the torture, but had told de Taillebourg everything. He was a failure, lost in the dark, dying.

Then, one day, he did not know how many days it was since he had been taken down to the Guêpier's cellars, de Taillebourg's two servants came and fetched him. They put a rough woollen shirt on him, pulled dirty woollen breeches over his soiled legs and then they carried him up to the castle yard and threw him into the back of an empty dung cart. The tower's gate creaked open and, accompanied by a score of men-at-arms in the Lord of Roncelets's livery and dazzled by the pale sun light, Thomas left the Guêpier. He was hardly aware of what was happening, he just lay on the dirty boards, hunched in pain, the stink of the cart's usual cargo sour in his nostrils, wanting to die. The fever had not gone and he was shaking with weakness. 'Where are you taking me?' he asked, but no one answered; maybe no one even heard him for his voice was so feeble. It rained. The cart rumbled northwards and the villagers crossed themselves and Thomas drifted in and out of a stupor. He thought he was dying and he supposed they were taking him to the graveyard and he tried to call out to the cart's driver that he still lived, but instead it was Brother Germain who answered him in a querulous voice, saying he should have left the book with him in Caen. 'It's your own fault,' the old monk said and Thomas decided he was dreaming.

He was next aware of a trumpet calling. The cart had stopped and he heard the flapping of cloth and looked up and saw that one of the horsemen was waving a white banner. Thomas wondered if it was his winding sheet. They wrapped a baby when it came into the world and they wrapped a corpse when it went out and he sobbed because he did not want to be buried, and then he heard English voices and he knew he was dreaming as strong hands lifted him from the remnants of dung. He wanted to scream, but he was too weak, and then all sense left him and he was unconscious.

When he woke it was dark and he was in another

cart, a clean one this time, and there were blankets over him and a straw mattress beneath him. The cart had a leather cover on wooden half-hoops to keep out the rain and sunlight. 'Will you bury me now?' Thomas asked.

'You're talking nonsense,' a man said and Thomas recognized Robbie's voice.

'Robbie?'

'Aye, it's me.'

'Robbie?'

'You poor bastard,' Robbie said and stroked Thomas's forehead. 'You poor, poor bastard.'

'Where am I?'

'You're going home, Thomas,' Robbie said, 'you're going home.'

To La Roche-Derrien.

He had been ransomed. A week after his disappearance and two days after the rest of the raiding party had returned to La Roche-Derrien a messenger had come to the garrison under a flag of truce. He brought a letter from Bernard de Taillebourg that was addressed to Sir William Skeat. Surrender Father Ralph's book, the letter said, and Thomas of Hookton will be delivered back to his friends. Will Skeat had the message translated and read to him, but he knew nothing of any book so he asked Sir Guillaume if he had any idea what the priest wanted and Sir Guillaume spoke to Robbie who, in turn, talked to Jeanette and next day an answer went back to Roncelets.

Then there was a fortnight's delay because Brother Germain had to be fetched from Normandy to Rennes.

De Taillebourg insisted on that precaution because Brother Germain had seen the book and he could confirm that what was exchanged for Thomas was indeed Father Ralph's notebook.

'And so it was,' Robbie said.

Thomas stared up at the ceiling. He vaguely felt it had been wrong to exchange him for the book, even if he was grateful to be alive, to be home and among his friends.

'It was the right book,' Robbie went on with indecent relish, 'but we added some stuff to it.' He grinned at Thomas. 'We copied it all out first, of course, and then we added some rubbish to mislead them. To confuse them, see? And that shrivelled old monk never noticed. He just pawed at the book like a starving dog given a bone.'

Thomas shuddered. He felt as if he had been stripped of pride, strength and even manhood. He had been utterly humiliated, reduced to a shivering, whining, twitching thing. Tears ran down his face though he made no sound. His hands hurt, his body hurt, everything hurt. He did not even know where he was, only that he had been brought back to La Roche-Derrien and carried up a steep flight of stairs to this small chamber under a roof's steep rafters where the walls were roughly plastered and a crucifix hung at the head of the bed. A window screened with opaque horn let in a dirty brown light.

Robbie went on telling him about the false entries they had added to Father Ralph's book. It had been his idea, he said, and Jeanette had copied out the book first, but after that Robbie had let his imagination run wild. 'I put some of it in Scots,' he boasted, 'how the Grail is really in Scotland. Have the bastards searching the heather, eh?' He laughed, but could see that Thomas was not listening. He went on talking anyway, and then another person came into the room and wiped the tears from Thomas's face. It was Jeanette.

'Thomas?' she asked, 'Thomas?'

He wanted to tell her that he had seen and spoken to her son, but he could not find the words. Guy Vexille had said Thomas would want to die while he was being tortured and that had been true, but Thomas was surprised to find it was still true. Take a man's pride, he thought, and you leave him with nothing. The worst memory was not the pain, nor the humiliation of begging for the pain to stop, but the gratitude he had felt towards de Taillebourg when the pain did stop. That was the most shameful thing of all.

'Thomas?' Jeanette asked again. She knelt by the bed and stroked his face. 'It's all right,' she said softly, 'you're safe now. This is my house. No one will hurt you here.'

'I might,' a new voice said and Thomas shook with fear, then turned to see that it was Mordecai who had spoken. Mordecai? The old doctor was supposed somewhere in the warm south. 'I might have to reset your finger and toe bones,' the doctor said, 'and that will be painful.' He put his bag on the floor. 'Hello, Thomas. I do hate boats. We waited for the new sail and then when they'd finished sewing it up they decided there wasn't enough caulking between the planks and when that was corrected they decided the rigging needed work and so the wretched boat is still sitting there. Sailors! All they ever do is talk about going to sea. Still, I shouldn't complain, it gave me the time to concoct some new material for your father's notebook and I rather enjoyed doing that! Now I hear you need me. My dear Thomas, what have they done to you?'

'Hurt me,' Thomas said and they were the first words he had spoken since he had come to Jeanette's house.

'Then we must mend you,' Mordecai said very calmly. He peeled the blanket back from Thomas's scarred body and, though Jeanette flinched, Mordecai just smiled. 'I've seen worse come from the Dominicans,' he said, 'much worse.'

So Thomas was again tended by Mordecai and time was measured by the clouds passing beyond the opaque window and the sun climbing ever higher in the sky and the noise of birds plucking straw from the thatch to make their nests. There were two days of awful pain when Mordecai brought a bone-setter to rebreak and splint Thomas's fingers and toes, but that pain went after a week and the burns on his body healed and the fever passed. Day after day Mordecai peered at his urine and declared it was clearing. 'You have the strength of an ox, young Thomas.'

'I have the stupidity of one,' Thomas said.

'Just brashness,' Mordecai said, 'just youth and brashness.'

'When they . . .' Thomas began and flinched from remembering what de Taillebourg had done. 'When they talked to me,' he said instead, 'I told them you had seen the notebook.'

'They can't have liked that,' Mordecai said. He had taken a spool of cord from a pocket of his gown and now looped one end of the line around a spur of wood that protruded from an untrimmed rafter. 'They can't have liked the thought of a Jew being curious about the Grail. They doubtless thought I wanted to use it as a pisspot?'

Thomas, despite the impiety, smiled. 'I'm sorry, Mordecai.'

'For telling them about me? What choice did you have? Men always talk under torture, Thomas, that is why torture is so useful. It is why torture will be used so long as the sun goes on circling the earth. And you think I am in more danger now than I was? I'm Jewish, Thomas, Jewish. Now, what do I do with this?' He was speaking of the cord, which now hung from the rafter and which he evidently wished to attach to the floor, but there was no obvious anchor point.

'What is it?' Thomas asked.

'A remedy,' Mordecai said, staring helplessly at the cord, then at the floor. 'I was ever unpractical with matters like this. A hammer and nail, you think?'

'A staple,' Thomas suggested.

Jeanette's idiot servant boy was sent out with careful instructions and managed to find the staple that Mordecai asked Thomas to hammer into the floorboard, but Thomas held up his crooked right hand with its fingers bent like claws and said he could not do it, so Mordecai clumsily banged the staple in himself and then tightened the cord and tied it off so that it stretched taut from floor to ceiling. 'What you must do,' he said, admiring his handiwork, 'is pluck it like a bowcord.'

'I can't,' Thomas said in panic, holding up his crooked hands again.

'What are you?' Mordecai asked.

'What am I?'

'Ignore the specious answers. I know you're an

Englishman and I assume you're a Christian, but what are you?'

'I was an archer,' Thomas said bitterly.

'And you still are,' Mordecai said harshly, 'and if you are not an archer then you are nothing. So pluck that cord! And keep on plucking it until your fingers can close on it. Practise. Practise. What else do you have to do with your time?'

So Thomas practised and after a week he could tighten two fingers opposite the thumb and make the cord reverberate like a harp string, and after another week he could bend the fingers of both hands about the cord and he plucked it so vigorously that it finally broke under the strain. His strength was coming back and the burns had healed to leave puckered welts where the poker had scored his skin, but the wounds in his memory did not heal. He would not talk of what had been done to him for he did not want to remember it, instead he practised plucking the cord until it snapped and then he learned to grip a quarterstaff and fought mock battles in the house yard with Robbie. And, as the days had lengthened out of winter, he went for walks beyond the town. There was a windmill on a slight hill that lay not far from the town's eastern gate and at first he could hardly manage the climb because his toes had been broken in the vice and his feet felt like unyielding lumps, but by the time April had filled the meadows with cowslips he was walking confidently. Will Skeat often went with him and though the older man never said much his company was easy. If he did talk it was to grumble about the weather or complain because the food was strange or, more likely, because he had heard nothing from the Earl of Northampton.

'You think we should write to his lordship again, Tom?'

'Maybe the first letter didn't reach him?'

'I never did like things written down,' Skeat said, 'it ain't natural. Can you write to him?'

'I can try,' Thomas said, but though he could pluck a bowcord and hold a quarterstaff or even a sword he could not manage the quill. He tried but his letters were scratchy and uncontrolled and in the end one of Totesham's clerks wrote the letter, though Totesham himself did not think the message would do any good.

'Charles of Blois will be here before we get any reinforcements,' he said. Totesham was awkward with Thomas, who had disobeyed him by riding to Roncelets, but Thomas's punishment had been far more than Totesham would have wanted and so he felt sorry for the archer. 'You want to carry the letter to the Earl?' he asked Thomas.

Thomas knew he was being offered an escape, but he shook his head. 'I'll stay,' he said, and the letter was entrusted to a shipmaster who was sailing the next day.

The letter was a futile gesture and Totesham knew it for his garrison was almost certainly doomed. Each day brought news of the reinforcements reaching Charles of Blois, and the enemy's raiding parties were now coming within sight of La Roche-Derrien's walls and harassing the forage parties that searched the countryside for any cattle, goats and sheep that could be driven back to the town to be slaughtered and salted down. Sir Guillaume enjoyed such foraging raids. Since losing Evecque he had become fatalistic and so savage that already the enemy had learned to be wary of the blue jupon with its three yellow hawks. Yet one evening, coming home from a long day that had yielded only two goats, he was grinning when he came to see Thomas. 'My enemy has joined Charles,' he said, 'the Count of Coutances, God damn his rotten soul. I killed one of his men this morning and I only wish it had been the Count himself.'

'Why's he here?' Thomas asked. 'He's not a Breton.'

'Philip of France is sending men to help his nephew,' Sir Guillaume said, 'so why won't the King of England send men to oppose him? He thinks Calais is more important?'

'Yes.'

'Calais,' Sir Guillaume said in disgust, 'is the arsehole of France.' He picked a shred of meat from between his teeth. 'And your friends were out riding today,' he went on.

'My friends?'

'The wasps.'

'Roncelets,' Thomas said.

'We fought half a dozen of the bastards in some benighted village,' Sir Guillaume said, 'and I put a lance clean through a black and yellow belly. He was coughing afterwards.'

'Coughing?'

'It's the wet weather, Thomas,' Sir Guillaume explained, 'it gives men a cough. So I left him alone, killed another of the bastards, then went back and cured his cough. I cut his head off.'

Robbie rode with Sir Guillaume and, like him, amassed coins taken from dead enemy patrols, though Robbie also rode in hope of meeting Guy Vexille. He knew that name now because Thomas had told him that it was Guy Vexille who had killed his brother just

404

before the battle outside Durham and Robbie had gone to St Renan's church, put his hand on the altar's cross and sworn revenge. 'I shall kill Guy Vexille and de Taillebourg,' he vowed.

'They're mine,' Thomas insisted.

'Not if I get to them first,' Robbie promised.

Robbie had found himself a brown-eyed Breton girl called Oana who hated to leave his side and she came with him whenever he walked with Thomas. One day, as they set out for the windmill, she appeared with Thomas's big black bow.

'I can't use that!' Thomas said, frightened of it.

'Then what bloody use are you?' Robbie asked and he patiently encouraged Thomas to draw the bow and praised him as his strength returned. The three of them would take the bow to the windmill and Thomas would drive arrows into the wooden tower. The shots were feeble at first for he could scarcely pull the cord halfway and the more power he exerted the more treacherous his fingers seemed to be and the more wayward his aim, but by the time the swallows and swifts had magically reappeared above the town's roofs he could pull the cord all the way back to his ear and put an arrow through one of Oana's wooden bracelets at a hundred paces.

'You're cured,' Mordecai told him when Thomas told him that news.

'Thanks to you,' Thomas said, though he knew it was not only Mordecai, any more than it was the friendship of Will Skeat or of Sir Guillaume or of Robbie Douglas that had helped him recover. Bernard de Taillebourg had wounded Thomas, but those bloodless wounds of God had not just been to his body, but to his soul, and it was on a dark spring night when the lightning was flickering in the east that Jeanette had climbed to her attic. She had not left Thomas until the town's cockerels greeted the new dawn and if Mordecai understood why Thomas was smiling the next day he said nothing, but he noted that from that moment on Thomas's recovery was swift.

Thereafter Thomas and Jeanette talked every night. He told her of Charles and of the look on the boy's face when Thomas had mentioned his mother; Jeanette wanted to know everything about that look and she worried that it meant nothing and that her son had forgotten her, but eventually she believed Thomas when he said the boy had almost wept when he heard news of her. 'You told him I loved him?' she asked.

'Yes,' Thomas said, and Jeanette lay silent, tears in her eyes, and Thomas tried to reassure her, but she shook her head as if there was nothing Thomas could say that would console her. 'I'm sorry,' he said.

'You tried,' Jeanette said.

They wondered how the enemy had known Thomas was coming and Jeanette said that she was sure that Belas the lawyer had had a hand in it. 'I know he writes to Charles of Blois,' she said, 'and that horrid man, what did you call him? *Épouvantail*?'

'The Scarecrow.'

'Him,' Jeanette confirmed, '*l'épouvantail*. He talks to Belas.'

'The Scarecrow talks to Belas?' Thomas asked, surprised.

'He lives there now. He and his men live in the storehouses.' She paused. 'Why does he even stay in the town?' Others of the mercenaries had slipped away to find employment where there was some hope of victory rather than stay and endure the defeat that Charles of Blois threatened.

'He can't go home,' Thomas said, 'because he has too many debts. He's protected from his creditors so long as he's here.'

'But why La Roche-Derrien?'

'Because I'm here,' Thomas said. 'He thinks I can lead him to treasure.'

'The Grail?'

'He doesn't know that,' Thomas said, but he was wrong because the next day, while he was alone at the windmill and shooting arrows at a wand he had planted a hundred and fifty paces away, the Scarecrow and his six men-at-arms came riding out of the town's eastern gate. They turned off the Pontrieux road, filed through a gap in the hedge and spurred up the shallow slope towards the mill. They were all in mail and all with swords except for Beggar who, dwarfing his horse, carried a morningstar.

Sir Geoffrey reined in close to Thomas, who ignored him to shoot an arrow that just brushed the wand. The Scarecrow let the coils of his whip ripple to the ground. 'Look at me,' he ordered Thomas.

Thomas still ignored him. He took an arrow from his belt and put it on the string, then jerked his head aside as he saw the whip snake towards him. The metal tip touched his hair, but did no damage. 'I said look at me,' Sir Geoffrey snarled.

'You want an arrow in your face?' Thomas asked him.

Sir Geoffrey leaned forward on his saddle's pommel, his raw red face twisted with a spasm of anger. 'You are an archer' – he pointed his whip handle at Thomas

– 'and I am a knight. If I chop you down there's not a judge alive who would condemn me.'

'And if I put an arrow through your eye,' Thomas said, 'the devil will thank me for sending him company.'

Beggar growled and spurred his horse forward, but the Scarecrow waved the big man back. 'I know what you want,' he said to Thomas.

Thomas hauled the string back, instinctively corrected for the small wind rippling the meadow's grass, and released. The arrow made the wand quiver. 'You have no idea what I want,' he told Sir Geoffrey.

'I thought it was gold,' the Scarecrow said, 'and then I thought it was land, but I never understood why gold or land would take you to Durham.' He paused as Thomas shot another arrow that hissed a hand's breadth past the distant wand. 'But now I know,' he finished, 'now at last I know.'

'What do you know?' Thomas asked derisively.

'I know you went to Durham to talk with the churchmen because you're seeking the greatest treasure of the Church. You're looking for the Grail.'

Thomas let the bowcord slacken, then looked up at Sir Geoffrey. 'We're all looking for the Grail,' Thomas said, still derisive.

'Where is it?' Sir Geoffrey growled.

Thomas laughed. He was surprised the Scarecrow knew about the Grail, but he supposed that gossip in the garrison had probably let everyone in La Roche-Derrien know. 'The best questioners of the Church asked me that,' he said, holding up one crooked hand, 'and I didn't tell them. You think I'll tell you?'

'I think,' the Scarecrow said, 'that a man searching

for the Grail doesn't lock himself into a garrison that only has a month or two to live.'

'Then maybe I'm not looking for the Grail,' Thomas said and shot another arrow at the wand, but this shaft was warped and the arrow wobbled in flight and went wide. Above him the great sails of the mill, furled about their spars and tethered by ropes, creaked as a wind gust tried to turn them.

Sir Geoffrey coiled the whip. 'You failed the last time you rode out. What happens if you ride again? What happens if you ride after the Grail? And you must be going soon, before Charles of Blois gets here. So when you ride you're going to need help.' Thomas, incredulous, realized that the Scarecrow had come to offer him help, or perhaps Sir Geoffrey was asking for help. He was in La Roche-Derrien for only one reason, treasure, and he was no nearer to it now than he had been when he first accosted Thomas outside Durham. 'You daren't fail again,' the Scarecrow went on, 'so next time take some real fighters with you.'

'You think I'd take you?' Thomas asked, astonished.

'I'm an Englishman,' the Scarecrow said indignantly, 'and if the Grail exists I want it in England. Not in some scab of a foreign place.'

The sound of a sword scraping from its scabbard made the Scarecrow and his men turn in their saddles. Jeanette and Robbie had come to the meadow with Oana at Robbie's side; Jeanette had her crossbow cocked and Robbie, as though he did not have a care in the world, was now slashing the tops from thistles with his uncle's sword. Sir Geoffrey turned back to Thomas. 'What you don't need is a damned Scotchman,' he said angrily, 'nor a damned French bitch. If you look for the

Grail, archer, look for it with loyal Englishmen! It's what the King would want, isn't it?'

Again Thomas did not answer. Sir Geoffrey hung the whip on a hook attached to his belt, then jerked his reins. The seven men cantered down the hill, going close to Robbie as if tempting him to attack them, but Robbie ignored them. 'What did that bastard want?'

Thomas shot at the wand, brushing it with the arrow's feathers. 'I think,' he said, 'that he wanted to help me find the Grail.'

'Help you!' Robbie exclaimed. 'Help you find the Grail? Like hell. He wants to steal it. That bastard would steal the milk from the Virgin Mary's tits.'

'Robbie!' Jeanette said, shocked, then aimed her crossbow at the wand.

'Watch her,' Thomas said to Robbie. 'She'll close her eyes when she shoots. She always does.'

'Damn you,' Jeanette said, then, unable to help it, closed her eyes as she pulled the trigger. The bolt slapped out of the groove and miraculously clipped the top six inches from the wand. Jeanette looked at Thomas triumphantly. 'I can shoot better than you with my eyes closed,' she said.

Robbie had been on the town's walls and had seen the Scarecrow accost Thomas and so he had come to help, but now, with Sir Geoffrey gone, they sat in the sun with their backs against the mill's wooden skirt. Jeanette was staring at the town's wall which still showed the scars where the English-made breach had been repaired with a lighter-coloured stone. 'Are you really nobly born?' she asked Thomas.

'Bastard born,' Thomas said.

'But to a nobleman?'

'He was the Count of Astarac,' Thomas said, then laughed because it was strange to think that Father Ralph, mad Father Ralph who had preached to the gulls on Hookton's beach, had been a count.

'So what's the badge of Astarac?' Jeanette asked.

'A yale,' Thomas told her, 'holding a cup,' and he showed her the faded silver patch on his black bowstave that was engraved with the strange creature that had horns, cloven hooves, claws, tusks and a lion's tail.

'I'll have a banner made for you,' Jeanette said.

'A banner? Why?'

'A man should display his badge,' Jeanette said.

'And you should leave La Roche-Derrien,' Thomas retorted. He kept trying to persuade her to leave the town, but she insisted she would stay. She doubted now she would ever get her son back and so she was determined to kill Charles of Blois with one of her crossbow's bolts, which were made of dense yew heartwood tipped with iron heads and fledged, not with feathers, but with stiff pieces of leather inserted into slits cut crosswise into the yew and then bound up with cord and glue. That was why she practised so assiduously, for the chance to cut down the man who had raped her and taken her child.

Easter came before the enemy arrived. The weather was warm now. The hedgerows were full of nestlings and the meadows echoed with the shriek of partridges and on the day after Easter, when folk ate up the remnants of the feast that had broken their Lenten fast, the dreaded news at last arrived from Rennes.

That Charles of Blois had marched.

*　　*　　*

More than four thousand men left Rennes under the white ermine banner of the Duke of Brittany. Two thousand of them were crossbowmen, most wearing the green and red livery of Genoa and bearing the city's badge of the Holy Grail on their right arms. They were mercenaries, hired and prized for their skill. A thousand infantrymen marched with them, the men who would dig the trenches and assault the broken walls of the English fortresses, and then there were over a thousand knights or men-at-arms, most of them French, who formed the hard armoured heart of Duke Charles's army. They marched towards La Roche-Derrien, but the real aim of the campaign was not to capture the town, which was of negligible value, but rather to draw Sir Thomas Dagworth and his small army into a pitched battle in which the knights and men-at-arms, mounted on their big armoured horses, would be released to smash their way through the English ranks.

A convoy of heavy carts carried nine siege machines, which needed the attentions of over a hundred engineers who understood how to assemble and work the giant devices that could hurl boulders the size of beer barrels further than a bow could drive an arrow. A Florentine gunner had offered six of his strange machines to Charles, but the Duke had turned them down. Guns were rare, expensive and, he believed, temperamental, while the old mechanical devices worked well enough if they were properly greased with tallow and Charles saw no reason to abandon them.

Over four thousand men left Rennes, but far more arrived in the fields outside La Roche-Derrien. Country folk who hated the English joined the army to gain revenge for all the cattle, harvests, property and virginity their families had lost to the foreigners. Some were armed with nothing more than mattocks or axes, but when the time came to assault the town such angry men would be useful.

The army came to La Roche-Derrien and Charles of Blois heard the last of the town's gates slam shut. He sent a messenger to demand the garrison's surrender, knowing the request was futile, and while his tents were pitched he ordered other horsemen to patrol westwards on the roads leading to Finisterre, the world's end. They were there to warn him when Sir Thomas Dagworth's army marched to relieve the town, if indeed it did march. His spies had told Charles that Dagworth could not even raise a thousand men. 'And how many of those will be archers?' he asked.

'At most, your grace, five hundred.' The man who answered was a priest, one of the many who served in Charles's retinue. The Duke was known as a pious man and liked to employ priests as advisers, secretaries and, in this case, as a spymaster. 'At most five hundred,' the priest repeated, 'but in truth, your grace, far fewer.'

'Fewer? How so?'

'Fever in Finisterre,' the priest answered, then smiled thinly. 'God is good to us.'

'Amen to that. And how many archers are in the town garrison?'

'Sixty healthy men, your grace' – the priest had Belas's latest report – 'just sixty.'

Charles grimaced. He had been defeated by English archers before, even when he had so outnumbered them that defeat had seemed impossible, and, as a result, he was properly wary of the long arrows, but he was also an intelligent man and he had given the problem of the English war bow a deal of thought. It was possible to defeat the weapon, he thought, and on this campaign he would show how it could be done. Cleverness, that most despised of soldierly qualities, would triumph, and Charles of Blois, styled by the French as the Duke and ruler of Brittany, was undeniably a clever man. He could read and write in six languages, spoke Latin better than most priests and was a master of rhetoric. He even looked clever with his thin, pale face and intense blue eyes, fair beard and moustache. He had been fighting his rivals for the dukedom almost all his adult life, but now, at last, he had gained the ascendancy. The King of England, besieging Calais, was not reinforcing his garrisons in Brittany while the King of France, who was Charles's uncle, had been generous with men, which meant that Duke Charles at last outnumbered his enemies. By summer's end, he thought, he would be master of all his ancestral domains, but then he cautioned himself against over-confidence. 'Even five hundred archers,' he observed, 'even five hundred and sixty archers can be dangerous.' He had a precise voice, pedantic and dry, and the priests in his entourage often thought he sounded very like a priest himself.

'The Genoese will swamp them with bolts, your grace,' a priest assured the Duke.

'Pray God they do,' Charles said piously, though God, he thought, would need some help from human cleverness.

Next morning, under a late spring sun, Charles rode around La Roche-Derrien, though he kept far enough away so that no English arrow could reach him. The defenders had hung banners from the town walls. Some of the flags displayed the English cross of St George, others the white ermine badge of the Montfort Duke that was so similar to Charles's own device. Many of the flags were inscribed with insults aimed at Charles. One showed the Duke's white ermine with an English arrow through its bleeding belly, and another was evidently a picture of Charles himself being trampled under a great black horse, but most of the flags were pious exhortations inviting God's help or displaying the cross to show the attackers where heaven's sympathies were supposed to lie. Most besieged towns would also have flaunted the banners of their noble defenders, but La Roche-Derrien had few nobles, or at least few who displayed their badges, and none to match the ranks of the aristocrats in Charles's army. The three hawks of Evecque were displayed on the wall, but everyone knew Sir Guillaume had been dispossessed and had no more than three or four followers. One flag showed a red heart on a pale field and a priest in Charles's entourage thought it was the badge of the Douglas family in Scotland, but that was a nonsense for no Scotsman would be fighting for the English. Next to the red heart was a brighter banner showing a blue and white sea of wavy lines. 'Is that . . .' Charles began to ask, then paused, frowning.

'The badge of Armorica, your grace,' the Lord of Roncelets answered. Today, as Duke Charles circled the town, he was accompanied by his great lords so that the defenders would see their banners and be awed. Most were lords of Brittany; the Viscount Rohan and the Viscount Morgat rode close behind the Duke, then came the lords of Châteaubriant and of Roncelets, Laval, Guingamp, Rougé, Dinan, Redon and Malestroit, all of them mounted on high-stepping destriers, while from Normandy the Count of Coutances and the lords of Valognes and Carteret had brought their retainers to do battle for the nephew of their King.

'I thought Armorica was dead,' one of the Norman lords remarked.

'He has a son,' Roncelets answered.

'And a widow,' the Count of Guingamp said, 'and she's the traitorous bitch flying the banner.'

'A pretty traitorous bitch, though,' the Viscount Rohan said, and the lords laughed for they all knew how to treat unruly but pretty widows.

Charles grimaced at their unseemly laughter. 'When we take the town,' he ordered coldly, 'the dowager Countess of Armorica will not be hurt. She will be brought to me.' He had raped Jeanette once and he would rape her again, and when that pleasure was done he would marry her off to one of his men-at-arms who would teach her to mind her manners and to curb her tongue. Now he reined in his horse to watch as more banners were hung from the ramparts, all of them insults to him and his house. 'It's a busy garrison,' he said drily.

'Busy townspeople,' the Viscount Rohan snarled. 'Busy goddamn traitors.'

'Townsfolk?' Charles seemed puzzled. 'Why would the townsfolk support the English?'

'Trade,' Roncelets answered curtly.

'Trade?'

'They're becoming rich,' Roncelets growled, 'and they like it.'

'They like it enough to fight against their lord?' Charles asked in disbelief.

'A disloyal rabble,' Roncelets said dismissively.

'A rabble,' Charles said, 'that we shall have to impoverish.' He spurred on, only checking his horse when he saw another nobleman's banner, this one showing a yale flourishing a chalice. So far he had not seen a single banner that promised a great ransom if its lord was captured, but this badge was a mystery. 'Whose is that?' he asked.

No one knew, but then a slim young man on a tall black horse answered from the rear of the Duke's entourage. 'The badge of Astarac, your grace, and it belongs to an imposter.' The man who had answered had come from France with a hundred grim horsemen liveried in plain black and he was accompanied by a Dominican with a frightening face. Charles of Blois was glad to have the black-liveried men in his army, for they were all hard and experienced soldiers, but he did feel somewhat nervous of them. They were somehow too hard, too experienced.

'An imposter?' he repeated and spurred on. 'Then we do not need to worry ourselves about him.'

There were three gates on the town's landward side and a fourth, opening onto the bridge, facing the river. Charles planned to besiege each of those gates so that the garrison would be trapped like foxes with their earths stopped. 'The army,' he decreed when the lords returned to the ducal tent, which had been raised close to the windmill that stood on the slight hill to the east of the town, 'will be divided into four parts, and one part will face each gate.' The lords listened and a priest copied down the pronouncement so that history would have a true record of the Duke's martial genius.

Each of the four divisions of Charles's army would

417

outnumber any relief force that Sir Thomas Dagworth could gather, but, to make himself even more secure, Charles ordered that the four encampments were to surround themselves with earthworks so that the English would be forced to attack across ditches, banks, palisades and thorn hedges. The obstacles would conceal Charles's men from the archers and give his Genoese crossbowmen cover while they rewound their weapons. The ground between the four encampments was to be cleared of hedges and other obstacles to leave a bare wilderness of grass and marsh.

'The English archer,' Charles told his lords, 'is not a man who will fight face to face. He kills from a distance and he hides behind hedges, thus frustrating our horses. We shall turn that tactic against him.' The tent was big, white and airy, and the smell inside was of trampled grass and men's sweat. From beyond the canvas walls came the sound of dull thudding as the engineers used wooden mallets to assemble the biggest of the great siege engines.

'Our men,' Charles further decreed, 'will stay within their own defences. We shall thus make four fortresses that will stand at the four gates of the town and if the English send a relief force then those men will have to attack our fortresses. Archers cannot kill men they cannot see.' He paused to make sure those simple words were understood. 'Archers,' he said again, 'cannot kill men they cannot see. Remember that! Our crossbows will be behind banks of earth, we will be screened by hedges and hidden by palisades, and the enemy will be out in the open where they can be cut down.'

There were growls of agreement for the Duke made sense. Archers could not kill invisible men. Even the fierce Dominican who had come with the soldiers in black looked impressed.

The midday bells rang from the town. One, the loudest, was cracked and gave a harsh note. 'La Roche-Derrien,' the Duke continued, 'does not matter. Whether it falls or not is of little consequence. What matters is that we draw our enemy's army out to attack us. Dagworth will probably come to protect La Roche-Derrien. When he arrives we shall crush him and once he is broken then only the English garrisons will be left and we shall take them one by one until, at summer's end, all Brittany is ours.' He spoke slowly and simply, knowing it was best to spell out the campaign for these men who, though they were tough as rams, were not renowned as thinkers. 'And when Brittany is ours,' he went on, 'there will be gifts of land, of manors and of strongholds.' A much louder growl of approbation sounded and the listening men grinned for there would be more than land, manors and castles as the rewards of victory. There would be gold, silver and women. Lots of women. The growl turned into laughter as the men realized they were all thinking the same thing.

'But it is here' – Charles's voice called his audience to order – 'that we make our victory possible, and we do it by denying the English archer his targets. An archer cannot kill men he cannot see!' He paused again, looking at his audience and he saw them nodding as the simple truth of that assertion at last penetrated their skulls. 'We shall all be in our own fortress, one of four fortresses, and when the English army comes to relieve the siege they will attack one of those fortresses. That English army will be small. Fewer than a thousand men!

419

Suppose, then, that it begins by attacking the fort I shall make here. What will the rest of you do?'

He waited for an answer and, after a while, the Lord of Roncelets, as uncertain as a schoolboy giving a response to his master, frowned and made a suggestion. 'Come to help your grace?'

The other lords nodded and smiled agreement.

'No!' Charles said angrily. 'No! No! No!' He waited, making sure they had understood the simple word. 'If you leave your fortress,' he explained, 'then you offer the English archer a target. It is what he wants! He will want to tempt us from behind our walls to cut us down with his arrows. So what do we do? We stay behind our walls. *We stay behind our walls.*' Did they understand that? It was the key to victory. Keep the men hidden and the English must lose. Sir Thomas Dagworth's army would be forced to assault earth walls and thorn hedges and the crossbowmen would spit them on quarrels and when the English were so thinned that only a couple of hundred remained on their feet the Duke would release his men-at-arms to slaughter the remnant. 'You do not leave your fortresses,' he insisted, 'and any man who does will forfeit my generosity.' That threat sobered the Duke's listeners. 'If even one of your men leaves the sanctuary of the walls,' Charles continued, 'we shall make sure that you will not share in the distribution of land at the end of the campaign. Is that plain, gentlemen? Is that plain?'

It was plain. It was simple.

Charles of Blois would make four fortresses to oppose the four gates of the town and the English, when they came, would be forced to assault those newly made walls. And even the smallest of the Duke's four forts would have more defenders than the English had attackers, and those defenders would be sheltered, and their weapons would be lethal, and the English would die and so Brittany would pass to the House of Blois.

Cleverness. It would win wars and make reputations. And once Charles had shown how to defeat the English here he would defeat them through all France.

Because Charles dreamed of a crown heavier than Brittany's ducal coronet. He dreamed of France, but it must begin here, in the flooded fields about La Roche-Derrien, where the English archer would be taught his place.

In hell.

The nine siege engines were all trebuchets, the largest of them capable of throwing a stone weighing twice the weight of a grown man for almost three hundred paces. All nine had been made at Regensburg in Bavaria and the senior engineers who accompanied the gaunt machines were all Bavarians who understood the intricacies of the weapons. The two biggest had throwing beams over fifty feet long and even the two smallest, which were placed on the far bank of the Jaudy to threaten the bridge and its barbican, had beams thirty-six feet long.

The biggest two, which were named Hellgiver and Widowmaker, were placed at the foot of the hill on which the windmill stood. In essence each was a simple machine, merely a long beam mounted on an axle like a giant's balance or a child's see-saw, only one end of the see-saw was three times longer than the other. The shorter end was weighted with a huge wooden box that was filled with lead weights, while the longer end, which actually threw the missile, was attached to a great windlass which drew it down to the ground and so raised the ten tons of lead counterweights. The stone missile was placed in a leather sling some fifteen feet long, which was attached to the longer arm. When the beam was released so that the counterweight slammed down, the longer end whipped up into the sky and the sling whipped even faster and the boulder was released from the sling's leather cradle to curve through the sky and crash down onto its target. That much was simple. What was hard was to keep the mechanism greased with tallow, to construct a winch strong enough to haul the long beam down to the ground, to make a container strong enough to thump down again and again and not spill the ten tons of lead weights and, trickiest of all, to fashion a device strong enough to hold the long beam down against the weight of the lead yet capable of releasing the beam safely. These were the matters on which the Bavarians were experts and for which they were paid so generously.

There were many who said that the Bavarians' expertise was redundant. Guns were much smaller and hurled their missiles with greater force, but Duke Charles had applied his intelligence to the comparison and decided on the older technology. Guns were slow and prone to explosions that killed their expensive gunners. They were also painfully slow because the gap between the missile and the gun's barrel had to be sealed to contain the powder's force and so it was necessary to pack the cannon ball about with wet loam, and that needed time to dry before the powder could be ignited, and even the most skilful gunners from Italy could not fire a weapon more than three or four times a day. And when a gun fired it spat a ball weighing only a few pounds. While it was true that the small ball flew with a velocity so great that it could not even be seen, nevertheless the older trebuchets could throw a missile of twenty or thirty times the weight three or four times in every hour. La Roche-Derrien, the Duke decided, would be hammered the old-fashioned way, and so the little town was surrounded by the nine trebuchets. As well as Hellgiver and Widowmaker, there was Stone-Hurler, Crusher, Gravedigger, Stonewhip, Spiteful, Destroyer and Hand of God.

Each trebuchet was constructed on a platform made of wooden beams and protected by a palisade that was tall and stout enough to stop any arrow. Some of the peasants who had joined the army were trained to stand close to the palisades and be ready to throw water over any fire arrows that the English might use to burn the fences down and so expose the trebuchets' engineers. Other peasants dug the ditches and threw up the earthen banks that formed the Duke's four fortresses. Where possible they used existing ditches or incorporated the thick blackthorn hedges into the defences. They made barriers of sharpened stakes and dug pits to break horses' legs. The four parts of the Duke's army ringed themselves with such defences and, day after day, as the walls grew and the trebuchets took shape from the pieces transported on the wagons, the Duke had his men practise forming their lines of battle. The Genoese crossbowmen manned the half-finished walls while behind them the knights and men-at-arms paraded on foot. Some men grumbled that such practices were a waste of time, but others saw how the Duke intended to fight and they approved. The English archers would be baffled by the walls, ditches and palisades and the crossbows would pick them off one by one, and finally the enemy would be forced to attack across the earth walls and the flooded ditches to be slaughtered by the waiting men-at-arms.

After a week of back-breaking work the trebuchets were assembled and their counterpoise boxes had been filled with great pigs of lead. Now the engineers had to demonstrate an even subtler skill, the art of dropping their great stones one after the other onto the exact same spot of the wall so that the ramparts would be battered away and a path opened into the town. Then, once the relieving army was defeated, the Duke's men could assault La Roche-Derrien and put its treasonous inhabitants to the sword.

The Bavarian engineers selected their first stones carefully, then trimmed the length of the slings to affect the range of their machines. It was a fine spring morning. Kestrels soared, buttercups dotted the fields, trout were rising to the mayflies, the wild garlic was blossoming white and pigeons flew through the new leaves of the green woods. It was the loveliest time of the year and Duke Charles, whose spies told him that Sir Thomas Dagworth's English army had yet to leave western Brittany, anticipated triumph. 'The Bavarians,' he told one of his attendant priests, 'may begin.'

The trebuchet named Hellgiver shot first. A lever was pulled that extracted a thick metal pin from a staple attached to the long arm of Hellgiver's beam. Ten tons of lead dropped with a crash that could be heard in Tréguier, the long arm whipped up and the sling whirled at the arm's end with the sound of a sudden gale and a boulder arched into the sky. It seemed to hang for a moment, a great stone lump in the kestrel-haunted sky, and then, like a thunderbolt, it fell.

The killing had begun.

The first stone, thrown by Hellgiver, crashed through the roof of a dyer's house close to St Brieuc's church and took off the heads of an English man-at-arms and the dyer's wife. A joke went through the garrison that the two bodies were so crushed together by the boulder that they would go on coupling throughout eternity. The stone which killed them, a rock about the size of a barrel, had missed the eastern ramparts by no more than twenty feet and the Bavarian engineers made adjustments to the sling and the next stone thumped just short of the wall, spewing up filth and sewage from the ditch. The third boulder hit the wall plumb and then a monstrous thump announced that Widowmaker had just shot its first missile and one after the other Stone-Hurler, Crusher, Gravedigger, Stonewhip, Spiteful, Destroyer and Hand of God added their contributions.

Richard Totesham did his best to blunt the assault of the trebuchets. It was evident that Charles was attempting to make four breaches, one on each side of the town, and so Totesham ordered vast bags to be sewn and stuffed with straw and the bags were placed to cushion the walls, which were further protected by baulks of timber. Those precautions served to slow the process of making the breaches, but the Bavarians were sending some of their missiles deep into the town and nothing could be done to shield the houses from those plunging boulders. Some townsfolk argued that Totesham should construct a trebuchet of his own and try to break the enemy's machines, but he doubted there was time and instead a giant crossbow was fashioned from ships' spars that had been brought upstream from Tréguier before the siege began. Tréguier was now deserted for, lacking walls, its inhabitants had either come to La Roche-Derrien for shelter, fled to sea in their ships or gone over to Charles's camp.

Totesham's springald was thirty feet in width and shot a bolt eight feet long propelled by a cord made from braided leather. It was cocked by means of a ship's windlass. It took four days to make the weapon and the very first time they tried to use it the spar-arm broke. It was a bad omen, and there was an even worse one next morning when a horse drawing a cart of night soil broke free from its harness and kicked a child in the head. The child died. Later that day a stone from one of the smaller trebuchets across the river plunged into Richard Totesham's house and brought down half the upper floor and very nearly killed his baby. Over a score of mercenaries tried to desert the garrison that night and some must have got clean away, others joined Charles's army and one, who had been carrying a message for Sir Thomas Dagworth concealed in a boot, was caught and beheaded. Next morning his severed head, with the letter fixed between his teeth, was hurled into the town by the trebuchet called the Hand of God and the spirits of the garrison plummeted even further.

'I am not sure,' Mordecai told Thomas, 'whether omens can be trusted.'

'Of course they can.'

'I should like to hear your reasons. But show me your urine first.'

'You said I was cured,' Thomas protested.

'Eternal vigilance, dear Thomas, is the price of health. Piss for me.'

Thomas obeyed, Mordecai held the liquid up to the sun, then dipped a finger in it and dabbed it onto his tongue. 'Splendid!' he said. 'Clear, pure and not too saline. That is a good omen, is it not?'

'That's a symptom,' Thomas said, 'not an omen.'

'Ah.' Mordecai smiled at the correction. They were in the small back yard behind Jeanette's kitchen where the doctor watched the house-martins bringing mud to their new nests beneath the eaves. 'Enlighten me, Thomas,' he said with another smile, 'on the matter of omens.'

'When our Lord was crucified,' Thomas said, 'there was darkness in daytime and a curtain in the temple was torn in two.'

'You are saying that omens are secreted at the very heart of your faith?'

'And yours too, surely?' Thomas asked.

Mordecai flinched as a boulder crunched down somewhere in the town. The sound reverberated, then there was another splintering crash as a weakened roof or floor gave way. Dogs howled and a woman screamed. 'They're doing it deliberately,' Mordecai said.

'Of course,' Thomas said. Not only was the enemy sending boulders to fall on the tight small houses of the town, but they sometimes used the trebuchets to lob the rotting corpses of cattle or pigs or goats to splatter their filth and stench through the streets.

Mordecai waited till the woman had stopped screaming. 'I don't think I believe in omens,' he said. 'We suffer some bad luck in the town and everyone assumes we are doomed, but how do we know there is not some ill fortune afflicting the enemy?'

Thomas said nothing. Birds squabbled in the thatch, oblivious that a cat was stalking just below the roof ridge.

'What do you want, Thomas?' Mordecai asked.

'Want?'

'What do you want?'

Thomas grimaced and held out his right hand with its crooked fingers. 'For these to be straight.'

'And I want to be young again,' Mordecai said impatiently. 'Your fingers are mended. They are misshapen, but mended. Now tell me what you want.'

'What I want,' Thomas said, 'is to kill the men who killed Eleanor. To bring Jeanette's son back. Then to be an archer. Just that. An archer.' He wanted the Grail too, but he did not like to talk of that with Mordecai.

Mordecai tugged at his beard. 'To kill the men who killed Eleanor?' he mused aloud. 'I think you'll do that. Jeanette's son? Maybe you will do that too, though I don't understand why you wish to please her. You don't want to marry Jeanette, do you?'

'Marry her!' Thomas laughed. 'No.'

'Good.'

'Good?' Thomas was offended now.

'I have always enjoyed talking with alchemists,' Mordecai said, 'and I have often seen them mix sulphur and quicksilver. There is a theory that all metals are composed of those two substances, did you know? The proportions vary, of course, but my point, dear Thomas, is that if you put quicksilver and sulphur into a vessel, then heat it, the result is very often calamitous.' He mimed an explosion with his hands. 'That, I think, is you and Jeanette. Besides, I cannot see her married to an archer. To a king? Yes. To a duke? Maybe. To a count or an earl? Certainly. But to an archer?' He shook his head. 'There is nothing wrong with being an archer, Thomas. It's a useful skill in this wicked world.' He sat silent for a few heartbeats. 'My son is training to be a doctor.'

Thomas smiled. 'I sense a reproof.'

'A reproof?'

'Your son will be a healer and I'm a killer.'

Mordecai shook his head. 'Benjamin is training to be a physician, but he would rather be a soldier. He wants to be a killer.'

'Then why —' Thomas stopped because the answer was obvious.

'Jews cannot carry weapons,' Mordecai said, 'that is why. No, I meant no reproof. I think, as soldiers go, Thomas, that you are a good man.' He paused and frowned because another stone from one of the bigger trebuchets had slammed into a building not far away and, as the echoing crash subsided, he waited for the screams. None came. 'Your friend Will is a good man, too,' Mordecai went on, 'but I fear he's no longer an archer.'

Thomas nodded. Will Skeat was cured, but not restored. 'It would have been better, I sometimes think —' Thomas began.

'If he had died?' Mordecai finished the thought. 'Wish death on no man, Thomas, it comes soon enough without a wish. Sir William will go home to England, no doubt, and your Earl will look after him.'

The fate of all old soldiers, Thomas thought. To go home and die on the charity of the family they served. 'Then I'll go to the siege of Calais when all this is over,' Thomas said, 'and see if Will's archers need a new leader.'

Mordecai smiled. 'You won't look for the Grail?'

'I don't know where it is,' Thomas said.

'And your father's book?' Mordecai asked. 'It didn't help?'

Thomas had been poring over the copy Jeanette had made. He thought his father must have used some kind of code, though try as he might he could not pierce the code's workings. Or else, in its ramblings, the book was merely a symptom of Father Ralph's troubled mind. Yet Thomas was sure of one thing. His father had believed he possessed the Grail. 'I will look for the Grail,' Thomas said, 'but I sometimes think the only way to seek it is *not* to search for it.' He looked up, startled, as there was a sudden scrabbling sound on the roof. The cat had made a rush and almost lost its footing as birds scattered upwards.

'Another omen?' Mordecai suggested, looking up at the escaping birds. 'Surely a good one?'

'Besides,' Thomas said, 'what do you know of the Grail?'

'I am a Jew. What do I know of anything?' Mordecai asked innocently. 'What would happen, Thomas, if you found the Grail?' He did not wait for an answer. 'Do you think,' he went on instead, 'that the world will become a better place? Is it just lacking the Grail? Is that all?' There was still no answer. 'It's a thing like Abracadabra, is that it?' Mordecai said sadly.

'The devil?' Thomas was shocked.

'Abracadabra isn't the devil!' Mordecai answered, equally shocked. 'It's simply a charm. Some foolish Jews believe if you write it in the form of a triangle and hang it about your neck then you'll not suffer from the ague! What nonsense! The only cure for an ague is a warm poultice of cow dung, but folk will put their trust in charms and, I fear, in omens too, yet I do not think God works through the one or reveals Himself through the other.'

'Your God,' Thomas said, 'is a very long way away.'

'I rather fear he is.'

'Mine is close,' Thomas said, 'and He does show Himself.'

'Then you're fortunate,' Mordecai said. Jeanette's distaff and spindle were on the bench beside him and he put the distaff under his left arm and tried to spin some thread from the wool bundled about its head, but he could make nothing of it. 'You are fortunate,' he said again, 'and I hope that when Charles's troops break in that your God stays close. As for the rest of us, I suppose we're doomed?'

'If they break in,' Thomas said, 'then either take refuge in a church or try and escape by the river.'

'I can't swim.'

'Then the church is your best hope.'

'I doubt that,' Mordecai said, putting down the distaff. 'What Totesham should do,' he said sadly, 'is surrender. Let us all leave.'

'He won't do that.'

Mordecai shrugged. 'So we must die.'

Yet, the very next day, he was given a chance to escape when Totesham said that anyone who did not want to suffer the privations of the siege could leave the town by the southern gate, but no sooner was it thrown open than a force of Charles's men-at-arms, all in mail and with their faces hidden by their helmets' grey visors, blocked the road. No more than a hundred folk had decided to go, all of them women and children, but Charles's men-at-arms were there to say they would not be allowed to abandon La Roche-Derrien. It was not in the besiegers' interest to have fewer mouths for the garrison to feed and so the grey men barred the road and Totesham's soldiers shut the town gate and the women and children were stranded all day.

That evening the trebuchets ceased their work for the first time since the stone had killed the dyer's wife and her lover and, in the strange silence, a messenger came from Charles's encampment. A trumpeter and a white flag announced that he wanted a truce and Totesham ordered an English trumpeter to respond to the Breton and for a white banner to be waved above the southern gate. The Breton messenger waited until a man of rank came to the walls, then he gestured at the women and children. 'These folk,' he said, 'cannot be allowed to pass through our lines. They will starve here.'

'This is the pity your master has for his people?' Totesham's envoy responded. He was an English priest who spoke Breton and French.

'He has such pity for them,' the messenger answered, 'that he would free them of England's chains. Tell your master that he has until this evening's angelus to surrender the town, and if he does he will be permitted to march out with all his weapons, banners, horses, families, servants and possessions.'

It was a generous offer but the priest did not even consider it. 'I will tell him,' the priest said, 'but only if

433

you tell your master that we have food for a year and weapons enough to kill all of you twice over.'

The messenger bowed, the priest returned the compliment and the parley was over. The trebuchets began their work again and, at nightfall, Totesham ordered the town gates opened and the fugitives were allowed back inside to the jeers of those who had not fled.

Thomas, like every man in La Roche-Derrien, served time on the ramparts. It was tedious work for Charles of Blois took great care to ensure that none of his forces strayed within bowshot of the English archers, but there was some diversion to be had in watching the great trebuchets. They were cranked down so slowly that it seemed the vast beams were hardly moving, but gradually, almost imperceptibly, the big wooden box with its lead weights would rise from behind the protective palisade and the long arm would sink out of sight. Then, when the long arm was winched as low as it could go, nothing would happen for a long time, presumably because the engineers were loading the sling and then, just when it seemed nothing ever would happen, the counterweight would drop, the palisade would quiver, startled birds flash up from the grass and the long arm would slash up, judder, the sling would whip about and a stone arc into the air. The sound would come then, the monstrous crash of the falling counterweight, followed a heartbeat later by the thump of the stone onto the broken ramparts. More straw-filled bags would be thrown onto the growing breach, but the missiles still did their damage and so Totesham ordered his men to begin making new walls behind the growing breaches.

Some men, including Thomas and Robbie, wanted to make a sally. Put together sixty men, they argued, and let them stream out of the town at first light. They could easily overrun one or two of the trebuchets, soak the machines in oil and pitch and throw burning brands into the tangle of ropes and timber, but Totesham refused. His garrison was too small, he argued, and he did not want to lose even a half-dozen men before he needed to fight Charles's men in the breaches.

He lost men anyway. By the third week of the siege Charles of Blois had finished his own defensive works and the four portions of his army were all protected behind earth walls, hedges, palisades and ditches. He had scoured the land between his encampments of any obstacles so that when a relieving army came its archers would have nowhere to hide. Now, with his own encampments fortified and the trebuchets biting ever bigger holes in La Roche-Derrien's walls, he sent his crossbowmen forward to harass the ramparts. They came in pairs, one man with the crossbow and his partner holding a pavise, a shield so tall, wide and stoutly made that it could protect both men. The pavises were painted, some with holy imprecations, but most with insults in French, English and, in some cases, because the crossbowmen were Genoese, Italian. Their quarrels battered the wall, whistled about the defenders' heads and smacked into the thatch of the houses beyond the walls. Sometimes the Genoese would shoot fire arrows and Totesham had six squads of men who did nothing except chase down fires in thatch and, when they were not extinguishing flames, they hauled water out of the River Jaudy and soaked the thatch roofs that were nearest the ramparts and thus most in danger from the crossbowmen.

The English archers shot back, but the crossbowmen

were mostly hidden behind their pavises and, when they did shoot, they exposed themselves for only a heartbeat. Some died all the same, but they were also bringing down archers on the town's walls. Jeanette often joined Thomas on the southern rampart and loosed her bolts from a crenellation by the gate. A crossbow could be fired from a kneeling position so she did not expose much of her body to danger, while Thomas had to stand to loose an arrow. 'You shouldn't be here,' he told her every time and she would mimic his words, then stoop to rewind her bow.

'Do you remember,' she asked him, 'the first siege?'

'When you were shooting at me?'

'Let's hope I'm more accurate now,' she said, then propped the bow on the wall, aimed and pulled the trigger. The bolt smacked into a pavise that was already stuck with feathered English arrows. Beyond the crossbowmen was the earth wall of the closest encampment above which showed the ungainly beams of two trebuchets and, beyond them, the gaudy flags of some of Charles's lords. Jeanette recognized the banners of Rohan, Laval, Malestroit, and Roncelets, and the first sight of that wasplike banner had filled her with anger and then she had cried for the thought of her son in Roncelets's distant tower. 'I wish they'd assault now,' she said, 'and I could put a bolt in Roncelets as well as Blois.'

'They won't attack until they've defeated Dagworth,' Thomas said.

'You think he's coming?'

'I think that's why they're here,' Thomas said, nodding towards the enemy, then he stood, drew the bow and launched an arrow at a crossbowman who had just stepped out from behind his shield. The man ducked back a heartbeat before Thomas's arrow hissed past him. Thomas crouched again. 'Charles knows he can pluck us whenever he wants,' he said, 'but what he really wants is to crush Dagworth.'

For when Sir Thomas Dagworth was crushed there would be no English field army left in Brittany and the fortresses would inevitably fall, one by one, and Charles would have his duchy.

Then, a month after Charles had arrived, when the hedges about his four fortresses were white with hawthorn blossom and the petals were blowing from the apple trees and the banks of the river were thick with iris and the poppies were a brilliant red in the growing rye, there was a drift of smoke in the south-western sky. The watchers on La Roche-Derrien's walls saw scouts riding from the enemy encampment and they knew that the smoke must come from campfires which meant that an army was coming. Some feared it might be reinforcements for the enemy, but they were reassured by others who claimed, truly, that only friends would be approaching from the south-west. What Richard Totesham and the others who knew the truth did not reveal was that any relieving force would be small, much smaller than Charles's army, and that it was coming towards a trap that Charles had made.

For Charles's ploy had worked and Sir Thomas Dagworth had taken the bait.

Charles of Blois summoned his lords and commanders to the big tent beside the mill. It was Saturday and the enemy force was now a short march away and, inevitably, there were hotheads in his ranks who wanted to strap on their plate armour, hoist up their lances and clatter off on horseback to be killed by the English archers. Fools abounded, Charles thought, then dashed their hopes by making it clear that no one except the scouts was to leave any of the four encampments. 'No one!' He pounded the table, almost upsetting the ink pot belonging to the clerk who copied down his words. 'No one will leave! Do you all understand that?' He looked from face to face and thought again what fools his lords were. 'We stay behind our entrenchments,' he told them, 'and they will come to us. They will come to us and they will be killed.'

Some of the lords looked disgruntled, for there was little glory in fighting behind earth walls and damp ditches when a man could be galloping on a destrier, but Charles of Blois was firm and even the richest of his lords feared his threat that any man who disobeyed him would not share in the distribution of land and wealth that would follow the conquest of Brittany.

Charles picked up a piece of parchment. 'Our scouts have ridden close to Sir Thomas Dagworth's column,' he said in his precise voice, 'and we now have an accurate estimate of their numbers.' Knowing that every man in the tent wanted to hear the enemy's strength, he paused, because he wanted to invest this announcement with drama, but he could not help smiling as he revealed the figures. 'Our enemies,' he said, 'threaten us with three hundred men-at-arms and four hundred archers.'

There was a pause as the numbers were understood, then came an explosion of laughter. Even Charles, usually so pallid, unbending and stern, joined in. It was risible! It was actually impertinent! Brave, perhaps, but utterly foolhardy. Charles of Blois had four thousand men and hundreds of peasant volunteers who, though not actually encamped inside his earthworks, could be relied on to help massacre an enemy. He had two thousand of the finest crossbowmen in Europe, he had a thousand armoured knights, many of them champions of great tournaments, and Sir Thomas Dagworth was coming with seven hundred men? The town might contribute another hundred or two hundred, but even at their most hopeful the English could not muster more than a thousand men and Charles had four times that number. 'They will come, gentlemen,' he told his excited lords, 'and they will die here.'

There were two roads on which they might approach. One came from the west and it was the most direct route, but it led to the far side of the River Jaudy and Charles did not think Dagworth would use that road. The other curled about the besieged town to approach from the south-east and that road led straight towards the largest of Charles's four encampments, the eastern encampment where he was in personal command and where the largest trebuchets pounded La Roche-Derrien's walls.

'Let me tell you, gentlemen' – Charles stilled the amusement of his commanders – 'what I believe Sir Thomas will do. What I would do if I were so unfortunate as to be in his shoes. I believe he will send a small but noisy force of men to approach us on the Lannion road' – that was the road that came from the west, the direct route – 'and he will send them during the night to tempt us into believing that he will attack our encampment across the river. He will expect us to reinforce that encampment and then, in the dawn, his real attack will come from the east. He hopes that most of our army will be stranded across the river and that he can come in the dawn and destroy the three encampments on this bank. That, gentlemen, is what he will probably attempt and it will fail. It will fail because we have one clear, hard rule and it will not be broken! No one leaves an encampment! No one! Stay behind your walls! We fight on foot, we make our battle lines and we let them come to us. Our crossbowmen will cut down their archers, then we, gentlemen, shall destroy their men-at-arms. But no one leaves the encampments! No one! We do not make ourselves targets for their bows. Do you understand?'

The Lord of Châteaubriant wanted to know what he was supposed to do if he was in his southern encampment and there was a fight going on in another of the forts. 'Do I just stand and watch?' he asked, incredulous.

'You stand and watch,' Duke Charles said in a steely voice. 'You do not leave your encampment. You understand? Archers cannot kill what they cannot see! Stay hidden!'

The Lord of Roncelets pointed out that the skies were clear and the moon nearly full. 'Dagworth is no fool,' he went on, 'and he'll know we've made these fortresses and cleared the land to deny them cover. So why won't he attack at night?'

'At night?' Charles asked.

'That way our crossbowmen can't see their targets, but the English will have enough moonlight to see their way across our entrenchments.'

It was a good point that Charles acknowledged by nodding brusquely. 'Fires,' he said.

'Fires?' a man asked.

'Build fires now! Big fires! When they come, light the fires. Turn night into day!'

His men laughed, liking the idea. Fighting on foot was not how lords and knights made their reputations, but they all understood that Charles had been thinking how to defeat the dreaded English archers and his ideas made sense even if they offered little chance for glory, but then Charles offered them a consolation. 'They will break, gentlemen,' he said, 'and when they do I shall have my trumpeter give seven blasts. Seven! And when you hear the trumpet, you may leave your encampments and pursue them.' There were growls of approval, for the seven trumpet blasts would release the armoured men on their huge horses to slaughter the remnants of Dagworth's force.

'Remember!' Charles pounded the table once more to get his men's attention. 'Remember! You do not leave your encampment until the trumpet sounds! Stay behind the trenches, stay behind the walls, let the enemy come to you and we shall win.' He nodded to show he was finished. 'And now, gentlemen, our priests will hear confessions. Let us cleanse our souls so that God can reward us with victory.'

Fifteen miles away, in the roofless refectory of a plundered and abandoned monastery, a much smaller group of men gathered. Their commander was a grey-haired man from Suffolk, stocky and gruff, who knew he faced a formidable challenge if he was to relieve La Roche-Derrien. Sir Thomas Dagworth listened to a Breton knight tell what his scouts had discovered: that Charles of Blois's men were still in the four encampments placed opposite the town's four gates. The largest encampment, where Charles's great banner of a white ermine flew, was to the east. 'It is built around the windmill,' the knight reported.

'I remember that mill,' Sir Thomas said. He ran his fingers through his short grey beard, a habit when he was thinking. 'That's where we must attack,' he said, so softly that he could have been talking to himself.

'It's where they're strongest,' a man warned him.

'So we shall distract them.' Sir Thomas stirred himself from his reverie. 'John' – he turned to a man in a tattered mail coat – 'take all the camp servants. Take the cooks, clerks, grooms, anyone who isn't a fighter. Then take all the carts and all the draught horses and make an approach on the Lannion road. You know it?'

'I can find it.'

'Leave before midnight. Lots of noise, John! You can take my trumpeter and a couple of drummers. Make 'em think the whole army's coming from the west. I want them sending men to the western encampment well before dawn.'

'And the rest of us?' the Breton knight asked.

'We'll march at midnight,' Sir Thomas said, 'and go east till we reach the Guingamp road.' That road approached La Roche-Derrien from the south-east. Since Sir Thomas's small force had marched from the west he hoped that the Guingamp road was the very last one Charles would expect him to use. 'It'll be a silent march,' he ordered, 'and we go on foot, all of us! Archers in front, men-at-arms behind, and we'll attack their eastern fort in the darkness.' By attacking in the dark Sir Thomas hoped he could cheat the crossbowmen of their targets and, better still, catch the enemy asleep.

So his plans were made: he would make a feint in

the west and attack from the east. And that was exactly what Charles of Blois expected him to do.

Night fell. The English marched, Charles's men armed themselves and the town waited.

Thomas could hear the armourers in Charles's camp. He could hear their hammers closing the rivets of the plate armour and hear the scrape of stones on blades. The campfires in the four fortresses did not die down as they usually did, but were fed to keep them bright and high so that their light glinted off the iron straps that fastened the frames of the big trebuchets outlined against the fires' glow. From the ramparts Thomas could see men moving about in the nearest enemy encampment. Every few minutes a fire would glow even brighter as the armourers used bellows to fan the flames.

A child cried in a nearby house. A dog whined. Most of Totesham's small garrison was on the ramparts and a good many of the townspeople were there too. No one was quite sure why they had gone to the walls for the relief army had to be a long way off still, yet few people wanted to go to bed. They expected something to happen and so they waited for it. The day of judgement, Thomas thought, would feel like this, as men and women waited for the heavens to break and the angels to descend and for the graves to open so that the virtuous dead could rise into the sky. His father, he remembered, had always wanted to be buried facing the west, but on the eastern edge of the graveyard, so that when he rose from the dead he would be looking at his parishioners as they came from the earth. 'They will need my guidance,' Father Ralph had said, and Thomas had made sure it had been done as he wished. Hookton's parishioners, buried so that if they sat up they would look eastwards towards the glory of Christ's second coming, would find their priest in front of them, offering them reassurance.

Thomas could have done with some reassurance this night. He was with Sir Guillaume and his two men-at-arms and they watched the enemy's preparations from a bastion on the town's south-east corner, close to where the tower of St Barnabé's church offered a vantage point. The remnants of Totesham's giant springald had been used to make a rickety bridge from the bastion to a window in the church tower and once through the window there was a ladder that climbed past a gaping hole torn by one of the Widowmaker's stones to the tower parapet. Thomas must have made the journey a half-dozen times before midnight because, from the parapet, it was just possible to see over the palisade into the largest of Charles's camps. It was while he was on the tower that Robbie came to the rampart beneath. 'I want you to look at this,' Robbie called up to him, and flourished a newly painted shield. 'You like it?'

Thomas peered down and, in the moonlight, saw something red. 'What is it?' he asked. 'A blood smear?'

'You blind English bastard,' Robbie said, 'it's the red heart of Douglas!'

'Ah. From up here it looks like something died on the shield.'

But Robbie was proud of his shield. He admired it in the moonlight. 'There was a fellow painting a new devil on the wall in St Goran's church,' he said, 'and I paid him to do this.'

'I hope you didn't pay him too much,' Thomas said.

444

'You're just envious.' Robbie propped the shield against the parapet before edging over the makeshift bridge to the tower. He vanished through the window then reappeared at Thomas's side. 'What are they doing?' he asked, gazing eastwards.

'Jesus,' Thomas blasphemed, because something was at last happening. He was staring past the great black shapes of Hellgiver and Widowmaker into the eastern encampment where men, hundreds of men, were forming a battle line. Thomas had assumed that any fight would not start until dawn, yet now it looked as though Charles of Blois was readying to fight in the night's black heart.

'Sweet Jesus,' Sir Guillaume, summoned to the tower's top, echoed Thomas's surprise.

'The bastards are expecting a fight,' Robbie said, for Charles's men were lining shoulder to shoulder. They had their backs to the town and the moon glinted off the espaliers that covered the knights' shoulders and touched the blades of spears and axes white.

'Dagworth must be coming.' Sir Guillaume said.

'At night?' Robbie asked.

'Why not?' Sir Guillaume retorted, then shouted down to one of his men-at-arms to go and tell Totesham what was happening. 'Wake him up,' he snarled when the man wanted to know what he should do if the garrison commander was asleep. 'Of course he's not asleep,' he added to Thomas. 'Totesham might be a bloody Englishman, but he's a good soldier.'

Totesham was not asleep, but nor had he been aware that the enemy was formed for battle and, after he had negotiated the precarious bridge to St Barnabé's tower, he gazed at Charles's troops with his customary sour

445

expression. 'Reckon we'll have to lend a hand,' he said.

'I thought you didn't approve of sorties beyond the wall?' Sir Guillaume, who had chafed under that restriction, observed.

'This is the battle that saves us,' Totesham said. 'If we lose this fight then the town falls, so we must do what we can to win it.' He sounded bleak, then he shrugged and turned back to the tower's ladder. 'God help us,' he said softly as he climbed down into the shadows. He knew Sir Thomas Dagworth's relieving army would be small and he feared it would be much smaller than he dared imagine, but when it attacked the enemy encampment the garrison had to be ready to help. He did not want to alert the enemy to the likelihood of a sortie from the battered gates and so he did not sound the church bells to gather his troops, but rather sent men through all the streets to summon the archers and men-at-arms to the market square outside St Brieuc's church. Thomas went back to Jeanette's house and pulled on his mail haubergeon, which Robbie had brought back from the Roncelets raid, then he strapped his sword belt in place, fumbling with the buckle because his fingers were still clumsy at such finicky things. He hung the arrow bag on his left shoulder, slid the black bow out of its linen cover, put a spare bowcord in his sallet, then pulled the sallet onto his head. He was ready.

And so, he saw, was Jeanette. She had her own haubergeon and helmet and Thomas gaped at her. 'You can't join the sortie!' he said.

'Join the sortie?' She sounded surprised. 'When you all leave the town, Thomas, who will guard the walls?'

'Oh.' He felt foolish.

She smiled, stepped to him and gave him a kiss. 'Now go,' she said, 'and God go with you.'

Thomas went to the marketplace. The garrison was gathering there, but they were desperately few in number. A tavern-keeper rolled a barrel of ale into the square, tapped it and let men help themselves. A smith was sharpening swords and axes in the light of a cresseted torch that burned outside the porch of St Brieuc's and his stone rang on long steel blades, the sound strangely mournful in the night. It was warm. Bats flickered about the church and dipped into the tangled moon-cast shadows of a house ruined by a trebuchet's direct hit. Women were bringing food to the soldiers and Thomas remembered how, just the year before, these same women had screamed as the English scrambled into the town. It had been a night of rape, robbery and murder, yet now the townsfolk did not want their occupiers to leave and the market square was becoming ever more crowded as men from the town brought makeshift weapons to help the foray. Most were armed with the axes they used to chop their firewood, though a few had swords or spears, and some townsmen even possessed leather or mail armour. They far outnumbered the garrison and would at least make the sally seem formidable.

'Christ Jesus.' A sour voice spoke behind Thomas. 'What in Christ's name is that?'

Thomas turned and saw the lanky figure of Sir Geoffrey Carr staring at Robbie's shield, which was propped against the steps of a stone cross in the market's centre. Robbie also turned to look at the Scarecrow who was leading his six men.

'Looks like a squashed turd,' the Scarecrow said. His

voice was slurred and it was evident he had spent the evening in one of the town's many taverns.

'It's mine,' Robbie said.

Sir Geoffrey kicked the shield. 'Is that the bloody heart of Douglas, boy?'

'It's my badge,' Robbie said, exaggerating his Scottish accent, 'if that's what you mean.' Men all about had stopped to listen.

'I knew you were a Scot,' the Scarecrow said, sounding even more drunk, 'but I didn't know you were a damned Douglas. And what the hell is a Douglas doing here?' The Scarecrow raised his voice to appeal to the assembled men. 'Whose side is bloody Scotland on, eh? Whose side? And the goddamn Douglases have been fighting us since they were spawned from the devil's own arsehole!' The Scarecrow staggered, then pulled the whip from his belt and let its coils ripple down. 'Sweet Jesus,' he shouted, 'but his goddamn family has impoverished good Englishmen. They're goddamn thieves! Spies!'

Robbie dragged his sword free and the whip lashed up, but Sir Guillaume shoved Robbie out of the way before the clawed tip could slash his face, then Sir Guillaume's sword was drawn and he and Thomas were standing beside Robbie on the steps of the cross. 'Robbie Douglas,' Sir Guillaume shouted, 'is my friend.'

'And mine,' Thomas said.

'Enough!' A furious Richard Totesham pushed through the crowd. 'Enough!'

The Scarecrow appealed to Totesham. 'He's a damned Scot!'

'Good God, man,' Totesham snarled, 'we've got Frenchmen, Welshmen, Flemings, Irishmen and Bretons in this garrison. What the hell difference does it make?'

'He's a Douglas!' the Scarecrow insisted drunkenly. 'He's an enemy!'

'He's my friend!' Thomas bellowed, inviting to fight anyone who wished to side with Sir Geoffrey.

'Enough!' Totesham's anger was big enough to fill the whole marketplace. 'We have fight enough on our hands without behaving like children! Do you vouch for him?' he demanded of Thomas.

'I vouch for him.' It was Will Skeat who answered. He pushed through the crowd and put an arm about Robbie's shoulders. 'I vouch for him, Dick.'

'Then Douglas or not,' Totesham said, 'he's no enemy of mine.' He turned and walked away.

'Sweet Jesus!' The Scarecrow was still angry. He had been impoverished by the house of Douglas and he was still poor – the risk he had taken in pursuing Thomas had not paid off because he had found no treasure – and now all his enemies seemed united in Thomas and Robbie. He staggered again, then spat at Robbie. 'I burn men who wear the heart of Douglas,' he said, 'I burn them!'

'He does too,' Thomas said softly.

'Burns them?' Robbie asked.

'At Durham,' Thomas said, his gaze on Sir Geoffrey's eyes, 'he burned three prisoners.'

'You did what?' Robbie demanded.

The Scarecrow, drunk as he was, was suddenly aware of the intensity of Robbie's anger, and aware too that he had not gained the sympathy of the men in the marketplace, who preferred Will Skeat's opinion to his. He coiled the whip, spat at Robbie, and stalked uncertainly away.

Now it was Robbie who wanted a fight. 'Hey, you!' he shouted.

'Leave it be,' Thomas said. 'Not tonight, Robbie.'

'He burned three men?' Robbie demanded.

'Not tonight,' Thomas repeated, and he pushed Robbie hard back so that the Scotsman sat on the steps of the cross.

Robbie was staring at the retreating Scarecrow. 'He's a dead man,' he said grimly. 'I tell you, Thomas, that bastard is a dead man.'

'We're all dead men,' Sir Guillaume said quietly, for the enemy was ready for them and in overwhelming numbers.

And Sir Thomas Dagworth was nearing their trap.

John Hammond, a deputy to Sir Thomas Dagworth, led the feint that came from the west along the Lannion road. He had sixty men, as many women, a dozen carts and thirty horses and he used them to make as much noise as possible once they were within sight of the westernmost of Duke Charles's encampments.

Fires outlined the earthworks and firelight showed in the tiny slits between the timbers of the palisade. There seemed to be a lot of fires in the encampment, and even more blazed up once Hammond's small force began to bang pots and pans, clatter staves against trees and blow their trumpets. The drummers beat frantically, but no panic showed on the earthen ramparts. A few enemy soldiers appeared there, stared for a while down the moonlit road where Hammond's men and women were shadows under the trees, then turned and went away. Hammond ordered his people to make even more noise

450

and his six archers, the only real soldiers in his decoy force, went closer to the camp and shot their arrows over the palisades, but still there was no urgent response. Hammond expected to see men streaming over the river that Sir Thomas's spies had said was bridged with boats, but no one appeared to be moving between the enemy encampments. The feint, it seemed, had failed.

'If we stay here,' a man said, 'they'll goddamn crucify us.'

'They goddamn will,' Hammond agreed fervently. 'We'll go back down the road a bit,' he said, 'just a bit. Back into deeper shadow.'

The night had begun badly with the failure of the feint assault, but Sir Thomas's men, the real attackers, had made better progress than they expected and arrived off the eastern flank of Duke Charles's encampment not long after the decoy group began its noisy diversion three miles to the west. Sir Thomas's men crouched at the edge of a wood and stared across the felled land to the shape of the nearest earthworks. The road, pale in the moonlight, ran empty to a big wooden gate where it was swallowed up by the makeshift fort.

Sir Thomas had divided his men into two parties that would attack either side of the wooden gate. There was to be nothing subtle in the assault, just a rush through the dark then a swarming attack over the earth wall and kill whoever was discovered on its farther side. 'God give you joy,' Sir Thomas said to his men as he walked down their line, then he drew his sword and waved his party on. They would approach as silently as they could and Sir Thomas still hoped he would achieve surprise, but the firelight on the other side of the defences looked unnaturally bright and he had a sinking feeling that the enemy was ready for him. Yet none showed on the embanked wall and no crossbow quarrels hissed in the dark, and so he dared to let his hopes rise and then he was at the ditch and splashing through its muddy bottom. There were archers to left and right of him, all scrambling up the bank to the palisade. Still no crossbows shot, no trumpet sounded and no enemy showed. The archers were at the fence now and it proved more flimsy than it looked for the logs were not buried deeply enough and they could be kicked over without much effort. The defences were not formidable, and were not even defended for no enemy challenged as Sir Thomas's men-at-arms splashed through the ditch, their swords bright in the moonlight. The archers finished demolishing the palisade and Sir Thomas stepped over the fallen timbers and ran down the bank into Charles's camp.

Except he was not inside the camp, but rather on a wide open space that led to another bank and another ditch and another palisade. The place was a labyrinth! But still no bolts flew in the dark and his archers were running ahead again, though some cursed as they tripped in holes dug to trap horses' hooves. The fires were bright beyond the next palisade. Where were the sentries? Sir Thomas hefted his shield with its device of a wheatsheaf and looked to his left to see that his second party was across the first bank and streaming over the grass towards the second. His own archers pulled at the new palisade and, like the first, it tumbled easily. No one was speaking, no one was shouting orders, no one was calling on St George for help, they were just doing their job, but surely the enemy must hear the falling timbers? But the second palisade was down and Sir Thomas jostled with the archers through the new gap and there was a meadow in front and a hedge beyond it, and beyond that hedge were the enemy tents and the high windmill with its furled sails and the monstrous shapes of the two biggest trebuchets, all of them lit by the bright fires. So close now! And Sir Thomas felt a fierce surge of joy for he had achieved surprise and the enemy was surely his, and just at that moment the crossbows sounded.

The bolts flickered in from his right flank, from an earth bank that ran between the second earthwork and the hedge. Archers were falling, cursing. Sir Thomas turned towards the crossbowmen who were hidden, and then more bolts came from the thick hedge in front and he knew he had surprised no one, that the enemy had been waiting for him, and his men were screaming now, but at least the first archers were shooting back. The long English arrows flashed in the moonlight, but Sir Thomas could see no targets and he realized the archers were shooting blindly. 'To me!' he shouted. 'Dagworth! Dagworth! Shields!' Maybe a dozen men-at-arms heard and obeyed him, making a cluster who overlapped their shields and then ran clumsily towards the hedge. Break through that, Sir Thomas thought, and at least some of the crossbowmen would be visible. Archers were shooting to their front and their side, confused by the enemy's bolts. Sir Thomas snatched a glance across the road and saw his other men were being similarly assailed. 'We have to get through the hedge,' he shouted, 'through the hedge! Archers! Through the hedge!' A crossbow bolt slammed into his shield, half spinning him round. Another hissed overhead. An archer was twisting on the grass, his belly pierced by a quarrel.

Other men were shouting now. Some called on St George, others cursed the devil, some screamed for their wives or mothers. The enemy had massed his crossbows and was pouring the bolts out of the darkness. An archer reeled back, a quarrel in his shoulder. Another screamed pitiably, hit in the groin. A man-at-arms fell to his knees, crying Jesus, and now Sir Thomas could hear the enemy shouting orders and insults. 'The hedge!' he roared. Get through the hedge, he thought, and maybe his archers would have clear targets at last. 'Get through the hedge!' he bellowed, and some of his archers found a gap closed up with nothing but hurdles and they kicked the wicker barriers down and streamed through. The night seemed alive with bolts, fierce with them, and a man shouted at Sir Thomas to look behind. He turned and saw the enemy had sent scores of crossbowmen to cut off his retreat and that new force was pushing Sir Thomas's men on into the heart of the encampment. It had been a trap, he thought, a goddamned trap. Charles had wanted him to come into the encampment, he had obliged and now Charles's men were curling about him. So fight, he told himself, fight!

'Through the hedge!' Sir Thomas thundered. 'Get through the damned hedge!' He dodged between the bodies of his men, pounded through the gap and looked for an enemy to kill, but instead he saw that Charles's men-at-arms were formed in a battle line, all armoured, visors down and shields up. A few archers were shooting at them now, the long arrows smacking into shields, bellies, chests and legs, but there were too few archers and the crossbowmen, still hidden by hedges or walls or pavises, were killing the English bowmen. 'Rally on the mill!' Sir Thomas shouted for that was the most prominent landmark. He wanted to collect his men, form them into ranks and start to fight properly, but the crossbows were closing on him, hundreds of them, and his frightened men were scattering into the tents and shelters.

Sir Thomas swore out of sheer frustration. The survivors of the other assault party were with him now, but all of his men were entangled in the tents, tripping on ropes, and still the crossbow bolts slammed through the dark, ripping the canvas as they hurtled into Sir Thomas's dying force. 'Form here! Form here!' he yelled, choosing an open space between three tents, and maybe twenty or thirty men ran to him, but the crossbowmen saw them and poured their bolts down the dark alleys between the tents, and then the enemy men-at-arms came, shields up, and the English archers were scattering again, trying to find a vantage point to catch their breath, find some protection and look for targets. The great banners of the French and Breton lords were being brought forward and Sir Thomas, knowing he had blundered into this trap and been comprehensively beaten, just felt a surge of anger. 'Kill the bastards,' he bawled and he led his men at the nearest enemy, the swords rang in the dark, and at least, now that it was hand to hand, the crossbowmen could not shoot at the English men-at-arms. The Genoese were hunting the hated English archers instead, but some of the bowmen had found a wagon park and, sheltered by the vehicles, were at last fighting back.

But Sir Thomas had no shelter and no advantage. He had a small force and the enemy a great one, and his men were being forced backwards by sheer pressure of numbers. Shields crashed on shields, swords hammered on helmets, spears came under the shields to tear through men's boots, a Breton flailed an axe, beating down two Englishmen and letting in a rush of men wearing the white ermine badge who shrieked their triumph and cut down still more men. A man-at-arms screamed as axes hacked through the mail covering his thighs, then another axe battered in his helmet and he was silent. Sir Thomas staggered backwards, parrying a sword blow, and saw some of his men running into the dark spaces between the tents to find refuge. Their visors were down and they could hardly see where they were going or the enemy who came to kill them. He slashed his sword at a man in a pig-snout helmet, back-swung the blade into a shield striped yellow and black, took a step back to make space for another blow and then his feet were tangled by a tent's guy ropes and he fell backwards onto the canvas.

The knight in the pig-snout helmet stood over him, his plate mail shining in the moon and his sword at Sir Thomas's throat.

'I yield,' Sir Thomas said hurriedly, then repeated his surrender in French.

'And you are?' the knight asked.

'Sir Thomas Dagworth,' Sir Thomas said bitterly and he held up his sword to his enemy who took the weapon and then pushed up his snouted visor.

'I am the Viscount Morgat,' the knight said, 'and I accept your surrender.' He bowed to Sir Thomas, handed back his sword and held out a hand to help the Englishman to his feet. The fight was still going on, but it was sporadic now as the French and Bretons hunted down the survivors, killed the wounded who were not worth ransoming and hammered their own wagons with crossbow bolts to kill the English bowmen who still sheltered there.

The Viscount Morgat escorted Sir Thomas to the windmill where he presented him to Charles of Blois. A great fire burned a few yards away and in its light Charles stood beneath the furled sails with his jupon smeared with blood for he had helped to break Sir Thomas's band of men-at-arms. He sheathed his sword, still bloody, and took off his plumed helmet and stared at the prisoner who had twice defeated him in battle. 'I commiserate with you,' Charles said coldly.

'And I congratulate your grace,' Sir Thomas said.

'The victory belongs to God,' Charles said, 'not to me,' yet all the same he felt a sudden exhilaration because he had done it! He had defeated the English field army in Brittany and now, as certain as blessed dawn follows darkest night, the duchy would fall to him. 'The victory is God's alone,' he said piously, and he remembered it was now very early on Sunday morning and he turned to a priest to tell the man to have a Te Deum sung in thanks for this great victory.

And the priest nodded, eyes wide, even though the Duke had not yet spoken, and then he gasped and Charles saw there was an unnaturally long arrow in the man's belly, then another white-fledged shaft hammered into the windmill's flank and a raucous, almost bestial, growl sounded from the dark.

For though Sir Thomas was captured and his army was utterly defeated, the battle, it seemed, was not quite finished.

Richard Totesham watched the fight between Sir Thomas's men and Charles's forces from the top of the eastern gate tower. He could not see a great deal from that vantage point for the palisades atop the earthworks, the two great trebuchets and the windmill obscured much of the battle, but it was abundantly clear that no one was coming from the other three French encampments to help Charles in his largest fortress. 'You'd think they'd be helping each other,' he said to Will Skeat who was standing next to him.

'It's you, Dick!' Will Skeat exclaimed.

'Aye, it's me, Will,' Totesham said patiently. He saw that Skeat was dressed in mail and had a sword at his side, and he put a hand on his old friend's shoulder. 'Now, you're not going to be fighting tonight, Will, are you?'

'If there's going to be a scrap,' Skeat said, 'then I'd like to help.'

'Leave it to the young ones, Will,' Totesham urged, 'leave it to the young ones. You stay and guard the town for me. Will you do that?'

Skeat nodded and Totesham turned back to stare into the enemy's camp. It was impossible to tell which side was winning for the only troops he could see belonged to the enemy and they had their backs to him, though once in a while a flying arrow would flash a reflection of the firelight as proof that Sir Thomas's men still fought, but Totesham reckoned it was a bad sign that no troops were coming from the other fortresses to help Charles of Blois. It suggested the Duke did not need help, which in turn suggested that Sir Thomas Dagworth did and so Totesham leaned over the inner parapet. 'Open the gate!' he shouted.

It was still dark. Dawn was two hours or more away, yet the moon was bright and the fires in the enemy camp threw a garish light. Totesham hurried down the stairs from the ramparts while men pulled away the stone-filled barrels that had formed a barricade inside the gateway, then lifted the great locking bar that had not been disturbed in a month. The gates creaked open and the waiting men cheered. Totesham wished they had kept silent for he did not want to alert the enemy that the garrison was making a sortie, but it was too late now and so he found his own troop of men-at-arms and led them to join the stream of soldiers and townsmen who poured through the gate.

Thomas went to the attack alongside Robbie and Sir Guillaume and his two men. Will Skeat, despite his promise to Totesham, had wanted to come with them, but Thomas had pushed him onto the ramparts and told him to watch the fight from there. 'You ain't fit enough, Will,' Thomas had insisted.

'If you say so, Tom,' Skeat had agreed meekly, then climbed the steps. Thomas, once he was through the gate, looked back and saw Skeat on the gate tower. He raised a hand, but Skeat did not see him or, if he did, could not recognize him.

It felt strange to be outside the long-locked gates. The air was fresher, lacking the stench of the town's sewage. The attackers followed the road which ran straight for three hundred paces before vanishing beneath the palisade which protected the timber platforms on which Hellgiver and Widowmaker were mounted. That palisade was higher than a tall man and some of the archers were carrying ladders to get across the obstacle, but Thomas reckoned the palisades had been made in a hurry and would probably topple to a good heave. He ran, still clumsy on his twisted toes. He expected the crossbows to start at any moment, but no bolts came from Charles's earthworks; the enemy, Thomas supposed, were occupied with Dagworth's men.

Then the first of Totesham's archers reached the palisade and the ladders went up, but, just as Thomas had reckoned, a whole length of the heavy fence collapsed with a crash when men put their weight on the ladders. The banks and palisades had not been built to keep men out, but to shelter the crossbowmen, but those crossbowmen still did not know that a sortie had come from the town and so the bank was undefended.

Four or five hundred men crossed the fallen palisade. Most were not trained soldiers, but townsmen who had been enraged by the enemy's missiles crashing into their houses. Their women and children had been maimed and killed by the trebuchets and the men of La Roche-Derrien wanted revenge, just as they wanted to keep the prosperity brought by the English occupation, and so they cheered as they swarmed into the enemy camp. 'Archers!' Totesham roared in a huge voice. 'Archers, to me! Archers!'

Sixty or seventy archers ran to obey him, making a

460

line just to the south of the platforms where the two biggest trebuchets were set. The rest of the sortie were charging at the enemy who were no longer formed in their battle line, but had scattered into small groups who were so intent on completing their victory over Sir Thomas Dagworth that they had not been watching behind them. Now they turned, alarmed, as a feral roar announced the garrison's arrival. 'Kill the bastards!' a townsman shouted in Breton.

'Kill!' An English voice roared.

'No prisoners!' another man bellowed, and though Totesham, fearful for lost ransoms, called out that prisoners must be taken, no one heard him in the savage roar that the attackers made.

Charles's men-at-arms instinctively formed a line, but Totesham, ready for it, had gathered his archers and now he ordered them to shoot: the bows began their devil's music and the arrows hissed through the dark to bury themselves in mail and flesh and bone. The bowmen were few, but they shot at close range, they could not miss, and Charles's men cowered behind their shields as the missiles whipped home, but the arrows easily pierced shields and the men-at-arms broke and scattered to find shelter among the tents. 'Hunt them down! Hunt them down!' Totesham released his archers to the kill.

Less than a hundred of Sir Thomas Dagworth's men were still fighting and most of those were the archers who had gone to ground in the wagon park. Some of the others were prisoners, many were dead, while most were trying to escape across the earthworks and palisades, but those men, hearing the great roar behind them, turned back. Charles's men were scattered: many were still hunting down the remnants of the first attack and those who had tried to resist Totesham's sortie were either dead or fleeing into shadows. Totesham's men now struck the heart of the encampment with the savagery of a tempest. The townsmen were filled with rage. There was no subtlety in their assault, just a lust for vengeance as they swarmed past the two great trebuchets. The first huts they encountered were the shelters of the Bavarian engineers who, wanting no part of the hand-to-hand slaughter that was finishing off the survivors of Sir Thomas Dagworth's assault, had stayed by their billets and now died there. The townsmen had no idea who their victims were, only that they were the enemy, and so they were chopped down with axes, mattocks and hammers. The chief engineer tried to protect his eleven-year-old son, but they died together under a frenzy of blows, and meanwhile the English and Fleming men-at-arms were streaming past.

Thomas had shot his bow with the other archers, but now he sought Robbie whom he had last seen by the two big trebuchets. Widowmaker had been winched down ready to launch its first missile in the dawn and Thomas stumbled over a stout metal spike that protruded a yard from the beam and acted as an anchor for the sling. He cursed, because the metal had hurt his shins, then he climbed onto the trebuchet's frame and shot an arrow above the heads of the men slaughtering the Bavarians. He had been aiming at the enemy still clustered at the foot of the windmill and he saw a man fall there before the gaudy shields came up. He shot again, and realized that his wounded hands were doing what they had always done and were doing it well, and so he plucked a third arrow from the bag and drove it into a firelit shield painted with a white ermine, then the English men-at-arms and their allies were climbing the hill and obscuring his aim so he jumped down from the trebuchet and resumed his search for Robbie.

The enemy was defending the mill stoutly and most of Totesham's men had veered away into the tents where they had more hope of finding plunder. The townsmen, their Bavarian tormentors killed, were following with bloody axes. A man in plate armour stepped from behind a tent and cut at a man with a sword, folding him at the belly, and Thomas did not think, but put an arrow on the cord, drew and loosed. The arrow went through the slit in the enemy's visor as cleanly as if Thomas had been shooting on the butts at home and moon-glossed blood, glistening like a jewel, oozed from the visor slits as the man fell backwards onto the canvas.

Thomas ran on, stepping over bodies, edging past half-fallen tents. This was no place for a bow, everything was too cramped, and so he slung the yew stave on his shoulder and drew his sword. He ducked into a tent, stepped over a fallen bench, heard a scream and twisted, sword raised, to see a woman on the ground, half hidden by bedding, shaking her head at him. He left her there, went out into the firelit night and saw an enemy aiming a crossbow at the English men-at-arms who attacked the mill. He took two steps and stabbed the man in the small of the back so that his victim arched his wounded spine and twisted and shook. Thomas, dragging the sword free, was so appalled by the noise the dying man made that he hacked the blade down again and again, chopping at the fallen, twitching man to make him silent.

'He's dead! Christ, man, he's dead!' Robbie shouted

at him, then snatched at Thomas's sleeve and pulled him towards the mill and Thomas took the bow from his shoulder and shot two men wearing the white ermine badge on their jupons. They had been trying to escape, running down the back side of the hill. A dog streaked across the shoulder of the slope, something red and dripping in its jaws. There were two great bonfires on the hill, flanking the mill, and a man-at-arms fell backwards into one, driven there by the strike of an English arrow. Sparks exploded upwards as he fell, then he began to scream as his flesh roasted inside his armour. He tried to scramble out of the flames, but a townsman thrust him back with the butt of a spear and laughed at the man's desperate squeals. The clash of swords, shields and axes was huge, filling the night, but in the strange chaos there was a peaceful area at the back of the windmill. Robbie had seen a man duck through a small doorway there and he pulled Thomas that way. 'He's either hiding or running away!' Robbie shouted. 'He must have money!'

Thomas was not sure what Robbie was talking about, but he followed anyway; he just had time to sling his bow again and draw the sword a second time before Robbie smashed the door down with his mail-clad shoulder and plunged into the darkness. 'Come here, you English bastard!' he shouted.

'You want to be killed?' Thomas roared at him. 'You're fighting for the goddamn English!'

Robbie swore at that reminder, then Thomas saw a shadow to his right, only a shadow, and he swung his sword that way. It clanged against another sword and Robbie was screaming in the dusty dark and the man was shouting at them in French and Thomas pulled back, but Robbie just slammed his sword down once, twice, and the blade chopped through bone and flesh and there was a crash as an armoured man fell onto the upper millstone. 'What the hell was he saying to me?' Robbie wanted to know.

'He was trying to surrender.' A voice spoke from across the mill and Thomas and Robbie both spun towards the sound, their swords banging against the wooden tangle of joists, beams, cogwheels and axles, and then the unseen man called out again. 'Whoa, boys, whoa! I'm English.' There was a thump as an arrow struck the outside wall. The furled sails tugged against their tethers and made the wooden machinery squeal and shudder. More arrows thumped into the boards. 'I'm a prisoner,' the man said.

'You're not now,' Thomas said.

'I suppose not.' The man climbed over the millstones and pushed open the door and Thomas saw he was middle-aged with grey hair. 'What's happening?' the man asked.

'We're gralloching the devils,' Robbie said.

'Pray God you are.' The man turned and offered his hand to Robbie. 'I'm Sir Thomas Dagworth, and I thank you both.' He drew his sword and ducked out into the moonlit night, and Robbie stared at Thomas.

'Did you hear that?'

'He said thank you,' Thomas said.

'Aye, but he said he was Sir Thomas Dagworth!'

'Then maybe he was?'

'So what the hell was he doing in here?' Robbie asked, before taking hold of the man he had killed and, with much effort and the clank of armour against stone and timber, dragged him to the door where the fires offered light. The man had discarded his helmet and Robbie's sword had split his skull, but under the gore there was the glint of gold and Robbie dragged a chain from beneath the man's breastplate. 'He must have been an important fellow,' Robbie said, admiring the gold chain, then he grinned at Thomas. 'We'll split it later, eh?'

'Split it?'

'We're friends, aren't we?' Robbie asked, then pushed the gold under his haubergeon before shoving the corpse back into the mill. 'Valuable armour that,' he said. 'We'll come back when it's over and hope no bastard has stolen it.'

There was tangled, bloody horror in the encampment now. Survivors of Sir Thomas Dagworth's attack still fought, notably the archers in the wagon park, but as the town's garrison swept through the tents they released prisoners or brought other survivors out of the dark places where they had been hiding. Charles's crossbowmen, who could have stemmed the garrison's attack, were mostly fighting against the English archers in the wagon park. The Genoese were using their huge pavises as shelters, but the new attackers came from behind and the crossbowmen had nowhere to hide as the long arrows hissed through the night. The war bows sang their devil's melody, ten arrows flying to every quarrel shot, and the crossbowmen could not endure the slaughter. They fled.

The victorious archers, reinforced now by the men who had been among the wagons, turned back to the shelters and tents where a deadly game of hide and seek was being played in the dark avenues between the canvas walls, but then a Welsh archer discovered that the enemy could be flushed out if the tents were set on fire. Soon there were smoke and flames spewing all across the encampment and enemy soldiers were running from the fires onto the arrows and blades of the incendiarists.

Charles of Blois had retreated from the windmill, reckoning his position on the hill made him conspicuous, and he had tried to rally some knights in front of his own sumptuous tent, but an overwhelming rush of townsmen had swept those knights underfoot and Charles watched, appalled, as butchers, coopers, wheelwrights and thatchers massacred their betters with axes, cleavers and reaping hooks. He had hastily retreated into his tent, but now one of his retainers unceremoniously pulled him towards the back entrance. 'This way, your grace.'

Charles shook off the man's hand. 'Where can we go?' he asked plaintively.

'We'll go to the southern camp, sir, and bring men back to help.'

Charles nodded, reflecting that he should have ordered that himself and regretting his insistence that none of his men leave their encampments. Well over half his army was in the other three camps, all of them close by and all of them eager to fight and more than capable of sweeping this disorganized horde aside, yet they were obeying his orders and standing tight while his encampment was put to the sword. 'Where's my trumpeter?' he demanded.

'Sir? I'm here, your grace! I'm here.' The trumpeter had miraculously survived the fight and stayed close to his lord.

'Sound the seven blasts,' Charles ordered.

'Not here!' a priest snapped and, when Charles looked

467

offended, made a hasty explanation. 'It will attract the enemy, your grace. After two blasts they'll be onto us like hounds!'

Charles acknowledged the wisdom of the advice with a curt nod. A dozen knights were with him now and they made a formidable force in this night of fractured battle. One of them peered from the tent and saw flames searing the sky and knew the Duke's tents would be fired soon. 'We must go, your grace,' he insisted, 'we must find our horses.'

They left the tent, hurrying across the patch of beaten grass where the Duke's sentinels usually stood, and then an arrow flickered from the dark to glance off a breastplate. Shouts were suddenly loud and a rush of men came from the right and so Charles retreated to his left, which took him back up the slope towards the firelit windmill, and then a shout announced that he had been seen and the first arrows slashed up the hill. 'Trumpeter!' Charles shouted. 'Seven blasts! Seven blasts!'

Charles and his men, barred from reaching their horses, now had their backs against the mill's apron, which was stuck with scores of white-feathered arrows. Another arrow spitted a man in the midriff, drilling through his mail, piercing his belly and the mail on his back to pin him to the mill's boards, then an English voice roared at the archers to stop shooting. 'It's their Duke!' the man roared, 'it's their Duke! We want him alive! Stop shooting! Bows down!'

The news that Charles of Blois was cornered at the mill prompted a growl from the attackers. The arrows stopped flying and Charles's battered, bleeding men-at-arms who were defending the hill stared down the slope to see, just beyond the light of the mill's two fires, a mass of dark creatures prowling like wolves. 'God help us,' a priest said in a scared voice.

'Trumpeter!' Charles of Blois snapped.

'Sir,' the trumpeter acknowledged. He had found his instrument's mouthpiece mysteriously plugged by earth. He must have fallen, though he did not remember doing so. He shook the last of the soil out of the silver mouthpiece, then put the trumpet to his mouth and the first blast sounded sweet and loud in the night. The Duke drew his sword. He only had to defend the mill long enough for his reinforcements to come from the other camps and sweep this impertinent rabble into hell. The second trumpet note rang out.

Thomas heard the trumpet, turned and saw the flash of silver by the mill, then he saw the reflection of flame-light rippling off the instrument's bell as the trumpeter raised it to the moon for the third time. Thomas had heard no order to stop shooting arrows and so he hauled his bow's cord back, twitched his left hand up a fraction and released. The arrow whipped over the heads of the English men-at-arms and struck the trumpeter just as he took breath for the third blast and the air hissed and bubbled out of his pierced lung as he spilled sideways onto the turf. The dark prowling things at the hill's base saw the man fall and suddenly charged.

No help came to Charles from the three remaining fortresses. They had heard two trumpet blasts, but only two, and they reckoned Charles must be winning; besides, they had his strict and constantly repeated orders to stay where they were on pain of losing out when the conquered lands were distributed among the victors. So they did stay, watching the smoke boil out of the flames and wondering what happened in the large eastern encampment.

Chaos was happening. This fight, Thomas reckoned, was like the attack on Caen: unplanned, disordered and utterly brutal. The English and their allies had been keyed up, nervous, expecting defeat, while Charles's men had been expecting victory – indeed they had gained the early victory – but now the English nervousness was being turned into a maddened, bloody, vicious assault and the French and Bretons were being harried into terror. A ragged clash sounded as the English men-at-arms slammed into Charles's men defending the windmill. Thomas wanted to join that fight, but Robbie suddenly pulled at his mail sleeve. 'Look!' Robbie was pointing back into the burning tents.

Robbie had seen three horsemen in plain black surcoats and with them, on foot, a Dominican. Thomas saw the white and black robes and followed Robbie through the tents, trampling over a collapsed spread of blue and white canvas, past a fallen standard, running between two fires and then across an open space that whirled with smoke and burning scraps of flying cloth. A woman with a dress half torn away screamed and ran across their path and a man scattered fire with his boots as he pursued her into a turf-roofed hut. For a moment they lost sight of the priest, then Robbie saw the black and white robes again: the Dominican was trying to mount an unsaddled horse that the men in black surcoats held for him. Thomas drew his bow, let the arrow fly and saw it bury itself up to its feathers in the horse's breast; the beast reared up, yellow hooves flailing, and the Dominican fell backwards. The men in black surcoats galloped away from the bow's threat and the priest, abandoned, turned and saw his pursuers and Thomas recognized de Taillebourg, God's torturer. Thomas screamed a challenge and drew the bow again, but de Taillebourg ran towards some remaining tents. A Genoese crossbowman suddenly appeared, saw them, raised his weapon and Thomas let the cord go. The arrow slashed the man's throat, spilling blood down his red and green tunic. The woman screamed inside the shelter, then was abruptly silenced as Thomas followed Robbie to where the Inquisitor had disappeared among the tents. The door flap of one was still swinging and Robbie, sword drawn, thrust the canvas aside and ducked into what proved to be a chapel.

De Taillebourg was standing at the altar with its white Easter frontal. A crucifix stood on the altar between two flickering candles. The camp outside was an uproar of screams and pain and arrows, of horses whimpering and men shouting, but it was oddly calm in the make-shift chapel.

'You bastard,' Thomas said, drawing his sword and advancing on the Dominican, 'you goddamn stinking turd-faced piece of priestly shit.'

Bernard de Taillebourg had one hand on the altar. He raised the other to make the sign of the cross. *'Dominus vobiscum,'* he said in his deep voice. An arrow scraped over the tent's roof with a high-pitched scratching sound and another whipped through a side wall and span down behind the altar.

'Is Vexille with you?' Thomas demanded.

'God's blessings on you, Thomas,' de Taillebourg said. He was fierce-faced, stern, eyes hard, and he made the sign of the cross towards Thomas, then stepped back as Thomas raised the sword.

'Is Vexille with you?' Thomas demanded again.

'Can you see him?' the Dominican asked, peering about the chapel, then smiled. 'No, Thomas, he's not here. He's gone into the dark. He rode to fetch help and you cannot kill me.'

'Give me a reason,' Robbie said, 'because you killed my brother, you bastard.'

De Taillebourg looked at the Scotsman. He did not recognize Robbie, but he saw the anger and offered him the same blessing he had given Thomas. 'You cannot kill me,' he said after he had made the sign of the cross, 'because I am a priest, my son, I am God's anointed, and your soul will be damned through all time if you so much as touch me.'

Thomas's response was to lunge his sword at de Taillebourg's belly, forcing the priest hard back against the altar. A man screamed outside, the sound faltering and fading, ending in a sob. A child wept inconsolably, her breath coming in great gasps, and a dog barked frantically. The light of the burning tents was lurid on the chapel's canvas walls. 'You are a bastard,' Thomas said, 'and I don't mind killing you for what you did to me.'

'What I did!' De Taillebourg's anger flared like the fires outside. 'I did nothing!' He spoke in French now. 'Your cousin begged me to spare you the worst and so I did. One day, he said, you would be on his side! One day you would join the side of the Grail! One day you would be on God's side and so I spared you, Thomas. I left you your eyes! I did not burn your eyes!'

'I'll enjoy killing you,' Thomas said, though in truth he was nervous of attacking a priest. Heaven would be watching and the recording angel's pen would be writing letters of fire in a great book.

'And God loves you, my son,' de Taillebourg said gently, 'God loves you. And God chastises whom he loves.'

'What's he saying?' Robbie interrupted.

'He's saying that if we kill him,' Thomas said, 'our souls are damned.'

'Till another priest undamns them,' Robbie said. 'There ain't a sin done on earth that some priest won't absolve if the price is right. So stop talking to the bastard and just kill him.' He advanced on de Taillebourg, sword raised, but Thomas held him back.

'Where's my father's book?' Thomas asked the priest.

'Your cousin has it,' de Taillebourg replied. 'I promise you, your cousin has it.'

'Then where is my cousin?'

'I told you, he rode away to fetch help,' de Taillebourg said, 'and now you must go too, Thomas. You must leave me here to pray.'

Thomas almost obeyed, but then he remembered his pathetic gratitude to this man when he had ceased the torture, and the memory of that gratitude was so shaming, so painful, that he suddenly shuddered and, almost without thinking, swung the sword at the priest.

'No!' de Taillebourg shouted, his left arm cut to the bone where he had tried to defend himself from Thomas's sword.

'Yes,' Thomas said, and the rage was consuming him, filling him, and he cut again and Robbie was beside him, stabbing with his sword, and Thomas swung a third time, but so lavishly that his blade got tangled with the tent roof.

De Taillebourg was swaying now. 'You can't kill me!' he shouted. 'I'm a priest!' He screamed that last word and was still screaming as Robbie chopped Sir William Douglas's sword into his neck. Thomas disentangled his own blade. De Taillebourg, the front of his robes soaked with blood, was staring at him with astonishment, then the priest tried to speak and could not, and the blood was spreading through the weave of his robes with an extraordinary swiftness. He fell to his knees, still trying to speak, and Thomas's sword blow took him on the other side of his neck, and more blood spurted out to slash drops across the white altar frontal. De Taillebourg looked up, this time with puzzlement on his face, then Robbie's last blow killed the Dominican, tearing his windpipe out of his neck. Robbie had to leap back to avoid the spray of blood. The priest twitched and in his death throes his left hand pulled the blood-drenched frontal off the altar, spilling candles and cross. He made a rattling noise, twitched and was still.

'That did feel good,' Robbie said in the sudden dark as the candles went out. 'I hate priests. I've always wanted to kill one.'

'I had a friend who was a priest,' Thomas said, making the sign of the cross, 'but he was murdered, either by my cousin or by this bastard.' He stirred de Taillebourg's body with his foot, then stooped and wiped his sword blade clean on the hem of the priest's robes.

Robbie went to the tent door. 'My father reckons that hell is full of priests,' he said.

'Then there's one more on his way down there now,' Thomas said. He picked up his bow and he and Robbie went back into the dark where the screams and arrows laced the night. So many tents and huts were now aflame that it might as well have been daylight and in the lurid glare Thomas saw a crossbowman kneeling

474

between two picketed and terrified horses. The crossbow was aimed up the hill to where so many English were fighting. Thomas put an arrow on his cord, drew, and at the very last second, just as he was about to put the arrow through the crossbowman's spine, he recognized the blue and white wavy pattern on the jupon and he jerked his aim aside so that his arrow hit the crossbow instead and knocked it out of Jeanette's hands. 'You'll get killed!' he shouted at her angrily.

'That's Charles!' She pointed up the hill, equally angry with him.

'The only crossbows are with the enemy,' he said to her. 'You want to be shot by an archer?' He picked up her bow by its crank and tossed it into the shadows. 'And what are you goddamn doing here?'

'I came to kill him!' she said, pointing again at Charles of Blois who, with his retainers, was warding off a desperate assault. He had eight surviving knights with him and they were all fighting savagely even though they were hugely outnumbered and every one of them was wounded. Thomas led Jeanette up the slope just in time to see a tall English man-at-arms hack at Charles who caught the blow on his shield and slid his own sword under its rim to stab the Englishman in the thigh. Another man attacked and was slashed down by an axe, a third pulled one of Charles's retainers away from the mill and hacked at his helmet. There seemed to be a score of Englishmen trying to reach Charles, smashing their shields into his retainer's weapons, thrusting swords and chopping with big war axes.

'Give him room!' an authoritative voice shouted. 'Give him room! Back away! Back away! Let him yield!'

The attackers reluctantly moved back. Charles had

his visor up and there was blood on his pale face and more blood on his sword. A priest was on his knees beside him.

'Yield!' a man shouted at the Duke, who seemed to understand because he impulsively shook his head in refusal, but then Thomas put an arrow on his cord, drew and pointed it at Charles's face. Charles saw the threat and hesitated.

'Yield!' another man shouted.

'Only to a man of rank!' Charles called in French.

'Who has rank here?' Thomas called in English, then again in French. One of Charles's remaining men-at-arms slowly collapsed, first to his knees, then onto his belly with a crash of plate armour.

A knight stepped out of the English ranks. He was a Breton, one of Totesham's deputies, and he announced his name to prove to Charles that he was a man of noble birth and then he held out his hand and Charles of Blois, nephew to the King of France and claimant of the Duchy of Brittany, stepped awkwardly forward and held out his sword. A huge cheer went up, then the men on the hill divided to let the Duke and his captor walk away. Charles expected to be given his sword back and looked surprised when the Breton did not make the offer, then the defeated Duke walked stiffly down the hill, ignoring the triumphant English, but suddenly checked for a black-haired figure had stepped into his path.

It was Jeanette. 'Remember me?' she asked.

Charles looked her up and down and flinched as though he had been struck when he recognized the badge on her jupon. Then he flinched again when he saw the anger in her eyes. He said nothing.

476

Jeanette smiled. 'Rapist,' she said, then spat through his open visor. The Duke jerked his head away, but too late, and Jeanette spat into his face again. He shivered with anger. She was daring him to strike her, but he restrained himself and Jeanette, unable to do the same, spat a third time. '*Ver*,' she said scornfully and walked away to an ironic cheer.

'What's *ver*?' Robbie asked.

'Worm,' Thomas said, then smiled at Jeanette. 'Well done, my lady.'

'I was going to kick his goddamn balls,' she said, 'but I remembered he was wearing armour.'

Thomas laughed, then stepped aside as Richard Totesham ordered a half-dozen men-at-arms to escort Charles back into La Roche-Derrien. Short of capturing the King of France, he was as valuable a captive as any to be had in the war. Thomas watched him walk away. Charles of Blois would now be joining the King of Scotland as England's prisoner and both men would have to raise a fortune if they wished to be ransomed.

'It isn't finished!' Totesham shouted. He had seen the crowd of jeering men following the captured Duke and hurried to pull them away. 'It isn't done! Finish the job!'

'Horses!' Sir Thomas Dagworth called. 'Take their horses!'

The fight in Charles's encampment was won, but not ended. The assault from the town had hit like a storm and driven clean through the centre of Duke Charles's carefully prepared battle line and what was left of his force was now split into small groups. Scores were already dead, and others were fleeing into the darkness. 'Archers!' a shout went up. 'Archers to me!' Dozens of archers ran to the back of the encampment, where the escaping French and Bretons were trying to reach the other fortresses, and the bows cut the fugitives down mercilessly.

'Clean them out!' Totesham shouted. 'Clean them out!' A rough kind of organization had emerged in the shambles as the garrison and the townsmen, augmented by the survivors of Sir Thomas Dagworth's force, hunted through the burning encampment to drive any survivors back to where the archers waited. It was slow work, not because the enemy was making any real resistance, but because men were constantly stopping to pillage tents and shelters. Women and children were pulled out into the moonlight and their men were killed. Prisoners worth a huge ransom were slaughtered in the confusion and darkness. The Viscount Rohan was chopped down, as were the lords of Laval and of Châteaubriant, of Dinan and of Redon.

A grey light glimmered in the east, the first hint of dawn. Whimpering sounded in the burned camp.

'Finish them off?' Richard Totesham had at last found Sir Thomas Dagworth. The two men were on the encampment's ramparts from where they stared at the southern enemy fortress.

'Can't leave them sitting there,' Sir Thomas said, then held out a hand. 'Thanks, Dick.'

'For doing my job?' Totesham responded, embarrassed. 'So let's scour the bastards out of the other camps, eh?'

A trumpet called the English to assemble.

Charles of Blois had told his men that an archer could not shoot a man he could not see, and that was true, but the men of the southern encampment, who formed the second largest portion of Charles's army, were crowding onto their outer rampart in an effort to see what was happening in the eastern encampment about the windmill. They had lit fires to give their own cross-bowmen illumination, but those fires now served to outline them as they stood on the earth bank, which had no palisade, and the English archers, given such a target, could not miss. Those archers were in the cleared ground between the encampments, shadowed by the loom of the long earthworks, and their arrows flickered out of the night to strike the watching French and Bretons. Crossbowmen tried to shoot back, but they made the easiest targets for few of them possessed mail, and then, with a roar, the English men-at-arms were charging over the defences and the killing began again. Townsmen, eager for plunder, followed the charge and the archers, seeing the earthwork stripped of defenders, ran to catch up.

Thomas paused on the earth rampart to shoot a dozen arrows into the panicked enemy who had made this encampment where the English siege camp had stood the previous year. He had lost sight of Sir Guillaume and, though he had told Jeanette to go back to the town, she was still with him, but now armed with a sword she had taken from a dead Breton. 'You shouldn't be here!' he snarled at her.

'Wasps!' she called back, and pointed to a dozen men-at-arms wearing the black and yellow surcoats of the Lord of Roncelets.

The enemy here made small resistance. They had been unaware of the disaster that had overcome Charles, and they had been surprised by the sudden assault from the darkness. The surviving crossbowmen now retreated panicking into the tents and the English again snatched brands from the great fires and hurled them onto the canvas roofs to flare bright and garish in the predawn darkness. The English and Welsh archers had slung their bows and were grimly working their way through the tent lines with axes, swords and clubs. It was another slaughter, fuelled by the prospect of plunder, and some of the French and Bretons, rather than face the screaming mass of maddened men, took to their horses and fled east towards the thin grey light that now leaked a touch of red along the horizon.

Thomas and Robbie headed for the men wearing Roncelets's waspish stripes. Those men had attempted to make a stand beside a trebuchet that had the name Stonewhip painted on its big frame, but they had been outflanked by archers and now they were trying to escape and in the chaos they did not know which way to go. Two of them ran at Thomas and he skewered one with his sword while Robbie stunned the other with a massive blow to his helmet, then a rush of archers swept the men in black and yellow aside and Thomas scabbarded his wet sword and unslung his bow before running into a big unburned tent that stood beside a pole flying the black and yellow banner and there, between a bed and an open chest, was the Lord of Roncelets himself. He and a squire were scooping coins from the chest into small bags and they turned as Thomas and Robbie entered and the Lord of Roncelets snatched up a sword from the bed just as Thomas dragged back the bowcord. The squire lunged at Robbie, but Thomas loosed the arrow and the squire jerked back as if tugged by a massive rope and the blood from the wound in his forehead pattered red on the tent roof. The squire jerked a few times and then was still, and the Lord of Roncelets was still three paces from Thomas when the second arrow was placed on the string. 'Come on, my lord,' Thomas said, 'give me a reason to send you to the devil.'

The Lord of Roncelets looked like a fighter. He had short bristly hair, a broken nose and missing teeth, but there was no belligerence in him now. He could hear the screams of defeat all about him, he could smell the burning flesh of the men trapped among the tents and he could see the arrow on Thomas's bow that was aimed at his face and he simply held out his sword in instant surrender. 'You have rank?' he asked Robbie. He had not recognized Thomas and, anyway, presumed that any man carrying a bow had to be a commoner.

Robbie did not understand the question, which had been asked in French, and so Thomas answered for him. 'He's a Scottish lord,' Thomas said, exaggerating Robbie's status.

'Then I yield to him,' Roncelets said angrily and threw his sword at Robbie's feet.

'God,' Robbie said, not understanding the exchange, 'but he scared quick!'

Thomas gently released the bowcord's tension and held up the crooked fingers of his right hand. 'It's a good job you surrendered,' he told Roncelets. 'Remember you wanted to cut these off?' He could not help smiling as first recognition, then abject fear showed on Roncelets's face. 'Jeanette!' Thomas shouted, his small victory gained. 'Jeanette!' Jeanette came through the tent flap and with her, of all people, was Will Skeat. 'What the hell are you doing here?' Thomas demanded angrily.

'You wouldn't keep an old friend from a scrap, would you, Tom?' Skeat asked with a grin and Thomas thought he could see his friend's true character in that grin.

'You're an old fool,' Thomas grumbled, then he picked up the Lord of Roncelets's sword and gave it to Jeanette. 'He's our prisoner,' he said, 'yours as well.'

'Ours?' Jeanette was puzzled.

'He's the Lord of Roncelets,' Thomas said, and he could not help another smile, 'and I've no doubt we can squeeze a ransom from him. And I don't mean that cash' – he pointed at the open chest – 'that's ours anyway.'

Jeanette stared at Roncelets and it slowly dawned on her that if the Lord of Roncelets was her prisoner then her son was as good as returned to her. She laughed suddenly, then gave Thomas a kiss. 'So you do keep your promises, Thomas.'

'And you keep good guard of him,' Thomas said, 'because his ransom is going to make us all rich. Robbie, you, me and Will. We're all going to be wealthy.' He grinned at Skeat. 'You'll stay with her, Will? Look after him?'

'I'll stay,' Will agreed.

'Who is she?' the Lord of Roncelets asked Thomas.

'The Countess of Armorica,' Jeanette answered for him and laughed again when she saw the shock on his face.

'Take him back to the town now,' Thomas told them, and he ducked outside the tent where he found two townsmen searching for plunder among the nearest tents. 'You two!' he snapped at them, 'you're going to help guard a prisoner. Take him back to the town and you'll be well rewarded. Guard him well!' Thomas pulled the two men into the tent. He reckoned the Lord of Roncelets could not escape if Jeanette, Skeat and the two men were watching him. 'Just guard him,' he told them, 'and take him to your old house.' This last was to Jeanette.

'My old house?' she was puzzled.

'You wanted to kill someone tonight,' Thomas said, 'and you can't kill Charles of Blois, so why don't you go and murder Belas?' He laughed at the look on her face, then he and Robbie slammed down the chest lid and covered it with blankets from the bed in hope of hiding it for a few moments and then they went back to the fight.

All through the flame-lit battle Thomas had caught glimpses of men in plain black surcoats and he knew that Guy Vexille must be nearby, but he had not seen him. Now there were shouts and the clash of blades from the encampment's southern edge and Thomas and Robbie ran to see what the commotion was. They saw that a group of horsemen in black surcoats were fighting off a score of English men-at-arms. 'Vexille!' Thomas shouted. 'Vexille!'

'It's him?' Robbie asked.

'It's his men, anyway,' Thomas said. He guessed his cousin had been in the eastern encampment with de Taillebourg and that he had come here in hope of bringing a relief force to Charles's aid, but he had been too late and now his men were fighting a rearguard battle to protect other men who were fleeing.

'Where is he?' Robbie demanded.

Thomas could not see his cousin. He shouted again. 'Vexille! Vexille!'

And there he was. The Harlequin, Count of Astarac,

armoured in plate, visor lifted, mounted on a black destrier and carrying a plain black shield. He saw Thomas and raised his sword in an ironic salute. Thomas unslung his bow, but Guy Vexille saw the threat, turned away and his horsemen closed protectively about him. 'Vexille!' Thomas yelled and he ran towards his cousin. Robbie called a warning and Thomas ducked as a horseman swung a blade at him, then he pushed against the horse, smelling leather and sweat, and another horseman banged into him, almost throwing him off his feet. 'Vexille!' he bellowed. He could see Guy Vexille again, only now his cousin was turning back, spurring towards him, and Thomas drew the bow-cord, but Vexille held up his right hand to show he had scabbarded his sword and the gesture made Thomas lower the black bow.

Guy Vexille, his visor raised and his handsome face lit by the fires, smiled. 'I have the book, Thomas.'

Thomas said nothing, but just raised the bow again.

Guy Vexille shook his head in reproof. 'No need for that, Thomas. Join me.'

'In hell, you bastard,' Thomas said. This was the man who had killed his father, had killed Eleanor, had killed Father Hobbe, and Thomas drew the arrow fully back and Vexille took a small knife that had been concealed in his shield hand and calmly leaned forward and cut the bowcord. The broken string made the bow jump violently in Thomas's hand and the arrow spewed away harmlessly. The cord had been cut so swiftly that Thomas had been given no time to react.

'One day you'll join me, Thomas,' Vexille said, then he saw that the English archers had at last noticed his men and were beginning to take their toll and so he turned his horse, shouted at his men to retreat and spurred away.

'Jesus!' Thomas swore in frustration.

'*Calix meus inebrians*!' Guy Vexille shouted, then he was lost among the horsemen galloping south. A flight of English arrows followed them, but none struck Vexille.

'Bastard!' Robbie swore at the retreating figure.

A woman's scream sounded from the burning tents.

'What did he say to you?' Robbie asked.

'He wanted me to join him,' Thomas said bitterly. He threw away the slashed cord and took the spare from under his sallet. His clumsy fingers fumbled as he restrung the bow, but he managed to do it on the second try. 'And he said he's got the book.'

'Aye, well, much good that will bloody do him,' Robbie commented. The fight had died and he knelt by a black-dressed corpse and began searching for coins. Sir Thomas Dagworth was shouting for men to assemble at the encampment's western edge to assault the next fortress where some of the defenders, realizing that the battle was lost, were already running away. Church bells were ringing in La Roche-Derrien, celebrating that Charles of Blois had entered the town as a prisoner.

Thomas stared after his cousin. He was ashamed because one small part of him, one small and treacherous part, had been tempted to take the offer. Join his cousin, be back in a family, look for the Grail and harness its power. The shame was sour, like the shame of the gratitude he had felt towards de Taillebourg when the torture ceased. 'Bastard!' he yelled uselessly. '*Bastard.*'

'Bastard!' It was Sir Guillaume's voice that cut across Thomas's. Sir Guillaume, with his two men-at-arms, was prodding a prisoner in the back with a sword. The captive wore plate armour and the sword scraped on it with every prod. 'Bastard!' Sir Guillaume bawled again, then saw Thomas. 'It's Coutances! Coutances!' He pulled off his prisoner's helmet. 'Look at him!'

The Count of Coutances was a melancholy-looking man, bald as an egg, who was doing his best to appear dignified. Sir Guillaume poked him again. 'I tell you, Thomas' – he spoke in French – 'that this bastard's wife and daughters will have to whore themselves to raise this ransom! They'll be swiving every man in Normandy to buy this gutless bastard back!' He jabbed the Count of Coutances again. 'I'm going to squeeze you witless!' Sir Guillaume roared and then, exultant, marched his prisoner onwards.

The woman screamed again.

There had been many women screaming that night, but something about this sound cut through Thomas's awareness and he turned, alarmed. The scream sounded a third time and Thomas began to run. 'Robbie!' he shouted. 'To me!'

Thomas ran across the remnants of a burning tent, his boots throwing up sparks and embers. He swerved round a smoking brazier, almost tripped on a wounded man who was vomiting into an upturned helmet, ran down an alley between armourers' huts where anvils, bellows, hammers, tongs and barrels full of rivets and mail rings were spilt on the grass. A man in a farrier's apron with blood streaming from a head wound staggered into his path and Thomas shoved him aside to run towards the black and yellow standard that still flew outside the Lord of Roncelets's burning tent. 'Jeanette!' he called. 'Jeanette!'

But Jeanette was a prisoner. She was being held by a huge man who had pressed her spine against the windlass of the trebuchet called Stonewhip that stood just beyond the Lord of Roncelets's tent. The man heard Thomas shouting and looked round, grinning. It was Beggar, all beard and rotted teeth, and he shoved Jeanette hard as she struggled to escape him.

'Hold her, Beggar!' Sir Geoffrey Carr shouted. 'Hold the bitch!'

'The pretty ain't going anywhere,' Beggar said, 'going nowhere, darling,' and he tried to haul up her coat of mail, but it was too heavy and awkward and Jeanette was struggling too frantically.

The Lord of Roncelets, still without his sword, was sitting on Stonewhip's frame. He had a red mark on his face, suggesting he had been struck, and Sir Geoffrey Carr with five other men-at-arms was standing over him. The Scarecrow stared defiantly at Thomas. 'He's my prisoner!' he insisted.

'He belongs to us,' Thomas said, 'we took him.'

'Listen, boy,' the Scarecrow said, his voice still slurred by drink, 'I am a knight and you are a turd. You understand me?' He staggered slightly as he stepped towards Thomas. 'I am a knight,' he said again, louder, 'and you are nothing!' His red face, made lurid by the flames, was twisted in derision. 'You are nothing!' he shouted again, then whipped round to make sure that his men were guarding the Lord of Roncelets. Such a wealthy captive would solve all Sir Geoffrey's problems and he was determined to hold onto him and take the ransom for himself. 'She can't take a captive,' he said, pointing his sword at Jeanette, 'because she's got tits, and you can't take him because you're a turd. But I'm a knight! A *knight*!' He spat the word at Thomas who, goaded by the insults, drew his bow. The new string was slightly too long and he could feel the lack of power in the black stave because of it, but he reckoned there was enough strength for his purpose. 'Beggar!' the Scarecrow shouted, 'if he looses that bow, kill the bitch.'

'Kill the pretty,' Beggar said. He was drooling spittle, which ran down his big beard as he stroked the mail rings above Jeanette's breasts. She still fought, but he had her bent painfully back across the windlass and she could hardly move.

Thomas kept the bow drawn. The trebuchet's long beam, he saw, had been winched down to the ground though the engineers must have been interrupted before they could load a stone because the great leather sling was empty. A heap of stones stood off to the right and a sudden movement there made Thomas see there was a wounded man leaning against the boulders. The man was trying to stand, but could not. There was blood on his face. 'Will?' Thomas asked.

'Tom!' Will Skeat tried to push himself upright again. 'It's you, Tom!'

'What happened?' Thomas asked.

'Not what I was, Tom,' Skeat said. The two townsmen who had been helping to guard the Lord of Roncelets were dead at Skeat's feet, and Skeat himself seemed to be dying. He was white-faced, feeble and every breath was a struggle. There were tears on his face. 'I tried to fight,' he said pitiably, 'I did try, but I'm not what I was.'

'Who attacked you?' Thomas asked, but Skeat seemed unable to answer.

'Will was just trying to protect me,' Jeanette shouted, then she screamed as Beggar thrust her back so hard that at last she was forced onto the top of the windlass and Beggar could push her mail skirts up. He gabbled excitedly just as Sir Geoffrey roared in anger.

'It's the Douglas bastard!'

Thomas loosed the cord. With a new bowcord he liked to shoot a couple of arrows to discover how the new hemp would behave, but he had no time for such niceties now, he just loosed the arrow and it sliced through the tangles of Beggar's beard to cut his throat, the broad arrow head slitting his gullet as cleanly as a butcher's knife, and Jeanette screamed as the blood spurted across her jupon and face. The Scarecrow bellowed in rage and ran at Thomas who rammed the horn-tipped bowstave into the red face then let the weapon fall as he drew his sword. Robbie ran past him and thrust his uncle's sword at the Scarecrow's belly, but even drunk Sir Geoffrey was quick and he managed to parry the blow and strike back. Two of his men-at-arms were running to help – the others were guarding the Lord of Roncelets – and Thomas saw the two men coming. He went to his left, hoping to put the big frame of Stonewhip between himself and the men wearing Sir Geoffrey's badge of the black axe, but Sir Geoffrey almost cut him off and Thomas gave a desperate back-swing with his newly drawn sword that slammed against the Scarecrow's blade with a force that numbed Thomas's arm. The blow rocked the Scarecrow back, then he recovered and leaped forward and Thomas was desperately defending himself as the Scarecrow rained blows down on him. Thomas was no swordsman and he was being beaten down to his knees and Robbie could not help him because he was fending off Sir Geoffrey's two followers, and then there was an almighty crash, a bang that sounded as though the gates of hell had just opened, and the ground shook as the Scarecrow screamed in utter agony. His howl, trailing blood, seared into the sky.

Jeanette had pulled the lever that released the long beam. Ten tons of counterweight had thumped to the ground and the thick metal pin that held the sling had jerked up between Sir Geoffrey's legs and torn a bloody hole from his crotch to his belly. He should have been hurled halfway to the town by the trebuchet's beam, but instead the pin had been trapped in his entrails and he was caught on the beam's end where he writhed in agony, his blood pouring down to the ground.

His men, seeing their master dying, stepped back. Why fight for a man who could offer no reward? Robbie gaped up as the Scarecrow twisted and jerked, and somehow the dying man managed to tear himself free of the great iron stake and he fell, trailing intestines and spraying blood. He hit the ground with a thump, bounced bloodily, yet still he lived. His eyes were twitching and his mouth was drawn back in a snarl. 'Goddamn Douglas,' he managed to gasp before Robbie stepped to him, lifted his uncle's sword, and rammed it down once, straight between the Scarecrow's eyes.

The Lord of Roncelets had watched it all happen with disbelief. Now Jeanette was holding a sword to his face, daring him to run away, and he dumbly shook his head to show that he had no intention of risking his life among the drunken, screaming, savage men who had

490

come out of the night to destroy the greatest army the duchy of Brittany had ever raised.

Thomas crossed to Sir William Skeat, but his old friend was dead. He had been wounded in the neck and he had bled to death on the stone pile. He looked strangely peaceful. A first shaft of the new day's sun cut across the world's edge to light the bright blood at the top of Stonewhip's beam as Thomas closed his mentor's eyes. 'Who killed Will Skeat?' Thomas demanded of Sir Geoffrey's men and Dickon, the young one, pointed at the wreckage of mail, flesh, entrails and bone that had been the Scarecrow.

Thomas inspected the dents in his sword. He must learn to use one, he thought, or else he would die by the sword, then he looked up at Sir Geoffrey's men. 'Go and help the attack on the next fort,' he told them. They stared at him. 'Go!' he snapped and, startled, they ran westwards.

Thomas pointed his sword at the Lord of Roncelets. 'Take him back to town,' he told Robbie, 'and guard him well.'

'What about you?' Robbie asked.

'I'm going to bury Will,' Thomas said. 'He was a friend.' He thought he must shed some tears for Will Skeat, but there were none. Not now, anyway. He sheathed the sword, then smiled at Robbie. 'You can go home, Robbie.'

'I can?' Robbie seemed puzzled.

'De Taillebourg's dead. Roncelets will pay your ransom to Lord Outhwaite. You can go to Eskdale, go home, go back to killing Englishmen.'

Robbie shook his head. 'Guy Vexille lives.'

'He's mine to kill.'

'And mine,' Robbie said. 'You forget he killed my brother. I'm staying till he's dead.'

'If you can ever find him,' Jeanette said softly.

The sun was lighting the smoke of the burning encampments and casting long shadows across the ground where the last of Charles's army abandoned their earthworks and fled towards Rennes. They had come in their great splendour and now they scuttled away in abject defeat.

Thomas went to the engineers' tents and found a pickaxe, a mattock and a shovel. He dug a grave beside Stonewhip and tipped Skeat into the damp soil and tried to say a prayer, but he could not think of one, and then he remembered the coin for the ferryman and so he went to the Lord of Roncelets's tent and pulled the charred canvas away from the chest and took a piece of gold and went back to the grave. He jumped down beside his friend and put the coin under Skeat's tongue. The ferryman would find it and know from the gold that Sir William Skeat was a special man. 'God bless you, Will,' Thomas said, then he scrambled out of the grave and he filled it in, though he kept pausing in hope that Will's eyes would open, but of course they did not and Thomas at last wept as he shovelled earth onto his friend's pale face. The sun was up by the time he finished and women and children were coming from the town to look for plunder. A kestrel flew high and Thomas sat on the chest of coins and waited for Robbie to return from the town.

He would go south, he thought. Go to Astarac. Go and find his father's notebook and solve its mystery. The bells of La Roche-Derrien were ringing for the victory, a huge victory, and Thomas sat among the dead and knew he would have no peace until he had found his father's burden. *Calix meus inebrians. Transfer calicem istem a me. Ego enim eram pincerna regis.*

Whether he wanted the job or not he was the King's cupbearer, and he would go south.

Historical Note

The novel begins with the battle of Neville's Cross. The name of the battle is derived from the stone cross that Lord Neville erected to mark the victory, though it is possible there was another cross already on the site which Lord Neville's memorial replaced. The battle, fought by a large Scottish army against a small scratch force hastily assembled by the Archbishop of York and the northern lords, was a disaster for the Scots. Their King, David II, was captured as described in *Vagabond*, trapped under a bridge. He managed to knock out some of his captor's teeth, but then was subdued. He spent a long time at Bamburgh Castle recovering from his facial wound, then was taken to London and put into the Tower with most of the other Scottish aristocracy captured that day, including Sir William Douglas, the Knight of Liddesdale. The two Scottish Earls who had previously sworn fealty to Edward were decapitated, then quartered, and the parts of their body displayed around the realm as a warning against treachery. Later that year Charles of Blois, nephew to the King of France and would-be Duke of Brittany, joined David II in the Tower of London. It was a remarkable double by the English who will, in another decade, add the King of France himself to the haul.

The Scots invaded England at the request of the French to whom they were allied, and it is probable that David II truly believed England's army was all in northern France. But England had foreseen just this kind of trouble and certain northern lords were charged with staying at home and being ready to raise forces if the Scots ever marched. The backbone of those forces was, of course, the archer, and this is the great age of English (and, to a lesser extent, Welsh) archery. The weapon used was the longbow (a name that was coined much later) which was a yew bow at least six feet in length with a draw weight of over a hundred pounds (more than double the weight of modern competition bows). It is a mystery why England alone could field armies of lethal archers who did, indeed, become kings of the European battlefield, but the likeliest answer is that mastery of the longbow was an English enthusiasm, practised as a sport in hundreds of villages. Eventually laws were passed making archery practice obligatory, presumably because the enthusiasm was fading. It was, certainly, an extraordinarily difficult weapon to use, requiring immense strength, and the French, though they tried to introduce the weapon into their ranks, never mastered the longbow. The Scots were accustomed to these archers and had learned never to attack them on horseback, but in truth there was no answer to the longbow until firearms were deployed on the battlefield.

Prisoners were important. A great man like Sir William Douglas would only be released on payment of a vast ransom, though Sir William was given early parole to help negotiate the ransom of the King of Scotland and when he failed he dutifully returned to his imprisonment in the Tower of London. The ransoms for men like Charles of Blois and King David II were massive and might take years to negotiate and raise. In David's case the ransom was £66,000, a sum that has to be multiplied at least a hundred times to get even a rough approximation of its modern value. The Scots were allowed to pay it in ten instalments and twenty noblemen had to be surrendered as hostages for the payment before David was released in 1357 by which time, ironically, his sympathies had become entirely pro-English. Sir Thomas Dagworth was officially the captor of Charles of Blois and he sold him to Edward III for the much smaller sum of £3,500, but doubtless it was better to have that money in hand than wait while a larger ransom was collected in France and Brittany. King David's captor had been an Englishman called John Coupland who also sold his prisoner to Edward, in Coupland's case for a knighthood and land.

Charles's defeat at La Roche-Derrien is one of the great unsung English triumphs of the period. Charles had faced archers before and had worked out, rightly as it happened, that the way to defeat them was to make them attack well-protected positions. What the archer could not see he could not kill. The tactic worked against Sir Thomas Dagworth's assault, but then came Richard Totesham's frenetic sortie from the town and, because Charles had insisted that the four parts of his army stay behind their protective earthworks, he was overwhelmed and the other parts of his army were then defeated in turn. His defeat and capture were an immense shock to his allies, the French, who were failing to relieve the siege of Calais. I must record my debt to Jonathan Sumption whose book, *Trial by Battle*, the first volume of his superb history of the Hundred Years War, was of particular use to me. The errors in the novel are entirely mine, of course, though in the interests of lightening my post bag may I gently point out that Durham Cathedral only possessed two towers in 1347 and that I placed the Hachaliah reference in the book of Esdras, instead of in Nehemiah, because I was using the Vulgate and not the King James Bible.